ETERNAL FRONTIER

ETERNAL FRONTIER

JAMES H. SCHMITZ

EDITED BY
ERIC FLINT &
GUY GORDON

ETERNAL FRONTIER

This is a work of fiction. All the characters and events portrayed in this book are fictional, and any resemblance to real people or incidents is purely coincidental.

"The Big Terrarium" was first published in *Saturn*, May 1957. "Summer Guests" was first published in *IF*, September 1959. "Captives of the Thieve-Star" was first published in *Planet Stories*, May 1951. "Caretaker" was first published in *Galaxy*, July 1953. "One Step Ahead" was first published in *IF*, April 1974. "Left Hand, Right Hand" was first published in *Amazing*, November 1962. "The Ties of Earth" was first published in *Galaxy*, November–December 1955. "Spacemaster" was first published in *New Writings in SF 3* in 1965. "The Altruist" was first published in *Galaxy*, September 1952. "Oneness" was first published in *Analog*, May 1963. "We Don't Want Any Trouble" was first published in *Galaxy*, June 1953. "Just Curious" was first published in *Alfred Hitchcock's Mystery Magazine*, December 1968. "These Are the Arts" was first published in *The Magazine of Fantasy & Science Fiction*, September 1962. "Would You?" was first published in *Fantastic*, December 1969. "Clean Slate" was first published in *Amazing*, September 1964. "Crime Buff" was first published in *Alfred Hitchcock's Mystery Magazine*, August 1973. "Ham Sandwich" was first published in *Analog*, June 1963. "Where the Time Went" was first published in *IF*, November 1968. "An Incident on Route 12" was first published in *IF*, January 1962. "Swift Completion" was first published in *Alfred Hitchcock's Mystery Magazine*, March 1962. "Faddist" was first published in *Bizarre Mystery*, January 1966. *The Eternal Frontiers* was first published by G.P. Putnam's Sons in 1973.

Afterword, © 2002 by Eric Flint; James H. Schmitz Chronography, © 2002 by Guy Gordon.

A Baen Books Original

Baen Publishing Enterprises
P.O. Box 1403
Riverdale, NY 10471
www.baen.com

ISBN: 0-7434-3559-1

Cover art by Bob Eggleton

First printing, September 2002

Library of Congress Cataloging-in-Publication Data

Schmitz, James H., 1911-
    Eternal frontier / by James H. Schmitz ; ed. by Eric Flint & Guy Gordon
        p. cm.
    "A Baen Books original"—T.p. verso.
    ISBN 0-7434-3559-1 (pbk.)
    1. Space colonies—Fiction. I. Flint, Eric. II. Gordon, Guy, 1951- III. Title.

PS3569.C5175 E84 2002
813'.54—dc21

                                                    2002071206

Distributed by Simon & Schuster
1230 Avenue of the Americas
New York, NY 10020

Production by Windhaven Press, Auburn, NH
Printed in the United States of America

10   9   8   7   6   5   4   3   2   1

Contents

Adventures in Time and Space

JAMES H. SCHMITZ was one of the finest writers of light-hearted adventure stories in the history of science fiction. His most familiar works, the Hub and Vegan Confederacy tales and his novel *The Witches of Karres*, were almost all of that nature.

But he wrote a number of other stories which were quite similar, which are much less well known—and, often, simply due to the vagaries of the publishing industry. To give an example, the opening tale of this volume ("The Big Terrarium") is as good a story as almost anything Schmitz ever wrote. Alas, it was published in a magazine called *Saturn*, which folded after four issues. So, unlike the stories published in *Analog*, which were usually reissued several times in various anthologies, "The Big Terrarium" vanished from sight. To the best of our knowledge, this anthology is the first time it has been reissued since it first appeared in that little-known and short-lived magazine in May of 1957. To one extent or another, the same fate befell many of the stories in this section of our anthology.

One of these stories is of particular interest, for anyone familiar with the history of science fiction. Schmitz's most famous single work, his novel *The Witches of Karres*, was published at the height of his career in 1968. But what few people know is that, at the beginning of his career—in the late 40s, twenty years earlier—he wrote a story which served as the prototype for the later novel. His "trial run," you might call it.

It's all very complicated . . .

Schmitz wrote the story "Captives of the Thieve-Star" sometime very early in his career, and then decided it was unpublishable and set it aside. The original title of the story was "What Threbus Said." Then, in 1949, he published the novelette "The Witches of Karres," which he would later expand into the novel by that name. Deciding

1

that his earlier story was in fact sellable, he hauled it out of the dustbin—but, of course, having already used the name "Threbus" in "The Witches of Karres," had to change the name of the heroine's father and the title "What Threbus Said" to "Captives of the Thieve-Star."

And that's how it all happened, honest.

That story, "Captives of the Thieve-Star," is included here. We think any reader will enjoy it for its own sake. But those of you familiar with *The Witches of Karres* will also enjoy seeing how Schmitz transmuted the protagonists of the earlier story into the familiar figures of Captain Pausert and Goth. And will chuckle, perhaps, at seeing the origins of the mysterious and mighty witches of Karres—as disreputable a clan of space gypsies as you could ask for.

The Big Terrarium
· · · · · · · · · · · · · · · · · · · ·

THE THIRD MORNING Fred Nieheim woke up in the Little Place, he no longer had to prove to himself that he wasn't dreaming. He knew where he was, all right, along with the rest of them—Wilma and Ruby and Howard Cooney and the Cobrisol. But knowing it didn't make him any happier.

He remained lying on his back, gazing moodily out through the bedroom window, while he wondered how one went about getting back to Earth from here—specifically, to the Nieheim farm twenty-two miles south of Richardsville, Pennsylvania, U.S.A. It wasn't apparently just a matter of finding a way out through the very odd sort of barriers that fenced in the area. According to the Cobrisol, a local creature which appeared to be well-informed, they would then simply be in something known as "Outside," which was nowhere near Earth. At least, the Cobrisol had never heard of Earth, and still wasn't entirely convinced that it existed.

"Sometimes, Fred," it had hinted gently only last evening while they sat together on the front porch, watching a rather good production of an Earth-type sunset above the apple orchard, "sometimes, the memory and other mental functions are deranged by transfer from one Place to another. Don't let it worry you, though. Such effects almost always wear off in time. . . ."

Fred felt Wilma stir quietly in bed beside him, and he raised himself cautiously on an elbow to look at her. The bed creaked.

Ruby went "Chuck-chuck!" sharply from the corner of the bedroom, where she slept in a basket. She was a middle-aged hen pheasant of belligerent nature, who regarded herself as the

3

watchdog of the Nieheim farm. Basket and all, she'd been transferred along with them to the Little Place.

Fred remained quiet until Ruby stuck her head back under her
wing. Wilma was still asleep, and only a rounded, smooth shoulder and a mop of yellow hair were visible at the moment above
the blankets. They had been married less than two years, and if
he and Wilma and Ruby had been set down here alone, he mightn't
have minded it so much. The Cobrisol had assured him that one
ordinarily received the best of care and attention in the Little Places;
and the Cobrisol itself, though disconcerting in appearance until
you got used to it, seemed to be as agreeable a neighbor as anyone could want.

Unfortunately, there was also Howard Cooney. . . .

Out in the kitchen, precisely as Fred's reflections reached that
point, a metallic clatter announced that Howard Cooney was
manipulating Wilma's big iron skillet on the stove again.

Fred scowled thoughtfully. For a recent acquaintance, Howard
certainly was making himself at home with them! He was a
tramp who had happened to select the night of their transfer
to sleep in the shed back of the Nieheim farmhouse; and so
he'd been picked up and brought along, too. Unfortunately,
whoever or whatever had constructed a reasonably accurate
duplicate of a section of the Nieheim farm in the Little Place,
hadn't bothered to include the shed. The first night, at Wilma's
suggestion, Howard had moved into the living room. After that,
he'd stayed there.

Fred felt he couldn't reasonably object to the arrangement under
the circumstances, but he suspected that Howard was an untrust-
worthy character. He'd already begun to ogle Wilma when he
thought nobody was noticing—and there was the disturbing fact
that he was considerably bigger and huskier than Fred. . . .

He'd better, Fred decided uneasily, work out a method of getting them all back to Earth before Howard got the wrong kind
of ideas.

"Morning," Howard Cooney said hospitably, as Fred came into
the kitchen. "Sit down and have some hoot. Where's Wilma?"

Fred said Wilma was still sleeping.

"Me," said Howard, "I'm up with the sun! Or what goes for the
sun around here. Know what? I'm going to build a still!" He
explained that he'd discovered a maze of piping under the front

porch which wasn't connected to anything and which he could use for the purpose.

Fred doubted Howard would have any success with his dubious project, but he didn't comment on it. The piping wouldn't be missed. The duplicated house functioned just as well as the house back on Earth had; but it was operated on different and—so far—incomprehensible principles. Hot and cold water ran out of the proper faucets and vanished down the drains, but neither faucets nor drains appeared to be connected to anything but the solid walls! Similarly, the replicas of the electric stove and refrigerator performed their normal duties—but Fred had discovered by accident that they worked just as well when they weren't plugged into the electric outlets. It was all a little uncanny, and he preferred not to think about it too much.

He tried a slice of the hoot Howard had been frying. Hoots came in various flavors, and this one wasn't at all bad—quite as good as ham, in fact. He said so.

"Could have been a famous chef back on Earth if I'd wanted to," Howard admitted carelessly. "This is last night's hoot, by the way. There weren't any fresh ones floating around this morning."

"Howard," said Fred, "I'm trying to think of a way to get us back to Earth—"

"You are?" Howard looked startled and then frowned. "Look, Buster," he said in a confidential tone, leaning across the table, "let's face it. We got it soft here. Once I get the liquor situation straightened out, we'll have everything we need."

Fred's mouth opened in surprise. "You don't mean you want to stay here all your life, do you?"

Howard eyed him speculatively. "You ought to wise up. You never been in stir, have you? Well, that's where you are now."

"It's more like a zoo," said Fred. "And—"

"Call it a zoo," the tramp interrupted. "Same principle." He shrugged his massive shoulders. "Trying to break out is a good way to get killed, see? And it's likely to make it rough on everyone else. You wouldn't want something worse than being shut up here to happen to Wilma, would you?" He grinned amiably at Fred, but the little gray eyes were shrewd and, at the moment, a trifle menacing.

There was just enough sense in what he'd said to make Fred uncertain. Howard seemed to have had some experiences which could be of value now. "What do you think we ought to do?" he inquired.

However, at that point, Howard became rather vague. In stir, he said, one had to take things easy until one had figured out the system. And then one made use of the system. The danger was in getting whoever was in charge of the Little place riled up by thoughtless action. . . .

Going in search of the Cobrisol after breakfast, Fred admitted to himself that he couldn't quite make out what Howard Cooney was after. The tramp seemed to have something definite in mind, but apparently he wasn't willing to reveal it at this time.

At any rate, he'd made it clear that he didn't intend to be helpful about getting them back to Earth.

He found the Cobrisol coiled up at the head of a sloping section of ground which apparently was intended to represent the upper half of the south meadow of the Nieheim farm on Earth. As such, it was a few hundred yards out of place, and the grass that grew there wasn't exactly grass either; but Fred didn't pay much attention to such arbitrary rearrangements of his property any more.

"Nice day, isn't it?" he remarked, coming up.

"If you're speaking of the weather, yes!" said the Cobrisol. "Otherwise, I'll reserve my opinion."

Fred sat down beside it. "Something wrong?"

The Cobrisol nodded. "Possibly . . ." It was a quite odd-looking creature, with a snaky, ten-foot body, brick-red in color and with a rubbery feel to it, and a head that was a little like that of a pig and a little more like that of an alligator. No arms or legs, but it didn't seem to miss them. When it moved slowly, it extended and contracted itself like an earthworm; when it was in a hurry, it slithered about in sideways loops like a snake. "Take a look around," it invited significantly.

Fred gazed about. There was the usual, vague sort of sun-disk shining through the overhead haze, and the morning was pleasantly warm. At the end of the meadow was a huge, vertical something with indefinite borders called a "mirror-barrier," inside which he could see the Cobrisol and himself sitting in the grass, apparently a long distance away, and the duplicated farmhouse behind them. To the left was a rather accurate reproduction of the Nieheim apple orchard—though the trees were constructed more like firs— complete with a copy of the orchard section of the Nieheim trout stream. Unfortunately, no trout appeared to have been transferred.

Beyond the orchard was a thick, motionless mist which blended into the haze of the sky. The mist was another barrier; the Cobrisol called it a "barrier of confusion." The first day, Fred had made a determined attempt to walk out of the Little Place at that point; it had been a confusing experience, all right!

There wasn't much more to the Little Place. Behind the house, the ground sloped uphill into another wall of mist. He could hear Wilma and Howard Cooney talking in the back garden; and a number of small, circular objects that looked as if they might be made of some shiny metal floated about here and there in the air. The Cobrisol had explained that these were Eyes, through which the goings-on in the Little Place were being observed. Their motion seemed aimless, but Fred hadn't been able to get close enough to one to catch it.

"Everything looks about the same to me," he admitted at last.

"*Every*thing?" repeated the Cobrisol.

Its long toothy jaws and rubbery, throat moved slightly as it spoke, though it wasn't actually pronouncing human words. Neither had Fred been talking in the Cobrisol's language, whatever that was. It was a little hard to understand. They hadn't been suddenly gifted with telepathy; it was just that when you were set down in a Little Place, you knew what the other intelligent creatures there wanted to say. And it sounded as if they were using your kind of speech.

Fred had given up trying to figure it out....

"Well, there aren't any hoots in sight this morning," he acknowledged. "Or robols either," he added, after a brief search of the meadow grass. "Howard Cooney mentioned the hoots were gone at breakfast."

"Very observant of the Cooney person," the Cobrisol stated drily. It and Howard had disliked each other on sight. "Fred, there are a few matters I feel I should discuss with you."

"Now's a good time for a chat," Fred said agreeably.

The Cobrisol darted its head about in a series of rapid, snaky motions, surveying the area.

"The Eyes," it remarked then, "have assumed an unusual observational pattern this morning. You will note that two are stationed directly above us. Another cluster has positioned itself above the roof of the house. Early in the morning, an exceptionally large number were gathered among the trees of the orchard. These have now largely transferred themselves to the opposite side of the Little Place, near the maze-barrier."

"I see," said Fred, wondering what it was driving at.

"The One who maintains this Place is showing a remarkable degree of interest in us today," the Cobrisol concluded.

Fred nodded.

"Very well," the creature resumed. "Life in a Little Place is usually very satisfactory. The Ones who maintain them can be regarded as hobbyists who take a benevolent interest in the life-forms they select to inhabit their creations. Whereas Big Places, of course, are designed for major scientific projects. . . ." The creature shuddered slightly throughout its length. "I've never been in one of those, but—well, I've heard stories! Until this morning, Fred, I was inclined to regard us here as exceptionally fortunate life-forms."

"Well," Fred said, frowning "I don't quite agree with . . . what do you mean, 'until this morning'?"

"There are indications that this Place is being maintained, shall we say, carelessly? Nothing conclusive, as yet, you understand. But indications!" The Cobrisol jerked its head in the direction of the mirror-barrier. "That barrier, for instance, Fred, and one or two others have been permitted to go soft overnight!"

"Go soft?" Fred repeated.

"They're no longer operating as barriers. If we chose to, we could go right through them now—and be Outside! An almost unheard-of example of slip-shod maintenance—"

Fred brightened. "Well, say!" He got hurriedly to his feet. "Let's try it then!" He hesitated. "I'll go get Wilma and Ruby first though. I don't like to leave Wilma alone with that Cooney character."

The Cobrisol hadn't moved.

"I'm afraid you don't have the picture," it remarked. "You assume that once you're outside you'll be able to find your way back to the place you call Earth?"

"Not exactly," Fred said cautiously. He didn't like to be evasive with the Cobrisol, but he wasn't sure it would want them to leave—and it might be in a position to make their departure more difficult. "We could just step through and look around a little. . . ."

"Even if we weren't under observation at the moment," the Cobrisol pointed out, "you wouldn't live very long if you did. No life-form—as we know life-forms—can exist Outside. The barriers are set up to keep us where it's safe. That's why it's so irresponsible, of the One—"

Fred abandoned the idea of taking Wilma with him. He'd have

to make a careful check first. "About how long," he inquired, "could I stand it out there, safely?"

"Forget it, Fred!" the creature advised him earnestly. "Unless you knew exactly what to do to get back into the Little Place, you'd be worse than dead as soon as you stepped out there. And you don't."

"Do you?" Fred challenged it.

"Yes," said the Cobrisol, "I do. But I won't tell you. Sit down again, Fred."

Fred sat down thoughtfully. At least, he'd learned a few new facts, and the knowledge might come in handy.

"A few moments ago," the Cobrisol said, "you made an interesting statement. It appears that you don't wish to leave Wilma alone with the other human?"

Fred glanced at it in surprise. "No," he said shortly, "I don't."

The Cobrisol hesitated. "I don't wish to be tactless," it remarked. "I understand many species have extremely rigid taboos on the subject—but might this have something to do with the process of procreation?"

Fred flushed. He hadn't got quite that far in his thoughts about Wilma and Howard. "In a general sort of way," he admitted.

The Cobrisol regarded him judiciously. "Wilma is a charming life-form," it stated then, somewhat to Fred's surprise, "whereas the Cooney is as offensive as he is ignorant. I approve of your attitude, Fred! How do you intend to kill him?"

Shocked, Fred protested that he didn't intend to kill Howard Cooney. Human beings didn't act like that—or, at least, they weren't supposed to.

"Ah," said the Cobrisol. "That is unusual." It reflected a moment. "To get back, then, to our previous subject—"

"What previous subject?" By now, Fred was getting a little confused by the sudden shifts in the conversation.

"Hoots and robols," the Cobrisol said tersely. "They don't just fade away and there were enough around last evening to have kept us all supplied for another week. What may we deduce from their sudden disappearance, Fred?"

Fred considered. "They got sick and died?"

"Try again!" the Cobrisol told him encouragingly. "We could still *see* a dead hoot, couldn't we?"

"Something ate them," Fred said, a trifle annoyed.

"Correct! Something," added the Cobrisol, "with a very large appetite—or else a number of perhaps less voracious somethings.

Something, further, that was transferred here during the night, since there was no shortage in the food supplies previous to this morning. And, finally—since it's given no other indications of its presence—something with secretive habits!"

Fred looked around uneasily. "What do you think it is?"

"Who knows?" The Cobrisol had no shoulders to shrug with, but it employed an odd, jerky motion now which gave the same impression. "A Gramoose? An Icien? Perhaps even a pack of Bokans. . . ." It indicated the observing Eyes above the house with a flick of its snout. "The point is, Fred, that the One appears curious to see what we shall do in the situation. Taken together with the softening of the barriers, this suggests a deplorable—and, for us, perhaps very unfortunate—degree of immaturity in our particular hobbyist!"

Feeling his face go pale, Fred got to his feet. "I'm going to go tell Wilma to stay in the house with Ruby," he announced shakily.

"A wise precaution!" The Cobrisol uncoiled and came slithering along beside him as, he strode rapidly towards the house. "The situation, incidentally, does have one slight advantage for you personally."

"What's that?" Fred inquired.

"I have noticed that the Cooney individual is considerably larger and more powerful than you. But you can emphasize to him now that, since we are in a state of common danger, this is no time to indulge in procreational disputes. . . ."

Before Fred could answer, there was a sudden furious squawking from Ruby in the back garden. An instant later, he heard a breathless shriek from Wilma and a sort of horrified bellowing from Howard Cooney. He came pounding up to the front porch just as the house door flew open. Howard dashed out, wild-eyed, leaped down the porch stairs, almost knocking Fred over, and charged on.

Fred's impression was that the big man hadn't even seen him. As he scrambled up on the porch, there was a thud and a startled "Oof!" behind him, as if Howard had just gone flat on his face, but he didn't look back. Wilma came darting through the door in Howard's tracks, Ruby tucked firmly under her left arm and a big iron skillet grasped in her right hand. Her face looked white as paper under its tan.

"Run, Fred!" she gasped. "There's something at the back door!"

"You're mistaken, Wilma," the Cobrisol's voice informed them from the foot of the stairs. "It's now coming around the house. Up on the front porch, everyone! You, too, Cooney! No place to run to, you know!"

"*What's* coming?" Fred demanded hoarsely. He added to Wilma, "Here, I'll hold Ruby!"

Nobody answered immediately. Howard thumped up the steps, closely followed by the Cobrisol. It struck Fred then that it probably had been a flip of the Cobrisol's tail that halted Howard; but Howard wasn't complaining. He took up a stand just behind Wilma, breathing noisily.

The Cobrisol coiled up on Fred's left.

"It's an Icien. . . . Well, things could be worse—listen!"

Ruby clasped under his left arm, Fred listened. A number of Eyes were bobbing about excitedly in front of the porch. Suddenly, he heard footsteps.

They were heavy, slow, slapping steps, as if something were walking through mud along the side of the house. Fred turned to the edge of the porch where Howard had been pulling up plankings to find material for his still. A four-foot piece of heavy pipe lay beside the loose boards, and he picked that up just as Wilma and Howard uttered a gasp of renewed shock. . . .

Something—the Icien—was standing behind the south end of the porch.

"Ah!" it said in a deep voice, peering in at the group through the railings. "Here we all are!"

Fred stared at it speechlessly. It stood on two thick legs, and it had a round head where a head ought to be. It was at least seven feet tall, and seemed to be made of moist black leather—even the round, bulging eyes and the horny slit of a mouth were black. But the oddest thing about it was that, in addition, it appeared to have wrapped a long black cloak tightly around itself.

It marched on to the end of the porch and advanced towards the stairs, where it stopped.

"Are all the intelligent inhabitants of the Place assembled here?" the inhuman voice inquired.

Fred discovered that his knees were shaking uncontrollably. But nobody else seemed willing to answer.

"We're all here," he stated, in as steady a voice as he could manage. "What do you want?"

The Icien stared directly at him for a long moment. Then it addressed the group in general.

"Let this be understood first! Wherever an Icien goes, an Icien rules!" It paused. Fred decided not to dispute the statement just now. Neither did anyone else.

"Splendid!" The Icien sounded somewhat mollified. "Now, as all intelligent beings know," it went on, in a more conversational tone, "the Law of the Little Places states that a ruling Icien must never go hungry while another life-form is available to nourish it. . . ." The black cloak around it seemed to stir with a slow, writhing motion of its own. "I am hungry!" the Icien added, simply but pointedly.

Unconsciously, the humans on the porch had drawn a little closer together. The Cobrisol stayed where it was, motionless and watchful, while the monster's black eyes swiveled from one to the other of the petrified little group.

"The largest one, back there!" it decided shortly.

And with that, what had looked like a cloak unfolded and snapped out to either side of it. For a blurred, horrified second, Fred thought of giant sting-rays on an ocean bottom, of octopi— of demonish vampires! The broad, black flipper-arms the creature had held wrapped about it were lined with row on row of wet-toothed sucker-mouths. From tip to tip, they must have stretched almost fifteen feet.

Howard Cooney made a faint screeching noise and fainted dead away, collapsing limply to the porch..

"Ah!" rumbled the Icien, with apparent satisfaction. "The rest of you may now stand back—" It took a step forward, the arms sweeping around to reach out ahead of it. Then it stopped.

"I said," it repeated, on a note of angry surprise, "that you may now stand back!"

Ruby clacked her beak sharply; there was no other sound. Fred discovered he had half-raised the piece of pipe, twisting it back from his wrist like a one-handed batter. Wilma held the big skillet in front of her, grasping it determinedly in both hands. Her face wasn't white any more; it was flushed, and her lips were set. And the Cobrisol's neck was drawn back like that of a rattlesnake, its jaws suddenly gaping wide.

"What is this?" The Icien glanced at some of the Eyes floating nearby, as if seeking support. "Are you defying the Law?" it demanded.

No one answered; but Fred realized, in a rush of relief which left him almost weak enough to follow Howard's example, that the monster was licked! It withdrew its horrid flippers slowly, letting them trail on the ground, while it shifted its weight uncertainly from one thick leg to the other.

And then Ruby burst into a series of raucous, derisive sounds that made everyone start nervously, including the Icien. The Cobrisol closed its long jaws with a snap. The Icien snorted, wrapped its flipper-arms back about itself, turned and stalked off toward the apple orchard. Its feet were huge and flat like the flippers of a seal, Fred noticed, which seemed to account for the odd, floppy sounds it made with each step.

At the edge of the trees, it turned again.

"This matter is not settled!" it rumbled menacingly. "But for the time being, the stream back here and the trees are my personal area. You will enter it at your own risk!"

Its voice and appearance still made Fred's skin crawl. "We'll agree to that," he answered hoarsely. "But you'll leave that area again at *your* own risk!"

The Icien gave him, a final, silent stare before it moved on into the orchard.

They began to revive Howard Cooney. . . .

Oddly enough, Howard seemed more sullen than grateful when he woke up finally and realized the Icien was gone.

"If it hadn't been for my weak heart," he growled, "I'd have clobbered the devilish creature!"

"An excellent suggestion," the Cobrisol remarked approvingly. "You'll find it sitting in the trout stream, Cooney. . . ."

Howard grunted and changed the subject. Within an hour after their encounter with the new neighbor, all the Eyes had disappeared from the area, indicating that whoever was using them didn't expect anything of interest to happen now. But the hoots and robols were back in normal numbers.

Apparently, a crisis had been passed. The only thing remarkable about the next day was that the weather turned hot and dry. The night wasn't much of an improvement, and by noon of the day that followed, it looked as if they were in for a regular Earth-style heat wave.

Wondering whether this meant that summer was now on the Little Place's calendar, Fred rigged up a makeshift hammock on the front porch, which seemed to be the coolest spot around the house. While Wilma gratefully napped in the hammock and Ruby drooped in a corner with a pan of water near her half-open beak, he sat on the front steps putting an edge to their two largest kitchen knives. He'd fastened the knife-handles into longish pieces of piping the afternoon after the Icien showed up; they made quite formidable looking weapons.

But he wished they were all safely back home again.

Glancing up presently, he discovered the Cobrisol in the meadow, moving slowly toward the house. Howard Cooney hadn't been in sight for the past two hours, which was one of the reasons Fred was maintaining informal guard duty until Wilma woke up. There'd been some trouble with Howard the evening before, and he suspected the tramp was still in a sulky mood, which wouldn't be improved any by the heat.

Twice, on its way to the house, the Cobrisol reached up languidly to snap a low-fluttering hoot out of the air; and each time, Fred winced. He'd convinced Wilma—and nearly convinced himself—that the olive-brown hoots and the pinkish, hopping robols were merely mobile vegetables; but, he still didn't like the way they wriggled about hopefully inside the Cobrisol's elastic gullet, as if they were trying to poke their way out again.

"Wilma's sleeping," he cautioned the creature, as it came sliding up to the foot of the stairs.

"Fine," said the Cobrisol in a low, pensive voice. "I don't imagine you've made any progress in your plans to return to Earth?"

"Well, no. . . . Why?"

"It's unlikely that there is any way of doing it," the Cobrisol admitted. "Very unlikely. However, if you think of something, I'd appreciate it if you invited me to go along."

Surprised, Fred, said he'd be happy to do that. "I think you'd like it on a real farm," he added, a little doubtfully.

"Cobrisols are adaptable creatures," it assured him. "But there are limits!" It glanced indignantly up at their simmering source of heat and light overhead. "Do you realize, Fred, that there've been no Eyes around for nearly two full days? The One has simply gone away, leaving the temperature on high! It's inexcusable."

Fred hadn't considered the possibility that the heat-wave might be due to an oversight on the part of the supervisor. "In that case," he said hopefully, "he might be back any minute to turn it down, mightn't he?"

"He might," said the Cobrisol. "Even so, I feel wasted here! But one thing at a time. There's fresh trouble coming up, Fred."

"If it's from the Icien," Fred remarked, a trifle complacently, "I wouldn't worry." He held up one of his weapons. "These are Icien spears!"

The Cobrisol inspected the spears. "Very ingenious," it acknowledged. "However, am I right in assuming, Fred, that the procreational problem involving the Cooney individual has come into the open?"

Fred reddened again and glanced at the hammock. "Howard did make a pass at Wilma after dinner last night," he said then, lowering his voice a trifle more. "I told him off!" He had, as a matter of fact, picked up one of the spears he was working on and threatened to run Howard out into the Icien-haunted night. Howard had gone white and backed down hurriedly.

"Ah?" said the Cobrisol. "A pass?"

Fred explained about passes.

"The Cooney is certainly easily frightened by the threat of physical destruction," the Cobrisol remarked. "But a frightened being is dangerously unpredictable!"

It paused, significantly.

"What are you driving at?" Fred inquired.

"An hour or so ago," said the Cobrisol, "I saw Cooney stealing into that section of the apple orchard that extends behind the house. I found him presently engaged in conversation with the Icien"

"What?" Fred was stunned. "Why, Howard's scared to death of that thing!" he protested.

"I believe that fear of it was one of his motivations," the Cobrisol agreed. "His attitude was a propitiating one. Nevertheless, they have formed an alliance. The Cooney is to rule over all humans that are now in this Place or that may be transferred to it eventually, while he acknowledges the Icien as the supreme ruler of all beings here, and as his own superior. . . . It was decided that, as the first step in this program, Cooney is to devise a means whereby the Icien can come upon you unawares, Fred, and eat you!"

Fred didn't tell Wilma of Howard's gruesome plotting with the Icien. She wouldn't be able to conceal her feelings well enough; and the conclusion he'd come to with the Cobrisol was that Howard must not suspect that they knew what he had done. Now and then, looking at the man—who, since his meeting with the Icien, had assumed a conciliatory and even mildly jovial attitude with the Nieheims—he had to suppress twinges of a feeling akin to horror. It was like living under the same roof with a ghoul!

But one had to admit, he thought, that Howard Cooney was being consistent. He had figured out the system here, and he intended to make use of it, just as he had announced he would do. If it hadn't been for the Cobrisol's alertness, he probably would have gotten away with it. In spite of the heat, Fred shivered.

After another two days, the meadow and orchard looked as if they had passed through an extreme summer's drought on Earth. It didn't get *much* hotter; it simply wouldn't cool down again at all, and the Little Place seemed to have forgotten how to produce rain. In the middle of the third night, Fred was lying awake when the Cobrisol slid its rubbery snout up on the pillow, next to his ear, and murmured, "Awake, Fred?"

"Yes," he whispered. It must have come sliding in by the window, though he hadn't heard a sound.

"The kitchen," it muttered. Then it was gone again. Moving cautiously, Fred managed to get out of the bedroom without rousing either Wilma or Ruby and locked the door quietly behind him. He stood a moment in the almost pitch-black little hallway, grasping the larger of the two Icien spears. In the living room, Howard snored loudly and normally, as if he hadn't a thing on his conscience.

The Cobrisol was waiting beside the door that opened from the kitchen into the garden. That was the weak spot in the house. The windows were all too high and narrow for a creature of the Icien's build to enter, the front door was bolted and locked, and at night Fred kept the key under his pillow. But the back door was secured only by a bolt which Howard, if he wanted to, could simply slide back to let the monster come inside....

"The Icien left its pool in the stream a short while ago," the Cobrisol whispered. "It's prowling about the house now. Do you hear it?"

Fred did. There wasn't a breath of breeze in the hot, black night outside; and no matter how carefully the Icien might be placing its great, awkward feet, the back garden was full of rustlings and creakings as it tramped about slowly in the drying vegetation. Presently, it came up to one of the kitchen windows and remained still for a while, apparently trying to peer inside. Fred couldn't even make out its silhouette against the darkness; but after a few seconds, an oily, alien smell reached his nostrils, and his hair went stiff at the roots....

Then it moved off slowly along the side of the house.

❊   ❊   ❊

"Going to wake up Cooney now." The Cobrisol's voice was hardly more than a breath of sound in the dark.

This was how they had expected it would happen; but now that the moment was here, Fred couldn't believe that Howard was going to go through with the plan. Aside from everything else, it would be as stupid as forming a partnership with a man-eating tiger! There came two faint thumps—presumably the Icien's flipper slapping cautiously against the frame of the living room window. Howard's snoring was cut off by a startled exclamation. Then there was dead silence. After what seemed a long time, Fred heard the Icien return along the outside of the house. It stopped in front of the back door and stayed there. It wasn't until then that he realized Howard already had entered the kitchen. There was a sound of shallow, rapid breathing hardly six feet away from him.

For a time, the tramp simply seemed to stand there, as motionless as the Icien outside the door. Finally, he took a deep, sighing breath, and moved forward again. As Cooney's hand touched the door, groping for the bolt, Fred dropped his spear and flung both arms around him, pinning his arms to his sides and dragging him backwards.

Howard gasped and went heavily to the floor. Fred guessed that the Cobrisol had tripped him up and flung itself across his legs, He wasn't trying to struggle.

"Be quiet or we'll kill you!" he breathed hastily. Then they waited. Howard kept quiet.

What the Icien made of the brief commotion inside the kitchen and the following silence was anybody's guess. It remained where it was for perhaps another ten seconds. Then they heard it move unhurriedly off through the garden and back to the orchard again.

In the bedroom, Ruby started clucking concernedly. . . .

"Now that his criminal purpose has been amply demonstrated," the Cobrisol argued, "the neat and reasonable solution would be for me to swallow Cooney." It eyed Howard appraisingly. "I'm quite distensible enough for the purpose, I think. If we stun him first, the whole affair will be over, in less than ten minutes—"

Howard, lying on the floor, tied hand and foot, burst into horrified sobs.

"We're not going to hurt you," Fred assured him quickly. He wasn't feeling too sorry for Howard at the moment, but Wilma's face had gone white at the Cobrisol's unpleasant suggestion. "But we're not giving you a chance to try any more tricks on us either. You're really in stir now, Howard!"

He explained to Wilma that they were going to use the bedroom as a temporary jail for Howard, since it was the only room in the house with a separate key.

"I know you were only joking," she told the Cobrisol. "But I wish you wouldn't talk about swallowing anybody again!"

"The jest was in bad taste," the Cobrisol admitted penitently. It winked a green, unrepentant eye at Fred. "Almost a pun, eh, Fred?"

In the end, they tied Howard up a little more comfortably and took turns watching him till morning. Then Fred cleared out the bedroom, nailed heavy boards across the window, leaving slits for air and light, and locked the prisoner inside.

He'd just finished with that when the Cobrisol called him into the back garden.

"The other half of our criminal population is behaving in an odd fashion," the creature announced. "I wish you'd come along and help me decide why it's digging holes in the streambed. . . ."

"Digging holes?" Fred hesitated. "It doesn't sound dangerous," he pointed out.

"Anything you don't understand can be dangerous!" the Cobrisol remarked sententiously. "Better come along, Fred."

Fred sighed and told Wilma to call him back if Howard showed any inclination to try to break out of the bedroom. From the edge of the orchard, they heard the Icien splashing around vigorously in one of the pools of the shrunken stream; and presently they were lying on top of the bank, peering cautiously down at it. Using its feet and flipper-tips, it was making clumsy but persistent efforts to scoop out a deep hole in the submerged mud.

"Iciens," whispered the Cobrisol, "are so rarely brought into contact with more civilized species that not much is known of their habits. Can you suggest a purpose for this activity, Fred?"

"Think it could be trying to dig its way out of the Little Place?" Fred whispered back.

"No. It's not that stupid."

"Well," Fred whispered, "I read about fish once, or it could have been frogs—those are Earth animals—that dig themselves into the mud of a creek that's drying out, and sleep there until it fills up with water again."

The Cobrisol agreed that it was a possibility. "Though it's already dug a number of holes and covered them again. . . ."

"Might still be looking for a soft spot," Fred suggested.

At that moment, they heard Wilma call Fred's name once, in a high, frightened voice.

Howard Cooney was waiting for them outside the kitchen door. Wilma stood in front of him, one arm twisted up behind her back, while Howard held the point of a small steak knife against the side of her neck. The two Icien spears leaned against the wall beside him.

"Slow to a walk!" he shouted in a hoarse, ragged voice, as they came in sight.

They slowed. The Cobrisol gliding beside him, Fred walked stiffly as far as the center of the garden, where Howard ordered him to stop again. Wilma's chin was trembling.

"I'm sorry, Fred!" she gasped suddenly. "I let him trick me!"

Howard jerked at her wrist. "Keep your mouth shut!" His eyes looked hot and crazy, and the side of his face kept twitching as he grinned at Fred.

"I'm in charge now, Buster!" he announced. "See how you like it!"

"What do you want me to do?" Fred kept his voice carefully even and didn't look at Wilma.

"The snake," said Howard, "doesn't come any closer, or this knife goes right in! Understand?"

"Certainly, I understand," said the Cobrisol. It began to curl up slowly into its usual resting position. "And, of course, I shall come no closer, Cooney. As you say, you're in charge now. . . ."

Howard ignored it. He jerked his head at the door. "You, Buster—you go right through the kitchen and into the bedroom! Go to the other side of the bedroom and look at the wall. We'll come along behind you, and I'll lock you in. Get it?"

Crazy or not, he had it figured out. Walking slowly toward the door, Fred couldn't think of a thing he could do fast enough to keep that knife from going through Wilma's throat. And once he was locked in—

Wilma's eyes shifted suddenly past him. "*Ruby!*" she screamed. "*Sic him!*"

Fred was almost as shocked as Howard, as the pheasant, her feathers on end, came half-running, half-flying past him, went up like a rocket and whirred straight at Howard's face.

Howard screeched like a woman, dodged and slashed wildly and futilely at Ruby. Wilma twisted free of his grasp and threw herself to the ground as Fred flung himself forwards.

He went headlong over the Cobrisol, which was darting in from the side with the same purpose in mind, and rolled almost to Howard's feet. For a moment, the tramp's white, unshaven face seemed to hang in the air directly above him, glaring down at him; and light flashed from the edge of the knife. It was another wild swipe, and it missed Fred by niches. Then Howard had jumped back into the kitchen and slammed the door behind him.

By the time they got around to the front of the house, Cooney was racing down the meadow like a rabbit, heading for the orchard. He dodged in among the trees and turned toward the trout stream.

Fred stopped. "We're not going to follow him there just now!" he panted. He glanced down at the spear he'd grabbed up before charging off in pursuit, and wondered briefly what he would have done with it if they'd caught up with Howard. The Little Place seemed to bring out the more violent side in everybody's nature.

"Come on," he said, a little shaken by the thought. "Let's get back to Wilma—"

"A moment, Fred," The Cobrisol had lifted its head off the ground, peering after Howard. "Ah!"

A harsh, furious roar reached them suddenly from the orchard, mingled with a human yell of fright and dismay. Howard Cooney came scampering out into the meadow again, glancing back over his shoulder. Close behind him lumbered the black, clumsy form of the Icien, its flipper-arms outstretched. . . .

"The confederates," murmured the Cobrisol, "are no longer in complete accord. As I suspected! Come on, Fred!"

It darted down into the meadow in its swift, weaving snake-gait. Fred ran after it, a little surprised by its sudden solicitude for Howard.

Everything happened very quickly then.

The Icien, to Fred's relief, stopped near the edge of the orchard when it saw them coming. The Cobrisol, well ahead of Fred, called suddenly, "Cooney! Wait!"

Howard looked round and saw two other deadly enemies hurrying toward him, apparently cutting off his escape from the Icien. He gave a scream of wild terror, turned and plunged toward the mirror-barrier.

A warning yell was gathering in Fred's throat, but he didn't have time to utter it. Howard reached the barrier and simply went on into it. Except that there wasn't the slightest ripple, he might have vanished in the same way beneath the surface of a quietly gleaming lake of quicksilver.

The Cobrisol turned and came gliding back to Fred.

"The barrier is still soft," it remarked. "Well, that's the end of Cooney."

Fred stared down at it, a little dazed. He was almost certain now that it had deliberately chased Howard into the barrier. "Is there anything we can do?" The Cobrisol curled up comfortably in the rustling dead grass. The green eyes stared blandly up at him far a moment.

"No," it said. "There is nothing we can do. But in a while there may be something to see, and I think you should see it, Fred. Why don't you go back to Wilma? I'll call you when it happens."

Fred glanced at the tall, shining thing that had silently swallowed up a man. It was a very hot morning, but for a moment he felt chilled.

He turned round and went back to Wilma.

What had occurred, according to Wilma, was that, shortly after Fred left the house, Howard Cooney began to groan loudly behind the bedroom door. When Wilma asked him what was wrong, he gasped something about his heart and groaned some more. Then there was a heavy thump inside the room, as if he'd fallen down; and, after that, silence.

Remembering he'd said he had a bad heart, Wilma hurriedly unlocked the door, without stopping to think. And Howard, of course, was waiting behind the door and simply grabbed her.

Wilma looked too remorseful for Fred to make any obvious comments. After all, he thought, he hadn't married her because of anything very remarkable about her brains, and Howard was—or had been—a pretty good actor. He decided not to tell her just yet what had happened to Howard; and when he heard the Cobrisol call him, he went out alone.

He's trying to get out now," the Cobrisol told him. "Take a good look, Fred. If you ever go Outside, you'll know why you don't want to get lost there, like he did!"

Fred stared apprehensively at the barrier which was changing as he looked at it. Now it no longer reflected the meadow and the house; its strange surface had became like a sheet of milky glass, stretching up into the artificial sky, and glowing as if from a pale light behind it. There was also a pattern of shifting and sliding colors inside it, which now coalesced suddenly into the vague outlines of Howard Cooney's shape. Only the shape looked about forty feet tall! It stood half turned away from them, in an attitude as if Howard were listening or watching.

"He's got everything aroused out there," said the Cobrisol, "and he's begun to realize it. . . ."

Fred's mouth felt suddenly dry. "Listen," he began, "couldn't we—that is, couldn't I—"

"No," said the Cobrisol. "You couldn't! If you went Outside, you still couldn't find Cooney. And," it added cryptically, "even if I told you how to get back, they're alert now and they'd get you before you could escape—"

Fred swallowed. "Who are *they*?"

"Nobody knows," said the Cobrisol. "There are a number of theories—rank superstition, for the most part— Watch it, Fred! I think they've found him. . . ."

The shape inside the barrier had begun to move jerkily as if it were running in short sprints, first in one direction, then in another. Its size and proportions also changed constantly, and for a few seconds Howard Cooney's fear-crazed face filled the whole barrier, his eyes staring out into the Little Place.

Then the face vanished, and there were many tiny figures of Cooney scampering about in the barrier.

Then he was no longer scampering, but crawling on hands and knees.

"They have him now," the Cobrisol whispered.

There was only a single large figure left, lying face down inside the barrier, and to Fred it seemed to be slowing melting away. As it dwindled, the odd inner light of the barrier also dimmed, until it suddenly went out. A few seconds later, the milkiness vanished from it, and it had become a mirror-barrier again.

That appeared to be the end of it.

What actually had happened to Howard Cooney was something the Cobrisol was either unwilling or unable to explain to Fred. He didn't question it too persistently. He had an uneasy feeling that he wouldn't really like to know. . . .

The morning the kitchen faucets stopped delivering water from their unknown source of supply wasn't noticeably hotter than the preceding few mornings had been. But when Wilma called from the kitchen to complain of the trouble, Fred was appalled. He didn't dare finish the thought that leaped into his mind; he shut it away, and went hurriedly into the bathroom without replying to Wilma.

A thin, warm trickle ran from the tub faucet there, and that was all.

He shut it off at once, afraid of wasting a single drop, and started for the kitchen. Wilma met him in the hall.

"Fred," she repeated, "the water—"

"I know," he said briskly. "We'll take all the pots and pans we have and fill them with water from the bathtub. It's still running there, but not very strong. They might turn it on again any moment, of course, but we want to be sure. . . ."

He'd felt he was being quite casual about it, but as he stopped talking, something flickered in Wilma's eyes; and he knew they were both thinking the same thought.

She reached out, suddenly and squeezed his hand. "It's too hot to kiss you, but I love you, Freddy! Yes, let's fill the pots and pans—"

"Or you do that, while I go talk to the Cobrisol," Fred said. He added reassuringly, "The Cobrisol's had a lot of experience with these Places, you know. It'll know just what to do."

What he had in mind, however, when he left Wilma in charge of the pots and pans in the bathroom, picked up a spear and went quietly outdoors, wasn't conversation with the Cobrisol. There had been no reason to dispute the Icien's appropriation of the entire trout stream; but now a more equitable distribution of the water rights in the Little Place seemed to be in order.

If it hadn't been so breathlessly still, the scene around the house might have been an artistic reproduction of the worst section of the Dust Bowl—or it could have been one of the upper and milder levels of hell, Fred thought. He looked around automatically to see if the Eyes had returned—they hadn't—and instead caught sight of the Cobrisol and the Icien down near the mirror-barrier, at the orchard's edge.

He stopped short in surprise. So far as he could see at that distance, the two creatures were engaged in a serious but not unfriendly discussion. There was about twenty-five feet of space between them, which was probably as close as the Cobrisol, fast as it was, cared to get to the Icien. But it was coiled up in apparent unconcern.

He walked slowly down the dried-out meadow toward them. As he approached, both turned to look at him.

"Fred," said the Cobrisol, "the Icien reports there isn't even a drop of moist mud left in the trout stream this morning."

The Icien stared balefully at Fred and said nothing; but he realized a truce had been declared to cope with the emergency. Somewhat self-consciously, he grounded the spear—it was useless now—and told them about the kitchen faucets. "What can we do about it? In this heat—"

"In this heat, and without water," the Cobrisol agreed soberly, "none of us will be alive very many hours from now! Unless—"

"Fred!" Wilma's call reached them faintly from the porch.

He turned, with a sinking feeling in his chest. "Yes?"

"The—bathtub—just—quit!" Her distant, small face looked white and strained.

Suddenly, Fred was extraordinarily thirsty. "It's all right, honey!" he shouted back. "We're going to fix it!" She hesitated a moment, and then went back into the house. He turned to the other two. "We *can* fix it, can't we?" he pleaded.

"There is a way, of course," the Icien rumbled. "But—" It shrugged its black leather shoulders discouragedly.

"We've been discussing it," said the Cobrisol. "The fact is, Fred, that the only one who can remedy this situation is yourself. And, undoubtedly, the attempt would involve extreme risk for you personally. . . ."

Fred guessed it then. "One of us has to go Outside to fix it; and neither of you can do it. Is that it?"

The two creatures stared at him.

"That's it," the Cobrisol agreed reluctantly. "I can't explain, just now, why it would be impossible for either of us to go Outside but between us we can tell you exactly what to do there. The risk, of course, is that what happened to Cooney will also happen to you. But if you make no mistakes—"

"He'll panic," the Icien growled darkly. "They all do!"

"No," said the Cobrisol. "It's been done before, Fred. But not very often."

Fred sighed and wiped a film of dirty sweat off his forehead with a hand that shook a little, but not too much. It seemed to him they were making a great deal of conversation about something that couldn't be helped!

"Dying of thirst," he pointed out reasonably, "gets to be pretty dangerous, too! What am I supposed to do?"

❀   ❀   ❀

As soon as he'd stepped Outside, he realized that, though the Cobrisol and the Icien had warned him of this particular problem, his real difficulty would be to remember exactly what he was supposed to do.

Basically, it was very simple— but he didn't want to do it!

Irrelevant thought-pictures were streaming through his mind. Wilma's white, tear-stained face as he'd seen it last, just a moment ago—but that moment was darting off into the past behind him as if a week passed with every heart-beat here. Clusters of bright, flickering memory-scenes of their farm, back home on Earth, swirled next through his head. . . . The reason for this kind of disturbance, the two creatures had told him, was that he didn't want to know what was going on Outside.

It was too different. Different enough, if he hadn't been warned, to hold him here shocked and stunned, trying to blind himself mentally to the strangeness around him, until it was too late—

That thought frightened Fred enough to drive the little escape-pictures out of his head as if a sudden gust of wind had swept them up and away together. He'd just recalled that he had very little time here!

He looked around.

It wasn't, he thought, really as bad as he'd expected. He got the instant impression—partly, at least, because of what he'd been told—that he was standing in the middle of the audible thought-currents of a huge mechanical mind. Not audible, exactly; the currents seemed to be tugging at him or pulsing rhythmically through and about him, in all directions. Most of them, as the Cobrisol had explained, appeared to be connected in some way or another with the upkeep of the Little Place. But there were others, darkly drifting things or very deep sounds—it was hard to distinguish really just what they *were* most like—that were completely and terrifyingly incomprehensible to Fred. . . .

Some of those were the dangerous ones. He wasn't to give them any attention. He waited.

The moment none of those dark, monstrous waves seemed to be passing anywhere near him, he quickly verbalized the first of the three things they had told him to think here:

"The Little Place has become too dry for the life-forms in it! There should be water and rain again in the Little Place!"

He held the thought, picturing rain coming down in, sheets all over the Little Place, the trout stream running full again, and water pouring freely from all the faucets in the house. Then he let the pictures and the thoughts go away from him. For an instant, there seemed to be a tiny shifting, a brief eddy of disturbance passing through all the mental flows about him.

Hurriedly, he formed the second thought:

"The temperature has become too high for the life-forms in the Little Place! The temperature must be adjusted to normal living requirements!"

This time, he'd barely finished the thought before it seemed to be plucked out of his mind by a sudden agitated swirling in the living currents about him. Then he had a sense of darkening, and something huge and deadly and invisible went flowing closely past, trailing behind it a fluttering apparition that brought a sound-less scream of terror into Fred's throat. It was a shape that looked exactly as Howard Cooney had looked in life, except that it was no thicker than a sheet of paper! For an instant, as Howard's eyes glared sightlessly in his direction, he had the impression that somewhere far overhead Howard had called his name. Then the thing that brought darkness with it and the fluttering shape were gone.

The other disturbances continued. In some way, the outside was growing aware of his presence and beginning to look for him.

The next order he hadn't discussed with the others, since he was certain they would have tried to talk him out of giving

"The life-forms in the Little Place that were taken away from Earth must be returned unharmed to Earth!"

Hastily, thinking of the Cobrisol, he added:

"Including any other life-forms that would like to come along except Iciens!"

Something like a long crash of thunder went shaking all through him—apparently, that last set of instructions had upset the entire Outside!

Fred didn't bother to think out the final thought. He shouted with all his strength: "And I should *now* be standing on the other side of the mirror-barrier inside the Little Place!"

Instantly, he was there. Rain was slamming down in sheets all about him, like an Earthly cloud-burst, as Wilma, laughing and crying, grabbed him by an arm. Hand in hand, they ran through the soaking meadow toward the house, the Cobrisol streaking ahead of them. The Icien was nowhere in sight.

❊　　　❊　　　❊

I didn't say exactly how *much* rain and water," Fred admitted. They had discovered they couldn't turn the faucets off now! It didn't matter much, since the surplus water vanished down through the drains as usual. But, two hours after Fred's return to the Little Place, the cloud-burst outdoors was continuing in full strength.

The Cobrisol lay in a corner of the kitchen, its teeth chattering, as if it were chilled. Wilma had shoved blankets under it and piled more blankets on top, and they had lit the stove. Actually the temperature had dropped only to the equivalent of a rather warm, rainy spring day on Earth.

"I should have cautioned you," the creature remarked, between fits of chattering, "to limit your order for water. You had no way of knowing that Cobrisols react unfavorably to excessive atmospheric moisture. . . ."

"This capsulating you mentioned," Wilma inquired concernedly, "does it hurt?"

"Not at all, Wilma," the Cobrisol assured her. "I shall simply shrivel up rather suddenly—it's a completely automatic process, you see, and not under my control—and form a hard shell around myself. As soon as things dry out sufficiently, the shell splits, and there I am again!"

Fred had offered to go back Outside and rephrase the order concerning the water, but he was rather relieved when everyone told him not to be foolish. At worst, the Cobrisol would simply go dormant for a while, and the disturbance caused by his visit obviously hadn't settled out yet.

From time to time, strange lights went gliding about erratically inside the mirror-barrier, as if the Little Place's mechanical wardens were persisting in their search for the intruder. Occasional faint tremors passed through the foundations of the house, and there were intermittent rumblings in the air, which might have been simulated Earth-thunder, to accompany the rain.

"There's a good chance," the Cobrisol explained, "that all this commotion may return the One's attention to the Little Place, in which case we can expect normal weather conditions to be reestablished promptly. Otherwise—well, I'm sure you agree with me now, Fred, that only an absolute emergency would justify going Outside again."

And, of course, Fred did agree. He hadn't gone into specific details concerning his experience there, since he knew it would be disturbing to Wilma. And neither had he mentioned his order to get them transferred back to Earth—almost anything seemed justified to get away from a place where your future depended entirely on somebody else's whims—but he was guiltily certain that that was the cause of most of the uproar.

Now and then they looked out from a window to see if the Eyes had reappeared; but none had. Towards evening, Fred observed the Icien wandering about the lower end of the meadow, trailing its flipper-arms through rivulets of water and stopping now and then to stare up into the streaming sky, as if it enjoyed getting thoroughly soaked. Unlike the Cobrisol, it was, of course, an aquatic sort of creature to begin with.

Just as he went to sleep that eight, Fred almost managed to convince himself that when he next woke up, he would discover they were all safely back on Earth. However, when he did awaken, he knew instantly the Outside hadn't acted upon that order. They were still in the Little Place—and it was raining harder than ever.

The Cobrisol had elected to sleep in the kitchen, but it wasn't lying on the chair before the stove where they had left it. Fred was wondering where it had crawled to, when another thought struck him. Expectantly, he separated the blankets on the chair.

The shell was lying there, a brown, smooth, egg-shaped shell— but hardly bigger than a healthy goose-egg. It was difficult to imagine the Cobrisol shrinking itself down to that size; but it couldn't be anything else. Feeling as if he were handling an urn containing the remains of a friend, Fred carried the shell carefully into the bedroom and laid it down on the bed.

"He said it was practically impossible to damage these shells," he reminded Wilma. "But it might better not to let Ruby peck at it."

"I'll watch her," Wilma promised, big-eyed. From the way she kept staring at the shell, Fred gathered that Wilma, too, felt as if the Cobrisol somehow had passed away, even if it was only a temporary arrangement.

"He'll probably be hatching again pretty soon," he said briskly. "I'll go check on the weather now. . . ."

He opened the front porch door and stopped there, appalled. A sheet of water covered the entire meadow and lapped up to within forty feet of the house! In the orchard, half the trees were submerged. Considering the slope of the ground, the water would be at least ten yards deep where it stood against the mirror-barrier. And the rain still drummed down furiously upon it.

He checked his first pulse to call Wilma. News as bad as that could wait a little. The barrier stood there, placidly mirroring the scene of the flood. Except for eerie rumbling sounds that still echoed in the upper air, the Outside seemed to be back to normal.

So, if he swam across now, Fred thought, before it rose any higher—

The order would be a quite simple one: "Reduce rainfall and water-level to meet the normal requirements of the life-forms within the Little Place."

And if he did it immediately, Wilma wouldn't have a chance to get all upset about it.

Of course, if he got caught Outside this time—

She and Ruby would be just as badly off one way as the other, he decided. He wasn't going to get caught! It would only take him a few minutes. . . .

He closed the porch door quietly behind him, stripped hurriedly to his shorts and started down towards the water, mentally rehearsing the order he would give, to fix it firmly in his mind. Intent on that, he almost overlooked the slow, heavy swirling of the water surface to his left as he began to wade out. A big fish, a section of his mind reported absently, had come up out of deep water into the shallows, turned sharply and gone out again—

He stopped short, feeling a sudden burst of icy pricklings all over him. A fish? There weren't any fish here!

He turned, slipping and almost stumbling on the submerged grass, and plunged back toward the higher ground. There was a sudden tremendous splash just behind him, and a surge of water round his knees. Then he was on solid ground; he ran on a few yards and slowed, looking back.

The Icien hadn't tried to follow him out of the water. It stood upright, black and dripping, in the rain-whipped shallows, probably furious at having missed its chance at him.

They stared silently at each other. He might have guessed it, Fred thought, looking at the great flat flipper-arms. The first time he'd seen it, it had reminded him of a huge stingray. It was an aquatic creature by choice, and this flood suited it perfectly.

And it was intelligent enough to know why he would want to swim back to the mirror-barrier.

He thought of the speed with which it had come driving after him, and knew that even with his spears he didn't have a chance against that kind of creature in deep water.

The Icien knew it, too. But it might expect him to make a final desperate attempt before the water came lapping into the house....

Fred walked back to the porch and pulled his clothes on again. When he looked round before going inside, the Icien vanished.

Less than three minutes later, Fred stepped quietly out the back door, carrying his spear. He heard Wilma lock and bolt the door behind him as he splashed carefully through the big puddles in the garden. Then he was trotting up the rain-drenched rising ground behind the house towards a wall of misty nothingness a few hundred yards away.

He wished the Cobrisol hadn't been obliged to capsulate itself so quickly; he could have used that knowledgeable creature's advice just now. But it had mentioned that there were a number of soft spots in the barriers around the Little Place. All he had to do was to find one that the rising flood hadn't made inaccessible, step through it, and give one quick order to the huge mechanical mind that was the outside.

That was the way he had explained it to Wilma. He had a notion the Icien wouldn't attempt to stop him outside the water, even if it knew what he was up, to. Spear in hand and in his own element, he didn't intend to be stopped by it, anyway.

He had covered half the distance between the house and the nearest barrier when a new inhabitant of the Little Place stood up unhurriedly behind a rock twenty yards ahead of him, blocking his advance.

Fred stopped, startled. For a moment, he had thought it was the Icien. But then he saw it was much closer than he had thought and quite small, hardly four feet high; though in every other respect it was very similar to the black monster. It spread its flipper-arms wide, opened a black gash of a mouth and snarled at him, fearless and threatening.

He thought: *It's a young one!*

The Icien had started to breed....

Holding the spear in both hands, Fred walked rapidly towards it. Iciens at any age appeared to be irreconcilably hostile, and he didn't care to wait until the big one came along to join the dispute. If it didn't get out of his way—

At the last moment, with a hiss of fury, the Icien cub waddled aside. Fred stepped cautiously past it and stopped again.

❀   ❀   ❀

An army of the little horrors seemed to be rising up in front of him! They sprouted into view behind boulders and bushes, and came hurrying in from right and left. There was a burst of ugly, hoarse Icien voices, which sounded very much like a summons to their awesome parent.

For a second or two, Fred was chiefly bewildered. Where had that horde arrived from so suddenly? Then a memory of the big Icien, scooping out holes in the mud of the half-dried trout stream, flashed up; it must have been sowing its brood then, in some strange, unearthly fashion. Obviously their growth rate simply wasn't that of Earth creatures.

He half turned and speared the first one as its flipper-tip gripped his leg. The blade sank into its body, and it snarled hideously, striking at him while it died. He pulled out the spear and slashed at another which had rushed in but stopped now, just out of reach.

Three had moved in behind him, apparently with the intention of cutting off his retreat to the house. But he was still headed for the barrier. He dodged to the left and turned uphill again; another line of them confronted him there!

As Fred hesitated, he heard Wilma cry out to him. He glanced back and saw. she had come out of the kitchen, carrying the other spear and that the big Icien was striding ponderously along the side of the house, on its way up from the flooded meadow. . . .

He turned back.

He had to spear two more of the ugly young before he got down to the garden; and the second of the two clung howling and dying to the spear-shaft. He dropped the spear, bundled Wilma into the kitchen and slammed and bolted the door almost in the big Icien's face. Seconds later, the black pack was roaring and banging against the outside wall. A flipper slapped and tore at the window-screen, and he jabbed at it with the tip of Wilma's spear until it vanished.

Wilma was shouting in his ear. "What?" he yelled dazedly.

"The Eyes!" she shouted. "They're back!"

"The Eyes?" Then he saw she was pointing up out the window into the rain.

More than a dozen of the odd shiny gadgets drifted there in the air. As Fred stared, a huge one—almost ten feet across—sailed slowly and majestically past the window. The roaring outside the house stopped suddenly, and there were splashing sounds every-where from the garden, as if the Icien and its brood were departing in great haste.

But the thundering racket in the upper air was growing louder by the second—and changing now in a manner Fred couldn't immediately define. He stood listening, and suddenly a wild notion came to him. He turned to Wilma.

"Quick! Get into the bedroom!"

"The bedroom?" Shy looked startled. "Why?"

"Don't ask!" He hustled her down the hall ahead of him. Ruby was screeching her head off behind the closed door. "Grab Ruby—make her shut up! I'll be right back."

Recklessly, he tore open the front door and looked out. Young Iciens were still streaming past on either side of the house, hurrying awkwardly to the water's edge and plunging in. The big Eye—or another one like it—was stationed in front of the porch now, turning slowly as if anxious to take in everything. For a moment, it seemed to Fred that it was focusing itself directly on him. . . .

He closed the door and hurried back into the bedroom. Wilma was sitting on the bed with Ruby in her lap and the shell of the Cobrisol under one hand. He sat down beside her.

"What do we do now, Fred?"

"We just wait!" He was trembling with exhaustion and excitement.

"Those noises—" she said.

"Yes?"

"It sounds to me," Wilma told him wonderingly, "exactly like two people were having themselves a big fight next door!"

"Or up in the attic," Fred nodded. "And it sounds even more like one person is being told off good by another one, doesn't it?"

"By a much bigger one!" Wilma agreed. She was watching him shrewdly. "You know something you haven't told me yet. What's going to happen?"

"I'm not sure," Fred admitted. "But I think in a minute or two—"

The world suddenly went black.

It was still black when Fred found he was thinking again. He decided he must have been unconscious for some while, because he felt stiff all over, Now he was lying on his back on something hard and lumpy and warm. Wilma's head, he discovered next, was pillowed on his arm, and she was breathing normally. Somewhere near the top of his head, Ruby clucked away irritably as she tended to do when she was half awake.

"Wilma?" he whispered.

"Yes, Fred?" she said sleepily. And then, "Where are we? It's awfully dark here!"

He was wondering himself. "It'll probably get light soon," he said soothingly. Wilma was sitting up, and now she gave an exclamation of surprise.

"We're outdoors somewhere, Fred! This is grass we're lying on—"

"It was magnificently done!" another voice remarked, startlingly close to Fred's ear. It was a small, rather squeaky voice, but it seemed familiar.

"Who was that?" Wilma inquired nervously.

"I think," said Fred, "it's the Cobrisol." He groped about cautiously and found the shell lying next to his head. It appeared to be cracked down the long side, and something was stirring inside it. "Are you uncapsulating again?" he inquired.

"Correct," said the Cobrisol. "But allow me to continue my congratulations, Fred. You appear to have resolved successfully a situation that had baffled even a Cobrisol! Need I say more?"

"I guess not," said Fred. "Thanks—"

"Wilma," the Cobrisol resumed, "you seem concerned about this darkness—"

"I'm glad you're back, Cobrisol!" she told it.

"Thank you," said the creature. "As I was about to explain, the appearance of darkness about us is a common phenomenon of transfer. Nothing to worry about! And—ah!"

They all cried out together, a chorus of startled and expectant voices. Around them, like black curtains whisking aside, like black smoke dispelled by a blower, the darkness shifted and vanished. Yellow sunlight blazed down on them, and the two humans threw up their hands to shield their eyes.

Then they lowered them again. It was, after all, no brighter than was normal for a clear summer day. They were sitting at the top of a sloping green meadow. They looked out over it, blinking. . . .

"Why!" Wilma said, in a small, awed voice. "Why, Fred! We're home!"

Then she burst into tears.

Some hours later, sitting on the front porch of the farm house—the *real* front porch of the *real* farm house—Fred remarked, "There's one thing I just don't get."

"What's that, Fred?" The Cobrisol lifted its head inquiringly out of the hammock. It was about the size of a healthy rattlesnake by now and accepting a sandwich or two from Wilma every half hour.

Fred hesitated and then told the Cobrisol quietly about the gruesome, fluttering thing he'd seen Outside that looked like Cooney.

"There are various theories about what happens to those who get lost Outside," the Cobrisol said thoughtfully. "There is no reason to provide you with additional material for nightmares, so I won't tell you what I think you saw. But it was the fact that the Icien and I were acquainted with some of those theories that made it quite impossible for either of us to do what you did."

It paused. "Otherwise, everything seems clear enough now. The One who collected you and Wilma and Ruby and the Cooney was obviously as immature as I suspected. He had no right to do it. Your interference with the mechanisms of the Outside created enough disturbance to attract the attention of a mature One, who then chastised the offender and returned you to Earth where you belonged—"

The Cobrisol sniffed the air greedily. "That's another bacon-and-egg sandwich Wilma is fixing!" it remarked with appreciation. "Yes, I'm sure I'll like it on Earth, Fred. But your hypothesis that my shell came along by accident is highly debatable. For one thing, you've noticed, of course, that we have retained the ability to understand each other's speech-forms—which, I gather, is not the rule among different species on Earth."

"Well—" The fact had escaped Fred's attention till now. "That could be an accident," he pointed out. "They just forgot to switch it off, or whatever they do."

"Possibly," the Cobrisol acknowledged. "I believe, however, that having become aware of our cooperative efforts in the Little Place, the mature One decided to utilize the special talents of a Cobrisol in whatever Project is being conducted on Earth. Had you thought of going into politics, Fred?"

Fred chuckled. "No! And I don't blame you for not being able to get rid of the feeling you're still in some Place or other. But this is Earth and nobody else has any Projects here! You'll realize all that, by and by."

"No doubt," said the Cobrisol. "What's that passing way up high above the apple orchard, Fred?"

Fred looked, and leaped excitedly out of his chair. "Hey, Wilma! Come quick!" he shouted. "No—it's gone now! Boy, they *are* fast. . . ."

Then his voice trailed off, and he felt his face go pale, as he turned to stare at the Cobrisol.

"A flying saucer," he muttered.

"Oh?" said the Cobrisol. "Is that what they call the Eyes here, Fred?"

Summer Guests
· · · · · · · · · · · · · · · ·

ALL THROUGH THAT Saturday night, rain drummed down mercilessly and unseasonably on Sweetwater Beach. Thunder pealed and lightning flared. In between, Mel Armstrong heard the steady boom of the Pacific surf not a block from his snug little duplex apartment. Mel didn't mind any of it. He was in bed, slightly smacked and wholly comfortable. He dozed, and now and then woke up far enough to listen admiringly to the racket.

At nine A.M., when he opened his eyes once more, he discovered the room was full of summer sunshine. Beyond his window gleamed a cloudless sky, and only the occasional gusts of wind indicated there had been anything like a storm during the night.

An exceptionally beautiful Sunday morning—made more beautiful, perhaps, by the fact that it marked the beginning of Mel Armstrong's annual two-week paid vacation. Mel was a salesman for Marty's Fine Liquors, a wholesale house. He was twenty-eight and in fairly good shape, but his job bored him. This morning, for the first time in months, he was fully aware of that. Perhaps it was the weather. At any rate, he had a sense, almost a premonition, of new and exciting events approaching him rapidly. Events that would break down the boundaries of his present humdrum existence and pitch him into the life of romantic adventure that, somehow, he seemed to have missed so far . . .

Recognizing this as a daydream, but unwilling to give it up completely, Mel breakfasted unhurriedly in his pajamas. Then, struck by a sudden, down-to-earth suspicion, he stuck his head out of his living room window.

As he'd guessed, there were other reminders of the storm in the narrow courtyard before the window. Branches and assorted litter had blown in, including at least one soggily dismembered Sunday paper. The low rent he paid for his ground-floor apartment in the Oceanview Courts was based on an understanding with the proprietor that he and the upstairs occupant of the duplex would keep the court clean. The other five duplexes that fronted on the court were bulging with vacationing visitors from the city, which made it a real chore in summer.

Unfortunately he couldn't count on his upstairs neighbor, a weird though rather amiable young character who called herself Maria de Guesgne. Maria went in for painting abstractions, constructing mobiles, and discussing the works of Madame Blavatsky. She avoided the indignity of manual toil.

Mel made himself decent by exchanging his pajamas for swimming trunks. Then he got a couple of brooms and a hose out of a garage back of the court and went to work.

He'd cleared the courtyard by the time the first of the seasonal guests began to show up in their doorways, and went on to inspect another, narrower court behind his duplex, which was also his responsibility. There he discovered Maria de Guesgne propped on her elbows on her bedroom window sill, talking reproachfully to a large gray tomcat that was sitting in the court. Both turned to look at Mel.

"Good morning, Mel!" Maria said with unusual animation. She had long black bangs which emphasized her sallow and undernourished appearance.

"Morning," Mel replied. "Scat!" he added to the cat, which belonged to somebody else in the neighborhood but was usually to be found stalking about the Oceanview Courts.

"You shouldn't frighten poor Cat," said Maria. "Mel, would you look into the bird box?"

"Bird box?"

"The one in the climbing rose," said Maria, leaning precariously from the window to point. "To your left. Cat was trying to get at it."

The bird box was a white-painted, weather-beaten little house set into a straggly rose bush that grew out of a square patch of earth beside Mel's bedroom window. The box was about ten feet above the ground.

Mel looked up at it.

"I'm sure I heard little birds peeping in it this morning," Maria explained sentimentally.

"No bird in its senses would go into a thing like that," Mel assured her. "I don't hear anything. And besides—"

"Please, Mel! We don't want Cat to get them!"

Mel groaned, got a wobbly stepladder out of the garage and climbed up. The gray cat walked over and sat down next to the ladder to watch him.

He poked at the box and listened. No sound.

"Can't you open the top and look in?" Maria inquired.

Holding the box in one hand, Mel tentatively inserted his thumbnail into a crack under its top and pushed. The weathered wood splintered away easily.

"Don't break it!" Maria cried.

Mel put his eye to the crack he'd made. Then he gasped, jerked back, letting go of the box, teetered wildly a moment and fell over with the stepladder. The cat fled, spitting.

"Oh, my!" said Maria, apparently with some enjoyment. "Poor Mel! Are you hurt?"

Mel stood up slowly. The bright morning world seemed to be spinning gently around him but it wasn't because of his fall. "Of course not," he said. His voice quavered somewhat.

"Oh?" said Maria. "Well, then—*are* there any little birds in the nest?"

Mel swallowed hard. "No," he said. He bent over and carefully picked up the ladder and placed it against the wall. The action made it unnecessary to look at her.

"Eggs?" she asked in a hopeful tone.

"No eggs either! No nothing!" His voice was steady again, but he had to get rid of Maria. "Well, I'll clean up this court now, I guess. Uh—maybe you'd like to come down and lend a hand?"

Maria replied promptly that she certainly would like to, but she hadn't had breakfast yet; and with that she vanished from the window.

Mel looked round stealthily. The cat was watching from the door of the garage, but no one else was in sight.

Hurriedly he replaced the stepladder under the bird nest and climbed up again.

Setting the box carefully down on the table in his living room, he locked the apartment door and closed the Venetian blinds. All this had been done in a sort of quiet rush, as if every second counted, which it did in a way. Mel wasn't going to believe, even for a moment, that what he thought he'd seen in that box could be really there; and he couldn't disprove it fast enough to suit him. But something warned him that he wouldn't want to have any witnesses around when he did take his second look.

Then, as he turned from the window, he heard a thin piping cry, a voice as tiny as the peeping of a mouse, coming from the table, from the box.

An instant fright reaction froze him where he stood. The sounds stopped again. There was a brief, faint rustle, like the stirring of dry parchment, and then quiet.

The rustling, he thought, must have been the wings—he'd been *sure* they had wings. Otherwise—

It could all have been an illusion, he told himself. An illusion that transformed a pair of featherless nestlings into something he still didn't want to give a name to. Color patterns of jade and pink flashed into his memory next, however, which made the bird theory shaky. Say a rather small green-and-pink snake then, or a lizard—

Except, of course, for the glassy glitter of the wings. So make it instead, Mel thought desperately, a pair of big insects, like dragonflies, only bigger . . .

He shook his head and moistened his lips. That wouldn't explain that tiny voice—and the more he tried to rationalize it all, the more scared he was getting. Assume, he took the mental jump, he really had seen the figures of two tiny, naked, green-and-pink people in there—with wings! One didn't have to drag in the supernatural to explain it. There were things like flying saucers, presumably, and probably such beings might exist on other worlds.

The thought was oddly reassuring. He still felt as if he'd locked himself in the room with things potentially in the class of tarantulas, but there was excitement and wonder coming up now. With a surge of jealous proprietorship, he realized that he didn't want to share this discovery with anybody else. Later, perhaps. Right now, it was *his* big adventure.

The room was too dim to let him distinguish anything inside the box as he had outdoors, and he was still reluctant to get his face too close to it. He gave it a gingerly rap with his knuckle and waited. No sound.

He cleared his throat. "Hello?" he said. Immediately, that seemed like an idiotic approach. Worse than that, it also brought no reaction.

For the first time, Mel had a sense of worry for the occupants of the box. There was no way of guessing how they'd got in there, but they might be sick or dying. Hurriedly he brought a lamp over to the table and tried to direct light inside, both through the round hole in its side and through the opening he'd made in the top. It wasn't very effective and produced no stir within.

With sudden decision, he shoved one hand into the opening, held the box with the other and broke off the entire top. And there they were.

Mel stared at them a long time, his fears fading slowly. They were certainly alive! One was green, a tiny body of luminous jade, and the other was silkily human-colored, which was why he had been confused on that point. The wings could hardly be anything else, though they were very odd-looking, almost like thin, flexible glass.

He couldn't force himself to touch them. Instead, he laid a folded clean towel on the table and tilted the box very slowly over it. A series of careful tappings and shakings brought the two beings sliding gently out onto the towel.

Two delicately formed female figurines, they lay there a moment, unmoving. Then the green one passed a tiny hand over her forehead in a slow, completely human gesture, opened slanted golden eyes with startled suddenness and looked up at Mel.

He might still have thought he was dreaming, if his attention hadn't been caught just then by a detail of undream-like realism. The other, the human-colored one, seemed to be definitely in a family way.

They were sitting on the folded bath towel in a square of afternoon sunlight which came in through the kitchenette window. The window was high enough up so nobody could look in from outside, and they seemed to want the warmth of the sun more than anything else. They did not appear to be sick, but they were still rather languid. It wasn't starvation, apparently. Mel had put bits of a variety of foods on a napkin before them, and he changed the samples as soon as his guests indicated they weren't interested. So far, canned sardine was the only item that had attracted them at all, and they hadn't done much more than test that.

Between moments of just marveling at them, assuring himself they were there and not an illusion, and wondering what they were and where they'd come from, Mel was beginning to get worried again. For all he knew, they might suddenly die on the bath towel.

"Miss Green," he said in a very low voice—he didn't want to

give Maria de Guesgne any indication he was in the house—"I wish you could tell me what you like to eat!"

Miss Green looked up at him and smiled. She was much more alert and vivacious than the other one who, perhaps because of her condition, merely sat or lay there gracefully and let Miss Green wait on her. The relationship seemed to be about that of an elf princess and her personal attendant, but they were much too real-seeming creatures to have popped out of a fairy tale—though their appearance did arouse recurrent bursts of a feeling of fairy tale unreality, which Mel hadn't known since he was ten. But, tiny as they were, Miss Green and the princess primarily gave him the impression of being quite as functional as human beings or, perhaps, as field mice.

He would have liked to inspect the brittle-seeming wings more closely. They seemed to be made up of numerous laminated, very thin sections, and he wondered whether they could fly with them or whether their race had given up or lost that ability.

But touching them might have affected their present matter-of-fact acceptance of him, and he didn't want to risk that...

A door banged suddenly in the apartment overhead. A moment later, he heard Maria coming down the hall stairs.

Mel stood up in sudden alarm. He'd known for some time that his neighbor had supplied herself with a key to his apartment, not to pry but with the practical purpose of borrowing from the little bar in Mel's living room when she was out of both money and liquor. She rarely took much, and until now he'd been more amused than annoyed.

He went hurriedly into the living room, closing the door to the kitchenette behind him. If Maria knocked, he wouldn't answer. If she decided he was out and came in to steal his liquor, he would pretend to have been asleep in the chair and scare the hell out of her!

She paused before the apartment door a moment, but then went out into the court.

Mel waited until her footsteps died away, going toward the street. As he opened the door to the kitchenette, something buzzed noisily out of the living room past his shoulder—a big, unlovely looking horsefly. The apartment screens didn't fit too well, and the fly probably had been attracted by the smell of food.

Startled, he stopped to consider the new problem. There was a flyswatter hanging beside the door, but he didn't want to alarm his guests—and then, for the first time, he saw Miss Green's wings unfold!

She was up on her feet beside the princess, who remained sitting on the towel. Both of them were following the swift, erratic course of the big fly with more animation than they'd shown about anything so far.

Miss Green gave a sudden piping cry, and the glassy appendages on her back opened out suddenly like twin transparently gleaming fans, and blurred into motion too swift for Mel to follow.

Miss Green rose into the air like a tiny human helicopter, hands up before her as if she were praying.

It wasn't till the horsefly swerved from the kitchenette window and came buzzing back that Mel guessed her purpose.

There was a sharper, fiercer drone like a hornet's song as she darted sideways into the insect's path. Mel didn't see her catch it. Its buzzing simply stopped, and then she was dropping gently back to the towel, with the ugly black thing between her hands. It looked nearly as big as her head.

There was an exchange of cheerful piping cries between the two. Miss Green laughed up at Mel's stupefied face, lifted the motionless fly to her mouth and neatly bit off its head.

Mel turned hurriedly and went into the living room. It wasn't, he told himself, really so *very* different from human beings eating a chicken. But he didn't feel up to watching what he knew was going to be a dismemberment and a feast.

At any rate, the horsefly had settled the feeding problem. His guests could take care of themselves.

That night, Miss Green hunted down a few moths. Mel woke up twice with the sudden sharp drone in his ears that told him she had just made her catch. Both times, it was a surge of unthinking physical fright that actually roused him. Awake, and remembering the disproportion in size between himself and the huntress, his reaction seemed ridiculous; but the second time he found he was reluctant to go back to sleep until it would appear that Miss Green was done with her foraging.

So he lay awake, listening to the occasional faint indications of her continuing activity within his apartment, and to more familiar sounds without. A train rattled over a crossing; a police siren gave a sudden halloo and faded into silence again. For a long time, there was only the whispering passage of distant cars over wet pavements, and the slow roll and thump of the surf. A haze of fog beyond

the window turned the apartment into a shut-off little world of
its own.

Miss Green moved about with no more than a whisper of air
and the muted pipe of voices from the top of the kitchenette
cupboard to show where she was. Mel had put a small carton up
there, upholstered with the towel and handkerchiefs and roofed
over with his best woolen sweater, to make a temporary home for
his guests. The princess hadn't stirred from it since, but Miss Green
remained busy.

He started suddenly to find her hovering directly over his bed,
vaguely silhouetted against the pale blur of the window. As he
stared, she settled down and came to rest on the blanket over his
chest, effortlessly as a spider gliding down along its thread. Her
wings closed with a faint snap.

Mel raised his head carefully to squint down along the blanket at her. It was the first time either of them had made anything
resembling a friendly advance in his direction; he didn't want to
commit any blunders.

"Hello," he said quietly.

Miss Green didn't reply. She seemed to be looking up at the
window, disregarding him, and he was content to watch her. These
strange creatures seemed to have some of the aloofness of cats in
their manner, and they might be as easily offended.

She turned presently, walked up over the blanket and perched
herself on Mel's pillow, above his head and somewhat to his right.
And there she stayed silently. Which seemed catlike, too: the grant-
ing of a reserved and temporary companionship. He would not
have been too surprised to hear a tiny purring from above his ear.
Instead, drowsily and lulled in an odd way by Miss Green's presence, he found himself sinking back into sleep.

It wasn't surprising either that his mind should be filled for a
time with vague pictures of her, but when the room about him
seemed to have expanded into something like a faintly luminous
fishbowl, he knew he was dreaming. There were others present.
They were going somewhere, and he had a sense of concern, which
had to do either with their destination or with difficulties in getting
there. Then a realization of swift, irrevocable disaster—

There were violent lurchings as the luminosity about him faded
swiftly into blackness. He felt a terrible, energy-draining cold, the
wet clutch of death itself, then something like a soundless explosion about him and anguished cryings. The motion stopped.

Blackness faded back to gray, but the cold remained. Icy water was pounding down on him now, as if he were fighting his way through a vertical current carrying somebody else. A desperate hunt for refuge and finding it suddenly, and slipping inside and relaxing into unconsciousness, to wait for the return of warmth and life . . .

Mel's eyes opened. The room was beginning to lighten with morning. He turned his head slowly to look for Miss Green. She was still there, on the pillow beside his head, watching him; and there was something in her position, in the unwinking golden eyes, even in her curious fluff of blue-white hair, that reminded him now less of a cat than a small lizard.

He didn't doubt that she had somehow enabled him to share the experience that in part explained their presence here. Without thinking, he asked aloud, "What happened to the others?"

She didn't move, but he was aware of a surge of horrified revulsion. Then before his open eyes for a moment swam a picture of a bleak, rain-beaten beach . . . and, just above the waterline, in a cluster of harsh voices, jabbing beaks and beating wings, great gulls were tearing apart a strange jetsam of tiny bodies too weakened to escape—

A small, plaintive crying came from the kitchenette. The picture faded as Miss Green soared into the air to attend to her princess.

Mel breakfasted in the living room, thoughtfully. He couldn't quite understand that luminous vehicle of theirs, or why it should have succumbed to the rain storm of Saturday night, which appeared to be what had happened. But his guests obviously were confronted with the problem of getting back to wherever they'd come from— and he didn't think Miss Green would have confided in him if he wasn't somehow expected to be helpful in solving the problem.

There was a thump on the sill outside his bedroom window, followed by an annoyed meowing. The gray cat that had been spying on the bird box seemed to suspect he was harboring the refugees. Mel went out into the little courtyard through the back door of the duplex and chased the animal away. The fog, he saw, was thinning out quickly; in an hour or so it would be another clear day.

When he came in, Miss Green fluted a few soft notes, which Mel chose to interpret as gratitude, from the top of the cupboard and withdrew from sight again.

One couldn't think of them, he decided, as being exactly like any creatures of Earth. The cold rain had been very nearly deadly to them, if the memory Miss Green had transmitted to him was accurate—as destructive as it had been to their curious craft. Almost as if it could wash right through them, to drain vital energies from their bodies, while in the merely foggy air of last night she had seemed comfortable enough. It indicated different tolerance spans with more sharply defined limits.

The thought came into his mind:

Another planet?

It seemed possible, even if it left a lot to explain. Mel got up in sudden excitement and began to walk about the room. He had a conviction of being right. It struck him he might be involved in an event of enormous historical significance.

Then, stopping for a moment before the window, he saw it—

Apparently high in the gray sky overhead, a pale yellow circle moved, much smaller than the sun, but like the disk of the sun seen ghost-like through clouds. Instantly, another part of his dream became clear to him.

He lost his head. "Miss Green! Come here, quick!"

A buzz, the swift drone of wings, and she was beside him, perching on his shoulder. Mel pointed.

She gave a lamenting little cry of recognition. As if it had been a signal, the yellow circle darted sideways in a long streaking slant, and vanished. Miss Green fled to report to the princess, while Mel stayed at the window, and quickly returned to him again. Evidently she was both excited and distressed, and he wondered what was wrong. If that apparition of pale light had been one of their vessels, as her behavior indicated, it seemed probable that its mission was to hunt for survivors of the lost globe.

Miss Green seemed either less sure of that, or less confident that the rescue would be easily effected. Some minutes later, she pointed to a different section of the sky, where the yellow circle—or another very like it—was now moving slowly about. Presently it vanished again, and when it reappeared for the second time it was accompanied by two others.

Meanwhile, Miss Green might have been transmitting some understanding of the nature of her doubts to Mel, because the ghostly vagrants now gave him an immediate impression of insubstantiality: not space-spanning luminous globes but pictured shapes projected on the air. His theory of interplanetary travelers became suddenly much less probable.

In the next few moments, the concept he was struggling with abruptly completed itself in his mind, so abruptly, in fact, that there was no longer any question that it had originated with Miss Green. The rescue craft Mel thought he was seeing actually were just that.

But the pictures in the sky were only signals to possible survivors that help was approaching. The globes themselves were elsewhere, groping their way blindly and dangerously through strange dimensions that had nothing to do with the ones Mel knew.

And they were still, in some manner his imagination did not even attempt to clarify, very, very "far away."

"I was wondering what you'd done with the bird box," Maria de Guesgne explained. "It's not there in the bush any more."

Mel told her annoyedly that the bird box had been damaged by the storm, and so he'd thrown it into the incinerator.

"Well," Maria said vaguely, "that's too bad." Her handsome dark eyes were shifting about his living room meanwhile, not at all vaguely. Mel had left the apartment door partly open, and she had walked right in on her way to the market. When she wasn't drinking or working herself up to a bout of creative painting, which seemed to put her into a tranced sort of condition, Maria was a highly observant young woman. The question was now how to get her out of the apartment again before she observed more than he wanted her to.

"How does it happen you're not at work on Monday afternoon?" she inquired, and set her shopping bag down on the armchair.

Keeping one eye on the kitchenette door, Mel explained about his vacation. Miss Green hadn't been in sight for almost an hour; but he wasn't at all sure she mightn't come out to inspect the visitor, and the thought of Maria's probable reactions was unnerving.

"Two weeks?" Maria repeated chattily. "It'll be fun having you around for two weeks—unless you're going off to spend your vacation somewhere else. Are you?"

"No," Mel said. "I'm staying here—"

And at that moment, Miss Green came in through the kitchenette door.

At least, Mel assumed it was Miss Green. All he actually saw was a faint blur of motion. It went through the living room, accompanied by a high-pitched hum, and vanished behind Maria.

"Good Lord!" she cried, whirling. "What's that? *OH!*" The last was a shrill yelp. "It stung me!"

❀ ❀ ❀

Mel hadn't imagined Miss Green could move so fast. Rising and falling with furious menace, the sound seemed to come from all points of the room at once, as Maria darted out of the apartment. Clutching her shopping bag, Mel followed her out hastily and slammed the door behind them. He caught up with Maria in the court.

She was rubbing herself angrily.

"I'm not coming into that apartment again, Mel Armstrong," she announced, "until you've had it fumigated! That thing kept stinging me! What was it, anyway?"

"A wasp, I guess." Mel felt weak with relief. She hadn't really seen anything. "Here's your bag. I'll chase it out."

Maria stalked off, complaining about screens that didn't even protect people against giant wasps.

Mel found the apartment quiet again and went into the kitchenette. Miss Green was poised on the top edge of the cupboard, a gold-eyed statuette of Victory, laughing down at him, the laminated wings spread and raised behind her like iridescent glass fans. Mel looked at her with a trace of uneasiness. She had some kind of small white bundle in her arms, and he wondered whether it concealed the weapon with which she'd stung Maria.

"I don't think you should have done that," he told her. "But she's gone now."

Looking rather pleased with herself, Miss Green glanced back over her shoulder and piped a few questioning notes to the princess. There was a soft reply, and she soared down to the table, folded her wings and knelt to lay the bundle gently down on it. She beckoned to Mel.

Mel's eyes popped as she unfolded the bundle. Perhaps he really shouldn't have been surprised.

He was harboring four guests now—the princess had been safely delivered of twins.

At dusk, Miss Green widened the biggest slit in the bedroom screen a little more and slipped out to do her own kind of shopping, with a section of one of Mel's handkerchiefs to serve as a bag.

Mel left the lights out and stayed at the window. He felt depressed, but didn't quite know why—unless it was that so many odd things had happened since Sunday morning that his mind had given up trying to understand them.

He wasn't really sure now, for example, whether he was getting occasional flash-glimpses of those circular luminous vessels plowing through another dimension somewhere, or whether he was half asleep and imagining it. Usually it was a momentary glow printed on the dark air at the edge of his vision, vanishing before he could really look at it.

He had a feeling they had managed to come a good deal closer during the day. Then he wondered briefly whether other people had been seeing strange light-shapes, too, and what they might have thought the glimpses were.

Spots before their eyes, probably.

Miss Green was back with a soft hum of wings, on the outer window sill, six feet from where he sat. She pushed the knotted scrap of cloth through the screen. There was something inside it now; it caught for a moment on the wires. Mel started up to help, then checked himself, afraid of feeling some bug squirming desperately inside; and while he hesitated, she had shoved it through. She followed it, picked it up again and flew off to the living room. After a moment she returned with the empty cloth and went out again.

She made eight such trips in the next hour, while night deepened outside and then began to lighten as a half-moon shoved over the horizon. Mel must have dozed off several times; at least, he suddenly found himself coming awake, with the awareness that something had just landed with a soft thump on the window sill outside.

It wasn't Miss Green. He saw a chunky shadow at one corner of the window, and caught the faintest glint of green eyes peering into the room. It was the cat from the courtyard.

In the same moment, he heard the familiar faint hum, and Miss Green appeared at the opposite end of the sill.

Afterward, Mel realized he'd simply sat there, stiffening in groggy, sleep-dazed horror, as the cat-shadow lengthened and flowed swiftly toward the tiny humanoid figure. Miss Green seemed to raise both arms over her head. A spark of brilliant blue glowed from her cupped hands and extended itself in an almost invisible thread of fire that stabbed against the cat's forehead. The cat yowled, swung aside and leaped down into the court.

Mel was on his feet, shaking violently, as Miss Green slipped in through the screen. He heard Maria open her window upstairs to peer down into the court, where the cat was making low, angry sounds. Apparently it hadn't been hurt, but no wonder Maria had suspected that afternoon she'd been stung by a wasp! Or that Miss Green's insect victims never struggled, once she had caught them!

He pulled down the shade and stood undecided in the dark, until he heard her piping call from the living room. It was followed by an impatient buzzing about the standing lamp in there, and Mel concluded correctly that he was supposed to turn on the light.

He discovered her on the living room table, sorting out the plunder she had brought back.

It wasn't a pile of electrocuted insects as he had expected, but a puzzlingly commonplace collection—little heaps of dry sand from the beach, some small white pebbles, and a sizable bundle of thin twigs about two inches in length. Since she was disregarding him, he shifted the lamp over to the table to see what this human-shaped lightning bug from another dimension was going to do next.

That was the way he felt about Miss Green at the moment . . .

What she did was to transport the twigs in two bundles to the top of the cupboard, where she left them with the princess. Then she came back and began to lay out a thin thread of white sand on the dark, polished surface of the table.

Mel pulled up his armchair, poured himself a glass of brandy, lit a cigarette and settled down to watch her.

By the time Miss Green indicated to him that she wanted the light turned out again, he had finished his second drink and was feeling rather benevolent. She had used up all her sand, and about a square foot of the table's surface was covered now with a confusingly intricate maze of lines, into which she had placed white pebbles here and there. Some of the lines, Mel noticed, blended into each other, while others stopped abruptly or curved back on themselves. As a decorative scheme, it hardly seemed worthwhile.

"Miss Green," he told her thoughtfully, "I hope it makes sense to you. It doesn't to me."

She piped imperiously, pointing: the light! Mel had a moment of annoyance at the way she was ordering him around in his own apartment.

"Well," he said, "I'll humor you this time."

For a moment after he had pulled the switch, he stood beside the table to let his eyes adjust to the dark. However, they weren't adjusting properly—a patch of unquiet phosphorescent glimmering floated disturbingly within his field of vision, and as the seconds passed, it seemed to be growing stronger.

Suddenly, Mel swore in amazement and bent down to examine the table.

"Now what have you done—?" he began.

Miss Green fluted soothingly at him from the dark and fluttered up to his shoulder. He felt a cool touch against his ear and cheek, and a burst of oddly pleasant tinglings ran over his scalp.

"Stop that!" he said, startled.

Miss Green fluted again, urgently. She was trying to tell him something now, and suddenly he thought he understood.

"All right," he said. "I'll look at it. That's what you want me to do, isn't it?"

Miss Green flew down to the table again, which indicated agreement. Mel groped himself back into the chair and leaned forward to study the curiously glowing design she had created of sand and pebbles.

He discovered immediately that any attempt to see it clearly merely strained his vision. Details turned into vaguely distorted, luminous flickerings when he stared at them and the whole pale, spidery pattern made no more sense than it had with the light on. She must have some purpose in mind with it, but Mel couldn't imagine what.

Meanwhile, Miss Green was making minor adjustments in his position which Mel accepted without argument, since she seemed to know what she was doing. Small tugs and pushes told him she wanted his hands placed on the table to either side of the design. Mel put them there. His head was to be tilted forward just so. He obliged her again. Then she was back on the table, and the top two-thirds of the pattern vanished suddenly behind a blur.

After a moment, he realized she had opened her wings and blotted that part from his sight.

In the darkness, he fastened his puzzled gaze on the remaining section: a quivering, thinly drawn pattern of blue-white light that faded periodically almost to the limits of visibility and slowly grew up again to what was, by comparison, real brilliance. His head was aching slightly. The pattern seemed to tilt sideways and move upward, as if it were creeping in a slow circle about some pivot-point. Presently, it turned down again to complete the circle and start on another round. By that time, the motion seemed normal.

When a tiny shape of light suddenly ran across the design and vanished again as it reached the other side, Mel was only moderately surprised. The figure had reminded him immediately of Miss Green. After a while, it crossed his field of vision in another direction, and then there were two more . . .

He seemed to be swimming forward, through the pattern, into an area of similar tiny figures like living silhouettes of light, and of entrancingly delicate architectural designs. It was like a marionette setting of incredible craftsmanship, not quite real in the everyday sense, but as convincing as a motion picture which was spreading out, second by second, and beginning to flow about him—

"Hey!" Mel sat up with a start. "You're trying to hypnotize me!"

Miss Green piped pleadingly. Clearly, she had only been trying to show him something. And wasn't it beautiful? Didn't he want to see more?

Mel hesitated. He was suspicious now, but he was also curious. After all, what could she do to him with her tricks?

Besides, he admitted to himself, the picture had vanished as soon as he shifted his eyes, and it *was* beautiful, like moving about through a living illustration of a book of fairy tales.

He yielded. "All right, I do want to see more."

This time, the picture grew up out of the design within seconds. Only it wasn't the same picture. It was as if he had turned around and was looking in another direction, a darker one.

There were fewer of the little light-shapes; instead, he discovered in the distance a line of yellow dots that moved jerkily but steadily, like glowing corks bobbing on dark water. He watched them for a moment without recognition; then he realized with a thrill of pleasure that he was getting another view of the luminous globes he had seen before—this time an other-dimensional view, so to speak.

Suddenly, one of them was right before him! Not a dot or a yellow circle, but a three-foot ball of fire that rushed toward him through the blackness with hissing, sputtering sounds!

Mel surged up out of the chair with a yelp of fright, and the fireball vanished.

As he groped about for the light, Miss Green was piping furiously at him from the table.

Then the light came on.

She was in a rage. Dancing about on the table, beating the air with her wings, she waved her arms over her head and shook her tiny fists at him. Mel backed off warily.

"Take it easy!" he warned. He could reach the flyswatter in the kitchenette with a jump if she started shooting off miniature electric bolts again.

She might have had the same idea, because she calmed down suddenly, shook her wings together and closed them with a snap. It was like a cat smoothing down its bristling back fur. There was a whistling query from the princess now, followed by an excited elfin conversation.

Mel poured himself a drink with a hand that shook slightly, and pretended to ignore the disturbance of his guests, while he tried to figure out what had happened.

Supposing, he thought a trifle guiltily, settling down on the couch at a safe distance from the table—supposing they simply had to have his help at this point. The manner in which one of the rescue globes suddenly had seemed to shift close to him suggested it. Was he justified in refusing to go on with it? In the directionless dark through which the globes were driving, they might have been reacting to his concentrated awareness of them as if it were a radio signal from the human dimensions. And it would explain Miss Green's rage at the sudden interruption of the contact.

But another thought came to him then, and his guilty feelings vanished in a surge of alarmed indignation.

Well, and just supposing, he thought, that he *hadn't* broken the contact. And that a three-foot sputtering fireball materialized right inside his living room!

He caught sight of Miss Green eying him speculatively and rather slyly from the table. She seemed composed enough now; there was even the faintest of smiles on that tiny face. The smile seemed to confirm his suspicions.

Mel downed his drink and stood up.

"Miss Green," he told her evenly, choosing his words with care, "I'm sorry to disappoint you, but I don't intend to be the subject of any more of your experiments. At least not until I've had time to think about it."

Her head nodded slightly, as if she were acknowledging his decision. But the smile remained; in fact, Miss Green had begun to look rather smug. Mel studied her uneasily. She might be planning to put something else over on him, but he knew how to stop that!

Before he turned out the light and went to bed, Mel methodically and somewhat grimly swallowed four more shots of brandy.

With that much inside him it wouldn't matter what Miss Green tried, because he wouldn't be able to react to her suggestions till he woke up again in the morning.

Actually it was noon before he awoke—and he might have gone on sleeping then if somebody hadn't been banging on his apartment door.

"Wake up, Mel!" he heard Maria de Guesgne shouting hoarsely. "I can hear you snoring in there!"

He sat up a little groggily and looked at the clock. His guests weren't in sight.

"You awake, Mel?" she demanded.

"Wait a minute!" he yelled back. "Just woke up and I'm not decent."

When he opened the door, she had vanished. He was about to close it quietly and gratefully again, when she called down the stairway. "That you, Mel? Come on up! I want to show you something."

He locked the door behind him and went upstairs. Maria received him beamingly in her living room. She was on one of her rare creative painting sprees, and this spree, to judge by the spattered appearance of the room and the artist, was more riotous than usual. A half dozen fair-sized canvases were propped on newspapers against the wall to dry. They were turned around, to increase the shock effect on Mel when he would get his first look at them.

"Ever see a salamander?" Maria inquired with anticipation, spreading a few more papers on the table.

Mel admitted he hadn't. He wished she'd given him time to have coffee first. His comments at these private showings were usually regarded as inadequate anyway.

"Well," Maria invited triumphantly, selecting one of the canvases and setting it abruptly up on the table before him, "take a look at one!"

Mel gasped and jerked back. "Holy Judas!" he said in a weak voice.

"Pretty good, eh?" For once, Maria appeared satisfied with his reaction. She held it away from her and regarded it. "One of my best!" she cried judiciously.

About three times life-size, it was a quite recognizable portrait of Miss Green.

❈   ❈   ❈

It didn't occur to Maria to offer Mel coffee but he got a cigarette from her. Fortunately, he wasn't called upon to make any more comments; she chattered away while she showed him the rest of the series. Mel looked and listened, still rather shaken. Presently he began to ask questions.

A salamander, he learned, was a fire elemental. Maria glanced at her fireplace as she explained this, and Mel noticed she seemed to have had a fire burning there overnight, which wasn't too unusual for her even in the middle of summer. Listening to the bang-haired, bright-eyed oddball rattling off metaphysical details about salamanders, he became aware of a sort of dread growing up in him. For Miss Green was pictured, wings and arms spread, against and within furling veils of yellow-white flame . . .

"Drawn from life?" he inquired, grinning to make it a joke. He pointed at the picture.

Without looking directly at her, he saw Maria start at the question. She stared at him intensely for a moment, and after that she became more reticent.

It didn't matter because it was all on the canvases. She had seen as much as he had and more, and put it down with shocking realism. Seen through somebody else's eyes, Miss Green's world was still beautiful; but now it was also frightening. And there was what Maria had said about salamanders.

"Maria," he said, "what actually happened last night?"

She looked at him sullenly. "I don't know what you're talking about, Mel."

"I imagine," he suggested casually, "you were just sitting there in front of the fire. And then—"

"Gosh, Mel, she was beautiful! It's *all* so beautiful, you know . . ." She recovered quickly. "I fell asleep and I had a dream, that's all. Why? What makes you ask?"

She was beginning to look rather wild-eyed, but he had to find out. "I was just wondering," he said, "whether they'd left."

"Why should they leave— Look, you oaf! I called you in to give you the privilege of looking at my paintings. Now get out. I've got to make a phone call."

He stopped at the door, struck by a sudden suspicion. "You're not going to try to sell them, are you?"

"*Try* to sell them!" She laughed hoarsely. "There are circles, Mel Armstrong, in which a de Guesgne original is *understood*, shall we say? Circles not exactly open to the common herd . . . This series," she concluded, rather prosaically, "will get me two thousand bucks as soon as I let one or two of the right people have a look at them!"

Brewing himself a pot of coffee at last, Mel decided that part of it, if true, wasn't any of his business. He had always assumed Maria was living on a monthly check she got from an unidentified source in Chicago, but her occasional creations might have a well-heeled following at that. As for the way Miss Green had got in to sit for her portrait—the upstairs screens weren't in any better shape than the downstairs ones. The fiery background, of course, might have been only in Maria's mind.

There was a scratching on top of the cupboard and whispery voices. Mel ignored the slight chill that drifted down his spine. Up to that moment, he'd been hoping secretly that Maria had provided a beacon for the rescue team to home in on while he slept, and that his guests had been picked up and taken home.

But Miss Green was peering down at him over the edge of the cupboard.

"Hi, salamander!" he greeted her politely. "Had a busy night? Too bad it didn't work."

Her head withdrew. In the living room Mel stopped to look at the design of sand and pebbles, which was still on the table. Touching one of the thread-like lines, he discovered it was as hard and slick as lacquer. Otherwise the pattern seemed unremarkable in daylight, but Mel dropped a cloth across it to keep it out of sight.

Miss Green fluttered past him to the sill of the bedroom window. He watched her standing on tiptoe against the screen, apparently peering about at the sky. After a while, it began to seem ridiculous to let himself become obsessed by superstitious fears about this tiny and beautiful, almost jewel-like creature.

Whatever abilities she might have, she and the princess were only trying to get home—and, having seen their home, he couldn't blame them for that.

He had a return of the fairy-tale nostalgia his glimpse of those eerily beautiful places had aroused in him the night before, a pleasantly yearning sensation like an awareness of elfin horns blowing far away to send faint, exciting echoes, swirling about the commonplace sky of Sweetwater Bay. The feeling might have been resurrected from his childhood, but it was a strong and effective one.

He recalled how bored he'd been with everything before they appeared . . .

He walked softly through the bedroom and stopped behind Miss Green. She was making an elaborate pretense of not having noticed his approach, but the pointed ears that could follow the passage of a moth in the dark were tilted stiffly backward. Mel actually was opening his mouth to say, "Miss Green, I'll help you if I can," when it struck him sharply, like a brand-new thought, that it was an extremely rash promise to make, considering everything that had happened so far.

He wondered how the odd impulse ever had come to him.

In sudden suspicion, he began to trace the last few minutes through again. He had started with a firm decision not to let his guests involve him in their plans any more than was healthy for him, if at all—and the decision had been transformed, step by step, and mental twist by mental twist, into a foolish willingness to have them make use of him exactly as they pleased!

Miss Green, still maliciously pretending to watch the sky, let him think it all out until it became quite clear what she had done and how she had done it. And then, as Mel spluttered angrily at this latest interference with his freedom of thought and action, she turned around and laughed at him.

In a way, it cleared the air. The pressure was off. Maria had proved a much more pliable subject than Mel; the rescuers had their bearings and would arrive presently. Meanwhile, everybody could relax.

Mel couldn't help feeling relieved as he grew sure of that. At the same time, now that the departure was settled, he became aware of a certain amount of belated regret. Miss Green didn't seem to know the exact hour; she was simply watching for them well ahead of their arrival.

Where would they show up? She waved her arms around in an appealingly helpless gesture at the court outside and the sky. Here, there—somewhere in the area.

It would be a fire globe. At his question, she pointed at the opposite wall of the court where a picture of one formed itself obligingly, slid along the wall a few feet, and vanished. Mel was beginning to enjoy all this easy last-minute communication, when he heard Maria come downstairs and open the door to the other court. There was conversation, and several sets of footsteps went up to her apartment and down again.

Cautioning Miss Green, he took a look around the shutters of the living room window. A small panel truck stood in the court;

Maria was supervising the careful transfer of her paintings into its interior. Apparently she didn't even intend to let them dry before offering them for sale!

The truck drove off with Maria inside with her paintings, and Mel discovered Miss Green doing a little spying of her own from the upper edge of the shutters. Good friends now, they smiled at each other and resumed their guard at the bedroom window.

The princess joined them around five in the afternoon. Whether she had been injured in the accident or weakened by the birth of her babies, Mel couldn't tell, but Miss Green carried her friend down from the cupboard without visible effort, and then went back for a globular basket of tightly woven tiny twigs, which contained the twins.

It was a masterfully designed little structure with a single opening about the thickness of a pencil, and heavily lined. Mel had a notion to ask for it as a souvenir, but decided against it. He lifted it carefully to his ear, to listen to an almost inaudible squeaking inside, and his expression seemed to cause Miss Green considerable silent amusement.

All in all, it was much like waiting patiently in pleasant company for the arrival of an overdue train. Then around seven o'clock, when the room was already dark, the telephone rang abruptly and returned Mel with a start to the world of human beings.

He lifted the receiver,

"Hello, oaf!" said Maria de Guesgne in what seemed for the moment to be an enormous, booming voice.

Mel inquired agreeably whether she'd succeeded in selling her paintings. It was the first thing that occurred to him.

"Certainly I sold them!" Maria said. He could tell by now that she was thoroughly plastered again. "Got a message to give you," she added.

"From whom?"

"Maybe from me, ha-ha!" said Maria. She paused a moment, seemed to be muttering something to herself, and resumed suddenly, "Oaf, are you listening?"

Mel said bluntly that he was. If he hung up on her, she would probably ring back.

"All right," Maria said clearly. "This is the message: 'The fiery ones do not tolerate the endangering of their secrets.' Warning, see? Goo'bye."

She hung up before he could say anything.

❈   ❈   ❈

Hers had been a chilling sort of intrusion. Mel stood a while in the darkening room, trying to gather up the mood Maria had shattered, and discovering he couldn't quite do it. He realized that all along, like a minor theme, there had been a trace of fear underlying everything he did, ever since he had first looked into that bird box and glimpsed something impossible inside it. He had been covering the fear up; even now he didn't want to admit it, but it was there.

He could quite simply, of course, walk out of the room and out of the apartment, and stay away for a week. He didn't even ever have to come back. And, strictly speaking, this was the sort of thing that should have happened to somebody like Maria de Guesgne, not to him. For him, the sensible move right now would be to go quietly back into the normal world of reality he had stepped out of a few mornings ago. It was a simple physical act. The door was over there . . .

Then Mel looked back at his guests and promptly reversed his decision. They were certainly as real as any living creatures he'd ever seen, and he felt there weren't many human beings who would show up as well as Miss Green had done in any comparable emergency. His own unconscious fears meant only that he had run into a new and unpredictable factor in a world that had been becoming increasingly commonplace for a number of years now. He could see that once you'd got settled into the idea of a commonplace world, you might be startled by discoveries that didn't fit that notion—and he felt now, rather hazily, that it wasn't such a bad thing to be startled like that. It might wake you up enough to let you start living again yourself.

He took the receiver off the phone and laid it on the floor, so there wouldn't be any more interruptions. If he ran off now before seeing how the adventure ended, he knew he would never quit regretting it.

He went into the bedroom and pulled his chair back up to the window. The shadowy silhouette that was Miss Green turned and sounded a few fluting notes at him. He had the immediate impression that she was worried.

What was the matter?

She pointed.

Clouds!

The sky was still full of the pastel glowings of the sunset. Here and there were patches of black cloud, insignificant-looking, like ragged crows swimming through the pale light.

"*Rain,*" the thought came. "*The cold rain—the killing rain! Another storm!*"

Mel studied the sky uneasily. They might be right. "Your friends are bound to get here first," he assured them, looking confident about it.

They smiled gratefully at him. He couldn't think of anything he might do to help. The princess looked comfortable on the towel he had laid along the screen, and Miss Green, as usual, looked alert, prepared to handle anything that had to be handled. He wondered about asking her to let him see how the globes were doing, and, instantly, a thought showed clear in his mind: "*Try it yourself!*"

That hadn't occurred to Mel before. He settled back comfortably in the chair and looked through the screen for them.

Four or five fiery visualizations quivered here and there in the air, vanished, reappeared, vanished . . .

Mel stopped looking for them, and there was only the sky.

"Closer?" he said aloud, rather pleased with himself. It had been easy!

Miss Green nodded, human fashion, and piped something in reply. Closer, but—

He gathered she couldn't tell from here how close, and that there was trouble—a not quite translatable kind of trouble, but almost as if, in their dimension, they were struggling through the radiant distortions of a storm that hadn't gathered yet here on Earth.

He glanced up at the sky again, more anxiously now. The black clouds didn't seem to have grown any larger.

By and by, because he had not had any awareness of going to sleep, Mel was surprised to find himself waking up. He knew immediately that he had been asleep a long time, a period of hours. There was grayness around him, the vague near-light of very early morning, and he had a sense of having been aroused by a swirling confusion of angry sounds. But all was silent at the moment.

Her answer was instantly in his mind. The storm had caused a delay—but a great globe was almost here now!

A curious pause followed. Mel had a sense of hesitation. And then, very swiftly and faintly, a wisp of thought, which he would have missed if that pause had not made him alert, showed and vanished on the fringe of his consciousness.

"*Be careful! Be very careful.*"

Miss Green turned back to the window. Beside her now, Mel saw the princess sitting as if asleep, with one arm across the twig basket and her head resting on her arm. Before he could frame the puzzled question that was struggling up in his mind, there was a series of ear-splitting yowls from the court outside. It startled Mel only for a moment, since it was a familiar sort of racket. The gray cat didn't tolerate intruding felines in its area, and about once a month it discovered and evicted one with the same lack of inhibition it was evidencing right now. It must have been the threatening squalls which usually preceded the actual battle that had awakened him.

The encounter itself was over almost instantly. There were sounds of a scampering retreat which ended beyond the garage, and, standing up at the window, Mel saw the gray shape of the win-ner come gliding back down the court. The cat stopped below him and seemed to turn up its head. For a moment, he felt it was staring both at him and at Miss Green, very much like a compe-tent little tiger in the gusty, gray night; then it made a low, menacing sound and moved on out of sight. Apparently it hadn't yet forgotten its previous meeting with Miss Green.

Mel looked down at her. "Why should I be careful?"

There was a pause again, and what came then hardly seemed an answer to his question. The princess was very weak, Miss Green indicated; he might have to help.

He was still wondering about that—and wondering, too, whether he'd really had something like a warning from her—when a sud-den wavering glare lit up the room behind them.

For a moment, he thought the fireball was inside the building. But the light was pouring in through the living room window; its source was in the opposite court, out of his line of sight. There was a crackling, hissing sound, and the light faded.

Miss Green came darting at him. Mel put his hand up instinc-tively and felt her thrust the basket into it. Almost instantly, she had picked up the princess and was outside the screen—

Then the cat attacked from below in a silent, terrible leap, a long, twisting shadow in the air, and they seemed to drop out of sight together.

Mel was out in the court, staring wildly around. In the swim-ming grayness nothing stirred or made sound. A cool, moist wind thrust at his face and faded. Except for the toy basket of twigs in his hand, he might have been awakening from a meaningless dream.

Then a lurid round of light like a big, wavering moon came out over the top of the building, and a sharp humming sound drove down through the air at him. Instinctively again, he held out the basket and felt it plucked away. He thought it was Miss Green, but the shape had come and gone much too swiftly to be sure of that.

The light grew brilliant, a solid white—intolerable—and he backed hurriedly into the shelter of the garage, his heart hammering in excitement and alarm. He heard voices from the other court; a window slammed somewhere. He couldn't guess what was happening, but he didn't need Miss Green's warning now. He had an overwhelming urge to keep out of sight until the unearthly visitor would be gone—

And then, running like a rabbit, the gray cat appeared from behind a box halfway down the court and came streaking for the garage. Mel watched its approach with a sort of silent horror, partly because it might be attracting undesirable attention to him—and partly because he seemed to know in that instant exactly what was going to be done to it.

It wasn't more than twenty feet away when something like a twisting string of fiery white reached down from above. The animal leaped sideways, blazed and died. There was a sound very like a gunshot, and the court was instantly dark.

Mel stayed where he was. For half a minute or so, he was shaking much too violently to have left his retreat. By the end of that time, he knew better. It wasn't over yet!

Pictures forming in the moist, dark air . . . delicate, unstable outlines sliding through the court, changing as they moved. Elfin castles swayed up out of grayness and vanished again. Near the edge of his vision other shapes showed, more beautiful than human . . .

Muttering to himself, between terror and delight, Mel closed his eyes as tightly as he could, which helped for a moment. But then the impressions began drifting through his mind. The visitors were still nearby, hanging somewhere outside the limits of human sight in their monstrous fireball, in the windy sky. They were talking to him in their way.

Mel asked in his mind what they wanted, and the answer showed immediately. The table in his living room with the pattern of glassy sand and pebbles Miss Green had constructed. The pattern was glowing again now under the cloth he had thrown over it. He was to go in and look at the pattern . . .

"No!" he said aloud. It was all terror now.

"*Go look at the pattern . . . Go look at the pattern . . .*"

The pictures burst round him in a soundless wild flowering of beauty, flickering rains of color, a fountain of melting, shifting forms. His mind drowned in happiness. He was sinking through a warmth of kindness, gratitude and love . . .

A drift of rain touched his cheek coldly—and Mel found himself outside the garage, moving drunkenly toward the apartment door. Then, just for a moment, a picture of Miss Green printed itself on his mind.

She seemed to be standing before him, as tall now as he was, motionless, the strange wings half spread. The golden unhuman eyes were looking past him, watching something with cold malice and contempt—and with a concentration of purpose that made a death's mask of the perfectly chiseled green face.

In that second, Mel understood the purpose as clearly as if she had told him. In the next, the image disappeared with a jerky, complete abruptness—

As if somebody were belatedly trying to wipe it out of his memory as well! But he knew he had seen her somehow—somewhere—as she actually was at that moment. And he knew what she had been watching. Himself, Mel Armstrong, staggering blindly about in his other-dimension, down in the court!

He hadn't stayed in the court. He was back in the garage, backed trembling against a wall. She—*they*—weren't trying to show him gratitude, or reward him somehow; before they left, they simply wanted to destroy the human being who had found out about them, and whom they had used. The table and the pattern were some sort of trap! What he couldn't understand was why they didn't simply come down in their fireball and kill him as they had the cat.

They were still pouring their pictures at him, but he knew now how to counteract that. He stared out through the garage window at the lightening sky—looked at, listened to, what was there, filling his mind with Earth shapes and sounds!

And he promptly discovered an ally he hadn't been counting on. He hadn't really been aware of the thumping wind before, and the sketchy pattering of raindrops, like a sweeping fall of leaves here and there. He hadn't even heard, beyond the continuous dim roar of surf from the beach, the gathering mutter of thunder.

They couldn't stay here long. The storm was ready to break. They weren't willing to risk coming out fully into the Earth dimension to hunt him down. And he didn't have to go to their trap . . .

Rain spattered louder and closer. The sweat chilled on Mel's body as his breathing grew quieter. They hadn't left him yet. If he relaxed his eyes—and his mind, there was an instant faint recurrence of the swirling unearthly patterns. But he could keep them out by looking at what was really here. He only had to wait—

Then the rain came down in a great, rushing tide, and he knew they were gone.

For a few seconds, he remained where he was, weak with relief. Over the noise of the storm, he heard human voices faintly from the other court and from neighboring houses. That final crash must have awakened everybody—and someone had seen the great globe of fire when it first appeared.

There should be some interesting gossip in the morning!

Which concerned Mel not at all. After drinking in the sweet certainty of being still alive and safe, he had become aware of an entirely unexpected emotion, which was, curiously, a brief but sharp pang of grief at Miss Green's betrayal. Why, he must have been practically in love with that other-dimensional, human-shaped rattlesnake! Mulling it over in moody amazement at himself, it struck Mel suddenly then that one could interpret her final action somewhat differently, too.

Because she could have planted that apparently revealing picture of herself deliberately in his mind, to stop him from stumbling into the trap the others had set for him. She might have been planning to save him from the beginning or merely relented at the last moment. There was no way of ever really knowing now, but Mel found he preferred to believe that Miss Green's intention was good.

In the driving rain, he hesitated a moment beside the blackened lump that had been the cat, but he couldn't force himself to pick it up and remove it. If someone else found it, it might add to the gossip, but that wasn't any business of his any more. Everyone knew that lightning did funny, selective things. So far as he was concerned, the matter was all over.

He opened the duplex door and stood staring.

His apartment door was open and the room beyond was dark, as he had left it, But down the little stairway and out of Maria's upstairs apartment, light poured in a quiet flood.

❊　　　❊　　　❊

She must have returned during the night while he was sleeping, probably drunk as a hoot-owl. The commotion downstairs hadn't been enough to arouse her. But something else had—she'd come down following swirling, beautiful, unearthly pictures, hunting the pattern that would guide her straight into a promised delight.

Mel didn't have to reach into the apartment to switch on the light. Lightning did funny, selective things, all right, and from where he stood he could smell what had happened. They hadn't wasted that final bolt, after all.

Oddly enough, what was uppermost in his mind in those seconds, while he continued to put off seeing what he was going to have to look at very soon, was the final awareness of how he must have appeared in their eyes:

A stupid native, barely capable of receiving training and instruction enough to be a useful servant. Beyond that, they had simply had no interest in him.

It was Maria they had worried about. The mental impressions he'd picked up in the court had been directed at her. Miss Green had been obliged to stop him finally from springing a trap which was set for another.

For Maria, who might have endangered their leaving.

Captives of the Thieve-Star

. . . .

I

THE CELEBRATION OF the wedding of Peer and Channok had to be cut a little short, because a flock of police-boats from Irrek showed up at detector-range about midway. But it was carried off with a flourish nevertheless.

The oxygen-bubble in the small mooncrater was filled with colorful solidographs, creating the impression of an outdoor banquet hall. The best bands playing in the Empire that night unwittingly contributed their efforts, and food and drink were beyond reproach.

Though somewhat dazed throughout, Channok was startled to discover at one point that the thick carpets on which he stood were a genuine priceless Gaifornaab weave—and no solidographs either! The eighty-four small ships of the space-rat tribe—or voyageurs, as they distinctly preferred to be called—lined up along the outer edges of the banquet hall looked eerily out of place to him; but Peer didn't seem to mind. Her people rarely did go far away from their ships, and the lawless, precarious life they led made that an advisable practice.

It would be up to him now, Channok reflected, beaming down on Peer, to educate her into customs and attitudes more fitting for the wife of a regular citizen of the Empire and probable future member of the Imperial Secret Service—

And then, suddenly, the whole ceremony seemed to be over! A bit puzzled by the abruptness with which everybody had begun to pack up and leave, Channok was standing beside the ramp of

65

his own ship, the *Asteroid*—an honest, licensed trader—when Santis strolled over to talk to him. Santis was Peer's father and the pint-sized chieftain of the tribe.

"Didn't tell you before, son," he remarked, "because you were already nervous enough. But as soon as they finish collapsing the bubble, you'll have about six minutes to get your *Asteroid* aloft and off this moon before the cops from Irrek arrive."

"I heard you, Pop, and everything's packed!" Peer called down from the open lock of the *Asteroid*. "Come up and kiss me goodby and we'll seal her up!"

Frowning suspiciously, Channok followed Santis up the ramp. "Why should I worry about cops?" he inquired, looking down at the two little people while they briefly embraced. Peer came about up to his shoulder, though perfectly formed, and Santis was an inch or two shorter. The tribe didn't run to bulk. "Nobody's hunting for me."

"Not yet, son," Santis conceded. He twirled his fierce brown mustache-tips thoughtfully and glanced at Peer.

"If you're passing anywhere near Old Nameless, you might cache that special cargo you're carrying for me there," he told her. "Around the foot of the Mound. Too bulky for the ships I've got here! I put a dowser plate in with it, and I'll come pick it up with a transport sometime in the next four months."

"Yes, Pop," said Peer.

"The Fourth Voyageur Fleet will rendezvous at New Gyrnovaan next Terra spring. If you can talk this big lug into it, try to make it there, daughter!"

"We'll be there," promised Peer.

Channok cleared his throat impatiently. Not if he could help it, they wouldn't!

"Those cops are looking for the missing Crown jewels of Irrek," Santis resumed, looking at him. "After they've opened you up from stem to stern to make sure you're not hiding them, they might apologize. And again they might not."

"Holy Satellites!" Channok said, stunned. "Did you actually—"

"Not I, son. I just master-mind these things. Some of the boys did the job. There goes the oxygen-bubble! Now will you get going?"

They got going, Channok speechless for once.

Some two months later, he stood in the *Asteroid*'s control room, watching a pale blur creep up along the starboard screen.

"That's not just one ship—that's at least a hundred," he announced presently, somewhat startled. "Looks like they've turned out the entire Dardrean war-fleet! Wonder what's up?"

Peer laid the cargo list she was checking down on the desk and came over to look at the screen..

"Hm," she said.

"It couldn't possibly have anything to do with us, could it?" he inquired, on a sudden alarming hunch. Being unfamiliar with the dialect used on Dardrea, he had left most of the bargaining there to her.

Peer shrugged. She showed the bland, innocent look of a ten-year-old child, but that was habitual with her. On one occasion she'd been mistaken for his daughter, and at times he even had to remind himself that she'd been eighteen and a student at the Imperial Institute of Technology when he first met her there—and then unwittingly became Santis' tool in the abstraction of a small but important section of the IIT's top-secret experimental files! He'd been trying to counteract that little brigand's influence on Peer ever since, but he wasn't too sure of his degree of success so far.

"We took the Merchants Guild for plenty on our auction," she admitted.

"Well," Channok frowned, "they'd hardly send a fleet after us for that."

"And, of course," added Peer, "we got the Duke of Dardrea's fabulous Coronet. Forgot to mention that. Perfectly legal, though! Some local-crook swiped it and we took it in trade."

Channok winced. As a matter of fact, fencing was a perfectly legitimate business on Dardrea. But a man who planned to enter the Imperial Secret Service, as soon as he could save up the money to pay his way through the Academy, couldn't afford any stains on his past. Throughout the Empire, the Service was renowned in song and story as the one body of men who stood above the suspicion of reproach.

"The Duke won't know it's gone for another week," Peer consoled him. "Anyway, it looks to me as if those ships are beginning to pull off our course."

There followed some seconds of tense observation.

"So they are," Channok acknowledged then. He mopped his forehead. "But I wish you wouldn't be quite so technical in your interpretation of local laws, Peer! Those babies are really traveling. Wonder who or what they're chasing?"

Three days later, as the *Asteroid* approached the area of the red giant sun of Old Nameless, where they were going to cache Santis' cargo for him—hot cargo, probably; and it would be a load off Channok's mind to get rid of it—they picked up the trail of the foundering spaceship *Ra-Twelve* and found part of the answer on board.

II

"It seemed to me," Channok remarked, watching the *Ra-Twelve*, in the viewscreen before them, "as if her drives had cut off completely just then. But they're on again now. What do you think, crew-member Peer?"

"Let's just follow her a bit," Peer suggested. "I've seen ships act like that that were just running out of juice. But this one won't even answer signals."

"It could be," Channok said hopefully, "a case of fair salvage! You might keep working the communicators, though . . ."

However, the *Ra-Twelve* continued to ignore them while she plodded on towards the distant red glare of the Nameless System like a blind, thirsty beast following its nose to a water-hole. Presently, she began a series of quavering zigzag motions, wandered aimlessly off her course, returned to it again on a few final puffs of invisible energy and at last went drifting off through space with her drives now obviously dead.

The *Asteroid* continued to follow at a discreet distance like a chunky vulture, watching. If there was anyone on board the *Ra-Twelve*, it almost had to be a ghost. Her rear lock was wide open, and the hull showed deep scars and marks of some recent space-action.

"But she wasn't really badly hurt," Channok pointed out. "What do you suppose could have happened to her crew?"

Peer gave him a nervous grin. "Maybe a space-ghost came on board!"

"You don't really believe those spooky voyageur stories, do you?" he said tolerantly.

"Sure I do—and so will you some day," Peer promised him. "I'll tell you a few true ones just before your next sleep-period."

"No, you won't," Channok said firmly. "Aside from space-ghosts, though, that crate has a downright creepy look to her. But I suppose I'd better go over and check, as soon as she slows down enough so we can latch on. And you're going to stay on the *Asteroid*, Peer."

"In a pig's eye, I am!" Peer said indignantly. And though Channok wished to know if she had forgotten that he was the *Asteroid*'s skipper, it turned out that this was one time he'd have to yield.

"Because, Channy dear," Peer said, her big dark eyes welling slow tears, "I'd just die if something happened to you over there and I was left all alone in space!"

"All you'd have to do," Channok said uncomfortably, "is to head the *Asteroid* for New Gyrnovaan, and you know it. Well—you've got to promise to stay right behind me, anyway."

"Of course," promised Peer, the tears vanishing miraculously. "Santis says a wife should always stick with her husband in space, because he might lead her into a jam, all right, but nothing like the !!****!; !**!! jams she's likely to run into if she strays around by herself."

"Whereas Ship's Regulation 66-B says," said Channok with grim satisfaction, "that crew-member Peer gets her mouth washed out with soap just before the next sleep-period because of another uncontrolled lapse into vituperous profanity—and what was that comment?"

"That one was under my breath," said Peer, crestfallen, "so it doesn't count."

Without making any particular remarks about it, both of them had fastened a brace of guns to their jet-harnesses. At close range— held thirty feet away against the *Asteroid*'s ring-bumpers by a set of dock grapnels—the *Ra-Twelve*'s yawning lock looked more than ever like the black mouth of a cavern in which something was lurking for them.

Channok went over first, propelled by a single squirt of his jets, and landed. a little heavier than he had intended to. Peer, following instructions to keep right behind him, came down an instant later in the middle of his back. They got untangled hurriedly, stood up and started swiveling their helmet beams about the *Ra-Twelve*'s storage lock.

It was practically empty. So was the big rack that had held the ship's single big lifeboat. There were some tools scattered around. They kicked at them thoughtfully, looked at each other and started forward through an open door up a dark passageway, switching their lights ahead and from side to side.

There was a locked door which probably led into the *Ra-Twelve*'s engine section, and then four cabins, each of which had been used by two men. The cabins were in considerable disorder, but from what one could tell in a brief look-around, each of the occupants had found time to pack up about what you would expect a man to take along when he was planning on a lifeboat trip. So whatever had happened probably hadn't been entirely unexpected.

The mess-room, all tidied up, was next; two locked doors were at the back of it, and also an open entrance to the kitchen and food storage. They glanced around at everything, briefly, and went on to the control-room.

It was considerably bigger than the one on the *Asteroid* and luxuriously equipped. The pilot's section was in a transparently walled little office by itself. The instruments showed both Dardrean and Empire markings and instructions. Channok switched the dead drives off first and then reached out, quite automatically, for the spot above the control desk where a light button ought to be—

Light instantly flooded the interior of the *Ra-Twelve*.

The intruders jumped a foot. It was as if the ship had suddenly come alive around them! Then they looked at each other and grinned.

"Automatic," Channok sighed.

"Might as well do it the easy way," Peer admitted. She slid the Ophto Needle she'd half-drawn back into its holster.

The *Ra-Twelve* had eighteen fully charged drive batteries still untouched. With some system of automatic power transfer working, she could have gone cruising along on her course for months to come. However, she hadn't been cruising, Channok discovered next; the speed controls were set to "Full Emergency".... An empty ship, racing through space till the battery she was operating on went dead—

He shook his head. And then Peer was tapping his arm.

"Look what I found! I think it's her log!"

It was a flat steel box with an illuminated tape at its front end, on which a date was printed. A line of spidery Dardrean script was engraved on a plate on the top of the box.

"*Ra-Twelve*," Peer translated. "That's her name."

"So it's a Dardrean ship! But they're using the Empire calendar," Channok pointed out, "which would make it an Empire crew . . . How do you work this thing? If it is her log, it might give us an idea of what's happened."

"Afterwards, Channy! I just found another door leading off the other end of the control room—"

The door opened into a second passage, parallel to the one by which they had come forward, but only half as long and very dimly lit. Filled with uneasy speculations, Channok forgot his own instructions and let Peer take the lead.

"More cabins," her voice said, just as he became aware of the wrecked door-frame out of which the light was spilling ahead of her.

A woman had been using that cabin. A woman who had liked beautiful and expensive things, judging by what was strewn about. It looked, Channok thought, as if she hadn't had time to finish, her packing.

"Her spacesuit's gone, though," Peer's voice announced from the interior of a disordered closet.

Channok was inspecting the door. This was the first indication that there had been any violence connected with whatever had happened on the *Ra-Twelve*. The door had been locked from without and literally ripped open from within by a stream of incandescence played on it by a gun held probably not much more than a foot away. That woman had wanted out in an awful hurry!

Peer came over to watch him. He couldn't quite read her expression, but he had a notion she wanted to bawl.

"Let's take a quick look at the rest of it and get back to the *Asteroid*," he suggested, somewhat disturbed himself. "We ought to talk this over."

The one remaining cabin lay just beyond the point where the passage angled back into the ship. There was light in that one, too, and the door was half open. Channok got there first and pushed it open a little farther. Then he stood frozen in the door-frame for a moment.

"What's stopping you?" Peer inquired impatiently, poking his ribs from behind.

He stepped back into the passage, pulled the door shut all the way, scooped her up and heaved her to his shoulder. His space-boots felt like iron anchors as he clunk-clunked hastily back through the passages to the derelict's lock. There was nothing definite to run from any more; but he knew now what had happened on the *Ra-Twelve*, and he felt nightmare pacing after him all the way.

He crossed to the *Asteroid's* control room lock in a jump, without bothering with his jets.

❀   ❀   ❀

"Close the outer lock!" he told Peer hoarsely, reaching up for the switch marked "Decontaminant" above him.

A fourfold spray of yellowish Killall was misting the trapped air in the lock about them an instant later.

"What was it?" Peer's voice came out of the fog.

"Antibiotic," Channok said, his scalp still crawling. "What you—what voyageurs call a lich, I think. I don't know that kind. But it got the guy in that last cabin."

The occupant of the last cabin had looked as if somebody had used a particularly vicious sort of acid gun on him, which somehow had missed damaging his clothing. To the grisly class of life-forms that produced that effect, an ordinary spacesuit offered exactly no resistance.

"A lich can't last more than an hour or so in space, Channy," Peer's voice came shakily after a pause. "It's a pretty awful way to get it, but that stuff over there must have been dead for a long time now."

"I know," said Channok. He hesitated and then cut off the Killall spray and started the blowers to clear the lock. "I guess I just panicked for a moment. But I'm going to go over that ship with decontaminant before we do any more investigating. And meanwhile you'd better get in a few hours of sleep."

"Wouldn't hurt any," Peer agreed. "How do you suppose the lich got on board?"

He could tell her, that. He'd seen a heavy, steel-framed glassite container in a corner of the cabin, opened. They must have been transporting some virulent form of antibiotic; and there might have been an accident—

Five hours later, they had come to the conclusion that it had been no accident. Four hours of that time, Channok had been engaged in disinfecting the *Ra-Twelve*, even her engine sections. He'd given the one man left on board space-burial in one of the *Asteroid*'s steel cargo crates. The crate hadn't been launched very far and presently hung suspended some eighty yards above the two ships, visible as a black oblong that obscured the stars behind it.

It and its contents were one of the reasons Channok was anxious to get done with the job of salvaging the *Ra-Twelve*. She was a stream-lined, beautiful ship; but after what had happened, he knew he would never be able to work up any liking for her. She seemed to be waiting sullenly and silently for a chance to deal with the two humans who had dared come on board her again.

He sealed her up presently, filled her with a fresh airmix and, having once more checked everything he could think of, let Peer come over again for a final briefing on their run to Old Nameless.

Peer wandered promptly into the cabin where the dead man had been and there discovered the wall-safe.

III

She called him. He couldn't imagine how he had overlooked it. Perhaps because it was so obviously *there*. It was an ordinary enough safe, from what they could see of the front of it; and there was a tiny key in its lock.

They looked at it thoughtfully.

"You didn't try to open it, did you?" Channok inquired.

"No," said Peer; "because—"

"That's what I was thinking," Channok admitted.

There had been, they had decided, at least two groups working against each other in the ship. The dead man had been in charge of the antibiotic. Perhaps the woman had been on his side, perhaps not. But the eight other men had acted together and had controlled the ship. What action or threat of theirs had caused the dead man to release his terrible weapon would be hard to discover now. But he had done it, and the eight men had abandoned the *Ra-Twelve* promptly, leaving the woman locked in her cabin

It looked pretty much as if she had been the one who had switched the drives to full speed—before jumping out into space. A pretty tough, desperate lot all around, in Channok's opinion. The *Ra-Twelve*'s log offered the information that they had left Dardrea three calendric days earlier, but had been of no further help in identifying crew or passengers. That most of them were professional criminals, however, seemed a pretty safe bet—as Peer had pointed out, in voyageur terms, amateurs didn't play around with taboo-weapons like a bottled lich.

Also, amateurs—Peer and Channok, for example—could have sense enough not to blunder into a booby-trap . . .

"He'd know, of course," Channok said reflectively, "that everybody would be wondering what's hidden in that safe. And it could be anything up to and including full instructions on how to set up an artificial culture of antibiotics. Plenty of governments would pay twenty times what the *Ra-Twelve* is worth as salvage for that kind of information. But it's nothing we need to know."

"Not that bad," Peer agreed.

"And the guy who opens that wall-safe had better be an armaments expert! Which we're not. But now, crew-member Peer, if we want to get Santis' cargo cached on Old Nameless before I fall asleep, we ought to get started. Idle curiosity is something we can satisfy some other time."

"Two hours past your sleep-period right now." said Peer, glancing at her wristwatch. "Tsk, tsk! That always makes you so grouchy."

Half an hour later, they were on their way—Channok in the *Ra-Twelve*, Peer in the *Asteroid* keeping as close to each other as two ships in flight could safely get. With the red glare of the Old Nameless sun a trifle off-center before him, Channok settled down in the most comfortable pilot-seat he'd ever found on any ship and decided he could relax a trifle. Peer was obviously having a wonderful time doing her first solo-piloting job on a ship of the *Asteroid*'s size; and since she'd run and landed the *Asteroid* any number of times under his supervision, he wasn't worried about her ability to handle it. However, he continued to check in on her over the communicators every five minutes or so, and grinned at the brisk, spacemanlike replies he got in return. Crew-member Peer was on her best behavior right now!

By and by, then—he couldn't have said just when it started—Channok began to realize that some very odd things were happening around him—

It appeared that the Thing he had put out for burial in a space-crate hadn't like the idea of being left alone. So it was following him.

Channok decided uneasily that it might be best to ignore it. But it kept coming closer and closer until, finally, the crate was floating just outside the *Ra-Twelve*'s control room port, spinning slowly like a running-down top.

The crate stayed shut, but he knew the Thing inside it was watching him.

"That's my ship," the Thing remarked presently.

Channok ignored it.

"And you're all alone," said the Thing.

"No, I'm not!" said Channok. "Peer's with me."

"Peer's gone back to Santis," said the Thing. "You're all alone. Except," it added, "for me."

"Well, good-bye!" Channok said firmly. There was no point in getting too chummy with it. He punched the *Ra-Twelve*'s drives down as far as they would go, and the crate vanished.

How that ship could travel! Nothing could hope to keep up with him now—except, Perhaps, that round, red glare of light just behind the *Ra-Twelve*.

That was actually overtaking him, and fast. It was coming up like a cosmic police-ship, with a huge, hollow noise rushing before it. Channok listened apprehensively. Suddenly, there were words:

"WHOO-WHOOO!" it howled. *"This is the Space Ghost!"*

He shot up out of his chair like a jabbed cat, knocking it over, and glared around.

The *Ra-Twelve*'s control room lay brightly lit and silent behind him.

"Ha-ha!" Peer's chuckle came from the communicator. "That woke you up, I bet! Was that you that fell over?"

"Aw-awk!" breathed Channok. Articulation came back to him. "All right, crewmember Peer! just wait till we get to Old Nameless! I'll fix you good!"

"Shall I tell you the story now about the Horror Ship from Mizar?" Peer inquired intrepidly.

"Go right ahead," Channok challenged, righting his chair and settling back into it. "You can't scare me with that sort of stuff." He began checking their position.

He must have been asleep for quite a while! The Nameless System was less than two hours ahead now. He switched on the front screen; and the sun swam up like a big, glowing coal before him. He began checking for the seventh planet.

"Well," he reminded the communicator grimly, "you were going to tell me a story."

The communicator remained silent a moment.

"I don't think I will, anyway," Peer said then, rather quietly.

"Why not?" Channok inquired, getting his screen-viewer disentangled from a meteor-belt in the Nameless System.

"I made that Space Ghost too good," whispered Peer. "I'm getting scared myself now."

"Aha!" said Channok. "See what behaving like that will get you?" He got Old Nameless VII into the viewer.

The communicator remained still. He looked over at it.

"Of course, there's really nothing to be scared of," he added reassuringly.

"How do you know?" quavered Peer. "I'm all alone."

"Nonsense!" Channok said heartily. "I can see the *Asteroid* right over there on the screen. You can see me, can't you?"

"Sure," said Peer. "That's a long way off, though. You couldn't do anything!"

"It's not safe for two ships to travel much closer together," Channok reminded her. "We're only two hours from Old Nameless right now—I'm already focussed on it."

"I've been focussed on it for an hour," said Peer. "While you were snoring," she added. "Two hours is an awful long time!"

"Tell you what," suggested Channok. "I'll race you to it. The *Ra-Twelve*'s a mighty fast boat—" He checked himself. He'd only dreamed that, after all.

"Let's go," Peer said briefly.

He let Peer stay just ahead of him all the way in, though the streamlined derelict probably could have flown rings around the *Asteroid*, at that. Just an hour later, they went around Old Nameless VII twice, braking down, and then coasted into its atmosphere on their secondary drives.

"That's the place," Peer's voice said suddenly. "I can see the old Mound in the plain. In the evening strip, Channy—that straight-up cliff."

He set the *Ra-Twelve* down first, at the base of a mountain that reared up almost vertically for eighteen thousand feet or so out of a flat, dimly-lit stretch of rocky desert land.

The *Asteroid* came down in a very neat landing, two hundred yards away. He got there on the run, just as the front lock opened. Peer came tumbling out of it into his arms and hung on fiercely, while her skipper hugged her.

"Let that scare be a lesson to you!" he remarked when he set her down.

"It certainly will," said Peer, still clutching his arm as they started over to the *Ra-Twelve*. "That old Space Ghost had me going!"

"Me, too," he confessed; "just for a moment, anyway. Well, let's get busy."

They went over the *Ra-Twelve* again from bow to stern, to make sure there was nothing they would want to take along immediately, and found there wasn't. They gave the unopened wall-safe a last calculating regard, and decided once more that they'd better not. Then they shut off everything, closed the front lock behind them and safetied it with the dock bolts.

The plain was darkening when they came out, but the top of the mountain still glowed with red light. They climbed into the *Asteroid*, and Channok closed the lock. He started for the control desk then; but Peer beat him to it and anchored herself into the seat of command with hands, knees and feet. It became apparent almost at once that he couldn't get her out of it without running the risk of pulling off her head.

"Now look here, crew-member Peer," he said persuasively, "you know good and well that if these top-heavy cargo crates have one weakness, it's the take-off."

"It could be the pilot, too," Peer said meaningly. "I've been studying the manual, and I've watched you do it. It's my turn now."

He considered her thoughtfully.

"Suppose you die of old age, all of a sudden?" argued Peer. "Wouldn't want me to sit here alone without knowing even how to take her off, would you?"

That did it.

"Go ahead," said Channok with dignity, taking a position back of the chair. "Go right ahead! This decrepit old man of twenty-eight is going to stand right here and laugh himself sick!"

"You'll be sick, all right," promised Peer. "But it won't be from laughing! I'll read that chapter out of the manual to you sometime."

She *had* studied it, too, he decided. She sat perched forward on the edge of the chair, alert and cocky, and went through the starting operations without hitch or hesitation. The *Asteroid* rumbled beneath them, briefly building up power . . .

Channok braced himself—

IV

For the next few seconds, the question seemed to be whether they'd pile into the plain or the mountain first; and, for another improbable moment, they were distinctly skidding along upside down. Then Peer got them straightened out, and they soared up rapidly into the night sky above Old Nameless.

Channok's hair settled slowly back into place.

Peer looked around at him, puzzled and rather pale.

"That's not the way it said in the manual!" she stated.

Channok whooped. Then he sat down on the floor, bent over and yelled.

When he got around to wiping the tears from his eyes, Peer was looking down at him disgustedly from the control chair.

"It wasn't the way it said in the manual!" she repeated firmly. "We're going to have this old crate overhauled before she'll be safe to fly—and if you weren't my husband, I'd really let you have it now!"

He stood up, muttering some sort of apology.

"I've done some just as bad," he assured her.

"Hum," said Peer coldly, studying Old Nameless in the screen below them. It seemed safe to pat her on the head then, but he kept his hand well out of biting range.

"We'd better get back to that mountain and bury the *Ra-Twelve* before it gets too dark to find the spot," he suggested.

"It's still just in sight," said Peer. "You get the guns ready, and I'll run us past it slowly."

Spaceships being what they were, there wasn't much ceremony about caching the *Ra-Twelve*. Channok got the bow-turret out; and as Peer ran the *Asteroid* slowly along the mountainside a few hundred feet above the *Ra-Twelve*, he cut a jagged line into the rock with the gun's twin beams. A few dozen tons of rock came thundering down on the *Ra-Twelve*.

They came back from the other side, a little higher up, and he loosened it some more. This time, it looked as if a sizable section of the mountain were descending; and when the dust had settled the *Ra-Twelve* was fifty feet under a sloping pile of very natural-looking debris. To get her out again, they'd only have to cut a path down to her lock and start her drives. She'd come out of the stuff then, like a trout breaking water . . .

Satisfied, they went off and got the *Asteroid* on an orbit around Old Nameless, not too far out. Peer had assured Channok that Santis' investigations had proved the planet safe for human beings, so it probably was. But he knew he'd feel more comfortable if they put in their sleep-periods outside its atmosphere. Bathed in the dismal light of its giant sun, old Nameless looked like a desolate backyard of Hell. It was rocky, sandy, apparently waterless and lifeless and splotched with pale stretches of dry salt seas. Incongruously delicate auroras went crawling about its poles, like lopsided haloes circling a squat, brooding demon. It wasn't, Channok decided, the kind of planet be would have stopped at of his own accord, for any purpose.

The cliff against which they had buried the *Ra-Twelve* was the loftiest section of an almost unbroken chain of mountains, surrounding the roughly circular hundred-mile plain, which was littered with beds of boulders and sand-hills, like a moon crater. What Peer had referred to as the "Mound" lay approximately at the center of the plain. It turned out, next morning, to be a heavily weathered, dome-shaped structure half a mile high and five miles across, which gave the impression that all but the top tenth of a giant's skull had been buried in the sand, dented here and there with massive hammers, and sprinkled thickly with rock dust. It was obviously an artifact—constructed with hundred-foot bricks! As the *Asteroid* drifted down closer to it, Channok became interested.

"Who built it?" he asked.

Peer shrugged. She didn't know. "Santis spent a few hours jetting around the edges of it once," she said. "But he wouldn't tell us much; and, afterwards, he wouldn't let us get nearer than a mile to it. He didn't go back himself, either—said it was dangerous to get too close."

It didn't look dangerous. But fifty thousand years ago, it might have been a fortress of some sort.

"You oughtn't to be flying so low over it, even!" Peer said warningly. "Right in the middle on top is where it's the most dangerous, Santis said!"

Channok didn't argue the matter—they had to get Santis' special cargo cached and off their hands first, anyway. He lifted the *Asteroid* a mile or so and then brought her down a couple of miles beyond the Mound, at the point Peer had designated.

They got out of the ship and gazed about the broken, rocky plain. The red light of the Nameless Sun was spilling across it in what passed for morning on this world. In it, the black mountain chains rearing about the horizon and the craggy waves of flat land had the general effect of a bomb-shattered and slowly burning city. Far off to their left, he could see the upper half of the towering precipice which marked the *Ra-Twelve*'s resting place.

"How long a time did you say you spent here?" he asked.

Peer reflected. "About two Terra-months, I guess. I'm not sure, though. That was a long time ago. My youngest brother Dobby wasn't born yet."

He shook his head. "What a spot for a nice family picnic!"

"It wasn't a picnic," Peer said. "But my kid brother Wilf and I had a lot of fun anyway, just running around and teasing the ghouls. I guess you don't notice so much what a place looks like when you're little."

"Teasing the what?"

"Ghouls," said Peer carelessly.

He looked at her suspiciously; but she seemed to be studying the nearby terrain for a good spot to start digging.

"And what were Santis and your mother doing?" he inquired.

"They were looking for some sort of mineral deposit on Old Nameless; I forget just what. How about that spot—just under that little overhang? It looks like good, solid top-rock."

Channok agreed it was just the place. He'd got a drilling attachment mounted to the *Asteroid*'s small all-purpose tractor; and now he went back and ran the machine down the ramp from the storage lock. He ordered Peer, who wanted to help, up a rock about twenty feet overhead, where she perched looking like an indignant elf, out of reach of any stray puffs of the drill-blast. Then he started running a slanting, narrow tunnel down under the overhang.

Half an hour later, when he backed the tractor out of the tunnel, pushing a pile of cooking slag behind him, he saw her standing up on the rock with a small stungun in her hand. She beckoned to him.

Channok pulled off his breather-mask, shut off the tractor, and jumped from the saddle.

"What is it?" he called anxiously, trotting towards her, while the machine's clacking and roaring subsided.

"Some of those ghouls!" Peer called back. "Climb up here and I'll show you." She didn't seem worried.

"They've ducked behind those rocks now," she said as he clambered up beside her; "but they won't stay there long. They're curious, and I think some of them remember the time we were here before."

"Are they dangerous?" he inquired, patting his bolstered set of heavy-duty Reaper guns.

"No," said Peer. "They look sort of awful, but you mustn't shoot them! If they get inside of thirty feet I'll hit them in the stomach with a stunner. They grunt then and run. Santis said that was the right way to teach them not to get too nosey."

They waited a moment in silence, scanning the rocks.

Then Channok started violently.

"Holy !!**?** Satellites!" he swore, his hair bristling.

A big, dead-white shape had popped up springily on a rock

about fifty feet away, stared at him for an instant out of eyes like grey glass-platters, and popped down out of sight again. Awful was right!

"Aha!" crew-member Peer gloated, grinning. "You shouldn't have said that! Tonight you've got to let me soap out your mouth!"

A light dawned gradually.

"You did it on purpose!" he accused her. "You knew I'd say something like that the first time I saw one!"

Peer didn't deny it.

"It's the soap for you, just the same," she shrugged. "People ought to have some self-control—that's what you said. Look, another one now—no, two!"

V

When he came up for lunch, he found about fifty ghouls collected around the area. By that time he had dug the cache, steel-lined it, disinfected it and installed preservatives, a humidifier and a dowser plate. Loading it up would take most of the rest of the day.

He avoided looking at the local population as much as he could while he ate. However, the occasional glimpses he got suggested that the Nameless System had made a half-hearted and badly botched attempt at developing its own type of humanoid inhabitant. They had extremely capable looking jaws, at any rate, and their wide, lipless mouths were wreathed in perpetual idiot grins. The most completely disagreeable parts of them, Channok decided, were the enormous, red-nailed hands and feet. Like fat, white gargoyles, they sat perched around the tops of the rocks in a wide circle and just stared.

"Sloppy-looking things," he remarked, noticing Peer's observant eyes on him. "But at least they're not trying to strike up a conversation."

"They never say anything until you hit them in the stomach with a stunner," she informed him. "Then they just grunt and run."

"Sure they mightn't get mean about that? The smallest of this lot looks plenty big enough to take us both apart."

Peer laughed. "All of them together wouldn't try it! They're real yellow. Wilf got mad at a couple of 'em once and ran 'em halfway over to the Mound before mother caught up with him and stopped him. Wilf had his blood up, that time!"

"Maybe the ghouls built the Mound." Channok suggested. "Their great-great-ancestors, anyway."

"They won't go near it now," Peer said, following his gaze. "They're scared of that, too."

They studied the rugged, ungainly slopes of the huge artifact for a moment. There was something fascinating about it, Channok thought. Perhaps just its size.

"Santis said the plain was the bottom of a sea a while ago," Peer offered. "So it could have been some sort of sea-things that built it."

"Any entrances into it?" he asked casually.

"Just one, right at the top."

"You know," he said, "I think I'd like to go over and have a look at that thing before we leave."

"No!" said Peer, alarmed. "You'd better not. Santis said it was dangerous—and there *is* something there! We saw a light one night."

"What kind of a light?"

"Like someone walking around the top of it, near that entrance, with a big lamp in his hand," Peer remembered. "Like he might have been looking for something."

"Sounds a bit like your old friend, the Space Ghost," Channok murmured suspiciously.

"No," Peer grinned. "This was a *real* light—and we took off the next evening. Santis said it might be as well if we moved somewhere else for a while."

Channok considered a moment. "Look," he said finally, "we can do it like this. I'll jet myself over there and stroll around it a bit in daylight; and if you're worried, you could hang overhead in the *Asteroid* with a couple of turrets out. Just in case someone gets tough."

"I could, maybe," said Peer, in a tight voice, "but I'm not going to. If you're going to go walking around there, after all Santis said, I'm going to be walking right behind you."

"Oh, no, you're not," Channok said.

"Oh, yes, I am!" said Peer. "You can't make me stay here!"

He looked at her in surprise. Her eyes were angry, but her lower lip quivered.

"Hey," he said, startled. "Maybe I'm being a pig!"

"You sure are!" Peer said, relieved. The lip stopped quivering. "You're not going over there, then?"

"Not if you feel that way about it," Channok said. He paused.

"I guess," he admitted awkwardly, "I just didn't like the idea of Santis flitting around space, Holy Aynstyn knows where, and still putting in his two millicredits worth every so often, through crew-member Peer."

Peer blew her nose and considered in turn. "Just the same," she concluded, "when Santis says something like that, it's a lot better if people do it. Is 'Holy Aynstyn knows where' a swear-word?"

"No," said Channok. "Not exactly."

He'd finished his lunch and was just going to suggest they run the tractor out of the cache and back the few hundred yards to the *Asteroid* for the first load of Santis' cargo, when he noticed that all the ghouls had vanished.

He called Peer's attention to the fact.

"Uh-huh," she said in an absent-minded tone. "They do that sometimes . . ."

Channok looked at her. She was staring at a high boulder a short distance away, with a queer, intent expression, as if she were deep in thought about something: He hoped she wasn't still brooding about their little argument—

Then she glanced at him, gave him a sudden grin, swung herself around and slid nimbly off the rock.

"Come on down quick!" she said. "I want to show you something before you get back to work. A ghoul-burrow!"

"A ghoul-burrow?" Channok repeated unenthusiastically.

"Yes, sure!" said a Peer impatiently. "They're cute! They're all lined with glass or something." She spread her arms wide. "Jump, and I'll catch you!"

Channok laughed, flopped over on his stomach with his legs over the edge of the rock, and slid down in a fair imitation of Peer's nonchalant style of descent, spraining his ankle only a little. Well, he hadn't grown up skipping from craggy moon to asteroid to heavy-planet to whatnot like she had . . .

They threaded their way about the rocks to the spot she had been studying. She explained that he'd have to climb into the burrow to get a good idea of what it was like.

"Well, look now, Peer!" Channok protested, staring into the big, round hole that slanted downwards under a big boulder—it did seem to be lined with black glass or some similar stuff. "That cave's got 'No Trespassing' written all over it. Supposing I slide down a half a mile and land in a mess of ghouls?"

"No, you won't," Peer said hurriedly. "It goes level right away, and they're never more than thirty feet long. And the ghoul's out—there's never more than one to a burrow; and I saw this one pop out and run off just before we started here. You're not scared, are you? Wilf and I crawled in and out of hundreds of them!"

"Well, just for a moment then," said Channok resignedly.

He got down on hands and knees and crept into the tunnel. After about six feet, he stopped and found he could turn around without too much trouble. "Peer?" be called back.

"Yes?" said Peer.

"How can I see anything here," Channok demanded peevishly, "when it's all dark?"

"Well, you're in far enough now," said Peer, who had sat down before the entrance of the tunnel and was looking in after him. "And now—I've got to ask you to do something. You know how I always promptly carry out any orders you give me, like getting in my full sleep-period and all?" she added anxiously.

"No, you do not!" Channok stated flatly, resting on his elbows. "Half the time I practically have to drag you to the cabin. Anyway, what's that got to do with—"

"It's like this," Peer said desperately. She glanced up for a moment, as if she had caught sight of something in the dim red sky overhead. "You've got to stay in there a while, Channy."

"Eh?" said Channok.

"When those ghouls pop out of sight in daytime like that, it's because there's a ship or something coming."

"Peer, are you crazy? A ship! Who— I'm coming right out!"

"Stay there, Channy! It's hanging over the *Asteroid* right now. A big lifeboat with its guns out—it must be those men from the *Ra-Twelve*. They must have had a tracer of some sort on her."

"Then get in here quick, Peer!" Channok choked, hauling out one of the Reapers. "You know good and well that bunch would kill a woman as soon as a man!"

"They've already seen me—I wanted them to," Peer informed him. She was talking out of the side of her mouth, looking straight ahead of her, away from the cave. "I'm not going to be a woman. I'm going to be a dumb little girl, ordinary size. I can pull that one off any time."

"But—"

"They'll want to ask questions. I think I can get them to send that lifeboat away. We can't fight that, Channy; it's a regular armed launch. Santis says you can always get the other side to split its forces, if you're smart about it."

"But how—"

"And then, when I yell 'Here we go!' then you pop out. That'll be the right moment—" She stood up suddenly. "We can't talk, any more. They're getting close—" She vanished with that from before the mouth of the burrow.

"Hold on there!" a voice yelled in the distance a few seconds later, as Channok came crawling clumsily up the glassy floor of the tunnel, hampered by the Reaper he still clutched in one hand. It seemed to come from up in the air, and it was using the Empire's universal dialect.

Peer's footsteps stopped abruptly.

"Who you people?" her voice screeched in shrill alarm. "You cops? I ain't done nothing!"

VI

"And just look at those guns she's carrying!" the deeper of the two strange voices commented. "The real stuff, too—a stunner and an Ophto Needle! Better get them from her. If it isn't a baby Flauval!"

"I didn't shoot nobody lately!" Peer said, trembly-voiced.

"No, and you ain't going to shoot nobody either!" the other strange voice mimicked her. That one was high-pitched and thin, with a pronounced nasal twang to it. "Chief, if there're kids with them, it's just a bunch of space-rats that happened along. It couldn't be Flauval!"

"I'd say 'it couldn't be Flauval', if we'd found her dead in her cabin," the deep voice said irritably. "But that door was burned out from inside—and *somebody* ditched the *Ra-Twelve* on this clod." It sounded as if the discovery of Peer had interrupted an argument between them.

"I still can't see how she got out," Nasal-voice Ezeff said sullenly. "She must have been sleeping in her spacesuit. We were out of the ship thirty seconds after I slap-welded that lock across her door. She must have felt the boat leaving and started burning her way out the same instant—"

"It doesn't matter how she did it," said the deep voice. Apparently, it belonged to someone with authority. "If Flauval could think and move fast enough to switch the drives to Full Emergency and still get alive out of a ship full of the Yomm, she could cheat space, too! She always did have the luck of the devil. If we'd had just that minute to spare before leaving, to make sure—"

It paused a moment and resumed gloomily: "That stubborn old maniac of a Koyle—'I'm the Duke's man, sir!' Committing suicide like *that*—so no one else would get control of the Yomm! If we hadn't managed to start the launch's locators in time . . . Well, I hope I'll never have to sweat out another four days like the last. And now we still have to find whoever got Koyle's records."

"Flauval ain't here," Peer offered at that point, brightly.

There was a pause. It seemed that the two newcomers must have almost forgotten their prisoner for a moment.

"What was that you said, kid?" Nasal-voice inquired carefully.

"Those space-rats are all half crazy," the deep voice said contemptuously. "She doesn't know what we're talking about."

"Sure I know!" Peer said indignantly. "You was talking about Flauval. It's Wilf that's the crazy one—I ain't! And she ain't here. Flauval."

"She ain't, eh?" Nasal-voice said, with speculative alertness.

"No, sir," Peer said, timid again. "She's went with the rest of'm."

Both voices swore together in startled shock.

"Where are they?" the deep voice demanded. "Hiding on the ship?"

"No, sir," quavered Peer. "It's just me on the ship, till they come back."

"You mean," the deep voice said, with strained patience "you're supposed to be on the ship?"

"Yes, sir," said Peer. She added in a guilty mutter, "Sleepin' . . ."

"Where did the others go?" Nasal-voice inquired sharply.

"But I ain't tired," said Peer. "Well, with the boxes and stuff! What Flauval wants buried."

There was another duet of exclamations which Channok, at almost any other time, would have considered highly unsuitable for Peer's ears. Right now, it escaped his attention.

"She's got Koyle's records," stated the deep voice then.

"What's in those boxes?" Nasal-voice snapped.

"D-d-don't shake me!" wept Peer. "Papers and stuff—I don't know. They don't never tell me nothing," she wailed, "because I'm just a little girl!"

"Yes, you're just a little girl," said Nasal-voice, exasperated. "You're not going to get much bigger either."

"Cut that," said the deep voice. "No sense scaring the kid."

"Well, you're not figuring on taking them back, are you?" Nasal-voice inquired.

"No. Just Flauval. The colonel will be glad to chat with Flauval a bit, now that she's turned up alive again. Koyle may have told her plenty before we soured him on her. But there's no point in making the rest of them desperate. It's easier when they surrender."

There was a short pause. Then the deep voice addressed Peer with a sort of amiable gruffness:

"So they all went off to bury the boxes, but you don't know where they went—is that it, little girl?"

"Oh, sure!" Peer said, anxious to please. "Yes, sir! I know that!"

"WHERE?" said both voices together, chorusing for the third time.

"It's that big Mound over there," Peer said; and Channok started nervously. "It's got a big door on top. No," she added, "I guess you can't see from down here—and you can't see from the ship. That's why I came out. To watch for'm. But you can see it plain from the top of the rocks."

"That would be the old reservoir or whatever it was we passed back there," said the deep voice.

"That's right," said Peer. "That's just what Flauval called it at lunch! The word you said. There was water there oncet, she said. They flew the boxes over with jets, but they'll be back before it's dark, they said."

There was a brief silence.

"Scares me when it's dark, it does," grumbled the idiot-child.

"Well, that ties it up," the deep voice said, satisfied. "It's the exact kind of stunt Flauval would try. But she's outsmarted herself, this time."

"How do you figure on handling it?" Nasal-voice inquired.

"Get up on one of those rocks with the kid where you can watch both that 'mound' and the lock of their ship. Yes, I know it's more trouble that way—but don't, ah, do anything conclusive about the—uh—aforementioned, before we've corralled the rest. Much more useful while capable of inhaling. Hostage possibilities. Inducement to surrender."

"Uh-huh," Nasal-voice said, comprehendingly.

"Yes, sir!" added Peer.

There was another short pause.

"Might as well skip the circumlocutions," the deep voice continued. "Barely human! I'll send a couple of men through the ship and, if it's empty, I'll leave one of them in the forward lock where you can see him. That's just in case anyone slips past us and comes back. The rest of us will go over to the reservoir in the launch. If the entrance is where she says it is, we've got them bottled. If it looks right, we'll go in."

"That'll be only four of you," said Nasal-voice. "No; three—you're keeping one at the launch-guns, aren't you?"

"Yes, of course. Hey, little girl—how many are with Flauval?"

"Of us, you mean?" Peer asked.

"Of what else?" snarled Nasal-voice.

"Now don't get her so scared she can't talk," the deep voice reproved. "That's right, little girl—how many of you?"

"Well, there's me," sniffled Peer, "and my old man, and my big brother Dobby. And then there's Wilf—that's all. But I don't like Wilf!"

"I don't like Wilf either," agreed Nasal-voice. "Four against three, chief. It might be safer to bring over the two from the *Ra-Twelve* first—no point in searching her anyway, now that we know where the records are."

"No," said the deep voice. "Flauval could just happen to decide to come out in the few minutes we're gone. It's sewed up too neatly right now. We'll have the heavy guns from the launch and we'll give them a chance to surrender. Flauval's too intelligent to pass that up—she never stops hoping. The chances are there won't be any shooting, till afterwards."

"Any friends of hers are likely to be tough," Nasal-voice warned.

"Very tough," said his chief. "Like the kid there! You worry at the wrong times, my boy. A parcel of space-rats that happened along." He swore again. "That woman's unbelievable luck! Well, take care of yourself, Ezeff. I'm off. Keep your eyes open both ways. Just in case—"

VII

There was silence for a moment. Then footsteps came crunching over the rocks towards the ghoul-burrow, and Channok got set. But the footsteps halted a few yards away.

"That's the one I was sitting on," Peer volunteered. "Nice, easy one to climb."

"Yeah, I never saw a nicer looking rock," Nasal-voice said sourly. "We've got to climb it, too. I'm not trying any point-landings with jets. Get on up there then, before I boot you up!"

There were sounds of scrambling.

"Don't you move now!" Peer said suddenly.

"What are you talking about?" demanded Nasal-voice.

"Durn rock come loose," muttered Peer. "Near flung me off!"

But Channok, meanwhile, had got the idea and settled back. It was not yet the Right Moment . . .

There were more scrambling sounds and some breathless swearing from Ezeff, who obviously had not spent his formative years in asteroid-hopping either. But at last all become quiet.

"And here we are!" Peer's voice floated down clearly. A small chunk of rock dropped right in front of the burrow's entrance, like a punctuation mark.

"Sit still, blast you!" said Nasal-voice, badly out of breath.

A large, dim shadow swept silently over the ground before the ghoul's burrow just then. That would be the launch, going towards the Mound. A prolonged silence overhead confirmed the impression.

"They want to give Flauval a surprise?" Peer inquired meekly at last.

Rather startlingly, Nasal-voice laughed.

"They sure do," he agreed. "That's a good one! Yes, sir, they sure do."

"Flauval's nice, don't you think?" continued Peer conversationally, picking up courage.

"Depends a lot on how you look at it," Nasal-voice said dreamily. "She's a real pretty thing anyhow, that Flauval. Luck of the devil she's had, too. But it's got to run out sometime."

There was another silence. Then Peer remarked:

"Boy, he set that launch down nice! Right quick spang on top of the—what the big guy said it was. On the Mound."

"We've got a good pilot," Nasal-voice agreed. "Flauval's going to get her surprise in just a minute now."

"And there they come out of the launch," continued Peer. "One, two, three, four. All four of them. Marching right down into the Mound."

"You've got sharp eyes," Nasal-voice acknowledged. "But that's funny!" he continued worriedly. "One of them was to stay with the guns."

"And now look at the launch!" cried Peer in a high, bright voice. "Getting *pulled* right into the Mound!"

Nasal-voice was making loud, choking sounds.

"What was that?" he screamed then. "What's happened? What's that over there?"

"Let go my arm!" cried Peer. "Don't pull it—you're pushing me off! *Here we go!*"

A small avalanche of weathered rock came down before the burrow's mouth as Channok shot out through it into the open. He looked up. In what looked like an inextricable tangle of arms and legs, Peer and Nasal-voice were sliding and scuffling down the steep side of the rock together. Nasal-voice was trying to hang on to the rock, but Peer was hanging on to him and jerking like a hooked fish whenever he got a momentary hold.

She looked down and saw Channok, put her boots into the small of Nasal-voice's back, pushed off and landed two yards from Channok on hands and feet. He flattened himself back against the boulder, while Nasal-voice skidded down the rest of the way unaided, wisely refraining from triggering his jets. In the position he was in, they simply would have accelerated his descent to a fatal degree.

He arrived more or less on his feet. Peer bounced up and down before him, her finger pointed, like a small lunatic.

"Surprise!" she screamed. "Surprise! Like Flauval got! When you locked her in her cabin and ran off with the launch, so she'd have to jump out into space!"

"That's right, kid," Nasal-voice panted softly, fumbling for his gun without taking his eyes off her. He looked somewhat like a white-faced lunatic himself just then. "Don't get scared, kid! Don't run off! I won't shoot."

He pulled the gun out suddenly.

But Channok had taken two soft steps forward by then, and he had only to swing. The Reaper was clubbed in his right hand, and he brought the butt end down on the top of Nasal-voice Ezeff's skull-tight flying cap as if he were trying to ram a stake through the surface rock of Old Nameless.

"What happened over there on the, Mound?" he inquired, in a voice that kept wanting to quaver. He was hurriedly pulling on Nasal-voice's flight suit

"Here's his goggles," said Peer, also shakily. "Tell you tonight about the Mound. But Santis was right!"

"That's what it sounded like," Channok admitted. He slipped on the goggles. "Do I look like this Ezeff now?"

"Not very much," Peer said doubtfully. "You still got that nose and that jaw. Better hold me close up to your face! I'll put on a good act."

"All right. As soon as I set you down in the lock, jump past the guard and yell, or something. If he looks after you, we mightn't have to kill this one." He held out his arms. "Hop up! We'd better get started before those last two on the *Ra-Twelve* decide to come over."

Peer hopped up. Channok wrapped his right arm carefully around her. They looked at each other thoughtfully for a moment.

"All set?" he asked.

"Sure," said crew-member Peer. She smiled faintly.

He triggered the jets with his left hand, and they shot upwards. Peer drew a deep breath.

"Quit bossing me around all the time, you big lug!" she yelled suddenly. She reached up for that nose and gave it a good yank.

"All right," Channok muttered, startled. "You don't have to be so realistic! He can't even see us yet."

"Just because you're bigger'n me!" shrieked Peer, as they soared over the top of the rocks into view of the *Asteroid*'s lock. She hooked a smart right to Channok's left ear.

"Cut that out now, Peer," he ordered futilely.

He was lightly battered all around by the time they reached the *Asteroid*'s lock, though the act did get them in safely. But then—whether it was the nose or the jaw—the instant he dropped Peer to her feet, the guard stopped laughing and brought a gun out and up, faster than Channok ever had seen a man produce one before. However, the Reaper had been ready in his hand all the time; so, with a safe fraction of a second to spare, it talked first—

The glare of the discharge seemed about fifty times brighter than normal.

"Hit the floor, Channy!" he heard Peer's shout.

He hit it without thought, dropping over the dead guard's legs.

Sound rammed at him enormously, roared on and began banging itself about and away among distant mountains. The *Asteroid*'s floor had surged up ponderously, settled back, quivered a bit and become stable again.

"An earthquake," Channok muttered, sitting up dazedly, "was exactly all we needed right now!"

"That wasn't any earthquake!" said Peer, standing pale-faced above him. "Get up and look!"

Long veils of stuff, presumably solid chunks of mountain, were drifting down the distant, towering face of the cliff at the foot of which they had buried the *Ra-Twelve*. Rising to meet them, its source concealed beyond the horizon of the plain, was the slow, grey cloud of some super-explosion.

"I guess," he said slowly, "one of those two must have got curious about Koyle's wall-safe!"

"We were pretty smart about that," nodded Peer.

"We were, for once!" Channok agreed. He was looking around for something to sit down on quietly when he caught sight of the dead guard again. He started violently.

"Almost forgot about him! I guess now I'll have to bury him, and that Ezeff, the first thing. Maybe this one is carrying something that will show who they were."

He found something almost instantly and he was glad then that Peer was still watching the oily writhings of the cloud across the plain. It was in a flat steel case he took out of one of the dead man's pockets: the identification disk of a member of the Imperial Secret Service—

The Service!

And they would have murdered us, he thought, shocked. They were going to do it!

He turned the guard over on his back. A big muscular young man with a look of sudden purpose and confidence still fixed on his face. It was the same face as the one on the disk.

Channok put the disk back in its case and shoved the case into the dead man's pocket. He stood up, feeling rather sick. Peer turned around from the lock and regarded him reflectively for a moment.

"You know, Channy," she stated carefully, "if you can't help it, it doesn't count."

He looked back at her. "I guess not," he said—and suddenly, for a moment, he could see four men marching one after the other down into the Mound. "Of course, it doesn't count!" he told her firmly.

VIII

They worked hard at shifting the cargo into the cache, but the Nameless Sun was beginning to slide down behind the mountains before they were finished. And by the time Channok had rammed the tunnel full of rocks with the tractor and cemented them into a glassy plug with the drill-blast, and scattered a camouflaging mess of boulders over everything, only a foggy red glow over the mountain crests, half obscured by the lingering upper drifts of the explosion of the *Ra-Twelve*, remained of the day.

There was no moon, but the sky had come full of stars big and little over the opposite section of the plain; and so there was light enough to make out the dark bump of the Mound in the distance. Every time Channok looked in that direction, the low, sinister pile seemed to have edged a little closer; and he looked as often as his work gave him a chance to do it. Santis might have been right in stating that the Mound wasn't dangerous if you didn't get too close to it—but the instant he suspected there might be something going on over there, Channok was going to hop off the tractor, grab up Peer and get off Old Nameless at the best speed he and the *Asteroid* could produce.

However, the Mound remained quiet. With everything done, he gave Peer a last ride back to the *Asteroid* on the tractor, ran it up the ramp into the storage section and closed the rear lock. Then they discovered they'd left their lunch containers lying among the rocks.

If he'd been alone, Channok would have left them there. But Peer looked so matter-of-fact about it that he detached the tractor's headlight and started back with her on foot. It was only a couple of hundred yards, and they found the containers without any difficulty. The Mound seemed to have moved a little closer again, but not too much. He gave it only a casual glance this time.

"Where are your friends, the ghouls?" he inquired, shining the light around the rocks as they started back. The grisly creatures had put in a few cautious appearances during the afternoon, but their nerves seemed to have suffered even more than his own from all that had happened.

"The ghouls always hit their burrows at sundown," Peer explained. "They're not like the story ones."

"What do they find to eat around here?" Channok inquired.

"Some sorts of rocks. They've got no real teeth but their mouth is like a grinder inside. Most of the rest of their insides, too, Santis said. I had a tame one I used to pitch stones at and he'd snap 'em up. But all that weren't blue he'd spit out. The blue ones went right down—you could hear them crunching for about a foot."

"What a diet!" Channok commented. Then he stopped short. "Say, Peer! If they bite like that, they could chew right into our cache!"

"They won't," said Peer. "Come on."

"How do you know?" Channok asked, following her.

"They can't bite through a good grade of steel-alloy. And they don't like its taste anyhow. Santis said so."

Well, it had been Santis this and Santis that for quite a while now! Peer's father seemed to be on record with a definite opinion on just about everything. And what made him think he knew what a ghoul liked to chew on?

Perhaps Channok couldn't be blamed too much. He was dog-tired and dirty and hungry. He'd killed his first two men that day, and not in fair fight either but with an assassin's sneak thrusts, from behind and by trickery; and he'd buried them, too. He'd seen the shining ISS disclose itself in action as something very tarnished and ugly, and a salvaged ship worth a fortune go up in a cloud of writhing grey smoke . . .

There had been a number of other things—close shaves that had felt too close, mostly.

At any rate, Channok stated, in flat unequivocal terms, that he didn't wish to hear anything else that Santis had said. Not ever!

"You're taking the wrong attitude," Peer informed him, frowning. "Santis is a very smart man. He could teach you a lot!"

"What makes you think I want to learn anything from a space-rat?" Channok inquired, exasperated.

Peer stopped short. "That was a dirty thing to say!" she said in a low, furious voice. "I'm not talking to you any more."

She drew away till there was a space of about six feet between them and marched on briskly towards the *Asteroid*, looking straight ahead.

Channok had to hurry to keep abreast of her. He watched her in the starlight for a few moments from the corners of his eyes. He probably shouldn't have used that term—the half-pint did look good and mad!

"Tsk! Tsk!" he said, disturbed.

Peer said nothing. She walked a bit faster. Channok lengthened his stride again.

"Who's my nice little girl friend?" he inquired wheedlingly.

"Shuddup," growled Peer.

She climbed into the *Asteroid* ahead of him and disappeared while he sealed the locks. The control room was dark, but he felt she was around somewhere. He switched on the power and the instruments. Familiar dim pools of green and pink gleamings sprang up in quick sequence like witchfire quivering over the control desk. Perhaps it wasn't an exceptionally beautiful sight, but it looked homelike to Channok. Like fires lighting up on a hearth.

"Well, let's see you handle this take-off," he invited the shadows around him briskly. This time there weren't any mountains nearby to worry about.

"You handle it," Peer said from behind his shoulder. "It's my turn to laugh."

She did, too, a few minutes later—loud and long. After he'd got over the first shock of narrowly missing the Mound, Channok gave a convincing imitation of a chagrined pilot and indignantly blamed the *Asteroid* . . .

He'd guided them halfway out of the Nameless System when she came behind the control chair in the dark, wrapped her arms in a stranglehold around his neck, and fondly bit his ear.

"Cut it out," Channok choked.

"Just the same," stated Peer, loosening her grip a trifle, "you're *not* so smart, like Santis is."

"I'm not, eh?"

"No," said Peer. "But Santis said you would be some time. 'That Channok's going to make a real spacer,' he said. 'Just give him a chance to catch on.'"

"Well," Channok muttered, secretly flattered, "we'll hope he was right."

"And, anyway," said Peer, "I *LOVE* you just as much!"

"Well, that's something, too," Channok admitted. He was beginning to feel very much better.

"And guess what I've got here," Peer said tenderly.

"What?"

"A nice, soapy cloth. For what you said when you saw the first ghoul. So just open that big trap right up now, Channy!"

He couldn't tell in the dark; but it tasted like she'd taken the trouble to mix something extra foul into the soap lather, too.

"And after you've stopped spitting bubbles," said crew-member Peer, who was switching on all lights to observe that part of the business, "I'll tell you what I saw on the Mound."

Channok shuddered.

"If you don't mind, Peer," he suggested soapily, "let's wait with that till we're a lightyear or two farther out!"

Caretaker
· · · · · · · · · · ·

"TELL HIM," SAID COMMANDER Lowndes' voice, speaking from the great exploration ship stationed on the other side of the world, "that we're recording it officially as Hulman's Planet. I think that might please him."

Marder hesitated with his reply. Through the viewport of the parked little scout flier, he looked out at the vast, shadowy valley before him, at green and scarlet swamps, at gleaming dark waters threaded through them. A huge, blue-wooded wave of mountains rose beyond, the setting sun just touching their crest. In a quarter of an hour, it would be completely dark. His glance turned, almost reluctantly, to the substantial but incongruous reality of Hulman's house nearby, its upper story and roof mirrored in the tiny swamp lake.

"No, it wouldn't please him," he said. "Boyce suggested it during our first visit with Hulman today. He wants us to record it instead as—I'll spell it—C-r-e-s-g-y-t-h. Cresgyth. That's his phonetic interpretation of the name given it by the people here."

"Fair enough," Commander Lowndes agreed, "if that's how he wants it." He inquired whether Marder had anything to add to the present report.

"Not now," Marder said. "I'll call you back after we've met his woman."

"His wife," Lowndes corrected him carefully. "I'm glad it happened to be you and Boyce who found Hulman. You're reliable men; you in particular, Marder. I don't need to emphasize that Hulman's chance discovery of what appears to be the first genuine human race ever encountered outside of Earth is of primary importance...." He continued to emphasize that obvious fact at some length. "Boyce might be inclined to hurry through the—ah, diplomatic overtures," he concluded. "You'll be careful about that part of it, Marder?"

"Very careful," Marder promised.

"On the two continents we've scanned so far, we've found no traces of human inhabitants, present or past. It's possible that Hulman's acquaintances are the sole survivors of humanity here. If we frighten the tribe into hiding, there may never be another contact—and within a hundred years or less, they may have become extinct."

"I understand."

"Fine. Now, then—what about these other creatures? What did Hulman have to say about them?"

"In the twenty years he's been marooned in this valley, he's had only three or four actual encounters with them—rather violent encounters, on his side. Apparently, they learned to avoid him after that. He seems," Marder added thoughtfully, "to have an almost psychopathic hatred for them."

"Not very surprising!" Lowndes' tone was reproving, reminding Marder that Hulman had been, for the past forty years, one of the great, legendary names of stellar exploration. "Deems' scout reports it bagged a couple of specimens a few hours ago and is bringing them in. The description checks with what Hulman gave you—a wormlike, blue body with a set of arms, legs, and a head. Out of water, they appear to wear some kind of clothes, presumably to conserve body moisture."

Marder agreed that it checked.

"We've found them remarkably elusive otherwise," Lowndes went on. "There seems to have been a widespread rudimentary civilization along the seas and major lake coasts—amphibious cave-builders is what they were originally. But all the caves we examined have been deserted for centuries, at least, which indicates major migratory movements of the species inland. The seas and lakes are almost completely barren of life above the plankton level."

There had been, according to Hulman, some kind of planetary catastrophe, Marder said. Hunger had driven the "snakes," as he called them, out of the great lake chains of their origin, up into the valley swamp lands and along the river courses, forcing the remnants of the mysterious human race ahead of them in their slow migration and gradually reducing the human living area. Hulman had killed six of the bluish, wormlike creatures in this section of the valley, in the first few years after he had crashed on the planet; after that, they had ceased to show up here. But, until now, he had been unable to give the humans more effective help.

After Lowndes cut contact, Marder remained sitting in the scout for a time, gazing out at the vast, darkening valley with troubled, puzzled eyes. For twenty-two years after the destruction of his ship, Hulman had lived here, separated from the humanity of his origin by an enormity of light-years, by the black abyss of space, but in the company of a woman who was of an alien, dying race.

"My wife!" Hulman had said, not defiantly but proudly, in speaking of her. "I called her Celia from the start, and she liked the name."

Hidden somewhere in the shadowed swamps, the woman he'd called Celia was watching Hulman's great log house until she could overcome her timidity of the visitors from space.

"She'll show up some time during the night," Hulman had laughed. "I'm leaving the doors open for her. I'll talk to her a little first, to reassure her, and you can meet her then. Meanwhile, why don't you have a look at her picture."

Years ago, as a boy, Marder had first seen Hulman's early paintings of the outer worlds and, like countless thousands of others before and since, he had felt his imagination swell and grow wide with the cosmic grandeur of Hulman's vision of universal life. In the fifty or so paintings he had seen in the log house that day, the great sweep of space had dwindled to something apparently much more commonplace. Hulman's imagination seemed to have shrunk to correspond to the physical limitations of the valley that confined him. However, he had retained a characteristic and extraordinary precision of lifelike detail, particularly in regard to the human beings he had found here.

They were beautiful creatures; but the paintings aroused a revulsion in Marder, in which he recognized a vague flavouring of terror. In the one painting Hulman showed them of the woman Celia, that effect was particularly pronounced. Marder found it difficult to explain to himself. Boyce seemed insensitive to it, and there was nothing in Hulman's words or attitude to provide additional clues.

Re-entering the house, Marder glanced back with more than a trace of uneasiness at the swamp from the doors Hulman had left open. After twenty years, Hulman should know whether danger threatened him from there; but for a visitor on a strange world,

"it" and "they" were always present in the unknown dark outside—
fears that usually were imaginary, but sometimes were not.

Marder smiled a little grimly at his own present apprehensions
and went in.

He found Hulman and Boyce in a cavernous cellar level beneath
the house itself. It was well lit and showed familiar and reassuring features: power plants, storage rooms, even a hydroponic
garden. The two men stood beside the opening of a deep fresh-
water well, twenty feet across, which took up the left side of the
main cellar hall.

"Sixty feet down, it's ten degrees Celsius," Hulman was stating,
with a disarming houseowner's pride. He was a big man, rather
heavy now, with a square-cut brown beard that showed only a few
traces of grey. "I got the idea from Celia's people. Swamp water's
none too healthy here at various seasons, but the well taps an
underground river that's as pure as you could wish—" He caught
sight of Marder. "Any news?" His face had become suddenly
anxious.

"They're going to wait over there with the ship," Marder said,
"a week or more, if required. We're to follow your judgment in
every way in establishing contact with the Cresgythians."

"Good!" Hulman was obviously relieved. "We can't do anything
till Celia comes in—and we'll have to be very tactful then. But
I'm sure it won't take a week."

"What makes them so shy of us?" Boyce inquired. A shadow
passed over Hulman's face. "It's not you," he said. "It's me . . .
Or it's an impression I gave them of the Earth kind of human
beings."

Back upstairs, with the three of them settled comfortably in the
big living-room, he explained. He'd given Boyce and Marder a room
together on the top floor of the house, across a small hall from
his own room and that of his wife.

"I've never asked Celia much about her people," he said. "There's
some kind of very strong taboo that keeps her from talking about
them. When I tried to press her for details at first, it was almost
as if I were committing some sort of gross indecency. But I do
know they hate violence, insanity—anything unbeautiful! And, you
see . . ."

When his ship crashed into the valley, he was the only man
left alive on her out of the original crew of four. "Banning went
insane two days before that and killed Nichols and Dawson," he
said, his face drawn and taut, remembering it again over a period

of twenty-two years. He paused. "And so I killed Banning before he could wreck the ship completely." He looked from one to the other of them. "It was unavoidable. But they never understood that, these people of Celia's."

"How did they find out?" Marder stirred uncomfortably.

Hulman shrugged. "I was unconscious for about a month and completely blind for six months afterward. They got me out of the wreck and nursed me back to life, but as soon as I was out of danger, only Celia would stay with me. She and I were alone for weeks before I regained my sight. How did they find out? They're sensitive in a number of ways. And there were those bodies in the ship. They—withdrew from me," he said with a grimace, "as soon as I no longer needed their help."

"Then in all this time," Marder said slowly, "you never were able to gain their confidence?"

Hulman stared at him a moment, apparently weighing the words. "It's not a question of confidence," he said finally. "It's a question of—well, I'm trying to tell you! I didn't mind being alone with Celia." He grinned suddenly, almost boyishly. "The others stayed in a small lake village they had a couple of miles up the valley, across the swamps. Celia went up there every few days, but she never brought anyone back with her. I suspected it was simply because I was an alien. I thought they'd get over that in time. Celia seemed happy enough, so it wasn't a very acute problem—"

He paused a few seconds, frowning. "One day, when she'd slipped away again, I remembered a pair of field glasses I'd taken off the ship, and I got them and trained them on the village. That was a very curious experience—I never have found a complete explanation for it. For just one instant, I had everything in the clearest possible focus. There were children playing on the platforms above the water; a few adults standing in the doorway of a house. And, suddenly, everything blurred!" Hulman gave a short hacking laugh. "Can you imagine that? They didn't want me to look at them, so they just blurred my vision!"

"Eh?" Boyce was frowning.

Marder sat still, startled, feeling the uneasiness growing up in him again.

Hulman smiled crookedly. "That's all I can tell you. The glasses had a four-mile range and they were functioning perfectly, but the instant I turned them on the village, the field blurred. I'd never felt so wholeheartedly—and successfully—snubbed before."

Boyce laughed uncomfortably and glanced at Marder. He was

still more than a little in awe of Hulman, of the shining legend miraculously resurrected from the black tomb of space; but he, too, Marder decided, had the vague sense of something disturbing and out of order here. Well, so much the better. There would be two of them to look out for trouble, if trouble came.

"I'll admit the trick annoyed me," Hulman said, "as soon as I'd got over my first surprise at it. Next day, I announced to Celia that I was going over to the village. She made no objection, but she followed me at a distance—probably to make sure I didn't drown on the way. It's wet going around here. At last I came over a rise and found myself a hundred yards from the village, on the land side. Almost immediately, I realized they had abandoned it. I walked around it a while and found cooking fires still glowing; but nobody had waited to receive me. So I went home, insulted and very sulky—I wouldn't even talk to Celia until the next morning!"

He laughed. "I got over that in a hurry. And then I settled down to building us a house of our own, much bigger and better than anything they had in the village; and that took up all my time for several months. For that whole period, I ignored our neighbours quite as thoroughly as they had ignored me."

He grinned at his guests a little shamefacedly. "But you know, I couldn't keep it up then. There was something so curiously happy and peaceful about them, even if they were giving me the cold shoulder. And the one good look I'd had of them had showed me they were physically the most beautiful people I'd ever seen. One day, when Celia was gone, I made another trip to the village—with exactly the same results as the first one. So I decided to look around for a less exclusive neighbourhood.

"I'd got the little flier of my ship repaired enough to take it off the ground and set it down again; and I calculated I'd salvaged enough fuel for at least one twenty-four-hour trip. Celia watched me take off. I flew high over the village and could see them down there, ignoring me as usual. Then I flew down the valley for almost fifty miles before I came across the first colony of the other ones—the snakes!"

Marder remembered something Lowndes had said. "Do the snakes live in caves?"

"No," Hulman said distastefully. "That's what fooled me. It was a village of snake houses set into the head of a little lake, almost like the one here. I set down on the lake, coasted up to the village, climbed up a ladder, and saw them!"

He shuddered. "They just stood there, very quietly, watching me from the doors and windows. What made it worse somehow. was that they wore clothes—but the clothes didn't cover enough. Those weaving, soft, blue bodies and staring eyes! I backed off down the ladder, with my gun ready, in case they rushed me; but they never moved . . ."

He had found eight more colonies of the snakes farther down the valley, but no trace of another tribe of his beautiful human-oids. He flew up the valley then, high up into the mountains, almost exhausting his fuel; and beside a glacier-fed mountain lake was a tiny stake village, built into the water. And they were snakes again.

"At the time, I didn't know just what to make of it. There was the possibility that my village represented an advance troop of human beings into a land of snakes. But I suspected—I felt even then, that it was the other way around; that it was the snakes that were encroaching on the humans. So I swore to myself that as long as I lived, at least, human beings were going to hold this section of the valley undisturbed and in safety.

"When I came back, I said to Celia—she was standing at the same spot I'd seen her last, as if she'd never left it—'Celia, I must speak to your people. Go tell them I will come again tomorrow and that they must not run away.' She looked at me silently for a long time, and then she turned and left in the direction of the village. She came back late at night and crept into my arms and said, 'They have promised to wait for you.'

"I set out next morning, full of great plans. The snakes lived in widely scattered settlements, after all. The villagers and I could wipe out those settlements one by one, until we'd cleared the land about us. That was the natural solution, wasn't it? I didn't real-ize then how different, in some ways, Celia's people were from us!"

Boyce asked uneasily, "What happened?"

"What happened?" Hulman repeated. "Well, I came over that rise, and there the village was. This time I knew they'd stayed at home! Then, not twenty feet off my path, I saw two of the snakes standing in the bushes, one watching me, the other looking at the village. Each had a kind of chunky crossbow over his shoulders; and they couldn't be seen from the village . . ."

He paused and shook his head. "So I shot them both down, before they got over their surprise. That was all." He looked from one to the other again. "It was the natural thing to do, wasn't it?"

Boyce nodded uncertainly. Marder said nothing.

Hulman leaned forward. "But apparently, from the point of view of the villagers, it wasn't! Because when I was done with the snakes—one of them took three shots before it would lie still—the village was empty again. When I got back home, I was actually sick with disappointment. And then I discovered that Celia was gone."

"That was a bad three days. But she came back then. And on the morning she came back, I discovered they'd broken up the village overnight and moved on. I think they're not more than ten or twenty miles distant from here, but I never tried to look them up again."

Boyce said puzzled, "But I don't see—"

"Neither did I," Hulman interrupted, "until it was too late." He gave his short bark of laughter again; there was, Marder realized, a sort of suppressed fury in it. "They won't kill their enemies—they're too polite for that! So their enemies are gradually squeezing them out of existence."

The three men studied each other in silence for a moment. Then Marder asked slowly, "Captain Hulman, what do you expect us to do in this situation?"

"Kill the snakes!" Hulman said promptly. "As many as we can find. If the human beings of this world won't defend themselves we'll have to defend them. As long as I've been here, no party of snakes has come past this point of the valley. A few of them have tried!" His eyes glittered with open hatred. "But I can't be on guard here forever. It's up to you and the other men on the ship to do the job right!"

Though Boyce was sleeping uneasily, Marder hadn't yet shut his eyes. The uneasiness was in him, too; and in him it was strong enough to offset the fatigue and excitement of the day. Vague night sounds came into the room they shared, a plaintive, thin calling like the distant cry of a bird. Not too different from the sounds on many other worlds he had known, and, as on all worlds that were new and strange, faintly tinged with the menace that was largely in the imagination.

But it was Hulman himself who was the principal cause of Marder's uneasiness.

The face of the explorer, the rumbling, angry voice, his monomaniacal devotion to the strange humanoids kept recurring in his mind. Nothing Hulman had done previously to stimulate the imagination of Earthmen toward the laborious exploration of space could equal this final accidental achievement: to have encountered the first other human beings Earthmen had yet discovered in the Universe. Men had looked out from their world like children staring into a great, dark, forbidding room. They had found space to be peopled sparsely with intelligent life—life that was sometimes horrible, sometimes merely odd, sometimes beautiful in weird, incomprehensible ways. But never enough like Man to be acceptable!

Hulman's fierce insistence on protecting what seemed to be the dying remnants of a human race against its own wishes was something Marder could understand well enough. He did not doubt that Boyce and the others would respond wholeheartedly to that insistence. Here was the proof that human life could rise spontaneously and endlessly throughout all the galaxies, that the Universe was not a darkened room, after all, but one lighted forever by the fires of humanity.

They had to protect that proof...

Strangely enough, though Boyce was asleep and he awake, it was Boyce who first seemed aware of motion in the house. Marder heard him breathe and stir unquietly, and then come awake and grow still, listening, waiting. He smiled faintly at the familiar signs, the tense alertness, the silent questioning of the strange world about them: "What is it? Who moves?" On many other strange, dark worlds, he had been among Earthmen as they came awake, asking that question. And he with them....

He grew aware of it then: there was motion in the house now, beyond the walls. Gradually, it resolved itself into slow, heavy steps on the carpeted flooring; and the picture of Hulman leaving his room to peer down the stairs came so convincingly into his mind that at once he relaxed again. And he was aware that Boyce was relaxing too.

Neither of them spoke. After a time, Hulman went back to his room, walking carefully so as not to disturb his guests; and the house was still. Presently, Boyce was sleeping again. Marder tried to pick up the train of thoughts he had been following before the disturbance; but they eluded him now. Fatigue grew up in him like waves of mental darkness, smothering the remnants of uneasiness; and reluctantly he let himself drift off.

The blast that roused him seemed to have gone off almost beside his head.

He found himself standing in the centre of the room, gun in

one hand, flashbeam in the other. Boyce's wide back was just disappearing through the door into the dark hall beyond; and Boyce's shout was in his ears:

"Hulman! They've got Hulman!"

Marder halted a fraction of a second, checked by the ridiculous hesitation of a man who doesn't want to go out into a strange house undressed; then he was following Boyce. As he plunged down the broad staircase to the lower floor of Hulman's house, a memory flashed into his mind: the guns that Hulman, cut off from standard power sources, had manufactured for himself here and shown them earlier in the evening. It had been the report of a missile gun that had awakened him; one of Hulman's own.

He lost Boyce's light for a moment when he reached the lower floor, and stood in indecision until he heard a muffled shouting to his left and remembered the descent into the cellars. As he reached the door, there was another angry shout from Boyce, and a blaze of pink light from below. Boyce had cut loose with his gun, so he was in contact with the intruders; and things would have to be finished very quickly now—a thermion spray was not designed to be an indoor weapon!

Marder reached the bottom of the cellar stairs seconds later.

A hedge of flame to their right, steady, impenetrable and soundless, slanted from the wall half around the great well. It cut them off from further advance; presumably it had cornered their antagonists.

Boyce, dressed in nightshorts, turned a furiously contorted face to him.

"One of them ducked around the corner over there; it can't get out. It was carrying Hulman!"

"Where is Hulman?"

"Over there—dead!"

Marder squinted against the reflected glare of the fire. Something dark lay hunched against the wall beyond the well; that was all he could make out.

"Sure he's dead?" His voice carefully matter-of-fact.

"Of course!" Boyce said beside him. The hand that held the gun was shaking. "When it dropped him—when I snapped a bolt at it—I saw he'd been shot through the head with his own gun!"

"The natives?" Marder asked, still carefully.

"No. Something—those snakes he was afraid of—some animal. It whipped around the corner before I saw it very clearly—"

His voice had gone dull. Marder glanced at him quickly. Boyce was in a state of semi-shock, and they had only a few minutes before the fire ate far enough into the walls to threaten their retreat upstairs and out of the house. He had no personal qualms about leaving Hulman's body and Hulman's slayers to roast together—the coincidence of murder on that particular night was something one could figure out more conveniently later—but Boyce might present a problem.

A voice addressed them from out of a passage beyond the well.

"You who were his friends," it said, "will you listen to me?" Marder felt his scalp crawling. "Who are you?" he called back.

"He called me his wife."

Boyce started violently, but Marder waved him to silence. It was a rich, feminine voice, a trifle plaintive; it was not difficult to fit it mentally to the painting of Hulman's wife.

"Why did you kill him?" There was a pause.

"But I thought you understood," the voice said. "Your medical men would say that he had been insane for twenty years, as he counted time. They would have forced him back into sanity. I could not bear the thought that he should suffer that."

Marder swallowed hard. "Suffer what?"

"Are you all fools? He was a fool, though I loved him. He could not see behind the shape of things. So—here among us—he saw shapes he could bear to see. In those moments when sanity came to him and he really saw what was there—then he killed. Are you all like that?"

Boyce stared at Marder, his mouth working. "What is she talking about?" he whispered hoarsely. "Is the snake with her?"

"Go upstairs, Boyce! Wait for me outside!"

"Are you going to kill the snake?"

"Yes, I'll kill the snake."

Boyce disappeared up the stairs.

"The house is burning, but there is some time left," Marder told the voice then. "Is there any way you can save yourself?"

"I can leave by the river that flows under the well," the voice said, "if you do not shoot at me."

"I won't shoot at you."

"May I take his body?"

Marder hesitated. "Yes."

"And you will all leave with your ship? I loved him, though my people thought it strange almost beyond their tolerance. They are foolish, too, yet not as foolish as you are. They saw what was in his mind and not beyond that, and so they were afraid of him.

But he is dead now and there is nothing that your people and mine could share. We are too different. Will you leave?"

Marder moistened his lips. "We'll leave," he said, seeing it all now, and glad he had sent Boyce upstairs. "What did you see beyond what was in his mind?"

"A brave spirit, though very frightened," the voice said slowly.

"He ventured far and far and far into the dark of which he was afraid. I loved him for that!" It paused. "I am coming now," it added, "and I think you had better look away."

Marder did not intend to look away, but at the last moment, when there was movement at the corner of the passage, he did. He saw only a swift undulating shadow pass along the wall, pause and stoop quickly, rise again with a bulky burden clasped to it, glide on and vanish.

He stood staring at the blank wall until there was a faint splash in the well far below him.

The great ship was drifting slowly above the night side of the world it was leaving, when Commander Lowndes joined Marder at the observation port.

"Boyce will make out all right," he said moodily. "He only guessed part of the truth, and that bit is being taken from his mind." He studied Marder thoughtfully. "If you'd looked squarely at the thing, we might have had to give you the same treatment. Our pickled specimens are pretty damned hideous."

Marder shrugged. Lowndes sat on the edge of a table.

"Selective hysterical blindness maintained for twenty-two years— with his own type of artistic hallucinations thrown in! I can't help wishing it hadn't happened to Hulman."

"He didn't maintain it throughout," Marder said slowly. "And whenever he saw them clearly, he killed them . . ."

"Who wouldn't? I almost feel," Lowndes said, "like getting out of space and staying out, for good!"

Which was giving it the ultimate in emphasis.

"What are you reporting?" Marder asked.

"That Hulman died here, quite peacefully, about a year before we found him—leaving a diary of inspiring courage and devotion to space exploration behind him. We'll have time enough to work up the diary. That should keep everybody happy. Marder," he said suddenly, waving his hand at the observation port, "do you think there actually are—well, people out there. Somewhere?"

Marder looked out at the vast, star-studded, shining black immensity.

"I hope so," he said.

"Do you think we'll ever find them?"

"I don't know," Marder said thoughtfully. "They've never found us."

One Step Ahead

· · · · · · · · · · · · · · · ·

PROGRAMMED CORPS LEAVING RIDZIN!

So the newscast machines roared that morning. Many added grimly: SKANDER WAR IMMINENT!

To well-informed citizens of Ridzin it came as no surprise. For fifteen years, the Programmed Corps, the mightiest war-machine ever known, had been developing on their world, lending Ridzin a significance unique in the Terrestrial League. Second-rate in most respects, Ridzin had been a logical base for the formation of the Corps. No one doubted that the League Central Government on Great Xal would have preferred the Corps to be assembled under its immediate supervision. But the jealousy of other powerful League worlds made it impossible—the Corps simply would not have come into being as a joint effort of the League if Great Xal had insisted on the point. On the other hand, the central government wouldn't have permitted its establishment on worlds like Hannaret or Lorcia, for example, worlds not too inferior to Great Xal in military strength and perennially on the verge of open rebellion. The Programmed Corps—its awesome manpower and appalling technical equipment drawn from all fourteen League worlds—must bring about, it was agreed by those in the know, in one direction or another a decisive shift in the balance of power in the League.

As it would also bring about a decisive shift in the balance of power between the Terrestrial League and that despised, remote, alien race called the Skanders. That, as all League citizens understood—having been told it regularly during the past fifteen

110

years—was the basic and vital reason for the Programmed Corps' existence. And because its personnel were conditioned to absolute unquestioning obedience to whomever knew the commands by which to direct them, the Corps could be brought into being only on a world like Ridzin, a world which by no stretch of the imagination could be regarded as a menace to anyone else.

And now the Programmed Corps—completed only after fifteen years of sustained effort, armed, trained, single-minded, irresistable—was shipping out!

"The fellow," visiting Inspector General Mark Treffry of Great Xal remarked in a tone of absorbed interest, as he peered through a window into the compound several stories below, "is magnificent!"

Dexter Monte, Treffry's Technical Advisor, standing a prudent dozen steps farther back in the room, cleared his throat.

"You really," the Inspector General went on, "should come over here and watch him! What incredible reaction speed!"

"I prefer," Dexter Monte said firmly, "not to expose myself at a window while a Programmed assassin is in the area. If I might suggest—"

Treffry chuckled.

"Don't you trust your own precautions?" he inquired. "The shields, the fields, the what-not? They've functioned perfectly so far."

"So far!" Monte repeated meaningfully.

Treffry grunted.

"Thinking of poor Ulbrand, I suppose?"

"Yes."

"Ah, well," said Treffry. "Ulbrand was no doubt a rather better than average Technical Advisor. But let's face it, Monte . . . he simply was not in your class! I'm not surprised they got him— whoever it is doesn't want us on Ridzin." He paused, added smugly, "And we have a pretty fair idea of who that is, don't we?"

"Yes," Monte said.

"Now as for you," Treffry went on, "I have complete confidence in your devices. That fellow down there is in a trap. But he's certainly handling himself well while we close it! On the average how many do we lose in these attacks?"

"Seventeen-point-two men."

"Well, our present would-be assassin seems to have accounted for at least two dozen by now. And—good heavens!" Treffry went silent a moment, staring down through the window.

"What's going on?" Dexter Monte inquired in an uneasy tone.

"I'm sure I don't know!" Treffry told him. "There were some odd glitters of extremely bright light. Almost like the scintillation of a diamond as you turn it."

"Ah!" Monte said. "The assassin was near it?"

"He *was* near it. He's *nowhere* now. What was it?"

Joining Treffry at the window, Monte said in great relief, "An adaptation of the Welban Vortex. I wasn't sure it would work on a Programmed mind."

"It worked," Treffry assured him. He gave the Advisor a side-long glance full of admiration. "This is the sixteenth or seventeenth such attack we've undergone, isn't it?"

"The twenty-first," Monte said.

"And always by Programmed Soldiery. They're unbelievable! I'll trust your traps while only one of them is involved. But when the entire Programmed Corps goes into action—" The Inspector General shook his head.

"Yes," Dexter Monte said slowly. "A fearful thought."

"Clearly, somebody else—somebody not at all authorized—knows at least a few of the key commands to their minds," Treffry said. "Well, we'll be rid of these problems soon enough. When is the first carrier scheduled to lift?"

Dexter Monte glanced at his watch. "In sixteen hours, thirty-two minutes and ten seconds."

He looked at Treffry, added, "If you want to hear Governor Vinocur's official announcement of the Programmed Corps' departure from the Planet of Ridzin, he's about to go on the air."

"By all means," said Treffry. "I think I'll really enjoy hearing our good and loyal friend Vinocur explain the situation to the public."

Planetary Governor Frank Vinocur was an old-time politician; while his speech, to which most of the adult population of Ridzin was tuned that morning, was a review of facts with which his listeners had been familiar for over a dozen years, he made them sound like news. There were friction points between the Terrestrial League and the alien Skanders. Though widely separated in space, they had overlapping spheres of influence—overlapping only slightly so far; but the situation was bound to become more serious as time went on. Unlike other spacefaring aliens men had encountered, the Skanders did not prudently withdraw when confronted by the mighty race of Terra—had, in fact, been known on occasion to attack first. They were savage and treacherous enemies, and showed, in addition, repulsively amebic physical characteristics.

Space, Governor Vinocur declared, was not large enough for the Terrestrial League and such as the Skanders! An eventual showdown with the creatures was inevitable . . . and, as all knew, it was for this showdown that the Programmed Corps had been created. Ridzin could proudly say in this hour of parting that it had earned its place in history as the home of the Corps. By the wise planning of the Central Government on Great Xal, the time to strike at the Skander vermin—strike first, strike hard!—had arrived. The Programmed Corps was prepared . . . and victory was certain!

The speech went over well—since Ridzin clearly would be remote from the battle zones. Throughout the day patriotic anti-Skander fervors grew in the population, reaching a high pitch when Governor Vinocur's press attaches let it become known that at the official leave-taking banquet that evening the Governor would be publicly appointed a Programmed Corps General by the Inspector General from Great Xal, Mark Treffry, who had been on Ridzin for the past year to arrange for the Corps' transfer. And when the last of the automatic transspace carriers lifted from the planet during the night hours, General Frank Vinocur would leave with it in the company of the Inspector General, to represent Ridzin and its people at the front in this stirring period of history.

That afternoon cheering crowds lined the routes along which the Programmed Corps convoys rolled toward the planet's three Transspace Stations. They surrounded the stations themselves where giant carriers, all bearing the insignia of Great Xal, lay in dense rows like vast steel sausages. Into them marched the Programmed Corps. Eighteen thousand men with full equipment were assigned to each carrier; the men would lie in rigid, frozen sleep during the long spaceflight to Great Xal. One by one, the carriers were loaded and closed their locks . . .

Some of Ridzin's citizens, noting that only the central government appeared to be involved in the operation, speculated that they might be witnessing a dramatic new turn in the Terrestrial League's internal politics. But no public mention was made of such possibilities and by the time the official banquet began the planet was in a festive mood, almost as if the war against the Skanders were already won. Governor Vinocur was duly appointed a General of the Programmed Corps while Ridzin followed the event on their tri-di screens; laudatory speeches were exchanged between him and the Inspector General; toasts and countertoasts were offered . . . Dexter Monte, the Inspector General's Technical Advisor, created a minor diplomatic flurry when, in full view of the entire planet, he refused to empty his glass in Ridzin's honor, explaining that he was not a drinking man, that alcohol had deleterious effects on his metabolism. However, he was quickly coaxed into it by Mark Treffry and Governor Vinocur, and thereafter drank dutifully, if sourly, to every toast proposed.

Then the official rituals were over, except for the final scene on the steel loading dock within the maw of the last giant carrier left on the planet, where Governor Vinocur bade Ridzin farewell. Inspector General Treffry stood smiling at his side, Dexter Monte standing a few feet behind the two, belching every few seconds and generally showing the effects of having been forced into participating in the toasts. Vinocur spoke briefly into the tri-di cameras, concluded with a formal salute; then camera crews withdrew, glancing with silent awe at the huge bulkheads to either side of the dock behind which eighteen thousand men lay frozen in sleep. As the last of them left the carrier the loading locks slid shut with a heavy steel boom. The three men standing on the dock were alone. There was a dim humming in the air as the ship computers readied the engines for lift-off and the long flight during which there would be no waking human being to guide them. Treffry looked at his watch.

"Still half an hour," he said. "But we might as well get to our tanks at once. Feeling any better, Monte?"

"No," Dexter Monte muttered. "Worse! I'll be more than happy to settle into that tank. I'm beginning to have some difficulty holding myself together, I can tell you!"

Treffry and Vinocur glanced at each other and laughed, more loudly than the remark called for, almost as if each were enjoying a private joke; Monte blinked in brief, bleary surprise at them as he turned to follow them off to the sleep tanks.

Five minutes later, Inspector General Mark Treffry heard the sharp click with which his sleeping tank sealed itself above him. He switched on the intercom connecting the three tanks. With no attendants left awake in the carrier, it was essential that he and his companions monitor one another through the steps required to ensure that they would awaken safely after the trip. Governor Vinocur acknowledged at once, and some seconds later, Dexter Monte also replied. The preparations were carried out, checked, and then Treffry settled back comfortably. He already felt a faint, not unpleasant numbness in legs and arms, which was the anesthetic's first effect. By the time the sleepcold touched him, he would not feel anything at all. But his mind was still awake and active; and the private joke which had made him laugh aloud a short while ago seemed too good now to keep to himself.

"Vinocur?" he said to the intercom.

"Yes, Treffry?" Vinocur's voice responded.

"Before we drop off," Treffry said, "I thought I'd thank you for a highly enjoyable experience." He could hardly refrain from laughing again.

"You're referring to your stay on Ridzin?" Vinocur asked politely. "We tried to make it as pleasant as possible, of course."

"I'm sure you did!" And now Treffry did laugh, huffing and snorting helplessly for almost a minute before he was able to stop. He dabbed at his eyes, and sensed that the sleep-heaviness had begun to edge into his hands.

"Why do you laugh, Treffry?" Vinocur's voice asked.

That almost set Treffrey off again. But he choked the laughter down. If he kept giving way to it, he would be asleep before he made sure that whatever dreams came to Frank Vinocur during the long trip would not be pleasant ones. He said, "Let me tell you—"

While the Programmed Corps was being forged into a magnificent, automatically functioning weapon on Ridzin, it became obvious that its completion was awaited with as much anxiety as eagerness by a number of the worlds of the Terrestrial League. The question, of course, was who in the end would control it.

"We didn't try to stop the plotting and bargaining that went on," Treffry said. "And we didn't become involved in it. We merely took measures to ensure that the central government and Great Xal would remain always one step ahead of the conspirators."

"Conspirators?" Vinocur's voice repeated carefully over the intercom.

"Hannaret and Lorcia from the beginning, naturally!" Treffry told him. "Then, during the past two years, the governing body of Ridzin. We did our intelligence work thoroughly. Great Xal held the margin of power, so nothing else was needed. We could let the thing ripen.

"My dear fellow, that was what has made the final stages of this game so amusing! The ingenuity! The intricate patterns of deception! War fleets from Lorcia and Hannaret combining suddenly for 'joint maneuvers' in an open threat to Great Xal—and on Ridzin, in apparent desperation, ineffectual gestures at sabotage, including a series of attempted assassinations by mysteriously malfunctioning Programmed soldiers! They were not intended to succeed, of course; murdering me could not have held up the transfer of the Corps by a day. I imagine poor Ulbrand got killed by accident—or, more correctly, by the ineptness of his defenses.

"And to what end? Why, to divert our attention. Nothing more. To draw us away from the one plan which did, in fact, have a chance to succeed. But that plan has failed, too, Vinocur!"

Treffry paused a moment. When the intercom remained silent, he went on complacently. "The Hannaret warships which were to intercept and halt our carriers on their way to Great Xal have been allowed to take up position midway on our course. But they will be joined a few days from now by twice their number of central government ships. There will be no interception, Vinocur!

"And now, with the Programmed Corps to enforce its orders, Great Xal deals once and for all with the malcontent worlds! The Terrestrial League will be hammered into a unit. That is the corps' only urgent and immediate task. Time enough later to turn to settling our score with the Skanders. Why we owe those obscene aliens some gratitude, as a matter of fact—if they hadn't been such a visible threat to the League it would have been impossible to bring the Corps into existence. So now, as I bid you good-night, 'General' Vinocur, I shall leave it to you to picture for yourself the warm reception awaiting you on Great Xal!"

There was silence again for a moment. Then Vinocur said, "Treffry?"

"Yes?" Treffry said, pleased. He had not really expected Vinocur to reply,

"You omitted mentioning one of our diversion attempts," the intercom told him.

"I did?" Treffry said. "What was that?"

"The interception of the carriers, of course. Too many people knew of that plan. It was almost inevitable that your intelligence would get wind of it."

Treffry started to speak, checked himself, suddenly chilled.

"To stay one step ahead in this game," Vinocur's voice told him blandly, "that, as you've indicated, was the great necessity here. To bedazzle, mislead, confuse with a variety of elaborate schemes and dodges—when, all the time, only some very simple plan, one known to the fewest possible planners, could be successful. And that plan has succeeded, Treffry! To this moment only four men have known about it. You will now be the fifth.

"The Programmed Corps is not on its way to Great Xal, you

see. Instead, the course of the carriers will take them to transspace stations on Hannaret."

Impossible, Treffry thought in instant, scornful relief. What was the fellow attempting to accomplish with such a lie? Only Ulbrand and Monte—

"Ulbrand's death," Vinocur's voice was continuing, "was no accident. He and Dexter Monte controlled the master programs of the carrier fleet's computers. We had to get Ulbrand out of the way."

"Ridiculous!" Treffry realized he had shouted, his voice thick and distorted, wondered briefly whether it was the anesthetic which made his mouth feel numb and stiffened now-or fear. "Monte!" he shouted again at the intercom.

Some seconds passed silently—as Vinocur, too, waited for Dexter Monte to respond.

"Monte!" Treffry bellowed once more. Slurred, mumbling noises issued from the speaker then, followed by a heavy belch.

"I couldn't answer at once," Dexter Monte explained in a weak, complaining voice. "I had to pull myself together. I don't feel at all well! If you two hadn't made me swallow those atrocious alcoholic concoctions—" He muttered indistinctly, added, "What is it?"

"You heard what that fool was saying?" Treffry demanded.

"You needn't speak so loudly!" Monte protested. "Yes, I heard him."

"Well?"

"Oh, I agreed almost a year ago to program the carriers to go to Hannaret when the time came. Is that what you want to know? It's true enough. They guaranteed me wealth, power, influence. The usual approach. Including direct blackmail, I must say! Ulbrand, incidentally, wasn't so stupid. I had to loosen his defenses to let the assassin get to him." Dexter Monte belched explosively, groaned in polite dismay. "Excuse me, gentlemen! Your infernal alcohol . . ."

Vinocur was laughing now. Treffry's thoughts seemed to whirl in confusion. Then he remembered something. He snorted.

"Monte, you're a miserable coward and a monstrous liar!" he stated. "I can believe they blackmailed you into agreeing to do what they wanted. But you're safe from them now, so you can give up the pretense! Because of course you didn't go through with it."

Vinocur abruptly stopped laughing. "He went through with it," he growled.

Treffry chuckled. "He couldn't, Vinocur! He simply couldn't!

Monte, like every other key man brought to Ridzin, was put through secret security tests once a month—and *I* supervised that operation—always. So Monte couldn't have harbored any real intentions to betray us: No human mind can deceive the testing machines . . . eh, Monte?"

Monte wearily mumbled a sentence or two.

"What did you say, Monte? Speak up!"

"I said I agree with you." Dexter Monte's voice was distinct again but quite faint. He sighed. "No human mind can deceive the testing machines."

Treffry swallowed with difficulty. The anesthetic definitely was affecting his tongue and throat now. "Are you listening, Vinocur?" he demanded. "So the Programmed Corps isn't going to Hannaret, is it, Monte?"

"No," Monte said. He added peevishly, "But you gentlemen *must* excuse me now! I really can't keep myself together any longer."

"Treffry—" Vinocur's voice had thickened, sounded heavily slurred.

"Yes?"

"Ask him—ask him whether the Programmed Corps is . . . going to Great Xal."

"What?"

"We . . . had him on . . . testing machines, too, Treffry!"

A monstrous thought swam up slowly in Treffry's mind.

"Monte!" he cried. "*Monte!*"

Odd watery whistling noises responded for some seconds from the intercom. Nothing else.

Could it be? Could the most awesome weapon ever devised, the irresistible Programmed Corps, be hurtling now, not toward Great Xal but, out of control, toward some immensely distant point in space? From which it presently would return, under new instructions, to wipe out the race which had created it?

"Monte!" This time, only Treffry's mind formed the word. The sound that came from his mouth was a heavy groan—the cold-sleep process was moving along its irreversible course. Moaning noises in the intercom indicated Vinocur was experiencing similar difficulties. Treffry's thoughts began to swirl in slow and awful confusion, revolving about one fact repeatedly mentioned in the speeches that day: the Skanders' repulsive amebic quality, their ability to force themselves out of their basic shape into another of their choosing and to maintain it for an indefinite period . . .

Perhaps for as long as fifteen or twenty years? Long enough to—

That thought, all thought, faded. The moaning in the intercom went on for almost another minute. Then it, too, stopped. In a silence which would remain unbroken for many months the great carrier fleet rushed toward its destination.

Left Hand, Right Hand

. . . .

JERRY NEWLAND was sitting up on the side of his bunk, frowning at the floor, when Troy Gordon came quietly into the room and stopped at the entrance to watch him. Not too good, Troy thought after a moment, studying Newland's loose mouth, the slow blinking of the eyes and the slumped immobility of position. Not too bad either—not for a man who, in most practical respects, had been dead for the better part of three years and come awake again only the day before.

But the question was whether Newland was going to recover quickly enough now to be of any use as an ally.

Troy moved forward a few steps into the room, stopped again as Newland raised his head in a sluggish motion to stare at him. For a few seconds, the man's face remained blank. Then he grinned. A strained, unpleasant-looking grin, but a grin.

Troy waited. Newland cleared his throat, said, "I . . . I recognized you almost immediately this time! And . . . I remembered that this same thing had happened before."

Troy grinned, too, guardedly. "My coming into the room this way?"

Newland nodded.

"It happened yesterday," Troy said. "What's my name?"

"Troy Gordon."

"And yours?"

"Jerry Franklin Newland."

"What do you do?"

"Do? . . . Oh!" Newland drew a deep breath. "I'm courier pilot for the . . . for the . . ." He stopped, looking first surprised, then dismayed. Then his face wrinkled up slowly, like that of a child about to cry.

"That part's gone again, eh?" Troy asked, watching him.

"Yes. There's some . . . there's . . ."

"You are—or you were—courier pilot for the Cassa Expedition," Troy said. He thumped his heel on the floor. "That's Cassa One, underneath us. We've been away from Earth for three years and eight months." He paused. "Does that help?"

Newland reflected, frowned. "Not much. I . . . it seems to be true when you say it." He hesitated. "We're prisoners, aren't we?"

"Uh-huh," he answered, flatly.

"I had that feeling. And you're hiding me here?"

"That's right," Troy agreed.

"Why?"

"Because nobody else knows you're still alive. It's better if they don't, right now."

Newland shook his head, indicated a sign fastened to the ceiling above the bunk in such a way that a man lying in the bunk on his back would catch sight of it as soon as he opened his eyes. "That," he said, "made sense as soon as I saw it just now! I remembered having read it before and what it meant. But otherwise everything's still badly blurred."

Troy glanced up at the sign. It read:

RELAX AND TAKE IT EASY, JERRY! YOU WERE IN A BAD SMASHUP, AND YOU'VE JUST FINISHED A LONG STRETCH IN THE EMERGENCY TANK OF YOUR SHIP. EVERYTHING'S BOUND TO SEEM A LITTLE FOGGY, BUT YOU'RE GOING TO BE OKAY. DON'T TRY TO LEAVE THE ROOM. IT HAS TO BE KEPT LOCKED, BUT SOMEONE WILL BE ALONG TO SEE YOU IN TWO OR THREE HOURS AT THE MOST.

Troy said, "Your memory will start coming back fast enough. You've made a good start." He sat down, took his cigarette case from his pocket. "I'll go over some of the things that have happened with you. That tends to bring them . . . and other things . . . back to mind. Care to smoke?"

"Yes, I'd like to smoke."

Troy tossed the cigarette case over to the bunk, watched the pilot reach for and miss it, then bend forward awkwardly to fumble for it on the floor. Reflexes still very bad, he thought. But when Newland had the case in his hand, he flicked it open without hesitation, took out a cigarette and closed the case, then turned it over and pressed the button which snapped on the concealed light. The day before, he had stared at the case helplessly until Troy showed him what to do. So his body had begun to recall more of its learned motion patterns.

Troy said, "I told you the main parts twice yesterday. Don't let that worry you . . . you've retained more than most would be likely to do after a quarter of the time you spent in the tank. You weren't in very good shape after the smash-up, Jerry."

Newland said wryly, "I can imagine that." He drew on the cigarette, coughed, then tossed the case back to Troy who caught it and put it in his pocket.

"Have you got back any recollection at all of what the aliens that caught us are like?" Troy asked.

Newland shook his head.

"Well," Troy said, "they're downright cute, in a way. More like big penguins than anything else. Short little legs. The heads aren't so cute . . . a hammerhead shark would be the closest thing there, which is why we call them Hammerheads—though not when we think some of them might be listening.

"They don't belong here any more than we do. They came from another system which is a lot closer than Sol but still a long way off. Now, we aren't the first Earth people to get to Cassa. There was an Earth survey ship poking around the system about twenty years ago, and it seems that the Hammerheads also had an expedition here at the time. They spotted our survey ship but weren't spotted themselves, and the survey ship eventually went back to Earth short two of its men. Those two were supposed to have got lost in the deserts on Cassa. Actually, the Hammerheads picked them up . . . Jerry?"

The pilot's head was beginning to nod. He straightened now and took a puff on the cigarette, grinning embarrassedly. "S'all right, Troy!" he muttered. "Seemed to get . . . sort of absent-minded there for a moment."

Which was, Troy knew, one of the symptoms of the re-awakening period. Newland's mind had been shut away from reality for a long time, wrapped in soothing, vaguely pleasant dreams while the emergency tank went about the business of repairing his broken body. The habit of unconscious retreat from his surroundings could not be immediately discarded, and particularly not when the surroundings were as undesirable as those in which Newland now found himself. It would be better, Troy thought, to skip some of the uglier details . . . and yet he had to tell the man enough to make him willing to cooperate in what would be, at the very least, a desperately dangerous undertaking.

He said, "You're still only three-quarters awake, Jerry. We have to expect that. But the closer you listen and the more information you can absorb, the faster you'll shake off the cobwebs. And that's important. These Hammerheads are a tough breed, and we're in a bad spot."

Newland nodded. "I understand that much. Go ahead."

"Well," Troy said, "whatever that first Earth survey ship had to report about the Cassa system looked good enough so that the administration put Cassa down for a major expedition some day. Twenty years later, we got here again—the interstellar exploration carrier *Atlas* with eight hundred men on board. I'm one of her engineers. And we found the Tareegs—that's what the Hammerheads call themselves—waiting for us. Not another bunch of scientists and assistants but a war-party. They'd learned enough from the two survey ship men they'd caught to figure out we'd be coming back and how to handle us when we got here.

"Now get straight on a few things about the Hammerheads, Jerry. Their weapons systems are as good or better than ours. In other ways, they're behind us. They've got a fair interstellar drive but can't make the same use of it we do, because they've still a lot to learn about inertial shielding. They have a couple of robot-directed interstellar drones standing in a hangar a few hundred yards from here which can hit half the speed of your courier, but no Hammerhead or human being could ride 'em up and live. The two big carriers that brought them to Cassa One are dead-slow boats compared to the *Atlas*. And that's about the best they have at present.

"Just the same, they're out to get us. War is the best part of living as far as they're concerned, and they're plenty good at it. So far they've only been fighting among themselves but they're itching for a chance at another race, and now we're it. Capturing an Earth expedition in the Cassa System was only part of the plan to take Earth by surprise."

Newland blinked, said slowly, "How's that? You'd think that might tip their hand. We'll be missed, won't we?"

"Sure we'll be missed," Troy said. "But when? We were to stay here eight years . . . don't remember that either, eh? The Hammerheads will have all the time they need to be set for who ever comes looking for us eventually."

"But would they know that?"

Troy said bitterly, "They know everything about Earth that our top brass scientists of the Cassa Expedition were able to tell them. Pearson and Andrews—those names mean anything? They were the Expedition Chiefs when we were captured. One of the first things the Hammerheads did was to have the science staff and other department heads look on while they tortured those two men to death. As a result, they've had all the cooperation they could ask for—more than any decent human being would think of giving them—from our present leadership, the senior scientists Dr. Chris Dexter and Dr. Victor Clingman. They're a couple of lousy traitors, Jerry, and I'm not sure they're even capable of realizing it. Clingman's in charge here at the ground base, and he acts as if he doesn't see anything wrong helping the Hammerheads."

"Helping the . . ." Vacancy showed for a moment in the pilot's expression; he frowned uncertainly.

"Try to stay awake, Jerry! There're just a few other things you should try to get nailed down in your memory this time. The Hammerheads are water animals. They can waddle around on land as long as they keep themselves moist, but they don't like it. They've got a religion based on a universal struggle between water and land. Cassa One's nothing but hot desert and rock and big salt beds, so it's no good to them. And the other two planets in the system have no oxygen to speak of.

"Now here's the thing that's hard to swallow. There's a huge lumped-up asteroid swarm in the system. The *Atlas* stopped for a few days on the way in to look around in it. Dexter and Clingman, after we'd been captured volunteered the information to the Hammerheads that a lot of that stuff was solid H_2O and that if they wanted Cassa One fixed up the way they'd like it— wet—the *Atlas* could ferry enough asteroid ice over here in billion-ton loads to turn most of the surface of the planet into a sea.

"You understand it wasn't the Hammerheads who had the idea. They don't have anything resembling the ship power and equipment to handle such a job; it hadn't even occurred to them that it could be possible. But you can bet they bought it when it was handed to them. It will give them a base a third of the way between their own system and Sol. That's what's been going on since we landed and were grabbed off . . . almost three years ago now.

"And these last weeks there've been, for the first time since we got here, a few clouds in the sky. It means the boys on the *Atlas* have as many of those mountains of ice riding on orbit as are needed, and they've started shoving them down into the atmosphere to break up and melt. So we . . . Jerry, wake up!"

Troy Gordon paused, watching Newland, then shrugged, stood up and went over to take the butt of the cigarette from the pilot's slack fingers. Newland had slid back into catatonic immobility; he offered no resistance as Troy swung his legs up on the bunk and straightened him out on his back.

How much would he remember the next time he awoke? Troy didn't know; he had no medical experience and was working on the basis of remembered scraps of information about the treatment given men recovering from an experience such as Newland's. There were people on the ground station who could have told him what to do, but he hadn't dared ask questions.

It was chiefly a matter of time now. Or of lack of time. What would happen when the giant hauling operation was concluded, when the water which had been carried in from space came creeping across the vast desert plateaus about the station, was something he didn't know. But it was almost certain that if his own plans hadn't been carried out by that time, they never would be.

"Jerry," he addressed the sleeping pilot softly, "if you've wondered why I'm risking my neck to bring you back to life and keep you hidden away from the Hammerheads and Clingman, it's because you're the one man I still can trust in this lousy expeditionary group. It's because you tried to do something about the situation on your own. You don't remember it yet, but when the Hammerheads took over the *Atlas* you made a break for it in the courier boat. You tried to get away and warn Earth. They shot you down before you could clear atmosphere; but then they couldn't find the wreck. They thought it was down in one of the salt beds and gave up looking for it.

"But I found it in the desert a couple of months later. You'd dropped through into the emergency tank and you were still more or less alive. I smuggled the tank into the station here as soon as I'd rigged up a place where I could keep it. I can use some help, and you'll be the best possible man for the job. . . ."

He stopped, surprised to see that Newland's mouth had begun

to work awkwardly as if he were trying to speak. Then a few words came, slow and slurred, but indicating that the pilot's mind had not sunk nearly as far from full wakefulness as during his previous relapses.

"Wha . . . want me . . . do?"

Troy didn't answer. Not yet, he thought. Not until Newland was no longer helpless. Because, in spite of all precautions, he might be discovered here at any hour; and if that should happen, Troy's secret must still be his own. He could act without Newland's help if necessary.

He waited a few seconds longer, while the pilot's face slowly smoothed out again into comatose blankness. Then Troy turned around quietly and left the room.

Troy Gordon's personal living quarters were on the lowest of the station's three underground levels, behind the central power plant and utilities section. Considerable privacy was their only attraction; and since the arrangement kept Troy, during his off-duty hours, close to his responsibilities as the station's maintenance engineer, neither Dr. Clingman nor the Hammerheads had objected to it. He was a useful man; and to the useful, minor privileges could be extended.

Troy had been able to take advantage of that circumstance. The room in which Newland was hidden lay behind his own quarters, forming an extension to them. The entrance to it was concealed, and while a careful search should have disclosed it, Troy—so far as he knew—had as yet given no one a reason to initiate such a search. The back room was not part of the station's original design; he had cut it secretly out of the rock. With the equipment at his disposal, it had been a relatively minor job.

But it involved a very ugly risk. Discovery would have meant death, and no easy one. With the exception of the cooperating chief scientists, the Hammerheads' attitude towards their captives was largely one of watchful indifference, so long as no one got out of line. But they had taken one measure which insured that, after a short time, there was very little inclination left among the prisoners to get out of line knowingly. At intervals of about a month, whether or not an overt offense had been committed, one more member of Earth's Cassa Expedition was methodically tortured to death by the aliens; and a group of his fellows, selected apparently at random, was obliged to witness the matter while fastened to a device which allowed them to experience the victim's sensations in modified form.

Troy had been included twice in the observing group. He hadn't known whether it implied a personal warning or not. In the Hammerheads' eyes, he was a useful servant; it might be that he was also a suspected one.

Troy left his rooms, locking the outer door behind him. Moving thirty feet down the narrow steel-floored passage behind the power plant, he entered one of the tool rooms, again closing and locking the door as he went through. It had been a much more difficult and lengthy undertaking to drill a tunnel from the station's lowest level up to the force-screened Hammerhead hangar outside than to carve an additional room out of the rock, but it had been completed months before. The tunnel's hidden station entrance was beneath the tool room floor, the other opening out of the polished rock base of the hangar twenty feet from one of the interstellar drones. The most careful human scrutiny would hardly have read any significance there into the hairline crack which formed an irregular oval on the rock; and since Troy hadn't been found out, he could assume that the Hammerheads' powers of observation were no more acute.

It had been night in the surrounding desert for some hours by now, but the hangar was brightly lit—a very unusual occurrence at such a time. Troy paused, momentarily disconcerted, studying the scene in the hangar through the vision screen installed in the tunnel just below the exit. If the Hammerheads—there were only Hammerheads—present—were initiating some major new activity in the next day or two, his plans might be, if not ruined, at least very dangerously delayed. He counted over a hundred of the creatures, mostly assembled near the far end of the hangar in three orderly groups. A few officers stood together, somewhat closer to him.

Troy chewed his lip anxiously, the moisture-conserving suits they wore for outside duty on Cassa One, which concealed the two sets of swim flippers along their sides and left the top pair of upper limbs . . . short, sturdy brown arms with hands larger than human hands, quite as capable and rather unpleasantly human in appearance . . . free for use. The transparent, inverted-triangle helmets were clamped down. As he looked on, one of their big atmospheric personnel carriers came gliding into sight behind the immobile ranks. There were commands, and the Tareegs turned and filed into the vehicle, moving with the rapid, awkward little waddle which was their method of progress on land. A minute or two later, the loaded carrier moved out of the hangar, and the lights in the vast structure slowly faded away.

Where were they going? They were carrying the usual weapons, but this was not some dryland drill. Troy could not remember seeing so large a group leave the station before. The uneasy conviction returned that the move must be connected with the fact that clouds had begun to show in Cassa One's skies, that the mile-thick boulders of ice which had been brought across space already were falling through the atmosphere of the dessicated world.

One or two more undisturbed days, Troy thought. In that time it would become clear whether Newland was going to recover sufficiently to be able to play a part in his plans. Only two sections of the shattered courier ship, the inertial shielding and the autonav, had been needed to transform the Hammerheads' interstellar drone twenty feet from the tunnel exit into a spaceship which men could ride and direct. Both those sections had been repairable, and everything else Troy had been able to steal or build in the station. Month after month passed as he brought it all together in the tunnel, familiarized himself with every necessary detail of the drones' mechanisms and fitted in the new installations ... first in theory, then in actual fact. A part of almost every night was spent in the darkened hangar, assembling, checking and testing one section or another, then disassembling everything and taking it back down into the tunnel before the moment came when the Tareeg watch-beams would sweep again through the hangar.

The beam-search was repeated each three hours and twenty-seven minutes throughout the night. Within that period of time, Troy would have to carry out a final complete assembly, let the drone roar into life and send it flashing up through the force-screen and into space.

By now, he knew he could do it. And if he had calculated the drone's capacity correctly, he would then be less than six months from Earth. The Hammerheads had nothing they could send after him.

But once in space, he needed Newland's experience. Everything else would be on board to get them to Earth, but without a trained pilot the probability of arriving only on autonav was something Troy couldn't calculate. With a great deal of luck, he thought, it still should be possible. Newland's skills, on the other hand, would give them something considerably better than an even chance.

But Newland would have to be recovered first. He was still under the ministrations of the emergency tank, embedded now in the wall of the back room beyond the bunk. The tank had to stay there; no amount of planning had shown a way it could be fitted into the drone besides everything else; there simply was no room left for it. And what Troy had learned made it clear that if he lifted into space with Newland before the pilot's behavior was very nearly normal, he would have a half-dead zombie on his hands before the trip was well begun.

That had been his reason for waiting. But the question was now whether he mightn't already have waited a little too long.

Troy checked his watch. Take a chance and begin the final installation at once? It would be an hour before the search-beams came back. The interior of the ships was inspected at irregular periods; he hadn't been able to establish any pattern for that. But to leave his equipment in place in the drone for one day, or two at the most, might not be stretching his luck too far. Then, if Newland shaped up, there would be that much less delay in leaving, that much less time to spend in the Tareeg hangar finishing the job at the end. And no one could tell what new developments the next few days might bring, or how much time they would find that they had left. . . .

He twisted the direction dials on the vision screen, swinging it slowly once more about the darkened hangar. Then he unlocked and shifted the exit switch, and the irregularly carved section of rock above him moved on its lifting rods out of the hangar floor. Troy swung up and out behind it, got to his feet and started over to the drone.

There was a thin, burring noise close to his ear.

Troy stopped in mid-stride, his face tight and wary. The noise meant that his room communicator was being called. Probably some minor technical emergency on the station, but . . . He counted off twenty seconds, then turned on the relay mike under his coat collar. Trying to make his voice thick with drowsiness, he said, "Gordon speaking. Who's it?"

"Reese," a carefully uninflected voice told him from the speaker. "Dr. Clingman wants you to come up to his office immediately, Gordon."

Troy felt a sudden sharp prickling of fear.

"At this time of night?" he demanded petulantly. "It's the middle of my sleep period! What's gone wrong now?"

"I wouldn't know," Reese said. "Our senior scientist"—he made the two words sound like a worn, habitual curse—"didn't go into details."

Dr. Victor Clingman was a large, untidy man inclined to plumpness, with stringy blond hair and protuberant pale eyes. His office adjoined that of the Tareeg station commandant—a Low Dsala, in Hammerhead terms—and it was permeated from there with a slightly salty, vaguely perfumed moistness. Rank had its privileges; only the Low Dsala enjoyed the luxury of keeping his station work quarters damp enough to make the wearing of a suit unnecessary. The other Hammerheads waddled about the cold, dry halls completely covered, breathing through humidifiers, and were only occasionally permitted, and then after much ceremony, to enter an area in their section called the Water Room and linger there for several hours.

Troy came into Clingman's office with his tool kit through the double doors designed to prevent moisture from escaping, shivering slightly as the sudden clamminess touched his skin. Clingman, engaged as usual in pecking out something on a writer, shirt sleeves rolled up on his plump arms, ranked piles of notes on the table beside him, turned a pale, unhealthy-looking face towards the door.

"Mister Gordon," he said mildly, dragging the "mister" out a little as was his habit. He nodded at the wall to Troy's left. "Our recording mechanisms became inoperative again . . . and just as I was in the process of noting down some very interesting fresh clues as to the probable origin of the Tareeg coup system. Will you try to attend to it?"

"Right away," Troy said, his vague fears dispelled. Clingman's recorders were a standard problem; the repair parts for such items were on the *Atlas* which had not come down into atmosphere for almost a year. There probably had been no reason to feel apprehensive about a night call to the office. It had happened on such occasions before.

He went to work, glancing over from time to time at the senior scientist who was frowning down pensively at the writer. Before the Hammerheads executed his predecessors, Dr. Victor Clingman had been head of the Biology Department on the Cassa Expedition, and his interest in the subject had not changed, though it was now centered exclusively on the life habits of their captors. The Tareegs did not seem to object to his preoccupation with them. Possibly it amused them; though Clingman had told Troy once, rather complacently, that his research already had proved to be of some usefulness to the Tareegs in answering certain questions they had had about themselves. That might also be true. On several occasions, at any rate, Troy had found either the Low Dsala or another Hammerhead officer in Clingman's office, answering the scientist's questions in high-pitched, reedy voices which always had the suggestion of a whistle in them. All of them apparently had been taught human speech, though they rarely chose to use it.

Clingman cleared his throat, asked without turning his head, "Did I tell you, Gordon, that the Tareegs' known history goes back to considerably less than a thousand years, by human time reckoning?"

"Yes, you did, doctor," Troy said. It had become almost impossible for him to do work for Clingman—and Clingman invariably called on him personally when he had some mechanical chore on hand—without listening to a lengthy, rambling discourse on the scientist's latest discoveries about the Tareegs. It was an indication, he thought, that Clingman had grown increasingly hungry for human companionship of any kind. He could hardly fail to know that the majority of the stations' human component was aware he had originated the suggestion made by the leading scientific group to the Hammerheads concerning the possibility of turning Cassa One into a Tareeg water world, and that he was generally despised for it. Troy's noncommittal attitude might have led him to believe that Troy either had not been informed of the fact or happened to be a man who saw nothing very objectionable in such an act.

Troy was, as it happened, less certain than some of the others that Clingman and the men like Dr. Chris Dexter, who had been directing the ice-hauling operations of the Atlas, had come to a deliberate, cold-blooded agreement among themselves to save their own skins by offering to help the Hammerheads against mankind. It was perhaps more likely that they had acted in unthinking panic, following the gruesome executions the Hammerheads had forced them to witness. That would be more forgivable, if only slightly so. It was difficult to be sure about Clingman in any way. He might be unpardonably guilty in his own mind and still no less frightened than before—for who knew, after all, what the Tareegs ultimately intended with their prisoners? On the other hand, he might actually have buried all such considerations beneath the absorbed, objective interest he appeared to take in them.

❊ ❊ ❊

Troy had paid no more attention than he could help at first to Clingman's scholarly monologues on his favorite theme. His own thoughts avoided the Hammerheads as far as possible. But as his personal plans began to develop and the chance that he might reach Earth grew into something more than a wildly improbable hope, he realized that the more he learned about the new enemy, the more valuable an eventual report would be. Thereafter he listened carefully, memorizing all of Clingman's speculations, and gradually developed some degree of detached interest of his own in the creatures. They had a curious history, short though it was, a history of merciless strife on twin water worlds of the same system in which any records of a common background had been long lost or destroyed. Then had come the shock of mutual discovery and renewed battling, now on an interplanetary scale, which ended in a truce of carefully guarded equality between the rival worlds.

"That situation, it seems possible," Clingman had said once, "may have led to the legend of the lost home-world of the Tareegs." It was a cautious reference to the obvious fact that neither Tareeg planet would have been willing to admit that it might be no more than an ancient colony of its twin. A remote and glorious ancestral world which had brought both colonies forth as equals was a much more acceptable theory. "And yet," Clingman went on, "the legend might well be based in fact. And it may be that we, with our skills, will enable the Tareegs to rediscover that world. . . ."

It sounded, Troy had thought, with something like amused disgust, as if the scientific brass had prudently worked out a new scheme to preserve itself after the Cassa One operation closed out.

"There also, of course," Clingman continued, blinking his pale eyes reflectively at Troy, "we have the origin of the parallel legend of the Terrible Enemy. What except the conquest of the home-world by a monstrous foe could have caused it to forget its colonies? In that light, it becomes a little easier to understand the . . . ah, well . . . the . . . cautious distrust the Tareegs have shown towards the first intelligent species they encountered in interstellar space."

And *that* sounded like an attempted apology—not so much for the Tareegs and their manner of expressing cautious distrust as for Dr. Victor Clingman's collaboration with them. But Troy said nothing. By then he was very eager to hear more.

He did. Almost week by week, something new was added to the Hammerhead data filed away in his mind. Much of it might be unimportant detail, but Earth's strategists could decide that for themselves. The Tareeg coup system Clingman was mulling over again tonight had been of significance at least to the prisoners; for it probably was the reason the majority of them were still alive. The two High Dsalas who, each representing one of the twin worlds, were in joint command of the Tareeg forces here would have gained great honor merely by returning to their system at once with the captured Earth expedition. But to have stayed instead, silently to have assumed personal responsibility for the creation of a new world fit for Tareeg use—that assured them honor and power beyond belief when the giant task was over and the announcement went out. . . .

The awareness that Clingman was speaking again broke into Troy's thoughts.

"Almost everything they do," the scientist observed musingly, "is filled with profound ceremonial meaning. It was a long while before we really understood that. You've heard, I suppose, that cloud formations have appeared on this side of the planet?"

Troy was about to answer, then checked himself, frowning down at the cleanly severed end of the lead he had been tracing. Severed? What . . .

"Gordon?"

"Uh . . . why, yes, I've seen them myself, doctor." Troy's mind began to race. The lead had been deliberately cut, no question of that. But why? He might have spent another hour checking over the recording equipment before discovering it—

"It means, of course," he heard Clingman saying, "that the dry sea basins of Cassa One gradually are filling with water. Now, we know the vital importance to the Tareegs of being able to immerse themselves in the—to them—sacred fluid, and how severely they have been rationed in that respect here. One might have thought that, from the High Dsalas down, all of them would have plunged eagerly into the first bodies of water to appear on the planet. But, no . . . so great a thing must not be approached in that manner! A day was set, months in advance, when it could be calculated that the water level would reach a certain point. At that hour, every Tareeg who can be spared from essential duty will be standing at the shore of the new sea. And together . . . ?"

Abruptly, the meaning of Clingman's words faded out of Troy's mind.

The sudden nighttime summons to Clingman's office—had it been no accident after all? Had he done something in the past few hours to arouse suspicion, and was he being detained here now while his rooms were searched? Troy felt sweat start out on his face. Should he say anything? He hesitated, then reached quietly into the tool kit.

"... and only then"—Clingman's voice returned suddenly to his consciousness—"will the word be prepared to go back, and the messenger ships filled with the sacred water so that it can be blended at the same moment with the twin worlds' oceans, to show that Cassa One has become jointly a part of each ..."

Messenger ships—the interstellar drones, of course. And the big troop of Hammerheads which had been taken from the station in the personnel carrier less than an hour ago ... His hands trembling a little, Troy quickly closed the recorder, picked up the toolkit.

Clingman checked himself. "Oh ... you've finished, Gordon?" He sounded startled.

Troy managed to work a grin on his face. "Yes, doctor. Just a broken lead. And now, if you'll excuse me. . . ." He started to turn away.

"Ah, one moment!" Clingman said sharply. "There was ... I ... now where ..." He gazed about the table, pushing fretfully at the piles of notes. "Oh, yes! Dr. Rojas ... Room 72. You were on your way up here when he attempted to reach you. Something that needed ... well, I forget now what he said. Would you mind going over there immediately?"

"Not at all." Troy's heart was pounding. If there had been any doubt he was being deliberately delayed, it would have vanished now. Dr. Rojas, of course, *would* have something waiting that "needed" Troy's attention before he got to Room 72. A call from Clingman would arrange for it.

But if they were suspicious of him, why hadn't he been placed under arrest? They don't want to scare me off, Troy thought. They're not sure, and if I'm up to something they don't want to scare me off before they know just what it is ...

He'd swung around to the hall, mind reaching ahead through the next few minutes, outlining quickly the immediate steps he would have to take—and so he was almost past the Hammerhead before he saw it. The door to the Low Dsala's offices had opened quietly, and the Low Dsala stood there five feet away, the horizontally stalked eyes fixed on Troy.

Troy started involuntarily. He might be very close to death now.

To approach a Hammerhead . . . let alone the station's ranking officer . . . unbidden within a dozen steps was a dangerous thing for a prisoner to do. The Dsala's left hand hung beside the ornament-encrusted bolt-gun all the officers carried—and those broad torturers' hands could move with flashing speed. But the creature remained immobile. Troy averted his eyes from it, keeping his face expressionless, walked on with carefully unhurried steps, conscious of the Dsala's stare following him.

It was one of the comparatively few times he had seen a Hammerhead without its suit. If one knew nothing about them, they would have looked almost comical—there was a decided resemblance to the penguins, the clown-birds of Earth, in the rotund, muscular bodies and the double set of swimming flippers. The odd head with its thick protruding eyelobes and the small, constantly moving crimson triangle of the mouth were less funny, as were the dark, human-shaped hands. Troy felt a chill on his back when he heard the Dsala break into sudden speech behind him: a high, quick gabble in its own language. Was it expressing anger? Drawing the door quietly shut, he heard Clingman begin to reply in the same tongue.

Reese looked briefly up from the intercom desk as Troy stopped before it. "Finished with Clingman?" he asked.

"Uh-huh," Troy said. "Any other little jobs waiting before I can get back to sleep?"

"Not so far," Reese told him sourly. "Pleasant dreams." He returned his attention to the panels before him.

So Dr. Rojas, as had seemed almost certain, had put in no call for him. But if he didn't show up at Room 72, how long before they began to wonder where he was? Perhaps four or five minutes . . .

Troy stepped out of the elevator on the maintenance level forty seconds after leaving Reese, went quickly on into the engine room. One Hammerhead guard stood watching him from the far end. As a rule, three of them were stationed here. They were accustomed to Troy's appearances, and he had been careful to establish as irregular a pattern as was practicable in attending to routine chores, so that in an emergency his motions would draw a minimum of attention. Ignoring the guard now, he carried out a desultory inspection of a set of wall controls, paused four times to remove four minor sections of machinery and drop them into his tool kit, and was leaving the big room again a minute and a half later.

Out in the passage, he reopened the kit, quickly snapped three of the small steel parts together. The carrying of firearms naturally was not a privilege the Tareegs extended to human beings; but the newly assembled device was a quite functional gun. Troy thumbed three dozen hand-made shells out of the fourth piece removed from the control equipment, loaded the gun and shoved it into his pocket.

The door to his quarters was locked, and there were no immediate signs inside that an inspection might have been carried out during his absence. Troy moved over to the rarely used intercom view-screen, changed some settings behind it, and switched it on. The hidden back room appeared in the screen, and—in spite of his near-certainty about Clingman's purpose in detaining him—Troy felt his face whiten slowly with shock.

Jerry Newland was no longer lying on his bunk, was nowhere in the room. A gaping opening in the wall behind the bunk showed where the emergency tank Troy had brought in from the crashed courier ship had been installed. So they not only had the pilot in their hands—they already were aware of his identity and of the condition he was in.

Troy felt a surge of physical sickness. Left to himself, Newland would have died in the desert without regaining consciousness as the tank's independent power source began to fail. Troy had saved him from that; but very probably it was the Tareeg death the pilot faced now. Troy switched off the screen, started back to the door, fighting down his nausea. Self-blame was a luxury for which he had no time. He couldn't help Newland, and there was not an instant to lose. Within a few hours, he could still be in space and take his chances alone at getting the warning to Earth.

But first the search for him must be directed away from the Tareeg hangar. And that, very fortunately, was an action for which he had long been thoroughly prepared. . . .

The Hammerhead guard at the station's ground-level exit also had been reduced to one soldier. And here the appearance of the maintenance engineer's groundcar on its way to one of the automatic installations out in the desert was as familiar an occurrence as Troy's irregular inspection visits in the engine room. The guard watched him roll past without moving and without indication of interest. Troy glanced at his watch as the exit closed behind him. Not quite six minutes since he'd left Clingman's office . . . they should already have begun to check on his whereabouts, and the fact that he alone of all the humans at the station had access to a groundcar would then be one of the first things to come to their minds.

He slowed the car near a tiny inspection door in the outer wall of the station, cut its lights, jumped out and watched it roll on, picking up speed as it swerved away to the east and rushed down into the dark desert. Months before he had installed the automatic guidance devices which would keep the car hurrying steadily eastwards now, changing direction only to avoid impassable obstacles. It might be that, at a time of such importance to the Tareegs, they would not attempt to follow the car. If a flier did discover it from the air, the vehicle would be destroyed . . . and it was rigged to disintegrate with sufficient violence then to conceal the fact that it had lacked a driver.

Troy opened the inspection door, then stopped for a moment, staring back at the Tareeg hangar beyond the station. Light had been glowing through its screens again when he came out; now the hazy translucence of the screens was drawing sideways and up from the great entrance rectangle. Another of the big personnel carriers nosed slowly out, moved up into the air and vanished against the night sky. If it was loaded as close to capacity as the one he had watched from inside the tunnel, almost two thirds of the Hammerhead force at the station had gone by now to attend the rites at Cassa One's new sea.

He waited while the force screen restored itself over the entrance. Immediately afterwards, the lights in the hangar turned dim and faded away. Troy climbed in through the inspection door, locked it and started back down to the maintenance level.

With a little luck, he thought, he might even be able to work undisturbed now inside the interstellar drone he had selected for his escape. He would have to be back in the tunnel when the search-beams came through again . . . he suspected they might be quite sensitive enough to detect the presence of a living being inside one of the ships. But the Hammerheads themselves might not show up again until he was prepared to leave. And then it wouldn't matter. If they did appear—well, he would get some warning from the fact that the hangar lights would begin to come on first. Not very much warning, but it might be enough.

The passage leading past his quarters was empty and quiet. Troy remained behind a corner for a minute or two listening. If Dr. Rojas had reported his failure to arrive at Room 72, the Tareegs must also have learned by now that he had left the station, and the last place they would think of hunting for him was here. But somebody—Hammerhead or human stooge—might be in his rooms, making a second and more thorough investigation there.

Everything remained still. Troy came quietly out into the passage, went down it to the tool room next to his quarters, opened the door, taking the gun from his pocket, and slipped inside. With the door locked, he stood still a moment, then turned on the lights.

A glance around showed that nobody was lurking for him here. He darkened the room again, crossed it, removed the floor section over the tunnel entrance and slipped down into the tunnel. Working by touch, he pulled the floor section back across the opening, snapped it into place and started up the familiar narrow passage he had cut through the desert rock.

He couldn't have said exactly what warned him. It might have been the tiny click of a black-light beam going on. But he knew suddenly that something alive and breathing stood farther up the passage waiting for him, and the gun came quickly from his pocket again.

His forehead was struck with almost paralyzing force. Stungun . . . they wanted him alive. Troy found himself on his knees, dizzy and sick, while a voice yelled at him. *Human*, he thought, with a blaze of hatred beyond anything he'd ever felt for the Tareegs. *Traitor human!* The gun, still somehow in his hand, snarled its answer.

Then the stungun found him again, in three quick, hammering blows, and consciousness was gone.

There came presently an extended period of foggy, groping thoughts interspersed with sleep and vivid nightmares. After a time, Troy was aware that he was in a section of the sick bay on the *Atlas*, and that the great carrier was in interstellar flight. So the operation on Cassa One was over.

He wondered how long he had been knocked out. Days perhaps. It was the shrill, rapid-fire voice of a Tareeg which had first jolted him back into partial awareness. For confused seconds, Troy thought the creature was addressing him; then came the click of a speaker and the sounds ended, and he realized he had heard the Tareeg's voice over the ship's intercom system. A little later, it occurred to him that it had been using its own language and therefore could not have been speaking to him.

During that first muddled period, Troy knew now and then that he was still almost completely paralyzed. Gradually, very gradually, his mind began to clear and the intervals of sleep which always ended with terrifying nightmares grew shorter. Simultaneously he found he was acquiring a limited ability to move. And that, too, increased. It might have been three or four hours after his first awakening before he began to plan what he might do. He had made a number of observations. There were three other men in this section with him. All seemed to be unconscious. He thought the one lying the bed next to his own was Newland, but the room was dim and he had been careful to avoid motions which might have been observed, so he wasn't certain. There was a single human attendant in the small room beyond the open doorspace opposite his bed. Troy didn't recall the man's face. He was in the uniform of a medical corpsman; but whatever else the fellow might be, he was here primarily in the role of a guard because he had a gun fastened to his belt. It classed him as a human being whose subservience to the Hammerheads was not in question. Twice, when the man in the bed at the far end of the room had begun to groan and move about, the guard came in and did something that left the restless one quiet again. Troy couldn't see what he used, but the probability was that it had been a drug administered with a hypodermic spray.

Getting his hands on the gun, Troy decided, shouldn't be too difficult if he made no mistakes. His life was forfeit, and to lie and wait until the Tareeg inquisitors were ready for him wasn't to his taste. Neither . . . though somewhat preferable . . . was personal suicide. A ship, even as great a ship as the *Atlas*, had certain vulnerabilities in interstellar flight—and who knew them better than one of the ship's own engineers? The prime nerve centers were the bridge and the sections immediately surrounding it. It might be, Troy thought, it just might be that the Hammerheads never would bring their prize in to the twin worlds to have its treasures of technological information pried out of it. And that in itself would be a major gain for Earth.

He turned various possibilities over in his mind with the detachment of a man who has acknowledged the inevitable fact of his own death. And he felt his strength flowing back into him.

The guard in the other room presently heard renewed groans and the slurred muttering of a half-conscious man. As he came in through the doorspace with the drug spray he walked into Troy's fist. It didn't quite put him to sleep, but the spray did thirty seconds later, and shortly he was resting, carefully bound and gagged since Troy didn't know how long the drug would retain its effect, in the back of large clothes locker.

The man in the next bed was Newland. He seemed uninjured but was unconscious, presumably drugged like the other two. Troy left the section in the corpsman's uniform, the gun concealed in his pocket. It was improbable that the guard's authority to carry it extended beyond the sick bay area. In another pocket—it might come in handy—was the refilled drug spray.

He was two decks closer to the bridge section when it struck him how deserted the *Atlas* seemed. Of course, he had avoided areas where he would be likely to run into sizable groups of either men or Tareegs. But he had seen only six humans so far, only two of the Hammerheads. These last had come out of a cross-passage ahead of him and vanished into another, two men following quietly behind, the high-pitched alien voices continuing to make a thin, complaining clamor in the otherwise empty hall seconds after they had disappeared. And the thought came to Troy: suppose most of the ship's complement was down in the sleepers?

It wasn't impossible. The *Atlas* must still be provisioned for years to come, but an excellent way to avoid human mutiny on the approach to the Hammerhead worlds would be to put any captives not needed for essential duty to sleep. And the *Atlas* hadn't been built for the convenience of water-creatures. To control a human skeleton crew would require a correspondingly small number of Tareegs. Most of their force, he thought, very well might be making the return in their own vessels.

The reflection literally stopped Troy in his tracks. Because that could change everything he'd had in mind, opened up possibilities he hadn't thought existed . . . including the one, still remote though it might be, of returning the *Atlas* to Earth. Perhaps the men now in charge of the ship would be almost as unwilling to allow that to happen as the Hammerheads; they had too much to answer for. But if the situation he had imagined did exist, his thoughts raced on . . . why then . . .

Troy's mind swam briefly with a wild premonition of triumph. There *were* ways in which it might be done! But because of that, there was also now the sudden need for much more caution than he had intended to use. What he needed first was somebody who could tell him exactly how things stood on board—preferably somebody in a position of authority who could be persuaded or forced to fall in then with Troy's subsequent moves.

The bridge deck was as quiet as the others. On the old *Atlas*, most of this area had been officers' country, reserved for the expedition heads and top ship personnel; and presumably that arrangement had been changed only by the addition of Tareeg commanders and guards. Troy kept to the maintenance passages, encountered no one but presently found unused crew quarters and exchanged the corpsman uniform there for less conspicuous shipboard clothes. This would make a satisfactory temporary base of operations. And now to get the information he wanted. . . .

The voice was coming out of the only door open on the dim hall. There were six staterooms on either side, and Troy remembered that the room beyond the open door had been occupied by Dr. Clingman on the trip out from Earth. The voice—preoccupied, mild, a little tired—was unmistakably Dr. Victor Clingman's.

Was he alone? Troy thought so. He couldn't make out the words, but it was a monologue, not a conversation. He had the impression of Clingman dictating another rambling dissertation on Tareeg ways into a recorder; and the conviction came to him, not for the first time, that the man was in some essential manner no longer sane, that he had come to believe that his observations on these deadly enemies some day really could be compiled into an orderly and valuable addition to human knowledge.

Sane or not, he was a frightened man, the perfect quarry for Troy's present purpose. With a gun on him, he would talk. And once having assisted Troy to any degree, he would be too terrified of Tareeg reprisals to do anything but switch sides again and go along with Troy, hoping that thereby the worst—once more—could be avoided. The worst for Victor Clingman. It would be impossible, Troy thought, to trust Clingman, but he could make very good use of him in spite of that.

He came quietly along the passage, his attention as much on the closed doors about him as on the one which was open. The guard's gun unfortunately wasn't a noiseless type, but he had wrapped a small cushion around its muzzle and across it, which should muffle reports satisfactorily if it came to that. Words became distinguishable.

"It is not a parasite in the ordinary sense," Clingman's tired voice said. "It is a weapon. It kills and moves on. A biological weapon limited to attack one species: the enemy. It is insidious. There is no warning and no defense. Unconsciousness and death occur painlessly within an hour after contact, and the victim has not realized he is being destroyed. The radius of infection moves out indetectably and with incredible swiftness. And yet there was a method of containing this agent. That knowledge, however, is now lost."

"As an achievement of the Tareeg genius for warfare, the weapon seems matched—in some respects surpassed—only by the one used to counteract it. And in that, obviously, there were serious faults. They . . ."

The man, Troy decided, was quite close, perhaps twelve feet to the right side of the door. He glanced back along the silent hall, slipped the cover from the gun—with Clingman, he would only need to show it—then came into the room in two quick strides, turning to the right and drawing the door shut behind him.

There was no one in sight. The voice continued: " . . . desperate, with no time to complete essential testing. A terrible gamble, but one which inevitably . . ." The meaning faded from Troy's mind as he discovered the wall-speaker from which the words were coming. His eyes darted across the room to a comfortable chair drawn up beside a table, to a familiar picture of untidily arrayed piles of notes on the table, a thread of smoke still rising from a cigarette in the tray among them. Clingman had been in the room within minutes, listening to one of his previous recordings as he worked. Troy's glance shifted to a closed door on his right. Bedroom and bath of the suite lay behind it. Clingman might be there. He might also . . . Troy reached back, quietly opened the door to the hall again, moved on and slipped out of sight behind an ornamental screen on the other side of the speaker.

Clingman could have left his quarters for some reason. In any event, it was obvious that he had intended to return to the room very shortly. If he brought someone with him, the situation might be more difficult. But hardly too difficult to be handled.

Troy worked the improvised silencer back over the gun muzzle, senses straining to catch either the opening of the door on his right or the sound of an approach down the hall.

"So it was possible," he heard the wall-speaker say, "to reconstruct, in almost every essential detail, what the concluding situation must have been on the world where the Tareeg species had its origin. The attacking section was safely screened, presumably by a form of energy barrier, against the deadly agent it had released.

The section under attack had no defense against an agent so nearly indestructible that it subsequently survived for over a thousand years in its inert, frozen condition without losing effectiveness in the least—"

Troy thought: What . . . WHAT HAD IT SAID?

He stepped out from behind the screen as the door on his right opened. Dr. Clingman stood in the door, mouth open, eyes bulging in surprise and alarm at the gun in Troy's hand. Then his gaze shifted to Troy's face, and his expression slowly changed.

"Mister Gordon," he murmured, smiling very cautiously, "you are really the most difficult man to keep stopped!"

Troy pointed a shaking finger at the speaker. "That!" he cried. "That . . . it said *a thousand years in the ice!*"

Clingman nodded. "Yes." His eyes returned, still rather warily, to the gun. "And I'm rather glad, you know, you happened to catch that particular part before I appeared."

Troy was staring at him. "That was their lost home world—the one you've kept talking about. That great asteroid cloud here. . . ."

"No, not here." Clingman came forward more confidently into the room, and Troy saw now that the left side of the scientist's face and head was covered with medical plastic. "The Cassa system is a long way behind us, Gordon," Clingman said. "We've been on our way back to Earth for more than two days."

"To Earth," Troy muttered. "And I . . ."

Clingman jabbed a stubby finger down on a control switch at the table, and the wall-speaker went silent. "It will be easier to tell you directly," he said. "You've already grasped the essential fact— our Tareeg captors, for the most part, are dead. They were killed, with some careful assistance from the men in charge of this expedition, by a weapon developed approximately twelve centuries ago on their ancestral world. A world which still circles today, though in a rather badly disintegrated condition, about the Cassa sun.

"But let's be seated, if you will. You gave me a very unpleasant fright just now." Dr. Clingman touched the side of his face. "I had an ear shot off recently by a man who didn't wait to have the situation explained to him. His aim, fortunately, was imperfect. And there is still a minor war in progress on the *Atlas*. Oh, nothing to worry about now—it's almost over. I heard less than twenty minutes ago that the last of the Tareeg guards on board had surrendered. About fifty of them have become our prisoners. Then there is a rather large group of armed men in spacesuits in one section of the ship with whom we have been unable to communicate. They regard us as traitors to the race, Dr. Dexter and myself in particular. But we have worked out a system of light signals which should tell them enough to make them willing to parley."

He settled himself carefully into the big chair, turning a white, fatigued face back to Troy. "That," he said, waving his pudgy hand at the wall-speaker, "is a talk I made up to explain what actually has happened to the main body of the mutineers. They comprised a large majority of the crew and of the expedition members, of course, but fortunately we were able to gas most of them into unconsciousness almost at once, so that no further lives have been lost. We have begun to arouse them again in small groups who are told immediately that the space ice we were bringing in to Cassa One carried a component which has resulted in the destruction of the Tareeg force, and who are then given as much additional information as is needed to answer their general questions and convince them that we are still qualified to command the Cassa Expedition. I believe that in a few more days normal conditions on the ship will have been restored."

Clingman glanced over at the smoldering cigarette in the tray, stubbed it out and lit another. "We had been aware for some time of your plan to escape back to Earth in one of the Tareeg drones," he said. "It was an audacious and ingenious scheme which might very well have succeeded. We decided to let you go ahead with it, since it was by no means certain until the very last day that our own plans would be an unqualified success. On the other hand, we couldn't let you leave too early because the Tareegs certainly would have taken the *Atlas* to the twin world then without completing the Cassa One operation. And we didn't care to let you in on our secret, for reasons I'm sure you understand."

Troy nodded. "If they'd got on to me, I might have spilled that, too."

"Exactly," Clingman said. "There was no question of your loyalty or determination but the Tareegs' methods of persuasion might cause the most stubborn man to tell more than he should. So no one who was not essential to the work was given any information whatever. Dr. Rojas applied certain medical measures which prevented Mr. Newland from recovering prematurely ... prematurely from our point of view, that is. It did not keep you from completing your other preparations but ensured that you would not actually leave unless we believed the move had become necessary, as a last resort."

Troy shook his head. He'd been working against some thing there had been no way of knowing about. "Was that Rojas waiting for me in the tunnel?"

"Yes. At that point, we knew we would win, and it had become safe enough to tell you. Unfortunately, you believed it was a trap."

Troy chewed his lip. "On that home world of the Tareegs when the two factions were fighting—the losing side did something which blasted the whole planet apart?"

"Not exactly," Clingman said. "The appearance of it is rather that the home world came apart in an almost gentle manner, section separating from section. How that could be done is something no one on Earth had worked out at the time we left. The original survey group brought back samples of the asteroid swarm for analysis. A good deal was learned from them."

He paused, frowning at his cigarette, said slowly, "The twin worlds have developed a new scientific Tareeg caste which was considered—or considered itself—too valuable to be risked on the interstellar expedition to the Cassa system. I think that was a very fortunate circumstance for us. Even before we left Earth, even when it was believed they were all dead, what had been deduced of the Tareeg genius for destruction was more than a little disturbing. The apparent purpose of that last defensive action on the home world was to strip the surface oceans from the hostile sections of the planet. Obviously, the process got out of hand; the entire planet was broken up instead. But one can't really doubt that—given more time—they would have learned to master the weapon.

"The killing agent developed by the opposing side evidently had been very thoroughly mastered. And again we can't say how they did it. It can be described as a large protein molecule, but its properties can be imagined only as arising out of a very complex organization, theoretically impossible at that level of life. It is confined to water, but its method of dispersion within that medium is not understood at all. At one instant, it is here; at the next, it apparently will have moved to a point perhaps several hundred miles away. It is life which has no existence, and cannot exist, except as a weapon. Unlike a parasite, its purpose is simply to kill, quickly and efficiently, and go on at once to another victim. Having exhausted the store of victims—a short process, obviously, even in an area of planetary dimensions—it dies of something like starvation within days.

"That, of course, was as practical a limitation to those employing it as the one that it attacks only Tareegs. They did not want to be barred indefinitely from an area which had been cleansed of their enemies, and neither did they want food animals in that area to be destroyed. They . . ."

His voice trailed off, and Troy stirred restlessly. Dr. Clingman was slumped farther down in his chair now, and the pale, protruding eyes had begun to blink drowsily. He seemed about to go to sleep. Troy said, "If the thing killed the Tareegs on Cassa One inside an hour after they'd gone into the sea, then they couldn't have had the time to start the interstellar drones back towards the twin worlds."

Clingman's head turned to him again. "No," Clingman said. "Of course not."

"And even," Troy went on, "if they had been able to ship a couple of loads of infected water back, it would have been harmless long before it reached their worlds."

Clingman nodded. "Quite harmless. As harmless as the new ocean on Cassa One would be by this time to Tareegs who entered it." He paused. "We'd thought, Gordon . . . as you might be thinking now . . . of sending the drones back instead with a load of asteroid ice containing the inert agent. That, of course, would not have reduced its effectiveness. Nevertheless, the scheme wouldn't have worked."

"Why not?" Troy asked.

"Because the drones, in the Tareeg view, were sacred messengers. They could be used only to announce in a certain prescribed manner that the Tareeg interstellar expeditionary force had discovered a water planet and taken possession of it, again with the required ceremony, for the twin worlds. The transmission of lumps of interplanetary ice would never have fitted that picture, would, in fact, have been an immediate warning that something very much out of order had occurred.

"That Tareeg insistence on exact ritualistic procedure—essentially a defensive measure in their dealings with one another—also happened to delay our own plans here very badly. Except for it, we would have been ready at least a year ago to flood Cassa One and entrap our captors."

Troy repeated, stunned, "You would have been ready . . ."

"Yes, but consider what might have resulted from that overhasty action. The Cassa system is much more readily accessible from the twin worlds than it is from Earth, and if we made some mistake with the drones, or if the Tareegs began to suspect for any other reason that their expeditionary force had met with disaster, they would be certain to establish themselves at once in a very strong manner here, leaving Earth confronted with a dangerously talented and implacable new enemy. No, we had to retain the appearance of helplessness until we had acquired an exact understanding of the manner in which the water-message must be prepared, and had discovered some substitute for the freezing effect on the lethal agent. That took an extra year."

Troy said carefully, "And during that year, as you knew would happen, another dozen or so men died very slow and painful deaths on the Tareeg execution benches. Any one of those men might have been you or I . . ."

"That is quite true," Clingman said. "But it was something that could not be avoided. In that time, we *did* learn the necessary ritual and we *did* find a numbing catalyst which will hold the protein agent inert until it loses its effect by being sufficiently diluted again. So now the drones have been dispatched. Long before this ship reaches Earth again, the agent will have been introduced to the twin worlds, and except for the specimens we carry on board, the Tareeg species will be extinct. It may not be a pleasant thing to have a pair of ghost worlds forever a little on our conscience— but one does not have to fight uncertain wars with ghosts."

Troy studied him in silence for some seconds.

"And I thought you were soft," he said at last. "I thought you were weak and soft. . . ."

Homo Excelsior

IN MANY OF SCHMITZ'S stories, especially his Telzey stories and the Agent of Vega quartet, the protagonists are people with extraordinary powers. Still, they are not supermen, and their powers and abilities are simply incorporated into "normal" societies rather than determining them. Unlike many other SF authors of his day—A.E. Van Vogt comes immediately to mind—Schmitz does not seem to have been particularly fascinated by the theme of what kind of societies "Homo Excelsior" might produce.

There are a few exceptions, however, and we've collected them together in this section of the anthology.

The Ties of Earth

· · · · · · · · · · · · · · · · · · ·

1

THE HAWKES RESIDENCE lay in a back area of Beverly Hills, south of Wilshire and west of La Brea. It was a big house for that neighborhood, a corner house set back from the street on both sides and screened by trellises, walls and the flanks of a large garage.

"That's the number," Jean Bohart said, "but don't stop. Drive on at least a block..."

Alan Commager pointed out that there was a parking space right in front of the house.

"I know," Jean agreed nervously, "but if we park there, somebody inside the house would notice us and that would spoil the main purpose of our trip."

"You mean," said Commager as he drove on obediently, "they'll fold the black altar out of sight, drop the remains of the sacrificed virgin through a trap door and hose out the blood, while we're stumbling across the dichondra? I thought we were expected."

"We're not expected till ten thirty," Jean said. "Ira didn't exactly make a point of it, but he mentioned they'd be doing other work till shortly after ten."

"Then I come on with the dice, eh? By the way, I didn't bring any along. Would these Guides keep sordid little items like that around?"

"It isn't going to be a crap game, silly," Jean informed him. "I told you Ira thinks these people can tell whether you were just

151

lucky last week or whether you've developed some sort of special ability. They'll test you—somehow."

Commager looked down at her curiously. Jean was a slim blonde who could look crisp as chilled lettuce after an afternoon of smashing tennis matches followed by an hour of diving practice off the high board. She wasn't intellectually inclined, but, understandably, Ira Bohart had never seemed to mind that. Neither did Commager. However, she seemed disturbed now.

"Are you beginning to get interested in that sort of thing yourself?" he inquired lightly.

"No," she said. "I'm just worried about that husband of mine. Honestly, Alan, this is as bad a metaphysical binge as he's ever been on! And some of those exercises he was showing me yesterday sort of scared me. If they do something like that tonight, I'd like to know what you think of it."

"It's just somebody else on the trail of the Bohart stocks and bonds, Jeannie. Ira will get disillusioned again before any harm is done. You know that."

"That's what I keep telling myself," Jean agreed unhappily. "But this time—"

Commager shook his head, parked the car and let her out, a block and a half from the Hawkes home. "Did you try any of those exercises yourself?"

"I'm not that loony," Jean said briefly. "Anyway, Ira advised me not to."

They walked back to the house in brooding silence. Between them, they'd seen Ira through a bout of Buddhism and successive experiences with three psychological fringe groups, in relentless pursuit of some form of control of the Higher Mind. After each such period, he would revert for a while to despondent normalcy.

Four years ago, it had seemed rather amusing to Commager, because then it had been Lona Commager and Ira Bohart who went questing after the Inexpressible together, while Alan Commager and Jean Bohart went sea-fishing or skin-diving off Catalina. But then Lona had died and the Inexpressible stopped being a source of amusement. Sometimes Ira bored Commager to death these days. But he still liked Jean.

"Why pick on me to expose these rascals anyway?" he asked as they came in sight of the house. "I may have surprised the boys at Las Vegas last week, but I couldn't tell a psychic phenomenon from a ringing in my ears."

She patted his arm. "That may be true, but you do intimidate people," she explained.

"Shucks!" Commager said modestly. It was true, though; he did. "So I'm to sit there and glare at them?"

"That's the idea. Just let them know you see through their little tricks and I'll bet they lose interest in Ira before the evening's out. Of course, you don't have to put it on too thick . . ."

Their host, Herbert Hawkes, for one, didn't look like a man who'd be easy to intimidate. He was as big as Commager himself and about the same age; an ex-football player, it turned out. He and Commager exchanged crushing hand-grips and soft smiles, as big men will, and released each other with mutual respect.

Ira, who didn't seem any more gaunt and haggard than usual, had appeared a little startled by their entry, possibly because they were early, but more likely, Commager thought, because of a girl who had coiled herself becomingly on the couch very close to Ira.

At first glance, this siren seemed no more than seventeen—a slender, brown-skinned creature in an afternoon dress the exact shade of her skin—but by the time they were being introduced, Commager had added twelve years to her probable age.

She was Ruth MacDonald, she told him, secretary of the Parapsychological Group of Long Beach. Had he heard of it? He said it sounded familiar, which was untrue, but it seemed to please Miss MacDonald.

The only other person present, a fifty-odd, graying teddy-bear of a man with very thick eyebrows, announced he was the Reverend Wilson Knox, president of the Temple of Antique Christianity. The Reverend, Commager realized, was pretty well plastered, though there was no liquor in sight.

Their interests might be unusual, but they hardly seemed sinister. Commager was practically certain he could identify Herbert Hawkes as the owner of one of the biggest downtown automobile agencies—which made him an unlikely sort of man to be a member of a group called the Guides. It was Hawkes' own affair, but it promised to make the evening more interesting than Commager had expected.

"Were we interrupting anything?" he inquired, looking around benevolently.

Ira cleared his throat. "Well, as a matter of fact, Alan, we were conducting a series of experiments with me as the guinea pig at the moment. Rather interesting actually—" He seemed a trifle nervous.

Commager avoided Jean's glance. "Why not just continue?"

"We can't," the Reverend Knox informed him solemnly. "Our high priestess was called to the telephone a few minutes ago. We must wait until she returns."

Ira explained hurriedly, "Mr. Knox is talking about Paylar. She's connected with the new group I'm interested in, the Guides. I suppose Jean told you about that?"

"A little." Commager waved his hand around. "But I thought you people were the Guides."

Hawkes smiled.

Wilson Knox looked startled. "Goodness, no, Mr. Commager! Though as a matter of fact—" he glanced somewhat warily at his two companions—"if someone here were a Guide, that person would be the only one who knew it! And, of course, Paylar. That's right, isn't it, Ruth?"

Miss MacDonald nodded and looked bored.

Jean said to Ira, "All I really told Alan was that some friends of yours would like to experiment with—well, whatever you think he was using in that crap game last week." She smiled brightly at the group. "Mr. Commager actually won eleven hundred dollars in fifteen minutes of playing!"

"Ah, anybody could if they kept the dice for fifteen minutes," Commager said airily. "Question of mind over matter, you know."

"Eleven hundred dollars? Phenomenal!" Wilson Knox came wide awake. "And may I ask, sir, whether you employ your powers as a professional gambler?"

Commager replied no, that professionally he was a collector, importer, wholesaler and retailer of tropical fish. Which was, as it happened, the truth, but the Reverend looked suspicious.

A door opened then and two other people came in. One was a handsome though sullen-faced young man whose white-blond hair had been trimmed into a butch haircut. He was deeply tanned, wore a tee-shirt, white slacks, sneakers and looked generally as if he would be at home on Muscle Beach.

The other one had to be Paylar: a genuine Guide or, at least, a direct connection to them. She was downright cute in a slender, dark way. She might be in her early twenties . . .

But for a moment, as Commager stood up to be introduced, he had the confused impression that jungles and deserts and auroras mirrored in ice-flows had come walking into the room with her.

Well, well, he thought. Along with Hawkes, here was another real personality.

They didn't continue with the experiments on Ira. Wilson Knox reported Commager's feat in Las Vegas to Paylar, who seemed to know all about it, and then went bumbling on into a series of anecdotes about other dice manipulators he had known or heard about.

Except for the Boharts, the others listened with varying expressions of polite boredom. But Ira seemed genuinely fascinated by the subject and kept glancing at Commager, to see how he was taking it. Jean became argumentative.

"Nobody can really prove that anyone has such abilities," she stated decisively. "Ira's been working around with this sort of thing for years and he's never shown me anything that couldn't have been a coincidence!"

Ira grinned apologetically. Wilson Knox sent a quick glance toward Paylar, who had settled herself in an armchair to Commager's left. The Reverend, Commager thought, seemed both miffed and curiously apprehensive.

Commager's own interest in the group became suddenly more lively.

"There are people in this world today, my dear young lady," Wilson Knox was telling Jean, "who control the Secret Powers of the Universe!"

Jean sighed. "When Ira tells me something like that, I always want to know why we don't hear what these mysterious people are doing."

Wilson Knox glanced at Paylar again. And this time, Commager decided, there was no question about it: the odd little man seemed genuinely alarmed. The bushy eyebrows were working in unconcealed agitation.

"We must consider," he told Jean helplessly, "that such people may have their own reasons for not revealing their abilities."

"Hm," sniffed Jean.

Commager laughed. "Mrs. Bohart has a point there, you know," he said to Paylar. "I understand the Guides imply they can, at any rate, train people to develop extrasensory abilities. Would you say they can produce some tangible proof for that claim?"

"Sometimes," she said. "With some people." She looked a little tired of the subject, as if it were something she had heard discussed often, as she probably had, so Commager was surprised when she added in the same tone, "I could, I think, produce such proofs very easily for you, Mr. Commager. To your own satisfaction, at least."

As she turned to look at him, her dark elfin face sober and confident, Commager was aware of a sudden stillness in the room. Wilson Knox started what seemed to be a protesting gesture and subsided again. And Jean was frowning, as if she had just discovered an unexpected uncertainty in herself.

"It's a fair offer," Commager acknowledged. "If you're suggesting an experiment, I'll be glad to cooperate."

For a moment, he saw something almost like compassion in the serious young face that studied him. Then Paylar turned to the others. "Would you arrange the lighting in the usual way? Mr. Commager, I should like you to sit here."

It was what they had come here for, Commager thought. Hawkes and the blond young man, whose name was Lex Barthold, went about the room adjusting the lights. Commager had a strong impression that Jean now would just as soon keep the experiment from being carried out, if she could think of a good enough reason.

But the experiment would be a flop anyway. No such half-mystical parlor games had worked on Commager since Lona had died.

2

In Commager's tropical fish store on Wilshire Boulevard, there were display tanks that were laid out with the casual stateliness of an English park and others that had the formal delicacy of a Chinese garden or that appeared to copy, in fantastic miniature detail, sections of some dreamland salt-water reef. These were the designs of two artistically minded girls who managed the store for Commager and they were often expensively duplicated by artists themselves in the homes of the shop's less talented patrons.

But the tanks that most interested Commager were the big ones in the back of the store, partitioned off from the plate-glass windows and the displays that faced the boulevard. Here fish and plants were bred, raised and stocked without regard for art, and the effect, when you sat down to watch them for a while, was that of being in the center of a secret, green-lit jungle out of which God knew what might presently come soaring, wriggling or crawling at you.

It wasn't a bad way, in Commager's opinion, to pass a few hours at night, when you didn't happen to be in a mood either for sleep or human company. In his case, that might happen once or twice a week, or perhaps less than once a month. When it happened more often, it was time to get organized for another one of those trips that would wind up at some warm and improbable point on the big globe of Earth, where people were waiting to help Commager fill his transport tanks with brightly colored little water-creatures— which, rather surprisingly, provided him with a very good income.

It was a pattern he had followed for most of the second half of his thirty-four years, the only two interruptions having been the second world war and the nineteen months he'd been married to Lona.

It was odd, he thought, that he'd never found anything more important to do with his life than that, but the personal games he could watch people play didn't seem to be even as interesting as the one he'd chosen for himself.

Also, he went on thinking half-seriously, if you got right down to it, probably all the important elements of life were contained right inside the big tank he was observing at the moment, so that if he could really understand what was going on in there, brightly and stealthily among the green underwater thickets, he might know all that could be known about the entire Universe.

Considered in that light, the tank became as fascinating as a stage play in a foreign language, in which the actors wore the bright masks of magic and played games that weren't so very unlike those being played by human beings. But any real understanding of the purpose of the play, human or otherwise, always had seemed a little beyond Commager's reach.

He yawned and shifted position in the chair he had pulled up for himself. Perhaps he was simply a bit more stupid than most. But there was a fretting feeling that this game playing, whether on a large scale or a small one, never really led to much, beyond some more of the same. There was, he conceded, a good deal of satisfaction in it for a time, but in the long run, the returns started to diminish.

It seemed that things—in some way Commager couldn't quite fathom—should have been arranged differently.

A car passing on the street outside sent a whisper of sound along the edge of his consciousness. With that came the awareness that it had been some time since he'd last heard a car go by and he found himself wondering suddenly what time of night it was.

He glanced at his wristwatch. Three-thirty. A little startled, he tried to compute how long he had been sitting there.

Then it struck him in a surge of panic that he couldn't remember coming to the store at all!

But, of course, his memory told him, you went with Jean to that house...

And Paylar had asked him to sit down and...

What kind of stunt had she pulled on him?

The blackness of terror burst into his consciousness as soon as his thoughts carried him that far—and it wiped out memory. He tried again:

A black explosion. He pushed at it and it retreated a little.

It had been between ten and eleven o'clock. Five hours or so ago. What was the last specific thing he could remember?

He had been sitting in a chair, his eyes closed, a little amused, a little bored. It had been going on for some time. Paylar, a quiet voice off to his left, was asking him a series of odd questions.

PAYLAR: But where are you, Mr. Commager?

COMMAGER: (tapping his forehead): Right here! Inside my head.

PAYLAR: Could you be more specific about that?

COMMAGER (laughing): I'm somewhere between my ears. Or somewhere back of my eyes.

PAYLAR: How far do you seem to be from the right side of your head? Do you sense the exact distance?

Commager discovered he could sense the exact distance. As a point of awareness, he seemed to be located an inch inside the right side of his skull. Simultaneously, though, he noticed that his left ear was less than an inch and a half away from the same spot—which gave him briefly an odd impression of the general shape of his head!

But he realized then that his attention was shifting around in there, rapidly and imperceptibly. His ears seemed to be now above him, now below and, for a moment, the top of his skull seemed to have moved at least a yard away.

He laughed. "How am I doing?"

Paylar didn't answer. Instead, she asked him to imagine that he was looking at the wall in front of him.

After a while, that wasn't too difficult; Commager seemed to be seeing the wall clearly enough, with a standing lamp in either corner, where Hawkes had placed them. Next, the voice told him to imagine that the same wall now was only a few inches in front of his face—and then that it suddenly had moved six feet behind him. It gave him an odd feeling of having passed straight through the wall in the moment of shifting it.

"Put it twenty feet in front of you again," she said. "And now twenty feet behind you."

Again the sensation of shifting in space, as if he were swinging back and forth, past and through the wall. Commager had become alert and curious now.

On the third swing, he went straight into the blackness . . . with panic howling around him! After that, everything was blotted out.

He couldn't, Commager discovered, close the gap any farther now. Somewhere near eleven o'clock in the evening, he'd gone into that mental blackout with its peculiarly unpleasant side-effects. His next memory might have been twenty minutes ago, when he found himself staring into the miniature underwater forest of the fish tank in his store.

He could phone the Bohart apartment, he thought, and find out what actually had happened. Immediately, then, he became aware of an immense reluctance to carry out that notion and he grimaced irritably. It was no time to worry about what the Boharts might think, but he could imagine Jean's sleepy voice, annoyedly asking who was calling at this hour.

And he'd say, "Well, look, I've lost my memory, I'm afraid. A piece of it anyway—"

He shook his head. They'd gone there to show up the Guides, after all! He'd have to work this out by himself. As if in response to his line of thought, the office telephone, up in the front of the store, began ringing sharply.

The unexpected sound jolted Commager into a set of chills. He sat there stiffly, while the ring was repeated four times; and then, because there was really no reason not to answer it, no matter how improbable it was that someone would be calling the store at this time of night, he got up and started toward the telephone down the long aisle of back-store tanks. Here and there, one of the tanks was illuminated by overhead lights, like the one before which he'd been sitting.

At the corner, where he turned from the aisle into the office, something lay in his path.

He almost stepped on it. He stopped in shock.

It was a slender woman, lying half on her side, half on her face, in a rumpled dress and something like a short white fur jacket.

Her loose hair hid her face.

The telephone kept on shrilling.

Commager dropped to one knee beside the woman, touched her and knew she was dead, turned her over by the shoulders and felt a stickiness on his hands. There was a slanting cut across her throat, black in the shadows.

"Well," a voice inside Commager's head said with insane calm, "if it isn't Miss MacDonald!" He felt no pity for her at the moment and no real alarm, only a vast amazement.

He realized that the telephone had stopped ringing and clusters of thought burst suddenly and coherently into his awareness again. Somebody apparently thought he was here, at three-thirty in the morning—the same somebody might also suspect that Miss MacDonald was here and even in what condition. And the phone could have been dialed quite deliberately at that moment to bring Commager out of the hypnotized or doped trance, or whatever it was that somebody knew he was trapped in.

In which case, they might be wanting him to discover Ruth MacDonald's body at about this time.

It would be better, he thought, not to get tangled up just now in wondering why anyone should want that to happen; or even whether, just possibly, it had been he himself who had cut Miss MacDonald's brown throat.

What mattered was that, at this instant, somebody was expecting him to react as reasonably as a shocked and stunned man could react in such a situation.

The only really reasonable course of action open to him was to call the police promptly—wherefore, if his curiously calm assumption was correct, he would be primarily expected to do just that. It would be much less reasonable, though still not too unlikely, to carry that ghastly little body far off somewhere and lose it.

Or he could just walk out of here and leave Miss MacDonald on the floor, to be discovered by the store's staff in the morning. That would be a stupid thing to do, but still something that might be expected of a sufficiently dazed and frightened man.

So he wouldn't do any of those things! The hunch was strong in him that the best way to react just now was in a manner unreasonable beyond all calculation.

He shoved Ruth MacDonald's body aside and flicked on his cigarette lighter. On the floor were gummily smeared spots, but she had bled to death somewhere else before she had been dropped here.

Commager's hands and clothes were clean, so it was very improbable that he had carried her in. The sensible thing, he thought, would be to clean up the few stains on the floor before he left, removing any obvious evidence that Miss MacDonald had been in the store at all.

Wherefore, he didn't bother to do it.

Nor did he waste time wondering whether a half dozen tanks in the back part of the store had been lit when he came in here or not. There was a variety of possible reasons why someone might have left a light on over some of them.

He picked up the slender stiffening body on the floor and carried it to the front door.

The door was unlocked and his Hudson was at the curb. He shifted Miss MacDonald to one arm, locked the store door behind him, then placed her in the back seat of the car.

Even Wilshire Boulevard was a lonely street at this hour, but he saw several sets of headlights coming toward him as he got into the car and started it. As far as he could make out, there hadn't been any blood spilled around inside the Hudson, either.

Twelve minutes later, he drove past the corner house he'd visited with Jean Bohart some time before ten in the evening. There was a light on in one of the rooms upstairs, which distinguished Herbert Hawkes's home from any other house in sight. A few blocks away, a dog began to bark.

Dogs might be a problem, he thought.

Commager parked the car a few hundred feet away and sat still for perhaps a minute, listening. The dog stopped barking. Headlights crossed an intersection a few blocks ahead of him.

He got out, lifted Miss MacDonald's body out of the car and walked unhurriedly back to the corner house and over the stepping stones of the dichondra lawn to the side of the house. Here was a trellis, with a gate in it, half open.

Commager eased his burden sideways through the gate. In the half-light of early morning, he set Ruth MacDonald down under a bush—which partly concealed her—in about the same position in which he'd found her. He had a moment of pity to spare for her now.

But there was motion inside the house. Commager looked at the door that opened into this side garden. A vague sequence of motions; somebody walking quietly—but without any suggestion of stealth—was coming closer to the door. Commager stepped quietly up to the wall beside the door and flattened himself against the wall.

A key clicked in the lock. The door swung open. A big shape sauntered out.

Commager's fist was cocked and he struck hard, slanting upward, for the side of the neck and the jaw . . .

He laid Herbert Hawkes down beside the body of Ruth MacDonald, one big arm draped across her shoulders.

Let the Guides figure that one out, he thought wearily. Not that they wouldn't, of course, but he was going to continue to react unreasonably.

Twenty minutes later, he was in his apartment and sound asleep.

3

The bedside phone buzzed waspishly. Commager hung for a moment between two levels of awareness. The blazing excitement of the fight was over, but he still hated to relinquish the wild, cold, clear loneliness of the blue—

The thin droning continued to ram at his eardrums. His eyes opened and he sat up, reaching for the telephone as he glanced at the clock beside it. 8:15.

"Alan? I think it worked! Ira had breakfast and drove off to the office, wrapped in deep thought. You were terrific, simply terrific! Just sitting there like a stone wall—"

Commager blinked, trying to catch up with her. Jean Bohart had an athlete's healthy contempt for lie-a-beds and felt no compunction about jolting them out of their torpor. She probably assumed he'd been up and around for the past two hours.

Then his waking memories suddenly flooded back. He sucked in a shocked breath.

"Eh?" She sounded startled.

"I didn't say anything," he managed. "Go ahead—"

He wouldn't, he realized presently, have to ask Jean any leading questions. There was a nervous tension in her that, on occasion, found its outlet in a burst of one-way conversation and this was such an occasion. The Boharts had left the Hawkes home shortly before twelve, Ira apparently depressed by the negative results of the evening. The Reverend Knox had made a phone call somewhat earlier and had been picked up within a few minutes by an elderly woman who, in Jean's phrasing, looked like a French bulldog.

"I think he was glad to get out of there!" she added.

Commager didn't comment on that. He himself had stayed on with the others. Ruth MacDonald, in Jean's opinion, was making a pretty definite play for him by that time, while Paylar—"What's her last name, anyway?"—had become withdrawn to the point of rudeness after Commager's spectacular lack of reaction to her psychological games.

"I think she knew just what we were doing by then!" Jean's voice held considerable satisfaction. "So did that Hawkes character. Did you know he's the Herbert Hawkes who owned the Hawkes Chrysler Agency on Figueroa? Well, there's something interesting about that—"

Hawkes had sold out his business about eight months before and it was generally known that his reason had been an imminent nervous breakdown. "What do you make of that, Alan?"

Offhand, Commager admitted, he didn't know what to make of it.

Well, Jean interrupted, she was convinced Hawkes had gone the way Ira would have gone if they hadn't stopped him. "Those Guides have him hypnotized or something!" She laughed nervously. "Does it sound as if I'm getting too dramatic about it?"

"No," he said, recalling his last glimpse of Hawkes and his horrid little companion much too vividly. "He doesn't strike me as acting like a man who's been hypnotized, though. Not that I know much about that sort of thing."

Jean was silent, thinking. "Did anything in particular develop between you and MacDonald?" she asked suddenly. There was a strange sharpness in her tone.

Commager felt himself whiten. "No," he said, "I just went home by and by." He tried for a teasing note. "Were you worrying about it?"

"She's poison, that's all!" Jean said sharply.

After she hung up, Commager showered, shaved, dressed and breakfasted, with very little awareness of what he was doing. He was in a frame of mind he didn't entirely understand himself; under a flow of decidedly unpleasant speculations was a layer of tingling, almost physical elation which, when he stopped to consider it, appeared a less than intelligent response to his present situation. But the realization didn't seem to affect the feeling.

The feeling vanished abruptly when he dumped the clothes he'd been wearing the night before out of the laundry bag into which he had stuffed them, along with the blanket on which he'd laid Ruth MacDonald's body in the car.

He had handled her with some caution and he couldn't discover marks on any of those articles now that seemed likely to incriminate him. But he had no doubt that a more competent investigation could reveal them.

The odd thing was that he still couldn't get himself to worry about such an investigation. He had no logical basis for his belief that unless he himself announced the murder of the secretary of the Parapsychological Group of Long Beach, nobody else was going to take that step. He couldn't even disprove that he hadn't, somewhere along the line last night, dropped into sheer criminal lunacy.

But, so far, nobody had come pounding at his door to accuse him of murder. And Commager retained the irrationally obstinate conviction that nobody would.

He had an equally strong conviction that he had become the target of the relentless hostility of a group of people, of whose existence he hadn't known until the day before—and that he wouldn't know why until he discovered the reason for his loss of conscious memory in a period during which he had, to Jean Bohart's discerning eyes, showed no noticeable change in behavior.

And, Commager decided finally, he'd better not let the lack of satisfactory conscious evidence for either certainty affect his actions just now.

He made two appointments by telephone and left the apartment an hour after he'd been wakened. A few minutes later, he was at the store, which would open for business at ten o'clock.

Commager unlocked the door and strolled inside. The store's staff had got there at nine and the floors, he noticed, had been thoroughly mopped. Nobody inquired whether he'd been in during the night, so it seemed he had guessed right in leaving the lights on over the big tanks.

He drove into Los Angeles then, to keep his first appointment, at Dr. Henry L. Warbutt's Psychology Center.

Henry was a stout, white-haired, energetic little man with the dark melancholy eyes of one of the great apes. "Thirty minutes for free is all I can spare, even for orphans," he informed

Commager. "But you're welcome to that, so come in and sit down, boy! Cup of tea, eh? What do you hear from the Boharts?"

Commager declined the tea, which was likely to be some nasty kind of disguised health-brew, and stated that the Boharts, when last heard from, had been doing fine. It wasn't his first visit to the Center. Both of his parents had been dead before he was twelve and Henry, who was a relative on his father's side, had been his legal guardian until he came of age.

"I want to find out what you know about a new local organization called the Guides," Commager explained. "They're on the metaphysical side, I'd say, but they seen to be doing some therapy work. They're not listed in the telephone book."

Henry looked slightly disturbed. "If you mean the Guides I'm thinking of, they're not so new. How did you hear about them? Is Ira messing around with that outfit now?"

Commager told him briefly of last night's earlier events, presenting Jean Bohart's version of his own role in them, as if that were the way he recalled it himself.

Henry became interested at that point. "Do you remember just what those exercises were that the woman put you through?"

When Commager had described them, he nodded. "They got those gimmicks from another group. I've used them myself now and then. Not on cash clients, of course, just as an experiment."

"The idea is to divert your attention away from your body-ego, if you know what I mean. No? Well, then—"

He made a steeple of his hands and scowled at his fingertips. "Metaphysically, it's sometimes used as a method to get you out of your physical body." He waved his hands vaguely around. "Off you go into the astral plane or something." He grinned. "Understand now?"

"More or less," Commager said doubtfully. "Did you ever see it happen?"

"Eh? Oh, no! With me, they usually just go to sleep. Or else they get bored and won't react at all, about like you did. There's no therapeutic value in it that I know of. But probably no harm, either."

"Would you say whether there's any harm in the Guides?"

"Well," said Henry thoughtfully, "they're certainly one of the more interesting groups of our local psychological fauna. Personally, I wouldn't go out of my way to antagonize them. Of course, Ira's such a damn fool, you probably had to do something pretty obvious to discourage him. Fifteen or twenty years ago, the Guides were working principally with drugs, as far as I could make out at the time. I don't know whether this is the same organization or not, but just lately—the last year or so—I've been hearing gossip about them again."

"What kind of gossip?"

"Well, you know a good many of the people who come into this Center for therapy are interested in metaphysics in one way or another," Henry explained. "Some of them have been telling me lately that the Guides are the latest thing in a True Group. And a True Group, in their language, means chiefly that the people in it have some honest-to-goodness supernatural abilities and powers."

He grimaced unhappily. "Another characteristic is that nobody else knows exactly who belongs to a True Group. In that way, your acquaintances seem to be living up to the legend."

Commager said he'd been under the impression that the Guides dealt in parapsychology.

Henry nodded. "Well, they'd use that, too, of course! Depending on the class of client—" He hesitated briefly. "By and large, I'd say the Guides were a very good outfit for fairly normal citizens like you and the Boharts to stay away from."

He'd also heard of the Reverend Wilson Knox and of the Temple of Antique Christianity, though not favorably.

"Knox has a crummy little sect back in one of the Hollywood canyons. They go in for Greek paganism. Strictly a screwball group." He didn't know anything of the Parapsychological Group of Long Beach. "You can't keep up with all of them."

4

Julius Savage was a lanky, sun-browned hypnotist who'd sometimes gone spear-fishing with Commager. On one such occasion— the last, if Julius had anything to say about it—Commager had been obliged to haul him half-drowned out of a kelp bed and thump him back into consciousness. Which made him the right man right now.

He clasped his hands behind his head, rocked himself back from his desk and looked first interested and then highly dubious, while Commager went on talking.

"You're about as lousy a hypnotic subject as I am myself, Alan!"

Julius protested finally. "I tried to put you under twice, remember? Anyway, how about sending you to my tame M.D. for a checkup first? Amnesia isn't anything to—No?" He considered. "Well, how long ago did this happen?"

The fact that it had happened only the night before reassured him somewhat. So presently Commager was sitting in an armchair being informed that his eyelids were getting heavier and heavier.

An hour later, Julius said discouragedly, "This isn't getting us anywhere and I've got another appointment at two o'clock! How bad do you want that information, Alan?"

"It's a matter of life and death!"

"Oh, hell!" said Julius. He went out of the room and came back with a small bottle, partly filled with a slightly oily, aromatic liquid. "I don't use this often, but—by the way, with the possible exception of last night, did anyone else ever try to hypnotize you?"

"Ira Bohart did, the first time I met him," Commager recalled. "It was at a party. No results."

"We'll make it two spoonfuls," Julius decided.

Ten minutes later, Commager got into the blackness. The next time he consciously opened his eyes, it was past three in the afternoon. Julius, looking pale and exhausted, stood at the desk watching him. He'd loosened his tie and hung his jacket over the back of a chair. His hair was disheveled.

"Brother!" he remarked. "Well, we got something, Alan. I'll play parts of it back to you." He jerked his head at a gently burbling percolator on a mantel. "Cup of coffee there for you. Better have some."

Commager sipped black coffee, yawned, and took note of the time. Too much of the day already was past, he thought uneasily; he wondered what the Guides had been doing meanwhile. "What happened to your appointments?"

"Canceled them," Julius said, fiddling with the tape recorder. "They'll keep." He glanced around at Commager. "Here's the first thing we got. Chronologically, it seems to fit in at the end of the period you can't remember. Symbolism, but I'm curious. We'll try it first."

Commager listened. After a while, there were pricklings of memory. When Julius stopped the recorder, he remarked, "I had a dream this morning that seems to tie in with that."

"Ah?" Julius looked professionally cautious. "Well, let's hear about it."

Commager hesitated. The dream seemed irrelevant and rather childish, like a fairy tale. He'd been flying around in a great open space, he began at last. And he'd been wondering why nobody else was up there with him, but he hadn't felt particularly concerned about it. Then a hawk came swooping at him, trying to knock him out of the air.

There was a long leash attached to the hawk's leg and Commager noticed that, far down below, a number of people were holding the leash and watching the battle. "That explained why there wasn't anyone else around, you see. When anyone tried it, they simply sent a hawk up after him."

"Hm!" said Julius. "Recognize the people?"

"No—" Commager checked himself and laughed. "Of course, it just struck me! Hawkes was the name of one of the people I met last night! That explains the dream!"

Julius nodded doubtfully. "Possibly. How did it continue?"

As Commager recalled it, there hadn't been much more to it. He couldn't damage the hawk and the hawk couldn't bring him down; finally it disappeared. Then he'd been up there alone . . . and then he'd been wakened by the telephone.

Julius tapped the desk with the eraser end of a pencil, looking thoughtful. "Well—" he sighed. He turned to the recorder. "Let's try another part of this now, Alan. The central part. Incidentally, we didn't get into what you were actually doing last night. These are your subjective impressions and they aren't necessarily an immediately recognizable reflection of real events, past or present. You understand that?"

Commager said he did. But he felt a stab of sharp apprehension. He was reasonably certain that whatever Julius heard or guessed in his office remained a private matter. But his own line of action had been based on the solid personal conviction that, whatever had happened last night, it hadn't been he who had killed Ruth MacDonald.

In view of the hypnotist's careful and almost formal phrasing, Commager was, for a few moments at least, not quite so sure about that.

There were a bad few moments . . .

Then the recorder was turning again.

"What do you make of it?" Julius asked. "It will help me formulate my own opinion."

Commager shrugged. He still felt shaken, after the intermittent waves of grief, rage and remorse that had pounded through him while a section of the tape rewound itself again—with a vividness and immediacy that dazed him, but still seemed rather unaccountable. After all, that had been over and done with almost four years ago!

"It's fairly obvious to me," he said reluctantly. At least his voice sounded steady enough. "A few months before my wife died, I'd begun to get interested in the ESP experiments she was playing around with. You remember Lona was almost as bad that way as Ira Bohart."

He managed a brief, careful grin. "It annoyed me at first, but, of course, I didn't let her know. I thought she'd drop it soon enough. When she didn't, I decided I'd experiment on the quiet by myself. Actually, I was after information I could use to convince Lona she was wasting her time with that sort of thing—and then she'd have more time to spare for the kind of fun and games I was interested in."

Julius smiled faintly and nodded.

"I started making lists of coincidences," Commager explained. "Occasions when I'd tell myself Lona would be home at six, say, and she'd actually show up about that time. Or I'd decide what dress she'd select to wear next morning—"

"Predictions, generally?" Julius drew a precise little circle on the desk blotter with his pencil and studied it critically.

"Yes. Or I'd put the idea into her head that she wanted to talk about some particular thing with me—and sometimes she would!" Commager smiled. "I was also, you see, keeping a list of the times these little experiments didn't work out, and they often didn't, at first. So that, when I told Lona about it finally, it would be obvious that the coincidences had been just that."

He hesitated. "I still think they were just that. But one day, it struck me I'd accumulated too many coincidences lately. It shook me."

"Did it stop your experimentation?" Julius remained intent on his art work.

"A few days later, it did," Commager said. He discovered suddenly that he was sweating. "Lona phoned me that afternoon that she was driving down to the beach to pick me up. After she hung up, I had a sudden positive feeling that if she drove her car that afternoon, she'd get killed! I almost called her back. But I decided I wasn't going to turn into another Ira Bohart. As of then, I was quitting all this ESP business and so was Lona! When she got there, I'd tell her—"

The sweat was running down his face now. "Well, you know that part of it. Lona had a heart attack while driving, the doctors thought, and crashed and got killed." He paused again, because his voice had begun to shake. "I don't know why that got on there"—he nodded at the recorder—"except that night was the first time since that I felt, even for a minute, that something might be going on that couldn't be explained in a perfectly normal way!"

"That," inquired Julius, "was while you were going through that peculiar set of exercises you were describing, wasn't it? Alan, how long ago has it been, exactly, since your wife died?"

"Not quite four years." Commager drove back a surge of impatience. "I suppose I've felt guilty enough about it ever since. But right now, Julius, I'm interested in finding out why I lost a few hours of memory last night and how to restore them. Are we getting any closer to that?"

"I think we are. Can you be at this office at 10 A.M. two days from tomorrow? That's Thursday morning."

"Why should I come here then?"

Julius shrugged. "Because that's the earliest appointment I could make for you with Dr. Ciardi. I phoned him just before you woke up. He's a friend of mine and an excellent psychiatrist, Alan. We do a lot of work together."

Commager said in angry amazement, "Damn you, Julius! I told you I didn't want anyone else to know about this!"

"I know," Julius admitted unhappily. "We've been fairly good friends for about eight years now, haven't we? We've been in and out of each other's homes and met each other's acquaintances, right?"

Commager's fingertips drummed on his right knee. He was still furious. "So what?"

"So hell, Alan! What you were telling me just now never happened! Your wife wasn't killed in an auto accident four years ago because, four years ago, you didn't have a wife! To the best of my knowledge, you've never been married!"

5

Commager had a rather early dinner at Tilford's. A mirror lined the entire wall on the opposite side of the room; now and then, he glanced at himself. For a sort of lunatic, he thought, the big, sun-tanned man sitting there looked remarkably calm and healthy.

He was still amazed, above all, at the apparent instantaneousness with which he had realized that what Julius had blurted out was true. He could picture Lona in a hundred different ways, very vividly, but he couldn't actually recall having ever mentioned her to anybody else. And he couldn't now remember a single time when he and she and any other person had been together.

It was almost as if the entire episode of Lona had been a story somebody had told him, illustrated out of his own imaginings. And now, in a few hours, the story was beginning to fade out. Specific scenes had dropped almost beyond the reach of memory. The image of Lona herself started to blur.

His immediate reaction had been an odd mixture of shocked self-disgust and profound relief, threaded with the feeling that actually he'd always known, without being consciously aware of it, that there wasn't any real Lona.

Even the emotions he'd felt while listening to the tape recorder were a part of the fabrication; almost at the instant of realization, they began to break away from him. Like the sudden shattering of a hard shell of alien matter, Commager thought, which he'd been dragging around, rather like a hermit-crab, under the pretense that it was a natural part of himself. The self-disgust became even more pronounced at that comparison.

But whatever his original motives had been for imposing that monstrous construction upon his mind, Commager couldn't see any further connection between it and the events of the past night.

Apparently he had thrust himself into a period of amnesia to avoid the full impact of an artificial set of emotions. In that period, there had been a very real and very unpleasant occurrence—a murder.

His main reason now for remaining convinced that he hadn't been the murderer was that the evening papers carried no indication that the body of Ruth MacDonald had been found.

Which certainly indicated guilt on the part of those who must have found her.

He could afford to wait until Thursday, Commager decided, to go digging after the causes of his delusion under Dr. Ciardi's guidance. But he probably couldn't afford to wait at all to find out what the Guides—he still had to assume it was the Guides—were preparing for him next.

And perhaps the best way to find out would be, quite simply, to ask.

He finished his dinner, walked up the street to a telephone booth and dialed the number of Herbert Hawkes's home. A man's voice informed him presently that it was the Hawkes residence, Lex Barthold speaking.

That, Commager recalled, was the name of the blond young man who had been an untalkative member of the party last night. He gave his own name and said he was trying to contact Miss Paylar— a piece of information which produced a silence of several seconds at the other end. But when Barthold spoke again, he sounded unshaken.

"Paylar isn't in at the moment. Shall I take your message, Mr. Commager?"

Commager said no, he'd try again, and hung up. Now that, he reflected, walking back to his car, seemed to be an interesting sort of household!

For the first time since leaving Julius's office, he wasn't too displeased with himself. If he saw Paylar alone, he might, as far as appearances went, be taking an interest in the well-being of Ira Bohart or, reasonably enough, in Paylar herself.

And things could start developing from that point.

Of course, she might avoid letting him see her alone. In any case, his call would give them something new to consider.

He drove to the beach and turned south toward San Diego. A half hour later, he parked before the cabin where, among bulkier items of fishing gear, he kept a 45-caliber revolver. He put that in the glove compartment of the car and started back to town.

The telephone rang a few minutes after he reached his apartment.

"I've called you twice in the last hour," Paylar said. "I understand you want to speak to me."

"I do," said Commager. "Do you happen to have the evening free?"

She laughed. "I've arranged to have it free. You can meet me at your aquarium store, Mr. Commager."

"Eh?" he said stupidly.

"At your store." Her voice still sounded amused. "You see, I may have a business proposition for you."

Then the line went dead.

Commager swore and hung up. When he turned into Wilshire

Boulevard not very many minutes later, he saw a long gray car, vague under the street lights, move away from the curb a hundred feet or so beyond his store and drive off. There was no sign of Paylar.

He parked and followed the car thoughtfully with his eyes. Then he got out. The store was locked, the interior dark. But in back of the office, behind the partition, was a shimmering of light.

He thought of the gun in his car. There had been one murder. It seemed a little early for another one.

He unlocked the door and locked it again behind him. This time, there were no bodies lying around the aisles. But at the back of the store, standing before a lighted fish tank and looking into it, Paylar was waiting for him.

He didn't ask her how she got in. It seemed a theatrical gesture, a boasting indication that his affairs could be easily invaded from without. Aside from that, the darkened store undoubtedly was a nice place for an ambush. Commager wondered briefly why he didn't feel more concerned about that and realized then that he was enormously angry. An ambush might have been a relief.

"Did you find out much about us today?" Paylar asked.

"Not enough," he admitted. "Perhaps you can tell me more."

"That's why I'm here."

Commager looked at her skeptically. She was wearing a black sweater and slacks that appeared wine-colored in the inadequate light from the big tank. A small, finely shaped body and a small, vivid face. The mouth smiled soberly; black eyes gleamed like an animal's as she turned her head toward him.

"We're an organization," she said, "that operates against the development of parapsychological abilities in human beings . . ."

Oddly enough, it made sense and he found himself believing her. Then he laughed. "Do you object to my winning a crap game?"

Paylar said seriously, "We don't object to that. But you're not stopping there, Mr. Commager."

Again there was an instant of inner agreement; an elation and anxiety. Commager hesitated, startled by his reaction. He said, "I'm not aware of any ambition along that line."

She shook her head. "I don't think you're being quite truthful. But it doesn't really matter how aware you are of it just now. The last twenty-four hours have indicated clearly that you can't be checked by any ordinary methods." She frowned. "The possibility had been foreseen—and so we hit you with everything that was immediately available, Mr. Commager. I was sure it was enough."

Commager felt a little bewildered. "Enough for what?"

"Why, almost anybody else would have done something sensible—and then refused to ever budge out of the everyday world again, even in his thoughts. Instead, you turned around and started to smoke us out—which, incidentally, saved you for the moment from an even more unnerving experience!"

Commager stared at her, appalled. That final comment had no present meaning for him, but she obviously was speaking about a murder of which she, at the very least, had known at the time. She considered it mildly amusing that it had back-fired on them!

He said harshly, "I'd enjoy breaking your neck. But I suspect that you're a little crazy."

She shrugged, smiling. "The trouble is that you're not going to go on thinking that, Mr. Commager. If you did, we could safely disregard you."

He looked down at his hands. "So what are you going to do?"

"There are others who say you can be stopped. It's certain you won't like their methods, though I'm not entirely sure they will be effective. I came here tonight to offer you an alternative."

"Go ahead and offer it."

"You can join us," she said.

Commager gave a short laugh of sheer astonishment. "Now why should I want to do that?"

"In the end," Paylar said soberly, "you may have very little choice. But there's another reason. You've been trying, all your life, to bring your abilities into your consciousness and under your control."

He shook his head. "If you mean wild talents, I haven't done anything of the sort."

"Unfortunately," she said, "you won't remain unaware of that trend in yourself very much longer. And, if you cooperate with us, we can and will help you to do just that. But we can't let you continue by yourself, without safeguards. You're too likely to be successful, you see. Those wild talents can become extremely wild!"

"You know," he said, almost good-humoredly, "I think you really believe what you say. But as far as I'm concerned, you're a group of criminal lunatics without any more secret ability than I have myself."

"That," Paylar replied undisturbed, "is precisely what we're afraid of. For the time being, though, we can use our abilities in ways that you cannot. What happened while you were doing those exercises last night, Mr. Commager?"

He looked at her and then away. "I got rather bored."

Paylar laughed. "You're lying! Exercises of that kind provide very convincing illusions, and very little else, for people who are hungry for illusion. But since you have an ability, it took no more than a word to bring it into action. That was when we knew you had to be stopped. However, I'm afraid you're still turning down my offer."

"You read my mind that time, lady! I'd turn you over to the police, too, if I thought it would do any good."

"It wouldn't," she assured him. Her head tilted a moment, with soft grace, into an attitude of listening. "I think my car is coming back for me. I'll leave that offer open, Mr. Commager—in case you survive long enough now to accept it."

He grinned. "You shouldn't frighten me like that."

"I've frightened you a little, but not nearly enough. But there is more than one way to shake a man to his senses—or out of them—so perhaps we can still change your mind. Would you let me out the front door now?"

Lights slid over the ceiling above her as she spoke, and the long gray car, its engine throbbing, stood at the curb when they came out. Paylar turned at the car door.

"You know where I'm staying," she said, looking up at him, "if you want to find me."

Commager nodded.

She smiled and then the door opened for her and light briefly filled the interior of the car.

Seconds later, he stood staring after it as it fled down the street. She'd been right about there being more than one way of shaking a man out of his senses.

The driver of the car—the very much alive driver—had been Ruth MacDonald!

Under what wasn't quite a full moon tonight, the Bay would have looked artificial if it hadn't been so huge. A savage, wild place, incongruous in this area with the slow thump and swirl and thunder of the tide.

A mile to the south was a cluster of cottages down near the water's edge. Commager's cabin was as close as anything could have been built to the flank of the big northern drop-off. He could look down at the sharp turn of the highway below him or out at the Bay. Nobody yet had tried to build on the rocky rises of ground behind him.

Without ordinary distractions, it was a good place for a few hours of painstaking reorientation. He wasn't exactly frightened, Commager told himself. But when he had recognized Ruth MacDonald, a wave of unreason inside him had seemed to rise to meet and merge with the greater wave of unreason rolling in from a shadow-world without. For that moment, the rules of reality had flickered out of existence.

An instant later, he'd had them solidly re-established. He was now simply a man who knew something had happened that he couldn't begin to explain rationally. It was a much more acceptable situation, since it included the obvious explanation of irrationality.

On Thursday morning, he could tell Dr. Ciardi, "Look, Doc, I'm having hallucinations. The last one was a honey. I thought I was carrying a dead woman all over town! What do we do about it?"

And they'd do whatever was done in such circumstances and it would be a sane, normal, active life for Alan Commager forever after—with a woman more or less like Jean Bohart to live it with, which would keep out the shadowy Lonas. With everything, in fact, that didn't fit into that kind of life, that belonged to the shadow-worlds, as completely obliterated and forgotten as they could become.

Commager wondered what made that picture look so unsatisfactory.

It struck him suddenly that, according to Paylar, this was exactly how the Guides had expected him to react as soon as her little games had steered him into a bout of amnesia and hallucinations. They'd wanted, she'd said, in approximately those words, to put him in a frame of mind that would make him refuse to ever budge out of the safe, everyday world again, even in his thoughts.

Commager grimaced. But they'd become convinced then that he wasn't going to do it!

He might do it all the same, he thought. But the reason it couldn't be a completely satisfactory solution was growing clear. One couldn't discount the probability that there was a little more to the shadow-worlds than lunacy and shadow. Perhaps only a very little more and perhaps not. But if he avoided looking at what was there, he would never find out.

And then he realized that he wasn't going to avoid looking at it, hadn't really been seriously considering it. He swore at himself, because avoidance did seem still the simple and rational solution, providing one could be satisfied with it.

He couldn't be satisfied with it and that was that. He could see now that if an organization such as Paylar had described the Guides to be existed, and if it were composed, at least in part, of people who really had developed an understanding and working knowledge of the possibilities of psi, it would be in a uniquely favorable position to control and check the development of similar abilities in others.

Its connections and its influence would be primarily with the psychological fringe groups here and with their analogs elsewhere; and the people who were drawn to such groups would be those who were dissatisfied with or incompetent in normal lines of activity, and had become abnormally interested in compensating for their lack of other achievement by investigating the shadowy, vague, ego-bolstering promise of psi.

And people frightened by the threat of total war, driven into a search for psychic refuge by the prospect of physical destruction.

In either case, because they were uncertain, less than normally capable people, they could be controlled without too much difficulty—and carefully diverted then, in groups or as individuals, from the thing they were seeking and might stumble upon.

The exercises she'd demonstrated to him, Paylar had said, were designed primarily to provide convincing illusions for those who were hungry for illusion.

She and her associates, Commager realized, might feel it was necessary. They might know just enough to be afraid of what such knowledge could lead to. If it were possible to encourage a pair of dice to bounce and spin in just the right pattern to win for you, it might, for example, also be possible to send a few buildings bouncing and spinning through a city! Of course, nobody ever seemed to have done it, but that might be due precisely to the existence of some controlling agency, such as the Guides claimed to be.

For a while, Commager regarded the possibility of accepting Paylar's invitation to join her group—and, a few seconds later, he knew he wasn't going to do that either.

However determined he might be to proceed with a painstaking and thorough investigation of this field of possibilities now, there was still a feeling of something completely preposterous about the entire business.

He could accept the fact that he had been shaken up mentally to the point where he might qualify without too much difficulty for the nearest insane asylum. But he wasn't ready to admit to anybody just yet that he, a grown man, was taking the matter of psi very seriously.

It was something you could try out for yourself, just as an experiment, behind locked doors and with the windows shaded.

So Commager locked the front door to his cabin and tried it out.

6

The telegram which had been shoved under his apartment door during the night gave a Hollywood telephone number and urgently requested him to call it. It was signed by Elaine Lovelock. So far as Commager could remember, Elaine was no one he knew. When he dialed the number, nobody answered.

He'd try to reach her again before he left for the store, he decided. It was eight-thirty now; he'd just got in from the Bay. The chances were somebody's deluxe fifty-gallon tropical fish tank had started to leak on the living room carpet, and it hadn't occurred to them immediately that this was what pails and pots were for.

He sat down to write a few notes on last night's experiment.

Nothing very striking had happened; he suspected he'd simply fallen asleep after the first forty minutes or so. But if he kept notes, something like a recognizable pattern might develop.

Item: The "Lona complex" hadn't bothered him much. It was beginning to feel like something that had happened to somebody else a long time ago. So perhaps the emotions connected with it hadn't been triggered by Paylar's exercises, as Julius seemed to assume. Or else, since he no longer believed in it, it was on its way out as a complex—he hoped.

Item: With his eyes closed, he could imagine very easily that he was looking through the wall of the room into another section of the cabin; also that he had moved there in person, as a form of awareness. In fact, he had roamed happily all around the Bay area for about ten minutes. For the present, that proved only that he had a much more vivid imagination than he'd thought—though whoever created Lona could be assumed to have considerable hidden talent along that line!

Item: When he'd tried to "read" specific pages of a closed book lying on a table near him, he had failed completely.

Item: He had run suddenly—he might have been asleep by then—into successive waves of unexplained panic, which brought him upright in his chair with his pulse hammering wildly.

Item: The panic had faded out of reach the instant he began to investigate it and he hadn't been able to recall it.

Item: Either shortly before or after that event, he'd had for a while the sensation of being the target of stealthy and malevolent observation. He had made an attempt to "locate" the observer and gained the impression that the other one unhurriedly withdrew.

Item: Briefly, he'd had a feeling of floating up near the ceiling of the room, watching his own body sitting in the armchair with its eyes closed. This had rocked him hard enough to awaken him again and he had concluded the experiments.

Item: After waking up, he hadn't found or imagined he'd found Ruth MacDonald or anybody else lying around the cabin, murdered or otherwise. He'd checked.

And that about summed it up, Commager decided. Not very positive results, but he was determined to continue the experiments.

He suspected Julius would feel very dubious about all this; but Julius wasn't going to be informed.

He himself was in a remarkably cheerful mood this morning.

Mrs. Lovelock had a magnificent, musical voice, rather deep for a woman.

"I'm so glad you called again, Mr. Commager," she said. "I was away on an unavoidable errand. Dr. Knox needs to see you immediately. How soon can you be here?"

"Dr. Knox?" Commager repeated. "Do you mean the Reverend Wilson Knox?"

"That is correct. Do you have the address of our Temple?"

Commager said he didn't. There was no immediate reason to add that he hadn't the slightest intention of going there, either. "What did he want to see me about?"

Mrs. Lovelock hesitated. "I couldn't explain it satisfactorily by telephone, Mr. Commager." A trace of anxiety came into her voice. "But it's quite urgent!"

Commager said he was sorry; he had a very full business day ahead of him—which was true—so, unless he could get some indication of what this was all about—

The melodious voice told him quaveringly, "Dr. Knox had a serious heart attack last night. He needs your help!"

Commager scowled. She sounded as off-beat as the rest of them and he had an urgent impulse to hang up.

He said instead, "I don't quite see how I could be of much help under those circumstances. I'm not a doctor, you know."

"I do know that, Mr. Commager," Mrs. Lovelock replied. "I also know that you haven't been acquainted with Dr. Knox for more than a few days. But I assure you that you may be saving a human life by coming out here immediately! And that is all I can tell you now—"

She stopped short, sounding as if she were about to burst into tears.

What she said didn't make sense. Also Commager hadn't liked the Reverend Knox, quite aside from the company he kept. But he could, he supposed resignedly, afford to waste a few more hours now.

"What was that address?" he asked, trying not to sound too ungracious about it.

On the way over, he had time to wonder whether this mightn't be part of some new little game the Guides wanted to play with him. He was inclined to discount Paylar's threats—psychologically, he suspected, they'd already tried everything they could do to him—and they didn't look like people who would resort readily to physical violence, though Hawkes could be an exception there.

When Commager came in sight of the Temple of Antique Christianity, physical violence suddenly looked a little more likely. He stopped a moment to consider the place.

It was in a back canyon beyond Laurel; the last quarter-mile had been a private road. A tall iron gate blocked the road at this point, opening into a walled court with a small building to the right. A sign over a door in the building indicated that this was the office.

Some distance back, looming over the walls of the court and a few intervening trees, was another structure, an old white building in the Spanish style, the size of a small hotel.

It looked like the right kind of setting for the kind of screwball cult Henry Warbutt had described. Depending on who was around, it also looked like a rather good place for murder or mayhem.

Should he just stroll in carelessly like a big, brave, athletic man?

Or should he be a dirty coward and get his revolver out of the glove compartment? It was bound to make an unsightly bulge in any of his jacket pockets—

He decided to be a dirty coward.

The gate was locked, but the lock clicked open a few seconds after Commager pushed a buzzer button beside it. The only visible way into the area was through the office door, so he went inside.

A pallid young man and a dark, intense-looking young woman sat at desks across the room from the door. The young man told Commager he was expected and went to a side door of the office with him, from where he pointed to an entrance into the big building, on the other end of what he called the grove.

"Mrs. Lovelock is waiting for you there," he said and went back to his desk.

The grove had the reflective and well-preserved air of a section of an exclusive cemetery, with just enough trees growing around to justify its name. There was a large, square lawn in the center, and a large, chaste bronze statue stood at each corner of the lawn, gazing upon it.

Back among trees to the left was a flat, raised platform, apparently faced with gray and black marble, but otherwise featureless. Commager had just gone past this when he realized that somebody had been watching him from the top of the platform as he passed.

That, at any rate, was the feeling he got. He hadn't actually seen anyone, and when he looked back, there was nobody there. But the feeling not only had been a definite and certain one—it resumed the instant he started walking on again. This time, he didn't look back.

Before he'd gone a dozen more steps, he knew, too, just when he'd experienced that exact sensation before. It was the previous night, while he was doing his parapsychological experiments at the Bay and had suddenly felt that he was under secret and unfriendly scrutiny.

He laughed at himself, but the impression remained a remarkably vivid one. And before he reached the entrance to the main building which the young man in the office had indicated to him, he had time for the thought that playing with the imagination, as he was doing, might leave one eventually on very shaky ground.

Then he was there, looking into a long hallway, and Mrs.

Lovelock's fine, deep voice greeted him before he caught sight of her.

"I'm so glad you could come, Mr. Commager!" she said.

She was standing in the door of a room that opened on the hall to the left, and Commager was a trifle startled by her appearance. He had expected a large handsome woman of about thirty, to match the voice. But Mrs. Lovelock was not only huge; she was shockingly ugly and probably almost twice the age he'd estimated. She wore a white uniform, so Commager asked whether she was Wilson Knox's nurse.

"I've been a registered nurse for nearly forty years, Mr. Commager," the beautiful voice told him. "At present, I'm attending Dr. Knox. Would you come in here, please?"

He followed her into the room and she closed the door behind them. Her big, gray face, Commager decided, looked both worried and very angry.

"The reason I wasn't more open with you over the telephone," she told him, "was that I was certain you wouldn't have taken the trouble to drive out here if I had been. And I couldn't have blamed you! Won't you sit down, please?"

Commager took a chair and said he was afraid he didn't understand.

Mrs. Lovelock nodded. "I shall give you the facts. Dr. Knox had a very severe heart attack at around two o'clock this morning. I have been a member of his congregation for twenty-four years, and I arrived with a doctor shortly afterward. Dr. Knox is resting comfortably now, but he is very anxious to see you. I must let him tell you why, Mr. Commager. But I should like to prepare you for what you will hear—"

Mrs. Lovelock stared gloomily at the carpet for a moment and then her face twisted briefly into a grimace of pure rage.

"Wilson—Dr. Knox—is a harmless old fool!" she told Commager savagely. "This Antique Christianity he worked out never hurt anybody. They prayed to Pan and they had their dances and chants. And there was the Oracle and he read out of the Book of Pan . . ."

"I don't know anything about Dr. Knox's activities," Commager said, not too politely.

She had thick, reddened, capable hands and they were locked together now on her lap, the fingers twisting slowly against one another, as if she were trying to break something between them.

"I was the Oracle, you see," she explained. "I knew it was foolish, but I'd sit up there on the dais in the smoke, with a veil over my head, and I'd say whatever I happened to think of. But this year, Wilson brought in that Ruth MacDonald—you know her, he said."

"I've met the lady," Commager admitted. "I wouldn't say I know her."

"She became the Oracle! And then she began to change everything! I told Wilson he was quite right to resist that. There are things, Mr. Commager, that a good Christian simply must not do!"

Which, Commager felt, was a remarkable statement, under the circumstances. Mrs. Lovelock came ponderously to her feet.

"Dr. Knox will tell you what remains to be told," she added rather primly. "And, of course, you cannot stay too long. Will you follow me now, please?"

The Reverend didn't look as if he were in too bad a condition, Commager thought when he saw him first. He was lying in a hospital bed which had been raised high enough to let him gaze down at the grove out of a window of his second-story room.

After he'd talked a few moments, Commager felt the man was delirious and he thought briefly of calling back Mrs. Lovelock or the other nurse who had been with Wilson Knox when they came in. But those two undoubtedly had been able to judge for themselves whether they should remain with the Reverend or not.

"Why should they want to kill you?" Commager asked. Knox had been speaking of the Guides and then had started to weep; now he blew his nose on a piece of tissue and made a groping motion for Commager's hand, which Commager withdrew in time.

"It was merely a matter of business as far as I was concerned, Mr. Commager. I certainly had no intention of blocking any activities of the Guides. In fact, I should prefer not to know about them. But when Miss MacDonald, who was employed by the Temple, upset our members, I protested to her, sir! Isn't that understandable?"

"Entirely," Commager agreed carefully. "What did Miss MacDonald do to upset them?"

"She predicted two of the congregation would die before the end of the year," Wilson Knox said shakily. "It caused a great deal of alarm. Many of our wealthier clients withdrew from the Temple at once. It is a considerable financial loss!"

The Reverend appeared rational enough on that point. Commager inquired, "Is Miss MacDonald one of the Guides, Dr. Knox?"

"It's not for me to say." Knox gave him a suddenly wary look. "When she spoke to me by telephone last night, I asked whether

I had offended anyone. I was, of course, greatly distressed!" His expression changed back to one of profound self-pity. "But she repeated only that it had become necessary for me to die this week and hung up."

It seemed an odd way at that for the Temple's new Oracle to have phrased her prediction, Commager thought. He regarded Dr. Knox without much sympathy. "So now you want me to simply tell her not to hurt you, eh?"

"It would be better, Mr. Commager," Knox suggested, "if you addressed yourself directly to the young woman called Paylar." He reached for his visitor's hand again. "I place myself under your protection, sir. I know you won't refuse it!"

Which was almost precisely what he had said as soon as the nurses left the room, and the reason Commager had believed the patient was in a state of delirium. Now it seemed more probable that he was merely badly mistaken.

Commager decided not to ask why it would be better to speak to Paylar. At any direct question concerning the Guides, the Reverend became evasive. He said instead, "What made you decide I could protect you, Dr. Knox?"

Knox looked downright crafty. "I have made no inquiries about you, sir, and I do not intend to. I am a simple man whose life has been devoted to providing a measure of beauty and solace for his fellow human beings. In a modest way, of course. I have never pried into the Greater Mysteries!"

He seemed to expect approval for that, so Commager nodded gravely.

"I speak only of what I saw," Wilson Knox continued. "On Sunday night, I saw them attempt to bring you directly under their sway. Forgive me for saying, sir, that they do not do this with an ordinary person! I also saw them fail and I knew they were frightened. Nevertheless, you were not destroyed."

He tapped Commager's hand significantly. "That, sir, was enough for me. I do not attempt to pry—I have merely placed myself under your protection!"

7

A man with Secret Powers, a man who could tell the Guides to go jump in the Pacific, might take a passing interest in the gimmicks of an organization like the Temple of Antique Christianity. So on his way out through the grove, Commager had turned aside to get a closer look at the dais.

He assumed, at least, that the gray and black marble platform was what Mrs. Lovelock had referred to as the seat of the Oracle, since nothing else around seemed suitable for the purpose.

Standing before it, he pictured her sitting up there in the night, veiled, a vast, featureless bulk, announcing whatever came into her mind in that stunning voice, and he could see that Wilson Knox's congregation might well have listened in pop-eyed fascination. Ruth MacDonald couldn't have been nearly as impressive.

Perhaps that was why she had started passing out death sentences.

Down on Sunset, he parked his car at the curb and remained in it, watching the traffic, while he tried to digest the information he had received—if you could call it information.

Wilson Knox and Mrs. Lovelock appeared to be people who had fabricated so much fantastic garbage for the clients of the Temple that they had no judgment left to resist the fabrications of others.

Commager's parting from Mrs. Lovelock had given him the impression that the huge woman also was sullenly afraid, though she hid it much better than the Reverend had. It could be simply that she felt her own position in the Temple would be lost if Knox died; but he thought that in her case, too, it was a more personal fear, of the Guides, or even of himself—

And he'd practically promised both of them to put in a word with Paylar to protect that revolting little man!

However, the Reverend's heart attack, at least, probably had been a real enough thing. And if Ruth MacDonald actually had telephoned a prediction of death to him earlier in the night, there was some cause for intervention. The practice of frightening people into their graves was something that anyone could reasonably insist should be stopped.

And that, of course, brought up the question of how he expected to stop it.

And the question, once more, of just what that odd group of people—who indicated they were the Guides or associated with them—was after.

Ruth MacDonald's activities concerning the Temple of Antique Christianity hardly seemed to lie on the lofty, idealistic level he'd been almost willing to ascribe to them in theory, even if he disliked their methods. She was a brassy, modern young witch, Commager thought, using the old witchcraft tools of fear and suggestion out of equally old motives of material gain and prestige.

But one couldn't account for Hawkes as simply as that, because Hawkes had had money and prestige.

Commager knew least of all about Paylar, except for the young man called Lex Barthold, whose connection with the others wasn't clear. The impression of Paylar was still mainly that she had a physical personality that would be hard to match if you liked them slender, dark and mysterious, and with a self-assurance that wasn't aggressive like Ruth MacDonald's, but that might be a great deal more difficult to crack. Among the three he'd had to deal with, she seemed to be the leader, though that wasn't necessarily true.

He found himself walking slowly down the street toward a phone booth.

Let's make a game of it, he thought. Assume that what Paylar had said and what the Reverend had suspected was true—at least in the Guides' own opinion—that he had turned out to be exceptionally tough material for their psychological gimmicks. That he had, in fact, abilities he didn't yet know about himself, but which, even in a latent state, were sufficient to have got the Opposition all hot and worried!

Even if the Guides only believed that—if they, like Knox and his mountainous registered nurse, had played around so long on the fringes of reality that they were as badly confused now as the people they'd been misleading—his intervention should still be effective. Particularly if he informed Mrs. Lovelock, with the proper degree of impressiveness, that he'd passed on the word.

A little play-acting didn't seem too much effort to put out to save a human life. Even a life like Wilson Knox's . . .

This time, it was Paylar who answered the telephone.

"You've disappointed me a little, Mr. Commager," she said. "When I first heard your voice, I was certain you were going to invite me out to dine and dance."

Commager assured her that this had been his primary purpose— and as soon as he'd said it, he began to wonder whether it wasn't true. But business came first, he added.

"Well, as to the business," Paylar told him demurely, "I'm not necessarily in control of Ruth's activities, you know. I hadn't been informed that the Reverend Knox was ill." She paused a moment. "I'll tell Ruth she isn't to frighten your friend again. Will that be satisfactory, Mr. Commager?"

"Why, yes, it is," Commager said and found himself flushing. Somehow, in her easy acceptance of his intervention, she'd managed to make him feel like a child whose fanciful notions were being humored by an adult. He put the idea aside, to be investigated later. "Now about where to have dinner—"

Paylar said she'd prefer to let him surprise her. "But I have a condition," she added pleasantly. "There'll be no shop-talk tonight!"

Putting him on the defensive again, Commager thought ruefully. He told her shop-talk had been far from his mind and would eight o'clock be about right?

It would be about right, she agreed. And then, arriving at the store finally, some fifteen minutes later, he found Jean Bohart waiting in his office.

"Hi, Alan," she greeted him gloomily. "You're taking me to lunch. Okay?"

In one way and another, Commager felt, Tuesday simply didn't look like a good day for business.

"I'm in a mood today," Jean announced. She picked without enthusiasm at a grapefruit and watercress salad. "But you're not talking to me, either!"

"I was thinking," Commager said, "that I was glad you didn't look like a certain lady I met this morning. What's the mood about?"

She hesitated. "I'm making my mind up about something. I'll tell you tomorrow. Who was the lady? Someone I know?"

"I doubt it. A Mrs. Lovelock."

"I don't know any Lovelocks. What's the matter with her looks?"

"Fat," Commager explained.

"Well," Jean said glumly, "I'm not that."

She was, in fact, in spite of her downcast expression, a model of crisp attractiveness as usual. A white sharkskin suit, with a lavender veil gathered lightly at her throat, plus a trim white hat to one side of a blonde head—neat, alert and healthy-looking as an airline hostess, Commager thought approvingly.

Jean mightn't care for the comparison, though, so he didn't tell her. And he wasn't going to press her about the mood, At the rare moments that she became reserved, probing made her sullen. Probably something to do with Ira again.

"I called off the Taylors for tomorrow," she told him suddenly, with some traces of embarrassment, "so we could talk. You don't mind, do you?"

"Of course not," Commager said hesitantly. Then it struck him suddenly: they'd had a date for an all-day fishing party Wednesday, Jean and he and the Taylor couple. He'd forgotten completely!

"That's all right then," Jean said, looking down at her plate. She still seemed curiously shy and Commager realized that this was no ordinary problem. "Will you sleep at your cabin tonight?"

"Sure," he said, concerned—he was very fond of Jean. His sleeping at the cabin was the usual arrangement on such occasions; he'd have everything ready there for the day before anyone else arrived and then they'd be off to an early start.

"I'll be there tomorrow at eight," said Jean. She gave him a quick, unhappy smile. "I love you, Alan—you never ask questions when you shouldn't!"

So he had two dates at eight now, twelve hours apart. If it hadn't been for the attendant problems, Commager decided, his social life might have looked exceptionally well-rounded at the moment to almost anybody.

But he didn't seem to be doing a very good job of keeping clear of attendant problems. It had struck him for the first time, while they were lunching, that Jean Bohart might easily have been the prototype of the figment of Lona. There were obvious general similarities, and the dissimilarities might have been his own expression of the real-life fact that Jean was Ira's wife.

But he felt himself moving into a mentally foggy area at that point. There had been occasional light love-making between them, too light to really count; but Jean certainly had remained emotionally absorbed with Ira, though she tended to regard him superficially with a kind of fond exasperation.

Commager didn't really know how he felt about Jean, except that he liked her more than any one else he could think of. There was a warning awareness that if he tried to push any deeper into that particular fog right now, he might get himself emotionally snagged again.

It didn't seem advisable to become emotionally snagged. There were still too many other doubtful issues floating around.

One of the other issues resolved itself—in a way—very shortly, with the ringing of the office telephone.

It was Elaine Lovelock once more.

"Mr. Commager," she said, "about the matter we were discussing—"

He began to tell her he had spoken to Paylar, but she interrupted him: "Dr. Knox died an hour ago!"

Some thirty minutes later, the first hot jolt of pain drove down from the center of Commager's throat to a point under the end of his breast-bone.

If it hadn't been so damned pat, he thought, he might have yelled for a doctor. The sensations were thoroughly convincing.

There was a section at the back of the store devoted to the experimental breeding of fish that were priced high enough to make such domestic arrangements worthwhile and exceptionally delicate in their requirements for propagation. The section had a door that could be locked, to avoid disturbances. Commager went in and locked it.

In the swampy, hot-house atmosphere, he leaned against one of the tank racks, breathing carefully. The pain was still there, much less substantial than it had been in the first few moments, but still a vertical, hard cramping inside his chest. It had shocked him—it did yet—but he was not nearly so much alarmed as angry.

The anger raged against himself—he was doing this! The suggestion to do it might have been implanted, but the response wasn't an enemy from outside, a phantom-tiger pressing cold, steely claws down through his chest. It was a self-generated thing that used his own muscles, his own nerves, his own brain—

It tightened suddenly again. Steel-hard, chilling pain, along with a bitter, black, strangling nausea in his throat. "I'm doing it!" he thought.

The clamping agony was part of himself; he had created it, structured it, was holding it there now.

And so he relaxed it again. Not easily, because the other side of himself, the hidden, unaware, responsive side was being stubborn about this! It knew it was supposed to die now, and it did its determined best.

But degree by degree, he relaxed the cramping, the tightness, and then suddenly felt it dissolve completely.

Commager stood, his legs spread apart, swaying a little drunkenly. Sweat ran from his body. His head remained cocked to the right as if listening, sensing, while he breathed in long, harsh gasps that slowed gradually.

It was gone.

And now, he thought, let's really test this thing! Let's produce it again.

That wasn't easy either, because he kept cringing in fear of its return.

But he produced it.

And, this time, it wasn't too hard to let it go, let it dissolve again.

He brought it up briefly once more, a single sharp stab—and washed it away.

And that, he thought, was enough of that kind of game. He'd proved his point!

He stripped off his shirt and hosed cold water over his head and shoulders and arms. He dabbed himself with a towel, put his wet shirt back on, combed his hair and went back to the office.

Sitting there, he thought of an old gag about a moronic wrestler who, practicing holds and grips all by himself, broke off his left foot and remarked admiringly, "Jeez, boss, nobody but me could have done that to me, huh?"

Which more or less covered what had happened. And now that he had made that quite clear, it seemed safe to wonder whether just possibly there mightn't have been some direct, immediate prompting from outside—something that told him to go ahead and break himself apart, just as the wrestler had done.

Though there needn't have been anything as direct as a telepathic suggestion. It could also have been done, quite as purposefully, by inducing the disturbed leaders of the Temple of Antique Christianity to bring their plight to his attention. By letting him become thoroughly aware of the shadowy, superstitious possibilities in the situation, opening his mind to them and their implications—and then hammering the suggestion home with the simple, indisputable fact of Wilson Knox's death.

If someone was clever enough to know Alan Commager a little better than he'd known himself so far—and had motive enough not to mind killing somebody else in order to soften him up—it could have been done in just that way. And Paylar had told him openly that the motive existed.

Commager decided that that was how it had been done; though now he didn't mind considering the possibility of a telepathic suggestion either. They might try something else, but he was quite sure that the kind of trick they had tried—whichever way it had been done—wouldn't work at all another time. They needed his cooperation for that, and he wasn't giving them any.

And still, aside from the fact that Wilson Knox had been threatened, nothing at all had occurred openly.

The anger in him remained. He couldn't bring himself to feel really sorry for Knox, or for Elaine Lovelock either. They were destructive mental parasites who'd had the bad luck to run into what might be simply a more efficient parasite of the same breed. In spite of their protests, they hadn't been any less ruthless with the people they controlled.

He could recognize that. But the anger stayed with him, a smoldering and dangerous thing, a little ugly. Basically, Commager knew, he was still angry with himself. For reasons still unknown, he had developed an area of soft rot in his thoughts and emotions; and he was reasonably convinced that, without that much to start on, the proddings and nibblings of—parasites—couldn't have had any effect. To have reduced himself to the level of becoming vulnerable to them seemed an intolerably indecent failing, like a filthy disease.

But anger, however honestly directed where it belongs, wants to strike outward.

For a parasite or whatever else she might be, Paylar looked flatteringly beautiful in a sheath of silver and black—and he didn't get a significant word out of her all evening.

Commager hadn't tried to talk shop, but he had expected that she would. However, in that respect, it might have been simply another interesting, enjoyable but not too extraordinary night out.

In other respects, it wasn't. He didn't forget at any time that here was someone who probably shared the responsibility for what he was now rather certain had been a deliberate murder. In retrospect, her promise to tell Ruth MacDonald not to frighten Knox any more hadn't meant anything, since Knox by then had been as good as dead.

The odd thing—made much odder, of course, by the other probability that he himself had been the actual target of that killing—was that, as far as Paylar was concerned, he seemed unable to feel any convincing moral indignation about the event. It was puzzling enough so that, under and around their pleasant but unimportant conversation, he was mainly engaged in hunting for the cause of that lack of feeling.

Her physical attractiveness seemed involved in it somehow. Not as a justification for murder; he wasn't even so sure this evening that he liked Paylar physically. He felt the attraction, but there was also a trace of something not very far from revulsion in his involuntary response to it. It wasn't too obvious; but she might have almost an excess of quiet vitality, a warmth and slender, soft earthiness that seemed almost more animal than human.

That thought-line collapsed suddenly. Rather, it struck Commager, as if he'd been about to become aware of something he wasn't yet prepared to see.

He suddenly laughed, and Paylar's short black eyebrows lifted questioningly.

"I just worked something out, Mabel!" he explained. He'd asked her earlier what her full name was, and she had told him gravely it was Mabel Jones, and that she used Paylar for business purposes only. He didn't believe her, but, for the evening, they had settled cosily on Mabel and Alan.

"The thing that's different about you," he went on, "is that you don't have a soul. So, of course, you don't have a human conscience either." He considered a moment. It seemed, at any rate, to reflect almost exactly how he felt about her. A cat, say, was attractive, pleasant to see and to touch; and one didn't blame a cat for the squawking bird it had killed that afternoon. One didn't fairly blame a cat either if, to avenge some mysterious offense, it lashed out with a taloned paw at oneself. He developed the notion to Paylar as well as he could without violating the rule against shop-talk.

The cat-woman seemed neither amused nor annoyed at his description of her. She listened attentively and then said, "You could still join us, Alan—"

"Lady," said Commager, astonished, "there are any number of less disagreeable suggestions you could have made at this hour!" He added, "Leaving out everything else, I don't like the company you keep."

Paylar shrugged naked tanned shoulders. Then her gaze went past him and froze briefly.

"What's the matter?" he inquired.

She looked back at him with a rueful smile. "I'm afraid you're going to see a little more of my company now," she remarked. "What time of night is it, Alan?"

Commager checked. It was just past midnight, he told her, so it wasn't surprising that this and that should have started crawling out of the woodwork. He turned his head.

"Hello, Oracle!" he said cordially. "What do you see in the tea leaves for me?"

Ruth MacDonald looked a little out of place here in a neat gray business suit. For a moment, she had also looked uncomfortably like a resurrected corpse to Commager, but she was alive enough.

She glanced at him. "I see your death," she said unsmilingly.

Commager told her that she appeared to be in a rut, but wouldn't she sit down and have a drink? The ice-faced young siren didn't share Paylar's immunity in his mind—she made his flesh crawl; she was something that should be stepped on!

Paylar stood up. "You're fools," she said to Ruth MacDonald without passion. She turned to Commager. "Alan, I should have told you I intended to drive back with Ruth—"

It was a lie, he thought, but he didn't mind. The expression of implacable hostility on Ruth MacDonald's face had been gratifying—Paylar's friends were becoming really unhappy about him!

The gray car stood almost at the far end of the dark parking lot where he had left his own. He walked them up to it and wished them both good night with some solemnity. "You, too, Miss MacDonald!" he said, which gained him another brief glance and nothing more. Then he stepped aside to let them back out.

When he stopped moving, there was no particular psychic ability required to guess what was pushing against the back of his spine. "We're taking the next car," Herbert Hawkes' voice announced gently behind him. "And I'm sure we can count on you to act reasonably this time, Mr. Commager."

It was rather neat, at that. The gray car was moving slowly away, racing its engine. If there had been anyone in sight at the moment—but there wasn't—a back-fire wouldn't have created any particular excitement.

"I'm a reasonable man," Commager said meekly. "Good evening, Mr. Barthold. I'm to take one of the back seats, I suppose?"

"That's what we had in mind," Hawkes admitted.

They might or might not be amateurs at this kind of thing, but they didn't seem to be making any obvious mistakes. Lex Barthold was driving, and Commager sat in the seat behind him. Hawkes sat beside Barthold, half-turned toward Commager. The gun he held pointed at Commager's chest lay along the top of the back-rest. From outside, if anyone happened to glance in, it would look as if the two of them were engaged in conversation.

Commager thought wistfully of his own gun, stacked uselessly away in his car. This was what came of starting to think in terms of modern witchcraft! One overlooked the simple solutions.

"I was wondering," he suggested, "what would happen if we passed a patrol-car."

Hawkes shrugged very slightly. "You might try praying that we do, Commager!"

Whether the possibility was bothering him or not, the big man didn't look happy. And there was a set tension about the way Lex Barthold drove which indicated an equal lack of enjoyment there. Witchcraft addicts themselves, they might feel that physical mayhem, if that was what they were contemplating, was a little out of their normal lines of activity.

Otherwise, they had brawn enough for almost any kind of mayhem, and while one needn't assume immediately that the trip was to wind up with outright murder, their attitude wasn't reassuring.

Meanwhile, he had been fascinated by the discovery that Hawkes sported a large, discolored bruise at the exact points of his neck and jaw where Commager had thought his fist had landed early Monday morning. Those "hallucinations" hadn't been entirely illusory, after all!

However, that made it a little harder again to understand what actually could have happened that night. Commager's thoughts started darting off after rather improbable explanations, such as the possibility of Ruth MacDonald's having a twin sister or a close double who had been sacrificed then—much as Knox had been—as part of the plot to drive Alan Commager out of his mind or into his grave. He shook his head. It just didn't seem very likely.

The one thing he could be sure of right now was that Hawkes, who mightn't be the most genial of men at best, hadn't appreciated that sneak punch.

They didn't pass any patrol-cars . . .

8

He killed Herbert Hawkes not a quarter of a mile away from his own Bayside cabin. The location wasn't accidental. Once they were past the point of possible interference, with the last fifty yards of a twisting, precipitous goat-path down to the Bay behind Commager and a gun still in front of him, Hawkes took time out to explain.

"We're counting on your being found," he said, "and this is your own backyard, so to speak. You've gone fishing now and then from that spot down there, Commager. Tonight, being a little liquored up, you decided to go for a swim. Or you slipped and fell from all the way up here and died instantly."

Commager looked at the gun. "With a couple of bullets in me?"

"I don't think it will come to that." Both of them, in spite of Hawkes's bland analysis of the situation, were still as nervous, Commager suspected, as a couple of cats in a strange cellar. "But if it does—well, you ran into a couple of rough characters out here, and they shot you and threw you in! Of course, we'd prefer to avoid that kind of complication."

He paused as if expecting some comment. They both stood about eight feet away, looking at Commager.

The Moon was low over the Bay, but it was big, and there was plenty of light for close-range shooting. This was a lumpy shelf of rock, not more than twenty by twenty feet, long and wide; the path dropped off to the right of it to another smaller shelf and ended presently at the water's edge, where there was a wet patch of sand when the tide was out.

The only way up from here was the path they'd come down by, and the two stood in front of that. He couldn't read Barthold's expression just now, but Hawkes was savagely tense—a big man physically confident of himself, mentally prepared for murder, but still oddly unsure and—expectant!

The explanation struck Commager suddenly: they were wondering whether he wasn't going to produce some witchcraft trick of his own in this emergency. It was such an odd shifting of their original roles that it startled a snort of rather hysterical mirth from him; and Hawkes, in the process of handing the gun to Barthold, tried to jerk it back, and then Commager moved.

He didn't move toward Hawkes but toward Barthold, who seemed to have a better hold on the gun. They might have thought he was after it, too, because Hawkes let go and swung too hastily at him, as Barthold took a step back. Commager slammed a fist into Barthold's body, swung him around between Hawkes and himself, and struck hard again. The gun didn't even go off.

He had no more time then for Barthold, because Hawkes rammed into him with disconcerting solidness and speed. In an instant, it was like fighting a baboon, all nails and muscles and smashing fists and feet. The top of Hawkes's skull butted his mouth like a rock. Commager hit him in the back of the neck, was free for a moment and hit again. Hawkes stepped back, straightening slightly, and Commager followed and struck once more, in the side. Then Hawkes disappeared.

It was as sudden as that. Realization that he was stumbling on the edge of the rock shelf himself came together with a glimpse of the thundering white commotion of surf almost vertically beneath him—a good hundred and fifty feet down.

With a terrible trembling still in his muscles, he scrambled six feet back on the shelf and glared wildly around for Lex Barthold. But his mind refused to turn away from the thought of how shockingly close he had come to going over with Hawkes; so a number of seconds passed before he grasped the fact that Barthold also was nowhere in sight.

Commager's breathing had slowed gradually, while he stared warily up the trail to the left. The noise of the water would have covered any sounds of either stealthy withdrawal or approach; but since Barthold seemed to have preferred to take himself and the gun out of the fight, it was unlikely he would be back.

On the other hand, there were a number of points on that path where he could wait for Commager to come within easy range, while he remained out of immediate physical reach himself.

To the right, the trail led down. Commager glanced in that direction again and, this time, saw the gun where it had dropped into the loose shale of the shelf.

Lex Barthold was lying on his back among the boulders of the next shelf down, his legs higher than his head, the upper part of his body twisted slightly to one side. He had fallen only nine feet or so, but he wasn't moving. They looked at each other for a moment; then Commager safetied the gun and put it in his pocket. He went on down.

"Hawkes went over the edge," he said, still rather dazed. "What happened to you?"

Barthold grunted. "Broke my back." He cursed Commager briefly. "But you're a dead man, too, Commager."

"Neither of us is dead yet," Commager told him. He felt physically heavy, cold and tired. He hesitated and added, "I'm going to go and get help for you."

Barthold shook his head slowly. "You won't get back up there alive. We've made sure of you this time..." He sounded matter-of-factly certain of it, and if he felt any concern about what would happen now to himself, there was no trace of it in his voice.

Commager stared down at him for a moment wondering, and then looked around.

Surf crashed rhythmically below them; the Moon seemed to be sliding fast through clouds far out over the Bay. Overhead, the broken, sloping cliffs might conceal anything or anybody. The feeling came strongly to him then that in this savage and lonely place anything could happen without affecting the human world at all or being noticed by it.

The night-lit earth seemed to shift slowly and giddily about him and then steadied again, as if he had, just then, drifted far beyond the boundaries of the reality he knew and were now somewhere else, in an area that followed laws of its own, if it followed any laws at all.

When he looked at Barthold again, he no longer felt the paradoxical human desire to find help for a man who had tried to kill him and whom he had nearly killed. He could talk in Barthold's own terms.

He bent over him. "What makes you so sure your friends have got me?"

Barthold gave him a mocking glance, but he didn't answer.

They weren't certain, Commager thought, straightening up. They were just hoping again! That something was preparing against him was an impression he'd gained himself, almost like the physical sensation of a hostile stirring and shifting in the air and the rocks about him, a secretive gathering of power. But they weren't certain!

"I think," he said slowly, "that I'll walk away from here when I feel like it." He paused, and added deliberately, "You people might last longer if you didn't try to play rough, Barthold. Except, of course, with someone like Wilson Knox."

Barthold spoke with difficulty. "The reason you're still alive is that Paylar and I were the only ones who would believe you were a natural of the new mind. The first one here in twenty-three years—" His breath seemed to catch; his face twisted into a grimace of pain. "But tonight they all know that ordinary controls won't work on you, Commager! That's what makes it too late for you."

Commager hesitated. He said gently, "When did you and Paylar discover I was a natural of the new mind?"

"Sunday night, of course!" Barthold was plainly anxious now to keep him here. He hurried on, "The mistake was made five years ago. You should have been destroyed then, before you had learned anything, not placed under control!"

Commager's eyes widened slightly. Until that statement, he had given only a fraction of conscious attention to what Barthold was saying, the greater part of his mind alert to catch those wispy, not-quite-physical indications that something unhealthy was brewing nearby in the night. But five years ago!

"Paylar made me an offer to join your group," he pointed out. "Wouldn't that have been satisfactory?"

Barthold stared up at him. His mouth worked, but for a few seconds he made no audible reply.

"Don't wait!" he said with startling, savage intensity. "Now, or . . ." The words thickened and slurred into angry, incomprehensible mutterings. The eyelids closed.

Commager bent down and prodded Barthold's shoulder with a forefinger. The man might be dying—those last words hadn't sounded as if they were addressed to him—but there were things he had to know now. "What are you, Barthold? Aren't you a natural, too?"

Barthold's eyes opened and rolled toward him, but remained unpleasantly unfocused. "Old mind—" the thick voice mumbled. And then clearly, "You're a fool, Commager! You didn't really know anything! If the others—"

The eyes closed again.

Old mind . . . That still told him nothing. "Are the others of the old mind?"

Barthold grinned tiredly. "Why don't you ask Hawkes?"

There was a sound behind Commager like the sloshing of water in the bottom of a boat. Then he had spun around and was on his feet, his hair bristling.

Hawkes stood swaying in the moonlight, twenty feet away. Water ran from his clothes to the rocks among which he stood. Water had smeared his hair down over his face. And the left side of his head looked horribly flattened.

He took a step forward, and then came on in a swaying rush.

For a long instant of time, Commager only stared. Hawkes was dead; quite obviously, even now as he moved, he was dead—so he hadn't come climbing back up the rocks out of the sweeping tug of the waves! He—

He was gone.

Commager walked over to the point where he had seen Hawkes. The rocks were dry. He went back to Barthold, his lips still stiff with horror.

"Tell me what this was!" he said hoarsely. "Or I'll kill you now!"

Barthold was still grinning, his eyes open and wickedly alert. "A picture I let you look at—but, you see, you learn too fast! You're a natural. You wouldn't believe a picture now, and the old mind couldn't do anything else to you. But there are others working for us—and now—"

There was a rumbling and a grinding and a rushing sound overhead. Commager leaped back, his eyes darting up. He heard Lex Barthold screaming.

The whole upper cliff-side was moving, sliding downward. A gray-black, turning, almost vertical wave of broken rock dropping toward them . . .

9

"People like us," Jean Bohart remarked, with an air of moody discovery, "are really pretty lucky!"

Commager went "Hm?" drowsily. Then he lifted his head to look at her. She stood beside the Sweet Susan's lashed wheel, shaded blue eyes gazing at him from under the brim of her yachting cap, hands clasped behind her. "What brought that to mind?" he inquired.

"I was thinking about my troubles," she said. "Then I started thinking they weren't really so bad! Comparatively—"

She was keeping her voice light. Commager sat up from where he'd stretched himself out beside the cabin, gathering his thoughts back out of the aimless diffusion of sleep. "Ready to talk about your troubles now?"

Jean shook her head. "Not yet." She frowned. "There's something about them I want to figure out by myself first—and I'm not quite done." The frown vanished. "If you've finished your nap, you might look around and see what a grand morning it is! That's what I meant by being lucky."

They were off Dana Point, he saw, so he'd slept a full hour since Jean had taken them out of the Newport Beach harbor. The Sweet Susan was running smoothly southward, through the Pacific's long smooth swells. Now that he was sitting up, the wind streamed cool about his head and neck and shoulders.

He said, "Yes, I guess we're lucky."

Jean grinned. "And since I've got you awake, I'll catch a nap myself! Not that I spent the night boozing and brawling."

Commager smiled at her. "Any time you feel like putting in a night like that, give me a ring."

Superficially, in her white slacks and thin sweater, Jean Bohart looked fresh as a daisy; only the tautness about her mouth and a controlled rigidity in the way she stood suggested that the "trouble" might be close to a complete emotional disaster.

He'd thought earlier that he would have liked to get out of this jaunt if he could; now he felt guilty and a little alarmed.

He moved over near the wheel while she lay down on the bench, pulling a pillow under her head and settling back with the cap-brim down over her eyes. He could tell that the muscles of the slim straight body weren't actually going to relax. But she would pretend now to be asleep and Commager let his thoughts shift away from Jean, promising himself to give her his full attention as soon as she was ready to talk.

There were a few problems of his own to be considered, though at the moment he had the sense of a truce, a lull. Last night, he had shaken the Guides badly; he had killed two of their members. But there were at least three left, and he hadn't crippled their power to act.

The truce, if it was that, was due in part to their fear of his reaction and in part to an entirely different kind of restraint—a restraint which he believed was self-imposed.

The reason he believed it was that he was now aware of being under a similar restraint himself. He thought he knew why it was an inescapable limitation, but impersonally he could agree with Paylar's opinion that, from the Guides' point of view, he should have been destroyed as soon as they became aware of him.

Left to himself—if in curiosity he had begun to investigate psi—he would have discovered the limitation quickly enough and abided by it. Even so, it appeared to permit an enormously extended range of effective activity. And Barthold had implied a conflict between an "old mind" and a "new mind."

It sounded like an esoteric classification of varying degrees of human psi potential—an ascendant individual "new mind" threatening the entrenched and experienced but more limited older group, which compensated for its limitation by bringing functioning members of the "new mind" under its control or repressing or diverting their developing abilities.

He, apparently, was a "natural of the new mind." He couldn't be permanently controlled. To the older group he represented an intolerable threat.

Some one, last night, had thrown a few thousand tons of stone at him! And he had deflected that missile from its course. Not by very much, but just enough to keep it clear of the frantically scrambling figure of himself, scuttling up the cliff path like a scared beetle.

He had done it—how?

Trying to restructure the action, Commager knew that the process itself hadn't been a conscious one. But it had been symbolized in his awareness by a cluster of pictures that took in the whole event simultaneously.

A visualization of himself and the long thundering of the rocks, the sideward distortion of their line of fall, and a final picture again of himself as he reached the top of the cliff unharmed.

It had all been there, in a momentary, timeless swirling of possibilities against the background of rock and shadow, the tilted, turning sky and moonlight glittering on racing waters.

Then, in an instant, the pattern had been set, decided on; and the event solidified into reality with the final thudding crash. Barthold lay buried under the rocks and perhaps, down in the water, the body of Hawkes also had been caught and covered.

He hadn't tried to save Barthold. Instead, automatically, he had flung out another kind of awareness, a flashing search for the mind that had struck at him. And he had been prepared, in a way he couldn't have described now, to strike back.

He "found" three of them; the one who had acted and two who merely observed. Almost, not quite, he knew where they were. But they were alert. It was as if something, barely glimpsed, had been flicked out of his sight, leaving a lifeless black emptiness for him to grope through if he chose.

Commager didn't choose to do any blind groping. He wasn't sure enough of himself for that.

The limitation that he—and, apparently, they—didn't dare to violate had to do with the preservation of appearances. It was a line of thought he didn't want to follow too far just now. But it seemed that the reality he knew and lived in was a framework of appearances, tough and durable normally but capable of being distorted into possibly chaotic variations.

The penalty seemed to be that to the degree one distorted the framework, he remained distorted himself. The smooth flow of appearances was quickly re-established, but the miracle-worker found himself left somehow outside. Commager suspected that he stayed outside.

He suspected also that a really significant distortion of appearances would thrust the life and mind that caused it so far out that, for all practical purposes, it ceased to exist.

He wasn't tempted to test the theory. Its apparent proof was that reality, by and large, did remain intact, while those who played around too consistently with even minor infringements notoriously failed to thrive.

To let a pair of dice briefly defy the laws of chance probably did no harm to anyone, but when you aimed and launched the side of a cliff as a missile of murder, you were very careful that the result was a rock-slide and not a miracle!

You didn't—ever—disturb the world of reality . . .

What he had to fear from them, if they broke the truce, was the ambush, the thing done secretly under the appearance of a natural series of events. It left an unpleasantly large number of possibilities open, but until something new happened, he couldn't know that they weren't ready to call it a draw. So far, his spontaneous reactions had been entirely effective; the obvious damage was all on the other side.

But since the damage wasn't all obvious, he had no present intention of forcing a showdown. "Natural" or not, he might be either not quite good enough at that kind of game, or much too good.

But meanwhile—Commager looked thoughtfully at Jean Bohart. She had fallen asleep finally, but she wasn't sleeping comfortably. Her mouth moved fretfully, and she made small whimpering sounds from time to time, almost like a puppy that is dreaming badly. If he'd become a miracle-worker on a small scale, Commager thought, if he'd already pushed himself to some degree beyond the normal limits of reality, he might as well get some use out of what he couldn't undo.

Looking at her, it wasn't too difficult to imagine the rigidities and tensions that kept Jean from finding any real physical rest. Nor—a step farther—was it hard to get a picture of her emotional disturbances shaping themselves into a scurrying and shifting dream-torment.

Carefully, Commager took hold of the two concepts. He waited until he could no longer be quite sure whether it was he or Jean who was really experiencing these things; and then, as he had done yesterday with the pain in his own body, he let dreams and tensions ebb away and cease to be.

In spite of everything else that had happened, he was still amazed, a few moments later, to realize that his experiment in therapy had been a complete success.

10

Clear blue bowl of the sky above. Black-blue choppy water of the Pacific all about.

The Sweet Susan drifted, throttled down and almost stationary. Near the kelp beds two miles to the south, eight other boats gradually changed their relative positions. In the north-east, toward which the Sweet Susan slowly moved, the dark jaws of the Bay opened out, still too far off to make out the scars of last night's rock-slide.

Jean had slept steadily for over an hour, and Commager had two lines trailing under superficial observation. Not even a mackerel had taken any interest so far, which probably wasn't due to the sinister influence of the Guides, but to the fact that the deep drop outside the Bay simply wasn't a very good fishing area.

Unconcerned about that, he'd been sitting there for some while, in a drowsy, sun-bright daydream composed of an awareness of physical well-being, his odd certainty that the truce still held, and enjoyment of the coincidence that the Sun was getting hotter to the exact degree that the breeze got brisker in compensation. For the hour, under such circumstances, the life of an unambitious, healthy animal seemed to be about as much as anybody reasonably could ask for.

He came out of it with a sort of frightened start. He had heard Jean stirring on the bench behind him. Now she yawned, just audibly, and sat up, and he knew she was looking at him.

Commager couldn't have said what kept him from turning his head. There was a momentary questioning alarm in him, which stiffened into cold watchfulness as Jean got up and went into the cabin. There had been another little shift in the values of reality while he was off-guard, he thought. Something was a shade wrong again, a shade otherwise than it had been an hour or so ago. But he didn't yet know what it was.

In a minute or so Jean came out again, and he guessed she'd changed into her swimsuit. He heard her come up behind him, and then a pair of smooth arms were laid lightly across his shoulders and a voice, from a point a little above and behind his head, inquired, "Had any luck, Alan? The Sun got a bit too hot for me."

It shocked him completely because it was Lona who touched him and spoke.

It was also, of course, Jean Bohart—and there was no longer any question that she'd served as the model for his imaginary woman. It had been out of just such scraps of illusion as this— voice sounds and touches, distorted seconds in time—that he'd built up that self-deception.

How he had been reached in the first place to get him started on the construction was something he couldn't yet recall, but the purpose was also completely obvious.

Five years ago, Lex Barthold had said, they'd taken him under control.

To divert a mind from a direction you didn't want it to follow, you gave it a delusion to stare at.

You drenched the delusion in violently unpleasant emotions, which kept the mind from any closer investigation of the disturbance—

Apparently, they'd expected the treatment to be effective for the rest of his lifetime. But when Ira reported on the minor sensation Commager had created in a Las Vegas club, they'd come alert to the fact that his developing psi abilities hadn't been permanently stunted. And then a majority of them had been afraid to attempt to kill a "natural."

Unconsciously, he'd resisted the next maneuver—drastic as it had been—to throw him into a delusive tizzy.

Then he'd begun to strike back at them.

It wasn't really surprising, he thought, that they'd become a little desperate. And they might have known of that dice game before Ira told them about it. Ira had been their means of contacting him directly.

As Jean had been the means of keeping the primary delusion reinforced and alive.

❈   ❈   ❈

"No luck, so far!" he told her, somewhat carefully. The momentary shock of recognition had faded, but some of the feeling he'd wasted on the delusion seemed to have transferred itself back to the model now! It didn't really surprise him, and it wasn't an unpleasant sensation; but, for a moment, at least, he didn't want it to show in his voice. "Did you get caught up on your sleep?"

It might have showed in his voice, because she moved away from him and leaned over the side of the boat, looking at the lines. "Uh-huh," she said casually. "I feel fine now. Better than I have in a long time, as a matter of fact."

Commager regarded her speculatively. The easy grace of her body confirmed what she said; the tensions were gone. He patted himself mentally on the back. Commager the Healer!

"Alan?"

"Yes?" he said.

"I'm leaving Ira." Her face flushed a little. "To be more exact about it, Ira's leaving me! For that MacDonald woman you met Sunday!"

Commager said softly that he'd be damned. His thoughts were racing as she went on, "He told me yesterday morning. It jolted my vanity, all right! But the funny thing is, you know, that as soon as I got over that, I found I actually didn't care. It was really a relief. Isn't that funny?"

He didn't think it was funny. It was a little too pat.

"For five years," she said, turning to face him, "I thought I loved that guy. And now I find I never did!" She shook her head. "I don't get it, Alan. How can anyone be so crazy?"

"What are you going to do?" he asked.

She stared at him for a moment, looking appealing, hurt and lovely. If he put his hand out to her now, she'd be in his arms.

"I'm going to Florida for a few months. Ira can settle it any way he wants to."

So that was the way it had been, Commager thought in astounded fury. He was the one they'd wanted to hold down, but it wasn't only his life they'd twisted and distorted to do it. They'd used Jean just as ruthlessly. And, perhaps, Ira—

For five years, he could have had his imaginary woman. She'd been within his reach in reality.

And, now that delusions were not working so well any more, they threw the reality at him!

Only now it was a little too late. He'd changed too far to be able to accept their gift.

"Jean," he said.

"Yes, Alan?"

"You're going to stop thinking for a while now," he told her gently. "You're going to just stand there for a while and not be aware of anything that happens."

A puzzled frown formed on her face as he started to speak, but it smoothed out again, and then she went on looking placidly at him. Perhaps her eyes had dulled a trifle.

This time, it didn't surprise Commager at all. Out beyond the Sweet Susan, he saw something like a faint haze beginning to shape itself over the moving surface of the water. He grinned a little.

Slowly and deliberately, he framed the cold thought in his mind: Do what you can for yourselves! The truce is over!

Their response was an instantaneous one. A long swell rose up behind the Sweet Susan, lifted the boat, passing beneath it, and dropped it again. The Sweet Susan was still rising as Commager picked up Jean Bohart and set her down beside the bench near the wheel; and it slapped down in a smash of spray as he cut the lashings of the wheel with the emergency knife and pulled out the throttle.

He glanced around. The haze was a thick fog about them, brilliant white against the blue of the sky overhead, while they ran through its wet, gray shade. The boat shuddered sideways behind the big swell, water roiling about it. Suddenly, with a kind of horror, Commager understood what was there.

He had seen pictures of it, or rather of a part of it, cast up on the coast years before: a house-sized chunk of rotten, oddly coarse-grained flesh, hurriedly disposed of and never identified. The drifted remnant of a nameless phenomenon of the Pacific deeps.

The phenomenon itself was underneath them now!

Still too far down to have done more than briefly convulse the surface as it turned, it was rising toward the boat. A thing of icy, incredible pressures, it was disrupted and dying as it rose, incapable of understanding the impulse that had forced it from the dark ocean up toward the coast hours before. But it was certain that, in the bright glare above it, it would find and destroy the cause of its pain.

So it came up with blind, hideous swiftness; and Commager discovered that rushing bulk could not be simply turned away from them as he had turned the rocks. It was driven by its own sick and terrible purpose. Neither could he reach the minds that guided it. This time, they were alertly on guard.

With seconds to spare then, he turned the boat.

In the fog to their left, the sea opened in a thundering series of crashes and settled again. Water smashed into the boat as it danced and drove raggedly away, and before it had gone very far it was lifted once more on a thrust of water from below.

The thing from the sea had followed, and it was terribly close! So close that the flickering dull glow of a mind as primitive as the monstrous body itself rose up in Commager's awareness.

He caught at it.

What he drove into the glow was like an insistence on its destruction. It seemed to blaze up in brief, white fury and then went black . . .

The Sweet Susan drove on through a curiously disturbed sea, surrounded by dissipating wisps of what might or might not have been an ordinary patch of fog. Probably, no one on any of the distant fishing boats even noticed that minor phenomenon.

A half-mile away, the water roiled once more; and that was all. The Pacific had gone back to its normal behavior.

11

It was sunset on the Bay, and Paylar was talking, at least most of the time. Sometimes Commager listened and sometimes he didn't.

It was a fairy-tale situation, he thought, somewhat amused at himself. Because he could feel the mood of it very strongly, a childlike one, a mood of enchantment around him and of terror along the fringes of the enchantment. Terror that was in part past, and in part still to come.

Far below the slope where they sat, sun-fires gleamed in the dark, moving waters, like fire shining out of the heart of a black jewel. Down there, as was not inappropriate near the end of a fairy tale, two of the bad ones lay dead and buried, unless one of them had been taken away by the water.

Much farther out, miles out, the body of a defeated dragon bumped slowly along the sea-bottom, back to the deeps, nibbled at, tugged at, pulled and turned by armies of hungry fish.

A blonde and beautiful princess was halfway to the far land of flowers called Florida by now, flying through the night skies, and released at last from an evil enchantment. She might still wonder at how oddly she'd acted the past few years, but she'd begun to look forward to new and exciting activities—and she was rapidly forgetting Alan Commager in the process.

It had been the only way to arrange it, because this was a trap of magic Jean had no business being in, and she'd been in it only because of him. He'd got himself the other one, the dark, beautiful, wicked witch, to keep company instead.

So Paylar talked of magical things, and he listened, pleasantly fascinated and willing for an hour to believe anything she told him. Earth turned under them, vast and ponderous, away from the Sun and into the night, a big, convincing stage background to what she was talking about.

All Earth life, she said, was a single entity, growing and developing from this great globe, and its conscious thinking processes went on mainly in that part of it that was human. Which was fine, she explained, while all humans were still Old Mind, as they had been at first, because they were aware of Earth and cared for it, knowing they were a part of it, and that it all belonged together. But then New Mind humans came along, as a natural development. They could think a little better than the others, but they were no longer aware of being a part of Earth life and didn't care about anything much but themselves, since they considered themselves to be individuals.

It didn't matter too much. They were still influenced by the purpose and patterns of Earth life, and had practically no conscious defenses against what seemed to them to be obscure motivations of their own. And there were always enough Old Mind people around who knew what was going on to direct the rather directionless New Minders patiently back to the old patterns, so that in the long run things tended to keep moving along much as they always had done.

It began to matter when New Minders developed a conscious interest in what was now called psi. That was an Earth life ability which had its purpose in keeping the patterns intact; and only the New Mind, which had intelligence without responsibility, was capable of using psi individualistically and destructively.

In most periods of time, the New Mind was kept from

investigating psi seriously by its superstitious dread of phenomena it couldn't rationalize. But when it did get interested—

In the Old Mind, adherence to the Earth life pattern was so complete that dangerous psi abilities simply didn't develop.

"So you see," she said, "we need New Mind psi to control New Mind psi."

Commager said he'd come to understand that finally. And also that they were able to keep control of the people they used by the fact that psi abilities tended to be as deadly to their possessor as to anyone else, when employed without careful restraint. "At best, I imagine there's a high turnover rate in the New Mind section of an organization like the Guides."

"There is," she agreed coolly. "Particularly since we select the ones that are potentially the most dangerous as recruits. The ones most hungry for power. Ruth, for example, is not likely to live out another year."

Privately and thoughtfully, Commager confirmed that opinion. "Doesn't that unusual mortality attract attention?" he inquired. It seemed a little tactless, but he added, "What about Hawkes and Barthold, for example? Aren't they going to be officially missed?"

"Hawkes was known to be nearly psychopathic," Paylar replied. "whatever happened to him will surprise no one officially. And no one but ourselves knew anything about Lex."

She had showed, Commager thought, an appalling indifference to the fate of her late companions. He studied her for a moment with interested distaste. "You know," he remarked then, "I don't feel any very strong urges for power myself. How does that fit in with your story?"

She shrugged. "A natural is always unpredictable. You have a blend of Old Mind and New Mind qualities, Alan, that might have made you extremely useful to us. But since you didn't choose to be useful, we can't take a chance on you."

He let that pass. "Where do people like you and Barthold come from?" he inquired curiously. "How did you get involved in this kind of thing?"

She herself came, she said, from a mountain village in northern Italy. Its name was as unimportant as her own. As for the role she was playing, in part she'd been instructed in it, and in part she'd known instinctively what she had to do. She smiled at him. "But none of that is going to concern you very much longer, Alan!"

She sounded unpleasantly certain about it. Although he thought he could foretell quite precisely what was going to happen tonight, Commager felt a little shaken. He suggested, "What would happen if people like myself were just left to do as they pleased?"

"Earth would go insane," she said calmly. The extravagance of the statement jolted him again, but he could see the analogue. The Old Mind was full of fears, too—the fear of chaos.

"That offer you made me to become one of the Guides—was that a trap, or was it meant sincerely?"

Her face abruptly became cautious and alert. "It was meant sincerely."

"How could you have trusted me?"

She said evasively, "There was a great deal you could have learned from us. You have discovered some of the things you can do by yourself, but you realize the dangers of uninstructed experimentation."

He looked at her, remembering the limitations of Old Mind and that, because of them, there couldn't be any real compromise. He didn't doubt they would have showed him what was safe to do and of use to them; but the only circumstances under which they really could trust him would be to have him so befuddled that he'd be almost completely dependent on their assistance and advice. So they would also have showed him things that were very much less than safe—for him.

He thought that Herbert Hawkes had followed that road almost to the end before he died, and that Ruth MacDonald was rather far advanced on it by now. Those two had been merely greedy and power-hungry people, utilizing talents which were more expensive than they'd been allowed to guess. Lex and Paylar had been the only leaders among the ones he'd met of that group.

He didn't bother to repeat his question; but Paylar said suddenly, "Why did you bring me out here this evening, Alan?"

"I thought I might find what was left of the Guides at Hawkes' place," Commager said. "I was a little annoyed, frankly, both because of something that happened today, and because of something that was done a while ago to somebody else. I was going to tell you to stop playing games around me and people I happen to like— or else!"

He grinned at her. "Of course, I realized you weren't going to risk a showdown right in the middle of town. It could get a little too spectacular. But since you were conveniently waiting alone there for me, I brought you out here."

"Supposing," Paylar said, "that we don't choose to accept a showdown here either?"

"Lady," he told her, "if it looks as if nothing is going to be settled, there are experiments I can start on with you that should have you yelling very quickly for help to any Guides remaining in the area. As I figure it, you see, a New Mind natural might be able to control an Old Mind expert very much as you intended to control me."

She went a little white. "That could be true. But you can't hope to survive a showdown, Alan!"

He spread his hands. "Why not? Logically, at least, I don't think there are very many of you left." He was almost certain he knew of one who hadn't openly played a part as yet, but he didn't intend to mention that name at the moment. "It wouldn't take more than a handful of developed New Mind psis to control an area like this. And you wouldn't want more than a handful around or you couldn't be sure of controlling them."

She nodded. "That's also true, of course. But you're still at a hopeless disadvantage, Alan. We—the Old Mind knows exactly how this situation can be resolved in our favor, if we're prepared to lose a few more of our controlled psis . . ."

"The psis mightn't feel quite so calm about it," Commager pointed out. He hesitated. "Though I suppose you might have them believing by now that I'm out to eat them!"

"They've been led to consider you a deadly threat to their existence," Paylar agreed with a touch of complacency. "They'll take any risk that's required, particular since they won't understand the full extent of the risk. And that isn't all, Alan. You're not the first New Mind natural we've dealt with, you know. If anything goes seriously wrong in this area, Old Mind all over the Earth will be aware of it."

He frowned doubtfully at her, because he'd been wondering about that. And then he let the thought come deliberately into the foreground of his consciousness that he would prefer to reach an agreement, if it could be done. The Guides' ability to grasp what was going on in his mind seemed to be a very hazy one; but in a moment, though Paylar's expression didn't change, he was certain she had picked up that intentional piece of information.

She said, with a slow smile, "How much do you remember of your parents, Alan?"

He stared at her in surprise. "Not very much. They both died when I was young. Why?"

She persisted, "Do you recall your mother at all?"

"No," he admitted warily. "She divorced my father about two years after I was born. I stayed with him and never saw her again. I understand she died about three years later."

"And your father?" she asked him insistently.

Commager gestured patiently toward the Bay. "My father drowned out there on a fishing trip when I was eleven. I remember him well enough, actually. Afterward I was raised by a guardian. Do you mind telling me what these questions are about?"

"Your father," she said, "was of the Old Mind, Alan. So he must have known what you might develop into almost since your birth."

Oddly enough, he found, he was immediately willing to accept that as valid information. "Why didn't he do something about his shocking little offspring?" he inquired.

"Apparently," Paylar said calmly, "he did. If he hadn't died, your special abilities might have been blocked away so completely that they would never have come to your attention—or brought you to our attention. As it was, what he did to check you was simply not sufficient."

Commager considered the possibility, and again it seemed that that was what had occurred. It was too long ago to arouse any particular emotion in him. He said absently, watching her, "What's all this supposed to prove, Paylar?"

"That we're not trying to control you out of malice. It seems as necessary to us now as it did to your father then."

He shrugged. "That makes no difference, you know. If more control is all you have to offer, I'm afraid we'll go right on disagreeing."

Paylar nodded. Then she just sat there, apparently unconcerned, apparently satisfied with what had been said and with things as they were, until Commager added suddenly, "I get the notion that you've just informed your little pals it's time for direct action. Correct?"

"Two of them are on their way here." She gave him her slight smile. "When they arrive, we'll see what occurs, Alan. Would you like me to show you some pictures meanwhile?"

"Pictures?" He stared at her and laughed. He was baffled and, for the moment, furious. He could, as she must realize and as he had once threatened to do, break her slim neck in one hand. The indications were that he could break her mind as easily if he exerted himself in that direction. But she seemed completely unconcerned about either possibility.

Her smile widened. "I caught that," she remarked. "You were really broadcasting, Alan! You won't try to hurt me—you're really incapable of it—unless you become very frightened. And you're almost sure you can handle all three of us anyway, so you're not yet afraid..."

And in that, for once, she might have given him more information than she knew. Because he had sensed there had been three of them involved, two actively and one as an observer, in the last two attempts against him. Paylar, he guessed, had been the observer—supervisor might be the better term.

If those three were the only Guides that remained active locally, she was quite right: he was convinced he could handle them. And if, as seemed likely, they were going to leave him no choice about it, he would.

What Old Mind elsewhere might think or do would be another matter then. He wasn't at all sure that he couldn't handle that problem also. Another piece of information Paylar had given him in the last minute or so was that sudden flares of emotion made him "legible" to those who had her own level of ability.

He would avoid such emotional outbursts in future.

"What kind of pictures did you intend to show me?" he inquired.

"You think I'm trying to trap you," she accused him.

"Aren't you?" Commager asked, surprised.

"Of course. But only by showing you what Earth-life really is like—while there is still time."

"Well," he said agreeably, "go ahead..."

So he sat there in the dark between sunset and moonrise and watched pictures, though that wasn't quite what they were. At first, it seemed as if time were flowing around him; the Moon would be overhead briefly and gone again, while the planes of the ground nearby shifted and changed. That, he thought, was to get him used to the process, condition him a little. The trickeries would come next.

But when they came, they weren't really trickery. He was simply, Commager decided, being shown life as Old Mind knew it and as, in a way, it was; though he himself had never thought to take quite so dramatic and vivid a view of it. Laughing and crying, thundering and singing, Earth life drifted past in terrors and delights, flows of brightness and piercing sound and of blackest silence and night.

At last, through all that tumult of light and fragrance and emotion, he began to grow aware of what to Old Mind, at least, was primarily there: the driving, powerful, unconscious but tremendous purpose. Earth dying and living, near-eternal . . .

In his mind, he found himself agreeing that it was a true picture of life and a good one.

He was a traitor to that life, Old Mind whispered to him. Earth needed him and had created him to help hold back the night and the cold forever! But the tiny, individual selfishness of the New Mind broke away from the flow of life and denied it.

So, in the end, all would die together—

The flow slowed. Into it crept the cold and the dark—a chill awareness of the approaching frozen and meaningless immobility of chaos.

It wasn't till then that Commager reached out carefully and altered the pictures a trifle. It had been a good show, he thought, though overly dramatic; and Paylar had timed the paralyzing emergence of chaos very nicely. The two for whom he'd been waiting had just reached the turnoff from the highway.

12

The headlights of the car glided swiftly down the Bay Road, as he brought his awareness back hurriedly to his immediate surroundings to check on the physical condition of his companion. She sat upright a few feet away from him, her legs crossed under her, her hands dropped laxly into her lap, while the black animal eyes stared in blind horror at the frozen picture of chaos.

She would keep, he decided. And he wasn't really worried about the other two . . . Ira Bohart and Ruth MacDonald.

He reached out for them, and as they flashed savagely back at him, he drew away, out of time, into the space that was open to New Mind only, where they would have to follow if they wanted to touch him.

They followed instantly, with a furious lust for destruction which wasn't unexpected but which shocked him nevertheless. They came like daggers of thought, completely reckless, and if they succeeded in touching him in the same way he had touched the sea-thing, the struggle would be over in an instant.

It became obvious immediately that he could prevent them from doing it, which—since he was a stronger, more fully developed specimen of their own class—was only to be expected. What concerned him was their utter lack of consideration for their own survival. The car they were in hadn't stopped moving; in less than half a minute now it would be approaching the sharp curve above the Bay.

He had counted on the driver's attention being forced away from him momentarily, either to stop the car or to manipulate it safely around the curve; in that instant, he would bring the other one under his control as completely as he had trapped Paylar, and he would then be free to deal at his leisure with the driver.

Individually, any one of the Guides was weaker than a New Mind natural; it had looked as simple as that. He wanted to save what was left of the group, to operate through them very much as Old Mind had been doing, but with a very different purpose.

The two who attacked should be withdrawing by now, dismayed at not having found him paralyzed by Paylar's "pictures," as they must have expected. They might be waiting for her to come to their assistance in some other manner, not knowing that she was no longer even aware of the struggle. However, within seconds the need of controlling the car would become urgent enough to settle the issue—

In an instant, he felt himself drawn down, blinded and smothered, in the grasp of a completely new antagonist! It was not so much the awareness of power immensely beyond that of the Guides that stunned him; it was a certainty that this new contact was a basically horrible and intolerable thing. In the fractional moment of time that everything in him was straining simply to escape from it, the New Minders drove through their attack.

Pain was exploding everywhere through his being, as he wrenched himself free. Death had moved suddenly very close! Because the third opponent wasn't Paylar, never had been Paylar. He had miscalculated—and so there had been one he'd overlooked.

Now they had met, he knew he wasn't capable of handling this third opponent and the two New Minders together.

Then without warning the New Minders vanished out of his awareness, like twin gleams of light switched off. Seconds later, from somewhere far out on the edge of his consciousness, as if someone else were thinking it, the explanation came: The car! They weren't able to stop the car!

With that, the last of them drove at him again; and for a moment he was swept down into its surging emotions, into a black wave of rage and terror, heavy and clinging. But he was not unprepared for it now, and he struck at the center of its life with deadly purpose, his own terrors driving him. Something like a long, thin screaming rose in his mind . . .

In that moment, complete understanding came.

As in a dream scene, he was looking down into the yard of the Temple of Antique Christianity. It was night-time now; and on the dais he'd investigated the day before, a bulky, shapeless figure twisted and shook under a robelike cloth which covered it completely.

The screaming ended abruptly, and the shape lay still.

13

Commager sat up dizzily. He discovered first that he was incredibly drenched with sweat, and that Paylar still sat in an unchanged position, as she stared at the thing he'd set before her mind to fix her attention. Down on the Bay Road, there was a faint shouting.

He stood up shakily and walked forward till he could look down to the point where the road curved sharply to the left to parallel the Bay. The shouting had come from there. A few people were moving about, two of them with flashlights. Intermittently, in their beams, he could see the white, smashed guard railings.

A brief, violent shuddering overcame him, and he went back to where Paylar sat, trying to organize his thoughts. The reason for her confident expectance of his defeat was obvious now.

The unsuspected opponent—the gross shape that had kicked about and died on the dais, the woman he'd known as Mrs. Lovelock—had been another New Mind natural. Or, rather, what had become of a New Mind natural after what probably had been decades of Old Mind control. But that part wasn't the worst of it.

I met her and talked to her! he thought in a flash of grief and horror. But I couldn't guess—

He drove the thought from his mind. If he wanted to go on

living—and he realized with a flicker almost of surprise that he very much did—he had other work to complete tonight. A kind of work that he'd considered in advance as carefully as the rest of it—

And this time, he thought grimly, he'd better not discover later that he'd miscalculated any details.

He sat down and rolled over on his side in the exact place and position in which he'd been lying before. Almost the last thing he saw was the sudden jerky motion of Paylar's body, as he dissolved the visual fixation he'd caught her attention in. Then, as she turned her head quickly to look at him, he closed his eyes.

When Commager's mind resumed conscious control of his body, there was a cloudy sky overhead and a cool gray wetness in the air. Paylar stood nearby, looking thoughtfully down at him. He looked back at her without speaking. The terrifying conviction of final failure settled slowly and dismally on him.

"You can wake up fully now," she told him. "It's nearly morning."

He nodded and sat up.

"What I shall tell you," her voice went on, "are things you will comprehend and know to be true. But consciously you will forget them again as soon as I tell you to forget. You understand?"

Commager nodded again.

"Very well," she said. "Somewhere inside you something is listening to what I am saying; and I'm really speaking now to that part of you—inside. Here and tonight, Alan, you very nearly won, though of course you could not have won in the final issue. But you must understand now, consciously and unconsciously, that you have been completely defeated! Otherwise, you would not stop struggling until you had destroyed yourself—as thoroughly as another one very like yourself, whom you met tonight, did years ago!"

She paused. "You know, of course, that the New Mind natural you killed tonight was your mother. We counted on the shock of that discovery to paralyze you emotionally, if all else failed. When it happened, for the few seconds during which the shock was completely effective, I was released by others of the Old Mind from the trap in which you had caught me."

She smiled. "That was a clever trap, Alan! Though if it hadn't been so clever, we might not have needed to sacrifice your mother. In those few seconds, you see, I planted a single, simple compulsion into your mind—that when you pretended afterward to become unconscious—as it appeared you were planning to do to deceive the Old Mind—your consciousness actually would blank out."

He tried to remember. Something like that had occurred. He had intended to act as if the struggle with the New Minders had exhausted him to the point where it was possible for Paylar to take him under complete control, since only in that way could he be safe from continuing Old Mind hostility. But then—

He had no awareness of what had happened in the hours that followed till now.

"You see?" Paylar nodded. There was a trace of compassion, almost of regret, in her expression. "Believe me, Alan, never in our knowledge has a functioning human mind been so completely trapped as you are now. I have been working steadily on you for the past six hours, and even now it would be impossible for you to detect the manner in which you are limited. But within minutes, you will simply forget the fact that any limitations have been imposed on you, and so you will remain free of the internal conflicts that destroyed your mother."

She paused. "And here is a final proof for you, Alan, of why this was necessary for us. You recalled that your father drowned in this Bay when you were a child. But as yet you seem to have blocked out of your memory the exact manner in which he died—"

Her voice changed, grew cold and impersonal. "Let that memory come up now, Alan!"

The memory came. With it came memory of the shocking conflict of emotion that had caused him to bury the events of that day long ago. But it aroused no emotional response in him now. It had been a member of an alien, hostile species he had compelled to thrust itself down into the water, until the air exploded from its lungs and it sank away and drowned . . . of the same hostile species as the one talking to him now.

"Yes," she said. "You drowned him, Alan, when you first became aware of the mental controls he had imposed on you. And then you forced yourself to forget, because your human conditioning made the memory intolerable. But you aren't truly human, you see. You are an evolutionary mistake that might destroy the life of all Earth if left unchecked!"

She concluded, "It has taken all these years to trap you again, under conditions that would permit us to impose controls that no living mind, even in theory, could break. But the efforts and the risks have been well worthwhile to Old Mind. For, you see, we can use your abilities now to make sure there will be no trouble from others of your kind for many years to come. And we can, as the need arises, direct you to condition others of your kind exactly as you have been conditioned . . . But now"—a flat, impersonal command drove at him again through her voice—"forget what I have told you! All of it!"

And, consciously, the mind of Commager forgot.

He had done, he thought, as he watched his body stand up and follow the woman up the path to his cabin, a superbly complete job of it.

What identity might be remained an intriguing problem for future research, though perhaps not one that he himself would solve. For practical purposes, at any rate, the identity of Alan Commager was no longer absorbed by the consciousness that rose from and operated through his brain and body.

And that was the only kind of consciousness Old Mind knew about. He was hidden from Paylar's species now because he had gone, and would remain permanently, beyond the limits of their understanding.

He directed an order to the body's mind, and the body stumbled obediently, not knowing why it had stumbled. Paylar turned and caught its arm, almost solicitously, steadying it.

"You'll feel all right again after a few hours rest, Alan," she told it soothingly.

Species as alien almost as a cat or a slender, pretty monkey, but with talents and purposes of her own, Paylar was, he thought, an excellent specimen of the second highest development of Earth evolution.

He reached very carefully now through the controls he had imposed on her consciousness to the core of her being, and explained gently to her what he had done.

For a few seconds, he encountered terror and resistance, but resignation came then, and finally understanding and a kind of contentment.

She would help him faithfully against Old Mind now, though she would never be aware of doing it.

And that, he thought, was really all for the moment. The next step, the development of New Mind psi in others, was an unhurried, long-term project. In all the area within his range, Old Mind control had stifled or distorted whatever promise originally had been present.

But the abilities were ever-recurring. And here and there, as he became aware of them now, their possessors would be contacted, carefully instructed and shielded against Old Mind spies. Until they had developed sufficiently to take care of themselves and of others. Until there were enough of them.

Enough to step into the role for which they had been evolved—and which the lower mind had been utterly unable to comprehend. To act as the matured new consciousness of the giant Earth life organism.

Spacemaster

THE DREAM was receding.

Haddan knew it was receding because he had insisted to himself it was a dream, a very vivid experience but untrue—a delusion which he should not attempt to retain. And he was forgetting the dream now as he woke up. There was a final memory of rainswept greenery, long peals of thunder and then, at the very end, the sound of Auris weeping wildly nearby. For a moment, Haddan hesitated, wanting to return to her. But she was part of the delusion. . . .

He came awake.

He was sitting alone in a room, at a table which projected like a wide shelf out of the blank wall before him. The wall was of some faintly gleaming material and in it Haddan could see his own dim reflection.

His mind seemed to recoil for an instant at that point, unwilling to acknowledge the bitter reality of being on the Spacemaster ship, of having become again a prisoner of the cynical overlords and debasers of mankind. And Auris and the others with him—detected in the act of violating the basic Spacemaster law.

He should find out soon enough what the penalty was for that. It seemed very improbable that he had simply fallen asleep and escaped into dreams immediately after the capture; he must have been drugged. And now Spacemaster had brought him awake. They intended to question him, of course. He had identified himself as the leader of the group, the man responsible for the construction of the spaceship which had secretly left the City of Liot two years before. It was the truth, and his statement might make things easier for the others.

But why was he sitting here alone? Was he being watched? The table on which his hands rested was bare and of the same material as the wall, satiny to the touch. Aside from the table and his chair, the room was unfurnished. Behind him, perhaps twenty feet away, was another blank wall. To right and left, at approximately the same distance where the walls began to curve smoothly towards each other, the space between ceiling and floor was filled by curtains of curling haze through which light and color moved in restless ripples. The stuff looked almost completely insubstantial, but Haddan realized he could not see into it. In spite of its lack of furnishing, the room gave the impression of cool elegance. And it was silent. There was not a whisper of sound except his own breathing.

They might be testing him, his nerve, his reactions. But he was gaining nothing by continuing to sit here.

Haddan attempted to shift the chair back and found it immovable, attempted to get out of it and instantly felt his body grow impossibly heavy. Some trick of gravity . . . they intended him to stay where he was. He settled back into the chair, felt his normal weight gradually return.

Perhaps two minutes later, a wave of light came gliding through the section of wall before him, suddenly enough to be startling. Then the wall vanished at that point. The table at which Haddan sat now extended on without visible support beyond the partition, a flat, square slab of dull-gleaming grey material, at the other side of which, with his eyes on Haddan, sat a man in a green and red uniform.

Haddan looked back without speaking. In his lifetime he had seen only a few dozen members of Spacemaster—all the others in the City of Liot, and most of those on various occasions before he became an adult. They showed a pronounced racial similarity: stocky, strong figures and broad, heavy-boned faces with slightly tilted grey eyes. This one, whose name was Vinence, had asked Haddan a half-dozen questions in an emotionless voice when they had been taken aboard the capturing Spacemaster vessel. What happened afterwards Haddan did not remember clearly, but it seemed to him now that it couldn't have been many more minutes before he had fallen asleep. Nor could he remember what the questions had been or how he had answered them. There was no reason to doubt that the Spacemaster had used some drug on him.

Vinence appeared in no hurry to speak at the moment. He continued to study Haddan thoughtfully. Haddan let his gaze shift about the other section of the partly divided big room. It was almost a mirror image of this one; but the wall on the far side was lined from floor to ceiling with what night have been individual cabinets, and the table section before the Spacemaster was covered with rows of small colored geometrical figures.

Vinence's flat voice asked suddenly, "What did you dream about, Haddan?"

That might not be as pointless a question as it seemed—and there was no immediate reason to be too truthful. Haddan shook his head. "I don't remember any dreams."

"I think you lie," Vinence told him after a pause, but almost as if he didn't care greatly whether Haddan was lying or not. The grey eyes retained their look of cool speculation. "There were certain records on your ship," he went on, "which you destroyed with other material when we paralyzed the drive and halted the ship. Those records—I refer now to the ones dealing with the sins of Spacemaster— have since been restored. I found them interesting reading."

Haddan felt the blood drain slowly from his face. To have been caught while escaping from Spacemaster bondage might be one thing. To have planned, as he and Auris had, to provide proof of the evil Spacemaster was for human beings wherever they could be found, and to work towards Spacemaster's destruction—perhaps not in their own lifetimes or even in the next century or two, but in time—that was quite another. He did not know whether Spacemaster actually was capable of restoring material objects which had been recently destroyed; but it seemed at least possible. They knew many things they had kept their subject cities from learning. Vinence might also have gained the knowledge of the records from Auris or himself while they were drugged. It would come, Haddan thought, to much the same thing in the end.

He said nothing. He watched Vinence's tanned hand move just above the table on his right and saw a rectangle of pale light appear in the surface of the table with the motion. Vinence's eyes shifted to the lighted area and remained there for some seconds. Haddan gained the impression that the Spacemaster was reading. Then Vinence looked back at him.

"Do you happen to know," Vinence asked, "when the City of Liot was built and stationed in orbit around the Liot Sun?"

"No," Haddan said. "There were no records of that period available."

Vinence said, "The records should still be in the city, though they would be difficult to find by now. Liot was built almost three thousand years ago. It was partly destroyed a number of times in inter-city wars, but the structure remains essentially intact today . . . one of the largest cities ever to be set into space."

Liot's inhabitants, Haddan thought, had not done as well with the passing of time as their city. And for that Spacemaster must be charged.

"The treaty between Spacemaster and the Eighty-two Cities," Vinence continued, almost as if he had caught the thought, "has been in effect a little less than four centuries. Under its terms the cities engaged themselves not to build space vessels either for war or peace, and to destroy the ones they had. Spacemaster in turn assumed the responsibility of providing means of transit and trade among the cities and elsewhere as required."

"I've seen a copy of the treaty," Haddan said drily. "It didn't look like one of the cities would have signed too willingly."

Vinence nodded. "Spacemaster encountered very considerable opposition to the terms during the first few decades. Nevertheless, the terms were enforced, and opposition eventually died away. But not entirely. From time to time during the next generations some group or other would attempt to regain the means of independent space travel, either openly or furtively. The necessary measures would then be taken, and the attempt would subside.

"Of late, matters have been very quiet. Prior to the current case—yours—it had been nearly a hundred and fifty years since the construction of spacecraft was last initiated in the City of Liot. On that occasion it was also a secret action and was partly successful. One small ship was completed and was launched unobserved from the city, carrying two members of the conspiracy. They had old star charts in their possession which were to guide them to the one world in this section of our galaxy reported to have natural conditions suitable for human life without the elaborate precautions of doming. Human settlers were, in fact, supposed to have lived there in that manner during one period of the distant past.

"In spite of their lack of experience, the two travelers succeeded in reaching their goal. They returned to the City of Liot several years later with the word that there was such a planet and that human beings still existed on it, though their number was small and they had retrogressed to a condition of almost unbelievably primitive savagery.

"The conspirators . . . several hundred in number . . . now hurried through their plans to complete the construction of a ship large enough to carry them and the equipment they would need to establish the nucleus of a new human civilization on this world. In that, they did not succeed. Spacemaster got wind of the affair, and the group committed mass suicide by barricading itself in a deserted building complex in Liot and detonating a bomb which disintegrated the complex. It was falsely assumed at the time that the ship they had been building and the material they had accumulated was destroyed with them. The ship and the other items actually were sealed away in another section of the city and remained undiscovered until a few years ago.

"Which brings us to you, Haddan. . . . The manner in which you became aware of the existence of this ship and of its original purpose is not important at the moment. You did learn of these things. You banded together with other malcontents, secretly finished the construction of the ship and eventually set forth on the voyage your predecessors failed to make. And you were apprehended two years later in the process of preparing for planetfall. . . ."

Vinence paused, glanced again at the glowing rectangle in the table surface and waved his hand across it. As the light faded out, he went on, "That, I believe, is essentially the picture presented by this case. Do you agree?" His voice and expression were still impassive.

Haddan remained silent for some seconds. There was a thickness of rage in his throat which would have made it almost impossible for him to speak. In its factual details, Vinence's account of what had occurred was correct. But it was very far from complete. And it was the Spacemaster's cynical omission of the circumstances which had driven two groups of people a century and a half apart to make the same desperate effort to escape from Liot that seemed appalling. Vinence and his kind were fully aware of what had been done to the cities. It had been a deliberate, completely planned thing. Long ago, Spacemaster must have suspected a competitor for power in Liot and her sister giants in this area of space. It had isolated them from one another first, then proceeded to break them down individually. In Liot, Spacemaster had assumed control step by step, over the decades, of all the great city's functions. In Haddan's lifetime, the process had long been completed. Only Spacemaster had any understanding now even of the vast machine complexes which powered and sustained Liot; and only it retained access to the city sections where the machinery was housed. When one began to look about and check, as Haddan had done, it became clear that not even the shadow of self-government had been left.

But that was not the real crime. The crime had been committed in a much more immediate manner against the city's inhabitants . . . but so quietly that it became noticeable only when one obtained, as Haddan again had done, an understanding of the differences between the population now and that of five or six generations ago—

He told Vinence, his voice held carefully even, "I can't agree that you've presented the significant part of the picture."

"No?" Variance said. "You believe that the emphasis should be placed on Spacemaster's misdeeds?"

Haddan looked at him, feeling the thickening in his throat again and his hands hungry to close on the throat of the unreachable man across the table. Misdeeds! When in a city, which could be calculated to have been built to contain fifteen million people, twenty thousand remained—twenty thousand at the most; more accurate figures were simply no longer available. And when the life-span average in Liot now did not appear to be even eighteen years. . . . When three out of four of the lingering descendants of the city's builders slouched past with slack-jawed, foolish faces and empty eyes—

Of what specific "misdeed" had Spacemaster been guilty there? He hadn't been able to find out; and neither—much better informed in such matters than Haddan—had Auris. They had wanted to know, to complete the record of humanity's case against Spacemaster. But too few others had been capable of giving any assistance. Whole fields of knowledge had faded from men's minds; and, in any event, that one area of knowledge might always have been Spacemaster's secret. There had not been enough time to make sure. But the condition of the people of Liot showed in itself that an enormity of some kind had been practiced on them, and Haddan and Auris had corroborating evidence for that.

Vinence's voice reached Haddan again. "I was referring to the fact that the restored records contain a number of interesting speculations about Spacemaster and its activities. These records were, I believe, compiled by yourself?"

Haddan nodded. "They were."

"They were designed to be brought eventually to the attention of galactic humanity?"

Haddan hesitated, said, "Yes, that was their purpose."

The tilted cool eyes considered him for a moment. "I should like," Vinence said slowly, "to hear by what reasoning you arrived at your conclusions. I might say that nothing you tell me now could affect in any way the measures that will be taken in regard to yourself and your companions. That is a settled thing." He paused, shrugged, added almost casually. "Some of you will lose all memory of the past. The others will live out the rest of their lives without ever quite awakening again from a not too unpleasant dream. We are not inhumane, you see. We simply do what is necessary. As these measures are."

Haddan stared at him helplessly. He felt cold. He had expected death for himself, though perhaps not for the others. He had, after all, been the ringleader. Without him, none of them would have left Liot. He had tried not to think of Auris.

But this was Spacemaster's way. Not outright death, but the slow quenching of the mind, the slow decay of the body. As they had done, in a somewhat different manner, in Liot.

"You must," Vinence said, "have made certain observations. Or perhaps Dr. Auris. . . ."

Haddan, suddenly, found himself speaking. The words came out quietly, icily, though there was fury behind them. It was, of course, quite pointless. Vinence knew what had happened, and he was not a man to be ruffled by a victim's accusations. But there was some satisfaction still in letting him know that Spacemaster had not been as successful as it believed in concealing the fact that it was engaged in systematic genetic destruction.

Some came to suspect it, though by that time there was very little they could do—except to avoid for themselves such obvious traps as the marvelous automatic medical centers Spacemaster began to install throughout the city—

Vinence interrupted almost irritably. "Nearly two hundred years ago the number of capable human physicians in Liot dropped to the point where those installations became necessary, Haddan. It was only one of the many steps taken during the period of the treaty to maintain life in the cities as well as was possible."

Only one of the many steps, no doubt, Haddan agreed. But hardly with the purpose of maintaining life. Accurate records must have been difficult to find in Liot even then, but there was some reason to speculate whether it mightn't be often the strongest and most intelligent who were reported to have succumbed in the Spacemaster centers. . . .

"You think they were killed there?" Vinence said.

"Or removed from the city."

"To further weaken the strain . . . yes, I see." Vinence spoke thoughtfully, as if this were a possibility he had considered for the first time. "How did you learn about things which happened so long ago, Haddan?"

"From a message left by one of the original designers of the ship we used," Haddan said.

"You discovered this message in what way?"

Haddan said, "Not by accident. The man committed suicide with the others so that Spacemaster would not learn that the ship hadn't been destroyed. I'm his lineal descendant. He arranged to make the information about the ship available again, provided the message eventually came into the hands of somebody who could understand it. The supposition was that such a person would then also be capable of acting on the information."

"The message was coded?"

"Of course."

"I find it curious," Vinence said, "that you didn't come to our attention before this."

Haddan shrugged. "My more immediate ancestors have followed the family tradition of staying out of your medical centers. I assume that's why the strain continued as long as it did. I've also observed that tradition . . . and the other one of not applying for passage out of Liot on a Spacemaster ship."

"You feel that's another of our traps?"

"I've discovered no evidence," Haddan said, "that anyone who met the physical requirements for space flight and was accepted for passage later returned to Liot."

"I see. It appears that you were remarkably busy in a number of areas during the years before you left the city. And I suppose you formed an acquaintance with Dr. Auris in order to confirm your ancestor's suspicions about procedures in our medical centers?"

Haddan had hoped to keep Spacemaster's interest away from Auris, but the records revealed very clearly the role she had played. He said, "Yes, I obtained some additional information in that manner."

Vinence nodded. "She is another unusual member of your generation," he said. "She applied for medical training while still almost a child—the first volunteer to appear in the centers for that purpose in a decade. She wanted to help the city . . . but you know about that. She was given instruction—"

"Carefully limited instruction," Haddan said.

"Yes, carefully limited. We were making a study of Dr. Auris. It seems that on your instigation she began to study us as well. When she disappeared, it was assumed she had died somewhere in the city. Haddan, you accuse us of the genetic destruction of the space civilization of the Eighty-two Cities. What benefit do you think Spacemaster derived from the act?"

It was a question Haddan had often asked himself, and he believed he knew the answer. But there was an undefinable vague uneasiness in his mind now when he said, "The cities were threatening to dispute that space mastery of yours. At the time they were forced to accept your treaty terms, they may not have been too far away from being your equals. But you still had certain technological advantages, so you broke them first. Then, not feeling strong enough to control them indefinitely simply by forbidding them to practice space flight, you decided on a program of deliberate, gradual extermination."

"And why," Vinence asked, "select that slow, almost interminable method? The effortless solution to such a problem would have been to open the cities to space."

"It would not have been a safe solution for Spacemaster," Haddan said, "if galactic mankind learned of the outrage." He hesitated, the sense of uneasiness stronger. For a moment, he seemed on the verge of recalling some very disturbing thing he had known once and forgotten about, and he felt sweat suddenly in the palms of his hands. Then those sensations faded. Vinence was still watching him, expression unchanged; and Haddan continued uncertainly, "You preferred to murder the cities in a manner which might, if necessary, be attributed to a natural process . . . something for which you could not be held responsible. You . . ."

He did not see Vinence move, but with that he was suddenly plunged into complete darkness. The Spacemaster and everything else had vanished. Haddan attempted automatically to surge up out of his chair but felt intolerable heaviness dragging him back. He waited, breathing with difficulty as the heaviness eased off again, for what would happen next.

Vinence spoke then, the voice coming now out of the dark above Haddan perhaps twenty feet off and a little to his right.

"The ship is moving, Haddan. We're returning to the planet at which you were intercepted—"

And abruptly there was light.

Not the light which previously had been in the room, but the rich, bright glow of a living world swimming under its sun. All the walls of the double room, the floor and ceiling, seemed to form a single continuous window through which the brightness poured. Haddan couldn't see Vinence, but there was a blurred, greyish area up towards the right which might be an energy block behind which the Spacemaster sat. And this, Haddan thought, could very well be—it hadn't occurred to him before—the control room of the ship.

The ship was stationary in atmosphere, well down. They must have been just off the planet to have arrived here in that nearly instantaneous manner, but the maneuver was still one which would have been flatly impossible to the space vessel so painstakingly completed in Liot. Haddan could make out forested hills below, lush dark-green rises about which three broad rivers curved, rain clouds scudding above them. Far to the left was the hazy expanse of a sea. The area seemed to be in the tropical zone, very similar in appearance to the one where he and Auris had come down in a small boat to decide where their ship should land. As it had done then, the scene brought a sudden, almost unbearable hunger to Haddan's throat, a sense of homecoming which, for an instant, drove out everything else.

"Rather different from the parks of the City of Liot," Vinence's voice commented. "More so than you knew, Haddan. Our tests of those you had on board show that the majority would not have lived long on an undomed world. You and Dr. Auris are fortunate in that respect. Many of the others are fortunate that Spacemaster found them before they could be seriously attacked by the infections you brought back to the ship with you. . . ."

Not so fortunate, Haddan thought; otherwise the statement might be true. It was one of the incalculable risks everyone in the group had taken knowingly and willingly. They had not been able to foretell either, what the impact of spaceflight on genetically weakened bodies might be; and nine men and four women of the eighty-five who left Liot died during the first quarter of the two-year voyage. And the irony was that they had taken such chances not knowing that Spacemaster regarded the world towards which they were fleeing as another of its possessions. If they had been able to land, and enough survived, it was still unlikely they would have escaped detection long enough to even begin to carry out their further plans.

"And now we shall look through the instruments at what might have been your new neighbors here," Vinence's voice went on. "An exceptionally large troop remains as a rule in this immediate area. . . . Yes, down at the bend in the northern river. . . . You see the cluster of golden sparks above the trees, Haddan? Its density indicates the presence of the troop, each spark representing one living human being."

Haddan's glance moved up the largest of the rivers, stopped at a firefly pattern of tiny, brilliant lights in the air on both sides of one of the bends. They would be invisible of course to the naked eye—a convenient method for Spacemaster to keep check on the scattered inhabitants of this planet and, if desired, even to conduct a head count. No, Haddan thought, he and the others from Liot couldn't have remained undiscovered here long.

The fireflies vanished; then the scene outside the ship darkened suddenly, becoming a blur of green and gold. As the blur cleared, Haddan saw that the devices Vinence was operating had produced a close-up view of the area of the river bend at ground level, and of fifty or sixty of the human "troop." It was a convincing illusion— he might have been sitting among them—and more than a view. His ears recorded babble of shrill calls from a group of children at the edge of the water; two women were shouting back and forth across the river. After a few seconds, Haddan realized there were also tactile sensations . . . a sense of warmth, of moving air; and, very faintly, odors of vegetation and water.

His gaze shifted about the group. They were not, he thought, remarkably handsome people, though there was a great deal of individual variance in that. All—even the bathing children—looked dirty; almost all were naked. They appeared to be chiefly engaged in grubbing around in reeds and thickets for edible substances, vegetable and animal. Only a few of the faces nearest him gave the impression of calculating intelligence. But there was, with very few exceptions, an air of alertness and robust energy about them which no group of corresponding size in Liot would have suggested. And the number of both grizzled oldsters and small children was startling. There had been *no* healthy old people in Liot.

It was a group which could have been retaught many things long forgotten here, Haddan thought, and which should have learned them quickly. The plan had not been a hopeless one in that respect; the possibility of developing a new civilization on this world had existed. And that made it the more strange that no civilization did exist here, that the descendants of the old-time settlers had regressed instead to this manner of living . . . almost exactly, except for the dexterous use of pieces of wood and rock in their varied pursuit of meals, the manner of a troop of animals. Vinence might have used the term contemptuously; but it was a correct one.

Spacemaster's work again? It very easily might be, Haddan decided, and it probably was. Why else should there be so *few* of these people on a world which obviously could have supported a far denser human population—even one which had lost every scrap of technological understanding. Yes, Spacemaster, almost certainly. A somewhat different form of degradation here, perhaps brought about for an entirely different purpose. But it had been done deliberately—

"Galactic humanity," Vinence's voice said from above him. "You're looking at a part of it here, you know, Haddan! As large a part, as a matter of fact, as you're likely to find in any one place on this world . . . and studying them at close range now, do you think Spacemaster would be really concerned about anything you could tell these people? It might be interesting to watch you trying to describe the City of Liot to them in the vocabulary of grunts which their use of speech amounts to.

"But, of course, you knew that. You understood it would take generations to bring about any significant change here, and that you and your companions could only begin the process. But this is one small, badly stunted twig on the great tree of mankind. You were planning to get word to the others. The number of them alone would make them unconquerable now. Only fourteen thousand years ago, they were still confined to a single planet not very different from this one. But then they drove out into the galaxy, established great civilizations on a thousand new worlds, scattered the self-sustaining giant cities through space. . . . *That's* the humanity Spacemaster would have to fear, isn't it, if it learned what we did to the Eighty-two Cities?"

"Or," Haddan said, "if it learned what you've done to this world! That alone would damn you—and in the end it will. You won't escape mankind's judgment for ever."

There was silence for some seconds, even the muted sounds of human activity at the river dwindling into nothing. Then Vinence spoke again.

"There's a very curious fact here, Haddan. You—and you're far from unique in it—have hypnotized yourself into believing certain facts about Spacemaster. By doing it, you were able to ignore another possible explanation for the way things have gone in Liot, though there are indications that it has never been very far from your awareness. Perhaps one can't blame you for the continuous self-deception, but it must end now. And I think that essentially you do want to know the true reason for what will be done with you and your friends."

The words seemed to just miss making sense. A queer, sharp surge of panic began to arise in Haddan. He heard himself blurt out thickly, "What are you talking about?"

There was no answer. Instead, complete darkness closed about him again. Haddan waited, his thoughts whirling, shifting drunkenly as if in shock. What *had* Vinence just said? He seemed unable to remember it clearly. What self-deception?

He realized that Vinence was speaking again.

"It took two years to cover the distance between Liot and the world we just left," the voice said. "But we are not called Spacemaster for nothing, so don't be too surprised now. What you will see is as real as it appears."

The thick darkness was lifting from the double room as he spoke, and through the surrounding endless window of walls and ceiling and floor the stars of space shone in. On Haddan's left was the harsh yellow-white glare of a nearby sun; and dead ahead, reflecting the glare like a blazing jewel, were the faceted walls of Liot. He recognized the city instantly, though he had seen this outside view before only in the instant after a long unused small lock opened to let out their ship. Then the drive immediately had hurled them away from the Liot Sun with almost the speed of light.

The city blurred now, reshaped itself, closer. The Spacemaster ship was gliding in towards a huge opened entry lock. Another blur, and it hung in the lock's mouth.

"What do you see, Haddan?"

He stared down the brilliantly lit, starkly empty lock. At the far end, a mile away, was another vast, gaping circle. Beyond it, more light. . . .

The thought came suddenly, numbing as death:

"The city is empty!"

Haddan didn't know he had said it. But he heard Vinence reply.

"Yes, empty . . . open to space. Liot was the last of the Eighty-two. It's been lifeless for nearly a year. And now"—the voice was flat and expressionless again—"we'll go to the worlds and cities of the galactic mankind on which you based your hopes. I think you've begun to understand consciously what we will find there."

And, in that instant, he had.

✸   ✸   ✸

Perhaps only hours later, Haddan stood at a window of a great globular structure floating less than half a mile above the surface of a world called Clell. A sense of heavy, almost paralyzing physical shock hadn't yet drained completely from his body. But his thoughts were clear again.

He had seen the dead worlds, the dead space cities of galactic mankind—enough of them; too many. Clell still lived, in a fashion. The glassy roofs of the flat, wide buildings stretching towards the horizon across the pleasant plain below Haddan sheltered eighty thousand human beings . . . the greater part of what was left of the proud species of Man. Clell was the next to last world he would see, and the last he would see while he still retained the knowledge of who and what he was.

Spacemaster's plans for his personal future in themselves were not distressing. They would take away his memories, but he would be living on the green world far away from Clell where there was thunder and rain, perhaps as a member of the band he had watched on the river's banks—not the most handsome of people on the whole, and somewhat soiled, but not unhappy. In Vinence's phrasing, he would have become a neoprimitive, one tiny, temporary, individual factor in Spacemaster's gigantic, centuries-spanning plan to obtain survival for the human race. And Auris would be there, though Haddan wouldn't be able to remember her, or she him. He recalled his feelings when he had looked down on that world and during the few hours he walked about on it, and he knew the other Haddan would be contented enough in his new existence. He certainly preferred that prospect to the drugged, comforting fantasies which would be the final life experience of the human majority on Clell . . . the majority which could not be employed in the plan.

But it was not what he wanted. And the immediate question was how far Spacemaster could be trusted.

Haddan's gaze shifted back to the table behind him. It was littered with maps, charts, masses of other informative material, much of it incomprehensible. But, added to what he had been shown from Vinence's incredible ship, there had been enough he understood to present the story of the genetic collapse of Man—or Spacemaster's version of it.

It was not too implausible. The death seed of multitudinous abnormal genes had been planted in the race before it set out to explore and inhabit the galaxy, and with the expansion their rate of development increased. For another long time, improving medical skills maintained the appearance of a balance; it had become very much less easy for civilized Man to die even under a heavy genetic burden. But since he continued to give short shrift to any government audacious enough to make the attempt of regulating his breeding preferences, that burden also continued to grow.

A point regularly came where medical knowledge, great as it might be, was suddenly shown to be no longer capable of the human repair work needed now to keep some specific civilization on its feet. The lethal genes, the innumerable minor mutations, had established at last a subnormal population, chronically sick and beginning to decrease rapidly in numbers. Spacemaster's charts indicated that this period, once entered, was not prolonged. When there were simply not enough healthy minds and bodies left to attend to the requirements of existence, the final descent became catastrophically swift and was irreversible. On Liot, Haddan had been living through the last years of such a period, modified only by Spacemaster's intervention.

Spacemaster, with its supermachines and superscience, had come into existence as an organization almost too late to act as more than humanity's undertakers. Liot had been the last of all islands of galactic civilization. In less than fifteen centuries, the race had gone everywhere from its peak of achievement and expansion to near-extinction. Spacemaster believed it could still be rebuilt from its remnants, but that the rebuilding required surgical ruthlessness and long-continued supervision.

That was the story Haddan had been given . . . and why, he thought, should they bother to lie to him? But there were puzzling features, and questions left unanswered. What was Spacemaster? Some superior genetic strain which had possessed the self-discipline and foresight to eliminate any threatening weaknesses in its ranks and to remain apart from deteriorated groups? Then why should they have undertaken the stupendous task of attempting to recreate the human race from the survivors of the foundering civilizations? They themselves, at an incomparable level of technological achievement, were the new humanity.

The reflection had raised eerie possibilities. There was the fact that he found it impossible to feel at ease in Vinence's presence. Something in the Spacemaster's appearance, the manner in which he moved, sent constant alert signals to Haddan's brain . . . a difference there, not too obvious but profoundly disturbing. It was as if his senses would not accept that Vinence was another human being, and the thought had come that perhaps on one of the dying worlds a race of robots had been brought into existence and given the task of saving mankind—that Vinence and his fellows were still attempting to carry out the task, with mechanical perseverance, mechanical lack of real interest and, actually, without too much intelligence.

Because Spacemaster's plan . . . or as much of it as Haddan had been allowed to see . . . contained obvious elements of sheer, senseless futility. . . .

Or Vinence might be, if not a robot, a member of a genuine alien species, one masquerading as human beings, and with very different designs on the survivors of humanity than Haddan had been told. There was the world Tayun to which he and Auris and such others of the Liot group as would not be retained on Clell were destined to go. It would be the last group Spacemaster could add to its sparse human breeding stock on Tayun. It had kept the City of Liot functioning for a year after Haddan's departure. Then it became obvious that there would be no more viable births in the city, that the last drop of genetic usefulness had been drained from the shrunken population. The survivors were transferred to Clell, and the city left open to space but intact . . . because eventually human beings should return to lay claim to it again.

That, Vinence said, was Spacemaster's purpose. For centuries it had drawn those who still seemed sufficiently sound out of the subnormal groups under its attention and moved them to Tayun, which of all known worlds came closest to matching the conditions which had existed on primitive Earth. Not too easy a world for human beings to live on without the tools and conveniences of civilization, and not too difficult. Which was exactly as it should be for Spacemaster's purpose. Tayun was the laboratory in which, over the course of generations, any concealed inherited weaknesses were to be worked very thoroughly out of the transplanted human strains. Throughout the long probationary period, they were therefore to have only their natural endowment to see them through the problems they encountered. This was the reason that transferred adults were not allowed to retain the memories of their previous life. Haddan, Auris and the rest would be left in the vicinity of some large group which could be counted on not to take too unamiable an attitude towards befuddled strangers. Since they were physically and mentally well above the present average on Tayun, it should not take them long to overcome their initial handicaps among the group's members. If their memories were left intact, it would be too difficult for them to avoid the temptation of introducing minor innovations to make life more easy for themselves and the others.

"It isn't intended that life should become more easy there for quite a few centuries," Vinence said, "except as the strain improves its natural ability to meet the conditions around it..."

He acknowledged that for a while it had appeared that the Spacemaster experiment on Tayun was too drastic and would fail. Diseases, shifts of climate, animal enemies, and their own latent genetic liabilities seemed to be killing the "neoprimitives" off faster than they could be brought in. But during the past sixty years, their number had first stabilized, and then had begun to increase detectably. The first crisis was over.

It all looked quite logical, so far. Haddan knew little of genetics as Spacemaster understood it; it had been among Liot's "lost" sciences. He was willing to accept that there were no effective gentler alternatives to letting a species cleanse itself in a world-wide natural framework of the individuals who lacked essential qualifications to survive. And having seen the neoprimitives of Tayun for himself, he had not been greatly surprised by Vinence's explanation.

But the further steps of Spacemaster's plan were—when one stopped to give them any thought at all—completely and unbelievably insane....

Hearing a door open and close behind him, Haddan turned and saw Vinence come across the room.

He stood silently, watching the stocky, strong-looking figure, the bland, impassive face with the tilted grey eyes. Every Spacemaster he had seen so far looked very much like Vinence. What *was* the wrongness about them? He couldn't have said exactly. Perhaps it was a hint of unevenness in the motion, the suggestion of a marionette propelled along by expert hands holding invisible strings. The smooth features and coolly calculating eyes... was this a robot? Haddan felt aversion, the concealed ripple of horror, crawl again over his skin.

Vinence stopped at the other side of the table, glancing at the materials scattered about it. He pulled out a chair and sat down.

"Did you get much out of this?" he asked Haddan.

"Not too much."

"It's a large subject," Vinence acknowledged. He stared thoughtfully at Haddan, added, "Our business on Clell has been concluded.

Besides Dr. Auris and yourself, four of your group chose Tayun. The others will remain here."

Haddan said incredulously, "Only four preferred Tayun?"

Vinence shrugged. "That's a very high average, Haddan. I did not expect so many. In the terminal generations of a culture like Liot almost nothing is left of the motivation to survive as a species. There were three of you of whom we felt nearly certain; but the majority of your group were intellectual rebels who faced the risks of leaving Liot without undue qualms largely because they have always been a little detached from living realities. For them there could be no compensation in beginning life again as a memoryless savage. The dreams of Clell held much more interest."

He added, "There was a time when Spacemaster might have taken another dozen from that particular group for Tayun, without their consent. The tests rate at least that many as qualified. But no combination of tests shows every essential. We learned that when we went only by them and our own judgment, and nothing else, we ended almost invariably by having weakened the Tayun strain."

"And what," Haddan asked, "are you going to accomplish finally by strengthening it?"

Something flickered for an instant in the Spacemaster's eyes. Then his expression changed slowly, became mocking, watchful, perhaps menacing; and the certainty grew in Haddan that his question had not come as a surprise.

Vinence said, "That is a curious thing to ask at this late moment." He nodded at the table before him. "Are you disagreeing with some of the conclusions you found there?"

Haddan looked at him. Why argue really? He would not change Spacemaster's plans . . . except perhaps unfavorably as regards to himself. Vinence's attitude of expectancy suggested he might be on the verge of entering a prepared trap. His reaction to the information allowed him, to the things he had been shown and told—without apparent good reason so far—could be the factor which determined what they did in his case. And it was quite possible that they preferred to exclude too questioning an attitude from man's new genetic pattern.

Why not accept Tayun? For him as an entity, there certainly would be compensations for becoming absorbed by the living racial strain. At the very least, it was better than to spend the rest of his days in the sterile dream-halls of Clell—

He heard himself say, "It was a logical question. The charts show what you've told me. Eventually Tayun Man is to be allowed to develop his own civilization. During that period, he should be a trifle hardier physically, a trifle more mentally competent, than the species was perhaps twenty thousand years ago. Serious genetic defects will have been burned out. But in every essential it will be the same species. Spacemaster will have provided mankind with a fresh start. That's what it amounts to, isn't it?"

Vinence nodded. "Very nearly."

Haddan said "Your helpfulness does go a little further, of course. The redevelopment of civilization when it begins will not be haphazard. Man will automatically come across prepared information in some concealed form or other at the moment he can best put it to use. So this second time he should advance very rapidly. But will some super-organization like Spacemaster still be in control of him then?"

"Hardly," Vinence said. "And not at all after they begin to spread through the galaxy again. That would be not only undesirable but impossible. We've learned that much."

"Then it seems," Haddan said, "that Spacemaster is committing an act of lunacy. If there's to be nothing but a fresh start, the whole cycle should be repeating itself a few thousand years from now. They'll have made the same mistakes and again be well advanced in the process of self-destruction. There's no reason to expect anything else—and of course you're aware of that. But unless you already know how to keep it from occurring . . ."

Vinence shook his head. "We don't." He hesitated. "There is a vast difference between restoring the health of a species and attempting to change its natural attitudes in any significant manner. The last is an enormously complex process which contains a much greater likelihood of doing harm than good. I'm engaged myself in Spacemaster's investigations of possible means to prevent renewed racial suicide, and have been for a long time. We are not at all certain that even a theoretical solution can be found." The tone was bland, the grey eyes still fixed unblinkingly on Haddan.

Haddan said doggedly, "A solution will have to be found, or the plan is almost meaningless. And until it is found, Spacemaster is wasting anyone like Dr. Auris or myself on Tayun . . . anyone capable of independent abstract thinking, which certainly isn't a vital requirement in Tayun Man at present. The strain can get along without our kind for a while. You should be putting every functioning mind you can reach to use in looking for the answers you don't have. That should be our assignment in Spacemaster's plan. Anything else is indefensible."

Vinence was silent for some moments. Then he shrugged, said, "There is one thing wrong with that assumption, Haddan. I mentioned that there are complexities in such a project. They are much greater than you realize. Certainly neither you nor Dr. Auris are stupid—but your individual remaining life expectancies are less than fifty years. You would be dead before you could learn half of what you would need to know to begin to be useful to us in such work. There is simply too much to be understood."

Haddan stared at him. "But you were capable of understanding it?"

"Yes, I was."

"Then what—"

Haddan's voice died in his throat. Vinence had raised his hands to his face, cupping the sides off his jaw in his palms, fingers pressed vertically along the cheeks. The hands seemed to make a slight tugging motion; then they lifted the Spacemaster's head from the sturdy neck and placed it unhurriedly upright on the table, a little to one side.

Haddan felt incapable of breathing or moving. He stared in a fascination of repugnance at the head, at the eyes—still fixed on him—at the grey, glistening, jellylike surface of the sectioned neck. Then the head's mouth moved.

"The Spacemaster's body," Vinence's voice said, with no change in tone or inflection—it seemed to be still coming out of the head—"is an interesting biological machine, Haddan. As a matter of fact, it represents a partial solution to the problem we were discussing, though not a very satisfactory one. There are pronounced disadvantages. This body, for example, couldn't exist for minutes if exposed to the open air of even so gentle a world as Clell. If you happened to touch me, I would die almost at once. And if you hadn't been enclosed in a screen of filtering energies since the instant we met, there would have been the same regrettable result. The 'Spacemasters' you may have seen in the City of Liot were manipulated automatons—displayed occasionally to produce some specific effect on the population. A Spacemaster body can tolerate very few of the realities of life as you know them. It experiences almost everything through instruments, at second hand. It uses no food, cannot sleep, cannot reproduce its kind.

"But we are human, and have had wholly human bodies. What

you see is the result of a fusion with something which is nearly, but not quite, another form of life, and with the non-living instrumentation which allows us to move, see, sustain normal gravity and—as you notice—to speak at considerable length. Nevertheless, we remember what human realities were like, and at times we miss them excruciatingly. We experience remorse, frustration, the sense of failure; and we are often too vividly aware of the artificial monstrosities we have become. As I said, there are disadvantages to this kind of living.

"The other side of the matter is that the Spacemaster body lives for a very long while, though eventually it does wear out along with its human component. So there's time to learn and understand some of those very complicated matters one must know in order to do what is necessary . . . which is what Spacemaster has been doing for the past two thousand years."

Haddan said hoarsely, "How long have you . . ."

"Not quite half that period. It was roughly nine hundred years ago that I faced the same choice as you do today. I'm a little shopworn by now, though it hardly shows yet."

Vinence's hands reached down, lifted the head, replaced it on the neck, twisted deftly, quickly and withdrew. "This may seem an overly dramatic demonstration," the Spacemaster went on, "but it has its uses. More than one apparent candidate has lost all interest in further discussion around this point."

Haddan drew in a deep breath, asked, "You're offering me a body of that kind?"

"Why else would we be talking about it?"

Something stirred in the back of Haddan's mind—a soft confusion of light and color, whispering rain, and Auris's sweetly intelligent face. Then it all faded.

He said, "I accept, of course."

"Of course you do," Vinence agreed. "There's been almost no question of that. But we've learned to wait until a potential recruit sees the need for membership and demands it, as his right, before we reveal the conditions. In the past, too many who were persuaded to become Spacemasters on the basis of our judgment of their qualifications eventually found it was a burden they no longer wanted to carry. And it's so very easy for any of us to step out on a pleasant planet, and breathe its air and die.

"But you've made your choice. We won't lose you. Neither are we afraid of losing Dr. Auris, who made the same decisions some hours before you."

In spite of everything, that came as a shock. After a moment, Haddan asked, "Then when . . . do we begin?"

Vinence said, "There are no formalities. You'll be inoculated at once. There will be a few uncomfortable months then until the fusion is complete. But afterwards . . . we build better bodies now than this one of mine . . . you should both have a full twelve hundred years ahead of you to work on Spacemaster's great problem, and Man's. And who knows? That may be the period in which the answer is finally found."

The Altruist

· · · · · · · · · · · · ·

"I PUT THEM right there!" Colonel Olaf Magrumssen said aloud.

He was referring to his office scissors, with which he wanted to cut some string. The string, designed for official use, was almost unbreakably tough, and Colonel Magrumssen had wrapped one end of it around a package containing a set of reports of the Department of Metallurgy, which was to be dispatched immediately. The other end of the string led through a hole in the wall to an automatic feeder spool somewhere behind the wall, and the scissors should have been on a small desk immediately under the point where the string emerged, because that was where the colonel always left them. Just now, however, they weren't there.

There wasn't anything else on the desk that they might have slipped behind; they weren't lying on the floor, and the desk had no drawers into which he could have put them by mistake. They were simply and inexplicably gone.

"Damn!" he said, holding the package in both hands and looking about helplessly. He was all alone in the Inner Sanctum which separated his residential quarters from the general office area of the Department of Metallurgy. The Sanctum, constructed along the lines of a bank vault, contained Metallurgy's secret files and a few simple devices connected with an automatic transportation system between Metallurgy and various other government departments. There was nothing around that would be useful in the present emergency.

"Miss Eaton!" the colonel bellowed, in some exasperation.

Miss Eaton appeared in the doorway a minute later, looking slightly anxious and slightly resentful, which was her normal expression. Otherwise, she was a very satisfactory secretary and general assistant to the colonel.

"Your scissors, Miss Eaton!" he ordered, holding up his package. "Kindly cut this string!"

Miss Eaton's gaze went past him to the desk, and her expression became more definitely resentful.

"Yes, sir," she said. She stepped up and, with a small pair of scissors attached by a decorative chain to her belt, cut the string.

"Thank you," said the colonel. "That will be all."

"There's a Notice of Transfer regarding Charles E. Watterly lying on your desk," Miss Eaton said. "You were to pass on it early this morning."

"I know." The colonel frowned. "You might get out Watterly's record for me, Miss Eaton."

"It's attached to the Notice of Transfer," Miss Eaton told him. She went out without waiting for a reply.

The colonel dropped the package into a depository that would dispatch it to its destination untouched by human hands, and turned to leave the Inner Sanctum. Still irritated by the disappearance, he glanced back at the desk.

And there the scissors were, just where he remembered having left them!

The colonel stopped short. "Eh?" he inquired incredulously, of no one in particular.

A long-forgotten childhood memory came chidingly into his mind . . .

"*Lying right there!*" a ghostly voice of the past was addressing him again. "*If it were a snake,*" the voice added severely, rubbing the lesson in, "*it would bite you!*"

The colonel picked up the scissors rather gingerly, as if they might bite him, at that. He looked surprised and alert now, all distracting annoyances forgotten.

Colonel Magrumssen was a logical man. Now that he thought back, there was no significant doubt in his mind that, the evening before, he had left those scissors on that desk. Nor that, after opening the Sanctum and sealing the package this morning, he had discovered they were gone.

Nor, of course, finally, that they now had returned again.

Those were facts. Another fact was that, aside from himself, nobody but Miss Eaton had entered the Inner Sanctum meanwhile—and she hadn't come anywhere near the desk.

Touching a sticky spot on one of the blades of the scissors, the colonel dabbed at it and noticed something attractively familiar about the pale brown gumminess on his finger.

He put the finger to his mouth. Why, certainly, he told himself— it's just taffy.

His mind paused a moment. *Just taffy!* it repeated.

Now wait a minute, the colonel thought helplessly.

One could put it this way, he decided: at some time last night or this morning, an Unseen Agency had borrowed his scissors for the apparent purpose of cutting taffy with them, and then had brought his scissors back . . .

Perhaps it was the complete improbability of that explanation which made him want to accept it immediately. In the humdrum, hard-working decades following Earth's Hunger Years, Colonel Magrumssen had become a hobbyist of the Mysterious, and this was the most mysterious-looking occurrence he'd yet run into personally. He'd been trained in espionage during the last counter-revolution, and while the lack of further revolutions ultimately had placed him in an executive position in Metallurgy, his interests still lay in investigating the unexplained, the unpredictable, in human behavior, and elsewhere.

As a logical man, however, he realized he'd have to put in his customary day's work in Metallurgy before he could investigate the unusual behavior of a pair of office scissors.

He locked the double doors of the Inner Sanctum behind him— locked them, perhaps, with exceptional attention to the fact that they *were* being locked—and went into the outer offices, to decide on Charles E. Watterly's Notice of Transfer.

The Department of Metallurgy, this section of which was under Colonel Olaf Magrumssen's supervision, was as smoothly operating an organization as any government coordinator could want to see. So was every other major organization—the simple reason being that employees who couldn't meet the stiff requirements of governmental employment were dropped quietly and promptly into the worldwide labor pool known as Civilian General Duty. Once CGD swallowed you, it was rather difficult to get out again; and life at those levels was definitely unattractive.

Charles E. Watterly's standing in Metallurgy was borderline at best, the colonel decided after going briefly over his record—a rather incredible series of preposterous mistakes, blunders, slip-ups and oversights. Watterly's immediate superior had made up a Notice of Transfer as a matter of course and sent it along to the colonel's desk to be signed. Signing it would send Charles E. Watterly automatically to Civilian General Duty.

The colonel was a tolerant man. He didn't care a particular hang how the Department of Metallurgy fared, providing his own position wasn't threatened. But even colonels who failed to keep their subordinates in line could wind up doing Civilian General Duty.

He could afford to give the unfortunate Watterly one more chance, the colonel decided. A man who could operate so consistently against his own interests should be worth studying for a while! And since Watterly's superior had passed the buck by making out the Notice of Transfer, the colonel summoned Miss Eaton and instructed her to have Watterly placed on his personal staff, on probation.

Miss Eaton made no comment. The airtight organization which was beginning to haul humanity, uncomfortably and sometimes brutally enough, out of the catastrophic decline of the Hunger Years did not encourage comment on one's superior's decisions.

"Mr. John Brownson of Statistics is here to see you," she announced.

"The two per cent Normal Loss," John Brownson, a personal assistant of the Minister of Statistics, informed Colonel Magrumssen presently, "has shown striking variations of late, locally. That's the situation in a nutshell. The check we're conducting in your department is of a purely routine nature."

He was relieved to hear that, the colonel said drily. What did Statistics make of these variations?

Brownson looked surprised.

"We've made nothing of them as yet," he admitted. "In time, we hope, somebody will." He paused and looked almost embarrassed. "Now in your department, we have localized one area of deviation so far. It happens to be the cafeteria."

The colonel stared. "The cafeteria?"

"The cafeteria," Brownson continued, flushing a trifle, "shows currently a steady point three increase over Normal Loss. Processed foodstuffs, of course, are so universally affected by the loss that almost any dispersal point can be used conveniently to check deviations. Similar changes are reported elsewhere in the capital area, indicating the possible development of a local trend..."

"Trend to what?" the colonel demanded.

Brownson shrugged thoughtfully. He wasn't, he pointed out, an analyst; he only produced the statistics.

"Well, never mind," said the colonel. "Our poor little cafeteria, eh? Let me know if anything else turns up, will you?"

Now that was an odd thing, he reflected, still idly, while he gazed after Brownson's retreating back. When you got right down to it, nobody actually seemed to know why there should be a two per cent untraceable loss in the annual manipulations of Earth's commodities! People like Brownson obviously saw nothing remarkable in it. To them, Normal Loss had the status of a natural law, and that was that.

Why, he realized, his reaction hovering somewhere between amusement and indignation, he'd been fooled into accepting that general viewpoint himself! He'd let himself be tricked into accepting a "natural law" which involved an element of the completely illogical, the inexplicable.

The colonel felt a flush of familiar excitement. Look, he thought, this could be—*why, this is big! Let's look at the facts!*

He did. And with that, almost instantly, a breathtakingly improbable but completely convincing explanation was there in his mind.

Furthermore, it tied in perfectly with the temporary disappearance of his office scissors that morning!

Colonel Magrumssen conceded, however, with something like awed delight at his own cleverness, that it was going to be a little difficult to prove anything.

The problem suddenly had become too intriguing to put off entirely till evening, so the colonel sent Miss Eaton out to buy a bag of the best available taffy. And he himself made a trip to his private library in his living quarters and returned with a couple of books which had nothing to do with his official duties.

He proceeded to study them until Miss Eaton returned with the taffy, which he put in a drawer of his desk. Then, tapping the last page of the text he had been studying—the chapter was titled "Negative Hallucinations"—he reviewed the tentative conclusions he'd formed so far.

The common starting point in the investigation of any unusual occurrence was to assume that nothing just occurred; that everything had a cause. The next step being, of course, the assumption that anything that happened was part of a greater pattern of events; and that if one got to see enough of it, the greater pattern generally made sense.

The mysterious disappearance and reappearance of his office scissors certainly seemed unusual enough. But when one tied it in with humanity's casual acceptance of the fact that some two per cent of Earth's processed commodities disappeared tracelessly every year, one might be getting a glimpse of a possible major pattern.

The colonel glanced back over a paragraph he had marked in "Negative Hallucinations":

Negative hallucinations are comprehensive in the sense that they also negate the sensory registration of any facts that would contradict them. Install in a hypnotic subject the conviction that there is no one but himself in the room; he will demonstrate that he does not permit himself to realize that he cannot see when another person present places both hands over his eyes . . .

Assuming that it wasn't too logical of humanity to take Normal Loss for granted, one could conclude that humanity as a whole might be suffering from a very comprehensive negative hallucination—in which case, it wouldn't, of course, be permitting itself to wonder about Normal Loss.

It was a rather large assumption to make, the colonel admitted; but he might be in a position to test it now.

For one then could assume also that there was somebody around, some Unseen Agency, who was benefiting both by Normal Loss and by humanity's willingness to accept Normal Loss without further investigation.

An outfit who operated as smoothly as that shouldn't really have bungled matters by returning his scissors under such suspicious circumstances. But even that sort of outfit might be handicapped by occasional members who weren't quite up to par. Somebody, say, who was roughly the equivalent of a Charles E. Watterly.

The notion satisfied the colonel. He unlocked a desk drawer which contained a few items of personal interest to him. A gun, for one thing—in case life eventually turned out to be just a little too boring, or some higher-up decided some day that Colonel Magrumssen was ripe for a transfer and CGD. A methodical man should be prepared for any eventuality.

Beside the gun, carefully wrapped, was a small crystal globe, a souvenir from a vacation trip he'd made to Africa some years before. There had been a brief personal romance involved with the trip and the globe; but that part of it no longer interested the colonel very much.

The thing about the globe right now was that, when one pressed down a little button set into its base, it demonstrated a gradual succession of tiny landscapes full of the African sunlight and with minute animals and people walking about in it. All very lifelike and arranged in such a manner that one seemed to be making a slow trip about the continent. It was an enormously expensive little gadget, but it might now be worth the price he'd paid for it.

The colonel wrapped the globe back up and set it on the desk next to the bag of taffy. Then he went about finishing up the day's official business, somewhat amazed at the fact that he seemed to be accepting his own preposterous theory as a simple truth—that invisible beings walked the Earth, lived among men and filched their sustenance from Man's meager living supplies . . .

But he hadn't, he found, the slightest desire to warn humanity against its parasites. That had nothing to do with the fact that nobody would believe him anyway. So far, he rather approved of the methods employed by the Unseen Agency.

By the time the next twenty-four hours were over, he also might have a fair idea of its purpose.

He laughed. The whole business was really outrageous. And he realized that, for some reason, that was just what delighted him about it.

He was sitting in his study, shortly after nine o'clock that evening, when he had the first indication that his plans were beginning to work out.

Up till then, he had remained in a curiously relaxed frame of mind. Having accepted the apparent fact of the Unseen Agency's existence, the question was whether its mysterious powers went so far that it actually could read his thoughts and know what he intended to do before he got around to doing it. If it could, his tricks obviously weren't going to get him anywhere. If it couldn't, he should get results—eventually. He felt he lost nothing by trying.

He was aware of no particular surprise then when things began to happen. It was as if he had expected them to happen in just that way.

He had pushed away the papers he was working on and leaned back to yawn and stretch for a moment. As if by accident, his gaze went to the mantel above the study's electronic fireplace, where he had placed the little crystal globe showing Africa's scenic wonders. He had left it switched to the picture of a burned brown desert, across which a troop of lean, pale antelopes trotted slowly toward a distant grove of palm trees.

From where he sat, he could see that the crystal no longer showed the desert view. Instead, Kilimanjaro's snow-covered peak was visible in it, reflecting the pink light of an infinitesimal morning sun.

The colonel frowned slightly, permitting a vague sense of disturbance—an awareness of something being not quite as it should be—to pass through his mind. Presumably, that awareness would reflect itself to some degree in his expression and might be noticed there by a sufficiently alert observer.

He dismissed the feeling and turned back to his papers.

What he caught in that moment, from the corner of his eye, couldn't exactly be described as motion. It was hardly more than a mental effect, a fleeting impression of shifting shadows, light and lines, as if something had alighted for an instant on the farthest edge of his vision and been withdrawn again.

The colonel didn't look up. A chill film of sweat covered the backs of his hands and his forehead. That was the only indication he gave, even to himself, of feeling any excitement. Without moving his eyes, he could tell that the gleaming crystal globe had vanished from its place on the mantel.

How did they do it? In some way, they were cutting off the links of awareness that existed between all rational human beings. They were broadcasting the impression that they, and the things they touched, and the traces of their activities did not exist. Once the mind accepted that, it would refuse to acknowledge any contradictory evidence offered by its senses of reasoning powers.

He'd started out by assuming that there was something there, so the effect of the negative hallucination was weakened in him. Every new advance in understanding he made now should continue to weaken it—and there was one moment when the Unseen Agency's concrete reality must manifest itself in a manner which his mind, at this point, couldn't refuse to accept. That was the instant in which it was manipulating some very concrete item, such as the crystal globe, in and out of visibility.

It was obvious, at any rate, that the Agency couldn't read his thoughts. He'd tricked it, precisely as he'd set out to do, into making a hurried attempt to resolve his apparently half-formed suspicion that someone might have been playing with the globe behind his back. It showed a certain innocence of mind. But, presumably, people who had such unusual powers mightn't be accustomed to the sort of devious maneuvering and conscious control of emotion and thought which was required to survive at an acceptable level in the colonel's everyday world.

He became aware suddenly of the fact that the crystal globe had been returned to its place on the mantel. For that same instant, he was aware also of a child-shape, definitely a girl, standing on tiptoe before the mantel, still reaching up toward the globe—and then fading quickly, soundlessly, beyond the reach of his senses again.

That was considerably more than enough—

He'd been thinking of some super-powered moron, of the Charles E. Watterly type, not a child! But it made even better sense this way, and it took only a few seconds of flexibility to adapt his plans to include the new factor.

The colonel took two white cards and a lead pencil out of a drawer of the desk at which he was working. He unhurriedly printed three words on the first card and five on the second. Putting the cards into his pocket, he finally looked up at the globe

As he expected, it showed the scene he'd last been studying himself—brown desert, the grove of palms and the antelopes.

He gazed at it for a moment, as if absently accepting this correction of the Unseen Agency's lapse as any good hypnotic subject should. And then, still casually, he took the bag of fresh taffy he'd had Miss Eaton buy that afternoon out of the desk drawer. He opened it, opening his mind simultaneously to the conviction that the child-shape would come now to this new bait.

Almost instantly, he realized, with a sense of sheer delight, that she *was* there!

At any rate, there was an eagerness, an innocent greed, swirling like a gusty, soundless little wind of emotion about him, barely checked now by the necessity of remaining unseen. He took out a piece of the taffy and popped it solemnly into his mouth, and the greed turned into a shivering young rage of frustration, and a plea, and a prayer: *Oh, make him look away! Just once!*

The colonel put the paper bag into his pocket, walked deliberately to the mantel and propped one of the two cards up against the globe.

There was a fresh upsurge of interest, and then an almost physically violent burst of other emotions behind him.

For the three words on the card read:

I SAW YOU!

Whistling soundlessly, the colonel waited a moment and replaced that card with the next one. He scratched his jaw and, as an apparent second thought, produced three pieces of taffy from his pocket, which he arranged into an artistic little pyramid in front of the card. He turned and walked back to his desk.

When he looked around from there, the card was gone.

So were the three pieces of taffy.

He waited patiently for over a minute. Something white fluttered momentarily before the globe on the mantel and the card had reappeared. For a moment again, too, the child became visible, looking at him still half in alarm, but also half in laughter now, and then vanished once more.

Reading what was written on the card, the colonel knew he'd won the first round anyway. His reaction wasn't the feeling of alert, cautious triumph he'd expected, but a curious, rather unaccountable happiness.

The five words he'd printed on the card had been:

DON'T WORRY—I WON'T TELL

That message was crossed out now with pencil. Underneath it, two single words had been printed in a ragged slope, as if someone had been writing very hurriedly:

THANK YOU!

By two o'clock that night, the colonel was still wide awake, though he had followed his methodical pattern of living by going to bed at midnight, as usual. Whatever the Unseen Agency's reaction might be, it wouldn't be bound by any conventional restrictions.

There was the chance, of course, that they would decide it was necessary to destroy him. Since he couldn't protect himself successfully against invisible opponents, the colonel wasn't taking any measures along that line. He'd accepted the chance in bringing himself to their attention.

They also might decide simply to ignore him. He couldn't, he conceded, do much about it if they did. Everyday humanity had its own abrupt methods of dealing with anyone who tried to dispel its illusions, and he, for one, knew enough not to make any such attempt. But the Unseen Agency should have curiosity enough to find out how much he actually knew and what he intended to do about it. . . .

His eyes opened slowly. The luminous dial of the clock beside his bed indicated it was three-thirty. He had fallen asleep finally; and now there were—presences—in his room.

After his first involuntary start, the colonel was careful not to move. The channels of awareness that had warned of the arrival of the Unseen Agency seemed to be approximately the same he had used unwittingly in sensing the emotions of the child earlier that night. Under the circumstances, he might regard theirs as more reliable than his eyes or ears.

Apparently encouraged by his acceptance of the fact, his mind reported promptly that the child herself was among those present— and that there was a new quality of stillness and expectancy about her now, as if this were a very important event to her, too.

Of the others, the colonel grew aware more gradually. But as he did, he discovered the same sense of waiting expectancy about them, almost as if they were trying to tell him that the next move actually was up to him, not them. In the instant he formed that conclusion, his feeling of their general presence seemed to resolve itself into the recognition of a number of distinct personalities who were presenting themselves to him, one by one.

The first was a grave, aged kindliness, but with a bubble of humor in it—almost, he thought, surprised, like somebody's grandmother.

Two and Three seemed to be masculine, darker, thoughtfully judging.

And, finally, there was Four, who appeared to come into the room only now, as if summoned from a distance to see what her friends had found—a personality as clear and light as the child's, but an adult intelligence nevertheless. Four joined the others, observant and waiting.

Waiting for what?

That, the colonel gathered, was for him to experience in himself and understand. His awareness of their existence had been enough to attract their attention to him. Moving and living securely beyond the apparent realities of civilization, as if it were so much stage scenery which had hypnotized the senses of all ordinary human beings, they seemed ready to welcome and encourage any discoverer, without fear or hostility, as one of themselves.

He could sense dimly the quality of their strange ability, and the motives that had created it. The ruthless mechanical rigidity of the human society that had developed out of the Hunger Years had been the forcing factor. These curious rebels must have felt a terrible necessity to escape from it to have found and developed in their own minds a means of bypassing society so completely—

the means being, essentially, so perfect a control of the outgoing radiations of thought and emotion that they created no slightest telltale ripple in the ocean of the subconscious human mind and left a negative impression there instead.

But they were not hiding from anyone who followed the same path they had taken.

There was a sudden unwillingness in him to go any further in that direction at the moment. Full understanding might lie in the very near future; but it was still in the future.

As if they had accepted that, too, he could sense that the members of the Unseen Agency were withdrawing from him and the room. Four was last to go; lingering a moment after the others had left, as if looking back at him; a light, clear presence as definite as spoken words or the touch of a hand.

A moment after she had left, the colonel realized, with something of a shock, that for the first time in his adult life, he had fallen in love. . . .

First thing he did next morning was to have himself measured for a new uniform of the kind he'd always avoided—the full uniform of his rank, white and gold, and with the extra little flourishes, the special unauthorized richness of cloth that only a colonel-and-up could afford or get away with. It was the sort of gesture, he felt, that Four might appreciate. And he had a reason for wanting to stay away from Metallurgy that morning for the four hours or so it might take to complete the suit.

He was in the position of a strategist who, having made an important gain, can take time out to consolidate it and consider his next moves. He preferred to do that beyond the range of any too observant eyes—and mind.

That Four and her kind should be content to live—well, like mice, actually—behind the scenery of the world, subsisting on the crumbs of civilization, was ridiculous. They seemed to have no real understanding of their powers, and of the uses to which they could be put.

It was the most curious sort of paradox.

The colonel found a park bench and settled down to investigate the problems presented by the paradox.

He was, he decided, a practical man. As such, he'd remained occluded, till now, to their solution of the problems of a society with which he was basically no more contented than they had been. But he had adjusted effectively to the requirements of that society, while they had withdrawn from it in the completest possible fashion this side of suicide.

To put it somewhat differently, he had learned how to influence and manipulate others to gain for himself a position comfortably near the top. *They* had learned how to avoid being manipulated.

But if a man could do that—without losing the will to employ his powers intelligently!

The colonel checked the surge of excitement which arose from that line of reflection, almost guiltily. The structure of society might be—and was—more than ripe for an overhauling. But he was quite certain that Four's people would not be willing to follow his reasoning just yet. Their whole philosophy of living was oriented in the opposite direction of ultimate withdrawal.

But give me time, he thought, *Just give me time!*

Four showed herself to him that afternoon.

He'd returned to his office—the white-and-gold uniform had created a noticeable stir in the department—and instructed Miss Eaton to send someone out for a lunch tray from the cafeteria.

A little later, he suddenly realized that Four was standing in the door of the office behind him. He knew then that, for some reason, he had expected her to come.

He was careful not to look around, but he sensed that she both approved of the white uniform and was laughing at him for having put it on to impress her. The colonel's ears reddened slightly. He straightened his shoulders, though, and went on working.

Next, the child-shape slipped by before his desk, an almost visibility. He glanced up at it, and it smiled and disappeared as abruptly as if it had gone through a door in mid-air and closed the door behind it. A moment later Four stood just beyond the desk, looking down at the colonel, no less substantial than the material of the desk itself.

He stared up at her, unable to speak, aware only of a slow, strong gladness welling up in him.

Then Four vanished—

Someone had opened the door of the office behind him.

"Your lunch, sir," the familiar voice of Charles E. Watterly muttered apologetically.

The colonel let his breath out slowly. But it didn't matter too much, he supposed. Four would be back.

"Thank you, Watterly," he said, with some restraint. "Set it down, please."

Watterly's angular shape appeared beside him and suddenly seemed to teeter uncertainly. The colonel moved an instant too late. The coffee pot lay on its side in the brown puddle that filled the lunch tray on the desk. The rest of the contents were about evenly distributed over the desk, the carpet, and the white uniform.

On his feet, flushed and angry, the colonel looked at Watterly.

"I'm sorry, sir!" Watterly had fallen back a step.

Now, *this* was interesting, the colonel decided, studying him carefully. This was the familiar startled white face, its slack mouth twisted into an equally familiar, frightened grin. But why hadn't he ever before noticed the incredible, cold, hidden malice staring at him out of those pale blue eyes?

Not a bungler. A hater. The airtight organization of society kept it suppressed so well that he had almost forgotten how the underdogs of the world could hate!

He let the rage in him ebb away.

Anger was pointless. It was the compliment one paid an equal. To withdraw beyond the reach of human malice, as Four and the rest of them had done, was a better way—for the weak. For those who were not, the simplest and most effective way was to dispose of the malicious by whichever methods were handiest, and forget about them.

At seven in the evening, Miss Eaton looked in at the colonel's central office and inquired whether he would need her any more that day.

"No, thank you, Miss Eaton," said the colonel, without looking up. "A few matters I want to finish by myself. Good night."

There was silence for a moment. Then Miss Eaton's voice blurted suddenly, "Sometimes it's much better to finish such matters in the morning, sir!"

The colonel glanced up in surprise. Coming from Miss Eaton, the remark seemed out of character. But she looked slightly resentful, slightly anxious, as always, and not as if she attributed any importance to her words.

"Well, Miss Eaton," the colonel said genially, while he wondered whether it had been a coincidence, "I just happen to prefer not to wait till tomorrow."

Miss Eaton nodded, as though agreeing that, in that case, there was no more to be said. He listened to her heels clicking away through the glass-enclosed aisles of the general offices, and then the lights went out there, and Colonel Magrumssen was sitting alone at his desk.

It was odd about Miss Eaton. He was almost certain now it had been no coincidence. Her personality which, for a number of years, he'd felt he understood better than one got to understand most people, had revealed itself in a single sentence to be an entirely different sort of personality—a woman, in fact, about whom he knew exactly nothing! At any other time, the implications would have fascinated him. Tonight, of course, it made no difference any more.

His gaze returned reflectively to a copy of the Notice of Transfer by which Charles E. Watterly had been removed from Metallurgy some hours before, to be returned to the substratum of Earth's underdogs, where he obviously belonged.

It had seemed the logical thing to do, the colonel realized with a feeling of baffled resentment. What did one more third-rate human life among a few billions matter?

But it seemed his unseen acquaintances believed it did matter, very much. Somewhere deep in his mind, ever since he had signed the Transfer, a cold, dead area had been growing which told him, as clearly as if they had announced it in so many words, that he wouldn't be able to contact them again.

Notices of Transfer weren't revocable, but he felt, too, that it wouldn't have done him much good if they had been. One committed the unforgivable sin, and that was that.

He had pushed Watterly back down where he belonged. And he was no longer acceptable.

There was one question he would have liked answered, the colonel decided, as he went on methodically about the business of cleaning up his department's top-level affairs for his successor.

What, actually, *was* the unforgivable sin?

A half hour later, he decided he wasn't able to find the answer. Something involved with Christian charity, or the lack of it, apparently. He had sinned in degrading Watterly. Civilization similarly had sinned on a very large scale against the major part of humanity. And so they had withdrawn themselves both from civilization and from him.

He shook his head. He might still be misjudging their motives—because it still didn't seem quite right!

On the proper form and in a neat, clear hand, he filled out his resignation from Metallurgy and from life, to make it easy for the investigators. He frowned at the line headed REASONS GIVEN and decided to leave it blank.

He laid down the pen and picked up the gun and squinted down its barrel distastefully. And then somebody who now appeared to be sitting in the chair on the other side of his desk remarked:

"That mightn't be required, you know."

The colonel put the gun down and folded his hands on the desk. "Well, John Brownson!" he said, politely surprised. "You're one of them, too?"

The assistant to the Minister of Statistics shrugged.

"In a sense," he admitted. "In about the same way that you're one of them."

The colonel thought that over and acknowledged that he didn't quite follow.

"It's very simple," Brownson assured him, "once you understand the basic fact that we're all basically altruists—you and I and every other human being on Earth."

"All altruists, eh?" the colonel repeated doubtfully.

"Not, of course, always consciously. But each of us seems to know instinctively that he or she is also, to some extent, an irrational and therefore potentially dangerous animal. The race is developing mentally and emotionally, but it hasn't developed as far as would be desirable as yet."

"That, at any rate, seems to be a fact," the colonel conceded.

"So there is a conflict between our altruism and our irrationality. To solve it, we—each of us—limit ourselves. We do not let our understanding and abilities develop beyond the point at which we can trust ourselves not to use them against humanity. Once you accept that, everything else is self-explanatory."

Now how could Brownson hope to defend such a statement, the colonel protested after an astonished pause, after taking a look at history? Or, for that matter, at some of the more outstanding public personalities in their immediate environment?

But the assistant to the Minister of Statistics waved the objection aside.

"Growth isn't always a comfortable process," he said. "Even the Hunger Years and our present social structure might be regarded as forcing factors. The men who appear primarily responsible for this stage of mankind's development may not consciously look on themselves as altruists, but basically, as I said, that is the only standard by which we do judge our activities—and ourselves! Now, as for you—"

"Yes?" said the colonel. "As for me?"

"Well, you're a rather remarkable man, Colonel Magrumssen. You certainly gave every indication of being prepared to expand your understanding to a very unusual degree—which was why," John Brownson added, somewhat apologetically, "I first directed your attention to the possible implications of Normal Loss. Afterward, you appear to have fooled much more careful judges of human nature than I am. Though, of course," he concluded, "you may not really have fooled them. It's not always easy to follow their reasoning."

"Since you're being so informative," the colonel said bluntly, "I'd like to know just who and what those people are."

"They're obviously people who can and do trust themselves *very* far," Brownson said evasively. "A class or two above me, I'm afraid. I don't know much about them otherwise, and I'd just as soon not. You're a bolder man than I am, Colonel. In particular, I don't know anything about the specific group with which you became acquainted."

"We didn't stay acquainted very long."

"Well, you wouldn't," Brownson agreed, studying him curiously. "Still, it was an unusual achievement."

The colonel said nothing for a moment. He was experiencing again a hot resentment and what he realized might be a rather childish degree of hurt, and also the feeling that something splendidly worthwhile had become irretrievably lost to him through a single mistake. But, for some reason, the feeling was much less disturbing now.

"The way it seemed to me," he said finally, "was that they were willing to accept me as an equal—whatever class they're in—until I fired Watterly. That wasn't it, then?"

"No, it wasn't. They were merely acknowledging that you had accepted yourself as being in that class, at least temporarily. That seems to be the only real requirement."

"If I knew instinctively that I couldn't meet that requirement, on a completely altruistic basis," the colonel said carefully, "why did I accept myself as being in their class even temporarily?"

John Brownson glanced reluctantly at the gun on the desk. For a moment, the colonel was puzzled. Then he grinned apologetically.

"Well, yes, that might explain it," he admitted. "I believe I've had it in mind for some time. Life had begun to look pretty uninteresting." He poked frowningly at the gun. "So it was just a matter of satisfying my curiosity—first?"

"I wouldn't know what your exact motive was," Brownson said cautiously. "But I presume it went beyond simple curiosity."

"Well, supposing now," said the colonel, tapping the gun, "that on considering what you've told me, I decided to change my mind."

Brownson smiled. "If you change your decision, you'll do it for good and sufficient reasons. I'd be very happy—and, incidentally, there's no need to blame yourself for Watterly. Watterly knew he couldn't trust himself in any position above Civilian General Duty. If you hadn't had him sent back there, he would have found someone else to do it. Self-judgment works at all levels."

"I wasn't worrying much about Watterly," the colonel said. He reflected a moment. "What actually induced you to come here to talk to me?"

"Well," said Brownson carefully, "there was one who expressed an opinion about you so strongly that it couldn't be ignored. I was sent to make sure you had the fullest possible understanding of what you were doing."

The colonel stared. "Who expressed an opinion about me?'

"Your Miss Eaton."

"Miss Eaton?" The colonel almost laughed. For a moment, he'd had a wild, irrational hope that Four had showed concern about him. But Four hardly would have been obliged to go to John Brownson for help.

"Miss Eaton," Brownson smiled wryly, "has a wider range of understanding than most, but not enough courage to do anything about what she knows. The bravest thing she ever did was to speak to you as she did tonight. After that, she didn't know what else to do, so—well, she prayed. At any rate, it seemed to be a prayer to her."

"For me?"

"Yes, for you."

"Think of that!" said the colonel, astonished. "That was why you came?"

"That's it."

The colonel thought about Miss Eaton for a moment, and then of what a completely fascinating, interesting world it was—if one could only become really aware of it. It seemed unreasonable that people should be going thorough life in blind, uneasy dissatisfaction, never quite realizing what was going on around and behind them. . . .

Of course, a good percentage of them might drop dead in sheer fright if they ever got a sudden inkling of what was there. For one thing, quite enough power to extinguish nine-tenths of the human life on Earth between one second and the next.

And the thought of that power and various perhaps not too rational manipulations of it, he reflected truthfully, might have been the really fascinating part of it all to him.

"Well, thank you, Brownson," he said.

There was no answer.

When the colonel looked up, the chair on the other side of the desk was empty. Brownson seemed to have realized that he'd done the best he could. The others, being wiser, would have known all along there was nothing to be done. His self-judgment stood.

"Damn saints!" the colonel said, grinning. The trouble was that he still liked them.

Trying not to think of Four again, he picked up the gun and then a final thought came to him. He laid it down long enough to write neatly and clearly behind REASONS GIVEN on the resignation form: IF IT WERE A SNAKE, IT WOULD BITE YOU!

A slim hand moved the gun away and a light voice laughed, at the inscrutable message he had written. Then his own hand was taken and he smiled back at Four, while the room stayed substantial and he did not.

It was remarkable how easily and completely one could retreat from the world, clear to the point of invisibility. There had always been people like that, people who could lose themselves in a crowd or be totally unnoticeable at a party. They just hadn't carried their self-effacement far enough. Probably the pressure of reality hadn't been as savage as it was now, to compel both extremes of assertion and withdrawal.

Normal Loss would rise an infinitesimal amount, the colonel thought with amusement—he'd have to live, too. The world wouldn't know why, of course.

The devil with this world. He had his own to go to, and a woman of his own to go with.

"You didn't really think I was going to kill myself, did you?" he asked Four, feeling the need to make her understand and respect him. "It was only a trick to get your attention."

"As if you had to," she laughed tenderly.

Oneness
· · · · · · · · ·

MENESEE FELT EXCITEMENT surge like a living tide about him as he came with the other directors into the vast Tribunal Hall. Sixty years ago, inexcusable carelessness had deprived Earth of its first chance to obtain a true interstellar drive. Now, within a few hours, Earth, or more specifically, the upper echelons of that great political organization called the Machine which had controlled the affairs of Earth for the past century and a half, should learn enough of the secrets of the drive to insure that it would soon be in their possession.

Menesee entered his box between those of Directors Cornelius and Ojeda, immediately to the right of the Spokesman's Platform and with an excellent view of the prisoner. When Administrator Bradshaw and Spokesman Dorn had taken their places on the platform, Menesee seated himself, drawing the transcript of the day's proceedings towards him. However, instead of glancing over it at once, he spent some seconds in a study of the prisoner.

The fellow appeared to be still young. He was a magnificent physical specimen, tall and strongly muscled, easily surpassing in this respect any of the hard-trained directors present. His face showed alert intelligence, giving no indication of the fact that for two of the three days since his capture he had been drugged and subjected to constant hypnotic suggestion. He had given his name as Rainbolt, acknowledged freely that he was a member of the group of malcontent deserters known in the records of the Machine as the Mars Convicts, but described himself as being a "Missionary of Oneness" whose purpose was to bring the benefits of some of the principles of "Oneness" to Earth. He had refused to state

262

whether he had any understanding of the stardrive by the use of which the Mars Convicts had made their mass escape from the penal settlements of the Fourth Planet sixty years before, though the drive obviously had been employed in bringing him out of the depths of interstellar space to the Solar System and Earth. At the moment, while the significance of the bank of torture instruments on his right could hardly have escaped him, his expression was serious but not detectably concerned.

"Here is an interesting point!" Director Ojeda's voice said on Menesee's right.

Menesee glanced over at him. Ojeda was tapping the transcript with a finger.

"This Rainbolt," he said, "hasn't slept since he was captured! He states, furthermore, that he has never slept since he became an adult—"

Menesee frowned slightly, failing to see any great significance in the fact. That the fellow belonged to some curious cult which had developed among the Mars Convicts following their flight from the Solar System was already known. Earth's science had methods of inducing permanent sleeplessness but knew, too, that in most instances the condition eventually gave rise to very serious side effects which more than offset any advantages to be gained from it.

He picked up his transcript, indicating that he did not wish to be drawn into conversation. His eyes scanned quickly over the pages. Most of it was information he already had. Rainbolt's ship had been detected four days earlier, probing the outermost of the multiple globes of force screens which had enclosed Earth for fifty years as a defense both against faster-than-light missiles and Mars Convict spies. The ship was alone. A procedure had been planned for such an event, and it was now followed. The ship was permitted to penetrate the first two screens which were closed again behind it.

Rainbolt's ship, for all its incredible speed, was then a prisoner. Unhurriedly, it was worked closer to Earth until it came within range of giant scanners. For an instant, a large section of its interior was visible to the instruments of the watchers on Earth; then the picture blurred and vanished again. Presumably automatic anti-scanning devices had gone into action.

The photographed view was disappointing in that it revealed no details of the engines or their instruments. It did show, however, that the ship had been designed for the use of one man, and that it was neither armored nor armed. Its hull was therefore bathed with paralytics, which in theory should have left the pilot helpless, and ships of the Machine were then sent up to tow the interstellar captive down to Earth.

At that point, the procedure collapsed. The ship was in atmosphere when an escape capsule was suddenly ejected from it, which later was found to contain Rainbolt, alert and obviously not affected by the paralysis beams. A moment later, the ship itself became a cloud of swiftly dissipating hot gas.

The partial failure of the capture might have been unavoidable in any case. But the manner in which it occurred still reflected very poorly, Menesee thought, on the thoroughness with which the plans had been prepared. The directors who had been in charge of the operation would not be dealt with lightly—

He became aware suddenly that the proceedings of the day had begun and hastily put down the transcript.

Spokesman Dorn, the Machine's executive officer, sitting beside Administrator Bradshaw at a transparent desk on the raised platform to Menesee's left, had enclosed the area about the prisoner with a sound block and was giving a brief verbal resume of the background of the situation. Few of the directors in the Tribunal Hall would have needed such information; but the matter was being carried on the Grand Assembly Circuit, and in hundreds of auditoriums on Earth the first and second echelons of the officials of the Machine had gathered to witness the interrogation of the Mars Convict spy.

The penal settlements on Mars had been established almost a century earlier, for the dual purpose of mining the mineral riches of the Fourth Planet and of utilizing the talents of political dissidents with a scientific background too valuable to be wasted, in research and experimental work considered either too dangerous to be conducted on Earth or requiring more space than could easily be made available there. One of these projects had been precisely the development of more efficient spacedrives to do away with the costly and tedious maneuverings required for travel even among the inner planets.

Work of such importance, of course, was supposed to be carried out only under close guard and under the direct supervision of reliable upper-echelon scientists of the Machine. Even allowing for criminal negligence, the fact that the Mars Convicts were able to develop and test their stardrive under such circumstances

without being detected suggested that it could not be a complicated device. They did, at any rate, develop it, armed themselves
and the miners of the other penal settlements and overwhelmed
their guards in a surprise attack. When the next ship arrived from
Earth, two giant ore carriers and a number of smaller guard ships
had been outfitted with the drive, and the Mars Convicts had
disappeared in them. Their speed was such that only the faintest
and briefest of disturbances had been registered on the tracking
screens of space stations near Mars, the cause of which remained
unsuspected until the news came out.

Anything which could have thrown any light on the nature of
the drive naturally had been destroyed by the deserters before they
left; and the few Machine scientists who had survived the fighting were unable to provide information though they were ques-
tioned intensively for several years before being executed. What
it added up to was that some eighteen thousand sworn enemies
of the Machine had disappeared into space, equipped with an
instrument of unknown type which plainly could be turned into
one of the deadliest of all known weapons.

The superb organization of the Machine swung into action
instantly to meet the threat, though the situation became complicated by the fact that rumors of the manner in which the Mars
Convicts had disappeared filtered out to the politically dissatisfied on Earth and set off an unprecedented series of local upris-
ings which took over a decade to quell. In spite of such difficulties,
the planet's economy was geared over to the new task; and presently defenses were devised and being constructed which would
stop missiles arriving at speeds greater than that of light. Simultaneously, the greatest research project in history had begun to
investigate the possibilities of either duplicating the fantastic drive
some scientific minds on Mars had come upon—chiefly, it was
concluded, by an improbable stroke of good luck—or of matching its effects through a different approach. Since it had been
demonstrated that it could be done, there was no question that
in time the trained men of the Machine would achieve their goal.
Then the armed might of the Machine would move into space to
take control of any colony established by the Mars Convicts and
their descendants.

That was the basic plan. The task of developing a stardrive
remained a huge one because of the complete lack of information about the direction organized research should take. That
difficulty would be overcome easily only by a second unpredictable

twist of fortune—unless one of the Mars Convicts' FTL ships ventured close enough to Earth to be captured.

The last had now happened. The ship had been destroyed before it could be investigated, so that advantage was again lost. The ship's pilot, however, remained in their hands. The fact that he disclaimed having information pertinent to the drive meant nothing. So far as he knew, he might very well be speaking the truth. But he had piloted a ship that employed the stardrive, was familiar with instruments which controlled it, had been schooled in their use. A detailed investigation of his memories could not fail to provide literally hundreds of meaningful clues. And the Machine's scientists, in their superficially still fruitless search for the nature of the drive, had, in fact, covered basic possibilities with such comprehensive thoroughness that a few indisputably valid clues would show them now what it *must* be.

The prisoner, still demonstrating an extraordinary degree of obliviousness to what lay in store for him, appeared to welcome the opportunity to be heard by the directors of the Machine. Menesee, leaning back in his chair, studied the man thoughtfully, giving only partial attention to what was said. This was the standard opening stage of a Tribunal interrogation, an underplayed exchange of questions and answers. Innocuous as it seemed, it was part of a procedure which had become refined almost to an unvarying ritual—a ritual of beautiful and terrible precision which never failed to achieve its goals. Every man watching and listening in the Machine's auditoriums across the world was familiar with the swift processes by which a normal human being was transformed into a babbling puppet, his every significant thought becoming available for the upper echelons to regard and evaluate.

They would, of course, use torture. It was part of the interlocking mechanisms of interrogation, no more to be omitted than the preliminary conditioning by drug and hypnosis. Menesee was not unduly squeamish, but he felt some relief that it would not be the crude instruments ranked beside the prisoner which would be used. They were reserved as a rule for offending members of the organization, providing a salutary warning for any others who might be tempted to act against the interests of the Machine or fail culpably in their duties. This prisoner, as an individual, meant nothing to the Machine. He was simply a source of valuable information. Therefore, only direct nerve stimulation would be employed, in the manipulation of which Spokesman Dorn was a master.

So far the Spokesman had restricted himself to asking the prisoner questions, his voice and manner gravely courteous. To Menesee's surprised interest, he had just inquired whether two men of the last Earth ship to visit Mars, who had disappeared there, might not have been captured by Mars Convicts operating secretly within the Solar System.

"Yes, sir," Rainbolt replied readily, "they were. I'm happy to say that they're still alive and well."

Menesee recalled the incident now. After the mass escape of the Mars Convicts the penal settlements had been closed down and the mining operations abandoned. To guard the desert planet against FTL raiders as Earth was guarded was technically infeasible. But twice each decade a patrol ship went there to look for signs that the Mars Convicts had returned. The last of these patrols had been conducted two years before. The missing men were believed to have been inspecting a deserted settlement in a ground vehicle when they vanished, but no trace of them or the vehicle could be discovered.

Administrator Bradshaw, seated to the spokesman's left, leaned forward as if to speak, but then sat back again. Menesee thought that Rainbolt's blunt admission had angered him. Bradshaw, white-haired and huge in build, had been for many years the nominal head of the Machine; but in practice the powers of the administrator were less than those of the spokesman, and it would have been a breach of protocol for Bradshaw to intervene in the interrogation.

Dorn appeared to have noticed nothing. He went on. "What was the reason for capturing these men?"

"It was necessary," Rainbolt explained, "to find out what the conditions on Earth were like at present. At the time we didn't want to risk discovery by coming too close to Earth itself. And your two men were able to tell us all we needed to know."

"What was that?" the spokesman asked.

Rainbolt was silent a moment, then said, "You see, sir, most of the past sixty years have been spent in finding new worlds on which human beings can live without encountering too many difficulties. But then—"

Dorn interrupted quietly, "You found such worlds?"

"Yes, sir, we did," Rainbolt said. "We're established, in about equal numbers, on planets of three star systems. Of course, I'm not allowed to give you more precise information on that at present."

"Quite understandable," the spokesman agreed dryly.

Menesee was conscious of a stir of intense interest among the listening directors in the hall. This was news, indeed! Mingled with the interest was surprised amusement at the prisoner's artless assumption that he had any choice about what he would or would not tell.

"But now that we're established," Rainbolt went on, apparently unaware of the sensation he had created, "our next immediate concern is to resume contact with Earth. Naturally, we can't do that freely while your Machine remains in political control of the planet. We found out from the two captured men that it still is in control. We'd hoped that after sixty years government in such a form would have become obsolete here."

Menesee heard an astonished murmuring from the director boxes on his right, and felt himself that the fellow's impudent last remark might well have been answered by a pulse of nerve stimulation. Spokesman Dorn, however, replied calmly that the Machine happened to be indispensable to Earth. A planetary economy, and one on the verge of becoming an interplanetary and even interstellar economy, was simply too intricate and precariously balanced a structure to maintain itself without the assistance of a very tightly organized governing class.

"If the Machine were to vanish today," he explained, "Earth would approach a state of complete chaos before the month was out. In a year, a billion human beings would be starving to death. There would be fighting . . . wars—" He shrugged. "You name it. No, my friend, the Machine is here to stay. And the Mars Convicts may as well resign themselves to the fact."

Rainbolt replied earnestly that he was not too well informed in economics, that not being his field. However, he had been told and believed that while the situation described by the spokesman would be true today, it should not take many years to train the populations of Earth to run their affairs quite as efficiently as the Machine had done, and without loss of personal and political liberties.

At any rate, the Mars Convicts and their descendants did not intend to give up the independence they had acquired. On the other hand, they had two vital reasons for wanting to come to an agreement with Earth. One was that they might waste centuries in attempting to accomplish by themselves what they could now do immediately if Earth's vast resources were made available to them. And the other, of course, was the obvious fact that Earth would not remain indefinitely without a stardrive of its own. If an unfriendly government was in control when it obtained one, the

Mars Convicts would be forced either to abandon their newly settled planets and retreat farther into the galaxy or submit to Earth's superior strength.

Meanwhile, however, they had developed the principles of Oneness. Oneness was in essence a philosophy; but it had many practical applications; and it was in such practical applications that he, Rainbolt, was a trained specialist. He had, therefore, been dispatched to Earth to introduce the principles, which would in time bring about the orderly disintegration of the system of the Machine, to be followed by the establishment of an Earth government with which the Mars Convicts could deal without detriment to themselves.

Menesee had listened with a sense of growing angry incredulity. The fellow couldn't be as much of a fool as he seemed! Therefore, he had devised this hoax after he realized he would be captured, to cover up his real purpose which could only be that of a spy. Menesee saw that Administrator Bradshaw was saying something in a low voice to the spokesman, his face stony. Dorn glanced over at him, then looked back at the prisoner and said impassively, "So the goal of your missionary work here is the disintegration of the Machine?"

Rainbolt nodded, with an air almost of eagerness. "Yes, sir, it is! And if I will now be permitted to—"

"I am afraid you will be permitted to do nothing," Spokesman Dorn said dryly, "except, of course, to answer the number of questions we intend to ask you."

"But, sir I—"

Rainbolt checked himself, looking startled. The spokesman's hand had moved very slightly on the desk before him, and Rainbolt had just had his first experience with direct nerve stimulation. He stood kneading his right hand with his left, staring up at the spokesman, mouth half open.

Menesee smiled in grim amusement. It would have been a low-level pulse, of course; but even a low-level pulse, arriving unexpectedly, was a very unpleasant surprise. He had foreseen the spokesman's action; had, in fact, felt a sympathetic imaginary twinge in his own right hand as the pulse reached the prisoner.

Rainbolt swallowed, said in a changed voice, "Sir, we heard from the two captured men that the Machine has retained its practice of torture during interrogations. It isn't necessary to convince me that you are serious about this. Do the questions you referred to have to do with the stardrive?"

The spokesman nodded. "Of course."

Rainbolt said stubbornly, "Then, sir, it can do you no good at all to torture me. I simply don't have such information. We do plan to make the stardrive freely available to Earth. But not while Earth is ruled by the organization of the Machine."

This time, Menesee did not observe the motion of the spokesman's hand. Instead he saw Rainbolt jerk violently to the right. At the same moment, a blast of intense, fiery, almost unbearable pain shot up his own arm. As he grasped his arm, sweat spurting out on his face, he heard screams from the box on his left and realized it was Director Cornelius who screamed.

There were answering screams from around the hall.

Then the pain suddenly subsided.

Menesee stared about, breathing raggedly. The pain-reaction had been severe enough to affect his vision; the great hall looked momentarily darker than it should have been. And although the actual pain had ended, the muscles of his right arm and shoulder were still trying to cramp into knots.

There was no more screaming. From the right came Director Ojeda's gasping voice. "What happened? Did something go wrong with the stimulating devices? We might all have been killed—!"

Menesee didn't reply. Wherever he looked, he saw faces whitened with shock. Apparently everyone in the Tribunal Hall, from the administrator and Spokesman Dorn on down to the directors' attendants and the two guards flanking the prisoner's area, had felt the same thing. Here and there, men who had collapsed were struggling awkwardly back to their feet. He heard a hoarse whisper behind him. "Sir, Director Cornelius appears to have fainted!"

Menesee glanced around, saw Cornelius' attendant behind the box, then Cornelius himself, slumped forward, face down and motionless, sprawling half across his table. "Let him lie there and keep quiet, fool!" Menesee ordered the man sharply. He returned his attention to the center of the hall as Spokesman Dorn announced in a voice which held more of an edge than was normal but had lost none of its strength and steadiness, "Before any moves are suggested, I shall tell you what has been done.

"The Tribunal Hall has been sealed and further events in it will be monitored from without. No one will be able to leave until the matter with which we are now concerned here has been settled to the satisfaction of the Machine.

"Next, any of you who believe that an instrument failure was involved in the experience we shared can disabuse themselves. The same effect was reported immediately from two other auditoriums on the Great Circuit, and it is quite possible that it was repeated in all of them."

Rainbolt, grimacing and massaging his right arm vigorously, nodded. "It *was* repeated in all of them, sir!"

The spokesman ignored him, went on. "The Tribunal Hall has, therefore, been cut out of the Grand Assembly Circuit. How circuit energies could have been employed to transmit such physical sensations is not clear. But they will not be used in that manner again."

Menesee felt a flash of admiration. His own thoughts had been turning in the same direction, but he couldn't have approached Spokesman Dorn's decisive speed of action.

Dorn turned his attention now to Rainbolt. "What happened," he said, "apparently was caused by yourself."

Rainbolt nodded. "Yes, sir. It was. It was an application of Oneness. At present, I'm acting as a focal point of Oneness. Until that condition is changed, whatever I experience here will be simultaneously experienced by yourselves."

Menesee thought that the effects of the Machine's discipline became splendidly apparent at that point. No one stirred in the great hall though it must have been obvious to every man present that Rainbolt's words might have doomed them along with himself.

Rainbolt went on, addressing Spokesman Dorn.

"There is only one mistake in your reasoning, sir. The demonstrated effect of Oneness is not carried by the energies of the Grand Assembly Circuit, though I made use of those energies in establishing an initial connection with the other auditoriums and the people in them.

"You see, sir, we learned from the two men captured on Mars about your practice of having the two highest echelons of your organization attend significant hearings in the Tribunal Hall through the Assembly Circuit. Our plan was based on that. We knew that if anything was to be accomplished with the Oneness principles on Earth, it would have to be through a situation in which they could be applied simultaneously to the entire leadership of the Machine. That has now been done, and the fact that you had the Tribunal Hall taken out of the Assembly Circuit did not change the Oneness contact. It remains in full effect."

Spokesman Dorn stared at him for an instant, said, "We can

test the truth of that statement immediately, of course; and we shall!" His hand moved on the desk.

Menesee felt pain surge through his left arm. It was not nearly as acute a sensation as the previous pulse had been, but it lasted longer—a good ten seconds. Menesee let his breath out carefully as it again ebbed away.

He heard the spokesman saying, "Rainbolt's claim appears to be verified. I've received a report that the pulse was being experienced in one of the auditoriums . . . and, yes . . . now in several."

Rainbolt nodded. "It was a valid claim, believe me, sir!" he said earnestly. "The applications of our principles have been very thoroughly explored, and the effects are invariable. Naturally, our stratagem would have been useless if I'd been able to maintain contact only long enough to provide you with a demonstration of Oneness. Such a contact *can* be broken again, of course. But until I act deliberately to break it, it maintains itself automatically.

"To make that clear, I should explain that distance, direction and intervening shielding materials do not change the strength of the contact. Distance at least does not until it is extended to approximately fifty thousand miles."

"And what happens then?" the spokesman asked, watching him.

"At that point," Rainbolt acknowledged, "Oneness contacts do become tenuous and begin to dissolve." He added, almost apologetically, "However, that offers you no practical solution to your problem."

"Why not?" Dorn asked. He smiled faintly. "Why shouldn't we simply lock you into a spaceship and direct the ship through the defense fields and out into the solar system on automatic control?"

"I sincerely hope you don't try it, sir! Experiments in dissolving contacts in that manner have been invariably fatal to all connected individuals."

The spokesman hesitated. "You and every member of the Machine with whom you are now in contact would die together if that were done?"

"Yes, sir. That is certainly what the results of those experiments show."

Administrator Bradshaw, who had been staring coldly at Rainbolt, asked in a hard, flat voice, "If you do nothing to break the contact, how long will this situation continue?"

Rainbolt looked at him. "Indefinitely, sir," he said. "There is nothing I need to do about it. It is a static condition."

"In that case," Bradshaw said icily, "*this* should serve to break the contact through you!"

As his hand came up, leveling a gun, Menesee was half out of his chair, hands raised in alarmed protest. "Stop him!" Menesee shouted.

But Administrator Bradshaw already was sagging sideways over the armrest of his chair, head lolling backwards. The gun slid from his hand, dropped to the platform.

"Director Menesee," Dorn said coolly from beside Bradshaw, "I thank you for your intended warning! Since the administrator and the spokesman are the only persons permitted to bear arms in the Tribunal Hall, I was naturally prepared to paralyze Administrator Bradshaw if he showed intentions of resorting to thoughtless action." He looked down at Rainbolt. "Are Director Menesee and I correct in assuming that if you died violently the persons with whom you are in contact would again suffer the same experience?"

"Yes, sir," Rainbolt said. "That is implicit in the principles of Oneness." He shrugged. "Under most circumstances, it is a very undesirable effect. But here we have made use of it—"

"The situation," Spokesman Dorn told the directors in the Tribunal Hall some minutes later, "is then this. There has been nothing haphazard about the Mars Convicts' plan to coerce us into accepting their terms. Considering the probable quality of the type of minds which developed both the stardrive and the extraordinary 'philosophy' we have encountered today, that could be taken for granted from the start. We cannot kill their emissary here, or subject him to serious pain or injury, since we would pay a completely disproportionate penalty in doing it.

"However, that doesn't mean that we should surrender to the Mars Convicts. In fact, for all their cleverness, they appear to be acting out of something very close to desperation. They have gained no essential advantage through their trick, and we must assume they made the mistake of underestimating us. This gentleman they sent to Earth has been given thorough physical examinations. They show him to be in excellent health. He is also younger by many years than most of us.

"So he will be confined to quarters where he will be comfortable and provided with whatever he wishes . . . but where he will not be provided with any way of doing harm to himself. And then, I believe, we can simply forget about him. He will receive the best of attention, including medical care. Under such circumstances, we can expect his natural life span to exceed our own.

"Meanwhile, we shall continue our program of developing our own spacedrive. As the Mars Convicts themselves foresee, we'll gain it eventually and will then be more than a match for them. Until then the defense fields around Earth will remain closed. No ship will leave Earth and no ship will be admitted to it. And in the long run we will win."

The spokesman paused, added, "If there are no other suggestions, this man will now be conducted to the hospital of the Machine where he is to be detained for the remainder of his days."

Across the hall from Menesee, a figure arose deliberately in one of the boxes. A heavy voice said, "Spokesman Dorn, I very definitely do have a suggestion."

Dorn looked over, nodded warily. "Go ahead, Director Squires!"

Menesee grimaced in distaste. He had no liking for Squires, a harsh, arrogant man, notorious for his relentless persecution of any director or officer who, in Squires' opinion, had become slack in his duties to the Machine. But he had a large following in the upper echelons, and his words carried weight.

Squires folded his arms, said unhurriedly as if savoring each word, "As you pointed out, Spokesman Dorn, we cannot hurt the person of this prisoner. His immediate accomplices also remain beyond our reach at present. However, our hands are not—as you seem to imply—so completely tied that we cannot strike back at these rascals at once. There are camps on Earth filled with people of the same political stripe—potential supporters of the Mars Convicts who would be in fullest sympathy with their goals if they learned of them.

"I suggest that these people serve now as an object lesson to show the Mars Convicts the full measure of our determination to submit to no threats of force! Let this prisoner and the other convicts who doubtless are lurking in nearby space beyond Earth's defense fields know that *for every day* their obscene threat against the high officers of the Machine continues, hundreds of malcontents who would welcome them on Earth will be painfully executed! Let them—"

Pain doubled Menesee abruptly over the table before him. A savage, compressing pain, very different from the fiery touch of the nerve stimulators, which held him immobile, unable to cry out or draw breath.

It relaxed almost as instantaneously as it had come on. Menesee slumped back in his chair, shaken and choking, fighting down bitter nausea. His eyes refocused painfully on Rainbolt, gray-faced but on his feet, in the prisoner's area.

"You will find," Rainbolt was saying, "that Director Squires is dead. And so, I'm very much afraid, is every other member of the upper echelons whose heart was in no better condition than his. This was a demonstration I had not intended to give you. But since it has been given, it should serve as a reminder that while it is true we could not force you directly to do as we wish, there are things we are resolved not to tolerate."

Ojeda was whispering shakily near Menesee, "He controls his body to the extent that he was able to bring on a heart attack in himself and project it to all of us! He counted on his own superb physical condition to pull him through it unharmed. *That* is why he didn't seem frightened when the administrator threatened him with a gun. Even if the spokesman hadn't acted, that gun never would have been fired.

"Menesee, no precautions we could take will stop that monster from killing us all whenever he finally chooses—simply by committing suicide through an act of will!"

Spokesman Dorn's voice seemed to answer Ojeda.

"Director Squires," Dorn's voice said, still thinned by pain but oddly triumphant, "became a victim of his own pointless vindictiveness. It was a mistake which, I am certain, no member of the Machine will care to repeat.

"Otherwise, this incident has merely served to confirm that the Mars Convicts operate under definite limitations. They *could* kill us but can't afford to do it. If they are to thrive in space, they need Earth and Earth's resources. They are aware that if the Machine's leadership dies, Earth will lapse into utter anarchy and turn its tremendous weapons upon itself.

"The Mars Convicts could gain nothing from a ruined and depopulated planet. Therefore, the situation as it stands remains a draw. We shall devote every effort to turn it into a victory for us. The agreement we come to eventually with the Mars Convicts will be on our terms—and there is still essentially nothing they or this man, with all his powers, can do to prevent it."

The Missionary of Oneness swung his bronzed, well-muscled legs over the side of the hammock and sat up. With an expression of great interest, he watched Spokesman Dorn coming across the sun room towards him from the entrance corridor of his hospital suite. It was the first visit he'd had from any member of the organization of the Machine in the two years he had been confined here.

For Spokesman Dorn it had been, to judge by his appearance, a strenuous two years. He had lost weight and there were dark smudges of fatigue under his eyes. At the moment, however, his face appeared relaxed. It might have been the relaxation a man feels who has been emptied out by a hard stint of work, but knows he has accomplished everything that could possibly have been done.

Dorn came to a stop a dozen feet from the hammock. For some seconds, the two men regarded each other without speaking.

"On my way here," Dorn remarked then, "I was wondering whether you mightn't already know what I've come to tell you."

Rainbolt shook his head.

"No," he said. "I think I could guess what it is—I pick up generalized impressions from outside—but I don't really know."

Spokesman Dorn considered that a moment, chewing his lower lip reflectively. Then he shrugged.

"So actual mind-reading doesn't happen to be one of your talents," he said. "I was rather sure of that, though others had a different opinion. Of course, considering what you are able to do, it wouldn't really make much difference.

"Well . . . this morning we sent out a general call by space radio to any Mars Convict ships which might be in the Solar System to come in. The call was answered. Earth's defense fields have been shut down, and the first FTL ships will land within an hour."

"For what purpose?" Rainbolt said curiously.

"There's a strong popular feeling," Spokesman Dorn said, "that your colleagues should take part in deciding what pattern Earth's permanent form of government will take. In recent months we've handled things in a rather provisional and haphazard manner, but the situation is straightened out well enough now to permit giving attention to such legalistic details. Incidentally, you will naturally be free to leave when I do. Transportation is available for you if you wish to welcome your friends at the spaceport."

"Thank you," said Rainbolt. "I believe I will."

Spokesman Dorn shrugged. "What could we do?" he said, almost disinterestedly. "You never slept. In the beginning you were drugged a number of times, as you probably know, but we soon discovered that drugging you seemed to make no difference at all."

"It doesn't," Rainbolt agreed.

"Day after day," Dorn went on, "we'd find thoughts and

inclinations coming into our minds we'd never wanted there. It was an eerie experience—though personally I found it even more disconcerting to awaken in the morning and discover that my attitudes had changed in some particular or other, and as a rule changed irrevocably."

Rainbolt said, "In a sense, those weren't really your attitudes, you know. They were results of the conditioning of the Machine. It was the conditioning I was undermining."

"Perhaps it was that," Dorn said. "It seems to make very little difference now." He paused, frowned. "When the first talk of initiating changes began in the councils, there were numerous executions. I know now that we were badly frightened men. Then those of us who had ordered the executions found themselves wanting similar changes. Presently we had a majority, and the changes began to be brought about. Reforms, you would call them—and reforms I suppose they actually were. There was considerable general disturbance, of course, but we retained the organization to keep that within reasonable bounds."

"We expected that you would," Rainbolt said.

"It hasn't really been too bad," Spokesman Dorn said reflectively. "It was simply an extraordinary amount of work to change the structure of things that had been imposed on Earth by the Machine for the past century and a half. And the curious part of it is, you know, that now it's done we don't even feel resentment! We actually wouldn't want to go back to what we had before. You've obtained an incredible hold on our minds and frankly I expect that when at last you do relinquish your control, we'll commit suicide or go mad."

Rainbolt shook his head. "There's been just one mistake in what you've said," he remarked.

Spokesman Dorn looked at him with tired eyes. "What's that?" he asked.

"I said I was undermining the conditioning of the Machine. I did—and after that I did nothing. You people simply have been doing what most of you always would have preferred to do, Spokesman. I relinquished control of the last of you over six months ago."

Dark Visions

AS A GENERAL rule, Schmitz wrote stories which were basically lighthearted, and often humorous. Every single story in his Hub universe, or the Agent of Vega stories, or his novel *Witches of Karres*—in short, his best known work—is of that nature. Whatever perils and dangers his heroes (or, more often, heroines) experience, the ending is always what can be called a "happy" one. Most of the stories are cheerful in tone, and even the ones which have a sterner theme (such as "Attitudes") still display an optimistic confidence that The Right Will Prevail.

But he did occasionally write stories with a much darker hue. Some of them, such as "We Don't Want Any Trouble," are downright chilling. We've collected these in one place, and given this section of the volume the title "Dark Visions." It seems an appropriate one. . . .

Tales of alien invasions that *succeed,* a psi story that is also a horror story, a cold look at the real likelihood of a man changing his life if he had the chance, and a grim tale of an experiment gone wrong.

Have fun.

We Don't Want Any Trouble

. . . .

"WELL, THAT WASN'T a very long interview, was it?" asked the professor's wife. She'd discovered the professor looking out of the living room window when she'd come home from shopping just now. "I wasn't counting on having dinner before nine," she said, setting her bundles down on the couch. "I'll get at it right away."

"No hurry about dinner," the professor replied without turning his head. "I didn't expect we'd be through there before eight myself."

He had clasped his hands on his back and was swaying slowly, backward and forward on his feet, staring out at the street. It was a favorite pose of his, and she never had discovered whether it indicated deep thought or just daydreaming. At the moment, she suspected uncomfortably it was very deep thought, indeed. She took off her hat.

"I suppose you could call it an interview," she said uneasily. "I mean you actually talked with it, didn't you?"

"Oh, yes, we talked with it," he nodded. "Some of the others did, anyway."

"Imagine *talking* with something like that! It really *is* from another world, Clive?" She laughed uneasily, watching the back of his head with frightened eyes. "But, of course, you can't violate the security rules, can you? You can't tell me anything about it at all. . . ."

He shrugged, turning around. "There'll be a newscast at six o'clock. In ten minutes. Wherever there's a radio or television set on Earth, everybody will hear what we found out in that interview. Perhaps not quite everything, but almost everything."

281

"Oh?" she said in a surprised, small voice. She looked at him in silence for a moment, her eyes growing more frightened. "Why would they do a thing like that?"

"Well," said the professor, "it seemed like the right thing to do. The best thing, at any rate. There may be some panic, of course." He turned back to the window and gazed out on the street, as if something there were holding his attention. He looked thoughtful and abstracted, she decided. But then a better word came to her, and it was "resigned."

"Clive," she said, almost desperately, "what happened?"

He frowned absently at her and walked to the radio. It began to make faint, humming noises as the professor adjusted dials unhurriedly. The humming didn't vary much.

"They've cleared the networks, I imagine," he remarked.

The sentence went on repeating itself in his wife's mind, with no particular significance at first. But then a meaning came into it and grew and swelled swiftly, until she felt her head would burst with it. They've cleared the networks. All over the world this evening, they've cleared the networks. Until the newscast comes on at six o'clock . . .

"As to what happened," she heard her husband's voice saying, "that's a little difficult to understand or explain. Even now. It was certainly amazing—" He interrupted himself. "Do you remember Milt Caldwell, dear?"

"Milt Caldwell?" She searched her mind blankly. "No," she said, shaking her head.

"A rather well-known anthropologist," the professor informed her, with an air of faint reproach. "Milt got himself lost in the approximate center of the Australian deserts some two years ago. Only we have been told he didn't get lost. They picked him up—"

"*They?*" she said. "You mean there's more than one?"

"Well, there would be more than one, wouldn't there?" he asked reasonably. "That explains, at any rate, how they learned to speak English. It made it seem a little more reasonable, anyhow," he added, "when it told us that. Seven minutes to six . . ."

"What?" she said faintly.

"Seven minutes to six," the professor repeated. "Sit down, dear. I believe I can tell you, in seven minutes, approximately what occurred. . . ."

The Visitor from Outside sat in its cage, its large gray hands slackly clasping the bars. Its attitudes and motions, the professor had noted in the two minutes since he had entered the room with the other men, approximated those of a rather heavily built ape. Reporters had called it "the Toad from Mars," on the basis of the first descriptions they'd had of it—the flabby shape and loose, warty skin made that a vaguely adequate identification. The round, horny head almost could have been that of a lizard.

With a zoologist's fascination in a completely new genus, the professor catalogued these contradicting physical details in his mind. Yet something somewhat like this might have been evolved on Earth, if Earth had chosen to let the big amphibians of its Carboniferous Period go on evolving.

That this creature used human speech was the only almost-impossible feature.

It had spoken as they came in. "What do you wish to know?" it asked. The horny, toothed jaws moved, and a broad yellow tongue became momentarily visible, forming the words. It was a throaty, deliberate "human" voice.

For a period of several seconds, the human beings seemed to be shocked into silence by it, though they had known the creature had this ability. Hesitantly, then, the questioning began.

The professor remained near the back of the room, watching. For a while, the questions and replies he heard seemed to carry no meaning to him. Abruptly he realized that his thoughts were fogged over with a heavy, cold, physical dread of this alien animal. He told himself that under such circumstances fear was not an entirely irrational emotion, and his understanding of it seemed to lighten its effects a little.

But the scene remained unreal to him, like a badly lit stage on which the creature in its glittering steel cage stood out in sharp focus, while the humans were shadow-shapes stirring restlessly against a darkened background.

"This won't do!" he addressed himself, almost querulously, through the fear. "I'm here to observe, to conclude, to report—I was selected as a man they could trust to think and act rationally!"

He turned his attention deliberately away from the cage and what it contained, and he directed it on the other human beings, to most of whom he had been introduced only a few minutes before. A young, alert-looking Intelligence major, who was in some way in charge of this investigation; a sleepy-eyed general; a very pretty captain acting as stenographer, whom the major had introduced as his fiancée. The handful of other scientists looked for the most part like brisk business executives, while the two Important Personages representing the government looked like elderly professors.

He almost smiled. They were real enough. This was a human world. He returned his attention again to the solitary intruder in it.

"Why shouldn't I object?" the impossible voice was saying with a note of lazy good humor. "You've caged me like—a wild animal! And you haven't even informed me of the nature of the charges against me. Trespassing, perhaps—eh?"

The wide mouth seemed to grin as the Thing turned its head, looking them over one by one with bright black eyes. The grin was meaningless; it was the way the lipless jaws set when the mouth was closed. But it gave expression to the pleased malice the professor sensed in the voice and words.

The voice simply did not go with that squat animal shape.

Fear surged up in him again. He found himself shaking.

If it looks at me now, he realized in sudden panic, I might start to scream!

One of the men nearest the cage was saying something in low, even tones. The captain flipped over a page of her shorthand pad and went on writing, her blonde head tilted to one side. She was a little pale, but intent on her work. He had a moment of bitter envy for their courage and self-control. But they're insensitive, he tried to tell himself; they don't know Nature and the laws of Nature. They can't feel as I do how *wrong* all this is!

Then the black eyes swung around and looked at him.

Instantly, his mind stretched taut with blank, wordless terror. He did not move, but afterward he knew he did not faint only because he would have looked ridiculous before the others, and particularly in the presence of a young woman. He heard the young Intelligence officer speaking sharply; the eyes left him unhurriedly, and it was all over.

"You indicate," the creature's voice was addressing the major, "that you can force me to reveal matters I do not choose to reveal at this time. However, you are mistaken. For one thing, a body of this type does not react to any of your drugs."

"It will react to pain!" the major said, his voice thin and angry.

Amazed by the words, the professor realized for the first time that he was not the only one in whom this being's presence had aroused primitive, irrational fears. The other men had stirred restlessly at the major's threat, but they made no protest.

The Thing remained silent for a moment, looking at the major.

"This body will react to pain," it said then, "only when I choose to let it feel pain. Some of you here know the effectiveness of hypnotic blocks against pain. My methods are not those of hypnosis, but they are considerably more effective. I repeat, then, that for me there is no pain, unless I choose to experience it."

"Do you choose to experience the destruction of your body's tissues?" the major inquired, a little shrilly.

The captain looked up at him quickly from the chair where she sat, but the professor could not see her expression. Nobody else moved.

The Thing, still staring at the major, almost shrugged.

"And do you choose to experience death?" the major cried, his face flushed with excitement.

In a flash of insight, the professor understood why no one was interfering. Each in his own way, they had felt what he was feeling: that here was something so outrageously strange and new that no amount of experience, no rank, could guide a human being in determining how to deal with it. The major was dealing with it—in however awkward a fashion. With no other solution to offer, they were, for the moment, unable or unwilling to stop him.

The Thing then said slowly and flatly, "Death is an experience I shall never have at your hands. That is a warning. I shall respond to no more of your threats. I shall answer no more questions.

"Instead, I shall tell you what will occur now. I shall inform my companions that you are as we judged you to be—foolish, limited, incapable of harming the least of us. Your world and civilization are of very moderate interest. But they are a novelty which many will wish to view for themselves. We shall come here and leave here, as we please. If you attempt to interfere again with any of us, it will be to your own regret."

"Will it?" the major shouted, shaking. "Will it now?"

The professor jerked violently at the quick successive reports of a gun in the young officer's hand. Then there was a struggling knot of figures around the major, and another man's voice was shouting hoarsely, "You fool! You damned hysterical fool!"

The captain had dropped her notebook and clasped her hands to her face. For an instant, the professor heard her crying, "Jack! Jack! Stop—don't—"

But he was looking at the thing that had fallen on its back in the cage, with the top of its skull shot away and a dark-brown liquid staining the cage floor about its shoulders.

What he felt was an irrational satisfaction, a warm glow of pride in the major's action. It was as if he had killed the Thing himself.

For that moment, he was happy.

Because he stood far back in the room, he saw what happened then before the others did.

One of the Personages and two of the scientists were moving excitedly about the cage, staring down at the Thing. The others had grouped around the chair into which they had forced the major. Under the babble of confused, angry voices, he could sense the undercurrent of almost joyful relief he felt himself.

The captain stood up and began to take off her clothes.

She did it quickly and quietly. It was at this moment, the professor thought, staring at her in renewed terror, that the height of insanity appeared to have been achieved in this room. He wished fervently that he could keep that sense of insanity wrapped around him forevermore, like a protective cloak. It was a terrible thing to be rational! With oddly detached curiosity, he also wondered what would happen in a few seconds when the others discovered what he already knew.

The babbling voices of the group that had overpowered the major went suddenly still. The three men at the cage turned startled faces toward the stillness. The girl straightened up and stood smiling at them.

The major began screaming her name.

There was another brief struggling confusion about the chair in which they were holding him. The screaming grew muffled as if somebody had clapped a hand over his mouth.

"I warned you," the professor heard the girl say clearly, "that there was no death. Not for us."

Somebody shouted something at her, like a despairing question. Rigid with fear, his own blood a swirling roar in his ears, the professor did not understand the words. But he understood her reply.

"It could have been any of you, of course," she nodded. "But I just happened to like *this* body."

After that, there was one more shot.

The professor turned off the radio. For a time, he continued to gaze out the window.

"Well, they know it now!" he said. "The world knows it now. Whether they believe it or not— At any rate . . ." His voice trailed off. The living room had darkened and he had a notion to switch on the lights, but decided against it. The evening gloom provided an illusion of security.

He looked down at the pale oval of his wife's face, almost featureless in the shadows.

"It won't be too bad," he explained, "if not too many of them come. Of course, we don't know how many there are of them, actually. Billions, perhaps. But if none of our people try to make trouble—the aliens simply don't want any trouble."

He paused a moment. The death of the young Intelligence major had not been mentioned in the broadcast. Considering the issues involved, it was not, of course, a very important event and officially would be recorded as a suicide. In actual fact, the major had succeeded in wresting a gun from one of the men holding him. Another man had shot him promptly without waiting to see what he intended to do with it.

At all costs now, every rational human being must try to prevent trouble with the Visitors from Outside.

He felt his face twitch suddenly into an uncontrollable grimace of horror.

"But there's no way of being absolutely sure, of course," he heard his voice tell the silently gathering night about him, "that they won't decide they just happen to like *our* kind of bodies."

Just Curious

· · · · · · · · · · · ·

Roy Litton's apartment was on the eighteenth floor of the Torrell Arms. It was a pleasant place which cost him thirty-two thousand dollars a year. The living room had a wide veranda which served in season as a sun deck. Far below was a great park. Beyond the park, drawn back to a respectful distance from the Torrell Arms, was the rest of the city.

"May I inquire," Roy Litton said to his visitor, "from whom you learned about me?"

The visitor's name was Jean Merriam. She was a slender, expensive brunette, about twenty-seven. She took a card from her handbag and slid it across the table to Litton. "Will that serve as an introduction?" she asked.

Litton studied the words scribbled on the card and smiled. "Yes," he said, "that's quite satisfactory. I know the lady's handwriting well. In what way can I help you?"

"I represent an organization," Jean said, "which does discreet investigative work."

"You're detectives?"

She shrugged, smiled. "We don't refer to ourselves as detectives, but that's the general idea. Conceivably your talents could be very useful to us. I'm here to find out whether you're willing to put them at our disposal from time to time. If you are, I have a test assignment for you. You don't mind, do you?"

Litton rubbed his chin. "You've been told what my standard fee is?"

Jean Merriam opened the handbag again, took out a check, and gave it to him. Litton read it carefully, nodded. "Yes," he said, and laid the check on the table beside him. "Ten thousand dollars. You're in the habit of paying such sums out of your personal account?"

"The sum was put in my account yesterday for this purpose."

"Then what do you, or your organization, want me to do?"

"I've been given a description of how you operate, Mr. Litton, but we don't know how accurate the description is. Before we retain you, I'd like you to tell me exactly what you do."

Litton smiled. "I'm willing to tell you as much as I know."

She nodded. "Very well. I'll decide on the basis of what you say whether or not your services might be worth ten thousand dollars to the organization. Once I offer you the assignment and you accept it, we're committed. The check will be yours when the assignment is completed."

"Who will judge when it has been completed?"

"You will," said Jean. "Naturally there will be no further assignments if we're not satisfied with the results of this one. As I said, this is a test. We're gambling. If you're as good as I've been assured you are, the gamble should pay off. Fair enough?"

Litton nodded. "Fair enough, Miss Merriam." He leaned back in his chair. "Well, then—I sometimes call myself a 'sensor' because the word describes my experiences better than any other word I can think of. I'm not specifically a mind reader. I can't predict the future. I don't have second sight. But under certain conditions, I turn into a long-range sensing device with a limited application. I have no theoretical explanation for it. I can only say what happens.

"I work through contact objects; that is, material items which have had a direct and extensive physical connection with the persons I investigate. A frequently worn garment is the obvious example. Eyeglasses would be excellent. I once was able to use an automobile which the subject had driven daily for about ten months. Through some such object I seem to become, for a time which varies between approximately three and five minutes, the person in question." Litton smiled. "Naturally I remain here physically, but my awareness is elsewhere.

"Let me emphasize that during this contact period I *am*—or seem to be—the other person. I am not conscious of Roy Litton or of what Roy Litton is doing. I have never heard of him and know nothing of his sensing ability. I am the other person, aware only of what he is aware of, doing what he is doing, thinking what he is thinking. If, meanwhile, you were to speak to the body sitting here, touch it, even cause it severe pain—which has been done experimentally—I wouldn't know it. When the time is up, the contact fades and I am back. Then I know who I am and can recall my experience and report on it. Essentially, that's the process."

Jean Merriam asked, "To what extent do you control the process?"

"I can initiate it or not initiate it. I'm never drawn out of myself unless I intend to be drawn out of myself. That's the extent of my control. Once it begins, the process continues by itself and concludes itself. I have no way of affecting its course."

Jean said reflectively, "I don't wish to alarm you, Mr. Litton. But mightn't you be running the risk of remaining permanently lost in somebody else's personality . . . unable to return to your own?"

Litton laughed. "No. I know definitely that can't happen, though I don't know why. The process simply can't maintain itself for much more than five minutes. On the other hand, it's rarely terminated in less than three."

"You say that during the time of contact you think what the other person thinks and are aware of what he's aware?"

"That's correct."

"Only that? If we employed you to investigate someone in this manner, we usually would need quite specific information. Wouldn't we have to be extremely fortunate if the person happened to think of that particular matter in the short time you shared his mind?"

"No," said Litton. "Conscious thoughts quite normally have thousands of ramifications and shadings the thinker doesn't know about. When the contact dissolves, I retain his impressions and it is primarily these ramifications and shadings I then investigate. It is something like developing a vast number of photographic prints. Usually the information my clients want can be found in those impressions in sufficient detail."

"What if it can't be found?"

"Then I make a second contact. On only one occasion, so far, have I been obliged to make three separate contacts with a subject to satisfy the client's requirements. There is no fee for additional contacts."

Jean Merriam considered a moment. "Very well," she said. She brought a small box from the handbag, opened it, and took out a ring, which she handed to Litton. "The person in whom the organization is interested," she said, "was wearing this ring until four weeks ago. Since then it's been in a safe. The safe was opened yesterday and the ring taken from it and placed in this box. Would you consider it a suitable contact object?"

Litton held the ring in his palm an instant before replying. "Eminently suitable!" he said then.

"You can tell by touching such objects?"

"As a rule. If I get no impression, it's a waste of time to proceed. If I get a negative impression, I refuse to proceed."

"A negative impression?"

Litton shrugged. "A feeling of something that repels me. I can't describe it more definitely."

"Does it mean that the personality connected with the object is a repellent one?"

"Not necessarily. I've merged with some quite definitely repellent personalities in the course of this work. That doesn't disturb me. The feeling I speak of is a different one."

"It frightens you?"

"Perhaps." He smiled. "However, in this case there is no such feeling. Have you decided to offer me the assignment?"

"Yes, I have," Jean Merriam said. "Now then, I've been told nothing about the person connected with the ring. Since very few men could get it on, and very few children would wear a ring of such value, I assume the owner is a woman—but I don't know even that. The reason I've been told nothing is to make sure I'll give you no clues, inadvertently or otherwise." She smiled. "Even if you were a mind reader, you see, you could get no significant information from me. We want to be certain of the authenticity of your talent."

"I understand," Litton said. "But you must know what kind of information your organization wants to gain from the contact?"

Jean nodded. "Yes, of course. We want you to identify the subject by name and tell us where she can be found. The description of the locality should be specific. We also want to learn as much as we can about the subject's background, her present activities and interests, and any people with whom she is closely involved. The more details you can give us about such people, the better. In general, that's all. Does it seem like too difficult an assignment?"

"Not at all," Litton said. "In fact, I'm surprised you want no more. Is that kind of information really worth ten thousand dollars to you?"

"I've been told," Jean said, "that if we get it within the next twenty-four hours, it will be worth a great deal more than ten thousand dollars."

"I see." Litton settled comfortably in the chair, placed his clasped hands around the ring on the table, enclosing it. "Then, if you like, Miss Merriam, I'll now make the contact."

"No special preparations?" she inquired, watching him.

"Not in this case." Litton nodded toward a heavily curtained alcove in the wall on his left. "That's what I call my withdrawal room. When I feel there's reason to expect difficulties in making a contact, I go in there. Observers can be disturbing under such circumstances. Otherwise, no preparations are necessary."

"What kind of difficulties could you encounter?" Jean asked.

"Mainly, the pull of personalities other than the one I want. A contact object may be valid, but contaminated by associations with other people. Then it's a matter of defining and following the strongest attraction, which is almost always that of the proper owner and our subject. Incidentally, it would be advantageous if you were prepared to record my report."

Jean tapped the handbag. "I'm recording our entire conversation, Mr. Litton."

He didn't seem surprised. "Very many of my clients do," he remarked. "Very well, then, let's begin . . ."

"How long did it take him to dream up this stuff?" Nick Garland asked.

"Four minutes and thirty-two seconds," Jean Merriam said.

Garland shook his head incredulously. He took the transcript she'd made of her recorded visit to Roy Litton's apartment from the desk and leafed through it again. Jean watched him, her face expressionless. Garland was a big gray-haired bear of a man, coldly irritable at present—potentially dangerous.

He laid the papers down, drummed his fingers on the desk. "I still don't want to believe it," he said, "but I guess I'll have to. He hangs on to Caryl Chase's ring for a few minutes, then he can tell you enough about her to fill five typed, single-spaced pages . . . That's what happened?"

Jean nodded. "Yes, that's what happened. He kept pouring out details about the woman as if he'd known her intimately half her life. He didn't hesitate about anything. My impression was that he wasn't guessing about anything. He seemed to know."

Garland grunted. "Max thinks he knew." He looked up at the man standing to the left of the desk. "Fill Jean in, Max. How accurate is Litton?"

Max Jewett said, "On every point we can check out, he's completely accurate."

"What are the points you can check out?" Jean asked.

"The ring belongs to Caryl Chase. She's thirty-two. She's Phil Chase's wife, currently estranged. She's registered at the Hotel Arve, Geneva, Switzerland, having an uneasy off-and-on affair with one William Haskell, British ski nut. He's jealous, and they fight a lot. Caryl suspects Phil has detectives looking for her, which he does. Her daughter Ellie is hidden away with friends of Caryl's parents in London. Litton's right about the ring. Caryl got it from her grandmother on her twenty-first birthday and had worn it regularly since. When she ran out on Phil last month, she took it off and left it in her room safe. Litton's statement, that leaving it was a symbolic break with her past life, makes sense." Jewett shrugged. "That's about it. Her psychoanalyst might be able to check out some of the rest of what you got on tape. We don't have that kind of information."

Garland growled, "We don't need it. We got enough for now."

Jean exchanged a glance with Jewett. "You feel Litton's genuine, Mr. Garland?"

"He's genuine. Only Max and I knew we were going to test him on Caryl. If he couldn't do what he says he does, you wouldn't have got the tape. There's no other way he could know those things about her." Garland's face twisted into a sour grimace. "I thought Max had lost his marbles when he told me it looked like Phleger had got his information from some kind of swami. But that's how it happened. Frank Phleger got Litton to tap my mind something like two or three months ago. He'd need that much time to get set to make his first move."

"How much have you lost?" Jean asked.

He grunted. "Four, five million. I can't say definitely yet. That's not what bothers me." His mouth clamped shut, a pinched angry line. His eyes shifted bleakly down to the desk, grew remote, lost focus.

Jean Merriam watched him silently. Inside that big skull was stored information which seemed sometimes equal to the intelligence files of a central bank. Nick Garland's brain was a strategic computer, a legal library. He was a multimillionaire, a brutal genius, a solitary and cunning king beast in the financial jungle— a jungle he allowed to become barely aware he existed. Behind his secretiveness he remained an unassailable shadow. In the six years Jean had been working for him she'd never before seen him suffer a setback; but if they were right about Litton, this was more than a setback. Garland's mind had been opened, his plans analyzed, his strengths and weaknesses assessed by another solitary king beast—a lesser one, but one who knew exactly how to make the greatest possible use of the information thus gained—and who had begun to do it. So Jean waited and wondered.

"Jean," Garland said at last. His gaze hadn't shifted from the desk.

"Yes?"

"Did Litton buy your story about representing something like a detective agency?"

"He didn't seem to question it," Jean said. "My impression was that he doesn't particularly care who employs him, or for what purpose."

"He'll look into anyone's mind for a price?" It was said like a bitter curse.

"Yes . . . his price. What are you going to do?"

Garland's shoulders shifted irritably. "Max is trying to get a line on Phleger."

Jean glanced questioningly at Jewett. Jewett told her, "Nobody seems to have any idea where Frank Phleger's been for the past three weeks. We assume he dropped out of sight to avoid possible repercussions. The indications are that we're getting rather close to him."

"I see," Jean said uncomfortably. The king beasts avoided rough play as a matter of policy, usually avoided conflict among themselves, but when they met in a duel there were no rules.

"Give that part of it three days," Garland's voice said. She looked around, found him watching her with a trace of what might be irony, back at any rate from whatever brooding trance he'd been sunk in. "Jean, call Litton sometime tomorrow."

"All right."

"Tell him the boss of your detective organization wants an appointment with him. Ten o'clock, three days from now."

She nodded, said carefully, "Litton could become extremely valuable to you, Mr. Garland."

"He could," Garland agreed. "Anyway, I want to watch the swami perform. We'll give him another assignment."

"Am I to accompany you?"

"You'll be there, Jean. So will Max."

"I keep having the most curiously definite impression," Roy Litton observed, "that I've met you before."

"You have," Garland said amiably.

Litton frowned, shook his head. "It's odd I should have forgotten the occasion!"

"The name's Nick Garland," Garland told him.

Still frowning, Litton stared at him across the table. Then abruptly his face paled. Jean Merriam, watching from behind her employer, saw Litton's eyes shift to her, from her to Max Jewett, and return at last, hesitantly, to Garland's face. Garland nodded wryly.

"I was what you call one of your subjects, Mr. Litton," he said. "I can't give you the exact date, but it should have been between two and three months ago. You remember now?"

Litton shook his head. "No. After such an interval it would be impossible to be definite about it, in any case. I keep no notes and the details of a contact very quickly grow blurred to me." His voice was guarded; he kept his eyes on Garland's. "Still, you seemed familiar to me at once as a person. And your name seems familiar. It's quite possible that you have been, in fact, a contact subject."

"I was," Garland said. "We know that. That's why we're here."

Litton cleared his throat. "Then the story Miss Merriam told me at her first visit wasn't true."

"Not entirely," Garland admitted. "She wasn't representing a detective outfit. She represented me. Otherwise, she told the truth. She was sent here to find out if you could do what we'd heard you could do. We learned that you could. Mr. Litton, you've cost me a great deal of money. But I'm not too concerned about that now, because, with your assistance, I'll make it back. And I'll make a great deal more besides. You begin to get the picture?"

Relief and wariness mingled for an instant in Litton's expression. "Yes, I believe I do."

"You'll get paid your regular fees, of course," Garland told him. "The fact is, Mr. Litton, you don't charge enough. What you offer is worth more than ten thousand a shot. What you gave Frank Phleger was worth enormously more."

"Frank Phleger?" Litton said.

"The client who paid you to poke around in my mind. No doubt he wouldn't have used his real name. It doesn't matter. Let's get on to your first real assignment for me. Regular terms. This one isn't a test. It's to bring up information I don't have and couldn't get otherwise. All right?"

Litton nodded, smiled. "You have a suitable contact object?"

"We brought something that should do," Garland said. "Max, give Mr. Litton the belt."

Jean Merriam looked back toward Jewett. Garland hadn't told her what Litton's assignment was to be, had given her no specific instructions, but she'd already turned on the recorder in her handbag. Jewett was taking a large plastic envelope from the briefcase he'd laid beside his chair. He came over to the table, put the envelope before Litton, and returned to his place.

"Can you tell me specifically what you want to know concerning this subject?" Litton asked.

"To start with," Garland said, "just give us whatever you can get. I'm interested in general information."

Litton nodded, opened the plastic envelope, and took out a man's leather belt with a broad silver buckle. Almost immediately an expression of distaste showed in his face. He put the belt on the table, looked over at Garland.

"Mr. Garland," he said, "Miss Merriam may have told you that on occasion I'm offered a contact object I can't use. Unfortunately, this belt is such an object."

"What do you mean?" Garland asked. "Why can't you use it?"

"I don't know. It may be something about the belt itself, and it may be the person connected with it." Litton brushed the belt with his fingers. "I simply have a very unpleasant feeling about this object. It repels me." He smiled apologetically. "I'm afraid I must refuse to work with it."

"Well, now," Garland said, "I don't like to hear that. You've cost me a lot, you know. I'm willing to overlook it, but I do expect you to be cooperative in return."

Litton glanced at him, swallowed uneasily. "I understand—and I assure you you'll find me cooperative. If you'll give me some other assignment, I assure you—"

"No," Garland said. "No, right now I want information about this particular person, not somebody else. It's too bad if you don't much like to work with the belt, but that's your problem. We went to a lot of trouble to get the belt for you. Let me state this quite clearly, Mr. Litton. You owe me the information, and I think you'd better get it now."

His voice remained even, but the menace in the words was undisguised. The king beast was stepping out from cover, and Jean's palms were suddenly wet. She saw Litton's face whiten.

"I suppose I do owe it to you," Litton said after a moment. He hesitated again. "But this isn't going to be easy."

Garland snorted. "You're getting ten thousand dollars for a few minutes' work!"

"That isn't it. I . . ." Litton shook his head helplessly, got to his feet. He indicated the curtained alcove at the side of the room. "I'll go in there. At best, this will be a difficult contact to attempt. I can't be additionally distracted by knowing that three people are staring at me."

"You'll get the information?" Garland asked.

Litton looked at him, said sullenly, "I always get the information." He picked up the belt, went to the alcove, and disappeared through the curtains.

Garland turned toward Jean Merriam. "Start timing him," he said.

She nodded, checked her watch. The room went silent, and immediately Jean felt a heavy oppression settle on her. It was almost as if the air had begun to darken around them. Frightened, she thought, *Nick hates that freak . . . Has he decided to kill him?*

She pushed the question away and narrowed her attention to the almost inaudible ticking of the tiny expensive watch. After a while she realized that Garland was looking at her again. She met his eyes, whispered, "Three minutes and ten seconds." He nodded.

There was a sound from within the alcove. It was not particularly loud, but in the stillness it was startling enough to send a new gush of fright through Jean. She told herself some minor piece of furniture, a chair, a small side table, had fallen over, been knocked over on the carpeting. She was trying to think of some reason why Litton should have knocked over a chair in there when the curtains before the alcove were pushed apart. Litton moved slowly out into the room.

He stopped a few feet from the alcove. He appeared dazed, half-stunned, like a man who'd been slugged hard in the head and wasn't sure what had happened. His mouth worked silently, his lips writhing in slow, stiff contortions as if trying to shape words that couldn't be pronounced. Abruptly he started forward. Jean thought for a moment he was returning to the table, but he went past it, pace quickening, on past Garland and herself without glancing at either of them. By then he was almost running, swaying from side to side in long staggering steps, and she realized he was hurrying toward the French doors which stood open on the wide veranda overlooking the park. Neither Garland nor Jewett moved from their chairs, and Jean, unable to speak, twisted around to look after Litton as they were doing. She saw him run across the veranda, strike the hip-high railing without checking, and go on over.

❀　　❀　　❀

The limousine moved away from the Torrell Arms through the sunlit park, Jewett at the wheel, Garland and Jean Merriam in the back seat. There was no siren wail behind them, no indication of disturbance, nothing to suggest that anyone else was aware that a few minutes ago a man had dropped into the neatly trimmed park shrubbery from the eighteenth floor of the great apartment hotel.

"You could have made use of him," Jean said. "He could have been of more value to you than anyone else in the world. But you intended to kill him from the start, didn't you?"

Garland didn't reply for a moment. Then he said, "I could have made use of him, sure. So could anyone else with ten thousand dollars to spare, or some way to put pressure on him. I don't need somebody like Litton to stay on top. And I don't like the rules changed. When Phleger found Litton, he started changing them. It could happen again. Litton had to be taken out."

"Max could have handled that," Jean said. Her hands had begun to tremble again; she twisted them tightly together around the strap of the handbag. "What did you do to get Litton to kill himself?"

Garland shook his head. "I didn't intend him to kill himself. Max was to take care of him afterward."

"You did something to him."

Garland drew a long sighing breath. "I was just curious," he said. "There's something I wonder about now and then. I thought Litton might be able to tell me, so I gave him the assignment."

"What assignment? He became someone else for three minutes. What happened to him?"

Garland's head turned slowly toward her. She noticed for the first time that his face was almost colorless. "That was Frank Phleger's belt," he said. "Max's boys caught up with him last night. Phleger's been dead for the last eight hours."

Would You?

. . . .

AFTER DINNER MARKUS Menzies suggested he might show Geoffrey about the chalet. Geoffrey agreed. The place had belonged previously to some Liechtenstein, and Marcus had bought it five years ago. What a man like Menzies could want with an expensive antique in the heart of the Alps, Geoffrey couldn't imagine. It wasn't the proximity of the ski slopes which had drawn Geoffrey into the area for the season. Markus always had looked on sporting activities involving physical exertion or risk as an occupation for lunatics. And he was an old man now. Though, Geoffrey reminded himself, only fifteen years his senior.

And what, for that matter, had induced Markus to invite him here for dinner tonight? It had been eight years since they last met, considerably longer than that since they'd had any significant dealings with each other. There'd been a time, of course, when Markus Menzies and Geoffrey Bryant had made a great team . . . in aircraft, in textiles, in shipping, in one thing and another, legitimate for the most part, occasionally not quite so legitimate. They'd both made their pile in the process; and then they'd split up. Markus went on to become extremely wealthy; Geoffrey remained as wealthy as he wanted to be or saw any use in being. It made sense to start to enjoy what he had rather than continue maneuvering for more. He wasn't married, had no intention of getting married, had no dependents of any kind. The world waited to be savored at leisure.

He'd accepted the telephoned invitation to dinner mainly out of curiosity. Markus wasn't prone to nostalgic sentimentality; he should have something in mind, and it might be interesting to find out what it was. But nothing was said over dinner to give Geoffrey a definite clue. The talk ranged widely but comfortably. Markus had acquired a variety of hobbies; the chalet might be one of them. He seemed completely relaxed, which meant nothing. If he had a purpose, it would show when he intended it to show, not before.

"I had quite a start the other day," he was remarking. "I was coming through the village, and there was a tall slender woman who . . . well, for an instant I actually believed I was looking, over a space of not more than twenty feet, at Eileen Howard."

After a moment Geoffrey said soberly, "I've made similar mistakes more than once."

Markus glanced across the table at him. Briefly his face looked worn and tired, more so than his age indicated. "Not at all like seeing a ghost," he said, as if to himself. "A compellingly vivid impression of Eileen as she was then. All life, warmth!" He shook his head. "Immediately afterwards, I was unable to understand what could have given me the idea. There was some general resemblance, of course." His voice trailed off.

Something in a motion or gesture could be enough, Geoffrey thought. The glimpse of a finely drawn profile, the inflection in a laugh. It hadn't happened to him in some time. They'd both wanted Eileen; probably they'd both loved her. And because of that, between them in their maneuverings, they shared in a way the responsibility for her accidental death. They'd never talked about it, rarely mentioned Eileen again. But the other's presence soon became a growing irritation. It was a relief when their informal partnership ended.

It might have been simply that chance incident in the village which caused Markus to extend his invitation, some sudden urge to speak of Eileen. But he did not seem to want to pursue the subject farther. Geoffrey was glad of it.

The talk shifted to impersonal things. It was after the brandy that Markus suggested a tour of the chalet. For a while they moved unhurriedly about the big hall downstairs, along corridors, in and out of rooms. Markus had taken the house with its furnishings and left most of those untouched. Landscapes and portraits shared the walls with formidably antlered and horned heads. Markus kept up a line of talk about the chalet's history and the affairs of previous owners. Geoffrey found himself getting bored.

"Where's the mysterious chair you mentioned?" he asked.

Markus nodded towards the stairway. "Upstairs." He smiled. "I was saving it for the last. Would you like to see it now?"

Geoffrey said he would, hoping that would end the tour. He followed his host up a narrow flight of stairs to the third floor of the chalet. Markus stopped before a door, took out a key. Geoffrey looked at him curiously. "You keep the room locked?"

"Some of the servants know the story," Markus said. "They have a superstitious feeling about the chair. I think they're a little afraid of it. So the room remains locked mainly for their peace of mind." He opened the door, switched on overhead lights. "There it is."

The room was not large and the chair dominated it. It stood on a low dais, evidently constructed for the purpose. A sizable chair of smoothly polished wood, rather heavily built but in lines of flowing grace. The carvings were restrained, barely more than indicated, except for an animal head at the end of each broad armrest. The heads lifted out from the chair, pointing into the room. They were oblong and flattened, somewhat like the heads of lizards or snakes.

Well, it's a chair, Geoffrey thought. He realized Markus was watching him. "Markus," he said, "do you expect me to be impressed?"

Markus smiled. "Why not? You're looking at a mystery. Do you recognize the period?"

Geoffrey shook his head. "Period furniture isn't one of my interests."

"The chair is at least two hundred years old," Markus said. "Records show it was acquired that long ago. They don't show from whom it was acquired. But it belongs to no definable period."

He moved towards the chair, Geoffrey following him. "What would you call that wood?" Markus asked.

Geoffrey shrugged. "Oak, possibly." Markus stroked a finger along the armrest. "Touch it," he suggested.

Geoffrey laid the palm of his hand on the chair, moved it tentatively back and forth, frowned, and pressed down with his fingers.

"That's very odd! " he said.

"What impression do you get?"

"A smoothness, almost like velvet. Not only that. I had the feeling it was soft, that it was giving a little under my touch. But it obviously is quite solid."

He drew his hand away, looked at Markus with increased interest. "What was that story again? That anyone who sits in this chair can change his past life?"

"That's it. One sits in the chair. One places his hands"—Markus nodded at the armrests—"on those carved heads—"

"—and makes a wish, eh?" Geoffrey concluded.

"No. Not a wish. One is then able, quite literally, to edit the events in his past. Say you made a wrong decision twenty years ago. You can now undo that mistake, and remake the decision. Lost opportunities can be regained, and your life up to the present will have been changed correspondingly. Anything can be changed. Anything. That's the story."

Geoffrey smiled uncomfortably. "You sound almost as if you believed it!"

"Perhaps I do."

Now this was getting eerie. Geoffrey stared at his host. Had Markus gone out of his mind? "You've tried it?" he asked.

"Should I want to change my life? I have my health, my hobbies, my money."

"Isn't there anything you'd like to have done differently?"

Markus said slowly, "I'm not sure there is."

"How did the people who are supposed to have used the chair make out?" Geoffrey asked, smiling to indicate he wasn't taking this seriously.

Markus shook his head. "Whoever has tried it evidently preferred not to put the fact on record. Would you?"

"Probably not." Geoffrey laughed. "Well, it's a good story, Markus. And perhaps I'm a little sorry it isn't true. Because there might be things in my life I would prefer to be otherwise. That wood— it must be wood—is certainly odd! I can't imagine what kind of treatment was given it to produce that effect."

"Put your hand on one of the reptile heads," Markus said.

Geoffrey looked at him, then cupped his palm over the carved head nearest him. "Now what?" he asked.

"Leave it there a moment."

Geoffrey shrugged mentally, let his hand rest on the wood. After some seconds his expression changed. Perhaps a minute later, he removed his hand. "This is very curious!" he remarked.

"What did you experience?" Markus asked.

"Something like a current of energy. It built up gradually, then held at a steady level. Almost electric. But not at all unpleasant. I gather you've felt it."

"Yes, I've felt it."

"While I was sensing this," Geoffrey said. "I found myself beginning to believe that I *could* change the past. If I wanted to."

"If you'd like to experiment," Markus told him, "the chair is yours."

"How does it work?"

"The way it's been described," said Markus, "you will be in contact with your past as long as you are seated in the chair and keep your hands on the carved heads. You'll begin to remember past events in all detail and find yourself a part of them again. And if you wish to change them then, turn them into something other than you recall as having happened, you'll be able to do it. When you're ready to stop the process, simply lift your hands from the heads. That's all there is to it. . . ."

So Geoffrey sat in the chair. He gave Markus, standing near the center of the room, watching him, a final probing glance. Then he clasped his hands firmly about the snakelike or lizardlike heads.

For a few seconds there was nothing. Then came the sense of flowing power, faint and far away, but growing stronger as if he were being drawn towards it, until it seemed all about him and streaming through him.

Like a great recording tape unreeling in all his senses, the past burst in.

It was a swift blur of impressions at first. Glimpses of color and motion, the ghostly murmuring of voices, flicks of smell and taste, a sense of shifting physically, a jerking in the muscles. It all rushed past him, or he was rushing, being rushed, through it. There remained some awareness of the room dimly about, of the motionless shadowy shape of Markus Menzies. Emotions began to wash through Geoffrey, a hurrying tide of anxieties, grief, furious anger, high delight, changing from moment to moment. . . .

And then, somewhere in darkness, it all stopped. As if he'd touched a button or switch on a machine, bringing it to a standstill. The awareness arose that he could control this.

At that point he was caught midway between apprehension—because of the strangeness of the experience—and fascinated interest. Something in him kept insisting that his sensations had been simply sensations, without further significance. That the chair, whatever strange machine the chair might be, was stirring up memories and drawing on them to produce such effects, and that there was nothing else to it, no preternatural connection at all with the realities of the past. But there was also the growing sense of power, of almost godlike power, and of being in control of what occurred here.

So all right, he thought, let's try it out. Let's select some occasion when something went wrong, some very minor thing for a start, and see if I can edit out the mistakes I made.

And he found such an occasion.

And then another, and another—

Until presently he discovered he was sitting in the chair again. His hands were still closed on the carved heads, but the feeling of the flow of power was gone. Markus Menzies stood staring at him, his face set and tense.

Geoffrey pushed himself rather stiffly to his feet and stepped down from the dais.

"Well?" Markus said harshly. "What happened?"

Geoffrey shook his head. "Oh, I was back there all right," he said. "At least, that was my impression." He smiled carefully. "This is some kind of trickery, I think, Markus. But very clever trickery."

"It's no trick, you fool! Did you change anything?"

"No, I didn't change anything. Though I admit I was tempted. Oh, yes! Strongly tempted—" To Geoffrey's surprise, his voice shook for an instant. "In particular," he went on, "in that series of events which ended, as you recall, in Eileen's death."

Markus's face was white now. "You were *there*—and you did nothing?"

"I changed nothing," Geoffrey said irritably. "I felt I could do it. I believe now that feeling was part of the deception. But if it wasn't deception, if it would have been possible, then I think I was wise not to make the attempt."

"You wouldn't save Eileen?"

"Markus. Eileen is dead. Quite dead. How could she be made alive again? And assuming she still were alive, had never died, the recent years would not have been at all what they were. That was a consideration. I realized during this that I've been very fortunate. The decisions I made, right and wrong, brought me safely to this point in life and into not unfavorable circumstances. In retrospect I know now that the odds were against that, though day by day, as I lived it, I never was fully conscious of them. Think of the countless opportunities each of us is given to turn unawares into the wrong path, the less satisfactory path, even the fatal path . . . no, I don't care to gamble deliberately against those odds, to place what I am and have now at stake again. And if I had acted in any way, that's what I would have done. To force change on the past, even in one minor aspect, might alter all the subsequent past in unforeseeable ways. That very well could be disastrous."

Markus said, with intense bitterness, "You're a coward!"

"Aren't you?" Geoffrey asked.

"Yes. I am," Markus said. "I once sat in that chair as you have done."

"I was sure you had," Geoffrey said. "And I don't blame you entirely for trying to get me to do something for which you didn't have the courage. But to do it was quite out of the question. Perhaps I might have modified the past without affecting the present external world in any noticeable way. Even that would have brought an element of intolerable uncertainty into my personal existence. As things are, I believe I understand the world and its realities well enough. My life has been based on the feeling of understanding it and being able to deal with it. I want to retain the feeling. And I would have lost it if I had attempted to change the past and succeeded. If I knew that was possible, I could never be sure of the reality of anything about me again. The world would have become as insubstantial and meaningless as a madman's dream.

"I don't want that. I couldn't live that way. So I won't put your device to the test. If I haven't proved that it can do what it is supposed to do, I can continue to believe that it's impossible. I prefer to believe it." He added, after a moment, "And so, I think, do you."

Markus shrugged heavily. "Did you have the feeling that this was the one opportunity you would be given—that if you didn't change the past now, you wouldn't have another chance?"

"Yes, I had that feeling," Gregory said. "It was part of the temptation." He looked over at the dais, and his gaze stayed for a moment on the carved animalic heads lifting silently into the room. "It doesn't matter," he said, "whether it was a valid feeling or not. Because nothing would induce me to sit in that chair again."

He started out of the room. Markus followed and locked the door behind them. As they went down the stairs, Geoffrey said, "I imagine that was your purpose in inviting me here tonight."

"Of course it was," Markus said.

"When did you have the experience?"

"Shortly after I bought this place. Almost five years ago."

"Have you ever tried to repeat it?"

Markus shook his head.

These Are the Arts
. . . .

"Now the Seven Deadly Arts are: Music, Literature,
Painting, Sculpture, Architecture, Dancing, Acting. The
Mercy of God has luckily purified these once pagan
inventions, and transformed them into saving instruments of grace. Yet it behooves us to examine with the
utmost diligence the possible sources of evil latent in each
and every one of these arts. Then we shall consider some
of the special forms of sin that may develop from them.
St. Chrysostom warned the faithful . . ."

—the preacher, in Huneker's "Visionaries"

HUGH GROVER WAS SITTING in the TV room of an old but
spacious and luxuriously equipped bomb shelter located in a forested section of the rambling Grover estate. The shelter had been
constructed by Hugh's grandfather sixty years earlier and, while
never actually used as a place of refuge, had been kept in good
condition by various members of the Grover family, who retained
a strong touch of foresight and prudence in their habits even
through the easygoing early decades of the Twenty-first Century.
The entrance to the shelter was camouflaged, and only the Grover
household and their intimates were informed of its existence and
whereabouts.

Hugh, now a man of forty and the last living member of the
family, looked very thoughtful and puzzled as he switched off the
TV set and audiophile attachment and closed up a bull-roarer
recording he had placed on the table beside him. He pushed away
the tall mirror he had set up so he could watch the screen without

looking at it directly, and climbed out of his chair. He had intended mirror and recording to be precautionary devices, but they had turned out to be superfluous. He had seen and heard nothing of the Galcom Craze.

It was possible that the World Government—wonder of wonders!—had heeded his warnings, or perhaps somebody else's, and banned the stuff completely. In the past few hours, Hugh had dialed every major station on earth. From none of them had the improbably beautiful face of a Galcom Teacher looked out at him; no Galcom symbol appeared suddenly in the screen. Nor had the audiophile programs produced any of those curious little cross-ripples of sound which were not openly connected with Galcom, but which Hugh had considered to be definitely one of its devices.

The absence of these items in itself was, of course, all to the good. But it seemed odd that, in addition, there hadn't been the slightest mention of Galcom during the hours Hugh listened and watched. He was the reverse of a TV addict, but he felt it improbable that what had started as the biggest TV Craze of recent years could simply have dropped from the public's interest again during the two weeks he was living in the bomb shelter. It seemed much more likely that the lack of reference to it was due to an official taboo.

He had predicted that the embittered settlers of Mars Territory would carry out a space attack on Earth after first softening up the population through the Galcom Craze. Did this deliberate lack of mention of the Craze suggest that certain elements of the danger still existed? Hugh Grover could think of no other reason for it.

He frowned, his finger moving toward a button to summon his secretary, Andy Britton, who shared the shelter with him and was at present asleep in another section. Then he checked himself. Andy made a good listener when Hugh felt like airing his thoughts, but it might be better to ponder this curious situation by himself first.

It had been through Andy Britton that Hugh first learned of the Galcom Craze. They had come in by Atlantic rocket from the Jura Mountains that evening with a box of newly uncovered Bronze Age artifacts to add to Hugh's private museum. The Grover residence was on the fringes of the little village of Antoinette, three miles upriver from the bomb shelter, in the direction of the sizable town of South Valley. Hugh unpacked while Andy drove into Antoinette to buy dinner supplies. He came back laughing.

"A new advertising craze has started up," he said. "This one might interest you, Hugh!"

"Why should it?" Hugh asked.

"Symbols," Andy told him. "Primitive meditation brought up to date on TV! Practically every big station seems to be involved. They have overlapping Symbol Hours around the clock. You can't guess who's doing all this, so I'll tell you. It's the first representatives of the Galactic Community to reach the Solar System. How about that?"

Hugh grunted and asked him what he thought he was talking about. Galcom, it appeared, was short for Galactic Community. The representatives were inhumanly beautiful women or inhumanly handsome men. They were referred to as The Teachers. Their mission was to facilitate the adoption of Earth into the Community by instructing its inhabitants in a New Method of Thought and Communication, which would enable them to exchange ideas with other Galcom entities, and also one another, with the greatest of ease and speed. The New Method could be acquired by devoting a little study daily to the Galcom Symbols being presented on purchased TV time.

It was, of course, a promotion hoax of some sort. After the World Supreme Court established that to question publicly the truthfulness of statements made through an advertising medium was to act in restriction of trade, and hence illegal, the way had been open for the staging of truly colossal attention-getting tricks. Throughout his life, Hugh Grover had been vaguely aware of a constant succession of TV Crazes of varying magnitude. When he thought of them at all, he concluded that in the comfortable world-wide suburbanity of the period people grew increasingly hungry for sensations of even the most idiotic variety. And since no corner of Earth was without its quota of TV sets, a really big Craze could command virtually universal attention. As a rule, they built up for a month or two, while the more sophisticated speculated on who was behind it this time and what actually was to be promoted, and the less sophisticated—time after time, apparently—took the gag at face value and very seriously. Andy reported that the smart money had begun to settle on Mars Territory as the Galcom sponsor within the first week and that the Craze was expected to resolve itself eventually as a renewed bid for Unlimited Free Water from Earth for the Territory.

"They seem to have hooked an unusual percentage of Believers this time," Andy said—Believers being, of course, the people who again had bought the gag. He had run into five or six persons in Antoinette who assured him with some excitement that the Galactic Community really existed, that this Craze was no Craze at all but a perfectly sincere and earnest attempt to help Earth raise itself to Galcom's lofty standards. Two of Andy's informants by now had achieved moments of direct mental communication with a Galcom Teacher, an experience described as enthralling and spiritually satisfying.

Hugh felt mildly disgusted, as he not infrequently was with the ways of the society in which he found himself. But since the study of symbolism and its use by primitive societies was in fact one of his most intensively cultivated hobbies, he was curious enough to turn on the TV set after dinner.

Immediately, he found himself face to face with one of the Galcom Teachers.

This one was female, and there could be no disputing the flawless and—figuratively, at least—the unearthly quality of her loveliness. Women irritated Hugh Grover as a rule, and he tended to avoid their company; but the Teacher's impact was not lost on him. He had been staring at her for almost twenty seconds before he discovered that the melodious voice was repeating some of the things Andy had told him. The arts the station's viewers were being taught here, she said, were not designed to make them worthy of membership in the Galactic Community, as some appeared to have assumed. No—they were worthy indeed, and the intention was only to dissolve the barriers of linguistic difference, to do away with the awkwardness of spoken words which led so often and easily to misunderstandings. Words were not necessary when mind could speak to mind. And now, if the viewers would give their relaxed attention to the Galcom symbols they would be shown, they would find their minds begin to open out gently and softly . . . like beautiful flowers. . . .

In spite of this sweetly fluted lunacy, Hugh did not turn off the TV. He was still staring in fascination at the exquisite creature in the screen when she suddenly faded from view and he was looking instead at a Galcom symbol.

In almost the same instant, the screen went blank.

It took Hugh some seconds to realize that he himself had shut off the set. He was not in the least tempted to turn it on again. He had been badly startled. At the moment the symbol appeared, there had been a distinct sensation as if something were tugging at his thoughts . . . and then something else inside him went tight, closed up; and the sensation ended.

Once before, he'd had a very similar experience. A psychiatrist had attempted to hypnotize him; and while Hugh, consciously, had been completely willing to let it happen, the attempt ended in absolute failure. At that time, too, there had been, as Hugh floated along mentally, his attention only half on the medical man's words, a sudden awareness of shutting off their effect and remaining closed to it, of having become impenetrable now and secure. And there was nothing that Hugh—consciously again—could do about it. He could not be hypnotized.

And what could that mean here? Brief as his glimpse of the Galcom symbol had been, he could recall it distinctly—a pale-blue, glowing, rather intricate design of markings which reminded Hugh of nothing so much as some of the ideographic characters used in the written Chinese language of past centuries. In itself, there was nothing sinister or alarming about its appearance. But Hugh could remember very vividly the feeling of something pulling at his thoughts. . . .

Hugh Grover continued to sit before the dead set for a while, becoming increasingly disturbed. At last, he got up and put a call through to the home of an acquaintance in the East who was an advertising executive.

The acquaintance confirmed Andy Britton's report on the Galcom Craze. It was a big thing, a very big thing. After only a few days, it was beginning to edge into the top popularity spot. In his opinion, it was likely to develop into the most success-ful TV spectacular of the past twenty years. Yes, Mars Territory definitely was backing it. The acquaintance couldn't yet see just how the Territory planned to tie in its perennial demand for Earth water, but that certainly would turn out to be the angle. Hugh presumably had become interested in the program because of its use of symbols? One heard that there appeared to be a very deft adaptation of neo-Jungian techniques involved. What was Hugh's opinion?

Hugh replied cautiously that he hadn't yet seen a Galcom pro-gram, but that it seemed possible. What effect did the symbols produce on the viewers?

"They're euphoric," the acquaintance said. It was difficult to be more specific because of wide variations in individual response. It was a really remarkable approach, a unique accomplishment. Yes, he understood there'd been negative reactions but in such an insignificant number that they could not affect the progress of the Craze in any way . . . Oh, perhaps point five per cent. There were always cranks and alarmists who objected to genuine innovations in the programs.

After Hugh hung up, he did some more intensive thinking. He was now thoroughly concerned, but there were reasons to be cautious about any action he took. Officially, he could be fitted very well into his acquaintance's classification of cranks and alarmists. He was known to be a wealthy eccentric—wealthy enough to get away with a degree of eccentricity which a man of moderate means could hardly have afforded. He was an amateur scientist. Even his friends regarded his preoccupation with things of the past, things of the mind, as somewhat morbid. And there had been a period ten years before, after an ill-fated attempt at marriage, when he suffered a quite serious nervous breakdown and required extensive psychiatric treatment.

He had developed a considerable degree of self-awareness over the years. He knew that his interests and studies reflected his mental organization . . . an organization in which conscious and unconscious processes which in most men were kept much more neatly distinct tended to merge to an uncomfortable degree. He knew also that he had, in consequence, developed defensive reactions which the ordinary person simply did not have, and ordinarily had no need for. He could not be hypnotized. Drugs which were supposed to reduce resistance to hypnosis merely raised his own level. And he could not be affected by the Galcom symbols. But neither of those things would be true for the vast majority of Earth's population.

He had made a careful study of the connections between specific sensory impressions and mental effects. Form, color, motion— these things held unique meanings for the unconscious mind and aroused responses of which the conscious man might not be in the least aware.

His mind had produced an instantaneous, violent reaction to his first glimpse of a Galcom symbol. It had sealed itself away from something it regarded as a very dangerous threat.

What would the same impression be doing to the mind of the average man, which had never needed to learn such stringent measures of defense?

In Hugh Grover's opinion, it could plunge the possessor of that mind—after not too many encounters—into a state of psychotic helplessness.

And who would be interested in doing such a thing to the people of Earth?

Precisely Mars Territory, of course.

⚛   ⚛   ⚛

He had been on Mars some years before. Except for World Government officials, whose duties held them there, not many Earth citizens visited the Territory. It held no attractions for tourists. Hugh Grover's interest was drawn by reports that excavations had begun again in some of the ruins of the aboriginal Martian culture scattered sparsely about the Territory. Earlier archaeological efforts had produced insignificant results; the ruins were over a quarter of a million years old and usually buried, and there was no evidence that the native race had advanced beyond the level of walled villages before it died out. But Hugh decided he would like to visit some of the new digs in person.

It had been a frustrating experience which gave him a very different picture of the Territorial settlers and in particular of their ruling group than he had obtained on Earth. They were a hard, sullen breed of men, rulers of a barren empire with the potential of a great industrial development—a development still stalled by Earth's refusal to supply Mars Territory with the required amounts of water. Hugh thought he understood the reason for that. Martian technology, spurred by necessity, was at least on a par with Earth's. Given unlimited water it would forge ahead. And once it was sufficiently ahead, complacent suburban Earth would be virtually at the mercy of a society which had learned again to fight and work relentlessly for what it wanted. It was hardly surprising that the World Government was reluctant to go to enormous expense to help bring such a situation about.

But it made Earth's citizens very unpopular on Mars. Hugh's attempts to obtain permission to visit the ruins of the prehistoric culture continued to run into unaccountable difficulties and delays, and the local Earth officials at last advised him quietly to give the matter up. If he did succeed in getting into the Territorial backlands, they could not be responsible for his safety there.

At the time, Hugh had thought he was confronting simple malice. But there was another explanation. If an aboriginal symbol science had existed on Mars in the distant past, Territorial scientists might have been studying its principles in order to learn how to adapt them to produce effects on the human mind. In other words, the tools of the Galcom Craze were being prepared . . . and, naturally, an Earthman would not have been a welcome visitor. It was quite likely, Hugh decided, that he wouldn't have gotten out of Mars Territory alive if he had been too persistent in his efforts.

One could conclude further that Mars Territory was now at war with Earth.

The Galcom symbols would—in the opinion of the Territorials, at least—determine the issue. The derangement of the mental structure of the great majority of Earth's population could be far advanced before any outer evidence of general psychosis appeared. Then the Territorial space attack would be launched.

Mars Territory, Hugh thought, was making a mistake. Earth's material advantages would still be too great for them and in the end Earth would win out. But for the private citizens who retained their sanity, the interim period would be extremely unpleasant and dangerous.

Partway through his reflections, he had pressed the audiophile button on the TV set without giving the action much consideration, and the familiar muted flows of classical music were accompanying his thoughts. Now, suddenly, he sat bolt upright. There had been a subtle intrusion in the music, an odd, quick, light, up-and-down rippling, like the crossing of two threads of sound, which was not a proper part of the piece to which he was listening.

Almost with that thought came an internal reaction very similar to what Hugh experienced at his glimpse of the Galcom symbol— a sense of something pulling, tugging gently at his mind, a dream-like distortion; then the quick, solid block of mental resistance which shut the feeling off. Hugh reached out hastily and turned off the audiophile.

So they were not limited to visual channels in their attack on Earth's minds! Men like himself who ignored TV presentations could still be approached along other routes.

That decided him. This was no speculation but quite real, quite serious personal danger. He realized now that he had been getting sleepy for the past few minutes—and he could not be sure he had not heard that curious cross-ripple of sound several times before it penetrated into his awareness. When the attack was insidious enough, his subconscious watchdogs might be much less dependable than he had believed.

The important thing then was to look out for himself. Hugh was aware that he had no overwhelming or all-inclusive fondness for his fellow men; on the whole, they were there, and he could tolerate them. A few, like Andy Britton, he rather liked, when they weren't being irritating. Nevertheless, his decision now to take Andy to the old Grover bomb shelter with him was due primarily to the fact that Andy was a very capable young man whose assistance during the possibly trying period ahead might be invaluable.

As for the others, he would try to warn them in time to avert or modify the approaching disaster; but it would have to be done in a manner which could not affect his own safety. Though Mars Territory looked like the responsible agent for what was happening, it must have allies on Earth in positions where they could deal with interference . . . and with those who interfered. Hugh spent an hour outlining his conclusions about the Galcom Craze in every detail. He then made approximately fifty copies of the message and addressed them to various members of the government, to news agencies, and to a number of important people whose background indicated that they might give serious thought to such a warning. He was careful to mention nothing that could serve to identify him and left the messages unsigned. Andy Britton was dispatched to South Valley to drop them into the mailing system there. After the secretary returned, Hugh told him what he believed was occurring and what his plans were.

Andy kept his face carefully expressionless, but it was plain what his own theory was—old Hugh had cracked up at last. However, he had a highly paid job, and if Hugh wanted them to sit out the next few weeks in a bomb shelter, that would clearly be all right with Andy Britton. Before dawn, all preparations had been made. They closed up the town house in Antoinette again, and installed themselves unobtrusively in the forest shelter down the river.

The next two weeks passed—to all appearances—uneventfully. Andy Britton dutifully avoided the shelter's TV room, and he and Hugh took turns observing the air traffic above the river and the road gliders passing along the highway from the shelter lookout panel. There were no signs of disturbance of any kind. Andy, an active individual by nature, began to show some degree of restiveness but made no attempts to argue Hugh out of his ideas.

Hugh saw no reason to rush matters. For the time being, he had secured himself from the Galcom attack, both as to possible personal effects and the dangers that could arise from a demented populace. His warning might or might not be heeded. Others might see the threat and take steps to end it. Whatever was to occur, he had withdrawn to a position where he could wait events out with the greatest degree of safety.

He began to give his attention to methods whereby he could— without exposing himself—regain a more complete contact with the outer world than simple observation from the shelter provided.

Out of this came eventually the arrangement in the TV room with the mirror and the bull-roarer recording. The Galcom symbols, judging from the sample he had seen, were asymmetrical designs. If the specific visual image produced by them brought about some effect on the mind, the effect should be nullified by a reversal of the image. Hence the mirror through which he could observe the TV screen without looking directly at it. He was cancelling out the Gorgon's head. The bull-roarer recording was to smother Galcom's audible form of attack, the drowsiness-producing cross-ripplings of light sound. The switch which started the recording would be in Hugh's left hand whenever he turned on the set, his thumb pressed down on its release. At any loss of alertness, he would let go automatically. The election of a bull-roarer with its own ritual implications hadn't been necessary for this purpose; but the notion pleased Hugh and—the subconscious being the suggestible and superstitious entity it was—a little deliberate counter-magic should strengthen the effect of sheer noise.

In spite of these supporting devices, Hugh had intended to proceed very prudently with his investigation. He couldn't be sure they would actually give him more protection than his own resources could provide. He hadn't forgotten the disconcerting feeling of having been caught off guard by a barely perceptible sound pattern, and there might, after all, be more Galcom tricks than the two he had encountered. The lack of anything in the least abnormal then in the TV programs he scanned through was rather disconcerting in itself. Something, obviously, *had* happened—must have happened. The Galcom program hadn't vanished without cause.

The appearance of it was that Galcom had been banned from the networks by World Government edict. The entire business of symbol trickery and its effects might have been turned over meanwhile to some scientific group for orderly investigation. Mars Territory could have been put under an embargo. And it was conceivable that Territorial raiders were known or suspected to be in space; and that while the Earth fleets hunted for them, the whole affair was being toned down deliberately in the networks to avoid a panic. There was, after all, no effective way of protecting the population from space attack except by stopping a raider before he got too close.

The appearance of it then was a little mystifying, not necessarily alarming. It concurred with the undisturbed look of the countryside traffic outside the shelter.

But those reflections did not at all change Hugh's feeling about the situation. The feeling told him with increasing clarity that there was some hidden menace in the lack of mention about Galcom. That the silence covered a waiting trap. And that specifically he— Hugh Grover—was being threatened.

He could acknowledge that, theoretically, that presented the picture of a paranoid personality. But the hunch was too strong to be ignored. He didn't intend to ignore it. He could lose nothing—except for strengthening Andy's notions about his loss of mental competence, which was hardly important—by acting on the assumption that the hunch was correct. If it was correct, if there was a trap waiting outside, the trap could be sprung. Not by him, but by Andy Britton.

Hugh rubbed his chin thoughtfully. There was another place in the northern Andes which could be turned into at least as secure a hide-out as Grandfather Grover's bomb shelter. In some respects—the nearest neighbors would be many miles away—it should be a more dependable one. He could get there overnight with one of the pair of jet rigs hanging in the shelter storeroom. For the sake of obtaining definite information, which would either confirm or disprove his suspicions, he could, therefore, risk losing the bomb shelter.

And he could—though he hoped nothing would happen to Andy—risk losing Andy.

Andy Britton was in the kitchen section, having breakfast. He looked up rather blearily when Hugh came in. His red hair was still uncombed and he had obviously just come awake.

"Mind coming along to the TV room a moment?" Hugh asked. "I've found something, but I'm not quite sure what it means."

"What have you found?"

"I'd sooner let you see for yourself."

In the TV room, Andy looked at the mirror and recording with controlled distaste, asked, "Want me to use those?"

"It can't do any harm," Hugh said. "Here—I'll hold the switch for the bull-roarer myself. Now go ahead."

Andy studied his face quizzically, then turned on the TV set and clicked in a station at random. He watched the screen through the mirror, looked over at Hugh again.

"Try another one," Hugh suggested.

Ten minutes later, Andy, face very thoughtful, switched off the set, asked, "Same thing everywhere?"

"I've been going down through the list these last three hours,"

Hugh said. "I don't believe I missed a station of any significance.
I didn't hear a word about the Galcom Craze. Odd, isn't it?"

Andy agreed it was very odd indeed.

"What do you make of it?" Hugh asked.

Andy's lips quirked. "Isn't it obvious? Everyone in the world—
except you and I, of course—has learned by now how to communicate with the alien races of the Galactic Community. Last
Monday, the Solar System was elevated to full membership. Why
keep the thing going after that?" He pondered a moment, added,
"I owe you an apology, of course, Hugh."

"Why?"

"I thought you were tottering, and I guess I showed it. Now it
looks as if you were right. Something stopped the Craze in
midswing. And only our good old paternal World Government
could have done it."

"The Craze couldn't have simply run itself out . . . naturally?"

Andy shook his head. "I followed a lot of them when I was still
young and foolish. That Galcom deal was good for another six
weeks. It didn't run out naturally. It was stopped. And unless there
was something mighty wrong about those symbols—just like you
said—it wouldn't have been stopped." He grinned suddenly, his
face lightening. "Know something? When we walk out of here
now—when they find out who it was that shot off those warning messages all over the world two weeks ago—I'll be a hero's
secretary!"

Hugh hesitated, said, "I'm not so sure about that, Andy."

"Huh?" The grin faded from Andy's face, was replaced by a
cautious "Now what?" expression. He asked, "What do you mean,
Hugh?"

Hugh said, "I don't want to seem unduly apprehensive." He
indicated the TV screen. "But what we saw there does suggest
something like a conspiracy to me."

"A conspiracy?"

"Exactly. I told you I was sitting here for three hours checking
through the various stations. Why in all that time did no one even
mention the late Galcom Craze?"

"I wouldn't know," Andy said with a trace of exasperation. "But
the obvious way to find out is to get out of here and start asking questions. We can't spend the rest of our lives lurking in a
bomb shelter, Hugh."

Hugh smiled. "I don't intend to, believe me. But I do think we
should be a little careful about asking questions." He considered,

went on, "As a first step, let's wheel out the flitter and look things over from the air for a while."

Andy said with strained patience, "That isn't going to tell us what happened to the Galcom Craze. Now suppose I put the midget road glider in the back of the flitter and—"

"Why not?" Hugh looked at his watch. "It'll be getting dark in a few hours. If it seems safe to let you do a little reconnoitering on foot around South Valley, that would be the time to start out."

Shortly after sunset, Hugh brought the flitter down to a quiet stretch of the road leading from Antoinette to South Valley. Andy swung the glider out of the flitter's rear compartment, straightened it, and climbed into the saddle. He grinned at Hugh, said, "I'll be careful . . . don't worry! See you at the bomb shelter early in the morning."

Hugh nodded. "I'll wait for you inside."

He watched the road glider disappear around the bend toward South Valley, and took the flitter up again. From the air, nothing out of the ordinary appeared to have occurred, or to be occurring, in the South Valley district. In Antoinette and the other towns and villages over which they had passed, people plainly were going about their everyday activities with no suggestion of an emergency or of disturbances. But Hugh did not intend to change any part of his plans. His instincts still smelled a trap.

By nightfall, he had locked each section of the bomb shelter individually, then left it, locking the camouflaged entrance behind him. Carrying one of the jet rigs and a knapsack of camping equipment, and with a heavy automatic pistol fastened to his belt, he moved uphill through the trees surrounding the shelter until he reached a point some three hundred yards away, from where he could watch both the approaches from the river road half a mile below and the air above the forest. Here he took out a pair of powerful night glasses, laid his other equipment beside a tree, and settled down to wait.

If Andy showed up unaccompanied in the morning, he would be there to receive him and find out what had happened during the past two weeks. But if Andy did not come alone, or if the shelter was approached by others in the interval, Hugh would vanish quietly among the big trees behind him. Once over the crest of the hill, he would be in the thick timber of a government preserve. He was an expert outdoorsman and felt no concern about his ability to remain out of sight there. Before the next morning, the jet rig would have carried him to his new retreat while any searchers would still be engaged in attempting to open the last locked sections of the bomb shelter where he was supposed to be.

Any searchers. . . . Hugh admitted to himself that he could find no rational answer to the question of who should be searching for him or what their purpose might be. His hunch didn't tell him that. What it told him was to stay ready to run if he wanted to survive.

He intended to do just that.

Andy Britton appeared riding the road glider along the route from Antoinette around nine in the morning. Hugh watched him approach through the glasses. Nothing had happened during the night. Near morning, when he began to feel traces of drowsiness, he had taken wake-up pills and come alert again.

The glider could not be used in the rough natural terrain of the estate grounds. Hugh saw Andy bring it to a stop near the edge of the estate, push it out of sight among some bushes and start up toward the shelter. They had agreed that he should come on foot, rather than have Hugh bring the flitter down to the road to pick him up. Hugh remained where he was, continuing to scan the sky, the road in both directions and the woods below him as Andy came climbing higher, disappearing for minutes at a time among the trees, then emerging into open ground again.

There was no one with him, following him, or watching him from the air. Hugh stood up finally, settled knapsack and jet rig over his shoulders, and started downhill toward the shelter, still careful to remain out of sight himself.

He was standing concealed among the bushes above the shelter entrance when Andy appeared directly below him.

"Up here, Andy!" Hugh said.

Andy stopped in his tracks, stood peering about, as if in bewilderment.

Hugh repeated, "Up here. Right above you . . . see me? That's right. Now come on up."

Watching the secretary scramble awkwardly through the shrubbery toward him, Hugh felt a sharp thrill of renewed apprehension, for Andy was stumbling like a man who was either drunk or on the very edge of exhaustion. Then, as he came closer, Hugh could see that his face was pale and drawn. A dazed face, Hugh told himself . . . a shocked face. Caution!

He said sharply, the sense of danger pounding through him, "That's close enough to talk! Stop there."

Andy stopped obediently twelve feet away, stood staring at Hugh, then at the knapsack and jet rig Hugh had let slide to the ground, and at the pistol belted to Hugh's side. A look of growing comprehension came into his face.

"Yes," Hugh said coldly, "I'm ready to move out if necessary. Is it?"

Andy seemed to be struggling for words. Then he said, his voice thick and harsh, "I don't think that will do any good, Hugh. You were wrong, you know."

"About what?"

"Mars Territory. They weren't behind the Galcom Craze. . . ." His voice faltered.

"Go ahead. Then who was behind it?"

"Hugh, don't you see? The Galcom Teachers *were* aliens. They took over Mars Territory two months ago, before they ever showed up on Earth."

Staring at Andy's sweating, anguished face, Hugh felt a dryness come into his throat. He asked, "Are you trying to tell me there is such a thing as the Galactic Community—that those Teachers were its missionaries, just as they claimed to be?"

Andy shook his head. "No. It's worse than that. It's a lot worse than that. You were right about the symbols. They were doing things to people's minds through them. But it wasn't to teach us how to communicate with others. It's almost the other way around."

"The other . . . try to make sense, Andy!"

"I'm trying to. Those Teachers are the servants or slaves of another race. They were sent here because they can be made to look and sound like humans. The others are telepaths and the way they handle their servants is by telepathic orders. They're in control of whole planets, whole races. They couldn't ordinarily have got control of Earth because there were hardly any human beings with enough telepathic sensitivity to receive their orders and respond to them. So that's what was to be done through the Galcom Craze and the symbols . . . soften us up mentally to the point where we could understand the master race's orders."

"And it succeeded?"

"Of course it succeeded. They're already here. They arrived on Earth almost a week ago."

"Then why . . . ?"

"Why does everything look so peaceful?" Andy asked bitterly. "Why shouldn't it? When they give a human an order, the human obeys. He can't help it. They don't want our economy to break down. They don't want panics and anarchy. This is a valuable planet and their property. Everybody's been told to keep on with their regular activities, just as if nothing had happened. So that's exactly what they do.

"But they can *tell* you what's happened if you start asking them questions. Oh, Lord, can they tell you about it!" Andy's face wrinkled up and tears ran down his cheeks. "They've started taking people away in their ships now. Our surplus population, they say. Nobody knows what happens to . . ."

Hugh said, shocked, "But they couldn't have got control of everybody. Not so easily! Not so fast!"

"No, not everybody. There were the people like ourselves who just hadn't watched the programs. And what they call 'immunes'— anyone who doesn't react to a telepathic command and won't respond to conditioning. What's the difference? There weren't enough of either. The immunes are being rounded up and killed. The others get the treatment."

Take Andy or leave him? Andy could still be very useful. . . .

"Andy," he said, "we'll have to act quickly. If we stay here until they get everything organized, we won't be able to move without being spotted. Here are the shelter keys . . . catch them! That's right. Now get in there and get out your jet rig. We'll lock up the shelter and leave at once."

Andy nodded. "And then, Hugh?"

"There's another place I know of. Down south, up in the mountains. Nobody else around for miles. . . . We'll be safe there a long time. It's stocked up for years." Hugh bent for knapsack and rig, added, "After we get there, we'll see. It's quite probable that I'm an immune myself. We may locate others. I . . ."

There was a sudden noise behind him. Hugh turned sharply. Andy stood four feet away, the small gun in his hand pointing straight at Hugh's head.

"You *are* an immune, Hugh," he said, chokingly. "But I'm not— I'm not!"

The tears poured down his face as he pulled the trigger.

Clean Slate

• • • • • • • • • • • •

DR. EILEEN RANDALL put the telephone down, said to George Hair, "It will still be a few minutes, I'm afraid, Mr. Hair." She smiled ruefully. "It's very embarrassing that the Director of ACCED should have to let his own employer, the government's Administrator of Education, wait to see him! But Dr. Curtice didn't know you were coming until an hour ago, of course."

"I quite understand, Dr. Randall," George Hair said politely. Eileen Randall, he thought, was not in the least embarrassed by the situation; and it was not the first time he had waited here to see Curtice. But her attitude interested him. She was belligerently loyal to Curtice, and her manner toward himself, on the other occasions they had met, had been one of cool hostility.

Today, there was an air of excitement about her, and something else which had drawn Hair's attention immediately. She was a lean, attractive, black-haired woman in her thirties, normally quiet, certainly not given to coy ruefulness with visitors. But he would have said that during the fifteen minutes he had been here, Dr. Randall had been playing a game with him, at least from her point of view. Back of it was a new level of self-assurance. She felt, he decided, somewhat contemptuous of him today.

It meant the ACCED group believed they had gained some very significant advantage against him. . . .

"What did you think of the dog?" she asked, smiling.

"An amazing animal!" Hair said. "I would not have believed such a performance was possible. I'm taking it for granted, of course, that the uncanny intelligence it demonstrated in carrying out your instructions is again a result of combined SELAM and ACCED techniques. . . . Or perhaps Dr. Curtice has developed an entirely new educational approach?"

"New in the extent to which selective amnesia was carried in the dog, Mr. Hair," Dr. Randall told him. "In this case, the memory impressions of every experience it had had since its birth were deleted from its brain before retraining began. The training methods otherwise were exactly the ones we have used on dogs for the past six years. The results, as you saw, go far beyond anything we have accomplished with animals before, due to the preliminary complete amnesia."

"Indeed?" Hair said. "I'm sure I've had the impression from Dr. Curtice that it was impossible to induce a complete and permanent amnesia by the use of instruments without actually destroying brain tissue."

Dr. Randall gave him a look of gleeful malice. "It was impossible until early this year, Mr. Hair! That's when Dr. Curtice made the first full-scale tests of several new instruments he's had under development for some time. It's quite possible now." She put her hand out to the telephone. "Should I call the main laboratory again? Of course, they *will* let us know as soon as he . . ."

"Of course," George Hair said. "No, no need to call them again, Dr. Randall." He smiled. "And it isn't really necessary, you know, for you to entertain me while I'm waiting, although I appreciate your having taken the time for it. If there's something else you should be doing, please don't let the fact that I'm here interfere with your work."

This was, George Hair told himself, looking out of the fourth-story window of the ACCED Building at the river below, a bad situation. A very bad situation.

It was clear that Curtice intended to use the complete amnesia approach on human subjects next, and Eileen Randall would not have spoken and behaved as she had if the ACCED group weren't already certain they had Wirt Sebert's backing for their plan—possibly even Mallory's.

And he would have to voice his unequivocal opposition to it. He could not do anything else. ACCED had never served any useful purpose but that of a political tool and the purpose had been achieved at an inexcusable expense in distorted lives. When applied to human beings, it was a failure, a complete failure. And now the fact could no longer be covered up by new developments and accomplishments with dogs.

Politically, of course, a promising new development in the program, if it could be presented in a convincing manner, was almost required now. It would be a very poor time to acknowledge failure openly. Governor Wingfield had been using rumors about ACCED as another means of weakening the Administration's position and creating a general demand for new elections; and this year, for the first time in the fifteen years since the Takeover, the demand might grow too strong to be ignored. A public admission that the ACCED program had not produced, and could not produce, the results which had been expected of it might make the difference, as Wingfield understood very well.

ACCED—accelerated education—had been Wirt Sebert's idea to begin with. Or rather, many ideas for it had been around, but they had never been systematized, coordinated, or applied on a large scale; and Sebert had ordered all that done. After the Takeover, the need for a major evolution of the educational system was obvious. The working details of Earth's civilization had become so complex that not enough people were able to understand them well enough to avoid continuous breakdowns. Immediate changes in simplifying organization, in centralizing communication had been made, which had helped. But they could not be expected to remedy matters indefinitely. What was needed in the long run was an army of highly trained men and women capable of grasping the multifactored problems of civilization as they arose, capable of intelligent interaction and of making the best possible use of one another's skills and knowledge.

ACCED was to have been the answer to that. Find the way, Wirt Sebert had said, to determine exactly what information was needed, what was essential, and then find the way to hammer it into young brains by the hundreds of thousands. Nothing less would do.

So ACCED came into being. It was a project that caught the public's imagination. For three years, a succession of people headed it. Then Richard Curtice was brought in, a man selected personally by Sebert; and Curtice quickly took charge.

At that time, indications of weakness in the overall ACCED approach already were apparent to those conducting the project. George Hair didn't know about them then. He was still Secretary of Finance—in his own mind and that of the public the second man of the Big Four, directly behind President Mallory. True, Wirt Sebert was Secretary of State, but Hair was the theorist, the man who had masterminded the Takeover which Mallory, Sebert, and Wingfield, men of action, had carried out. He was fully occupied with other matters, and ACCED was Sebert's concern.

Sebert, no doubt, had been aware of the difficulties. ACCED, in the form which had been settled on for the project, was based on the principle of reward and punishment; but reward and punishment were expressed by subtle emotional conditions of which the subject was barely conscious. Combined with this was a repetitive cramming technique, continuing without interruptions through sleep and waking periods. With few exceptions, the subjects were college and high school students, and the ACCED process was expected to accomplish the purpose for which it had been devised in them within four to five years.

Throughout the first two years, extraordinary results of the process were reported regularly. They were still being reported during the third year, but no mention was made of the severe personality problems which had begun to develop among the subjects first exposed to ACCED.

It was at this point that Dr. Curtice was brought into the project, on Wirt Sebert's instructions. Curtice was then in his late thirties, a man with a brilliant reputation as a psychiatric engineer. Within a year, he was ACCED's director, had selected his own staff, and was engaged in the series of modifications in the project which, for the following decade, would keep the fact that ACCED was essentially a failure from becoming general knowledge. SELAM was Curtice's development, had preceded his appointment to ACCED. He applied the selective amnesia machines immediately to the treatment of the waves of emotional problems arising among ACCED's first host of recruits. In this, as George Hair learned later, SELAM was fairly effective, but at the expense of erasing so much of the ACCED-impressed information that the purpose of the project was lost.

Dr. Curtice and his colleagues had decided meanwhile that the principal source of the troubles with ACCED was that the adolescent and post-adolescent subjects first chosen for it already had established their individual personality patterns to a degree which limited the type of information which could be imposed on them by enforced learning processes without creating a destructive conflict. The maximum age level for the initiation of the ACCED approach therefore was reduced to twelve years; and within six months, the new phase of the project was underway on that basis, and on a greatly extended scale.

Simultaneously, Curtice had introduced a third phase—the transfer of infants shortly after their birth to ACCED nurseries where training by selected technicians could be begun under conditions which were free of distorting influences of any kind. The last presently was announced as the most promising aspect of the ACCED project, the one which eventually would produce an integrated class of specialists capable of conducting the world's economic affairs with the faultless dependability of a machine.

The implication that the earlier phases were to be regarded as preliminary experiments attracted little immediate attention and was absorbed gradually and almost unnoticed by the public.

It was during the seventh year of the ACCED project that George Hair's personal and political fortunes took a turn for which he was not in the least prepared. There had been a period of sharp conflict within the Administration, President Mallory and the Secretary of State opposing Oliver Wingfield, the perennial Vice President. Hair recognized the situation as the power struggle it essentially was. While his sympathies were largely with Mallory, he had attempted to mediate between the two groups without taking sides. But the men of action were not listening to Hair, the theorist, now. Eventually Wingfield was ousted from the government, though he had too strong and well-organized a following to be ousted from public life.

And shortly afterwards, Mallory explained privately to George Hair that his failure to throw in his full influence against Wingfield had created so much hostility for him, particularly in Sebert's group, that it was impossible to retain him as Secretary of Finance. Mallory made it clear that he still liked Hair as a person but agreed with Sebert that he should play no further major role in the Administration.

It was a bad shock to Hair. Unlike Wingfield and the others, he had developed no personal organization to support him. He had, he realized now, taken it for granted that his continuing value as an overall planner was so obvious to Mallory and Wirt Sebert that nothing else could be needed to secure his position beside them. For a time, he considered retiring into private life; but in the end, he accepted the position of Administrator of Education offered him by Mallory, which included among other matters responsibility for the ACCED Project.

Hair's first encounter with Dr. Curtice left him more impressed by ACCED's director than he had expected to be. He was aware that the project had been much less successful than was generally assumed to be the case, and his mental image of Curtice had been that of a glib operator who was willing to use appearances in place of facts to strengthen his position. But Curtice obviously had an immense enthusiasm for what he was doing, radiated self-assurance and confidence in ACCED's final success to a degree which was difficult to resist. There was nothing in his manner to suggest that he resented Hair's appointment as his superior; it was the attitude of Eileen Randall and, to a less extent, that of Dr. Longdon, Curtice's two chief assistants, which made it clear from the start that Hair was, in fact, resented.

There were also indications that Wirt Sebert was not pleased with the appointment; and Hair suspected there had been a touch of friendly malice in Mallory's move—a reminder to Sebert that Mallory, although he had agreed to Hair's ouster from Finance, was still the Big Man of the original Big Four. Hair himself had enough stubbornness in him to ignore Sebert's continuing antagonism and the lack of cooperation he could expect from Sebert's protégés in ACCED. He had been somewhat startled when his first survey of the new situation in which he found himself showed that other activities of the Department of Education were of no significance except as they pertained to the ACCED project. Dr. Curtice evidently had been running the Department very much as he pleased in recent years. It seemed time, George Hair thought, to establish whether ACCED was worth anywhere near the support it was getting from the government.

The Project was now in its seventh year. The initial experiment involving high school and college age groups was no longer mentioned and had almost dropped from the public mind. Hair's check brought him the information that a considerable number of the original subjects were still undergoing remedial psychiatric treatment at ACCED institutions. The others had merged back into the population. It was clear that the ACCED process had not had a single lasting success in that group.

Hair visited a number of the ACCED-run schools next where the process had been in use for the past three years. The age level here varied between ten and thirteen. He was shown records which indicated the ACCED students were far in advance of those to whom standard educational methods had been applied. The technicians assured him that, unlike their older predecessors, the present subjects were showing no undesirable emotional reactions to the process. Hair did not attempt to argue with the data given by their instruments. But he saw the children and did not like what he saw. They looked and acted, he thought, like small, worried grown-ups.

His inspection of two of the nursery schools was made against Dr. Randall's coldly bitter opposition: the appearance of a stranger among ACCED's youngest experimental subjects was unscheduled and would therefore create, a disturbance; nobody had been allowed there before. But Hair was quietly insistent. It turned into a somewhat eerie experience. The students were between two and four years old and physically looked healthy enough. They were, however, remarkably quiet. They seemed, Hair thought, slower than children at that age should be, though as a bachelor he admittedly hadn't had much chance to study children that age.

Then one of the taciturn attendants conducting him through the school caught his eye and indicated a chubby three-year-old squatting in a cubicle by himself, apparently assembling a miniature television set. Hair watched in amazement until the assembly was completed, tested, and found satisfactory; whereupon the small mechanic lay down beside the instrument and went to sleep.

They had another trump card waiting for him. This was a girl, perhaps a year older, who informed Hair she understood he had been Secretary of Finance and wished to ask him some questions. The questions were extremely pertinent ones, and Hair found himself involved in a twenty-minute defense of the financial policies he had pursued during the twelve years he held the office. Then his inquisitor thanked him for his time and wandered off.

One could not object to ACCED as an experiment, George Hair concluded. An approach capable of producing such remarkable results was worth pursuing, within sensible limitations. The trouble with ACCED was chiefly that it was neither regarded nor handled as a limited experiment. Curtice and his assistants seemed completely indifferent to the fact that by now the processes had been applied to well over fifty thousand cases, only a handful of which had been under their immediate supervision. The number was increasing annually; and if the second and third groups were to show delayed negative responses similar to those of the first, the damage might not become apparent for several more years but would then be enormously more significant than the development of a relatively few precocious geniuses.

Hair took his figures to Mallory, pointed out the political dangers of failure if ACCED was continued on its present scale, recommended cutting it back sharply to the level of a controlled experiment until Curtice's group was able to show that the current stages of their work would not bog down in the same type of problems as the first had done. This would release department funds for the investigation of other approaches to the educational problem which could be brought into development if it appeared eventually that ACCED had to be written off.

Mallory heard him out, then shook his head.

"I've been aware of what you've told me, George," he said. "The trouble is that neither you nor I have the background to understand fully what Curtice is up to. But the man has a fantastic mind. There's nobody in his field to approach him today. He feels he needs the kind of wide, general experimentation he's getting through ACCED and his work with SELAM to produce the information he's after. I've seen some of the results of both, and I'm betting on him!"

He added thoughtfully, "If you're right in suspecting that the approach has an inherent weakness in it which will make it ultimately unusable, it'll show up within another few years. Time enough then to decide what to do. But until we do have proof that it isn't going to work, let's let the thing ride."

He grinned, added again, "Incidentally, I'll appreciate being kept informed on what's going on in the department. ACCED is Wirt's baby, of course, but there's no reason it should be his baby exclusively. . . ."

Which made Hair's role clear. Mallory was curious about Sebert's interest in ACCED, had wanted a dependable observer who would be associated closely enough with the project to detect any significant developments there. Hair was now in a position to do just that. But he was not to interfere with Curtice because that would defeat Mallory's purpose.

Hair accepted the situation. He could not act against Sebert's wishes unless he had Mallory's authority behind him; and if Mallory had decided to wait until it was certain Curtice had failed, his role must remain that of an investigator. In time, the evidence would present itself. The reports he was receiving from the ACCED Building could not be considered reliable, but he was installing his own observers at key points in the project; and if that did not increase his popularity with Curtice and his colleagues, it would insure, Hair thought, that not too much of what was done escaped his attention. In addition, there was an obvious pattern to the manner in which the various project activities were stressed or underemphasized which should serve to guide him now.

❀   ❀   ❀

The emphasis during the next two years shifted increasingly to SELAM. After the first wave of acute psychoneurotic disturbances had subsided, Curtice's selective amnesia machines had played a limited role in the ACCED project itself; but they had been used experimentally in a variety of other ways. SELAM, when it was effective, produced a release of specific tensions by deleting related portions of the established neural circuitry and thereby modifying the overall pattern of the brain's activity. It had a record of successful applications in psychiatric work, the relief of psychosomatic problems, some forms of senility, in the rehabilitation of criminals, and finally in animal experiments where the machines could be used to their fullest scope. The present limiting factor, according to Curtice, lay in the difficulty and the length of time required to train a sufficient number of operators up to the necessary level of understanding and skill in handling the machines. Most of SELAM's more spectacular successes had, in fact, been achieved by himself and a handful of his immediate associates.

The story was now that this problem was being overcome, that a corps of SELAM experts soon would be available to serve the public in various ways, and that the average citizen could expect a number of direct benefits for himself, including perhaps that of a virtual rejuvenation, in the foreseeable future. George Hair did not give much attention to these claims. They were, he thought, another distraction; meanwhile, ACCED could receive correspondingly less publicity. And ACCED, as a matter of fact, if it had not yet encountered a renewed serious setback, was, at least, being slowed down deliberately in order to avoid one. A number of the teen-age schools had quietly closed, the students having been transferred to country camps where the emphasis was on sports and recreation, while accelerated education had been reduced to a few hours a day. Curtice admitted privately that certain general danger signals had been noted and that a pause in the overall program was indicated until the difficulties had been analyzed and dealt with. He did not appear unduly concerned.

It was during the third year following Hair's attempt to persuade Mallory to have ACCED cut back at once to the level of experimental research that Oliver Wingfield launched his first public attacks on the project. Wingfield was then campaigning for the governorship he was to win with startling ease a few months later, while continuing his crusade for the general elections he hoped would move him into the top spot in the Administration. The detailed nature of his charges against ACCED made it evident that he had informants among the project personnel.

It put George Hair in a difficult position. If it was a choice between supporting Wingfield and supporting Mallory, he much preferred to support Mallory. This was due less to his remaining feelings of friendship for Mallory than to the fact that Oliver Wingfield's policies had always had an aspect of angry destructiveness about them. As one of the Big Four, he had been sufficiently held in check; his pugnacity and drive had made him extremely useful then. If he was allowed to supplant Mallory, however, he would be a dangerous man.

In all reason, Hair thought, they should have closed out ACCED before this. The political damage would have been insignificant if the matter was handled carefully. To do it now, under Wingfield's savage criticism, would be a much more serious matter. The government would appear to have retreated under pressure, and Wingfield's cause would be advanced. But he was not sure the step could be delayed much longer.

Then he had his first reports of six-year-old and seven-year-old psychotics in several of the nursery schools. They were unofficial reports coming from his own observers; and the observers were not entirely certain of their facts; the local school staffs had acted immediately to remove the affected children, so that the seriousness of their condition could not be ascertained. It looked bad enough; it was, in fact, what Hair had expected and, recently, had feared. But he told himself that these might be isolated cases, that there might not be many more of them. If that turned out to be true, the matter conceivably could be ignored until the political climate again became more favorable to the government.

Unless, of course, Oliver Wingfield heard of it. . . .

Wingfield apparently didn't hear of it. His attacks during the next few weeks were directed primarily at the camps for ACCED's teen-age subjects. Curtice's group had volunteered no information on the incidents to Hair; and Hair did not press them for it. For a while, there was a lull in the reports of his observers.

Then the reports began to come in again; and suddenly it was no longer a question of isolated incidents. An epidemic of insanity was erupting in the ACCED nursery schools, and Hair knew he could wait no longer.

He had come to the ACCED Building expecting to find Curtice and his associates evasive, defensive, perhaps attempting to explain away what could no longer be explained away. That they might have the gall even now to think that giving the project another shift would avert the storm of public criticism due to burst over ACCED as soon as Wingfield's informants learned of the swiftly rising number of psychotic children in the nursery schools would never have occurred to him if he had not been warned by Eileen Randall's manner. Even so, he felt shocked and amazed.

The ACCED group might delude itself to that extent, he thought. But Wirt Sebert must be standing behind them in this. And how could Sebert show such incredibly bad judgment? Further, at so critical a time, Sebert would have conferred with Mallory before committing himself to giving Curtice further support, and Mallory must have agreed to it.

He could not believe that of Philip Mallory. Unless . . .

George Hair stood frowning out of the window of the ACCED Building at the river curving through the valley below. Unless, he thought, Curtice had, this time, come up with a genuine break-through, something indisputable and of great and exciting signifi-cance, something that could not be challenged. Because that might still do it, stifle Wingfield's declamations and dim the picture of lunatic children in the public's mind. The public forgot so easily again.

"Mr. Hair," Eileen Randall's voice purred from the doorway.

Hair turned. Her mouth curved into a condescending smile.

"Will you come with me, please? They're waiting to see you now. . . ."

A hundred feet down the hallway, she opened the door to Curtice's big office for him. As Hair stepped inside, he was barely able to suppress a start of surprise. Beside Curtice and Dr. Longdon, there was a third man in the office whose presence, for a moment, seemed completely incongruous.

"Good morning, Felix," Hair said. "I didn't expect to find you here."

Felix Austin, Chief Justice and President Mallory's right-hand man for the past five years, smiled briefly. He was tall and sparse, in his late fifties, almost exactly Hair's age.

"As a matter of fact, George," he said, "I hadn't expected to meet you today either. But I happened to be in the building, and when I heard you wanted to speak to Dr. Curtice, I thought I might sit in on the discussion. If you'd rather I'd leave, I shall do it at once, of course."

Hair shook his head. "No, you're quite welcome to stay." He took a seat, laid the briefcase he had brought with him on his knees. Eileen Randall sat down across the room from him, not far from Curtice.

Hair's fingers were trembling, though not enough to be noticed by anyone but himself, as he opened the briefcase and drew out three copies of a resume made up from the reports of his ACCED observers during the past six weeks. Austin's presence, of course, was not a coincidence; and he wasn't expected to believe that it was. He was being told that he should not count on Mallory backing him against Curtice today. He had suspected it, but the fact still dumbfounded him because he could not see Mallory's motive. He looked at Eileen Randall.

"Dr. Randall," he said, "I have here three copies of a paper I should like the group to see. Please give one each to Dr. Curtice and the Chief Justice. Perhaps you and Dr. Longdon will be willing to share the third."

Eileen Randall hesitated an instant, then stood up, came over and took the papers from him. Austin cleared his throat.

"We're to read this immediately, George?" he asked.

"Please do," Hair said.

He watched them while they read. Austin frowned thoughtfully; Curtice seemed completely uninterested. Longdon and Eileen Randall exchanged occasional glances. Curtice finished first, waited until the others put down their copies.

He said then, "These figures are remarkably accurate, Mr. Hair. Of course, we've known you had good men working for you. The current incidence is perhaps a trifle higher than shown." He looked over at Dr. Longdon. "About eight per cent, wouldn't you say, Bill?"

"Approximately," Longdon agreed.

"We understand and appreciate your concern, Mr. Hair," Curtice went on with apparent sincerity. "But as it happens"—his forefinger tapped the resume—"this is not a matter which need give any of us concern, although you were not in a position to know it. The situation was anticipated. We have been sure almost from the beginning that immature brains would not be able to absorb the vast volume of information forced on them by ACCED indefinitely, and that the final result would be the acute stress and confusion expressed in these figures."

"You were sure of it almost from the beginning?" Hair repeated.

"I became convinced of it personally within a few months after I was brought into the project," Curtice said.

George Hair stared at him. "Then, in Heaven's name, why—if you were certain of eventual failure—did you continue with these monstrous experiments for years?"

"Because," Curtice said patiently, "they were producing a great deal of information—information we absolutely needed to have, absolutely needed to test in practice."

"For what purpose?" Hair demanded. He looked over at Austin. "Felix, you're informed of what these people have been doing?"

Austin nodded. "Yes, I am, George." His voice and face were expressionless.

"Then supposing you. . . ."

"No, let Dr. Curtice tell it, George. He can answer your questions better than I can."

It appeared, Hair thought, that Austin was deferring deliberately to Curtice, to make it clear that Curtice was now to be considered the equal of either of them.

"We needed the information," Curtice continued, as if there had been no interruption, "for a purpose it would not have been advisable to make public at the time. It would have made much of the research we were planning virtually impossible, particularly since we had no way of proving, even to ourselves, that what we wanted to do could be accomplished. Even today, less than two dozen people are fully informed of the plan.

"Our purpose, Mr. Hair, was and is the creation of a genuine superman—a, man who will be physically and mentally as fully developed as his genetic structure permits. I have had this goal in mind for many years—it has been the aim of all my experiments with SELAM. When ACCED was formed, I saw the possibilities of incorporating its methods into my own projects. I went to Secretary Sebert and informed him of my plans. That was why I was made Director of the ACCED project. All ACCED's activities since that day have been designed solely to supply us with further information."

"And how," Hair asked, making no attempt to keep the incredulous distaste he felt out of his voice, "do you propose to go about creating your superman?"

Curtice said, "An adult brain, and only an adult brain, has the structural capacity to assimilate the information supplied by the accelerated educational processes as it streams in. A child's brain is not yet structured to store more than a limited amount of information at a time. It is developing too slowly to meet our purpose.

"But, as the first experiments with ACCED showed, an adult

brain, even the brain of a young adult, already has accumulated so much distorted information that the swift, orderly inflow of ACCED data again produces disastrous conflicts and disturbances. Hence the work with SELAM techniques during these years. We know now that a brain fully developed and mature, but with all memory, all residual traces of the life experiences which brought about its development removed from it, can be taught everything ACCED can teach, perhaps vastly more it will be able to absorb and utilize the new information completely."

There was a long pause. Then Hair said, "And that is the story you will tell the public? That you can delete all a man's present memories, subject him to the ACCED processes, and finally emerge with a new man, an ACCED-trained superman—who happens to have been the goal of the project all along?"

"Essentially that," Curtice said.

Hair shook his head. "Dr. Curtice," he said, "I don't believe that story! Oliver Wingfield won't believe it. And, this time finally, the public won't believe it. You're just looking for another lease of time to continue your experiments."

Curtice smiled without rancor, glanced at Austin.

"Felix," he said, "perhaps you'd better talk to him, after all."

Austin cleared his throat.

"It's true enough, George," he said. "Dr. Curtice has proof that he can do exactly as he says."

Hair looked back at Curtice.

"Does that mean," he asked, "that you actually have produced such a superman?"

"No," Curtice said. He laughed, apparently with genuine amusement now. "And with very good reason! We know we can remove all memory traces from a human brain and leave that brain in undamaged condition and in extremely good working order. We have done it with subjects in their seventieth year of life as well as with subjects in their fifth year of life, and with no greater basic difficulty. We also have applied modified ACCED methods to the five-year-old subjects and found they absorbed information at the normal rate of a newly born infant—much too slowly, as I have explained, for our purpose. but we have not applied ACCED methods of instruction to the adult memoryless subjects. We want supermen, but we want them to be supermen of our selection. That's the next and the all-important stage of the project."

"Then," George Hair said flatly, "I still do not believe you, and the public will not believe you. Your story will be put down as another bluff."

Curtice smiled faintly again.

"Will it?" he asked. "If the Director of ACCED becomes the first subject to undergo the total process?"

Hair's mouth dropped open. "You are to be. . . ."

"And if," Curtice went on, "Chief Justice Felix Austin has volunteered to be the second subject?"

Hair looked in bewilderment from one to the other of them. "Felix, is this true?"

"I fully intend to be the second subject," Austin told him seriously. "This is a big thing, George—a very big thing! The third and fourth subjects, incidentally, following Dr. Curtice and myself by approximately two years, will be President Mallory and Secretary Sebert. . . ."

George Hair sat in his study, watching the public reaction indicator edge up above the seventy-two mark on the positive side of the scale. Two hours before, just after the official announcement of the government's Rejuvenation Program was made, the indicator had hovered around forty. The response had been a swift and favorable one, though no more favorable than Hair had expected.

It was a little over five weeks since his meeting with Curtice and Felix Austin in the ACCED Building. Mallory's and Sebert's publicity staffs had been in full action throughout that time, operating indirectly except for an occasional, carefully vague release which no more than hinted at a momentous development to come. The planted rumors were far more direct. "Rejuvenation" was a fully established concept in the public mind days before the actual announcement; the missing details, however, were the sensational and unexpected ones—precisely the explosive touch required to swing the skeptical and merely curious over to instant support of the official program.

Curtice's goal of the ACCED-trained mental superman was being played down at present; it was less tangible, of far less direct interest, than the observable response of an aging body to the complete SELAM process. Hair had seen the seventy-year-old subjects of whom Curtice had told him. They were old men still, but old men from whom the physical and emotional tensions of a lifetime had been drained together with the memory traces of a lifetime. The relaxed, sleeping bodies had fleshed out again, become strong and smooth-skinned, presenting the appearance of young maturity. They gave credibility to Curtice's claim, based on comparable work with animals, that SELAM now offered humanity a life extension of at least sixty healthy years.

The public had seen those same rejuvenated bodies in the tridi screens today. It had listened while Curtice explained the developments in his SELAM machines which had brought about the miracle, and watched him walk smiling into the laboratory where he was to become the first human being to whom the combined SELAM and ACCED techniques would be fully applied.

Those were compelling arguments. The superman theme had been barely introduced but would grow in significance as the implications of Felix Austin following Curtice within a few months, and Mallory and Sebert following Austin within two years, were considered. What the leaders wanted for themselves, the public wanted. Unofficially, the word already was out that when the President and Secretary received the Rejuvenation treatment, a hundred deserving citizens would receive it with them, that SELAM and ACCED would become available to all whose personal records qualified them for the processes as quickly as Dr. Curtice's intricate machines could be duplicated and technicians trained in their use.

There was no question, George Hair thought, that the bait was being swallowed. And the thought appalled him. On the one occasion he'd spoken with Philip Mallory during the past weeks, he had brought up the subject of loss of individuality, of personality, by the SELAM process and in the subsequent period when, within a year and a half, a new mentality would be created by machines in the emptied, receptive brain, perhaps a vastly more efficient mentality but nevertheless. . . .

And Mallory had looked at him shrewdly, and laughed.

"The old Phil will be there again, George—don't worry!" he'd said. "I'm not suddenly rushing into this thing, you know. We can't talk about everything Dick Curtice has done with SELAM, but I've seen enough of his half-way jobs to go ahead." He gave Hair a conspiratorial dig with his elbow. "If Curtice weren't as far along as he is, Wingfield would have had our skins before summer! That's part of it. The other part of it is that I'm sixty-four and Sebert's sixty-six. You're fifty-eight yourself. We can all use some freshening up if we're to stay on top of the pile. . . ."

That had been the lure for Mallory. If it hadn't been for the pressures being built up by Wingfield, Hair thought, Mallory need have felt no concern about remaining on top for another twenty years. But he'd seen the developing threat and prepared quietly to more than match it with a bold, overwhelming move of his own. A new Big Four was in the making, a Big Four of supermen, with Curtice in Hair's position as thinker and theorist, Felix Austin in Wingfield's, while Mallory and Sebert remained the central two, the leaders. Hair had no illusions about his own prospects in the new era. As Administrator of Education, he had remained a popular, almost legendary figure; but it was clear now that it had been a popularity skillfully maintained by Mallory's publicity machine to give ACCED additional respectability in the transition period ahead. Thereafter, the legend would be allowed to fade away, and he with it.

He didn't, Hair decided, really want it otherwise. He did not share Mallory's will to stay on top at all costs ... definitely not at the cost of allowing his personality to be dissolved in Curtice's Rejuvenation process, even if the opportunity were offered him, although he was already quite certain it would not be offered. The new ruling group would have no further need of him.

He could resign now; but it would be awkward and change nothing. The psychotic children in ACCED's nursery schools were no longer an issue. They had been mentioned, casually, as a detail of the experiments, now concluded, which had been required to produce Rejuvenation, with the additional note that their rehabilitation would be undertaken promptly. The statement had aroused few comments ... He might as well, George Hair told himself finally, watch the thing through to the end.

During the next three months, he found himself involved frequently in the publicity connected with the Rejuvenation program, although he refused interviews and maintained the role of a detached spectator. Oliver Wingfield, stunned into silence no more than a few days, shifted his attack from ACCED to the new government program, lashed out savagely at Hair from time to time as one of the planners of what he described as an attempt to foist the rule of robot minds on normal men. Hair, not too sure he wasn't in some agreement with Wingfield on the latter point, held his peace; but Mallory's publicity experts happily took up the battle.

Despite Wingfield's best efforts, the Rejuvenation program retained its high level of popularity. The successful conclusion of the SELAM phase of the process on Richard Curtice was announced by Dr. Langdon. For the next sixty days, Curtice would be kept asleep to permit physical regeneration to be well advanced before ACCED was introduced by degrees to the case. Tridi strips taken at ten-day intervals showed the gradual transformation of a middle-aged scientist in moderately good condition to a firm-muscled athlete apparently in his early twenties. Attention began to shift to Felix Austin as the next to take the step, six weeks after Curtice's ACCED training had begun; and the continuing denunciations by Wingfield and his followers acquired a note of raging hysteria.

Three months and ten days after Curtice had submitted himself to his SELAM machines, George Hair came back to the ACCED Building, now the center of the new Rejuvenation complex. He was not at all sure why he should be there, but Longdon had called him that morning, told him there had been a very important development and asked him to come as soon as he possibly could. There had been a degree of urgency in the man's voice which had made it difficult to refuse. Hair was conducted to a part of the building he had not seen before and into a room where Longdon was waiting for him.

Longdon's appearance underlined the urgency Hair had sensed in his voice when he called. His eyes were anxious; his face looked drawn and tired. He said, "Mr. Hair, thank you very much for coming so promptly! Dr. Randall and I are faced with a very serious problem here which I could not discuss on the telephone. It's possible that you will be able—and willing—to help us. Let me show you what the trouble is."

He opened a door to another room, motioned to Hair to enter, and followed him inside, leaving the door open.

Hair recognized this room immediately. He had seen it several times in the tridi screen during demonstrations of the changes being brought about in Curtice's physical condition by SELAM. As he had been then, Curtice was lying now on a sunken bed in a twelve by twelve foot depression in the floor, his tanned, muscular body clothed only in white trunks. His face was turned toward the door by which they had entered and his eyes were half opened. Then, as they came toward him, his right hand lifted, made a slow, waving motion through the air, dropped to his side again.

"Our subject is exceptionally responsive today!" Dr. Longdon commented, an odd note of savage irony in his voice.

Hair looked quickly at him, frowning, asked, "What is the problem you wanted to discuss?"

❀   ❀   ❀

Longdon nodded at the figure sprawled across the sunken bed.

"There is the problem!" he said. "Mr. Hair, as you know, our calculations show that an adult brain, freed completely by SELAM techniques of the clutter of memories it has stored away, can absorb the entire volume of ACCED information within a period of less than two years. At the end of that time, in other words, we again would have a functioning adult, and one functioning in a far more integrated manner, far more efficiently, than is possible to the normally educated human being, and on the basis now of a vastly greater fund of accurate information than a normal human mind can acquire in a lifetime. . . ."

"I know, of course, that that was your goal," Hair said. "Apparently, something has gone wrong with it."

"Very decidedly!" Longdon said. "This is the forty-third day since we began to use ACCED training methods on Curtice. In child subjects—children whose memories were completely erased by SELAM at the age of five—forty-three days of modified ACCED produced a vocabulary equivalent to that of an average two-year-old. Curtice, in the same length of time, has acquired no vocabulary at all. Spoken words have no more meaning to him today than when we started."

A door had opened and closed quietly behind Hair while Longdon was speaking. He guessed that Eileen Randall had come into the room but did not look around. He was increasingly puzzled by Longdon's attitude. Curtice's failure to develop speech might be a very serious problem—might, in fact, be threatening the entire Rejuvenation program. But he did not see what it had to do with him, or how they expected him to help them.

He asked, "Have you discovered what the difficulty is?"

"Yes," Longdon said, "we know now what the difficulty is." He hesitated, scowling absently down at Curtice for a few seconds, went on. "A child, Mr. Hair, a young child, wants to learn. Not long after birth, it enters a phase where learning might appear to be almost its primary motivation. Later in life, it may retain the drive to learn or it may lose it. It has been assumed that this depended on whether its life experiences were of a nature to encourage the learning urge, or to suppress and eventually to stifle it.

"Now it appears that this is only partly true. Later life experiences may indeed foster and even create a learning urge of their own. But the natural drive, the innate drive, apparently is present only for a comparatively short time in childhood. It is not, in itself, a permanent motivation in man.

"Dr. Curtice's biological age is nearly fifty years. Before SELAM wiped the effects of his life experiences from him, he was, of course, a man intensely interested in learning, intensely curious. But his curiosity and interest were based on the experiences he has lost, and were lost with them. And he is decades past the age where the innate drive to learn could still motivate him.

"We can teach him almost nothing because he is inherently uninterested in learning anything. We have used every conceivable method to stimulate interest and curiosity in him. Intense pleasure or severe pain will produce corresponding reactions, but when the sensations end, he appears to forget them quickly again.

"There is, however, a barely detachable learning curve, which can be projected. In twenty years, by the consistent use of brutally drastic methods, we should be able to train Dr. Curtice's brain to the point where he could comprehend very simple instructions. By that time, of course, the training process itself would have produced such severe physical and emotional stresses that the rejuvenating effect of SELAM would have been lost, and he would be showing—at the very least—his actual physical age."

Dr. Longdon shrugged, spread his hands, concluded, "So at best, Mr. Hair, we might wind up eventually with a very stupid, very dull old man of seventy.

Eileen Randall's voice said harshly behind Hair, "Mr. Hair, it is not nearly as hopeless as that! Not nearly!"

She went on vehemently, as he turned to look at her. "We simply need time! Time to understand what really has happened here . . . to decide what must be done about it. If Richard weren't helpless, he would tell us what to do! He would never—" Her voice broke suddenly.

Longdon said patiently, giving Hair an apologetic glance, "Eileen, you know we've gone endlessly over all calculations, tried everything! We. . . ."

"We have not!" Eileen Randall began to weep.

George Hair looked in something like irritated amazement from one to the other of them. He said carefully, "This is, of course, a very serious matter, but I am hardly qualified to assist you in it. It's no secret to you that my connection with the program has been and is a purely figurative one. The only suggestion I can make is that President Mallory should be informed immediately of the problems you've encountered here."

Longdon said tonelessly, "President Mallory is aware of the problem, Mr. Hair."

"What?" Hair said sharply. "When was he told?"

"Over a month ago. As soon as it became evident that Dr. Curtice was not responding normally to the ACCED approach for dememorized subjects." Longdon cleared his throat. "President Mallory's instructions were to maintain absolute secrecy while we looked for a solution. Now, however...." He shrugged.

Over a month ago ... Hair's mind seemed to check for an instant at the words; then his thoughts were racing as Longdon went on. For more than a month after Mallory and Sebert had realized that the Rejuvenation program might end in humiliating public failure before it had well begun, the build-up had continued, Oliver Wingfield and his adherent were being scientifically needled into a crescendo of baffled rage, and Felix Austin—yes, only five days from now, Chief Justice Austin was scheduled to undergo the SELAM techniques which evidently had destroyed Curtice! Hair felt a sudden chill prickling the back of his neck....

"Mr. Hair, you *must* help us!" Eileen Randall was staring desperately at him, tears streaming down her face.

"There's no way I could help you, Dr. Randall."

"But you can—you must! They'll murder Richard if you don't! They've said so! You—your influence with President Mallory—his old friend...." The words drowned in a choked wailing.

Hair felt his breath shorten. Curtice had to die, of course—die plausibly and conveniently so that his condition need never be revealed. But Mallory and Sebert weren't stupid enough to think that Curtice's death alone would be sufficient.

"It isn't necessary!" Eileen Randall was babbling shrilly again. "Even—even if the program has to end, we could take him away quietly, take care of him somewhere. They could say he was dead— no one would ever know! We...." She clapped her hands to her face, turned and ran from the room, making muffled, squalling sounds.

"I should see she's taken care of, Mr. Hair," Longdon said shakily. "If you'll excuse me a minute...." He started for the door.

"Dr. Longdon!"

Longdon stopped, looked back. "Yes?"

"Who suggested to you that I should use my influence with President Mallory on Curtice's behalf?"

Longdon's eyes flickered. "Chief Justice Austin."

"I see," Hair said. "When did he suggest it?"

"This morning," Longdon told him, with a brief, frightened grimace. "He was here shortly before I called you. I could not avoid acknowledging that Dr. Curtice's case was hopeless. The Chief Justice advised us then that only your personal appeal to President Mallory could save Curtice's life, that we should attempt to get in touch with you immediately . . ."

He hurried out of the room. Hair stood staring after him a moment, then turned, glanced at the mindless thing on the sunken bed, went quickly over to the other door through which he and Longdon had entered. There had been, he recalled, a telephone in the outer room.

He dialed the number of his office, waited, listening to the soft purr on the line. Then, suddenly, the line went dead.

That was that, Hair told himself. He replaced the receiver, went over to the window and looked out at the newly erected buildings of the Rejuvenation complex. His thoughts seemed to be moving sluggishly. Perhaps it was fear; but perhaps it simply had been too long a time since he had been involved in an operation of this kind. After the Takeover, it no longer had seemed necessary; and he had a feeling that what was going on now was somehow unreal.

But it was real enough. Mallory, the man of action, the practical man who intended to remain on top, hadn't forgotten the lessons of the past. He might have been betting on Curtice's genius, but he had been preparing for years to hedge on the bet if necessary. Perhaps he'd never expected ACCED or the Rejuvenation program to come to anything. Either way, he could turn the projects to his advantage in the end.

Hair's gaze shifted for a moment to the sky above the buildings. It would come from there in all likelihood, and in an instant of ravening fury the Rejuvenation complex would be obliterated. The buildings, the personnel, the machines, the records, anything that would have left the slightest possibility of beginning the program again . . . and George Hair, the thinker, the theorist, the living legend, whom Mallory had not forgiven for failing to throw in his influence openly against Wingfield in their first struggle for control.

Wingfield would be blamed for it, and they could make it stick. Wingfield was finished. . . .

Hair turned at a sound behind him. Longdon had come into the room.

"Mr. Hair," he said, grinning apologetically, "you must forgive Eileen! She has always been in love with Curtice, of course. If she is only allowed to take care of him, she will be satisfied. I hope you can persuade President Mallory to leave her that much...."

Hair looked at Longdon's anxious eyes. Longdon hadn't grasped everything, of course, but he had grasped enough to be aware that not only Curtice's life was in danger.

For an instant, Hair wondered how Longdon would react if he were told that communications from the building to the world outside already were being intercepted, and that therefore neither of them—nor anyone else within half a mile of where they stood— could have more than a very few minutes still to live.

But although he had never liked Longdon in the least, that seemed a pointless cruelty now.

"I'll see what I can do, Dr. Longdon," he agreed.

Time for Crime

WE'VE SEPARATED OUT those of Schmitz's stories with a specific crime theme and have put them in here. Among these half dozen stories are the three stories which Schmitz wrote that have no science fiction element at all, but are purely "crime fiction." (Although, even there, the longest of the stories—"Crime Buff"— has a vaguely fantastical feeling about it, at least in the nature of the peculiar family which lies at the center of the tale.) But we've also included three others which, though technically SF, could also be described as crime stories with a twist.

With Schmitz, the distinction is somewhat artificial anyway. A large number of Schmitz's stories focused on crime, including some of his very best Hub stories—such as "The Searcher," to give just one example. For that matter, the first and longest story in "Homo Excelsior," "The Ties of Earth," is hard-boiled enough that we considered including it here and giving this section the alternate title "Schmitz Noir." "The Ties of Earth" is probably the closest science fiction has ever come to the spirit which infuses the writings of the great crime novelist Raymond Chandler. And "Just Curious," of course, is as much of a crime story as it is a psi horror story.

Still, making fine distinctions is part of what editors do, and so we put together the six stories which we think, taken as a whole, give the spectrum of Schmitz's approach to mixing crime and speculative fiction. In fact, the title of the section itself ("Time for Crime") was determined by one of the stories, which, in a whimsical manner, posits the idea that stealing time itself might someday be a crime.

Crime Buff
· · · · · · · · · · · ·

JEFF CLARY STOOD halfway down the forested hillside at the edge of a short drop-off, studying the house on the cleared land below. It was a large two-story house with a wing; Jeff thought it might contain as many as twenty-five to thirty rooms. There was an old-fashioned, moneyed look about it, and the lawns around it seemed well-tended. It could have been an exclusive sanitarium as easily as a private residence. So far, there'd been no way to decide what, exactly, it was. In the time he'd been watching it, Jeff hadn't caught sight of a human being or noticed indications of current human activity.

What had riveted his attention at first glimpse wasn't so much the house itself as the gleaming blue and white airplane which stood some two hundred yards to the left of it. A small white structure next to the plane should be its hangar. The plane was pointed up a closely mowed field. It seemed a rather short run-way even for so small a plane, but he didn't know much about airplanes. Specifically—importantly at the moment—he didn't know how to fly one.

That summed up the situation.

A large number of people were engaged today in searching for Jeff Clary, but the blue and white plane could take him where he wanted to go in a few hours, safely, unnoticeably. He needed someone to handle it.

That someone might be in the house. If not, there should be one or more cars in the garage adjoining the house on the right. A car would be less desirable than the plane, but vastly superior to hiking on foot into the open countryside. If he could get to the city without being stopped, he'd have gained a new head start on the searchers. If he got there with a substantial stake as well, his chances of shaking them off for good would be considerably better than even.

Jeff scratched the dense bristles on his chin. There was a gun tucked into his belt, but he'd used the last bullet in it eight hours ago. A hunting knife was fastened to the belt's other side. A knife and a gun—even an empty gun could get him a hostage to start with. He'd take it from there.

Shade trees and shrubbery grew up close to the sides of the building. It shouldn't be difficult to get inside before he was noticed. If it turned out there were dogs around, he'd come up openly—a footsore sportsman who'd got lost and spent half the night stumbling around in the rain-wet hills. As soon as anyone let him get close enough to start talking, he'd be as close as he needed to be.

He sent a last sweeping look around and started downhill, keeping to the cover of the trees. His feet hurt. The boots he wore were too small for him, as were the rest of his fishing clothes. Those items had belonged recently to another man who had no present use for them.

He reached the side of the house minutes later. No dogs had bayed an alarm, and he'd been only momentarily in sight of a few front windows of the building. He'd begun to doubt seriously that there was anybody home, but two of the upper-floor windows were open. If all the occupants had left, they should have remembered to close the windows on a day of uncertain weather like this.

He moved quickly over to a side door. Taking the empty gun from his belt, he turned the heavy brass doorknob cautiously. The door was unlocked. Jeff pushed it open a few inches, peering into the short passage beyond.

A moment later, he was inside with the door closed again. He walked softly along the tiled passageway, listening. Still no sound. The passage ended at a large, dimly lit central hall across from a stairwell. There were several rooms on either side of the hall, and most of the doors were open. What he could see of the furnishings seemed to match the outer appearance of the house— old-fashioned, expensive, well cared for.

As he stood, briefly undecided, he heard sounds at last, from upstairs. Jeff slipped back into the passage, watching the head of the stairway. Nobody went by there, but after a few seconds the footsteps stopped. Then music suddenly was audible. A TV or radio set had been switched on.

That simplified matters.

Jeff moved across the hall and up the stairs, then followed the music along a second-floor passage to the right. Daylight and the music spilled into the passage through an open doorway. He stopped beside the door a moment, listening. He heard only the music. Cautiously he looked in.

A girl stood at one of the bedroom's two windows, looking out, back turned to Jeff; a dark-haired slender girl of medium height, wearing candy-striped jeans with a white blouse. A portable TV set stood on a side table.

Jeff came soundlessly into the room, gun pointed at the girl, and drew the door shut behind him. There was a faint click as it closed. The girl turned.

"Don't make a sound," Jeff said softly. "I'd rather not hurt you. Understand?"

She stood motionless at sight of him. Now she swallowed, nodded, blue eyes wide. She looked younger than he'd expected, a smooth-featured teenager. There shouldn't be any trouble with her. He went to the TV, keeping the gun pointed at the girl, turned the set off.

"Come over here," he told her. "Away from the window. I want to talk to you."

She nodded again, came warily toward him, eyes shifting between his face and the gun.

"Be very good, and I won't have to use it," Jeff said. "Who else is in the house?"

"Nobody right now." Her voice was unexpectedly steady. "They'll be coming in later, during the afternoon."

"Who'll be coming in?"

She shrugged. "Some of my family. There's to be a meeting tonight. I don't know just who it'll be this time—probably seven or eight of them." She glanced at the watch on her wrist, added, "Tracy should be back in around an hour and a half—about two o'clock. The others won't begin to show up before five."

"So Tracy should be back by two, eh? Who's Tracy?"

"Tracy Nichols. Sort of my cousin by marriage."

"You and she live here?"

The girl shook her head. "Nobody lives here permanently now. My Uncle George owns the place. At least, I think it's his property. It's used for meetings and so on."

"Who looks after it?"

"Mr. and Mrs. Wells are the caretakers. They left yesterday after they got everything set up, and they won't be back till tomorrow night when we're gone again."

"Why did they clear out?"

"They always do. The family doesn't want other people around when they have a meeting."

Jeff grunted. "You got secrets?"

The girl smiled. "Oh, there's a lot of talk about business and so on. You never know what's going to come up."

"Uh-huh. What's your name?"

"Brooke Cameron."

"Where do you live?"

"Place called Renfrew College. Two hundred miles from here. You're Jeff Clary, aren't you?"

She'd added the question with no slightest change in inflection, and Jeff was jolted into momentary silence. Watching him, she nodded slowly, as if satisfied.

"Take away the beard—yes, that's who you are, of course!" Interest was kindling in her face. "Pictures of you were shown in the newscasts, you know. But you were supposed to be heading north."

Jeff had heard as much on a car radio ten hours ago.

"Pretty sharp, the way you walked out of that maximum security spot," Brooke Cameron went on. "They said it's only happened once before there."

"Maybe you talk a little too much," he told her. "If you know who I am, you should have sense enough not to play games."

Brooke shrugged. "I'm not playing a game. Of course, you *might* kill me, but I wouldn't be any use to you then. I'd like to help you."

"I bet you would."

"Really! I'm a sort of crime buff, and you're a very interesting criminal. That's not all, either!" Brooke smiled engagingly. "So, first, what do you need here? The plane's your best chance out, and it got a full tank this morning. Can you handle it?"

"No," Jeff said after a moment. "Can you?"

"Afraid not. They didn't want to let me learn how for another two years. But Tracy's flown it sometimes. She took it out today to get it gassed. You'll have to wait till she gets back."

"I could take your car," Jeff remarked, watching her.

"No car here now, Jeff. Tracy brought me in with her early this morning and went on to the city to pick up some stuff she ordered. Either way you want to go, you'll have to stay till she gets back. The only thing you'd find in the garage is an old bicycle, and that's probably got flat tires. You can go look for yourself."

"I might do that." Jeff studied her curiously. "You'd like to help me, eh?" She nodded. "Well, let's try you. This should be good hunting country. Any guns in the house?"

"Not sporting guns," Brooke said promptly. "But there could be a loaded revolver in Uncle George's desk. He usually keeps one there. His room's down the hall." Her gaze flicked over the gun in Jeff's hand. "Ammunition, too," she said. "But it won't fit the gun you have."

Jeff grunted. "You're wondering whether this one's empty?"

"Well, it might be." Her blue eyes regarded him steadily. "You put two bullets in the guard you shot, and you wouldn't have found any spare shells on him. There was more shooting, and then they must have been pushing you pretty hard for a time. If this isn't a gun the couple you kidnapped happened to have in their car, it could very well be empty."

Jeff grinned briefly. "Are you wondering now where that couple is?"

Brooke shook her head. "No, not much. I mean you're here by yourself, and I don't think you'd let them get away from you." She shrugged. "Let's go look in Uncle George's desk."

The revolver was in a desk drawer, a beautiful shop-new .38. Brooke looked on silently while Jeff checked it and dropped half a dozen spare shells into a jacket pocket.

"So now you have that," she remarked. "You want to shave and clean up next, or eat? A ham was sent in for dinner."

"What makes you think I want to do either?" Jeff asked dryly.

She shrugged. "We can go sit in a south room upstairs, of course," she said. "You can watch the road from there and wait for Tracy to drive up. But that'll be a while. She'll call, anyway, to let me know when she's ready to start back."

Jeff laughed. "That's convenient, isn't it? I'll try the ham."

He hadn't realized until he began to eat how ravenous he was. Then he concentrated savagely on the food, almost forgetting Brooke sitting across from him at the kitchen table. When he'd finished and looked over at her, he saw the worn brown wallet she'd laid on the table. Jeff stared at it, eyes widening.

"How—"

"I'm quite a good pickpocket," Brooke said absently. She frowned at the wallet. "Told you I'm a crime buff—and I don't just read about it." She touched one of three irregular dark stains on the wallet with a finger, looked at Jeff and pushed the wallet across the table to him. "I got it while we were going to Uncle George's room. So Mr. and Mrs. Rambow didn't get away, did they?"

"No, they didn't get away," Jeff said harshly. He hadn't noticed her brushing against him or touching him in any manner as they went along the passage, and the thought of her doing it without letting him catch her made him uneasy. "And they shouldn't have tried," he went on. "Their car got smashed up enough while they were about it that I couldn't use it anymore. It's down in a nice deep gully back in the hills where it isn't likely to be found very soon, and they're inside. Now you know."

Brooke brushed back her hair. "I really knew anyway," she said. "You have a sort of record, Jeff."

Anger faded into curiosity. "Aren't you scared?"

"Oh, yes, a little. But I'm useful to you—and I'm *not* trying to get away."

"I'd like to know what you are trying to do," Jeff admitted. "Whatever it is, there'd better be no more tricks like that."

"There won't be," Brooke said.

"All right." Jeff tugged at the shoulder of his jacket. "Are there clothes in this spooky house that could fit me?"

Brooke nodded. "Uncle Jason's just about your build. He's got a room upstairs, too. Let's go see."

Jeff stood up. "What kind of place is this?" be asked irritably. "A home away from home for any of you who happens to feel like it?"

"I guess it's used like that sometimes," Brooke said. "I don't know everything the family does."

Uncle Jason's room was at the south end of the house. It was equipped sparsely and with the neat impersonality of a hotel room. Several suits hung in plastic sheaths in the closet and two pairs of shoes stood in a plastic box on the closet shelf. The shoes would be a bit large for Jeff, but a relief after the cramping boots he'd been wearing. He decided any of the suits should fit well enough, and he found an electric shaver. He peered out a window. No vehicle was in sight, and anyone coming could be spotted minutes away. All good enough.

He hauled a straight-backed chair away from a table, turned it facing the window. "Come here and sit down," he told Brooke. She'd been watching him silently as he moved about, not stirring herself from the position she'd taken up near the passage door.

She came over now. "You want me to watch the road?"

"Just sit down."

She settled herself in the chair. Jeff said, "Now put your arms behind you." He fished a piece of rope out of a pocket.

"You don't have to do that," she said quickly.

"I'll be busy for a while," Jeff said. "I don't want to worry about you."

Brooke sighed, clasped her hands together behind the chair. Jeff looked down at her a moment. Brooke Cameron bothered him. The way she was acting didn't make sense. It wasn't just the matter of the wallet, though that had been startling. He'd suspected at first that she was trying to set a trap for him while pretending to be helpful, but he didn't see what she could attempt to do, and it didn't seem to fit in with telling him where he could find a loaded gun. Perhaps she was hoping help would arrive. He didn't feel too concerned about that possibility. He'd be ready for them.

He could put an abrupt end to anything she might have in mind by slipping the rope around her slender neck; but that would be stupid. If some unexpected trouble arose before he got out of here, a live hostage would be an immediate advantage, and he might still find her useful in other ways.

He fastened her wrists together, drawing the rope tight enough to make it hurt. She wriggled her shoulders a little but didn't complain. He knotted the end of the rope about a chair rung below the seat, grinned at her. "That'll keep you safe!"

He washed his hands and face, shaved carefully and put on Uncle Jason's suit and shoes, interrupting what he was doing several times to come back to the window and study the empty road. When he'd finished, he went downstairs and found a door that opened into the garage. There was a bicycle there, as she'd said, and no car, though the garage had space enough for three of them. Jeff returned to the top floor.

Brooke looked around as he came into the room.

"I suppose you'll be going to Mexico," she remarked.

His eyes narrowed. At it again—and she happened to be right. "Sounds like a good first stop, doesn't it?" he said.

She studied him. "You'll need a good paper man to fix you up once you're down there."

Jeff laughed shortly. "I know where to find a good paper man down there."

"You do? Got the kind of money he's going to want?"

"Not yet." There wasn't much more than a hundred dollars in the stained brown wallet. "Any suggestions?" he asked.

"Twenty-eight thousand in cash," Brooke said. "I keep telling you I want to help."

He stiffened. "*Twenty-eight*—where?"

She jerked her elbows impatiently. "Get me untied and I'll show you. It's downstairs." He didn't believe her. He felt an angry flush rising in his cheeks. If it was a lie, she'd be sorry! But he released her.

She got up from the chair, rubbing her bruised wrists, said, "Come along. Have to get keys from my room," and went ahead of him into the passage.

Jeff followed watchfully, close on her heels, looked on as she took two keys from a purse. They went back to the stairway, down it to the central hall on the ground floor. Brooke used the larger of the keys to open a closet behind a section of the hall's polished oak paneling. A sizable black suitcase stood inside. Brooke nodded at the suitcase.

"The money's in there." She offered Jeff the other key. "You'll have to unlock it."

Jeff shook his head.

"We'll take it to your Uncle Jason's room before we look at the money," he told her. "I'll let you carry it."

"Sure," Brooke said agreeably. "I carried it in here."

She picked up the suitcase, shut the closet, and walked ahead of Jeff to the stairs. The way she handled the suitcase indicated there was something inside, but something that wasn't very heavy. It could be twenty-eight thousand dollars, but a variety of rather improbable speculations kept crossing Jeff's mind as he followed her upstairs. Was the thing rigged? Would something unpleasant have happened if he'd unlocked it just now? He shook his head. It wasn't at all like him to engage in nervous fantasies.

Nevertheless, he found himself moving a few steps back from the suitcase when he told Brooke to put it on the carpet and open it. She knelt beside it and unlocked it, and nothing remarkable occurred. She opened the suitcase and Jeff saw folds of furry green material. "What's that?" he asked.

"My cape. Dyed muskrat. The money's under the clothes." Brooke took out the green cape, laid it on the floor, added several other items while Jeff watched her motions closely.

"There's the money," she said finally.

Jeff nodded. "All right. Take it out and put it on the table."

Brooke glanced over at him with a quick grin. "Don't trust me yet, do you?"

"Not much," Jeff agreed.

"You should. That's my money I'm letting you have."

"Your money, eh?"

"Well—sort of. I stole it."

"That I can believe," Jeff said. "Get it up on the table."

Brooke took six slender stacks of bills from the suitcase, laid them side by side on the table and moved back. "Count it!" she invited, then looked on as Jeff riffled slowly through the stacks.

"Where did you steal it?" he asked.

"Man named Harold Brownlee—city councilman. He has a home in the suburbs. The money was in his den safe. I picked it up two nights ago."

"Just like that, huh?"

"No, not just like that," she said. "It was worked out pretty carefully. Twenty-five thousand was bribe money on a land development racket. I don't know about the rest—probably just a little something Brownlee wanted to have on hand, like people do. We knew when the bribe payoff was to be and where he keeps that kind of cash between his trips out of town to get it deposited."

"How did you know?" Jeff put the last bundle down. It was twenty-eight thousand dollars and a little more.

She shrugged. "Family intelligence. How? They don't let me in on that kind of thing yet. But they did let me do the Brownlee job by myself—well, almost by myself. Tracy insisted on being a lookout at the country club where the Brownlees were that night. She'd have let me know if they started home before I finished." Brooke added with a trace of resentment, "It wasn't necessary. If they had come back early, they wouldn't have seen me."

Jeff was staring at her. An hour ago, he would have considered it a crazy story. Now he simply wasn't so sure. He was about to speak when he heard a tiny sound, like the tinkle of distant fairy chimes. "What was that?" he asked sharply.

"Just Tracy," said Brooke. "She wants to talk. I guess she's ready to start home." She tapped her wristwatch. "Two-way transmitter," she explained. "Tracy has one just like it. You want me to talk to her?"

Startled, Jeff hesitated. The chimes tinkled faintly again. Now it was clear that Brooke's little watch was producing the sound.

"Go ahead," he told her. He added, "You'd better remember what not to say."

Brooke smiled. "Don't worry! You'll have to stand close if you want to hear Tracy. They're made so you can talk privately." She slid a fingernail under a jeweled knob of the watch, lifting it a scant millimeter, gave it a twist. "Tracy?" she said, holding the watch a few inches from her ear. Jeff moved over to her.

"I'll be on my way back in just a few minutes," the watch whispered. "Have there been any calls?"

"No," Brooke said. "Didn't know you were expecting any." Her own voice was low but not a whisper.

"I'm not really expecting one," the ghostly little voice said from the watch. "But I remembered Ricardo wasn't sure he could make it tonight. He said he'd phone the house early if he couldn't come, so we'd be able to get someone else to give us a quorum."

Brooke winked at Jeff, said, "Well, he hasn't called yet, so he'll probably show up."

"Right. See you soon. 'Bye."

"'Bye," said Brooke. She pushed down the knob, told Jeff, "That switches it off again."

"Uh-huh." Jeff scratched his chin. "How long will it take Tracy to get here now?"

"Forty minutes probably. Not much more. It's a good road most of the way, and she drives fast."

"How old is she?"

"Twenty-four. Seven years eight months older than I am. Why?"

"Just wondering." Jeff held out his hand, "Let's see that thing."

"The two-way? Sure." Brooke slipped the instrument off her wrist, gave it to him. "Be careful with it," she cautioned. "It's mighty expensive."

"It should be!" Jeff turned it about in his fingers, studying it. A stylish little woman's wristwatch, and it was running. There was nothing at all to indicate it could be anything other than that, but he'd heard it in action. "Yes, very expensive!" he said thoughtfully. He placed the watch on the table beside the bills. "That sounds like a peculiar family you've got," he remarked. "You really weren't lying about the Brownlee job?"

Brooke smiled. "Take a look at what's inside the cape," she said. "That's my prowling outfit, or most of it."

Jeff laid the dyed muskrat cape on one end of the table, opened it, fur side down. There were a number of zippered pockets in the lining. Jeff located variously shaped objects in some of the pockets by touch, took them out and regarded them.

"Earphone," he said. "So this matchbox-sized gadget it's connected to should be another radio?"

Brooke nodded. "Local police calls."

"Yes, handy. And a fancy glass cutter. The two keys?"

"Duplicates of the ones Brownlee had for his den safe."

"Which made that part of it simple, didn't it?" Jeff remarked. "And a pocket flash could be useful, of course. Why the cigarette case, if that's what it is?"

"Open it," Brooke told him.

He pressed the snap of the case, looked at the long-tipped narrow cigarettes clasped inside, a brand he didn't know. "Imports?" he asked.

"Uh-huh."

Jeff sniffed at the cigarettes. "Anything special about them?"

"Just their length. They taste lousy." Brooke put out her hand. "There's a back section, you see. Let me—"

"Just tell me what to do," Jeff said.

Opening the hidden inner section of the case turned out to be a more complicated operation than switching the wristwatch over to its transmitter function, even under Brooke's guidance, but after some fumbling Jeff accomplished it. He pursed his lips, considered a silk-packed row of thin metal rods, in silence for a moment.

"Picks," he said then. "You any good at using them?"

"Pretty good, I think," Brooke said. "I should be able to open almost any ordinary lock with one or another of those."

"Look kind of light."

"Not too light, Jeff. That's beryllium—harder than steel."

"I suppose you know it can be worth ten years just to be found with a set of picks like those on you?"

"That's why it's a cigarette case," Brooke told him.

Jeff shook his head. "Where did you get all these things?"

"They were custom-made. For me."

Jeff snapped both sections of the cigarette case shut and put it down. "None of it really makes any sense!" he remarked. "Your people must have money."

"Plenty," Brooke agreed.

"Then why do you play around with stuff like this? Are you nuts who do it for kicks?"

"It's not for kicks," Brooke said. "It's training. The Brownlee job the other night was a test. It's a way of finding out if I can qualify for the fancy things the family does—that some of them do, anyway."

"And what do they do?" Jeff asked.

"I don't know that yet, so I can't tell you. The family operates on a theory."

"Okay. Let's hear the theory—"

"If you decide to stay legal," Brooke said, "you give away too much advantage to people who don't care whether they do or not. But if you do things that aren't legal, you can get yourself and others into trouble. It takes a knack to be able to do it and keep on getting away with it. So it's only those who show they have the knack who get into the nonlegal side of the family. The others don't break laws and don't ask questions, so there's nothing they can spill. The family keeps getting richer, but everything looks legitimate. And most of it is."

Jeff shook his head again. "Just who is this family?"

"Oh, the Camerons and the Achtels and some Wylers and a few on the Nichols side. There could be others I don't know about." Brooke added, "The Wylers and Nichols are kind of new, but the Camerons and Achtels have been working together a long time."

Jeff grunted. "Supposing you'd got caught at the Brownlee house?"

She shrugged. "That would have been *it* for me. Nothing much would have happened. The family's got pull here and there, and I'd have been a fool rich kid playing cops and robbers. But I'd never have got near a nonlegal operation after that. I'd have proved I didn't have the knack."

"What if it was just bad luck?"

"They've got no use for someone who has bad luck. It's too risky."

Jeff nodded. He watched her a moment, head tipped quizzically to the side. "Now, something else." He smiled. "Why are you pretending you want to help me?"

"I do want to help you." Brooke frowned. "After all, how likely is it you'd have come across the cash if I hadn't told you?"

"Then what do you figure on getting out of it?"

"You're to take me to Mexico with you."

"You're out of your mind!" Jeff was honestly startled. "From what you've been telling me, you have it made here."

"You think so." Brooke turned to the suitcase. "There's something you haven't seen yet."

"Hold it right there," Jeff said. "What's that something?"

"You can keep your gun pointed at me while I'm getting it out," she told him, half scornfully. "I picked up more than money at the Brownlee place."

He made no further move to check her then but kept close watch as she opened a side section of the suitcase and brought out a small leather bag. She loosened the bag's drawstrings and shook its contents out on the table. "What do you think of those?" she demanded.

Jeff looked at the tumbled, shining little pile and moistened his lips. "Nice stuff—if it's genuine."

"*If* it's genuine!" Brooke's eyes flashed. She reached for a string of pearls, swung it back and forth before his face. "If you knew pearls, you wouldn't be calling that just 'nice stuff!' You need someone like me, Jeff. For one thing, I do know pearls. They were in the safe with the money, and there was a very good reason for that."

She dropped the pearls back on the other jewelry. "But you know what would have happened if you hadn't come along today? The meeting at the house tonight was supposed to be about me. A quorum of the active side of the family was going to review the Brownlee job and decide if I was maybe good enough to go on to something a little bigger than I've been allowed to do so far. The job wasn't much for sure—I just went in and did what I was supposed to do—but I did everything *right*; there's nothing they can fault me on.

"So probably I'd pass. And then?" She waved her hand at the table. "I wouldn't see any of that again! Oh, sure, a third of what the haul's worth would be credited to my family account. When I'm twenty-one, I'll finally have a little something to say about that account. The rings and the watch and those lovely pearls and the rest of it would leave the house with Ricardo Achtel—he runs a jewelry firm for the family, imports, exports, manufacture. And they'd decide I could move up a notch. You know what that would mean?" She laughed. "I'd be working out with a lousy circus for a couple of years at least!"

Jeff blinked. "A circus?"

Brooke nodded. "Right! We've got one in Europe. It's a small circus, but putting in a hitch there while you're young is family tradition for active members. It goes back for generations." She grimaced. "There're all *kinds* of things you can learn at the circus that will be useful later on, they tell you."

Jeff grinned warily. "Well, there might be."

Brooke tossed her head. "I don't need all that discipline. I don't want to be thinking about the family in everything I do. They're so cautious! Now, you're somebody who doesn't mind cutting corners fast when it's necessary. We'd be a team, Jeff!"

Jeff felt a touch of amazed merriment. "What about Tracy?" he asked.

"What about her? She takes us there; we ditch her. I sort of like Tracy, but she's sold on the family. She won't make trouble for us afterward, and neither will the others. They're too careful for that. They know the kind of trouble I could make for them. You have a place to go to down there?"

Jeff nodded. "Uh-huh. Friendly old pot rancher, fifty miles from the border. Nice quiet place. You know, I've been thinking, Brooke."

"Yes?" she said eagerly.

"You've got these cute miniaturized gadgets. A cigarette case that isn't really one, and a watch that's something else besides." Jeff picked up the pencil flash he'd discovered in Brooke's cape. "This looks custom-built, too."

Her eyes might have flickered for an instant. "It is," she said. "It's the best."

"The best what, aside from being a light?"

"Well—nothing. I want a light I can rely on, naturally."

"Uh-huh. But it's thicker at this end than it really needs to be, isn't it? As if something might be built in there." Jeff fingered the pencil flash. "And this little hole, you'll notice, points wherever you point the light. I don't see how the thing can be opened either."

"Opening it is a little tricky," Brooke said. "If you'll let—"

"No, don't bother." Jeff smiled. "Here's where you switch on the light—fine! So it is a flashlight. What does this ring do?" He turned the flash up, pointing it at Brooke's face.

"Twist it to the left, and it dims the beam," Brooke said, watching him.

"To the right?"

"That brightens it, of course. And—" Her breath caught. "Don't twist it too far, Jeff."

"Why not?"

"Well, don't point it at me then." She smiled quickly. "I'll explain."

"Sure, explain." Jeff lowered the flashlight.

Brooke was still smiling. "I didn't really know about you. You can see that."

"Uh-huh. I understand."

"So I didn't want to tell you about it yet. It's a tranquilizer gun."

Jeff raised his brows. "Doesn't look much like one."

"Family specialty. You couldn't buy that kind of tranquilizer anywhere. I don't know what it is, of course, but we might be able to have it analyzed."

"Maybe we could," Jeff said. "What's its range?"

"You're not supposed to try to use it over thirty feet. Indoors, that's likely to be as much range as you'll want."

"You've used it?"

"No," Brooke said. "I saw it used once, but it's only for a real emergency. The family doesn't want it to get out that someone makes a gun like that."

"What was the effect?"

Brooke grimaced. "Worked so fast it scared me! The man didn't even know he'd been hit, and he didn't move for another two hours. But it won't kill anyone, and there isn't supposed to be much aftereffect. It's a little hollow needle."

Jeff nodded thoughtfully. "Very interesting. It seems we now have the explanation for your generous offer to finance me."

Brooke looked startled. "I told you—"

"You told me a lot of things. I'll even believe some of them— that this is a gun, for example. It's what you were working to get your hand on right from the start, wasn't it?"

Brooke said reluctantly, "I would have felt better if I'd had it. You see—"

"I know. You just weren't sure you could trust me. All right, obviously I can't be sure I can trust you either." Jeff raised the pencil flash, pointing it at her. "So why don't I see for myself what that little hollow needle does after it hits?"

Brooke shook her head. "You don't want to do that, Jeff."

"Why not?"

"Tracy's sort of slippery. If I'm awake and in the plane with you two, she'll be a lot easier to handle. I can keep her conned. Whether you believe it or not, I do want to go to Mexico with you."

Jeff grinned and dropped the pencil flash into a coat pocket.

"And you're getting your wish!" he told her. "Go sit down in your chair."

He tied Brooke's hands behind the chair back, secured the rope to a rung, testing all knots carefully. Then he checked the time and said, "Keep your month shut from now on unless I ask you something."

Brooke nodded silently. Her expression indicated she might be frightened at last, and she might have reason for it. Jeff went to the window, studied the valley road. Nothing to be seen there yet. Rain clouds drifted over the lower countryside though the sky remained clear above the house. There was a distant roll of thunder. Jeff left the room, returned with a silk scarf. He laid the scarf on the table, restored the bundled bills, the jewelry and Brooke's burglary equipment to the suitcase, except for the pencil flash, which stayed in his pocket along with the two-way watch. He covered the assortment in the suitcase with Brooke's cape, thinking there still might be stuff concealed in it that he hadn't discovered. If so, it could wait. He closed and locked the suitcase, pocketed the key. The clothes and boots he'd been wearing went into the closet from which he'd taken Uncle Jason's suit and shoes.

He returned to the window, stood looking out. He felt a little tense, just enough to keep him keyed up, which he didn't mind. He was always at his best when keyed up. He knew exactly what he was going to do, and it was unlikely that anything could go wrong. Even if Brooke happened to have lied about Tracy's ability to fly a plane, it wouldn't affect his plans seriously. He'd leave the two of them here, dead and stowed away where they shouldn't be found at once, and go off in Tracy's car. A few hours' start was all he needed now. The plane would be preferable, of course. If the two disappeared with him, he could work out a way to put heat on their precious family.

He'd been tempted to wait, to let that crew of cautious wealthy practitioners of crime start drifting in during the afternoon, nail them down as they arrived, and then see what he could make out of the overall situation, but that might be crowding his luck. He'd got a great deal more than he'd expected to get at the house, and he liked the way the setup looked now.

He inquired presently, "What color is Tracy's car?"

Brooke's tongue tip moistened her lips. "Red," she said. "Cherry red. Sports car. Is she coming?"

"In sight," Jeff said. "Still a few minutes away." He went to the table, picked up the silk scarf. "Let's make sure everything stays very quiet in here when she shows up!" He wrapped the scarf tightly around Brooke's mouth and jaw, knotted it behind her head and came back to the window.

He stood away from it a little, though there was no real chance the sharpest of eyes could have spotted him from the road. Tracy, he decided, did drive fast—and expertly. The little red car was flicked around curves, accelerated again on the straight stretches.

By the time the sound of the engine grew audible on the breeze, he could make out a few details about the driver: a woman, all right—goggled, bright green scarf covering her head, strands of blonde hair whipping out back of the scarf. She was coming to the house because there was nowhere else to go; the road stopped here. Satisfied, Jeff left the room, went unhurriedly downstairs.

He'd made up his mind a while ago about the place where he'd wait for Tracy, and he was there a minute later. A side door opened on the garden near the angle formed by the house with the garage. The angle was landscaped with thick dark-green bushes, providing perfect cover. For the moment, he remained near the door. The chances were that Tracy would come directly to the garage; and if she did, he'd have the gun on her as soon as she stepped out of the car. If, instead, she drove around to the front entrance of the building, he'd slip back into the house through the side door and catch her inside. The rest would be simple. It shouldn't take long to make her realize what she had to do for her own sake and Brooke's, that Jeff didn't really need either of them, and that if she didn't follow his orders, exactly, he'd shoot them both and leave with her car.

From his point of concealment, he watched the car turn up the driveway from the road. The section of driveway leading to the garage curved out of sight behind a stand of ornamental pines sixty yards away. The car swung into it, vanished behind the trees. There was a momentary squeal of brakes.

Jeff frowned, listening, Uncle George's .38 in his hand. He heard the purring throb of the engine, but the car obviously had stopped. It shouldn't make much difference if Tracy left it there; she still had to come to the house. But it wasn't the way Jeff had planned it, and he didn't like that.

He gauged the distance to the pines. He could reach them in a quick sprint and find out what she was doing. However, he didn't favor that idea either. If she had the car in motion again before he got there and caught sight of him in the open, he could have a real problem. Undecided, Jeff began to edge through the bushes toward the front of the garage.

He heard a sound then, a slight creaking, which he might have missed if his ears hadn't been straining for indications of what was delaying Tracy. He turned his head, and something stung the side of his neck. He swung around, startled, felt himself stumbling oddly as his gaze swept up along the side of the house.

A window screen in a second-floor room above him was being

quietly closed. Jeff jerked up the revolver. He was falling backward by then, and he fired two shots, wildly, spitefully, at the blurring blue of the sky before he was lying on the ground, the gun somehow no longer in his hand. He had a stunned thought: that Brooke couldn't possibly have done it, that he had her tranquilizing gadget in his coat. And besides—

He didn't finish the second thought. Tracy was standing next to him, holding a gun of her own, when Brooke came out through the side door.

"Well!" Tracy said. "So now I know why you were giving me the high sign from the window." She glanced down at Jeff's face, back at Brooke. "Tranquilizer?"

"No," Brooke said reluctantly. "He spotted that while we were talking and took it."

"So it was Last Resort, eh?"

"Yes."

Tracy grimaced. "Suspected it, by the way he looks." She shook her head. "Well, Brooke—curare. You know, the rules. You may have quite a bit of explaining to do."

"I *can* explain it."

"Yes? Start with me!" Tracy invited. "A sort of rehearsal. Let's see how it will stand up."

"You know who that is? Was, I guess."

Tracy looked at Jeff again. "No. I should?"

"Jeff Clary."

Tracy blinked. "Clary? The escaped convict they're hunting for? You're sure?"

"I'm sure," Brooke said. "They've been broadcasting his picture and I recognized him as soon as he turned up in the house. Anyway, he admitted it. He's killed three people in the past twenty-four hours, and he had plans for you and me after you'd flown him across the border."

"Now, that doesn't start the explanation off too badly," Tracy conceded. "Still—"

Brooke said, "He had to go anyway."

"Probably. But not at your discretion. If you had to let him take your sleepy-bye kit, what about mine? You know where I keep it. The bag's upstairs in my closet at present."

"I thought of that," Brooke said, "but I didn't think I'd have time to hunt around for the bag. He had me gagged and tied to a chair, and he stayed right there in the room with me until you were almost driving in. Last Resort was quicker. I grabbed it."

"Um!" Tracy tapped her nose tip reflectively. "Well, that really should do it! They can't give you too much of an argument." She smiled. "So the big bad convict ties you to a chair? Angelique the Eleven-Year-Old Escape Artist. Remember the howl you raised when they sent you off to the circus that summer?" She looked at the gun in her hand. "Might as well put this away, and we'll start tidying up."

"Hadn't you better use the gun first?" Brooke said.

"Huh?" Tracy looked thoughtful. "Yes!" she said then. "Good thinking, Brooke! They should prefer to let Clary be found if the coroner doesn't have reason to poke around too closely. We'll take away the reason."

She pointed the gun at a spot between Jeff's eyebrows.

There had been assorted activities in the house in the latter part of the afternoon and the early part of the evening, but around ten o'clock things were quiet again. The rain, after holding off to the south most of the day, had moved in finally, and there was a gentle steady pattering against the closed windows in Tracy's room. For the past half hour, Brooke and Tracy had been playing double slap solitaire at a small table. Neither was displaying her usual fierce concentration on the game.

Tracy lifted her head suddenly, glanced at Brooke. "I think the reporting committee's coming!"

Brooke listened. Footsteps were audible in the passage. "Well, it's a relief," she muttered. "They've been discussing it long enough."

She put down her card pack and went to the door.

"Here we are, George!" she called. "Tracy's room."

She came back and looked on as the tuxedoed committee filed in. George Cameron, president of Renfrew College and scholarly authority on the Punic Wars, entered first; then Ricardo Achtel, who handled Baldwin Gems, Imports and Exports, among other things. Finally came Jason Cameron, best known in some circles as big-game hunter and mountaineer. Three big guns of the family. All gave her reassuring smiles, which struck Brooke as a bad sign. She drew a deep breath.

"What's the verdict?" she asked.

"Let's not look on it as a verdict, Brooke," said George Cameron. "Sit down; we'll have to talk about it." He glanced around, noted the absence of free chairs. "Mind if we use your bed, Tracy?"

"Not at all," Tracy told him.

George and Jason sat down on the bed. Ricardo Achtel leaned against the wall, hands shoved into his trousers pockets. "There was a special news report some ten minutes ago," George remarked. "I don't believe you caught it?"

Brooke shook her head.

George said, "They've found the unfortunate Rambow couple in their car. Each had been shot from behind almost at contact range—a deliberate execution. Clary afterward ran the damaged vehicle off the road, as he told you. A highway patrol happened to notice smashed bushes, investigated and discovered the wreck and the bodies in a ravine."

"How far from where Clary was found?" Tracy asked.

"Less than four miles. We worked out his probable backtrail closely enough," George said. "And that should wind it up. The theory that Clary tried to kidnap another motorist, who was lucky or alert enough to shoot first, and may have sufficient reason for not wanting to identify himself, is regarded as substantiated. Either of the two bullets found in Clary's body should have caused almost instant death. Police will try to trace the gun. The usual thing."

There was a short pause. "All right, and now what about me?" Brooke asked. "I've flunked?"

"Not at all," George said. "On the whole, you did very well. You were dealing with a killer and stalled him off until you could create an opportunity to end the threat to yourself and Tracy. Naturally, we approve."

"Naturally," Tracy agreed dryly.

"However," said Jason Cameron, "there was a rather serious breach of secrecy."

"I've tried to explain that," Brooke told him. "I had to do something to keep Clary working to outfigure me. I couldn't think of a good enough set of lies on the spot. He didn't seem exactly stupid. So I told him the truth, or mostly the truth, which made it easy."

George scratched his jaw. "Yes, but there you are, Brooke! In doing it, you took a chance. Mind you, no one's blaming you. If there's any fault, it's in those responsible for your progress—which certainly must include myself. But as far as you knew, there was a possibility, however slight, that the police would trace Clary to the house and take him alive. We could have handled the resulting problem, but some harm might have been done. Further, in being frank with Clary, you made killing him almost a necessity—

thus reducing your options, which is never desirable."

Jason nodded. "There's a definite streak of candor in you, Brooke. It's been noticed. Your immediate inclination is to tell the truth."

"Not," observed Ricardo Achtel, "that there's anything essentially wrong with that."

"No, of course not," George agreed. "However, one can also argue in favor of facile dissimulation. Those who don't seem born with the ability—I had a good deal of early difficulty in the area myself—must acquire it by practice. It's felt you fall short on that point, Brooke."

"In other words," Brooke said, "I didn't flunk out, but I didn't get upgraded tonight either?"

"Not formally," George told her. "We believe you need more time. The matter will be brought up again at your next birthday."

"Seven months," said Brooke. She looked discouraged.

"They'll pass quickly enough for you," George assured her.

"In a sense, you see," Jason remarked, "circumstances did upgrade you today by presenting you with a difficult and serious problem, which you solved satisfactorily though in a less than optimum manner. It seems mainly a question of letting your experience catch up."

George nodded. "Exactly! So you'll continue your formal education at Renfrew, but you'll also start going to drama school."

"Drama school?" Brooke said, surprised.

"Ours. The training you receive there won't precisely parallel that given other students, but you should find it interesting. Tracy went through the process a few years ago."

Brooke looked over at Tracy.

"Uh-huh, so I did," Tracy said slowly. She shook her head. "Poor Brooke!"

Ham Sandwich

· · · · · · · · · · · · · ·

THERE WAS NO ONE standing or sitting around the tastefully furnished entry hall of the Institute of Insight when Wallace Cavender walked into it. He was almost half an hour late for the regular Sunday night meeting of advanced students; and even Mavis Greenfield, Dr. Ormond's secretary, who always stayed for a while at her desk in the hall to sign in the stragglers, had disappeared. However, she had left the attendance book lying open on the desk with a pen placed invitingly beside it.

Wallace Cavender dutifully entered his name in the book. The distant deep voice of Dr. Aloys Ormond was dimly audible, coming from the direction of the lecture room, and Cavender followed its faint reverberations down a narrow corridor until he reached a closed door. He eased the door open and slipped unobtrusively into the back of the lecture room.

As usual, most of the thirty-odd advanced students present had seated themselves on the right side of the room where they were somewhat closer to the speaker. Cavender started towards the almost vacant rows of chairs on the left, smiling apologetically at Dr. Ormond who, as the door opened, had glanced up without interrupting his talk. Three other faces turned towards Cavender from across the room. Reuben Jeffries, a heavyset man with a thin fringe of black hair circling an otherwise bald scalp, nodded soberly and looked away again. Mavis Greenfield, a few rows farther up, produced a smile and a reproachful little headshake; during the coffee break she would carefully explain to Cavender once more that students too tardy to take in Dr. Al's introductory lecture missed the most valuable part of these meetings.

368

From old Mrs. Folsom, in the front row on the right, Cavender's belated arrival drew a more definite rebuke. She stared at him for half a dozen seconds with a coldly severe frown, mouth puckered in disapproval, before returning her attention to Dr. Ormond.

Cavender sat down in the first chair he came to and let himself go comfortably limp. He was dead-tired, had even hesitated over coming to the Institute of Insight tonight. But it wouldn't do to skip the meeting. A number of his fellow students, notably Mrs. Folsom, already regarded him as a black sheep; and if enough of them complained to Dr. Ormond that Cavender's laxness threatened to retard the overall advance of the group towards the goal of Total Insight, Ormond might decide to exclude him from further study. At a guess, Cavender thought cynically, it would have happened by now if the confidential report the Institute had obtained on his financial status had been less impressive. A healthy bank balance wasn't an absolute requirement for membership, but it helped . . . it helped! All but a handful of the advanced students were in the upper income brackets.

Cavender let his gaze shift unobtrusively about the group while some almost automatic part of his mind began to pick up the thread of Dr. Al's discourse. After a dozen or so sentences, he realized that the evening's theme was the relationship between subjective and objective reality, as understood in the light of Total Insight. It was a well-worn subject; Dr. Al repeated himself a great deal. Most of the audience nevertheless was following his words with intent interest, many taking notes and frowning in concentration. As Mavis Greenfield liked to express it, quoting the doctor himself, the idea you didn't pick up when it was first presented might come clear to you the fifth or sixth time around. Cavender suspected, however, that as far as he was concerned much of the theory of Total Insight was doomed to remain forever obscure.

He settled his attention on the only two students on this side of the room with him. Dexter Jones and Perrie Rochelle were sitting side by side in front-row chairs—the same chairs they usually occupied during these meetings. They were exceptions to the general run of the group in a number of ways. Younger, for one thing; Dexter was twenty-nine and Perrie twenty-three while the group averaged out at around forty-five, which happened to be Cavender's age. Neither was blessed with worldly riches; in fact, it was questionable whether the Rochelle girl, who described herself as a commercial artist, even had a bank account. Dexter Jones, a grade-school teacher, did have one but was able to keep it barely

high enough to cover his rent and car payment checks. Their value
to the Institute was of a different kind. Both possessed esoteric
mental talents, rather modest ones, to be sure, but still very interesting, so that on occasion they could state accurately what was
contained in a sealed envelope, or give a recognizable description
of the photograph of a loved one hidden in another student's
wallet. This provided the group with encouraging evidence that
such abilities were, indeed, no fable and somewhere along the
difficult road to Total Insight might be attained by all.

In addition, Perrie and Dexter were volunteers for what Dr. Aloys
Ormond referred to cryptically as "very advanced experimentation."
The group at large had not been told the exact nature of these
experiments, but the implication was that they were mental exercises of such power that Dr. Al did not wish other advanced students to try them, until the brave pioneer work being done by
Perrie and Dexter was concluded and he had evaluated the
results . . .

"Headaches, Dr. Al," said Perrie Rochelle. "Sometimes quite bad
headaches—" She hesitated. She was a thin, pale girl with untidy
arranged brown hair who vacillated between periods of vivacious
alertness and activity and somewhat shorter periods of blank-faced
withdrawal. "And then," she went on, "there are times during the
day when I get to feeling sort of confused and not quite sure
whether I'm asleep or awake . . . you know?"

Dr. Ormond nodded, gazing at her reflectively from the little
lectern on which he leaned. His composed smile indicated that he
was not in the least surprised or disturbed by her report on the
results of the week's experiments—that they were, in fact, precisely
the results he had expected. "I'll speak to you about it later, Perrie,"
he told her gently. "Dexter . . . what experiences have you had?"

Dexter Jones cleared his throat. He was a serious young man
who appeared at meetings conservatively and neatly dressed and
shaved to the quick, and rarely spoke unless spoken to.

"Well, nothing very dramatic, Dr. Al," he said diffidently. "I did
have a few nightmares during the week. But I'm not sure there's
any connection between them and, uh, what you were having us
do."

Dr. Ormond stroked his chin and regarded Dexter with benevo-
lence. "A connection seems quite possible, Dexter. Let's assume it
exists. What can you tell us about those nightmares?"

Dexter said he was afraid he couldn't actually tell them anything.

By the time he was fully awake he'd had only a very vague impression of what the nightmares were about, and the only part he could remember clearly now was that they had been quite alarming.

Old Mrs. Folsom, who was more than a little jealous of the special position enjoyed by Dexter and Perrie, broke in eagerly at that point to tell about a nightmare *she'd* had during the week and which *she* could remember fully; and Cavender's attention drifted away from the talk. Mrs. Folsom was an old bore at best, but a very wealthy old bore, which was why Dr. Ormond usually let her ramble on a while before steering the conversation back to the business of the evening. But Cavender didn't have to pretend to listen.

From his vantage point behind most of the group, he let his gaze and thoughts wander from one to the other of them again. For the majority of the advanced students, he reflected, the Institute of Insight wasn't really too healthy a place. But it offered compensations. Middle-aged or past it on the average, financially secure, vaguely disappointed in life, they'd found in Dr. Al a friendly and eloquent guide to lead them into the fascinating worlds of their own minds. And Dr. Al was good at it. He had borrowed as heavily from yoga and western mysticism as from various orthodox and unorthodox psychological disciplines, and composed his own system, almost his own cosmology. His exercises would have made conservative psychiatrists shudder, but he was clever enough to avoid getting his flock into too serious mental difficulties. If some of them suffered a bit now and then, it made the quest of Total Insight and the thought that they were progressing towards that goal more real and convincing. And meeting after meeting Dr. Al came up with some intriguing new twist or device, some fresh experience to keep their interest level high.

"Always bear in mind," he was saying earnestly at the moment, "that an advance made by *any* member of the group benefits the group as a whole. Thus, because of the work done by our young pioneers this week I see indications tonight that the group is ready to attempt a new experiment . . . an experiment at a level I frankly admit I hadn't anticipated you would achieve for at least another two months."

Dr. Ormond paused significantly, the pause underlining his words. There was an expectant stirring among the students.

"But I must caution you!" he went on. "We cannot, of course, be certain that the experiment will succeed . . . in fact, it would be a very remarkable thing if it did succeed at a first attempt. But if it should, you will have had a rather startling experience! You will have seen a thing generally considered to be impossible!"

He smiled reassuringly, stepping down from the lectern. "Naturally, there will be no danger. You know me well enough to realize that I never permit the group or individuals to attempt what lies beyond their capability."

Cavender stifled a yawn, blinked water from his eyes, watching Ormond walk over to a small polished table on the left side of the room in front of the rows of chairs. On it Mavis Greenfield had placed a number of enigmatic articles, some of which would be employed as props in one manner or another during the evening's work. The most prominent item was a small suitcase in red alligator hide. Dr. Ormond, however, passed up the suitcase, took a small flat wooden plate from the table and returned to the center of the room.

"On this," he said, holding up the plate, "there rests at this moment the air of this planet and nothing else. But in a minute or two—for each of you, in his or her world of subjective reality—something else *will* appear on it."

The students nodded comprehendingly. So far, the experiment was on familiar ground. Dr. Ormond gave them all a good-humored wink.

"To emphasize," he went on, "that we deal here with practical, down-to-earth, *real* matters . . . not some mystical nonsense . . . to emphasize that, let us say that the object each of you will visualize on this plate will be—a ham sandwich!"

There were appreciative chuckles. But Cavender felt a twinge of annoyance. At the moment, when along with fighting off fatigue he'd been trying to forget that he hadn't eaten since noon, Dr. Al's choice looked like an unfortunate one. Cavender happened to be very fond of ham.

"Now here," Ormond continued, putting the plate down, "is where this experiment begins to differ from anything we have done before. For all of us will try to imagine—to visualize as being on this plate—*the same ham sandwich*. And so there will be no conflict in our projections, let's decide first on just what ingredients we want to put into it." He smiled. "We'll make this the finest ham sandwich our collective imagination can produce!"

There were more chuckles. Cavender cursed under his breath, his mouth beginning to water. Suggestions came promptly.

"Mustard?" Dr. Ormond said. "Of course—Not too sharp

though, Eleanor?" He smiled at Mrs. Folsom. "I agree! A light touch of delicate salad mustard. Crisp lettuce . . . finely chopped gherkins. Very well!"

"Put it all on rye," Cavender said helplessly. "Toasted rye."

"Toasted rye?" Ormond smiled at him, looked around. "Any objections? No? Toasted rye it shall be, Wally. And I believe that completes our selection."

He paused, his face turning serious. "Now as to that word of caution I gave you. For three minutes each of you will visualize the object we have chosen on the plate I will be holding up before me. You will do this with your eyes open, and to each of you, in your own subjective reality, the object will become, as you know, more or less clearly discernible.

"But let me tell you this. Do not be too surprised if at the end of that time, when the exercise is over, the object *remains visible to you* . . . does not disappear!"

There was silence for a moment. Then renewed chuckles, but slightly nervous ones, and not too many.

Dr. Ormond said sternly, "I am serious about that! The possibility, though it may be small tonight, is there. You have learned that, by the laws of Insight, any image of subjective reality, if it can be endowed with *all* the attributes of objective reality by its human creator, *must* spontaneously become an image in objective reality!

"In this case, our collective ham sandwich, if it were perfectly visualized, could not only be seen by you but felt, its weight and the texture of each of its ingredients perceived, their appetizing fragrance savored"—Cavender groaned mentally—"and more: if one of you were to eat this sandwich, he would find it exactly as nourishing as any produced by the more ordinary methods of objective reality.

"There are people in the world today," Dr. Ormond concluded, speaking very earnestly now, "Who can do this! There always have been people who could do this. And you are following in their footsteps, being trained in even more advanced skills. I am aware to a greater extent than any of you of the latent power that is developing—has developed—in this group. Tonight, for the first time, that power will be focused, drawn down to a pinpoint, to accomplish one task.

"Again, I do not say that at the end of our exercise a ham sandwich will lie on this plate. Frankly, I don't expect it. But I suggest very strongly that you don't let it surprise or startle you too much if we find it here!"

There was dead stillness when he finished speaking. Cavender had a sense that the lecture room had come alive with eerie little chills. Dr. Ormond lifted the plate solemnly up before him, holding it between the fingertips of both hands.

"Now, if you will direct your attention here ... no, Eleanor, with your eyes open!

"Let us begin ..."

Cavender sighed, straightened up in his chair, eyes fixed obediently on the wooden plate, and banned ham sandwiches and every other kind of food firmly from his thoughts. There was no point in working his appetite up any further when he couldn't satisfy it, and he would have to be on guard a little against simply falling asleep during the next three minutes. The cloudiness of complete fatigue wasn't too far away. At the edge of his vision, he was aware of his fellow students across the room, arranged in suddenly motionless rows like staring zombies. His eyelids began to feel leaden.

The three minutes dragged on, came to an end. Ormond slowly lowered his hands. Cavender drew a long breath of relief. The wooden plate, he noted, with no surprise, was still empty.

"You may stop visualizing," Ormond announced.

There was concerted sighing, a creaking of chairs. The students came out of their semi-trances, blinked, smiled, settled into more comfortable positions, waiting for Dr. Al's comments.

"No miracles this time!" Ormond began briskly. He smiled.

Mrs. Folsom said, "Dr. Al—"

He looked over at her. "Yes, Eleanor?"

Eleanor Folsom hesitated, shook her head. "No," she said. "Go on. I'm sorry I interrupted."

"That's all right." Dr. Al gave her a warm smile. It had been, he continued, a successful exercise, a very promising first attempt, in spite of the lack of an immediate materialization, which, of course, had been only a remote possibility to start with. He had no fault to find with the quality of the group's effort. He had sensed it ... as they, too, presently would be able to sense it ... as a smooth flow of directed energy. With a little more practice ... one of these days ...

Cavender stifled one yawn, concealed another which didn't allow itself to be stifled behind a casually raised hand. He watched Ormond move over to the prop table, put the wooden plate down beside the red suitcase without interrupting his encouraging summary of the exercise, hesitate, then pick up something else, something which looked like a flexible copper trident, and start back to the center of the room with it.

Mrs. Folsom's voice said shrilly, "*Dr. Al—!*"

Ormond looked patient.

"Yes, Eleanor? What is it?"

"Just now," Mrs. Folsom said, her voice still holding the shrill note, "just a moment ago, on the plate over there, I'm certain . . . I'm almost certain I saw the ham sandwich!"

She added breathlessly, "And that's what I was going to say before, Dr. Al! Right after you told us to stop visualizing I thought I saw the sandwich on the plate! But it was only for a moment and I wasn't sure. But now I'm sure, almost sure, that I saw it again on the plate on the table!"

The old woman was pointing a trembling finger towards the table. Her cheeks showed spots of hectic red. In the rows behind her, the students looked at one another, shook their heads in resignation, some obviously suppressing amusement. Others looked annoyed. They were all familiar with Eleanor Folsom's tendency to produce such little sensations during the meetings. If the evening didn't promise to bring enough excitement, Eleanor always could be counted on to take a hand in events.

Cavender felt less certain about it. This time, Mrs. Folsom sounded genuinely excited. And if she actually believed she'd seen something materialize, she might be fairly close to getting one of those little heart attacks she kept everyone informed about.

Dr. Al could have had the same thought. He glanced back at the prop table, asked gravely, "You don't see it there now, do you, Eleanor?"

Mrs. Folsom shook her head. "No. No, of course not. It disappeared again. It was only there for a second. But I'm sure I saw it!"

"Now this is very interesting," Ormond said seriously. "Has anyone else observed anything at all unusual during the last few minutes?"

There was a murmured chorus of dissent, but Cavender noticed that the expressions of amusement and annoyance had vanished. Dr. Al had changed the tune, and the students were listening intently. He turned back to Mrs. Folsom.

"Let us consider the possibilities here, Eleanor," he said. "For one thing, you should be congratulated in any case, because your experience shows that your visualization was clear and true throughout our exercise. If it hadn't been, nothing like this could have occurred.

"But precisely what was the experience? There we are, as of this moment, on uncertain ground. You saw something. That no one else saw the same thing might mean simply that no one else happened to be looking at the plate at those particular instants in time. I, for example, certainly gave it no further attention after the exercise was over. You *may* then have observed a genuine materialization!"

Mrs. Folsom nodded vigorously. "Yes, I—"

"But," Ormond went on, "under the circumstances, the scientific attitude we maintain at this Institute demands that we leave the question open. For now. Because you might also, you understand, have projected—for yourself only—a vivid momentary impression of the image you had created during our exercise and were still holding in your mind."

Mrs. Folsom looked doubtful. The flush of excitement began to leave her face.

"Why . . . well, yes, I suppose so," she acknowledged unwillingly.

"Of course," Ormond said. "So tonight we shall leave it at that. The next time we engage in a similar exercise . . . well, who knows?" He gave her a reassuring smile. "I must say, Eleanor, that this is a very encouraging indication of the progress you have made!" He glanced over the group, gathering their attention, and raised the trident-like device he had taken from the table.

"And now for our second experiment this evening—"

Looking disappointed and somewhat confused, Eleanor Folsom settled back in her chair. Cavender also settled back, his gaze shifting sleepily to the remaining items on the prop table. He was frowning a little. It wasn't his business, but if the old woman had started to hypnotize herself into having hallucinations, Dr. Al had better turn to a different type of meeting exercises. And that probably was exactly what Ormond would do; he seemed very much aware of danger signals. Cavender wondered vaguely what the red suitcase on the table contained.

There was a blurry shimmer on the wooden plate beside the suitcase. Then something thickened there suddenly as if drawing itself together out of the air. Perrie Rochelle, sitting only ten feet back from the table, uttered a yelp—somewhere between surprise and alarm. Dexter Jones, beside her, abruptly pushed back his chair, made a loud, incoherent exclamation of some kind.

Cavender had started upright, heart hammering. The thing that had appeared on the wooden plate vanished again.

But it had remained visible there for a full two seconds. And there was no question at all of what it had been.

For several minutes, something resembling pandemonium swirled about the walls of the lecture room of the Institute of Insight. The red suitcase had concealed the wooden plate on the prop table from the eyes of most of the students sitting on the right side of the room, but a number of those who could see it felt they had caught a glimpse of something. Of just what they weren't sure at first, or perhaps they preferred not to say.

Perrie and Dexter, however, after getting over their first shock, had no such doubts. Perrie, voice vibrant with excitement, answered the questions flung at her from across the room, giving a detailed description of the ham sandwich which had appeared out of nowhere on the polished little table and stayed there for an incredible instant before it vanished. Dexter Jones, his usually impassive face glowing and animated, laughing, confirmed the description on every point.

On the opposite side of the room, Eleanor Folsom, surrounded by her own group of questioners, was also having her hour of triumph, in the warmth of which a trace of bitterness that her first report of the phenomenon had been shrugged off by everyone—even, in a way, by Dr. Al—gradually dissolved.

Dr. Al himself, Cavender thought, remained remarkably quiet at first, though in the excitement this wasn't generally noticed. He might even have turned a little pale. However, before things began to slow down he had himself well in hand again. Calling the group to a semblance of order, he began smilingly to ask specific questions. The witnesses on the right side of the room seemed somewhat more certain now of what they had observed.

Dr. Ormond looked over at Cavender.

"And you, Wally?" he asked. "You were sitting rather far back, to be sure—"

Cavender smiled and shrugged.

"Sorry, Dr. Al. I just wasn't looking in that direction at the moment. The first suggestion I had that anything unusual was going on was when Perrie let out that wild squawk."

There was general laughter. Perrie grinned and flushed.

"Well, I'd have liked to hear *your* squawk," she told Cavender, "if you'd seen a miracle happen right before your nose!"

"Not a miracle, Perrie," Ormond said gently. "We must remember that. We are working here with natural forces which produce natural phenomena. Insufficiently understood phenomena, perhaps, but never miraculous ones. Now, how closely did this materialization appear to conform to the subjective group image we had decided on for our exercise?"

"Well. I could only see it, of course, Dr. Al. But as far as I saw it, it was exactly what we'd . . . no, wait!" Perrie frowned, wrinkling her nose. "There was something added!" She giggled. "At least, I don't remember anyone saying we should imagine the sandwich wrapped in a paper napkin!"

Across the room, a woman's voice said breathlessly, "Oh! A *green* paper napkin, Perrie?"

Perrie looked around, surprised. "Yes, it was, Mavis."

Mavis Greenfield hesitated, said with a nervous little laugh, "I suppose I did that. I added a green napkin after we started the exercise." Her voice quavered for an instant. "I thought the image looked neater that way." She looked appealingly at the students around her. "This is really incredible, isn't it "

They gave her vague smiles. They were plainly still floating on a cloud of collective achievement—if they hadn't created that sandwich, there could have been nothing to see!

It seemed to Cavender that Dr. Ormond's face showed a flicker of strain when he heard Mavis' explanation. But he couldn't be sure because the expression—if it had been there—was smoothed away at once. Ormond cleared his throat, said firmly and somewhat chidingly, "No, not incredible, Mavis! Although—"

He turned on his smile. "My friends, I must admit that you *have* surprised me! Very pleasantly, of course. But what happened here is something I considered to be only a very remote possibility tonight. You are truly more advanced than I'd realized.

"For note this. If even one of you had been lagging behind the others, if there had been any unevenness in the concentration each gave to the exercise tonight, this materialization simply could not have occurred. And that fact forces me now to a very important decision."

He went over to the prop table, took the suitcase from it. "Mavis," he said gravely, "you may put away these other devices. We will have no further need for them in this group. Dexter, move the table to the center of the room for me, please."

He waited while his instructions were hastily carried out, then laid the suitcase on the table, drew up a chair and sat down. The buzz of excited conversation among the students hushed. They stared at him in anticipatory silence. It appeared that the evening's surprises were not yet over—and they were ready for *anything* now!

"There is a point," Dr. Ormond began in a solemn voice, riveting their eager attention on him, "a point in the orderly advance towards Total Insight at which further progress becomes greatly simplified and accelerated, because the student has now developed the capability to augment his personal efforts by the use of certain instruments."

Cavender thoughtfully reached inside his coat, brought out a cigarette case, opened it and slowly put a cigarette to his lips. About to flick on a lighter, he saw Reuben Jeffries watching him with an expression of disapproval from across the aisle. Jeffries shook his head, indicated the NO SMOKING sign on the wall. Cavender nodded, smiling a rueful apology for his absent-mindedness, and returned the cigarette to its case. He shoved his hands into his trousers pockets, slouched back in the chair.

"I have told you," Ormond was saying, "that the contributions many of you so generously made to the Institute were needed for and being absorbed by vital research. Tonight I had intended to give you a first inkling of what that research was accomplishing." He tapped the suitcase on the table before him. "In there is an instrument of the kind I have mentioned. The beneficial forces of the Cosmos are harnessed by it, flow through it. And I believe I can say that my efforts in recent months have produced the most effective such device ever seen . . ."

"Dr. Al," Mrs. Folsom interrupted firmly, "I think you should let them know how the instrument cured my heart condition."

Faces shifted towards her, then back to Dr. Al. The middle-aged majority of the students pricked their ears. For each of them, conscious of the years of increasingly uncertain health to come, Mrs. Folsom's words contained a personal implication, one that hit home. But in spite of the vindication of her claim to have seen a materialized ham sandwich, they weren't quite ready to trust her about this.

Dr. Ormond's face was grave.

"Eleanor," he said reprovingly, "that was letting the cat out of the bag, wasn't it? I hadn't intended to discuss that part of the matter just yet."

He hesitated, frowning, tapping the table top lightly with his knuckles. Mrs. Folsom looked unabashed. She had produced another sensation and knew it.

"Since it was mentioned," Ormond said with deliberation at last, "it would be unfair not to tell you, at least in brief, the facts to which Eleanor was alluding. Very well then—Eleanor has served during the past several weeks as the subject of certain experiments connected with this instrument. She reports that after her first use of it, her periodically recurring heart problem ceased to trouble her."

Mrs. Folsom smiled, nodded vigorously. "I have not," she announced, "had one single touch of pain or dizziness in all this time!"

"But one should, of course," Dr. Ormond added objectively, "hesitate to use the word 'cure' under such circumstances."

In the front row someone asked, "Dr. Al, will the instrument heal . . . well, other physical conditions?"

Ormond looked at the speaker with dignity. "John, the instrument does, and is supposed to do, one thing. Providing, as I've said, that the student working with it has attained a certain minimum level of Insight, it greatly accelerates his progress towards Total Insight. Very greatly!

"Now, as I have implied before: as one approaches the goal of Total Insight, the ailments and diseases which commonly afflict humanity simply disappear. Unfortunately, I am not yet free to show you proof for this, although I have the proof and believe it will not be long before it can be revealed at least to the members of this group. For this reason, I have preferred not to say too much on the point . . . Yes, Reuben? You have a question?"

"Two questions, Dr. Al," Reuben Jeffries said. "First, is it your opinion that our group has now reached the minimum level of Insight that makes it possible to work with those instruments?"

Ormond nodded emphatically. "Yes, it has. After tonight's occurrence there is no further question about that."

"Then," Jeffries said, "my second question is simply—*when do we start?*"

There was laughter, a scattering of applause. Ormond smiled, said, "An excellent question, Reuben! The answer is that a number of you will start immediately.

"A limited quantity of the instruments—fifteen, I believe—are available now on the premises, stored in my office. Within a few weeks I will have enough on hand to supply as many of you as wish to speed up their progress by this method. Since the group's contributions paid my research expenses, I cannot in justice ask more from you individually now than the actual cost in material and labor for each instrument. The figure . . . I have it somewhere . . . oh, yes!" Ormond pulled a notebook from his pocket, consulted it, looked up and said, mildly, "Twelve hundred dollars will be adequate, I think."

Cavender's lips twitched sardonically. Three or four of the group might have flinched inwardly at the price tag, but on the whole they were simply too well heeled to give such a detail another thought. Checkbooks were coming hurriedly into sight all around the lecture room. Reuben Jeffries, unfolding his, announced, "Dr. Al, I'm taking one of the fifteen."

Half the students turned indignantly to stare at him. "Now wait a minute, Reuben!" someone said. "That isn't fair! It's obvious there aren't enough to go around."

Jeffries smiled at him. "That's why I spoke up, Warren!" He appealed to Ormond. "How about it, Dr. Al?"

Ormond observed judiciously, "It seems fair enough to me. Eleanor, of course, is retaining the instrument with which she has been working. As for the rest of you—first come, first served, you know! If others would like to have Mavis put down their names . . ."

There was a brief hubbub as this suggestion was acted on. Mavis, Dexter Jones and Perrie Rochelle then went to the office to get the instruments, while Dr. Ormond consoled the students who had found themselves left out. It would be merely a matter of days before the new instruments began to come in . . . and yes, they could leave their checks in advance. When he suggested tactfully that financial arrangements could be made if necessary, the less affluent also brightened up.

Fifteen identical red alligator-hide suitcases appeared and were lined up beside Ormond's table. He announced that a preliminary demonstration with the instrument would be made as soon as those on hand had been distributed. Mavis Greenfield, standing beside him, began to read off the names she had taken down.

Reuben Jeffries was the fifth to come up to the table, hand Ormond his check and receive a suitcase from the secretary. Then Cavender got unhurriedly to his feet.

"Dr. Ormond," he said, loudly enough to center the attention of everyone in the room on him, "may I have the floor for a moment?"

Ormond appeared surprised, then startled. His glance went up to Reuben Jeffries, still standing stolidly beside him, and his face slowly whitened.

"Why . . . well, yes, Wally." His voice seemed unsteady. "What's on your mind?"

Cavender faced the right side of the room and the questioning faces turned towards him.

"My name, as you know," he told the advanced students, "is Wallace Cavender. What you haven't known so far is that I am a police detective, rank of lieutenant, currently attached to the police force of this city and in temporary charge of its bunco squad."

He shifted his gaze towards the front of the room. Ormond's eyes met his for a moment, then dropped.

"Dr. Ormond," Cavender said, "you're under arrest. The immediate charge, let's say, is practicing medicine without a license. Don't worry about whether we can make it stick or not. We'll have three or four others worked up by the time we get you downtown."

For a moment, there was a shocked, frozen stillness in the lecture room. Dr. Ormond's hand began to move out quietly towards the checks lying on the table before him. Reuben Jeffries' big hand got there first.

"I'll take care of these for now, Dr. Al," Jeffries said with a friendly smile. "The lieutenant thinks he wants them."

Not much more than thirty minutes later, Cavender unlocked the door to Dr. Ormond's private office, went inside, leaving the door open behind him, and sat down at Ormond's desk. He rubbed his aching eyes, yawned, lit a cigarette, looked about in vain for an ashtray, finally emptied a small dish of paper clips on the desk and placed the dish conveniently close to him.

There had been an indignant uproar about Dr. Al's arrest for a while, but it ended abruptly when uniformed policemen appeared in the two exit doors and the sobering thought struck the students that any publicity given the matter could make them look personally ridiculous and do damage to their business and social standing.

Cavender had calmed their fears. It was conceivable, he said, that the district attorney's office would wish to confer with some of them privately, in connection with charges to be brought against William Fitzgerald Grady—which, so far as the police had been able to establish, was Dr. Ormond's real name. However, their association with the Institute of Insight would not be made public, and any proceedings would be carried out with the discretion that could be fully expected by blameless citizens of their status in the community.

They were fortunate, Cavender went on, in another respect. Probably none of them had been aware of just how much Grady had milked from the group chiefly through quiet private contributions and donations during the two years he was running the Institute. The sum came to better than two hundred thousand dollars. Grady naturally had wasted none of this in "research" and he was not a spendthrift in other ways. Cavender was, therefore, happy to say that around two thirds of this money was known to be still intact in various bank accounts, and that it would be restored eventually to the generous but misled donors.

Dr. Al's ex-students were beginning to look both chastened and very much relieved. Cavender briefly covered a few more points to eliminate remaining doubts. He touched on Grady's early record as a confidence man and blackmailer, mentioned the two terms he had spent in prison and the fact that for the last eighteen years he had confined himself to operations like the Institute of Insight where risks were less. The profits, if anything, had been higher because Grady had learned that it paid off, in the long run, to deal exclusively with wealthy citizens and he was endowed with the kind of personality needed to overcome the caution natural to that class. As for the unusual experiences about which some of them might be now thinking, these, Cavender concluded, should be considered in the light of the fact that Grady had made his living at one time as a stage magician and hypnotist, working effectively both with and without trained accomplices.

The lecture had gone over very well, as he'd known it would. The ex-students left for their homes, a subdued and shaken group, grateful for having been rescued from an evil man's toils. Even Mrs. Folsom, who had announced at one point that she believed she had a heart attack coming on, recovered sufficiently to thank Cavender and assure him that in future she would take her problems only to a reliable physician.

Footsteps were coming down the short hall from the back of the building. Then Reuben Jeffries' voice said, "Go into the office. The lieutenant's waiting for you there."

Cavender stubbed out his cigarette as Dexter Jones, Perrie Rochelle and Mavis Greenfield filed into the office. Jeffries closed the door behind them from the hall and went off.

"Sit down," Cavender said, lighting a fresh cigarette.

They selected chairs and settled down stiffly, facing him. All three looked anxious and pale; and Perrie's face was tear-stained.

Cavender said, "I suppose you've been wondering why I had Sergeant Jeffries tell you three to stay behind."

Perrie began, her eyes and voice rather wild, "Mr. Cavender . . . Lieutenant Cavender . . ."

"Either will do," Cavender said.

"Mr. Cavender, I swear you're wrong! We didn't have anything to do with Dr. Al's . . . Mr. Grady's cheating those people! At least, I didn't. I swear it!"

"I didn't say you had anything to do with it, Perrie," Cavender remarked. "Personally I think none of you had anything to do with it. Not voluntarily, at any rate."

He could almost feel them go limp with relief. He waited. After a second or two, Perrie's eyes got the wild look back. "But . . ."

"Yes?" Cavender asked.

Perrie glanced at Dexter Jones, at Mavis.

"But then what *did* happen?" she asked bewilderedly, of the other two as much as of Cavender. "Mr. Cavender, I saw something appear on that plate! I know it did. It was a sandwich. It looked perfectly natural. I don't think it could have *possibly* been something Mr. Grady did with mirrors. And how could it have had the paper napkin Mavis had just been thinking about wrapped around it, unless . . ."

"Unless it actually was a materialization of a mental image you'd created between you?" Cavender said. "Now settle back and relax, Perrie. There's a more reasonable explanation for what happened tonight than that."

He waited a moment, went on. "Grady's one real interest is money and since none of you have any to speak of, his interest in you was that you could help him get it. Perrie and Dexter showed some genuine talent to start with, in the line of guessing what card somebody was thinking about and the like. It's not too unusual an ability, and in itself it wasn't too useful to Grady.

"But he worked on your interest in the subject. All the other students, the paying students, had to lose was a sizable amount of cash . . . with the exception of Mrs. Folsom who's been the next thing to a flip for years anyway. She was in danger. And you three stood a good chance of letting Grady wreck your lives. I said he's a competent hypnotist. He is. Also a completely ruthless one."

He looked at Mavis. "As far as I know, Mavis, you haven't ever demonstrated that you have any interesting extrasensory talents like Dexter's and Perrie's. Rather the contrary. Right?"

She nodded, her eyes huge.

"I've always tested negative. Way down negative. That's why I was really rather shocked when that . . . Of course, I've always been fascinated by such things. And *he* insisted it would show up in me sometime."

"And," Cavender said, "several times a week you had special little training sessions with him, just as his two star pupils here did, to help it show up. You were another perfect stooge, from Grady's point of view. Well, what it amounts to is that Grady was preparing to make his big final killing off this group before he disappeared from the city. He would have collected close to thirty thousand dollars tonight, and probably twice as much again within the next month or so before any of the students began to suspect seriously that Dr. Al's instruments could be the meaningless contraptions they are.

"You three have been hypnotically conditioned to a fare-you-well, in those little private sessions you've had with him. During the past week you were set up for the role you were to play tonight. When you got your cue—at a guess it was Mrs. Folsom's claim that *she'd* seen the ham sandwich materialize you started seeing, saying, acting, and thinking exactly as you'd been told to see, say, act, and think. There's no more mystery about it than that. And in my opinion you're three extremely fortunate young people in that we were ready to move in on Grady when we were."

There was silence for a moment. Then Perrie Rochelle said hesitantly, "Then Mrs. Folsom . . ."

"Mrs. Folsom," Cavender said, "has also enjoyed the benefits of many private sessions with Grady. She, of course, was additionally paying very handsomely for them. Tonight, she reported seeing what she'd been told to report seeing, to set off the hypnotic chain reaction."

"But," Perrie said, "she said her heart attacks stopped after she started using the instrument. I really don't see how that could have been just her imagination?"

"Very easily," Cavender said. "I've talked with her physician. Mrs. Folsom belongs to a not uncommon type of people whose tickers are as sound as yours or mine, but who are convinced they have a serious heart ailment and can dish up symptoms impressive enough to fool anyone but an informed professional. They can stop dishing them up just as readily if they think they've been cured." He smiled faintly. "You look as if you might be finally convinced, Perrie."

She nodded. "I . . . yes, I guess so. I guess I am."

"All right," Cavender said. He stood up. "You three can run along then. You won't be officially involved in this matter, and no one's going to bother you. If you want to go on playing around with E.S.P. and so forth, that's your business. But I trust that in future you'll have the good sense to keep away from characters like Grady. Periods of confusion, chronic nightmares— even chronic headaches—are a good sign you're asking for bad trouble in that area."

They thanked him, started out of the office in obvious relief. At the door, Perrie Rochelle hesitated, looked back.

"Mr. Cavender . . ."

"Yes?"

"You don't think I . . . I need . . ."

"Psychiatric help? No. But I understand," Cavender said, "that you have a sister in Maine who's been wanting you to spend the summer with her. I think that's a fine idea! A month or two of sun and salt water is exactly what you can use to drive the last of this nonsense out of your mind again. So good night to the three of you, and good luck!"

Cavender snapped the top of the squat little thermos flask back in place and restored it to the glove compartment of Jeffries' car. He brushed a few crumbs from the knees of his trousers and settled back in the seat, discovering he no longer felt nearly as tired and washed out as he had been an hour ago in the lecture room. A few cups of coffee and a little nourishment could do wonders for a man, even at the tail end of a week of hard work.

The last light in the Institute building across the street went out and Cavender heard the click of the front door. The bulky figure of Detective Sergeant Reuben Jeffries stood silhouetted for a moment in the street lights on the entrance steps. Then Jeffries came down the steps and crossed the street to the car.

"All done?" Cavender asked.

"All done," Jeffries said through the window. He opened the door, eased himself in behind the wheel and closed the door.

"They took Grady away by the back entrance," he told Cavender. "The records in his files . . . he wasn't keeping much, of course . . . and the stuff in the safe and those instruments went along with him. He was very co-operative. He's had a real scare."

Cavender grunted. "He'll get over it."

Jeffries hesitated, said, "I'm something of a Johnny-come-lately in this line of work, you know. I'd be interested in hearing how it's handled from here on."

"In this case it will be pretty well standard procedure," Cavender said. "Tomorrow around noon I'll have Grady brought in to see me. I'll be in a curt and bitter mood—the frustrated honest cop. I'll tell him he's in luck. The D.A.'s office has informed me that because of the important names involved in this fraud case, and because all but around forty thousand dollars of the money he collected in this town have been recovered, they've decided not to prosecute. He'll have till midnight to clear out. If he ever shows up again, he gets the book."

"Why leave him the forty thousand?" Jeffries asked. "I understood they know darn well where it's stashed."

Cavender shrugged. "The man's put in two years of work, Reuben. If we clean him, he might get discouraged enough to get out of the racket and try something else. As it is, he'll have something like the Institute of Insight going again in another city three months from now. In an area that hasn't been cropped over recently. He's good in that line . . . one of the best, in fact."

Jeffries thoughtfully started the car, pulled out from the curb. Halfway down the block, he remarked, "You gave me the go-ahead sign with the cigarette right after the Greenfield girl claimed she'd put the paper napkin into that image. Does that mean you finally came to a decision about her?"

"Uh-huh."

Jeffries glanced over at him, asked, "Is there any secret about how you're able to spot them?"

"No . . . except that I don't know. If I could describe to anyone how to go about it, we might have our work cut in half. But I can't, and neither can any other spotter. It's simply a long, tedious process of staying in contact with people you have some reason to suspect of being the genuine article. If they are, you know it eventually. But if it weren't that men with Grady's type of personality attract them somehow from ten miles around, we'd have no practical means at present of screening prospects out of the general population. You can't distinguish one of them from anyone else if he's just walking past you on the street."

Jeffries brought the car to a halt at a stop light.

"That's about the way I'd heard it," he acknowledged. "What about negative spotting? Is there a chance there might be an undiscovered latent left among our recent fellow students?"

"No chance at all," Cavender said. "The process works both ways.

If they aren't, you also know it eventually—and I was sure of everyone but Greenfield over three weeks ago. She's got as tough a set of obscuring defenses as I've ever worked against. But after the jolt she got tonight, she came through clear immediately."

The light changed and the car started up. Jeffries asked, "You feel both of them can be rehabilitated?"

"Definitely," Cavender said. "Another three months of Grady's pseudo-yoga might have ruined them for good. But give them around a year to settle out and they'll be all right. Then they'll get the call. It's been worth the trouble. Jones is good medium grade—and that Greenfield! She'll be a powerhouse before she's half developed. Easily the most promising prospect I've come across in six years."

"You're just as certain about Perrie Rochelle?"

"Uh-huh. Proto-psi—fairly typical. She's developed as far as she ever will. It would be a complete waste of time to call her. You can't train something that just isn't there."

Jeffries grunted. "Never make a mistake, eh?"

Cavender yawned, smiled. "Never have yet, Reuben! Not in that area."

"How did you explain the sandwich to them—and Greenfield's napkin? They couldn't have bought your stage magic idea."

"No. Told them those were Dr. Al's posthypnotic suggestions. It's the other standard rationalization."

They drove on in silence for a while. Then Jeffries cleared his throat.

"Incidentally," he said. "I should apologize for the slip with the sandwich, even though it turned out to our advantage. I can't quite explain it. I was thinking of other matters at the moment, and I suppose I . . ."

Cavender, who had been gazing drowsily through the windshield, shook his head.

"As you say, it turned out very well, Reuben. Aside from putting the first crack in Mavis Greenfield's defenses, it shook up Dr. Al to the point where he decided to collect as much as he could tonight, cash the checks, and clear out. So he set himself up for the pinch. We probably gained as much as three or four weeks on both counts."

Jeffries nodded. "I realize that. But . . ."

"Well, you'd have no reason to blame yourself for the slip in any case," Cavender went on. "The fact is I'd been so confoundedly busy all afternoon and evening, I forgot to take time out for dinner. When that sandwich was being described in those mouth-watering terms, I realize I was really ravenous. At the same time I was fighting off sleep. Between the two, I went completely off guard for a moment, and it simply happened!"

He grinned. "As described, by the way, it *was* a terrific sandwich. That group had real imagination!" He hesitated, then put out his hand, palm up, before him. "As a matter of fact, just talking about it again seems to be putting me in a mood for seconds..."

Something shimmered for an instant in the dim air. Wrapped in its green tissue napkin, a second ham sandwich appeared.

Where the Time Went

. . . .

THIS BEGAN IN the office of John D. Carew, of the John D. Carew Literary Agency, New York City. Present in the room were John D. Carew and George Belk, one of his authors.

"George," Carew was saying, "please don't misunderstand me. When—rather long ago—I saw the first samples of your work, I was delighted. I told myself you might grow in time to be one of our most valuable properties. I still believe you retain that potential. But having represented you for over eight years, I begin to feel concerned. Your overall output remains regrettably slight."

George Belk sighed. "I know it."

"I can place almost anything you write," Carew went on, "for relatively good money. But over the years checks have been few and far between. You must be feeling the financial pinch from time to time."

"I get by," George said, looking despondent. "But barely."

Carew clucked in a sympathetic way. "If you'd like to confide in me, George—what seems to be your problem? "

George sighed again. "I wish I could define the problem! I can't. The effect is simply that I don't seem to have time to get more writing done."

Carew's eyebrows lifted for a moment "You are engaged in other work? Perhaps in intensive social activities?"

"No! Neither. I write full time. Of course I have chores to take care of around the house. I go shopping. And I try to reserve half an hour a day for physical exercise."

Carew nodded. "The last is commendable! One should keep fit. But is that all you do? Besides writing? "

"Yes," George said. "That's all."

"Then you must, in fact, be putting in a great deal of worktime during an average day. . . ."

"No, I don't," George said. "Let me try to explain it to you—though, as I said, I can't explain it myself. You may not believe this, but I'm a methodical and orderly man. I keep files and records. So I can't help noticing that I manage to waste an incredible amount of time."

"In what way?"

George scowled. "That's what I'd like to know! Take my half-hour of exercise in the morning. Nine to nine-thirty is the period I set aside for it. I shave at eight, right after breakfast. Then I drag some mats out into the living room and pull back the furniture. By then it's nine o'clock."

Carew looked very thoughtful., "Shaving and dragging out some mats and pulling back a few pieces of furniture consumes a full hour?"

"It doesn't seem reasonable, does it?" George said. "Well, that's part of what I mean. A small part . . . So then it's nine o'clock and I exercise. I time that—thirty minutes exactly."

"But before I've got dressed again and straightened out the living room and am ready to go shopping, it's usually close to eleven."

Carew grunted and stroked his chin. "When do you actually get to work?"

George looked embarrassed. "Well, around one-fifteen."

"You shop for two hours?"

"Yes, somehow it comes to that. I have to go to several stores. No one store ever seems to carry everything you want."

"I see. Then you work through the afternoon?"

"In principle. I may put in a short break now and then."

"Doing what?" Carew asked.

"Oh, I might have a snack and then of course I have to wash the dishes again. Oh I'll tidy up a room that's beginning to look too messy. That kind of thing."

"Umm. And in the evening?"

"Ordinarily I'm working. I take in an occasional TV show."

Carew leaned back in his chair. "And what is your average daily output under those circumstances?"

George hung his head. "Roughly—five hundred words."

Carew just blinked at him in silence.

❋　　❋　　❋

"That's the incredible part of it!" George said explosively. "Because I've timed myself on occasion. When I have, I've found I can turn out a page of perfectly usable material in around twenty minutes." He leaned forward, slammed his fist on the desk. "I tell you, sometimes I think this is going to drive me crazy! *Where does the rest of my time go?*"

"I'm not sure," said Carew, pulling open a desk drawer. "But it's possible that there is a solution to your problem. Yes, quite possible!"

"What kind of solution?" George asked hopefully.

Carew fished about in the drawer, took out a business card and slid it across the desk to George. "When you get home," he said, "call this number and get yourself an appointment. I'll have talked with their office meanwhile."

George read the card. The name on it was William W. Gordon, M.D.

"Now wait a minute!" he said suspiciously. "This Dr. Gordon doesn't happen to be a psychiatrist, does he?"

"No," said Carew. "Dr. Gordon is not a psychiatrist. He has medical and psychological degrees, but he isn't in general practice. He does research work."

"And just how is he supposed to research me?" George asked in a somewhat belligerent tone.

"He isn't going to research you George. He's going to research your problem."

"Well, I don't know," George muttered. He stared uneasily at the card, turning it around in his fingers.

"George," said Carew, "you exhibit the not uncommon fear of your ilk that if a headshrinker ever got his hooks on you, you'd be in for a fast trip to the funny farm. Let me assure you that you run no risk of that in doing as I suggest. Let me assure you further that I know of several cases in which a problem quite similar to yours was solved by Dr. Gordon to the applicants' great satisfaction."

"Could you give me a few names?" George said warily.

"I could, but I don't intend to," Carew told him.

Dr. Gordon was a big warm fuzzy man who seemed reluctant to voice even the most general sort of opinion about George's problem. "First, Mr. Belk," he said, "we must establish precisely what the nature of the trouble is. Only then can we begin to think in terms of corrective procedures."

George had to be satisfied with that. He sat rigid in a chair while Dr. Gordon fitted a mesh of metal bands about his skull and tightened them down gently with large stubby fingers.

"What's that for?" George asked

"It should give me some information about this and that going on inside your head."

George cleared his throat. "Carew told me you weren't a psychiatrist."

"I'm not," Dr. Gordon said, "though I started out in that direction. Think of me as an electronics specialist and don't worry about your mittful of neuroses and compulsions. I couldn't care less about them. Now, let's see how well you can let yourself relax for the next five minutes."

The five minutes passed eventually, and George was told he could stop relaxing. He twisted around in the chair and saw Dr. Gordon place some instruments into a drawer in his desk. He was frowning pensively.

"What did you find out, Doctor?" George asked.

Dr. Gordon looked up and stopped frowning. "Oh, about what I expected." He came over and began to remove the metal mesh from around George's head.

"Is it . . . serious?" asked George.

"Well, definitely it's something we must follow up. Now, Mr. Belk, I need your cooperation for the next step. It will hardly inconvenience you at all."

Dr. Gordon then turned to a wall closet and took from it a device which looked like one of the more expensive kinds of camera except that it had no lens and nothing visibly on it which would be twisted or pressed. "We'll put this in a case," Dr. Gordon said, placing the instrument in a case as he spoke, "and you'll set it up in your house for the next two days. You say you're not married. Do you have many visitors?"

"Very few nowadays," said George.

"You live alone?"

"Yes. Except for some cats."

"Cats don't count," said Dr. Gordon. "Very well. Set up this instrument—you can leave it in the case—somewhere near the center of your house. This is Tuesday. Between now and ten A.M. Friday, I'd like you to note down the occasions when somebody besides yourself is in the house or even comes to the door. The mailman, as an example. If you happen to forget, it won't matter too much. But try to remember. Note the time anybody arrives and the length of time he stays around. I'll see you again Friday at ten. Bring the instrument back with you."

Hesitantly George took the instrument case. "This is all rather mystifying!" he remarked uncomfortably.

"I'm sure it must seem that way to you," said Dr. Gordon. "But remember, Mr. Belk, that we live in a rapidly evolving scientific age!" He gave George a brief smile and a reassuring clap on the shoulder. "Put your trust in advanced electronics!"

During the next two days George forgot half the time that he had Dr. Gordon's device in the house. When he first got home with it, he'd taken it out of the case and looked it over carefully. That told him nothing. There were no settings, no concealed switches in it. He put it back in the case on a small table which stood approximately in the center of the house. He called John Carew, told him what Dr. Gordon had said and described the mysterious instrument. "Is that his usual procedure?"

Carew said he had no idea what Dr. Gordon's usual procedure was. However they could assume he knew what he was doing, and George should go along with instructions.

That part was easy. Only the mailman came to the house on Wednesday and Thursday, and George dutifully noted the time of day. Otherwise he went about his normal activities, still wondering now and then at the way time seemed to be slipping through his grasp. In spite of Carew's assurances, he found himself unable to develop much faith in the effectiveness of Dr. Gordon's approach.

At quarter to eleven on Friday morning his telephone rang. He picked up the receiver,

"Hello, Mr. Belk," Dr. Gordon's voice said. "It appears we've forgotten our appointment, heh?"

Abashed, George admitted that he had indeed forgotten it. "And I don't know how it happened," he said. "I definitely planned to be at your office by ten o'clock. It seems to me I was looking at my watch just a moment ago, and it was then barely past nine."

"I'm not surprised," Dr. Gordon said cryptically. "I'll see you as soon as you can make it here. Bring along the drainometer."

"The what?" asked George.

"The gadget," said Dr. Gordon, and hung up.

On reflection George decided that knowing the device was called a drainometer didn't really tell him much. He took it from its place on the table and set off, feeling unhappy and badly confused. At the office Dr. Gordon ushered him into a side room, provided him with some magazines to leaf around in, and disappeared with the drainometer. Some fifteen minutes later he came back into the room, closed the door, and stood staring at George.

"This is as bad a case as I've come across," he observed, shaking his head. "Worse even than I'd suspected."

"As bad a case of what?" George asked, alarmed.

"Of time drainage!" Dr. Gordon pulled a chair out from behind a table and sat down. "I'll explain the situation to you as well as I can, Mr. Belk, and I believe you'll see why it was necessary for me to remain silent until now."

He steepled his fingers. "I won't attempt to go into the math of this," he said. "For one reason, because I suspect that scientific math is not your forte."

"No, it isn't," George agreed.

"Then let me tell you in a more general way about time. There are two distinct kinds of time. There is TIME—time in capitals, so to speak—which is the time through which the world about all of us progresses. And then there is subjective, or individual, lower case time."

George nodded interestedly. "Einstein's theories have to do with that, don't they?"

"Not really. The science of time units is a different development. Picture to yourself that everybody generates and has available for his use a personal supply of time units or particles. Say, roughly, that for every fifty years of real time, or TIME, everybody generates and uses up fifty million time particles.

"When this process is operating normally, the individual is synchronal in TIME. He feeds out his time particles in a steady uniform stream which keeps him comfortably abreast of the passage of TIME in the world. However, problems may arise. You, for example, Mr. Belk, do not have as solid a contact with the flow of your time particles as you might have—we can assume that something in you withdraws to some extent from the outside world and TIME. As a result you're a natural time particle waster. At present there isn't much we can do about that condition. On the other hand, it's hardly a serious matter. I'd estimate that you normally lose about one time particle in twenty—not a significant percentage."

"I'm not sure I'm following all this," George admitted.

"It's not necessary for you to grasp it all," Dr. Gordon assured him. "I simply want you to have the general picture. Now look

at another aspect of the matter. People, as you know, have widely
varying feelings about the value of time. Some never get enough
of it. They have many things to do and many more things they'd
like to do and simply can't get around to doing. If they could
squeeze forty-eight full hours into a single workday, they'd be
delighted.

"And then there are people who have, as we say, time on their
hands. Often very heavily on their hands. It is a commodity for
which they can find no real use. If it were possible, they would
be glad to be relieved of a large part of it.

"And nowadays it is possible. That's the point here. There are
methods whereby a portion of the flow of one individual's time
particles can be diverted from him and integrated into the flow
of another person's time particles. The second person now has
subjectively more time available to him than he had before, and
the first person has subjectively less. It is an insidious process: the
loser in this transaction has no way of grasping what has happened. If he is a man who places no value on time and has time
to spare in that sense, he may not even notice that anything has
happened. He may feel quite comfortable—and less bored—within
the time particle flow left at his disposal.

"But when the victim is a busy man, a man who needs his time,
it is a different matter. Again, of course, he doesn't understand the
situation. He simply is aware that it seems to take him forever to
get anything done. He feels that the minutes and hours are slipping through his fingers, as in fact they are."

George stared at the doctor in shocked dismay. "That's what's
been happening to me?" he asked.

That's what's been happening to you, Mr. Belk."

"But," George cried, outraged, "this has been going on for years!

"Evidently."

"What can I do to stop it? You said—"

"I indicated that your problem could be solved, Mr. Belk," said,
Dr. Gordon. "And indeed it will be. You see, this situation is so
fraught with unethical possibilities that an organization exists which
is dedicated to policing the transfer of subjective time among
individuals. Such transactions may be quite legitimate. As I
explained, a good many people have more time than they know
what to do with, they have surplus time which is a nuisance to
them. People who need additional time are allowed to draw it from
such individuals, providing suitable compensation is made. Since

our organization operates with as much secrecy as possible, the donor frequently doesn't know there has been a transaction. But always he must be compensated. An unexpected stroke of good fortune comes his way; he may find a better job, more suitable to his unenergetic nature, suddenly open to him, and so forth. Both parties have benefitted."

"But why the secrecy?" George asked. "If everybody knew—"

"If everybody were aware of this, Mr. Belk, the situation might get completely out of hand. As I said, the process of extracting time particles from somebody else is very simple, once it is understood. We want no more people to know about it than we can help."

"I see." George hesitated. "Then you—this organization—will keep whoever has been stealing my time from doing it again?"

Dr. Gordon smiled. "We can do better than that. Much better. The drainometer recordings indicate that at various periods during the past two days as much as nine out of ten of your time particles have been surreptitiously diverted. This is a blatant crime. The fact that you are, as I previously indicated, inherently somewhat careless with your time has made you an easy victim. But now compensation must be made by those who took advantage of this. When you leave here, you will carry another instrument with you. The next attempt to tap the flow of your time particles will give us a direct line to the perpetrator. In all likelihood. we shall find then that you have been preyed upon not by one individual but by a criminal gang."

"A gang?" George repeated.

"Exactly. As I pointed out, Mr. Belk, time is a commodity. It has value. For some it has great value. Among such people there always will be a number who do not care whether the commodity they want can be obtained legally or ethically, provided only they get it. And there always will be criminal elements willing to supply the commodity for a price. We're constantly on the lookout for indications of such a situation."

"And you can make them compensate for what they've done?"

"Yes, we can," said Dr. Gordon. "The organization has very effective means of dealing with such criminals and those who benefit unethically by their crimes. We shall establish exactly how much time was diverted from you and by whom during the past years, and to the last particle this time will be drained from the guilty parties involved and restored. Not in a lump sum, so to

speak. But you will have established a time credit with the organization, on which you can draw as your requirements or wishes
dictate. In other words, if you should like to operate for a while
on the basis of a fully usable forty-eight-hour working day, or even
a hundred-hour day, you will be able to do it."

George was silent a moment. "I hardly know how to thank the
organization—and you, sir!" he said then. "There must be some
way I can repay you."

Dr. Gordon cleared his throat. "Well, as a matter of fact, it is
customary to charge a fee. The fee goes not to me but to the
organization. As I say, time is a commodity. We all can use it.
Would a fee of say ten per cent of the time you will regain seem
fair to you?"

"Eminently fair!" George declared.

He called John Carew next day to tell him of the outcome of
the matter.

"Exactly as I thought!" Carew said with evident satisfaction.

"So you knew all about this time drain stuff, eh?" said, George.

"I should," Carew's voice told him. "Quite a long while ago I
found myself in a pickle not unlike yours. Somebody steered me
to the organization, and they adjusted the matter very satisfactorily.
In fact, I'll still put in an occasional fifty hours day, though I found,
as I believe you will, that a fully available ordinary workday is quite
enough in the long run."

"I expect you're right," George agreed. "For a few months though
I intend to really live it up on my time account!"

"Fine," said John Carew. "In that case, I'll look forward to getting
a new novel from you within . . . oh, let's say the next two weeks."

And he got it.

An Incident on Route 12

PHIL GARFIELD WAS thirty miles south of the little town of Redmon on Route Twelve when he was startled by a series of sharp, clanking noises. They came from under the Packard's hood.

The car immediately began to lose speed. Garfield jammed down the accelerator, had a sense of sick helplessness at the complete lack of response from the motor. The Packard rolled on, getting rid of its momentum, and came to a stop.

Phil Garfield swore shakily. He checked his watch, switched off the headlights and climbed out into the dark road. A delay of even half an hour here might be disastrous. It was past midnight, and he had another hundred and ten miles to cover to reach the small private airfield where Madge waited for him and the thirty thousand dollars in the suitcase on the Packard's front seat.

If he didn't make it before daylight . . .

He thought of the bank guard. The man had made a clumsy play at being a hero, and that had set off the fool woman who'd run screaming into their line of fire. One dead. Perhaps two. Garfield hadn't stopped to look at an evening paper.

But he knew they were hunting for him.

He glanced up and down the road. No other headlights in sight at the moment, no light from a building showing on the forested hills. He reached back into the car and brought out the suitcase, his gun, a big flashlight and the box of shells which had been standing beside the suitcase. He broke the box open, shoved a handful of shells and the .38 into his coat pocket, then took suitcase and flashlight over to the shoulder of the road and set them down.

There was no point in groping about under the Packard's hood.

When it came to mechanics, Phil Garfield was a moron and well aware of it. The car was useless to him now...except as bait.

But as bait it might be very useful.

Should he leave it standing where it was? No, Garfield decided. To anybody driving past it would merely suggest a necking party, or a drunk sleeping off his load before continuing home. He might have to wait an hour or more before someone decided to stop. He didn't have the time. He reached in through the window, hauled the top of the steering wheel towards him and put his weight against the rear window frame.

The Packard began to move slowly backwards at a slant across the road. In a minute or two he had it in position. Not blocking the road entirely, which would arouse immediate suspicion, but angled across it, lights out, empty, both front doors open and inviting a passerby's investigation.

Garfield carried the suitcase and flashlight across the right-hand shoulder of the road and moved up among the trees and undergrowth of the slope above the shoulder. Placing the suitcase between the bushes, he brought out the .38, clicked the safety off and stood waiting.

Some ten minutes later, a set of headlights appeared speeding up Route Twelve from the direction of Redmon. Phil Garfield went down on one knee before he came within range of the lights. Now he was completely concealed by the vegetation.

The car slowed as it approached, braking nearly to a stop sixty feet from the stalled Packard. There were several people inside it; Garfield heard voices, then a woman's loud laugh. The driver tapped his horn inquiringly twice, moved the car slowly forward. As the headlights went past him, Garfield got to his feet among the bushes, took a step down towards the road, raising the gun.

Then he caught the distant gleam of a second set of headlights approaching from Redmon. He swore under his breath and dropped back out of sight. The car below him reached the Packard, edged cautiously around it, rolled on with a sudden roar of acceleration.

The second car stopped when still a hundred yards away, the Packard caught in the motionless glare of its lights. Garfield heard the steady purring of a powerful motor.

For almost a minute, nothing else happened. Then the car came gliding smoothly on, stopped again no more than thirty feet to Garfield's left. He could see it now through the screening bushes—

a big job, a long, low four-door sedan. The motor continued to purr. After a moment, a door on the far side of the car opened and slammed shut.

A man walked quickly out into the beam of the headlights and started towards the Packard.

Phil Garfield rose from his crouching position, the .38 in his right hand, flashlight in his left. If the driver was alone, the thing was now cinched! But if there was somebody else in the car, somebody capable of fast, decisive action, a slip in the next ten seconds might cost him the sedan, and quite probably his freedom and life. Garfield lined up the .38's sights steadily on the center of the approaching man's head. He let his breath out slowly as the fellow came level with him in the road and squeezed off one shot.

Instantly he went bounding down the slope to the road. The bullet had flung the man sideways to the pavement. Garfield darted past him to the left, crossed the beam of the headlights, and was in darkness again on the far side of the road, snapping on his flashlight as he sprinted up to the car.

The motor hummed quietly on. The flashlight showed the seats empty. Garfield dropped the light, jerked both doors open in turn, gun pointing into the car's interior. Then he stood still for a moment, weak and almost dizzy with relief.

There was no one inside. The sedan was his.

The man he had shot through the head lay face down on the road, his hat flung a dozen feet away from him. Route Twelve still stretched out in dark silence to east and west. There should be time enough to clean up the job before anyone else carne along. Garfield brought the suitcase down and put it on the front seat of the sedan, then started back to get his victim off the road and out of sight. He scaled the man's hat into the bushes, bent down, grasped the ankles and started to haul him towards the left side of the road where the ground dropped off sharply beyond the shoulder.

The body made a high, squealing sound and began to writhe violently.

Shocked, Garfield dropped the legs and hurriedly took the gun from his pocket, moving back a step. The squealing noise rose in intensity as the wounded man quickly flopped over twice like a struggling fish, arms and legs sawing about with startling energy. Garfield clicked off the safety, pumped three shots into his victim's back.

The grisly squeals ended abruptly. The body continued to jerk for another second or two, then lay still.

Garfield shoved the gun back into his pocket. The unexpected interruption had unnerved him; his hands shook as he reached down again for the stranger's ankles. Then he jerked his hands back, and straightened up, staring.

From the side of the man's chest, a few inches below the right arm, something like a thick black stick, three feet long, protruded now through the material of the coat.

It shone, gleaming wetly, in the light from the car. Even in that first uncomprehending instant, something in its appearance brought a surge of sick disgust to Garfield's throat. Then the stick bent slowly halfway down its length, forming a sharp angle, and its tip opened into what could have been three blunt, black claws which scrabbled clumsily against the pavement. Very faintly, the squealing began again, and the body's back arched up as if another sticklike arm were pushing desperately against the ground beneath it.

Garfield acted in a blur of horror. He emptied the .38 into the thing at his feet almost without realizing he was doing it. Then, dropping the gun, he seized one of the ankles, ran backwards to the shoulder of the road, dragging the body behind him.

In the darkness at the edge of the shoulder, he let go of it, stepped around to the other side and with two frantically savage kicks sent the body plunging over the shoulder and down the steep slope beyond. He heard it crash through the bushes for some seconds, then stop. He turned, and ran back to the sedan, scooping up his gun as he went past. He scrambled into the driver's seat and slammed the door shut behind him.

His hands shook violently on the steering wheel as he pressed down the accelerator. The motor roared into life and the big car surged forward. He edged it past the Packard, cursing aloud in horrified shock, jammed down the accelerator and went flashing up Route Twelve, darkness racing beside and behind him.

What had it been? Something that wore what seemed to be a man's body like a suit of clothes, moving the body as a man moves, driving a man's car . . . roach-armed, roach-legged itself!

Garfield drew a long, shuddering breath. Then, as he slowed for a curve, there was a spark of reddish light in the rear-view mirror.

He stared at the spark for an instant, braked the car to a stop, rolled down the window and looked back.

Far behind him along Route Twelve, a fire burned. Approximately at the point where the Packard had stalled out, where something had gone rolling off the road into the bushes.

Something, Garfield added mentally, that found fiery automatic destruction when death came to it, so that its secrets would remain unrevealed.

But for him the fire meant the end of a nightmare. He rolled the window up, took out a cigarette, lit it, and pressed the accelerator . . .

In incredulous fright, he felt the nose of the car tilt upwards, headlights sweeping up from the road into the trees.

Then the headlights winked out. Beyond the windshield, dark tree branches floated down towards him, the night sky beyond. He reached frantically for the door handle.

A steel wrench clamped silently about each of his arms, drawing them in against his sides, immobilizing them there. Garfield gasped, looked up at the mirror and saw a pair of faintly gleaming red eyes watching him from the rear of the car. Two of the things . . . the second one stood behind him out of sight, holding him. They'd been in what had seemed to be the trunk compartment. And they had come out.

The eyes in the mirror vanished. A moist, black roach-arm reached over the back of the seat beside Garfield, picked up the cigarette he had dropped, extinguished it with rather horribly human motions, then took up Garfield's gun and drew back out of sight.

He expected a shot, but none came.

One doesn't fire a bullet through the suit one intends to wear . . .

It wasn't until that thought occurred to him that tough Phil Garfield began to scream. He was still screaming minutes later when, beyond the windshield, the spaceship floated into view among the stars.

Swift Completion
· · · · · · · · · · · · · · · · · · ·

BEGINNING WITH MONDAY of that week, George Redfern—a healthy, athletic, but thwarted and frustrated young man—had been trying to maneuver his wife into a situation which would leave him an unimplicated widower. There was nothing haphazard about George's efforts. His preparations had been thorough; he had worked out not one scheme but several, including alternate steps he might take if, through no fault of his own, something should threaten to go wrong.

Now, around noon on Friday, George stood at the top of the flight of stairs in the Redfern's suburban residence, moodily watching Martha Redfern adjust a silk scarf about her shapely neck before a mirror in the entry hall below. None of his plans, somehow, appeared to be getting anywhere. Was his wife simply enjoying a remarkable run of good luck, or had she actually gained an inkling of what was in his mind?

"George?" Martha said abruptly without turning her gaze from the mirror.

George gave an involuntary start. He hadn't realized she knew he was watching. "Yes?" he replied.

Martha took some envelopes from the mirror stand and held them up.

"I'm afraid I forgot to stamp these," she told him. "The stamps are in the top left-hand corner of my desk in the study, George. I'll need six. Be waiting for you down by the car, dear."

She slipped the letters into her purse and went through the French doors to the terrace. Silently obedient, George started along the upstairs hall to the study. Martha was a member of the State

404

Legislature, now running for her second term; the study resembled an elegantly equipped business office, and Martha used it as her office when she was at home. This morning, her secretary, Joanne Brown, had not been in, and she had taken care of her mail herself. A portable typewriter and a wire basket with carbon copies of the letters she had written, stood on her desk. Catching sight of the letters, George glanced back towards the hall, then picked the letters up to look them over.

The one on top was addressed to a Mr. Donald H. Spurgeon—Martha's Uncle Don—of Spurgeon & Sanders, Attorneys at Law. It was marked PERSONAL. George read the first two sentences and felt the blood drain suddenly from his face. He gulped, and sat dizzily down at the desk, clutching the letter in his hand. Then, after inhaling deeply several times to compose himself, he smoothed the letter out, and hastily read through it, his feeling of incredulous shock increasing as he approached the end. It read:

Dear Uncle Don:
This letter is intended only for your confidential information. I am convinced that George has given up hope of getting his hands on any appreciable part of my money while I am alive, so he is now planning to do away with me. He would then be free to devote his attention to Cynthia Haley, of whom he has, I am sure, become enamored.

With elections coming up in a few weeks, you will readily see how awkward it would be for me to make an open issue of the matter. In this district, George's social background and personal good looks represent important assets. I cannot afford to give them up, particularly not during the present difficult campaign.

I foresee no great difficulty, however, in dealing with the situation on a personal level, and intend to take no other steps at this time. If, on the other hand, George should happen to succeed in his schemes, I want him to be punished. In the event of my death, this letter will open the question of his guilt. No more should be required. His motivations will be easy to establish; and, in any case, as you will agree, George has not the character to face a determined investigator for five minutes without going into a state of panic and convicting himself.

I intend to drive to the beach this evening—leaving

George at home—and shall spend the weekend at the Hamilton Hotel to rest up for the final campaign flurries. If you wish, you can reach me at the hotel by telephone in the morning.

Your affectionate niece,
MARTHA

George sat staring at the damning missive in complete consternation. It was immediately clear that Martha had sent him back after the stamps with the purpose of having him read it. Once that letter was in the mails to Uncle Donald Spurgeon—a dry-voiced, cold-eyed individual whom George found frightening even under ordinary circumstances—he wouldn't dare to lift a finger against her. And that, of course, was exactly what Martha meant when she wrote of 'handling the situation on a personal level.'

George's mind went racing through the few possibilities left open to him. If he could prevent Martha from mailing the letter . . . one of his schemes for her disposal involved that simple but effective instrument, a homemade sap. The sap was in his coat pocket; and the area about the garage was screened by hedges and trees from neighbors and passersby. So, assuming Martha was waiting by the car as she'd said. . . .

George puckered his lips thoughtfully. It *was* a possibility— nothing he could count on; but if Martha gave him the chance to rap her on the head in the next two or three minutes, he could proceed from there directly to the Alternate Plan 4 or 5. However, he was certain that she would now be very much on her guard against some desperate move on his part until she knew that the letter actually had been mailed, and that George was also aware of that. The confounded little gun she'd started carrying around during the week was almost certainly inside her purse at the moment. And even discounting the gun, a single feminine scream arising from the Redfern garden would be ruinous. . . . No, if a good opening presented itself, he would be prepared to make instant use of it; but that was all he dared to do.

Then there was something else he might be able to do. . . .

George quickly rolled an envelope into the typewriter, put Martha's return address on it, and addressed it to Donald H. Spurgeon. After a moment's reflection added PERSONAL in the lower left-hand corner, where Martha would have placed it, brought out a blank piece of letter paper, folded it, shoved it into the envelope and sealed the envelope.

That wasn't too bad, he thought. It would be preferable, of course, if no letter at all arrived in Uncle Don's office. But if, after Martha's death, George reluctantly admitted to having noticed signs of increasing mental and emotional instability in his wife during the past few months, her mailing of a letter with no message on it would provide corroborating evidence. Again, it was questionable whether Martha would give him a chance to switch the letter for the one in her purse. But again, too, if the opportunity came, he would be ready for it.

George scratched his head, hesitating. But he could think of absolutely nothing else which might be done at the moment, and if he delayed here any longer, it would only increase Martha's suspicious alertness.

He pulled open the stamp drawer, reached into it, then paused for a moment. His eyes narrowed briefly.

Right there in the drawer, he realized, was a method of keeping Martha's letter from reaching Uncle Don even after it was mailed. Here was a way of canceling her attempt to insure herself against getting murdered, without letting her know it had happened . . .

George began to feel a little better.

He was obliged to discard the first, and simplest, method of circumventing his wife's precautions when he was still thirty feet from the garage.

From beyond a thick hedge, he heard Martha speak animatedly; then there was a burst of laughter. George stopped for an instant, listening intently. He might have expected something like this. At least two other women were there with her. Her secretary, Joanne Brown . . . and . . . yes! Cynthia. The delectable Cynthia Haley. Martha must have invited both of them to accompany her on an afternoon shopping trip. And—deliberately, of course—she had refrained from telling George about the arrangement.

His suspicions were confirmed by the glance Martha gave him as he came around the hedge. It was bright with malicious amusement.

"Found it?" she asked, the twist of her mouth telling him that she wasn't referring to the stamp drawer.

"Uh-huh," George said blandly. "Six stamps . . . wasn't that what you said?" He gave the two other ladies his most boyishly winning grin, received two smiles in return. A timid one, accompanied by a faint blush, from Joanne Brown. A lazy, openly 'my-you're-handsome' sort of smile from the lovely Cynthia. Martha took the half-dozen letters from her purse and held them out to him.

She said, "If you'll put the stamps on like a good boy, we'll mail them on the way."

Their eyes met for an instant, then George shrugged with a trace of irritation and took the letters.

He heard the women settle themselves into the back of the car while he put a stamp on each of the envelopes. Try the switch with the fake letter? No; Martha probably was watching. The other method was safer anyway. She'd played right into his hand again by trying to show him that he was still under her thumb, that he'd better learn to like it. George finished stamping the letters and walked around to the driver's seat with them.

Martha said from the rear of the car, "I'll hold the letters while you're driving, dear."

He handed them back to her, the envelope addressed to Donald H. Spurgeon on top, then got in and started the motor. There was silence in the rear seat for a few seconds as he backed the car expertly into the turnaround, reversed direction and swung out into the driveway. George realized he was perspiring. Any instant now, he would hear Martha begin, her voice taut, "But, George, dear boy, you've . . ."

Instead, he heard her purse snap shut, the letters safely inside. George let his breath out carefully. Cynthia Haley inquired whether either of the others had been to Restow's, and wasn't it divinely . . .

The chatter went on. George took out a cigarette and lit it. So far, so good! It had been a smart move not to attempt to switch the letters. Martha very likely would have noticed it when she took the envelopes back.

Three blocks from the business district, she pointed out a mailbox and handed him the letters through the car window. At the mailbox, George paused and flicked a glance back at the car. Martha was watching him, an openly mocking look on her face. He deposited the letters, walked back to the car, his expression wooden.

He dropped the three women off at Martha's bank, drove around the corner and pulled in to the curb. Martha's car, the one she planned to use tonight, was in a garage a few blocks away; it had been picked up during the morning, for a check-up. Probably, George realized now, Martha had also wanted to prevent him from gimmicking the sedan in some manner before she set out. Of course this had been one of the possible methods of disposal on his agenda.

George scratched it mentally from the list. Martha was to stop by for the car in the evening, after she finished her shopping, and drive it home. There wouldn't be time to do a sufficiently careful job of gimmicking on it. He hadn't liked this idea much, anyway. An accident actually mightn't be difficult to arrange; but he had not been able to work out anything to make sure—or even to make it very probable—that the accident would be fatal to the sedan's occupants.

The sap in his pocket began to look like the best idea again. . . .

George moved the car back out into traffic, and drove home slowly through the warm summer afternoon, chain-smoking and thinking.

His introductory move, last Monday evening, had been to report a prowler on the grounds. The move had backfired because Martha, normally not easy to alarm, had begun locking her bedroom door each night. Now that George thought of it, she had also seen to it that her husband would have no opportunity to obtain a duplicate key to the bedroom during the days that followed. This afternoon was the first time he'd found himself alone in the house since Monday.

As it happened, that particular precaution of Martha's had made no real difference—except for knocking out the murder-by-prowler scheme which George originally had favored. He'd been in possession of a duplicate key to Martha's bedroom for the past two months. The fact now gave him an advantage which she didn't know about or considered. He let himself into the bedroom and looked around.

The little gun Martha had been keeping at her bedside this week, supposedly as protection against the prowler, wasn't in sight. He'd been right in assuming she had it with her. A partly packed suitcase lay beside the bed; another one, empty, stood against the wall. Martha's little bedroom bar was locked. She'd probably have a few drinks before leaving; that, at any rate, had been Martha's practice at the beginning of any long drive since George had known her. She was an excellent driver, and alcohol didn't affect her reactions perceptibly, but in drawing up his plans George had given the habit some consideration.

He peered into Martha's handsome adjoining bathroom, came back to the bedroom, and went over to the large built-in dress closet. Sliding one of the closet doors back, he glanced towards the vanity on the far side of the room, clicking his tongue reflectively against his teeth.

Martha would be back, she had stated, around six. It was a warm day. One of the first things she'd do would be to have herself some bourbon on the rocks, and then climb into the shower.

George nodded, pulled the closet door shut and left the bedroom, locking the door behind him. He went downstairs, whistling softly, and on into the rumpus room in the basement where he kept a variety of body-building equipment. Only a few minor preparations were required to see Alternate Plan 4 ready to roll.

He heard Martha's car come along the driveway at twenty minutes past six, and opened the door to the terrace for her when she walked up through the garden, carrying an assortment of paper bags. Martha went directly to her bedroom and locked the door behind her with a sharp, decisive click. She was making it plain, George realized, that there would be no more polite pretense about the situation in the Redfern house unless there was somebody around to impress.

He stood at the far end of the upstairs hall for a minute or two, listening. Then he removed his shoes and came quietly down the hall to his wife's room.

He could hear her moving around, pulling out drawers; then came the click of a suitcase lock. Paper rustled for a while; then there was a short silence followed by the clink of ice cubes into a glass and the brief burbling of a bottle. The wall closet's door opened next; hangers were slid about inside it. Presently the second suitcase snapped shut, and there was another short period of relative inactivity while Martha started on her second drink and lit a cigarette. Finally George heard her go into the bathroom.

The shower began to roar. When he heard Martha close the stall behind her, George brought out his key, opened the bedroom door and stepped inside. He looked quickly around.

The vanity lights were on, but she'd turned off the overhead light. The two packed suitcases stood at the foot of the bed. The purse Martha had been carrying lay on the bed, and a linen suit was laid out next to it. George pulled the door shut, went over to the purse. The gun was inside.

He slipped the gun into his pocket, and was behind the door of the closet when Martha came out of the bedroom. He heard her move about, fitting herself into her underclothes. Then she poured a third drink and settled down before the vanity mirror, humming to herself.

George gave her a minute or two, then came on stocking feet out of the closet. She was in her slip, putting on lipstick, her eyes intent on the mirror.

Six feet away from her, George said quietly, "You know, I'm afraid those letters I mailed for you will be returned to us."

Martha's whole body had jerked violently at the first sound of his voice. It must have had a shattering effect on her to discover her husband inexplicably inside her locked room, and George couldn't be sure whether she actually grasped what he said. Martha came half out of her chair like a cat, obviously with the idea of grabbing the gun from her purse; then, recognizing that George stood between her and the bed, she reached out quickly for a small pair of scissors on the vanity. In the mirror, George saw her mouth open wide as she sucked her breath in to scream. He stepped forward and brought the sap down with a solid swing.

It wasn't until Martha was lying face down on the carpet and he'd made certain she was dead that George realized just how intensely he had disliked his wife. Breathing a little heavily, he checked his watch . . . five minutes to seven, and getting dark enough now to put Alternate Plan 4 into immediate action.

He carried the two suitcases downstairs, placed them against the wall in the dark entry hall, then went on through the door opening into the dining room. He felt steady enough, but he could do with a drink—just one—himself. He brought out brandy, was filling a glass when the terrace doorbell rang.

George, starting almost as wildly as Martha had done, splashed brandy on the table. He set the bottle down with a shaking hand, stood dead still for an instant, staring towards the hall. Then he moved stealthily to a corner window and peered out on the terrace.

Joanne Brown stood under the doorlight; as George looked, the secretary was putting out her hand to ring the bell again. The ring came, a polite, brief little tinkle. George's glance shifted to the overnight bag and portable typewriter case standing beside her; and suddenly he understood. Martha had intended to take Joanne to the beach with her, and the girl had come over in her own car. If she'd come a few minutes later, and he'd already left with Martha's body when she arrived . . . sweat started out on George's face as he realized the narrowness of his escape.

Then he straightened his tie, put on the boyish smile, and went to open the French doors for little Joanne Brown.

By seven-thirty, George had Martha's sedan rolling up into the hills west of town towards a place he had selected a month before as a possible setting for her untimely end. The road was a winding, two lane affair which both he and Martha used occasionally as a shortcut to the coast highway; it permitted fast driving in some sections, but eventually it turned into a steep, hill-hugging grade which saw little traffic.

George was busy going over the details of his plan in his mind, so his thoughts turned only occasionally to the two bodies under the blankets in the back of the car. Joanne Brown's unexpected appearance, as much as it had startled him, actually had been a break for which he could be thankful. A man who proposes to kill his wife does not deliberately select a time which makes it necessary to kill his wife's secretary as well. Suspicion was even less likely to touch him now. In fact, with proper handling of the concluding steps of Alternate Plan 4, the whole thing looked simply perfect.

Coming around a curve, he saw the lights of traffic flowing along the highway across the valley towards which the hill road presently started turning down. Two miles beyond the top of the grade, a dirt path came winding down the hill from the left. George stopped the car and looked about to make sure no one was approaching; then he switched off his headlights and backed the sedan carefully a hundred feet up the dirt path.

He put on the hand brake, climbed out and went around to the rear of the car where he opened the trunk and brought out the bicycle which ordinarily formed part of an exercise stand in the basement rumpus room of the Redfern home. With tonight's use for it in mind, George had purchased a few accessories for the vehicle.

Strapped across the bicycle's carrier rack was a canvas roll. George quickly opened the roll, took out a pair of soiled tennis shoes and a beaked cap. He put these articles on, slipped out of his suit and shirt, and stood attired in shorts and a worn T-shirt. Wrapping his street clothes and shoes into the roll, he strapped it across the rack and wheeled the bicycle into the bushes where it was out of sight.

A minute or two later, he had moved Martha's body into the right front seat of the car. He trotted down to the point where the dirt path opened into the hill road and glanced about. Still no headlights coming from either direction. George hurried back to the sedan and got in for the final maneuver which he had been rehearsing so carefully in his mind.

On the opposite side of the road, for around a quarter-mile, the hillside dropped off vertically three or four hundred feet to the woods in the valley. George turned on the headlights, shifted the sedan into third gear and released the hand brake. As the car began to roll forward, he switched on the ignition and pressed the starter button.

The car picked up speed rapidly, coming down the path. George turned it into the road, and let it roll on a hundred feet along the grade. Then, heart hammering with excitement, he opened the door on his left, rose half out of the seat, gave the steering wheel a violent wrench to the right, and dove out through the door as the sedan veered towards the low fence guarding the drop to the valley.

He hit the pavement, arms, head and legs tucked in expertly, in a tumbler's roll. There was a crash behind him, a long screech of metal on rock. For a heart-stopping instant, George thought the car's momentum hadn't been enough to take it through the fence. But then the screeching ended, and after some moments there came other crashing noises, far below him . . . two, three, four in rapid succession, and then ominous silence. Shaken but triumphant, George climbed to his feet. The hill road lay dark and quiet, twenty feet of the guard fence torn away. Without waiting to look down at the wreck, he sprinted back to the dirt path, pulled the bicycle out of the bushes and began shoving it up the path towards the top of the hill.

He was trembling violently with excitement, but he knew he was safe. Apparently the wreck hadn't caught fire. But if it had, and attracted attention immediately, it would have taken at least an hour to get to it in the valley. As it was, it might easily be morning before someone reported a shattered guard fence on the hill road, or stopped to investigate,

In any event, in considerably less than an hour an anonymous cyclist would slip quietly through the back garden gate of the Redfern residence. The bicycle, cleaned and freed of such incongruous attachments as a lamp and a carrier rack, would be back in the exercise stand. And George Redfern, in pajamas and dressing gown, would be having a quiet drink before retiring, prepared to express adequate shock and grief if the telephone rang to inform him of a terrible accident in the hills which had snuffed out the lives of his wife and her unfortunate secretary.

Every detail, George thought jubilantly, played safely, just as he had planned it! Nothing, nothing at all, that could even begin to direct the finger of suspicion at Martha Redfern's husband. . . .

In the Redfern residence the telephone remained quiet all night.

Shortly before nine o'clock in the morning, the mailman came walking up through the garden towards George's front door. George came out on the porch and gave the man a boyishly happy grin.

"Morning," he observed. "Wonderful day!"

The mailman grunted and fished a small pack of letters out of his bag. "Looks like someone made a mistake here!" he said.

"Eh?" George took the letters, looked at the RETURNED FOR INSUFFICIENT POSTAGE stamp on the top one, shook his head irritatedly. "My wife's stupid secretary again! She . . ." He shuffled through the envelopes, said suddenly in a tight voice, "I believe— yes, I'm sure it was six letters Mrs. Redfern asked me to mail for her."

The mailman looked at him blankly.

George cleared his throat. "Only four, however, have come back."

The mailman shrugged, shifting bag on his shoulder. "So she stuck a four-cent stamp on the others like she should've."

"No! I . . ."

"Well, them letters just slipped through, then," the mailman explained patiently. "They'll collect the two cents at the other end. . . ." He checked himself, staring at George's face. "Why, you look pale!" he said, surprised. "Nothing that important about them two letters, is there?"

"No, no, not at all!" George attempted to smile, felt his mouth twitch into a lopsided grimace. "I was just wondering . . . that is, I . . ." His voice faded out.

"You ain't sick, are you, Mr. Redfern?" the mailman asked. "Maybe I should get you a glass of water?"

George didn't answer. Across the mailman's shoulder, he watched a police car turn quietly into the driveway. It came rolling on towards the house. The pale, implacable face staring at him out of the car's rear window belonged to Martha's Uncle Don Spurgeon.

A series of brilliantly clear pictures flashed for an instant through George's mind . . . Martha's letter arriving with the morning mail in the offices of Spurgeon & Sanders, with two cents to collect on it. Uncle Don calling the Hamilton Hotel immediately, hearing that Mrs. Redfern had not checked in and, alarmed, notifying the police, who had just finished establishing the identity of the two dead occupants of a savagely smashed automobile in the hills.

Cynthia Haley, who could testify it was George who had put the two-cent stamps on Martha's letters.

The mailman standing right here, wondering about Mr. Redfern's extraordinary reaction to the fact that two of the letters had not been returned. . . .

"Mr. Redfern," the mailman's voice was saying, "why, you're shaking all over now! Mr. Redfern?"

The police came to a stop.

Faddist
· · · · · · · ·

HE HAD PROMISED Elaine that he would tend her garden organically. And he kept his word.

Elaine's half-acre fruit and vegetable garden, Herman Broadbent told himself with a touch of somberness rather unusual in him, had never looked quite so lush, so deep-green-healthy, as it did today. Even the blood orange tree she used to worry about was responding nobly, with fruits and flowers, to the painstaking organic gardening methods in which his wife had schooled him, and formed a fitting centerpiece for the whole garden. It would have made Elaine very happy to see it.

With the edge of his fork, Herman broke a piece from the whipped-cream scone on the plate before him, and transferred it to his mouth. He was a plump, white-haired man, tanned and rosy-cheeked. Holding the morsel on his tongue for a moment, he half closed his eyes, appreciating the delicate combination of flaky pastry and almost ethereal cream, before closing his teeth slowly down on it. Munching, he let his gaze move over the other items on the porch table . . . cinnamon rolls and jam tarts, grouped about a majestic chocolate buttercream cake.

Elaine, Herman Broadbent admitted to himself with a rueful little smile, would not have been happy to see anything like that in her home! When he thought of his wife, as he often did when sitting on the back porch these pleasant summer evenings, Herman would concede only one fault in Elaine. She had been a health food faddist and had tried very hard, throughout their nineteen years of married life, to turn Herman into one.

Herman, a French pastry and whipped cream man by nature,

had gone along with her notions, in part because he was fond of Elaine, and in part because she was twice as strong-willed as he was. In time, he became habituated to wheat germ, yeast, desiccated liver, vegetarian beefsteaks, sunflower seeds, royal jelly, squawbush tea, and the long, long roster of nutritious growths, from apricots to zucchini squash, all exuberantly healthful, positively bursting with minerals and vitamins, which Elaine produced with relentless enthusiasm in her organic garden.

He grew used to this diet; but he never entirely forgot the devitalizing, unnatural, overprocessed goodies he had doted on before running into Elaine. Once, in their eighth year of marriage, as Herman recalled it now, he made the mistake of bringing a box of quite plain Vanilla Treats back from the market with him. Elaine had gone absolutely white. Without a word, she emptied the Treats into the garbage can, then wheeled on Herman.

"Are you trying to dig your grave with your teeth, Herman Broadbent?" she cried. "You *know* you like the wonderful, nutty flavor of homemade Brewer's Yeast cookies much better than that poisonous trash!"

Herman knew no such thing. But neither did he lapse again—except, on occasion, in his dreams. Nevertheless Elaine remained distrustful. When, in the nineteenth year of their marriage, she was invited to address the annual convention of the Association of Organic Garden Growers in Idaho, she hesitated, torn between delight at the prospect of being among kindred spirits for a whole week and a suspicion that Herman might go berserk in her absence. Finally, she exacted two solemn pledges from him. One, to take faithful care of the garden while she was gone; and the other, not to deviate by so much as a nibble from the list of menus she drew up for him.

Herman promised. Next afternoon, Elaine, having packed her bags and informed the neighbors of the honor awaiting her, drove off to the railway station.

Four days later, a telegram arrived from the Association asking why Mrs. Broadbent had not appeared to address them. Herman notified the police, and an investigation was instituted which led to nothing. Somewhere between the railroad station and Idaho, Elaine seemed to have vanished into thin air. In the eight months since that day, no trace of her ever had been reported.

He could say with full honesty, Herman reflected, gazing out on the garden, that he had kept the first of the two pledges. Two hours each afternoon, he toiled away in the garden, removing each intruding sprout of a weed as it appeared, spreading compost heap material about, spading, watering, and in the fullness of time harvesting each crop and shoving it carefully down the garbage disposal unit he'd installed in the kitchen sink. Elaine couldn't have found a word of fault with the garden's condition.

The other promise, of course, he hadn't kept. Not a single healthful, genuinely nourishing bite had he let pass his teeth since waving goodbye to Elaine from the front porch. For almost an hour after she left, he had held out while half-buried memories came crowding into his mind . . . hot apple strudels and shortcakes, pecan rolls and tarts . . . everything topped by snowdrifts of icing, by airy clouds of whipped cream. Finally, his mouth watering unbearably, Herman realized that the bakeries would soon be closed. His pledge forgotten, he rushed out. . . .

What had possessed Elaine that fateful day to make her change her mind? Was it intuition? Some telepathic warning? Or just the sudden realization that she was testing her husband beyond his power to resist? Herman would never know. Lost in an orgiastic rapture, he had been in the kitchen, slicing off his fourth piece of lemon chiffon cake, with the bread knife, when the door to the porch opened. Appalled, he stared at his wife framed against the darkening garden beyond.

Wordlessly Elaine had pulled the garbage can out from under the sink and begun sweeping the remaining components of Herman's unrestrained feast into it. Still clutching the bread knife, he watched her in stunned silence. Having cleared the table, Elaine shoved the garbage can back under the sink, stood staring stonily out the window, arms folded over her chest.

"I saw you from the garden," she said heavily. "It was . . . disgusting . . . incredible! And after all these years! I shall never be able to trust you out of my sight again, Herman Broadbent!"

Herman had looked at her back, many things rushing through his mind . . . yeast and steamed kale, sunflower seeds and wheat germ. Years and years of it still to come; for on such a diet he might well live to be over a hundred. And never, never in all that time, even one more spoonful of whipped cream!

Against that, there was the fact that he was really quite fond of Elaine.

One cannot have everything, Herman understood then. The time comes when one must decide.

Rather regretfully, but purposefully, he made his decision.

❀   ❀   ❀

So Elaine was gone, but her garden remained. He would tend it faithfully as long as he stayed here. And he would stay here all the rest of his days.

It would never do if, during his lifetime, some unsentimental new tenant decided to uproot Elaine's magnificently blooming, organically nourished blood orange tree.

The Eternal Frontiers

JAMES SCHMITZ WROTE only four novels in his career. Two of them, *Legacy* and *The Demon Breed*, were issued earlier in this series as part of the complete Hub stories. (*Legacy* as part of volume 3, *Trigger & Friends; The Demon Breed* as the concluding story in volume 4, *The Hub: Dangerous Territory.*) The longest and best-known of his novels, *The Witches of Karres*, will be published as the seventh and final volume in the Baen reissue.

Here is the fourth.

1
..

THE TWO SPACESKIFFS appeared out of thick cloud cover behind them, not much more than five miles away. Ilken spotted them in the car screens an instant before Crowell did, said quickly, "Looks like we're being jumped!"

For a moment, watching the skiffs hurtling toward them, Crowell didn't believe it was an attack, though Ragnor training took over as automatically with him as it did with Ilken. She was slipping into the shielded seat of the gun in the center of the aircar as he turned the car's nose down, sent it racing toward the patchy dark green of the Kulkoor forest below. His finger pressed a stud and his seat's shield closed about him. "In place!" her voice said. Another stud jammed down. The canopy unfolded abruptly above, snapped down into the walls.

Ready for action.

The skiffs had halved the distance between them by then, and Crowell saw they weren't aircars as he'd assumed at first glance. They were cutting speed sharply—space vehicles weren't normally designed for treetop level maneuverings, and forest growth swayed barely twenty feet below as he brought the car out of its dive. But he couldn't outrun them. It was a question of what kind of stuff they carried. There was no longer any question about their intentions.

The car's guns *brrumpped* out the short heavy stuttering of a triple defensive charge. Yellow shimmering abruptly veiled the rear screen. Lights blazed through the shimmer and ragged roars of sound shook the car. Spray torps. Neatly blocked.

Then a final flare of light to the left, too far off target to be in line with the filtering fields—and, barely audible, the momentary hard hiss of spray against plastic and metal. Crowell looked back quickly at Ilken. She grinned reassuringly through the gun shield. "Lousy shot!" her voice commented.

That, however, was precisely what had made it dangerous. Crowell was checking the controls, slowing the car, turning it into a wide circle. No immediate evidence of significant damage. They'd been at the limit of the torp's effective range. He said, "They may get the idea and start bracketing us. Where are they now?"

"Looping overhead. Be back in thirty seconds."

"Can you take them?"

"If they come in a bit closer this pass. You playing cripple?"

"Yes. Let's finish it before they change tactics."

Crowell heeled the car half over. "I'm watching the trees, not them. Give me directions."

"More to the left," Ilken's voice told him. "They're coming. Man, they *are* fast! Still more to the left—steady! Just drift . . . That's it!"

The gun erupted on the last word.

"Got them!" She half sang it.

Crowell heard explosion, righted the car and whipped it up above the wall of waving greenery toward which it had been sliding. He looked around. One skiff was a ball of boiling smoke. The other—Ilken swore furiously. "Only singed him!" The gun swiveled after the plunging vehicle.

"Hold it!"

"Why?"

"It's out of action. The pilot may still—there he goes!"

A bulky object, man-shaped, dwarfed by distance, had been ejected by the crippled skiff, began its own drift to earth as the skiff smashed slanting into the forest. The figure turned over, dropped more quickly toward the trees.

"He's alive!" Ilken's voice said thinly.

"I want him alive, you bloodthirsty Mailliard!" The aircar was hurtling toward the descending figure. "We have to find out who they are."

"You'll find out—if you catch him! He's going to make it down." Her voice was chilled with self-disgust.

The figure did make it down into the trees before they reached it. But, Crowell thought, that was strictly a temporary escape. The trees formed a detached small wood, a ragged oval of dense growth surrounded by open rocky ground. The skiff pilot was somewhere within the growth. Crowell brought the car to a halt above the center of the wood, inquired, "Didn't bring along a communicator, did you?"

"No." There was abrupt alertness in Ilken's voice. "Something wrong with the car comm?"

"Dead. Got hit evidently. I've been trying to raise the Base."

She said nothing. It could cause new problems. There was a spaceship around, which had sent the skiffs down to do a job. The ship might be carrying other skiffs, and if the people aboard realized the first attempt had failed, the other skiffs might soon appear. But the probability was that the ship would leave quickly and quietly. For all its crew knew, Crowell already was in communication with the Base, had reported the attack, commandeered reinforcements, alerted the Star Union sentinel ship. If the raider was above atmosphere, the sentinel ship should have it in its instruments—

"Let's get our man!" he said. He unsnapped the energy carbine beside the driver's seat, stood up. "Set me down on the other side of the trees, then get back up here . . ." He broke off. "You're hurt! Why didn't you—"

"Been hurt worse." Ilken had slipped out from behind the gun shield. Red wetness. She'd slit the left leg of her bush outfit from hip to knee, slapped two broad strips of sealing plastic to the side of her thigh.

"How bad is it?" He spoke almost brusquely, knowing she'd gone Mailliard on him. Any indication of anxiety here would be bad form. As it was, the short black brows above her pale eyes lifted slightly at the question. But she said, "Just my legs." She touched the plastic. "That's the two worst cuts. There's nothing that can't wait."

A ring of whiteness showed about her mouth; aside from that, her expression revealed only a trace of impatience. Crowell had never fully understood the Mailliard ability to push pain and shock to the edges of awareness as long as circumstances required it. But he did feel somewhat reassured. The skiff pilot almost certainly was a Star Union swimmer—picking him up, getting indisputable evidence that this had been a swimmer plot could be vitally important. It shouldn't take many minutes to do it. He asked, "Can you operate?"

"Yes." She proved it by walking past him, settling herself in the driver's seat. Her motions gave no evidence of discomfort. "That man's in a support suit, isn't he?" she said.

"That's what it looked like."

"He's probably armed."

"Handgun at most. They wouldn't have expected to have to get out of their skiffs."

"You want to drive him out of the trees?"

"Or get him to surrender," Crowell said. "If he bolts, try to pin him down in the open with the car. Don't kill him unless it looks like he's going to make it into one of the big forest patches."

Ilken nodded. "All right. You think he's a swimmer?"

"I'm almost sure he is."

"Supposing he's a Galestral? We're in their area. Might be something here they don't want us to stumble across."

"There just might be," Crowell agreed. "But then they wouldn't try to hit us while we are in their area. It would turn suspicion directly on them—which is what the swimmers would like."

"Yes, you're right."

Ilken set the car in motion. They circled the growth once, not far above the treetops. If the pilot sighted them, it should discourage him from attempting to cross open ground. Then the car dipped quickly to the edge of the wood. Crowell swung down, carbine in hand, and Ilken took the car up again to assume a watch position.

Crowell slipped in among the trees. He was reasonably certain that what they'd seen ejected from the skiff was an undamaged standard support suit. If so, the man inside was subject to no gravity pull. The suit was a one-man vehicle, fairly maneuverable. It could move at a respectable speed in the open, but in heavy growth like this its propulsion devices were almost useless. The pilot might be physically unharmed, but if he was a swimmer, his emotional condition should be less satisfactory. The odds were it was the first time he'd found himself on a planet without a gravity-shielded dome about him, at the bottom of a moving ocean of atmosphere, hiding in a tangle of restlessly stirring alien life. The suit sensors provided him with sight and sound, but what they had to report was unfamiliar. And he must expect that this shifting, uneasy environment concealed a hunter or hunters. He shouldn't feel much confidence in his position. It might very well be possible to get him to surrender.

Some half a dozen leggy quadrupeds, slate-gray in color, stepped out of dense undergrowth into Crowell's path and stood for a startled moment, staring at him. They might already have been alarmed by the noise and light flashes of the nearby air battle—

and they could serve a purpose here! Crowell sprang suddenly forward, throwing up his arms. The herd wheeled about with squeals of fright and pounded off through the brush.

Crowell stood still again, wondering what the skiff pilot had made of the abrupt commotion. Then he stepped back behind a tree trunk.

The support suit was coming into view. Any doubts he might have had about the identity of the attackers would have been discarded now. This was how a suited null-g swimmer moved on a planet's surface in places where his propulsion devices weren't usable. The legs tiptoed along through the brush, bulky torso swaying this way and that. The man inside wasn't walking but pushing himself forward and lifting briefly into the air with each step. His free hand reached ahead, grasping at whatever was available to help pull the body along. The other hand wasn't free because it held a gun.

The big rounded head section contained no viewplate, but the swimmer could keep simultaneous watch on the area about and above him through a set of screens inside. This was as close as Crowell was likely to get to his quarry without being seen. He leveled the carbine, stepped out from behind the tree, said sharply, "Drop the gun! Stay where you are!"

The swimmer twisted about—not at all awkwardly or uncertainly now, but in a swift powerful motion that brought the suit's legs off the ground, swung him around to point head on, lying flat in the air, toward Crowell. The handgun was firing as he moved, ejecting a thirty-foot needle of blue-white radiance which swept in toward Crowell from the right, scything through the growth. No need for careful aim from the swimmer's point of view . . . as the knife of fire flashed through the space where Crowell stood, Crowell would die.

It was standard practice with that type of weapon, simple and fast. Against a gun already aimed, it wasn't fast enough. Crowell squeezed the carbine's trigger briefly. The support suit jerked backward and the handgun's beam winked out. The suit began to turn, was caught by the undergrowth and slid slowly down through it to the ground.

Crowell came walking forward, eyes on the suit, chewing his lip. He'd sighted at the man's shoulder, but he'd seen the suit turn sideways as he fired. Only slightly, but too far! The bolt had ripped on into the torso. The pilot almost certainly was dead.

He picked up the handgun and pocketed it, then leaned the

carbine against a shrub, and unfastened the head section of the support suit. As he turned the section back, the pilot's head sagged to the side. The eyes were half closed. Crowell found no trace of throat pulse. He looked at the angle at which the beam had seared into the suit and the body within, shook his head and sealed the suit again. He moved back out of the trees the way he had come, towing the nearly weightless suit behind him.

The car settled to the ground. Ilken's tanned face looked out at him. "He's dead?"

"Quite dead. Couldn't help it. We'll take the body back to Base."

"Star Union type suit," she remarked, looking at it. "A swimmer?"

"Definitely. For the record, I want the null-g characteristics established by the medical department."

Ilken said, "There's an aircar upstairs watching us."

Startled, Crowell glanced up, saw only cloudy sky. "Not another of their skiffs?"

"Aircar. I had it in the screen. Not one from the Base, so it should be the Galestrals." She pointed suddenly. "Up there!"

Crowell gazed in the indicated direction, saw a pale speck drift out from among cloud veils. They'd been less than fifty miles from the Galestral survey team's ship position when the attack began. "I'll try to wave them down," he said.

"Think you can trust them?"

He shrugged. "About as much as we can trust anyone on Kulkoor at present. We've no quarrel with the Galestral Company, so far. If I can use their communicator to contact the Base, it'll save us a good deal of time."

He lifted the support suit and its contents into the back section of the car, moved thirty steps away, sealed his coat pockets, took off the coat and began swinging it back and forth through the air. Perhaps a minute passed. The car above was moving very slowly but seemed to be continuing on its course. "What makes you think they're watching us?" Crowell asked.

"'They're circling. What else would they be looking at?" Ilken added, "They're starting down now—they've seen you!"

Crowell continued to wave the coat until it became obvious that the aircar was, in fact, descending toward them. Then he slipped the coat on, fastened it. "They may have caught the shooting from a distance," he said.

"Probably did," Ilken agreed.

He looked over at her. "Legs bothering you?"

"Not as much as they will be."

"We want to get attention for them as soon as we can."

Ilken, eyes on the approaching aircar, remarked, "Legs might have become a problem if we'd had to walk back to Base—or even the fifty miles to the Galestral ship. But we'd probably have made it, either way."

"We'd—what are you talking about?"

She nodded at the console. "Power section took a hit. Gauge shows two minutes flight left—and it's dropping."

Crowell swore. "Why didn't you tell me before?"

"No sense worrying you with it until we found out whether the Galestrals would come down for us. You know, I'm looking forward to this! Always did want to meet a Galestral . . ."

2
..

CROWELL HAD SEEN a Cencom tape identifying the three people in the aircar which presently settled to the ground a dozen yards from him. They were the full complement of the Galestral heavy metals survey team on Kulkoor, and—supposedly, at least—three fourths of the entire current Galestral representation on the planet. Their names were Grant Gage, Ned Brock, Jill Hastings. They might range in age between Ilken and himself. When they stepped out of the car, each had one of the light Suesvant rifles of Galestral slung from the shoulder.

Crowell explained the situation briefly. They didn't seem surprised; no doubt they were well briefed on the political rivalries and tensions between the swimmer and walker factions of the Star Union. Grant Gage said they'd picked up energy bursts on a survey instrument from thirty-five miles away and come to investigate. They'd seen nothing of the aerial fight and hadn't realized Crowell was in trouble until they saw him waving at them in the ground screen.

Jill Hastings broke in. "You say Lieutenant Tegeler was hurt by torp spray . . ."

"Yes," Crowell said. He'd told Ilken to wait in the car. "She feels the damage isn't too significant, but I want to get our medical department here immediately to make sure."

"You're over two hours from your Base," Jill pointed out. "We can have her on our ship in ten minutes and start doing something about the spray."

Crowell studied her. Slender, blond, intelligent face, reflective blue eyes. Looking very competent in her bush outfit. However, torp spray injuries were messy things to handle—

Grant Gage said, "Jill's our surgeon, and a good one, Captain Witter. The ship's equipped for emergencies of that kind."

Crowell nodded. "I appreciate the offer! Let's see what Lieutenant Tegeler thinks."

Ilken thought it was a fine idea. She smiled at Jill. "Stuff's beginning to be something of a nuisance."

They completed arrangements quickly. Crowell used the Galestral car's communicator to contact the Base. Dr. Bates would come out at once. A technical crew was to collect all available evidence of the skiff attack, and guncars were to accompany the group in case of attempted interference.

Captain Bymer, of the sentinel ship, could not be reached immediately by the Base comm office. Crowell thought he might be in pursuit of the raider, said, "Get me in contact with him as soon as you can."

Guy Hansen next—

Hansen's voice said dryly from the communicator, "We've had some trouble here, too, Witter. The aerial surveillance system is inoperative."

"Inoperative in what way?"

"I haven't been able to determine either the cause or the extent of the damage as yet. But in view of your experience, sabotage seems a definite possibility."

"When did it happen?"

"About an hour ago."

That did make sabotage a definite possibility. Hansen was still in the process of establishing an aerial surveillance pattern about Kulkoor; at present, there would have been very little chance that the skiff attack on Crowell's car could be recorded by one of the system's units. But the people behind the attack wouldn't know that.

Crowell spoke last with Herrick, his security deputy. "We're not slapping secrecy on this," he said, "because I want you to watch for reactions. Now they've tried to hit me and missed, somebody might like to do away with evidence. The Public Servant Betheny and her two swimmer attendants are confined to her quarters. Take any steps necessary to make sure they stay there, regardless of what Betheny or others have to say about it. You have the authority under Cencom Seal."

"Yes, sir!" said Herrick cheerfully. "The Public Servant is to be allowed the use of a communicator?"

"Definitely. Let her get her sympathizers lined up. It will make it easier to handle them by the time I get back to Base. If there's any actual trouble before then, take care of it on the spot. You're my personal representative as of now."

Crowell switched off the communicator, climbed out of the car. The survey team, standing outside with Ilken, had been listening with unconcealed interest.

"Many thanks," he said to Grant Gage. "That's started things rolling. Now if you'd care to get the patient to your ship—"

Gage asked, "You're not coming with us?"

"No," Crowell said. "I'll be sitting at the gun in our car until the Base group gets here. I'm not entirely sure we're finished here with whoever sent down those skiffs."

Gage nodded. "I believe I'll stay with you, Captain Witter." He smiled briefly. "The Galestral Company has an obvious interest in seeing that your evidence remains intact. Ned can take Lieutenant Tegeler and Jill to the ship and come back with the car."

Ilken Tegeler lay stretched out, facedown, on a white surgical shelf in a small brightly lit cabin of the Galestral ship. Her clothing, slashed here and there by spent spray where it wasn't blood-soaked, was being cleaned and repaired elsewhere on the ship, and Jill Hastings was at work getting the torp spray particles back out of her. The nozzle of a shiny container behind the shelf adhered to the pit of Ilken's left elbow. What she got from it was a feeling of warmth spreading in a slow flow through her arm and on through her body. Actually, it was feeding something into her to act as a substitute for the blood she was losing. She'd lost plenty already, and was likely to lose a good deal more before Jill was done. The torp needles had struck deep here and there. Most of them were tiny, not easy to locate, and not at all easy to remove.

But she felt perfectly comfortable. More than comfortable. They had a marvelous sort of anesthetic, which couldn't really be called an anesthetic, since there was no insensitivity or numbness. What she felt, as Jill's instruments searched out the torp fragments, dug and sucked delicately at them, was a continuing series of soothing pleasure pulses. She decided her brain was recording pain, probably rather severe pain, but was being tricked into identifying it as something else.

"People could learn to *like* being cut to pieces this way!" she remarked presently.

"As a matter of fact," Jill said, "people have learned to like it.

The pleasure effect can be stepped up considerably. You have to be careful with the stuff."

Ilken frowned. "Mighty foolish people!"

"Yes. Very foolish."

"That was on Galestral?"

"Yes. I don't believe the drug's in use anywhere else."

Ilken was silent a moment. "Number of things I'd like to know," she said then. "Distract you to talk?"

"Not at all. But try not to move."

Ilken said, "There're legends about you Galestrals on backwoods planets like Ragnor. The way I used to hear it told when I was a child, all Galestrals stood ten feet tall—and there *weren't* any stupid ones."

Jill chuckled gently. "Too bad it's not true! I've known remarkably stupid Galestrals. And physically we average smaller than the Star Union's walker citizens—not to mention advanced swimmer types."

"It's because Galestral's near g and a half that you've cut down on size?"

"Uh-huh. Adaptation. The process seems to have leveled off in the past few generations."

"Noticed the way you people move at around norm-g here," Ilken remarked. "Real light and easy, like you didn't know how to stumble! You've been to the space cities?"

"No," Jill said. "I've worked with the Company's exploration and survey teams since I finished training. I've never been in Star Union territory."

"That rifle you carry—it's a Suesvant?"

"Yes."

"Same model they use against the superbeasts?"

"The very same." Jill's voice smiled. "Does it seem too light for that?"

"Just by looking at it, I'd have said so. More like something for small game, up to people. I've heard the Suesvants have an awful punch."

"They do, when that's what you need. But they can be used on small game, too, without tearing it up. It depends on the type of shell you select."

"Hm! Any secrets about the construction?"

Jill said there wasn't really—rifles of the general Suesvant type had been manufactured off and on in the Star Union. But they'd never become popular except on Galestral, where personal weapons of exceptional effectiveness had been a survival requirement until fairly recent times. If they were any good, they were complicated precision instruments, and very expensive. "The main point, though, is the amount of practice it takes to learn how to handle a Suesvant so that in an emergency you make the right moves automatically," she said. "It would be quite easy to make the wrong move with a Suesvant when there's no time to think about it."

"Because of the different kinds of shells?"

"Mostly. I limit myself to five standard types as a rule. But there are over a hundred to choose from for specific purposes."

"You've been in the . . . what do they call those places on Galestral?"

"The wildlands? Yes. I spent four months in them near the end of my training period. A sort of graduation test."

"And you've stopped superbeasts with the Suesvant?"

"A few. Most of them won't go up against humans anymore. But you can't ever be sure in their territories. Some will be watching you and pretending they aren't, while they lay traps and wait for you to get careless. The Company feels that in four months you'll be tested enough to qualify for the Space Exploration Corps. So I graduated . . . My turn now—when did you leave Ragnor?"

"Eh? Oh, a little more than half a year ago," Ilken said. "Captain Witter got a discharge from the Rangers, and I got one with him. We went to Halcolm. He was born there. First space city I'd seen—first *anything* I'd seen at that time except Ragnor."

"What did you think of it?"

"Halcolm was interesting, all right, but I wouldn't want to stay there much longer than we did. It's a mixed city, and the swimmers have been getting control of it. There's a big null-g section, and most of the rest of the city is quarter-g. You get warned when you come to a norm-g area, so nobody wanders in by accident and hurts himself! Most of Halcolm's walkers couldn't stand on their feet under norm-g. They get exercised in a box during their sleep periods, so they'll stay healthy."

"I've heard about that. The sleepex."

"Yes. And maybe they are healthy," Ilken said, "though they looked pretty flabby to me. But they mostly like quarter-g because it seems like less work, and they don't mind eating medicated food to make up for it because they can't taste the medication. The swimmers, anyway, exercise. I was taught null-g gymnastics while I was there. *That* is great!"

"Who taught you?"

"Captain Witter. He was born a swimmer."

Jill said, "He doesn't give one that impression."

"No. He got into a g-training program when he was eleven, to show he could be a norm-g walker if he felt like it. Still the walker type basically, so he made it, and became a walker then finally, politically. But all his relatives are swimmers, some of them pretty high up in the Swimmer League. I guess they think Captain Witter's a little odd, though he gets along with them all right."

"What do you think of the swimmers generally?"

"When they're not shooting at me?" Ilken asked dryly. "Well— I don't mind them being what they are. It's their business. But I wouldn't like to see them get the upper hand in the Star Union. They'd want to turn everybody into swimmers, and if you didn't want to be one, there aren't many places to go that seem worth going to."

"Two ways of life, with diverging technologies and diverging types of adaptive body chemistry," Jill's voice said thoughtfully. "Eventually, there should be two species. I've been told we already have them. Maintaining mixed populations in the space cities must be getting increasingly awkward for both sides. I can see why the swimmers want to settle it their way."

"So can I," Ilken said. "But I don't want that to be my way. They push it at you like it's a religion. We'd visit some of Captain Witter's people or swimmer friends and they'd hear I was a Mailliard of Ragnor, and pretty soon then one or the other would be explaining to me how Man started out as the primitive Earth walker and became spaceman who brought the Star Union into existence and was evolving now as the swimmer into *homo universalis*, who was the highest form of life ever known and would still go on evolving.

"But a planet walker who insisted on remaining a walker obviously couldn't evolve into anything. His or her descendants would still simply be walker primitives. I couldn't even get angry about it because they really were trying to make me see the light and welcome me into the fold. Freed of the ancestral gravitational bonds, is how they liked to put it. Captain Witter never argued with them, so I didn't either. I'd just smile nicely. Guess they decided I must be sort of dense!"

Jill laughed.

"But I couldn't stand living even as a walker in one of the norm-g cities," Ilken said. "Big as they are and even when you can look out through the walls and see the stars, they're still spaceships, and you're inside. From what I've heard of Galestral, you wouldn't think Ragnor was much of a world to brag about, but we were *outside* there, with the whole galaxy around us. Swimmers don't know what the feeling is like, being a planet walker! They're always inside *something*. Was that why the people who settled Galestral left the Star Union—to get away from the space cities?"

"In part," Jill's voice told her. "They seem to have had something like a religious drive, too, but it was to be back on the surface of a terroid world. And in part they wanted to be independent of Cencom and Star Union politics—not just away from the swimmers."

"Well, they made it. No one else around here now is really independent of Cencom."

"No, it seems nobody is."

There was a pause in the talk for some minutes after that. Jill's instruments remained busy. Ilken, ignoring them—ignoring also the feelings of pleasure they produced, which now seemed somewhat indecent—was thinking. She was inclined to like this helpful and friendly-seeming Galestral woman; but the Galestrals might be enemies. Not her enemies directly, but enemies of the Star Union. Therefore, here on Kulkoor, of Crowell Witter. Therefore again, her own.

No harm in fishing a little farther . . .

Ilken said, "Cencom records say it was you and Grant Gage who discovered that ghost mining camp in the mountains everybody's puzzled about."

"That's right. We did find it."

"Been back there lately?"

"No, not for some while. Why?"

"It's where we were headed when the swimmer skiffs jumped us. Captain Witter thought we might run across your man Farquhar there."

Silence for a moment. Then Jill's voice said, "It might be as good a place as any to look for Farquhar. But I doubt he'll be found if he doesn't choose to be found. He doesn't tell even us where he goes or what he's doing."

"Thought you three were supposed to be helping him look for . . . whatever it is he's looking for."

"That's what we thought," Jill said dryly. "Our instructions say we're his back-up team. If he asks for any kind of assistance in solving the so-called Kulkoor Problem, we're to give it to him. Technically, we're under his orders in that respect. So far, he hasn't asked for assistance. In fact, he's implied that at best we'd be in his way. I've seen him twice since he reached Kulkoor. He's conducting the investigation for the Company strictly on his own."

"That's all right with the Company?"

"Evidently. Farquhar's supposed to be the best biota analyst alive—and he does have a remarkable record in the Exploration Corps."

"Record for doing what?"

"For noticing things nobody else happened to notice. He's got his own mobile laboratory, his own supply of message drones, reports directly to the Galestral Company. He lets us know periodically that he's still alive. Otherwise, he ignores us as much as he can. Apparently he's working on a theory he doesn't want to discuss."

"Do you three have a theory?" Ilken asked.

"About why there was a mysteriously abandoned mining camp on Kulkoor a year before legitimate mining operations were to begin?"

"Yes."

"Well," Jill said, "it's not hard to guess why the miners came. Presumably a wildcat outfit from some terroid settlement heard of the Kulkoor find and was trying to make off with a fortune in ore while they had the opportunity. The question is how and why the men disappeared. We've done some theorizing about that like everyone else. There's always the possibility, of course, that the camp is a fake."

"Set up so someone would find it?"

"Yes."

"What for?"

"Conceivably," Jill's voice said amiably, "to justify measures the Star Union would like to take on Kulkoor."

"And Cencom," said Ilken, "seems to think the Galestral Company might have set up the camp. For the same general reason."

"Well, if Cencom isn't responsible, it could suspect that. It's logical."

"Um! What's another of your theories?"

"We haven't come up with anything that looks good. But there's an animal here that could make it seem a man had disappeared without trace. It's a flying animal."

"We saw some big flying things along the coast on the way out from the Base," Ilken said.

"That type seems mainly a carrion eater. But there's an inland species, probably related, that's strictly a hunter, and a powerful one. We've seen it a number of times in the mountain forests around the camp area. If a flock of those creatures had staged a surprise raid on the camp, they'd be physically capable of cleaning it out in a matter of moments. But it would take a level of intelligence Kulkoor's fauna doesn't appear to have reached. The fliers hunt individually and in pairs, not in flocks."

"Still doesn't sound like the worst theory to me," Ilken observed drowsily. "You mentioned it to Farquhar?"

"We dictated it to the communicator in his air cruiser. There was no sign he was listening, but it was recorded. We picked up his recorded reply a few days later. He thanked us for the suggestion—and said he felt we made an excellent heavy metals survey team."

Ilken said, "Guess I see now why he hasn't answered either to the comm calls Captain Witter's been sending him since we landed here four days ago. Odd thing about your other theory, you know! Swimmer League could have had the mining camp set up to push Cencom in their direction—null-g domes for the Kulkoor operations. Or Cencom could have done it. Captain Witter and I wouldn't have to know about that."

"No, you wouldn't."

Ilken yawned, slowly and luxuriously. "On the other hand," she said, "Galestral people could have set it up, and you three wouldn't have to know it . . . Farquhar might."

Jill's voice said something that faded out curiously. Ilken then had a prolonged sense of drifting gently away from everything here without being either inclined or able to do anything about it.

3
..

SOME TIME LATER—Ilken couldn't have said whether it was a long time or a short one—she became aware again of being in the Galestral ship's bright little sick bay, having torp spray pleasurably excised from her, while a shiny container behind the surgical shelf gently pumped its blood substitute into her arm. There was something else going on. Jill was asking questions, and she was replying to them.

Ilken felt a touch of grim amusement. The new drug affecting her now was in keeping with her other experiences here—beautifully efficient! She wanted to answer the questions; she enjoyed answering them; and she wasn't even able to remember what it could be like to feel opposed to answering them.

But it didn't make any difference. Crowell might have had secrets to spill under such circumstances; she didn't have any. There was nothing of real significance the Galestrals could learn through her . . . and actually Jill didn't seem to be digging for secrets, at least not at the moment. She was asking questions about the Ragnor Campaign. In particular, about Crowell's and Ilken's part in the final stages of it.

"Well, when Captain Witter went to Cencom and sold them on his plan," Ilken heard herself saying, "we'd been long beaten but didn't know it. There were only around forty-two thousand Mailliards left on Ragnor. The year we wiped out the Star Union's swimmer dome colony, there'd been easily five times that many. We didn't know the losses we'd taken. You didn't use a communicator much in those years because the Rangers had learned to zero in on them fast. So we thought there were a lot more of the groups still around but out of contact. At that stage, the Rangers could have finished us off in another six months if they'd pushed it. But they were holding back."

"Why?"

"Politics. After the Ragnor Campaign began, Cencom was able to build up its walker ground forces to over ten times what it'd had until then. We'd showed that swimmer troops weren't good at taking or holding planet territory, and as long as Mailliards were fighting on Ragnor, Cencom had a fine official reason to keep adding to its walker strength. We weren't to be wiped out too quickly. Of course, we didn't know that either. We could count, and what we saw was that it still usually cost the Star Union two to three dead Rangers to chalk up one dead Mailliard. We figured we weren't doing badly."

"How did Captain Witter change it?"

"He'd got the facts on Ragnor, and he didn't mind talking about them. He had proof. It wasn't the kind of story Cencom liked to have spread around the Star Union. And if he could get the Mailliards to become Star Union citizens, Cencom would have a new ready-made ground strike force of planet walkers born and bred at norm-g plus. Cencom saw it, particularly since enough Star Union people had begun to worry about you Galestrals by then to keep up the pressure for increasing walker strength. So when Captain Witter came back to Ragnor, he was still a Ranger officer, but he was also a Cencom investigator with instructions to bring the Ragnor Campaign to a negotiated end—and with the Cencom Seal to back him up, however he wanted to go about it.

"Of course, he still had to convince the Mailliards then, and *that* wasn't easy. We—my group—heard one day that a Ranger captain had got a Mailliard group to give up without a fight not fifty miles from us. Everyone figured it was some new Ranger trick, and Captain Witter became a prime sneak-hunter target. I was sixteen by then and my group's best sneak-hunter, so I went out to collect his head myself. Came pretty close to doing it, too—closer than anyone else before or after. But I got caught and—"

Ilken checked, blinked a few times, glanced around. The blood substitute container had been detached from her arm, and Jill Hastings sat in a chair a few feet away looking at her.

"Stuff's worn off, Jill," Ilken said.

"Has it?" said Jill.

"Yes. Just noticed I don't have to go on telling you any more."

Jill smiled, stood up. "All right. The drug does have a quite transitory effect. And the patch-up surgery's finished. I'll go get your clothes."

Half a dozen aircars and a transport from the Star Union Base reached the area of the attack some two hours after Crowell's call; and the Galestrals took their leave. Crowell had the on-the-spot technical investigation he'd wanted carried out, supervised by Guy Hansen. His damaged car, the wrecked spaceskiff and its dead pilot were then loaded on the transport. Within forty minutes, the Star Union group was on its way back to the Base.

It had become evident by that time that Crowell's instructions to Herrick had caused considerable disturbance among Base personnel. Dr. John Sutton, the expedition's director and scientific head, called twice to protest against the highhanded and insulting restriction of Public Servant Betheny of Varien to her quarters. He said he intended to record an official complaint with Cencom. Crowell told him he would be given an opportunity to do just that within the next few hours. Meanwhile, the Public Servant would remain under guard.

Crowell was driving one of the Base cars, Hansen beside him, Ilken and Dr. Bates in the rear of the car. After Dr. Sutton's second call, Crowell said to Hansen, "You've known Betheny for a number of years, haven't you?"

Hansen nodded. "I knew her rather well for a while." Born in Varien, newest and greatest of the Star Union's all-swimmer cities, Guy Hansen, like Crowell, had made an early decision to develop the capabilities of a norm-g walker. He'd been active nonetheless for a number of years in the Swimmer League. Cencom records listed him as being now politically uncommitted. It proved nothing in itself, but in the few days Crowell had been on Kulkoor, he'd decided Hansen was one of three men on the Base he'd trust completely in an emergency. Dr. Bates was another. Herrick, a veteran of the Ragnor Campaign and commander of the Base's small security force, was the third.

Crowell said, "When I was sent here to check into the problems the Base has been having, the League put heavy pressure on Cencom to allow Betheny to come out simultaneously. The argument was that the League's interests must also be officially represented on Kulkoor. I thought it a little odd at the time that they'd risk one of their leaders in what's regarded as an unpredictable and potentially dangerous situation."

Hansen glanced over at him. "Perhaps you're beginning to see why."

"Perhaps I am. She's been here four days and seems to have three fourths of our walker personnel eating out of her hand. Is arranging murders another specialty of hers?"

Hansen shrugged. "I never enjoyed the League leadership's confidence enough to answer that. But Betheny is *homo universalis* with a vengeance. In other words, completely ruthless when the League's interests are involved—and getting the domes contract on the Kulkoor project should be the League's biggest current goal. She'd hardly be here otherwise."

"Why not?"

"She detests being on or anywhere near the surface of a planet. I know that about her."

Crowell grunted. "So that's why she brought her private psychiatrist along . . ." He added, "Once I was out of the way, along with Lieutenant Tegeler—and probably with any evidence of the attack also safely out of the way—Betheny would have had authority at the Base as the ranking Star Union official on Kulkoor."

"Only for as much time as it would take Cencom to get another representative equipped with the Cencom Seal out here," Hansen remarked.

"Four weeks, more or less," said Crowell. "Completely ruthless— it's a safe guess that enough would have happened in that time to buy the League its domes contract."

Hansen looked uneasy. "What, actually, could Betheny do?"

"I'm thinking of a number of things I could be doing in that position." Crowell shrugged. "Further unexplained disappearances. More and increasingly serious problems with the quick-growth crops and food animals. A limited number of virus fatalities at the Base. It could be carried further, but too much wouldn't really be necessary. Cencom would be suspicious, of course, but by then it wouldn't have much choice. Betheny has Public Servant immunity, and there'd be no time for lengthy investigations."

Hansen said, "If it isn't a secret, what's the deadline for the decision on whether Kulkoor mining is to be carried out by walker outfits or under swimmer domes?"

"There's no secret as far as I'm concerned," Crowell said. "Eight weeks should be the limit, if operations are to start as agreed on by the end of the year. There's no reason to think the Galestral Company won't be ready to begin mining at that time. So Cencom can't wait. If there's any remaining doubt about the feasibility of walker operations, it will decide for the domes."

Hansen nodded. "I can see Betheny's motivation," he said. "But it seems to me she'd need more help than she'd get from the ship that brought her here if she's to do what you think she has in mind."

"She would," Crowell agreed. "So we'll assume the help's already here. Otherwise, having me killed wouldn't have made much sense. She took a longer chance than she should have, in any case, in trying to have it done in that particular manner."

Hansen said reflectively, "It may not have looked that way to her, or to her advisers. I'm no combat specialist—but logically those skiffs should have finished your car on the first pass, shouldn't they?"

"Ordinarily, two armed spaceskiffs will slap down a guncar, yes." The standard guncar, Crowell thought. As Cencom investigator on Ragnor, where some of his sincerest enemies had worn the Star Union's Ranger uniform, he'd taken the precaution of flying a car with nonstandard armament for four years. For three and a half of those years, Ilken had been his gunner. The car they'd used today was of the same type. The odds hadn't been what they seemed.

The Base comm office presently connected Captain Bymer of the sentinel ship with Crowell. Bymer had reported previously that the sentinel's automatic scanning devices had recorded no traces of another space vessel at the time of the attack by the skiffs. In the meantime, he'd carried out a search run about Kulkoor, with equally negative results. The raider evidently had withdrawn beyond scanning range after losing contact with the skiffs. The sentinel ship now had resumed its orbital station above the Star Union Base. It would remain alerted for immediate action.

When Crowell's airborne cavalcade arrived at the Base, he found a delegation waiting for him, headed by Dr. John Sutton, who came forward as soon as Crowell stepped down from the car. The rest of the group remained where they were, expressions indicating varying degrees of disapproval.

"Captain Witter," Dr. Sutton said, "we realize you have reason enough to be disturbed by the murderous attack on you. But such a matter hardly calls for hasty decisions! We suggest that you join us in my office, where the situation can be discussed and due consideration given to the measures that should be taken."

"Who is we, Dr. Sutton?" Crowell asked.

"Why—" Dr. Sutton looked surprised, glanced back at his companions. "Why, my senior department heads over there, of course!"

"Of course," said Crowell. "Well, it's an excellent suggestion! If you and the other gentlemen will go to the office, we—that's Dr. Bates, Mr. Hansen, Lieutenant Tegeler and I—will meet you there presently. There's some business to be taken care of first."

Dr. Sutton frowned. Crowell jerked his head up at the open car lock in the guard screens. "Six vehicles are lining up out there," he observed, "and in a few moments they'll start coming down exactly where you and your colleagues are standing."

The scientific body withdrew, looking disgruntled. The transport moved down through the lock, followed by the guncars. Herrick had appeared, and Crowell started issuing instructions. Hansen went to the mapping office. Dr. Bates had the skiff pilot's body taken to his laboratory. With Herrick in charge of the other work, Crowell turned to Ilken. "What's Bates' medical opinion on your legs?"

She grinned briefly. "Spray's been cleaned out. That part's all right. I'm to stay off them the next few days."

"Are you going to do it?"

"Not likely!"

"All right. Let's get to our quarters and pick up some equipment. Then we'll pay Betheny a visit."

They set off. There was a trace of stiffness in Ilken's walk. The advice given her by Dr. Bates was probably good. But there might be critical developments in the following hours, and if Ilken felt able to operate, Crowell wanted her beside him.

She said, "Think there's something wrong on Bymer's ship, don't you?"

"Bound to be," Crowell agreed. "We were tracked after we left the Base this morning. Those skiffs didn't come flying around the curve of the planet to look for us—they were dropped into atmosphere directly overhead. So the swimmer ship was showing in Bymer's scanners. He's lying to us, or somebody else has edited the scan tapes and lied to him. After things get straightened out enough around here, we'll go up in the shuttle and check. Until then, we won't mention that matter. What did you think of Jill Hastings, by the way?"

Ilken shrugged. "She's plenty smart. Otherwise, I'm not at all sure."

Crowell nodded. "About the impression I had of the three of them. I'd very much like to know exactly what Farquhar is doing on Kulkoor ... Biota analyst!" He scratched his jaw. "Well, we'd better not discount the Galestrals in anything that goes on here—even if there are only four of them on the planet."

"We don't know that's all there are," Ilken said.

"No, we don't."

4
..

THE SHORT ENTRY passage into the almost globular structure which enclosed the living quarters of Betheny of Varien on the Star Union Base was subject to the pull of Kulkoor's gravity. Betheny and her swimmer attendants came through it only in skim bubbles. Guide rods for the use of visitors hung from the walls. Crowell and Ilken equipped themselves with one as they came in.

They'd made some minor adjustments for the null-g visit. Loose clothing had been discarded, shirts tucked under belts. Ilken's dark hair was drawn into a tight smooth coil at the back of her head. The pair of Mailliard tarsh knives normally carried inside her jacket was fastened to her belt, one on each side.

At the end of the passage, gravity ended. So did any similarity to a norm-g residential dwelling. The structure had been brought along, collapsed, on the swimmer ship which carried Betheny to Kulkoor. Expanded, the globe took up eight times as much space as the quarters assigned to Crowell on the Base. Within, all earlier architectural rules had been swept aside by a design intended only to serve null-g's needs and pleasures. The curving walls of the section beyond the passage glowed softly; furnishings swam in barely visible spider webbing. It was a functional arrangement which had sweep and beauty. As Crowell and Ilken moved into the section on a guide current, day brightness grew up in it. Air stirred with cool freshness, and there was a blending of background sounds, barely noticeable until one began listening for them, which impressed the mind as the sounds of life.

It was a familiar pattern to Crowell; his childhood had been spent in such surroundings. He hadn't known then what it meant, but in time he'd felt something vaguely oppressive about it. Later he'd understood. Swimmer art, functional art in particular, was highly advanced. Through it the swimmer created, very skillfully, the illusion of his own universe, one he could take with him wherever he went. What had oppressed Crowell had been the almost unconscious sense of being barred by the illusion from the realities of the universe.

Having found his way out of the illusion, he no longer had such feelings about it. He'd drifted with Ilken toward the center of the section. In relationship to each other, they'd remained vertical, moving forward together on the entry current until it blended into other guide currents in the section. There were two round exits, a large one in front of them, another overhead, both veiled by the rippling tints of sight and sound barriers. They'd announced themselves from outside the structure, and the announcement had been acknowledged by Dr. Torres, one of Betheny's two companions. But Betheny appeared now in no hurry to receive them.

It was Dr. Torres who came in by the round opening over their heads some two minutes later. Crowell and Ilken shifted position to face her. The psychiatrist was a swimmer giant of the intermediate stage, aging but lithe, with the magnetic good looks and compelling personality almost characteristic of her type. She wore swimmer attire, a thin copper tunic which left her strong brown arms and legs uncovered. As she approached, the section's light gleamed for an instant from the bronze designs on her skull, depilated or perhaps hairless from birth.

"Captain Witter, Lieutenant Tegeler," she said. "Betheny will join us in a moment. Perhaps you'd like to tell me the reason for your visit."

"Dr. Sutton would refer to it as the situation," Crowell said.

"The situation? We were informed that an attempt was made to kill you some hours ago."

"It was."

Dr. Torres nodded. "Would you care to tell me about it in detail?"

"I'm sure you've already been told about it in as much detail as is necessary," Crowell said. "Betheny has made friends here."

"So she has." The psychiatrist's fine dark eyes regarded Crowell with the barest suggestion of mockery. "Captain Witter, you're acting under Cencom Seal, which at present gives you a certain degree of authority. But perhaps I should caution you not to become too zealous in your use of it. You seem to have formed a mental connection between the Public Servant's presence on the Base and the attack on you. I need hardly remind you that if you should violate the Public Servant's immunity in any way because of such suspicions, you'd be guilty of a capital crime."

"You needn't remind me," Crowell agreed. "And now, since I'm sure Betheny of Varien is listening to what's being said, perhaps she'll join us—or should we join her?"

Betheny's finely chiseled features suggested a curious blend of arrogance and outgoing warmth. On level ground, she would have stood four inches taller than Crowell. Her shoulders were wider; her weight might be almost twice his. For all her size, she remained a superbly feminine being—the current culmination of *homo universalis*, beautiful, maternal, infinitely appealing. It was a good part of the strength of the Swimmer League that its leaders were such parent figures, benevolent and magnificent. They were admired, desired, trusted. Even dedicated walkers surrendered to the attraction. And it had been, Crowell thought, a calculated move to send Betheny rather than a male counterpart to Kulkoor. The Star Union expedition's department heads were men.

He sensed the attraction himself when Betheny appeared, dressed as she would be when she went out among walkers, in a silver suit and helmet. She was accompanied by a young woman with short brown hair, an intermediate swimmer type like Dr. Torres—a bodyguard, carrying a sidearm.

Crowell said, addressing Betheny, "I have some reason to believe that there's a League conspiracy to defeat the purpose of the Star Union's expedition on Kulkoor. The immunities of a Public Servant will be respected if possible, but I can't allow you to interfere with an investigation of that possibility."

"How would you prevent it?" Betheny said.

"I've considered having the three of you put temporarily under sedation."

The bodyguard glanced at Betheny. Betheny shook her head.

"We have no intention of interfering with your investigation, Captain Witter," she said.

"Very well," Crowell said. "In that case, you'll remain with me while Lieutenant Tegeler goes over your quarters."

Betheny smiled. "What will she be looking for?"

"Evidence of the conspiracy," Crowell said.

When Crowell and Ilken arrived at Dr. Sutton's office, Dr. Sutton turned immediately to Crowell. He appeared again to be acting as spokesman for the group, to which Hansen and Dr. Bates had added themselves.

"The opinion's been expressed by several here," Dr. Sutton told Crowell, "that the incident this morning was staged by Galestrals, with the purpose of heightening the distrust which divides some of our Star Union citizens in the critical area of Kulkoor. Dr. Bates informs us that the man you shot shows null-g swimmer modifications. There is, of course, the possibility that the Galestrals have developed a swimmer type."

"Yes," Crowell agreed, "that does seem possible."

Dr. Sutton glanced at the others.

"They also could have obtained Star Union equipment to divert suspicion from themselves if the operation failed."

Crowell nodded. "Or they could have manufactured identical equipment. Why not? Mr. Hansen, have you told these gentlemen about the damage done to the surveillance instruments?"

"No," Hansen said. "I thought I should wait until this discussion got started."

"Please do it now."

Hansen said to the group, "A few of you have been aware that the aerial mapping system being established on the Base can be used as a form of continuous planetary surveillance. It would be random and incomplete, but it should disclose any significant violations of the Santrask Agreement, which was its purpose.

"A few hours ago—shortly before the attack on Captain Witter's aircar—the system became inoperative. We've established meanwhile that the damage was caused by miniaturized destructive devices, activated from outside the mapping section."

"And perhaps from outside the Base?" said Dr. Sutton who was listening closely.

Hansen shrugged. "That's possible. At any rate, it was sabotage—and the devices must have been installed by some trained member of our personnel."

"You're suggesting," one of the other men said, "that the surveillance system was put out of action to keep the details of the attack on Captain Witter from being recorded by an aerial unit. Would that have happened if the system had been operating?"

"Only by a rather unlikely coincidence," Hansen said. "Naturally, the saboteurs may not have realized that they'd run a smaller risk of arousing suspicion by leaving the system intact."

Dr. Sutton said, "All that might seem to prove is that there is, in fact, at least one saboteur on the Base. I'm not sure I consider it proved! But let's concede the point. The question remains then whether the agency behind the sabotage is the Swimmer League or the Galestral Company. Men can be bought, and I'm sure no one here assumes that some Star Union citizens couldn't be induced to turn traitor."

"That would be a thoughtless assumption, to say the least," Crowell agreed. "However, one might have expected a Galestral agent to do a more permanent job on the surveillance system— Mr. Hansen expects to have it back in operation in less than a week." He placed one of two boxed instruments he'd brought into the office on a table and opened it. "In any case," he went on, "if there's someone like that around, it won't be long before we establish the fact."

Dr. Sutton eyed the instrument. "What do you have there?"

"An interrogator," Crowell told him. "Developed originally for the Ragnor Rangers. Truthful information was often quite difficult to get by any other means from Mailliard prisoners. This device produced it regularly. There's nothing about it to fight because it doesn't seem to do anything."

"You intend to question the Base personnel?"

"Of course." Crowell smiled at the group. "Beginning with the assembled heads of the major departments here! After clearing you, we'll work down through the ranks. It's a short process. We'll have put everyone through it in less than three hours."

They'd stiffened. Then Hansen laughed. "The logical step! Start with me."

Crowell turned to Dr. Sutton. "What's behind that door?"

"My secretary's office."

"Is she occupying it at the moment?"

"No."

"Then I'll check you out there, one at a time. Now we must bear in mind the possibility that a hired Galestral spy or a League conspirator is a member of this group. You've observed that Lieutenant Tegeler and I are armed. We'll keep our weapons on hand throughout the interrogation. Lieutenant Tegeler will remain in this office to watch the group while I question you individually."

Dr. Sutton's color had heightened. "That hardly seems necessary!"

This time, he found no support among his fellows. Fifteen minutes later, Crowell came out of the side office with the last of them and announced, "All right—everyone in this room has proved to be free of evil intentions. We can now start going through your departments. With your permission, Dr. Sutton, I'll continue to use your offices for it."

Dr. Sutton said, "I don't understand how that device operates. It pronounced a few dozen words at random. Nothing else happened. And yet you seem confident that I'm innocent in the matter."

"The words weren't pronounced at random," Crowell said, "and the instrument was interpreting your reactions to them. All it really showed was that none of you is involved in a conspiracy to pervert the legitimate activities of the Base. But that's all we need to know at the moment." He opened the second case he'd brought in. "Here's something else. No doubt most of you can see what it is."

"A transmitter, of course," said Hansen. He frowned.

"You recognize the type?" asked Crowell.

"Yes." Hansen picked up the transmitter, turned it around, set it back again. "An extremely powerful transmitter!" He looked at Crowell. "Why are you showing it to us?"

"It's powerful enough," said Crowell, "to push a call halfway through the Kulkoor System. It's well enough shielded to make its use undetectable to anyone but the receiver. I'm showing it to you because Lieutenant Tegeler removed it from its place of concealment in the Public Servant's quarters just before we came here."

There was an abrupt disturbed murmur of voices. One of the men asked, "Exactly what are you suggesting, Captain Witter?"

"Draw your own conclusions. Betheny's immunity covers her personal attendants. I can't interrogate those three. But I hardly feel it's necessary. And, Dr. Sutton, I think we can agree it's most unlikely that the Public Servant will turn out to be a Galestral agent?"

Dr. Sutton shook his head, cleared his throat. "I'm beginning to think this is a very bad business!"

"Perhaps it is," said Crowell. "Now let's start running the departments through the quiz. I'm putting you all on your honor not to mention the purpose of the check to anyone." He looked at Ilken. "Tell Herrick to station two guards in the office. Somebody might suspect what we're doing anyway and become a little desperate."

5
. .

THERE WAS NO TROUBLE in Dr. Sutton's office, but somebody did become desperate. Herrick got a call from a storehouse clerk about unusual activity in the area. Supply Chief Willis, assisted by a man identified as Merriman, an aerial surveyor, was engaged in dumping unopened cases into the disposal; and Willis had ordered other storehouse personnel out of the structure. Herrick went there hurriedly with two security men. They met the two on the way out, and Willis and Merriman retreated into the disposal room. When Herrick's group forced its way through the door, the two stood before the activated disposal screen. Merriman was white-faced. Willis was grinning.

"Merriman would have surrendered," Herrick reported to Crowell. "But he didn't get the chance. Willis shoved him into the screen, then waved his hand at us and walked into the screen himself. We didn't have time to stop him."

There'd been two brief flashes of light, and the men were gone. Considerable speculation followed as to what Willis had been getting rid of, and why he'd preferred to murder an associate and kill himself to letting either be interrogated. Dr. Bates suggested that some of the cases might have contained biological agents. Experimental food crops and livestock, brought in to determine whether major projects on Kulkoor could become partly self-supporting, had been seriously affected by toxins of bacterial type, which hadn't yet been located in native life forms. The carriers could have been developed elsewhere, released here, to give further weight to arguments in favor of establishing a complete system of swimmer domes on Kulkoor. Laboratory-created diseases could

452

have been scheduled to strike personnel next. Willis was in a position to conceal the fact that such materials had been delivered to the Base; and Merriman could have distributed them outside while appearing to be going about his work.

Crowell wasn't giving much attention to theories. Having started the initial investigation, it was essential to carry it through as quickly as possible, identify those involved in the conspiracy and get them out of action. Details and proof could wait. By mid-afternoon, he'd finished checking out all personnel on the Base and those flown in from outlying stations for the purpose. He wound up with eight prisoners—fewer than he'd expected. The crew of the sentinel ship remained to be investigated. There'd been no communication between ship and Base in the interval.

Ilken inquired, "Be legal to take Betheny and those other two up to the ship and freeze them?"

"It should be legal in the circumstances," Crowell said. "I could call it another form of detention. But I'll keep her down here. If she has other moves to make, I'd rather she makes them as soon as possible. The ship might become our lifeline. I wouldn't feel easy about having Betheny on it even in a frozen state."

"Think somebody might decide to let her wake up?"

Crowell shrugged. "You saw the effect she's had on our Base administration in the few days she's been around. She's here because she carries an overcharge of the *universalis* appeal. We'd better not take chances with it."

He appointed Hansen to act as Cencom's representative in his absence, contacted Captain Bymer and told him to send down the landing shuttle to take material evidence of the attack by the spaceskiffs on board for storage. He didn't mention that he and Ilken also would arrive on the shuttle.

The body of the spaceskiff pilot was taken to the sentinel ship's freezer and placed in a compartment. Leaving the section with Captain Bymer and Ilken, Crowell said, "Captain, there's a chance that some members of your crew have notions about taking over the ship. We've brought the means of identifying them with us. How would you suggest going about it without tipping them off?"

Bymer studied him a moment, said, "Let's go to the instrument room."

They went there, and Bymer dismissed the two men on duty. After they'd left, he said coldly, "The instrument room controls the ship, and I've now sealed it. Please tell me specifically what you suspect."

"Since we talked last," Crowell said, "we've uncovered evidence of a swimmer conspiracy on the Base. It's not a minor matter—the Public Servant is involved. We've nabbed the conspirators and cleared the rest of the Base personnel. You'll understand that we must start here by clearing you."

Captain Bymer's face reddened slowly. He said, "I have no objection to that."

Ilken took the interrogator out of its case and placed it on a table.

"Thank you, Captain," Crowell said presently. "You're not a swimmer conspirator—but you certainly have people on board who are. Your area scanners were in operation at the time my car was attacked by the spaceskiffs, weren't they?"

"They're in continuous automatic operation while we're at station," Bymer acknowledged. He hesitated. "You feel the ship that dispatched the skiffs should have been recorded?"

"Yes." Crowell described the details which made it seem the ship must have been in space approximately above the point of ambush. Bymer nodded. His expression was now grim. "After your call, I checked the tapes supposedly covering that time period," he said. "They showed nothing. But tapes can be replaced. Lieutenant Jones was monitoring the scanning devices at the time. He was alone in the instrument room."

"Who assigned him to the duty?"

"First Officer Henderson." Bymer added, "Henderson's served with me for over four years."

"Well," Crowell said, "we'd better start with those two."

Lieutenant Alfred Jones was an apple-cheeked young man whose face remained respectfully puzzled as he listened to the disconnected string of words coming from a small instrument. The instrument disclosed to Crowell that the lieutenant reacted strongly to eight of those words. Without looking up, Crowell observed, "Good enough!"

Lieutenant Jones closed his eyes and slumped down on the table between them. Standing eight feet behind Jones, Captain Bymer shut off a small device and put it in his pocket. Together, he and Crowell carried the unconscious young man into an adjoining room and left him lying on the floor.

Summoned to the instrument room, First Officer Henderson strolled in smiling and pointing a gun at Bymer and Crowell. Then he dropped the gun with a gasp, looked down white-faced at the Mailliard tarsh transfixing his wrist, and fainted.

"Under the circumstances," Crowell remarked, as Ilken came forward from the door of the other room, "we'd better check out the ship's surgeon next . . ."

There were no further problems. The Second Engineer and two of the remaining members of Captain Bymer's crew reacted positively to the swimmer test. They, the First Officer and Lieutenant Jones went into the personnel freezer. So did the eight prisoners Crowell then had brought up from the Base in the shuttle.

"There's a strong probability," he said to Bymer, "that a swimmer group is hidden out somewhere on Kulkoor, waiting for instructions from Betheny. Without her cooperation, we're not likely to locate them until they make a move. But if we can put the swimmer ship out of commission, the planetside's group's activities will be sharply restricted. What do you think of our chances of finding the ship?"

Captain Bymer said, "You're assuming it's remained in the Kulkoor System?" The computer technicians had restructured the scanning tape sections Lieutenant Jones had deleted from the record. The raider, clearly visible for a full twenty-five minutes before vanishing behind the curve of the planet, had been identified as the vessel which brought Betheny and her retinue to Kulkoor four days before.

"Definitely," said Crowell. "Getting Lieutenant Tegeler and myself killed was simply to be one step in an overall plan designed to put the Swimmer League in effective control of the Kulkoor Project. Whatever that plan was, the ship has a role in it. They've no way of knowing yet that we've taken countermeasures and have Betheny isolated, so they're somewhere within maximum transmitter range, ready to pick up orders. But that's still a great deal of space to go hunting around in at random."

Captain Bymer blinked reflectively.

"We shouldn't have to hunt for them at random . . ."

He explained. The swimmer ship wasn't likely to be drifting in open space while it waited. The Kulkoor System was a dirty one— masses of debris circling the sun between and beyond the four planets. The edges of such a meteoric cloud were the place to look for the raider; and there were a number of large ones currently not far from Kulkoor. They could use the ship computers to determine the most promising spots to start looking.

Crowell got in touch with Guy Hansen on the Base. "We'll have a better chance to sneak up on them if we maintain transmitter silence," he said. "It may take a couple of days. You needn't mention why we're maintaining silence. Call us only if you think there's a genuine emergency building up. We'll respond then, and be available shortly thereafter."

6
..

GRANT GAGE SWITCHED off the message drone transcriber, leaned back in his chair, flipped on ship intercom. "Jill?"

"I'm in here," Jill's voice announced from the adjoining communicator room.

"Oh! Didn't hear you go in. What date was it that Farquhar last contacted us?"

"Eight planet days ago. Check it against the Galestral calendar."

Grant's gaze shifted to the console calendars. "Getting a response?"

"The usual kind. His truck's recording the call. Farquhar either isn't at home, or doesn't want to talk. I said one of the Zuron cameras had disappeared, and asked him to call back if he was interested in hearing the details." She'd come to the door as she spoke. Grant regarded her a moment. Survey Technician Second Class. Multilevel training. Four-year veteran of the Galestral Space Exploration Corps at age twenty-two. Three completed outworld tours. Jill Hastings. One of Galestral's more valuable employee-shareholders.

"I've finished the standard reports," he said. He tapped the intercom switch. "Ned?"

The intercom grunted. "About done."

"Got a report we can feed the drone?"

"Doing that now. Be there in three-four minutes."

Intercom off again. Grant said to Jill, "How about shaping up breakfast for three?"

"We're going back out?"

"Uh-huh. I want to make a run inland, up to the area of the

457

ghost camp. If it's my lucky day, there'll be neither fog nor rain on the hills and we'll find and bag one of those big birds."

Jill set her face in prim lines, recited in a good-girl voice, "Company orders state *clearly* that at present we are to concern ourselves with the quote Kulkoor Problem unquote *only* to the extent we are instructed to do so by Biota Analyst First Class Frank Farquhar! We have received no—"

"I'm aware of it. And the Biota Analyst may have good reasons for his games, but I'm beginning to get tired of them. Company orders don't say we can't go hunting. Go rustle up the grub, woman! You and Ned can catch up on sleep on the way."

Jill got busy in the mess. She heard Ned Brock come along the passage presently, on his way to the drone room. Her thoughts remained preoccupied with Frank Farquhar. Almost all they knew about him was what they'd learned since his arrival on Kulkoor, and that was chiefly that he was a loner by preference. He might find it an asset in his line of work, but he carried it to irritating extremes. He'd landed with his own supplies and equipment—a small aircar, an airtruck with a laboratory, a drone receiver and supply of message drones. His reports went separately to Galestral. It probably would be two days before they heard from him next; and the chances were it would be nothing but a recorded message then. He was supposed to check in with his back-up team every ten planet days, solely to let them know he was still around. So far, he'd done it. If two weeks went by without word from him and they couldn't make contact with him, they were to assume he'd run afoul of the Kulkoor Problem and was dead or disabled. They'd notify Galestral of the fact and start seeing what they could do about the problem themselves. If they failed in turn to solve it, the Galestral Company would take both failures into account in selecting the personnel who were to form its new front line on Kulkoor.

In the meantime, they ran routine checks, adjusted and repositioned survey instruments, stood by to carry out the occasional instructions Farquhar had for them, and maintained the security precautions called for by Condition Abnormal. The last meant that their ship was stationed six hundred feet in the air, moored by magnetic beam to Kulkoor's surface. They left the ship and returned to it by aircar, and their Suesvant rifles went wherever they went.

Until this morning, that had been all.

That morning, coming back from a dawn check of the survey devices, Ned and Jill discovered that one of the Zuron cameras set up in the vicinity of the hovering spaceship was gone. The Zurons, stilt-mounted twenty feet above the ground, swiveled toward, focused on and took pictures of any moving object more than six inches in diameter which came within a two-hundred-yard range. A large variety of Kulkoor fauna had been catalogued in this manner; but less than a dozen species turned out to be of interest to Farquhar, for whose benefit the cameras were being operated. During the past weeks, the survey team had collected a sample of each of those species for him; he'd be picking them up when he got around to it. He hadn't said why he was interested; and whatever the assorted animals had in common remained obscure to the team.

The missing camera introduced a new factor. The shaft supporting it had been snapped off near the upper end, and the broken section had vanished with the camera. The Zurons were protected by deterrent energy fields which discouraged large animals from running into the stilts and smaller ones from climbing them. Until now, they'd been effective. Ned Brock went over the surrounding ground with a tracker and picked up no indication that anything had come near the stilt during the night.

But something could have come flying up to it—something powerful enough to break the metal shaft—something which then hadn't simply let the Zuron fall to the ground but had carried it away.

They'd come across only one life form on Kulkoor that might be capable of doing both; and that was the big winged forest hunter who also—just possibly—could be responsible for the fact that there was a mysteriously abandoned mining camp on Kulkoor. It hadn't been observed so far down in the plains, but there was nothing to keep it from going there.

"Let's assume for now that's what it was," said Grant. "The question is why it did it."

That, indeed, was the question. It could have been an accident. A simple-witted predator, coming into the Zuron's range and catching the camera's motion as it swung toward it, might attack instinctively, wrench the Zuron off and carry it away, simply because it hadn't realized that what it grasped wasn't edible.

Ned Brock said, "That's how it almost has to have happened. But I keep thinking—"

"Ned, it's what we're all thinking," said Jill.

On Galestral, it wouldn't have been considered an accident. Too many of the indigenous life forms there, whipped back eventually out of the sections of the planet men wanted for themselves, had been intelligent enough to understand that man's instruments were his allies. Such a creature, approaching stealthily at night for a closer look at the floating ship and coming across the Zuron, might have broken the camera away and disposed of it to keep its presence from being reported, even though it couldn't know how the report would be made.

Until now, the only thing which might hint that any of Kulkoor's native life had reached that level of intelligence was whatever had occurred at the mining camp on the mountain slopes, months before. Jill could understand why Grant wanted to examine a specimen of the big flier they'd seen moving with shadowy quickness through the nearby forests.

A special report on the loss of the Zuron, and the circumstances under which it had been lost, was added to the contents of the message drone. Ned had calculated the degree of force required to snap the camera shaft; the figure should raise a few eyebrows on Galestral. The team kept its speculations to itself. Speculation in that area remained Farquhar's business at present.

They dispatched the drone, had their breakfast, set out.

Ned had taken Grant at his word and stretched out in the back of the car to catch up on sack time lost by the dawn patrol. Jill, not at all sleepy, took the seat behind Grant, Suesvant lying across her knees. Her thoughts roamed, tinged with discontent.

Galestral, the Galestral Company, and the Star Union . . . the only significant powers in this galactic region. Perhaps equal powers effectively, though Galestral maintained a stable population of thirty-two million people, while the Star Union's citizens numbered over half a billion—but half a billion scattered widely in space cities and mobile asteroid bases, divided further by political manipulations and walker and swimmer factions. Now that the Galestral Company had begun to move back into space, there'd been the risk of a serious clash of interests with the Star Union.

The Santrask Agreement, set up eight years before, had been designed to minimize that risk. It regulated the exploitation of uncolonized and unclaimed worlds for the benefit of any human government willing to abide by its terms. The discovery of a profusion of heavy metal pockets on Kulkoor had been the first significant test of the Agreement. Their value was immense and estimates of the value kept being increased as surveys continued. If it hadn't been immense, the exploitation of Kulkoor couldn't have been considered. It lay almost at the rim of explored space, as distant from the closest Star Union bases as from Galestral, still farther from most of the scattered colony worlds of the minor Santrask powers. Even message drones took weeks to reach it. Ferrying in and maintaining equipment for large-scale mining operations would be a project which should strain the resources of the Galestral Company and the Star Union. The lesser Santrask signatories couldn't begin to undertake such projects. The Star Union would act as their agent on Kulkoor.

And now the operations had been stalled before they began. Kulkoor had presented the human intruders with a riddle . . .

Superficially, it mightn't seem too significant. Grant and Jill had been among the first survey teams assigned to Kulkoor. Starting out on an uncharted area one morning, they'd spotted mining machinery and a space shuttle on a forested mountain slope below. Legitimate mining work wasn't scheduled to begin for more than another year. They'd notified other teams, dropped down to investigate.

Some surface mining had been done in the area. The shuttle was partly loaded with ore. But nobody was in sight; and the machines evidently hadn't been used recently. It wasn't until they'd landed that they discovered the camp, set up among trees nearby and concealed from the sky by a camouflage effect. The camp area was silent, appeared deserted, but they waited until another Galestral car was circling overhead before they approached it, Suesvants held fire-ready.

Jill could recall the growing eeriness of that experience. Brown forest mold, small clumps of dry vegetation, dead branches littered the camp, carried in by gusts of wind. A few small animals scuttled away from them. Nothing else stirred. They saw what should be the control shack some fifty yards from the point they'd entered. They went up to it, moving warily. The shack had no windows, and its door was closed. While Jill covered him from twelve feet away, Grant touched the door handle, shifted it cautiously. Unlocked. Holding the Suesvant in one hand, he threw the door back.

The interior of the shack was brightly lit and obviously unoccupied. They didn't enter immediately. From the door, their gaze shifted about the room. Office of the camp boss. Control panel along one wall. Glassy shimmer of a dust and small-vermin screen across the doorspace. The normal degree of disorder . . . From the appearance of it, whoever had worked here might have stepped out of the place ten minutes ago. Jill's skin was prickling; she wasn't sure why.

Grant went in, opened the camouflage field switch. Pools of pale sunlight appeared suddenly in the camp area between the trees. A third aircar had arrived by then. Its crew joined Grant and Jill, and they went through the rest of the camp. There was no one, living or dead, in the shelters, nothing to indicate that the eruption of some local plague had driven away the men. Nor was there anything to suggest violence or a planned departure. The camp looked normal except for the degree of disturbance which could be accounted for by prowling animals, wind and rain. The machinery was set up to work. The miners' personal belongings lay about in the shelters; it was possible to calculate from them that there had been forty-three men quartered here. Light and heating systems were functioning, and most of the force screens designed to keep vermin out of the shelters were powered. The camouflage field was nearly exhausted.

What had become of the men? The shuttle had been their only link with the ore carrier which had brought them to Kulkoor but presumably had come no closer than the flow of meteorite clouds nearest the planet where it would have been almost safe from chance detection. And the shuttle stood here, as enigmatic as the rest of it. Where had they gone? Why had they gone?

The questions remained unanswered. Biotracker readings indicated there had been no human beings in the camp area for at least a month before Grant and Jill arrived. The ore carrier presumably had left when the shuttle failed to return from the planet. Nothing was found to show from where it had come. The shuttle and most of the other machinery were Star Union manufacture, decades old. They could have been picked up almost anywhere. Personal belongings provided no clues. A ragtag outfit, probably from some regressed walker colony, which had got wind of the Kulkoor bonanza and considered it worth the long haul to slip in and load up what it could before authorized mining operations began and the planet came under a degree of surveillance which made private projects impossible.

That was the appearance of it.

It could have been a deliberate mystification. It could have been a number of other things, which might or might not turn out to have wider significance. In any case, every effort must be made to explain what had happened before major operations on Kulkoor were started. The Galestral Company and Cencom were agreed on that. They went about their efforts to obtain the explanation in different ways.

The Galestral Company proceeded by the book, by the disciplined rules established in the conquest of its own planet. It left three observers and a scout ship stationed on Kulkoor, hauled off its other personnel. Grant Gage and Jill Hastings were two of the observers. They were selected for the job because, of the people then on Kulkoor, they were, by their record, the best qualified to handle it. Because there was, also by their record, a streak of the nonconformist in both of them, they were joined by Ned Brock, almost as qualified and by nature a Company man, a stabilizing influence in the team. They were skilled, highly trained people; they weren't to stick out their necks in this matter. A specialist would be sent to do that. The Galestral Company was frugal in the use of human resources. Those it used were expendable when the purpose was worth the price, but they weren't expended if calculation could prevent it.

Cencom, with less direct experience in dealing with abnormal planetary conditions, set up a test project staffed with a hundred and fifty people, to subject Kulkoor to overall analysis during a planned ten-month period. The problem, if it existed, should be brought to light somewhere along the line. The peril, if it arose, would be met by conventional means; the Base was protected by defensive and offensive armament. The sentinel ship, stationed in synchronous orbit above the Base, was equipped to evacuate all personnel as a last resort.

The Star Union project was now beginning its third month. A mapping crew of two had been lost with their aircar. The indications were that they'd attempted to fly through a violent storm in mountainous country. No trace of car or crew had been found; but no one seemed inclined to blame the Kulkoor Problem for the disappearance. An occasional accident of that kind could be expected.

There'd been no other losses.

Jill sighed. The Star Union, by its own lights, was also going by the book on Kulkoor. And the book was getting old. Throughout its two hundred and sixty-three years of existence, Cencom, the tunneled planetoid, still the most formidable space fortress known, had been the Star Union's strategic center. The Galestral Company wasn't much younger.

Between them, they'd grown to dominate the area. You were a Star Union citizen—walker or swimmer; essentially space-oriented, space-housed, in either case. Or you were a working shareholder of the Galestral Company. Galestral was as magnificent a world as Earth ever could have been, but it was the only world like that around. Ragnor never had been able to support as much as half a million Mailliards; and the Mailliards had been regressing technologically for decades before they tangled with the Star Union. Scores of colonies on other worlds led a marginal existence, or dropped below it and failed. Kulkoor, though four fifths of its land surface was cold desert, might have made a better man home than almost all of them.

But that was the way it was at present. Men had moved away from Earth, come this far. Planets that weren't fit for human habitation remained inexhaustible sources of raw material. Motion had stopped; it was time for organization, for consolidation. The Star Union was formed; and presently the Galestral Company split away from the Star Union, conquered the almost unconquerable native terrors of Galestral, and held the planet against all human comers until no more felt tempted to come.

Consolidation continued. It became stagnation, Jill thought. There'd been no change in basic ship design in three hundred years. The ships were good—but only that. They didn't have the range to go unsupported out of this sterile area, far enough to leave the Star Union and the Galestral Company behind.

Far enough to break the strings.

7
..

IT TOOK ALMOST two days to locate the swimmer ship. As Captain Bymer had predicted, it was skimming the fringes of a dense meteor cloud when spotted. It might have spotted the sentinel simultaneously. It edged into the hurtling space avalanche, vanished from instrument detection. It didn't reappear.

Bymer said, "If he tries to cut through that sludge, he's had it! He won't try."

"So where is he?" said Crowell.

"He's put down somewhere—some big rock near the point of entry. He'll come out eventually. But if we wait for that, we may lose him."

"Then let's not wait." Crowell was beginning to like Captain Bymer.

They found the swimmer presently, sitting at the bottom of a deep ragged crevice in one of the larger meteorite chunks. When they signaled it, it drove up from the crevice, guns blazing. The action lasted barely twenty seconds. Then the swimmer was hulled, silenced and blinded, spinning through space. Captain Bymer held fire. A string of spacesuited figures spurted from the wreck. They made no attempt to escape; there was nowhere to go.

An hour later, a fresh load of prisoners was in the personnel freezer, and the sentinel ship was on its way back to Kulkoor. They hadn't tried to board the swimmer. With its power dead, it was being chewed up by the drift before the last survivor of its crew had been brought into the sentinel.

❋   ❋   ❋

Crowell had intended to interrogate some of the captured swimmers at length before returning to the Base. But when he got in contact with Guy Hansen to let him know the period of communicator silence was over, Hansen said, "I think you'd better come down as soon as you can, Crowell."

"Why?" Crowell asked.

"For one thing, you'll have an opportunity to meet that mysterious Galestral biota analyst. Farquhar's spending the night at Station Three."

"Good enough!" Crowell said. "We'll be there as quickly as Captain Bymer can get us back. Anything else?"

"Yes. The Zoology Department's lost a man. Alex Hays. We found his body today some five miles north of Station Three. He'd been killed by an animal—apparently a previously unrecorded species he was trying to collect. That, incidentally, is what brought Farquhar to view."

"How did Farquhar hear about it?"

Hansen said dryly, "It turns out that one person on the Base with whom he's been in fairly regular communicator contact is Dr. Freemont of Zoology. They've been exchanging information on Kulkoor fauna for the past month. It didn't occur to Freemont to mention it until now. He called Farquhar after the body was found, and Farquhar showed up at the Station some five hours later."

"He wants to look for the animal?" Crowell said.

"I'd assume it. He didn't tell Freemont his purpose.

"Do you know what general type of animal it's supposed to be?"

"A large fur-covered biped. Hays' initial report referred to it as a humanoid giant."

"A—when did he make that initial report?"

"Four planet days ago."

"And Dr. Freemont and the Zoology Department didn't think that was worth mentioning either?"

"It seems," said Hansen, "that the Zoology Department didn't take Alex Hays' story seriously."

"One might have called Alex a romantic, Captain Witter," Dr. Freemont was saying defensively a few hours later. "To put it more bluntly, he was an overly imaginative young man, and he let the characteristic interfere with his work. Zoology is understaffed, and on more than one previous occasion valuable department time was wasted in trying to follow up unsubstantiated reports made by him."

Crowell nodded. "I understand. Just what did he report on this occasion—and did he leave notes?"

"We've found no notes. But he did talk a good deal about his experience. Today I checked what he'd told me against what he'd told others, and found that his story was, in fact, rather consistent."

"You're inclined to believe it now?"

"I'm more inclined to believe it than I was. It's possible, after all, that the planet's fauna has developed a biped form, or, at any rate, a large animal which occasionally stands, even walks, on its hind legs. If so, it must be an exceedingly rare species, or it should have been sighted before. Hays was in an aircar, making a routine fauna count, when he saw it. He said he had the impression of looking down at a creature like the mythical ogres of Earth." Dr. Freemont's mouth quirked in distaste. "I took the time to question him about it. More factually then, he claimed it was a biped, with long straight legs, but massive and apelike in the upper part of the body. Its arms were long and heavy. It was apparently very large for that type of structure—Hays estimated it as eight feet in height, with a weight of well over five hundred pounds. It was furred, brown-black in color. Its head was relatively large, with pointed ears or earlike appendages. There were no weapons or other artifacts—in other words, no indications of more than animal intelligence."

Dr. Freemont reflected a moment. "I believe that sums up the description."

"It seems a quite specific one," Crowell said.

"Yes—perhaps more so than one should expect. Alex Hays evidently did see something. I'm not convinced that what he saw would match his description of it too closely."

"Why do you think that?"

The zoologist shrugged. "Hays said the creature moved quickly. He had it briefly in view at the edge of a stand of forest, saw it again some seconds later as it passed through an opening among the trees. He continued to circle above the forest for over an hour but saw no more of it. I feel he may have used his imagination to supply more than those glimpses actually showed him. He tried to persuade me to have Zoology organize a search for the biped, and collect it. I turned him down. I did call Gerson, who's in charge at Station Three, to check on the story. Gerson has worked together with Hays, and he simply laughed. He assured me there'd never been any indication of such a creature in that area, and, of course,

Station Three has gone over the entire vicinity rather thoroughly. Hays asked to be relieved of his regular duties so he could hunt the creature by himself, and I refused."

"So he went after it without authorization?" Crowell said.

"Yes. In part, I'm afraid, because his colleagues had been making something of a joke of the Hays Ogre. I didn't learn until this morning that he'd left the Base yesterday after checking out an aircar. He'd forged my signature on the permit. When he didn't reply to communicator calls, I informed Mr. Hansen that he was missing and might be in trouble."

Crowell looked over at Hansen. Hansen said, "Herrick and I went out in two cars to look for Hays. We found his car within half an hour. It was standing in the open in the general area where he'd reported seeing the biped. What was left of his body was under some bushes a hundred yards away. Part of it had been devoured. His energy carbine lay thirty feet from the body. It was almost fully charged but set to fire, and something like a fifteen-second burst had been fired from it. Apparently Hays missed."

"Apparently?" said Crowell.

Hansen said, "There were heavy rainstorms in that section during the night. They left no tracks, nothing at all to show what kind of creature killed Hays. We made a search of the surrounding ground, thinking it might have been hurt badly enough by the carbine to go into hiding nearby. We found nothing. The place is on the edge of a dense stretch of forest which extends up into the mountains, and to look further for it seemed useless."

Dr. Freemont remarked, "The condition of Hays' body, incidentally, is no proof that the killer was carnivorous. There are a number of scavenger species in the northern forests which quickly dispose of anything dead or dying."

"Was Hays a reasonably good shot?" Crowell asked.

"I would say so. He liked hunting and brought in many specimens for the department during our first weeks of operation on Kulkoor."

"I was thinking," Crowell said, "that it isn't really easy to miss something big that's coming at you with an energy carbine. He should have had it in his sights for most of those fifteen seconds."

"Unless he panicked," Hansen said.

"Yes, that's possible. What about Farquhar, Doctor? Did he comment in any way on what had happened?"

"He said only that he'd like to find out more about the creature

Hays had encountered, and asked me to arrange to have him stay over at Station Three tonight."

"You know he did show up there?"

"Yes, an hour or two after sundown. At the moment, I'm not sure of the exact time. Dan Gerson called me to say Farquhar had arrived."

Hansen said, "Would you like me to call the Station now and put you in touch with Farquhar""

Crowell shook his head, looked at his watch. "He may have reasons for not wanting to be in touch with me. The night's almost over anyway. Lieutenant Tegeler and I will fly out to the Station immediately and try to catch Farquhar before he wakes up."

It was barely first light when Crowell's repaired car came drifting down toward Station Three. The Station was a low wide structure, built against and partly into a rocky slope, two hundred feet below a dark line of forest along the crest of the slope. Ilken, watching the ground screen, said, "Two cars parked down there. Only one belongs to the Station. So Farquhar's still around."

Crowell didn't comment. Mists half veiled the slopes; he hadn't been able to distinguish the cars. A moment later, Ilken frowned. "There's—" Her voice paused; then she said, "Hold the car, Crowell!"

He checked their descent, looked quickly over at her. "Something wrong?"

"Hard to make out." She was adjusting the screen, nodded suddenly. "Take a look!" Her tone was flat.

The two cars were shadowy in the screen, but Crowell could make them out. There was something oddly distorted about their positions and outlines. He stared. "You'd think they'd been hit by a rock slide!"

"They've been smashed," Ilken agreed. "Smashed up bad!" They exchanged a glance, and she got to her feet, moved over to the gun and slipped into position there. Crowell was tapping out a number on the communicator. After a moment, he said, "Herrick? We're hanging above Station Three. See if you can raise them on Base comm in there. If there's no response, get out here fast with a couple of armed cars!"

8
..

"CAPTAIN WITTER," the voice of the Base comm operator said, "the three Galestral people have just arrived. They asked Dr. Bates to show them the bodies, and they're with him now. Mr. Hansen will come out to Station Three with them."

"Thanks," Crowell said. "I'll be waiting."

He switched off his wrist transmitter and glanced down the slope at Station Three. The smashed entry door was visible at this angle; and though he was upwind of the Station now, the stench of death still seemed to be in his nostrils. A shadow drifted over the rocks, and he looked up at his car moving slowly fifty feet above. It was a flat platform at present, its canopy collapsed. Ilken was at the gun, and Bill Tabor, one of the Base's car operators, at the controls. Their attention was on the forest at the top of the slope. Two other armed cars hung in the sky a quarter-mile up, scopes scanning the area. Crowell's hand brushed the gun holster on his hip, obeying a half-conscious need to make sure the weapon was there, though by itself it shouldn't be much protection if whatever had ravaged Station Three during the night chose to return.

Fifteen minutes later, the Galestral car settled to the ground farther up the slope. Hansen climbed out first, followed by the three members of the survey team. "I've told them the circumstances about Hays," Hansen said as they approached.

Crowell nodded, looking at the Galestrals. Their Suesvant rifles were slung across their backs; bandoliers crossed their chests. They'd been informed earlier that Frank Farquhar had disappeared and evidently hadn't been in the Station when it was attacked. "We'll

470

show you what it's like in there," Crowell said. "Then we can compare conclusions."

The three went matter-of-factly about their examination of the interior shambles of Station Three, faces showing sober alertness but almost nothing in the way of emotion. Crowell and Hansen, who had gone over the Station in detail before, looked on. Things had been left as they'd been found, except that the bodies of the four technicians who'd staffed the Station had been removed. Patches of stickily dried blood covered sections of the floor; insect-like creatures crawled and flew about the patches. The smells of violent death hung in the air.

Apparently, only one killer had come in. Two well-defined foot-prints showed on the smeared floor of the main room. They weren't unlike the impressions a naked human foot might have left, though larger and proportionately broader. Both were of the same foot— a foot sixteen inches long from the end of the heel to the most advanced of the four thick toe marks, six and a half inches across at the widest point. The kind of foot required to support the giant frame which had raised and swung a great rock, over three hundred pounds at an estimate, to drive the entry door back into the Station. The rock still lay across the door's shattered sections.

Smeared dark patterns of other footprints, very much smaller ones, were visible near the entrance, crossing through the short hall into the main area. They appeared to be those of scavenging animals which had come into the Station later at night, after the killer had left. Furnishings and equipment in the main room were knocked about and smashed. Two heavy-charge shock guns hung untouched on the wall near the entrance.

Ned Brock picked up a packed knapsack from behind an over-turned table and placed it on a chair.

"Farquhar's," he commented. He added after a moment, "So he just picked up his Suesvant and walked out . . ."

In the adjoining instrument room, the picture was much the same. One of the two station chronometers had been shattered. Crowell pointed it out, said, "It's indicating sixteen hours eight minutes Base Time. Which fixes the time of the attack at approxi-mately three hours after nightfall. They were still at work here." He nodded at a handgun on the floor. "That's been identified as Dan Gerson's. Gerson was the man who was dictating a report into the recorder in this room at the moment of the attack."

Grant Gage asked, "Has the gun been fired?"

"Yes," Crowell said. "We found it with its trigger locked down and its charge expended. There's still a measurable radiation residue in the room. His body was lying a few yards away from it."

"The others were killed in the main room?"

"Two of them were. Ray Cross and Edwin Raines." Crowell nodded at a shattered doorframe across the room. "The fourth, Wilma Howard, died in the sleeping section beyond that door."

Grant said, "Could we hear the recording of the attack?"

The recorder into which Gerson was dictating hadn't been damaged in the violent action in the room and was still running when Crowell, Ilken and Herrick came into the Station in the morning. As a result, they had an audible record of the attack and of the night hours that followed.

The significant section wasn't long. Biologist Gerson's voice was interrupted by the explosively abrupt shattering of the entrance door. He exclaimed something, the words drowned out by snarling roars, human yells, thudding noises. The roars swelled up, ended suddenly with the rest of the racket. Then, after some seconds, came a splintering crash which marked the destruction of the sleeping section door. The beast's snarls rose again, subsided. The last of its victims had died. Vague sounds continued to come from the machine—an intermittent deep rumbling, a wet slapping. Occasionally a piece of equipment crashed. The noises produced unpleasantly vivid impressions of the intruder prowling about, making a deliberate search for hidden survivors, pausing from time to time to tear at one of the bodies again. At last the Station grew quiet. It had gone.

Crowell shut off the recorder, said, "All four died within less than two minutes. I had the tapes scanned for the rest of the night. There's nothing to indicate that the creature came back to the Station. It broke up the two aircars with rocks, as you saw, and then apparently went away."

He added, "Unless there's something else you want to check here, shall we go outside and try to determine what this means, and what should be done about it?"

Everything indicated that the attacker was a creature of the type described by Alex Hays. In fact, it could very well have been the one he'd reported seeing and which probably had killed him not many miles from this point. It might have been watching Station Three from concealment for some time. It had known enough, at any rate, to select the entry door as its point of assault.

And it had—must have—some degree of immunity to energy weapons. Crowell said, "I've heard that a number of Galestral's superbeasts can absorb heavy charges without being stopped."

The three nodded. Grant said, "There are species which generate energy blasts for attack or defense. Others developed a corresponding tolerance for them. But nothing's been found on Kulkoor to explain why this biped should have the ability."

"No," Crowell said. "Of course, we may be finding the explanation before we're done. In any case, the biped does seem to have it. Going by the Galestral animals, could a creature like that stand up against guncar fire?"

Grant shook his head. "Not for a significant length of time—if you could get it to face a guncar."

"That might be a problem," Crowell conceded.

Ned Brock said, "A point that puzzles me is that there's a standard force screen control panel in the Station's entrance hall. The rock couldn't have damaged the door if the Station screen had been on. Why should it have been switched off—particularly when someone had been killed in the area two days before?"

And that was, as a matter of fact, a rather delicate point. Crowell said, "We have no explanation. The outlying stations have instructions to maintain protective screening except when personnel enters or leaves. The rule seems to have been violated here last night."

Grant said after a moment, "The screen can be opened from outside the Station?"

"Yes," Crowell said. "That's a necessary provision. But you have to know the coded key for an individual screen to do it."

Hansen added, "That's only one of several unexplained details. What do you make of Farquhar's interest in the biped and the fact that he wasn't in the Station when the thing showed up?"

"I could make a guess about that," Grant said. "He may already have been aware there was such a life form around. His immediate response to the information he got from your Base suggests it. And he may have attached some special significance to that life form."

Hansen said dryly, "Meaning he considered it a possible clue to the Kulkoor Mystery?"

"Or the Kulkoor Problem, as the Galestral Company calls it. Yes, he may have. Farquhar wouldn't have asked permission to make Station Three his temporary quarters for any minor reason. I'll carry that farther. The Station's area scanners are turned off. But Farquhar may have been using them before he left. He might have caught a glimpse of the biped prowling about, and gone out after it without telling the Station staff what he'd seen or what he intended. It would be in keeping with the way he preferred to operate—strictly by himself."

Grant added, "We can assume the biped ambushed and killed him before it attacked the Station."

9

HEAVY RAINS HAD fallen in the area again overnight, and any visible tracks around Station Three had been washed away before morning. But the Galestrals had brought along a device with which they expected to be able to follow both Farquhar's trail and that of the biped. Jill Hastings explained it briefly to Crowell while Ned Brock registered the biped's pattern on it in the main room. "He's screening out all but the strongest readings here and discarding the ones connected with human beings and nonliving materials," she said. "The biped's scent will be the most definite one left. Once it's registered, it can be picked up again anywhere. So can biped trails then as a class. Farquhar's individual pattern already is on record in the biotracker."

Guy Hansen had been flown back to the Star Union Base meanwhile, to keep an eye on developments in Crowell's continuing absence. There had been a moment of barely perceptible hesitation on the Galestrals' part when Crowell said he would accompany them on foot in their search for Farquhar. But they didn't argue the matter. He'd decided to carry one of the shock guns which had been part of Station Three's defensive equipment. Even for a man of his strength, they were awkwardly heavy weapons; and they had neither the sustained charge of energy guns or much range. But at close quarters their jolt supposedly would put almost anything that walked at least temporarily out of action.

Ned Brock's biotracker picked up Farquhar's trail readily outside the Station entrance. They set off up the slope. Ilken and the Base operator would attempt to accompany the ground party in Crowell's car, keeping close to the forest roof. Half a mile up, the crew of a second guncar was to scan the wider area for indications of anything that might be of significance, while another operator would follow with the Galestral car, his job being chiefly to keep the vehicle aloft and ready for use.

The invisible spoor led to the forest, turned there into a narrow game trail. It was more open under the trees than Crowell had expected. The thick canopies were frequently interlaced, but around the trunks the undergrowth was sparse. There were signs of minor life, small voice sounds near and far, sudden scuttlings, and bursts of whirring flight. The Galestrals moved silently, rather like searching hounds, Crowell thought—Ned Brock in the lead with the biotracker, Crowell some twenty-five feet behind him, and the other two on Crowell's right and left. After a few minutes, Crowell realized this was a formation into which he'd been quietly fitted, and that the purpose of the formation, however much it shifted because of the growth through which they passed, was to ensure that Ned Brock was covered at all times by the Suesvant of one of the others, while he himself remained covered by both. He felt a momentary flush of annoyance at the last, told himself to forget it. Personnel of the Galestral Space Exploration Corps reportedly received a lengthy conditioning among the formidable denizens of their planet's wildlands. His companions had some reason to regard him as an amateur in this business.

Ned Brock checked abruptly, slid the tracking device into a pocket. Crowell, stopping almost as abruptly, brought up the shock gun. Grant and the girl were immobile. A wide thicket of denser growth lay ahead and to the left, some forty feet away, a matted gray-green tangle, sodden from the rains. Crowell watched it, wondering what they had noticed. Ned had raised his Suesvant, and Jill was drawing off to the left, edging in toward the thicket. She stopped; and Ned was in motion, closing up on the growth from the right, while Grant came past Crowell. Crowell had a momentary impulse to join that stealthy advance, and again told himself to forget it; they were moving with absolute stillness, in a manner beyond his ability here—if he stirred, he might spoil their game. And if something did break from the thicket, he could get into the action from where he stood.

Moist coolness touched the back of his neck. Wind shift-blowing now toward the thicket. The Galestrals stood still.

Then the tops of the thicket shook; there were crashings inside the vegetation. Crowell had a glimpse of a large chunky body scuttling on four short legs away from the thicket on the far side of Jill. It was followed by another. In moments, both beasts had disappeared in the forest.

Crowell let his breath out with a sigh.

He realized he was drawing approving glances from the Galestrals as they resumed formation; and he felt curiously pleased.

Some ten minutes later, they found Farquhar's Suesvant rifle. Ned Brock again was leading the way, along an animal trail which followed a small stream. The forest was relatively open here, and Crowell had occasional glimpses of his car moving overhead. Evidently they were registering in the scanners frequently enough to be followed without difficulty. On the far side of the stream a steep bank rose to a height of around twenty to twenty-five feet above them; and Crowell was aware that Grant and Jill were giving the upper edge of the bank a good deal of attention.

Ned said quietly, "Here's where it got him!"

Farquhar's body wasn't there. But that this was in fact the place where he'd been killed became quickly obvious. Rocks had been the biped's weapon again—two large rocks hurled with what must have been remarkable accuracy from the top of the bank beyond the stream. Deep marks in the side of the bank showed where the creature had come sliding down then to finish off Farquhar if he hadn't been killed outright. It had left its footprints in the mud. The Suesvant lay nearby, barrel twisted and action smashed.

Ned cast about with the biotracker, and the story grew clear. Having drawn Farquhar here and killed him, the biped had gone to Station Three, done its work and returned to this point by another route to pick up Farquhar's body and carry it off.

They set out again. Crowell felt renewed tensions growing in him. The biped might not be far away, though it had been almost ten hours since it passed through here. This seemed to be its territory; they could come on it at any time. Ned lifted the tracker now and then, moved it along the bushes they were passing and checked the readings. Crowell realized he was picking up scent traces left by the biped or Farquhar's body where they had brushed against the growth. Then Ned glanced back, announced, "Open ground ahead!"

The trees thinned out. They emerged on a shallow rocky plateau leading to a wide, rushing stream. Ahead and to the left, on the far side of the stream, rose forested mountain slopes. On the right was a glacier lake, deep cold blue, perhaps two miles across.

"It headed straight for the stream," Ned said.

❀   ❀   ❀

And in the stream the trail was lost. The biotracker couldn't pick up scent traces half a day old from a swiftly moving body of water. The car crews had nothing to report. For the next hour, Ned Brock moved up and down both sides of the stream, covered by two car guns. But the tracker's readings showed neither human nor biped traces.

To the west, the stream poured out of a narrow mountain gorge, crowded with luxuriant vegetation. To the east, it emptied into the quiet lake. "What do you think's happened?" Crowell asked Grant Gage. They were by themselves at the moment, standing at the edge of the stream.

Grant shrugged. "The thing's either followed the water back into the mountains or into the lake. If it wasn't attempting to cover its trail, it may be naturally amphibious. It may have carried Farquhar's body on with it or buried it under rocks in the stream."

"In either case," said Crowell, "we're not very likely to recover the body now."

"No, we're not."

"You'll abandon the search?"

"No," Grant said, "we won't abandon the search."

Crowell was silent a moment, said, "If the particular biped we were following is located and killed eventually, its body may show indications that it's stopped previous radiation charges. That would prove it was in fact a biped which attacked Station Three and probably killed Hays before that. But we can already say as much. What else could be proved by continuing the hunt?"

"I don't know," said Grant. He rubbed his jaw reflectively. "We tried to contact you two days ago.

"I know. I was off-planet and out of communication at the time, getting the swimmer ship rounded up. We managed to do that. I came back early this morning because I'd been told Farquhar was in Station Three. So I went there to talk to him before he'd disappear again."

"Yes, I understand. The reason we were trying to contact you is that we thought *we* might have got a clue to the Kulkoor Mystery."

"What was that?" Crowell asked.

Grant told him about the vanished Zuron camera and their speculations. Mountain mists had covered the areas where the big fliers had been observed previously; they hadn't so far been able to kill and examine one. "If it was one of those creatures which broke off the camera, and if it was done deliberately," he said, "we've had, within a few days, demonstrations of calculated hostility against human beings by two different Kulkoor species."

Crowell was frowning. "A biped couldn't have taken the camera?"

"Not unless it was walking on air. Ned went over the surrounding area thoroughly with the biotracker. Whatever took the camera left no trace of itself."

"The biped certainly has given evidence of considerable intelligence," Crowell remarked.

"Yes. Perhaps at the level of the primitive human savage. Perhaps more than that."

"And if your flier is at a similar level of intelligence—"

"Then we seem to have a biologically unstable situation on Kulkoor," Grant said. "One of the two should be the planet's dominant species by now—and a relatively and obviously numerous one. The other should be extinct, or nearly so. Particularly here, where the fertile land forms something like a linked chain of large islands around the equatorial zone, surrounded by desert. There's no room for two competing intelligent species, unless there's something like an instinctive alliance or truce between them."

"As I understand there was among some of the more advanced native life forms on Galestral," Crowell said.

"Something like that. On Galestral it was hardly a truce since they preyed on one another. But they did maintain a balance and apparently had been doing it for a very long time. And they united against the human intruder."

"You think that might be happening here?"

"It could explain what's happened so far," Grant said. "Kulkoor's intelligent life may be trying to frighten us off, get rid of us, without revealing too much about itself."

Crowell said slowly, "If that's the case, it could delay large-scale operations for quite a while."

"Yes, it could," Grant said. "Here's how the situation will look to the Galestral Company. Before we left the ship, we sent off a drone to report Farquhar's disappearance and the general circumstances under which it occurred. We'll report now that we have evidence of his death. We've told you that we're stationed here as Farquhar's backup team. The fact that he didn't choose to make use of us in his work, and refused to give us any information about it, doesn't change that. We'll pick up where he left off—and, of course, we have new material to work on now. We'll report at regular intervals to the Company, which appears to be as much in the dark about any actual progress made by Farquhar as we are. So long as it seems that we might be able to solve the problem, the Company will wait. If we stop reporting, or if they hear from you that we've failed, they'll make their next move."

Crowell said, "Meaning they'll send out somebody else?"

"Yes. Who'll be sent and what the new group will be equipped to do is something I can't say."

"By failing you mean that the three of you will have been killed—"

"Yes. Since we don't know what we're up against, that's certainly a possibility."

"How will I know you've failed, and how would I get word to the Galestral Company about it?"

"We'll be in contact with you. If the contact is broken and you're unable to reestablish it, you can assume failure. We'll leave a message drone, set to Company coordinates, at your Base. Tell them as much as you can and dispatch it."

Crowell was silent a moment. "The Base setup is mainly a defensive one," he said then. "But I'd like to take a more active part in this. I'll have this general area and the one around the mining campsite kept under aerial surveillance. Can you think of anything else?"

"Not at present," Grant told him. "We'll be trying to find the biped, and a small hunting party is more likely to be successful in that than a large one. We don't want to drive the thing into hiding."

"Yes, I see." Crowell felt dissatisfied. Grant added, "The dangers of the situation aren't all here, of course. Kulkoor has become too valuable a prize. If the matter isn't cleared up quickly, there'll be new suspicions raised."

"No doubt there will be," Crowell agreed. "But there's no reason so far to start thinking in terms of a superbeast that might have been imported from Galestral."

"Not yet," said Grant. "There's no Galestral superbeast that matches the description of the biped. But that could be difficult to prove."

"Are there any that could account for the missing camera?"

"Several." Grant hesitated. "Captain Witter, we're aware that though you represent Cencom here, you haven't always found yourself in accord with Cencom's policies."

Crowell smiled briefly. "Lieutenant Tegeler told me your sick bay is equipped with a very effective truth drug."

"Yes, it's a dependable one. We're Galestral Company sharehold-ers and we work for the Company. But that also doesn't mean that we'd necessarily be in agreement with specific Company policies—or informed of them."

Crowell nodded. "Not when the stakes are large enough. I realize that. We'd better not tie ourselves down to any one theory . . ."

"And now," Ned Brock said as the survey team's car started back to their ship, "what will be the procedure? If the thing wanted to lose trackers, it picked a good place for it. It could go upstream or down. If it's at home in the water, the lake was less than half a mile away. If it likes the rocks, it had the mountains right there. Trying to pick up its trail again could turn into a long chore."

"So we won't try to pick up its trail," said Grant. "It was first seen in daylight—it's diurnal when it feels like it. When we get back, let's look around by car generally. We still might get a glimpse of the thing or another of its kind today. If we don't, we'll change tactics. Judging by what we know of it now, this is a creature which waits and watches quietly until it has the advantage. Then it goes in to kill. It doesn't bluster or bluff."

Ned said, "I see . . . and we know its general territory."

"And that it hates aircars," Jill added. She nodded. "If we make a nuisance of ourselves around the territory long enough, it should start looking for an opportunity to get to us."

They sent a drone report to the Galestral Company from the ship, returned to the Star Union Base with another drone for Crowell's use, if required, and, by mid-afternoon of the planet day, were back above the stream where the trail had been lost. They moved downstream and on along the fringes of the lake. For the most part, the lake walls were steep and rocky, but here and there forest growth spread to the water's edge. They saw assorted forms of animal life but nothing resembling a great brown biped.

Presently they came back, moved up the stream past the point where the biped's trail had entered the water. A mile on, the stream cascaded out of a deep narrow gorge in the mountain. The car slipped into the gorge. Luxuriant vegetation crowded the walls on both sides. Spray misted the air. There were endless hiding places here for even quite large creatures, and a man on foot would find difficult going. They lifted out of the gorge finally. The car circled above the area enclosing Station Three, the stream, the flanks of the mountains.

"All right, let's start being obnoxious," Grant said. "We'll be thorough about it! Then we'll give the thing—or things—an opening."

They went on shift from then on, one handling the car, one watching the scanners, one sleeping or resting. The car drifted about, almost aimlessly. It floated along open ground, hung close above the tops of trees, sometimes nosed in below the forest canopy for a few hundred yards. Repeatedly it visited the gorge, the edge of the lake, circled slowly about Station Three. Now and then they saw a Star Union aircar moving through the sky above them.

The day wore on.

10

. . .

"WHAT ARE YOU going to do?" Ilken asked Crowell.

He grunted. "Assume the worst."

"Why?"

"The thing smells. The picture's wrong! I don't like coincidences."

Her pale eyes studied him. "You don't think Farquhar's dead?"

"Oh, he's dead," Crowell said sourly. "That part—but I'd like to know why he's dead!" He added, "Something's being wound up tight here. I want to have all the room possible to move in when it's set off."

"You haven't got much of a story yet to sell the people."

"I'll sell them on it."

Crowell had Station Three sealed, its force screen locked from without, before returning to the Star Union Base. On the Base, he called the department heads to a meeting in Dr. Sutton's office.

They came eagerly, anxious to learn the details of what had occurred.

Crowell told them. It had been shown that an intelligent, dangerous life form existed on Kulkoor. Within three days, six human beings had been killed, apparently by a single specimen which had planned its attacks carefully and had demonstrated at least partial immunity to portable energy weapons.

"So far, we can't say what other qualities it has," he said. "The Galestral survey team is at present attempting to locate the biped which attacked Station Three and kill it for analysis. They're better equipped for that job than we are."

"In what way?" said one of the men.

"They have a sophisticated tracking instrument. They've been trained to hunt the most dangerous kinds of game known. And I believe most of you are aware that the Suesvant rifles they use as personal weapons were designed specifically to deal with superbeasts."

There was an uneasy stir. Dr. Sutton said, "You're not implying that this biped animal—dangerous as it evidently is—can be classed with some of the Galestral monsters?"

"No, I'm not implying it," Crowell said. "But until we know how it's to be classed, we'll act as if there were a species of superbeasts confronting us on Kulkoor. That involves giving the Galestral team all the support we can—chiefly by getting our guncars freed for action. It involves further putting this Base immediately on emergency status. The work parties operating off-Base today already are being recalled, and I want each of you to see to it at once that the outlying stations connected with your departments are closed down and the personnel returned to the Base before nightfall."

There were startled protests. Important work was being carried on in the stations. Much of it couldn't be transferred to the Base. Vital projects would be ruined if they didn't get continuous direct attention. So drastic a measure hardly seemed indicated—the stations were well-protected structures and the personnel now had been alerted to the possibility of danger.

Crowell listened briefly before he said, "Gentlemen, please keep one thing in mind! This Base—the entire Kulkoor Expedition—is itself an experimental Cencom project. Your scientific work is of great importance. I'd be the last to deny it. But the primary purpose of the Cencom project is to determine whether operations on Kulkoor can be carried out through semi-open bases such as this. It's by far the most economical approach. But you wouldn't be here now if there hadn't already been some question as to whether it's possible. You're drawing risk pay with good reason. Cencom wants to see if something's going to happen to you. If something does, it will be necessary to consider other methods."

"We're quite aware of being technically expendable, Captain Witter," Dr. Sutton said stiffly.

"Fine," Crowell said. "And if that turns out to be more than a technicality, I'm here, among other things, to try to keep casualties to a minimum. That again must override other considerations. It's quite possible that the next few days will bring proof that the biped is not an abnormally dangerous creature and that standard precautions will be all that's necessary to prevent a recurrence of what happened last night at Station Three. In that case, the stations will be reopened and the general work program resumed. But at present you'll regard yourselves as part of a defensive military operation. I'll allow no deviations from it. Anyone who refuses to go along will be frozen and sent back to Cencom on the next supply ship."

Dr. Sutton said, "We'll have to follow your instructions. But you show more confidence in the Galestrals than some of us feel. I think that's an aspect of the matter that requires further discussion."

Crowell nodded. "I agree. There'll be another meeting later in the day at which it will be discussed. We'll assemble again after you've carried out your orders."

Herrick already had put the Base on alert status. The defense screens were closed, guards stationed at the locks. The rotary gun towers which could sweep the surrounding area with devastating thoroughness were manned. A majority of Dr. Sutton's scientists might remain unhappy about the interruption of pet projects, but Crowell didn't much care. He dispatched a message drone to Administrator Ogilvy on Cencom, to report what had happened, what he was doing and intended to do, then checked to make sure the evacuation of the stations had begun and would be completed before dark. The departments evidently were cooperating, though grudgingly. The experimental ranch animals could shift for themselves in the enclosed areas set up for them for as much as several weeks.

Crowell said to Ilken, "Let's pay a call on Betheny."

"About the swimmer bunch that's on Kulkoor somewhere?" Ilken said.

"Yes. Now we've knocked out the ship, I'm less concerned about them. But I'd sooner have them out of the way."

"I can't see Betheny obliging you about that," Ilken said.

She was right. Betheny said, not too pleasantly, that she didn't know what Crowell was talking about.

Crowell shrugged. "You've been told what's going on," he said. "It's a situation that could work to the advantage of the Swimmer League as much as to Cencom's. Why not take your chances on it? Your men on Kulkoor can't do you much good now. I'll bring your transmitter here, and you can contact them and tell them to come in peaceably. There's no point in trying to fake up a menace on the planet when we seem to have one on hand that's real."

"As to that," said Betheny, "I may have a great deal to say presently. But not now, and not to you."

"You'll get your chance to do all the talking you want to in the next few hours," Crowell told her.

They left Betheny's null-g installation, went to Herrick's office. Herrick looked around from his desk as Crowell drew the door shut behind them.

"Herrick," Crowell said, "how many of our personnel would be required to maintain and, if necessary, fight the Base?"

Herrick didn't blink an eye. "Forty-eight," he said. "I've listed their names."

Captain Bymer's voice said from the communicator, "A total evacuation of the Kulkoor Base would, of course, require the services of a supply ship. The next one due—"

Crowell interrupted. "I'm talking about an emergency evacuation of personnel only. Some two thirds or possibly all of them. How long would it take you to shuttle between a hundred and a hundred and fifty people up to the sentinel and start feeding them into the freezers?"

There was a moment's silence.

"Perhaps four hours, once preparations for it have been made," Bymer said then.

"How much time do you need for the preparations?"

"That's a seventy-five-hour process, Captain Witter."

"How about cutting it to twenty hours?"

"A technical impossibility! We'd overload the standard life support systems and paralyze the ship."

"All right," Crowell said. "How much *can* you shave from those seventy-five hours?"

Another pause, a longer one, before Bymer's voice told him, "Conceivably the period might be reduced to forty hours before commencing to load. I can't recommend that unless there is a valid and pressing emergency."

Crowell looked at his watch, said, "I don't know that there'll be an emergency. But start preparations now, on the forty-hour schedule—and don't consider it a drill! As far as the Base is concerned, that's what it will be at present."

"For the record, Captain Witter," Bymer said, "these instructions have been given me under Cencom Seal?"

"They have."

❀   ❀   ❀

There were startled expressions when Betheny of Varien, in the saddle of a null-g bubble and escorted by Crowell and Ilken, came into Dr. Sutton's office to attend the second meeting of the expedition's leaders.

Crowell said, "The Public Servant remains under security arrest. But a number of you have indicated that, as the representative of the Swimmer League on Kulkoor, she should have the opportunity to express her opinion on the current situation. That seems reasonable. Dr. Sutton, at the end of our previous meeting you mentioned that there were aspects connected with the Galestral survey team which needed further discussion. Would you care to develop that thought now?"

"Yes," Dr. Sutton said. "I was referring to the fact that you seemed to place complete trust in the motivations of the Galestral Company as far as Kulkoor is concerned."

Several people began to speak at once, but Betheny's voice cut coolly through those of the others. "We certainly must consider the possibility," she said, "that the murder of Star Union people is in fact part of a continuing Galestral plan to mystify and discourage Cencom until Galestral is left in effective control of Kulkoor."

It crystallized what had been the essence of a number of rumors on the Base that day. Crowell asked Dr. Sutton, "Is that what you had in mind?"

Dr. Sutton glanced uncertainly at Betheny. "I wouldn't have put it in so definite a manner," he said. "But—yes. I feel it is at least a possibility which must be taken into account now in what we plan and do."

"Let me tell you, Captain Witter," Betheny said, "what Dr. Sutton and I and a good many other people in this room and on this Base really think. It's that the Galestral Farquhar's purpose in joining the staff at Station Three last night was not necessarily the hunting of a killer beast as he implied.

"He may as easily have directed the beast to attack our personnel and concealed himself, pretending to be one of its victims, in order to strengthen the effect of the occurrence on us, and through us on Cencom."

Complete silence for a moment. Crowell said thoughtfully, "A domesticated superbeast, imported to Kulkoor by the Galestrals, eh?"

Betheny said, "Let Dr. Freemont tell you whether that would be impossible."

The zoologist looked startled. Crowell said, "Let's assume it isn't impossible. What I'd like to ask Dr. Freemont is whether he knows of a Galestral superbeast resembling in the least the giant biped described by Alex Hays."

Dr. Freemont shook his head. "No—but, of course, only a relative handful of Star Union scientists has had an opportunity to study Galestral fauna at firsthand. Most of the information we have about it was supplied by the Galestrals themselves."

"Precisely. And note, please," Betheny said to the group at large, "that it would make no real difference if Captain Witter's Galestral friends could show us what they say is Farquhar's body or an executed biped. Nobody here knows what Farquhar looks like. The staff of Station Three, who could tell us, are dead. And Galestral could afford the loss of one of its monster pets to throw us off guard."

Crowell said mildly, "It will be only a matter of a few days before our newly installed surveillance equipment is operational again. If what happened at Station Three last night was part of a larger Galestral plot—in other words, if there are Galestral men, equipment, or superbeasts, in significant numbers on Kulkoor—the fact should soon become apparent. Mr. Hansen can assure you this. And if only one superbeast was smuggled in to commit a few murders, it's difficult to see much sense to it. We might already be able to state what the facts are if the surveillance equipment hadn't been sabotaged."

Eyes shifted questioningly again to Betheny. She smiled. "Let's not be naive," she said. "Major political goals are involved here. The Swimmer League has good reason to regard Captain Witter and his Mailliard assistant as unscrupulous enemies. They are, incidentally, no longer attached to the Ragnor Rangers. They're mercenaries. Cencom hired them to act against League interests on Kulkoor. But their loyalty even to Cencom can't be taken for granted. The Galestral Company is a liberal paymaster. I believe we should regard Captain Witter's willingness to work hand in hand with the so-called Galestral survey team in solving the problem of what happened at Station Three with some skepticism. I believe also we might be safer here today if he and Lieutenant Tegeler had in fact been eliminated."

Crowell shrugged. "It's true that Lieutenant Tegeler and I retain our Ranger rank only by Cencom's courtesy, and that we're now independent specialists who were hired by Cencom to do a job on Kulkoor," he acknowledged. "I don't mind admitting that we're being paid highly to do it, and I have no strong personal objection to being called a mercenary because of that. As to whether we're also in Galestral's pay, there's obviously no point in denying such an accusation. If we were Galestral agents, we'd hardly admit it."

Betheny, he thought, had now shot her bolt. She had, in fact, done approximately what he'd brought her to the meeting to do. And there was a momentary flicker in her eyes as he spoke which indicated she'd begun to suspect it.

"Let's look instead at the wider implications here," he went on. "There may be something on Kulkoor, whether it's Galestral superbeasts or a Kulkoor phenomenon, from which we have no real protection unless we remain behind energy screens. At the moment, we're simply trying to find out whether that's true. It's quite possible that in a day or two we may be able to establish that it isn't true.

"But if it is true, we're as useless on a base of this kind, as far as any actual utilization of the planet goes, as if we were lying in our sentinel ship's personnel freezer. Cencom won't consider ferrying in vast numbers of ground fighters to develop and maintain a foothold on this planet. Many of you must be aware of the enormous expense of the limited Ragnor Campaign. You'll realize that when it comes to Kulkoor, the logistics problems would be prohibitive. That's aside from the fact that the Star Union simply doesn't have enough ground fighters on hand to deal with either an invasion force of Galestrals or some local superfauna.

"What Cencom would be forced to do is to resort to the dome system on Kulkoor. Expensive enough in itself but feasible. The domes, of course, for reasons of efficiency, would be the newest class of null-g domes, swimmer staffed. Our job is now to find out whether that's necessary. If the biped type of creature turns out to be a minor menace, one that can be handled within the present framework of operations, it won't be necessary."

He concluded, "So regardless of inconveniences and the disruption of projects it involves, I'm asking for your full cooperation these next few days to help determine what the nature of the problem is and to find a means of dealing with it."

11
. . .

THROUGH THE EVENING and the moonless Kulkoor night, the Galestrals' aircar had continued to prowl. Its searchlight fingered the ground here and there, held sometimes on startled beast shapes staring up at unaccustomed brightness.

Toward morning, the car became almost stationary, drifting slowly back and forth along a rocky slope, rarely more than twenty feet from the ground. They'd made it clear, very clear, that they were in the area. It had been impossible to remain unaware of them. And now, if there was something around that resented their presence, had been watching from cover with anger and suspicion, it was time to give the watcher an opportunity to put an end to the nuisance.

The car lifted, floated over the crest of the slope, dropped into a grassy valley behind it.

They'd selected their site at first light an hour ago—the open bowl of the valley. On the far side was a broad belt of forest; and beyond the forest was the area into which they'd followed the biped the day before, the stream where its trail had ended between mountain and lake. On this side rose overhanging cliffs.

The aircar stood in the approximate center of the valley. It was their primary bait. Jill Hastings leaned against a slanted rock beneath the massive overhang, Suesvant resting on the rock and pointed into the valley through the foliage of a lopped-off tree branch which concealed her. She was secondary bait and hunter both. The Suesvant controlled the valley bowl. If the thing they hunted came to investigate the aircar, it would have to move out of cover. They expected the car to draw it from hiding, though perhaps not for some hours. If it had been watching, it knew where they'd descended.

It might suspect the humans weren't in the grounded aircar but somewhere nearby. So it might stalk about the wooded fringes of the valley, searching first for them. Jill's view to left and right was limited by the curve of the cliff; but those approaches were covered respectively by the Suesvants of Grant and Ned, sitting in trees. She was in danger only if the biped could do what none of the great beasts of Galestral could—absorb all the varied forms of violent death the Suesvant could spit out in fractions of a second, and still keep coming. They didn't believe it could. And if it could, then Grant and Ned, each dependent now only on his own senses to warn him of the creature's approach through the forest growth, were taking a greater risk than she.

So: a trap, doubly baited, with a good probability that in one way or the other, it would be sprung. The rest was a matter of waiting. The biped had shown it was good at the waiting game. So were they.

The minutes crept along. The morning brightened slowly, darkened again as black rain clouds massed overhead. There was a sudden heavy downpour, intermittent spatterings thereafter. Thunder rumbled along the mountains. Jill's gaze moved methodically along the far sides of the valley. Now and then she used the gun scope to study some area in magnified detail. Considerable animal life was astir; between rainfalls the air seemed full of small voices. Occasionally she saw more sizable creatures in the valley and along the forest's edge. Two long-legged striped brutes prowled about the car for several minutes, studying it with silent suspicion from every angle before moving off.

She had a clump of bushes directly across the valley from her in the scope when, quite suddenly, she was looking at a head. That was all she could see of the creature; the head had been raised cautiously out of the vegetation to peer into the valley. It was a big dark head with a short muzzle, silvery eyes, pointed black ears. A shivering went down her back. Anything with a head that size was too heavy to be supported by the undergrowth. The creature was standing on the ground . . . and it stood well above the height of a man.

That section of the forest's edge was out of the others' range of vision. Jill pressed the alert button on her wrist transmitter. Immediately her skin tingled twice under the transmitter band. All right—the men were informed . . .

Now, patience. She could fire at the head, but if it didn't belong to what she was almost certain it belonged, that would spoil the whole plan. She made a minute adjustment to the Suesvant's sight. Ready, now.

The head sank back into the growth and disappeared. Jill lifted her eyes above the scope, waited. A minute passed, another. Then something moved slowly into view under the trees, a hundred feet from the place where she'd seen the head. At once, she had it back in the scope—and that was it. The biped. The Kulkoor Beast. Bulky overall build; weight perhaps approaching a quarter of a ton. Black-brown color with moss-green markings. The animal head—nothing humanoid or apelike about that head—was set on a short thick neck. Oddly irregular ridgings, like deformities, on the great chest . . .

And while all this was registering, there was the slow, growing pressure of her finger on the trigger, cross-hairs centered on the thing's ridged upper torso. Then a great whip cracked, and the Suesvant had struck across the valley. Confined, the tremendous recoil would have lifted Jill from the rock, flung her back against the cliff with bone-breaking force. But the mechanisms dispersed it; what she felt, half consciously, was a momentary push on the shoulder. As the biped staggered back—only staggered back?—she placed a second bullet a dozen inches below the first, a third one below that. By then, the creature was turning sideways, stumbling, jaws stretched open; and she pumped a fourth shot at the head. An explosive, that one; there was a spout of white fire as it struck. Then the biped was out of sight in the vegetation.

"It went down," she announced unsteadily, fingers automatically flicking four new shells into the chamber. "Can't see it now. Hit it four times, but—"

"Just where was it?" Grant's voice from the transmitter.

Jill described the location. The Suesvant was pointed across the rock again, and her eyes kept scanning the forest. So far, the bipeds had appeared to be solitary hunters. But the maneuvers with the aircar might have drawn more than one to the area. However, nothing seemed to be stirring. The four reports had brought an outburst of startled animal sounds from the valley. That was fading now.

Jill concluded, "That creature is unbelievable! The first two penetrants only seemed to jolt it. It was the third one that started it down."

Silence for a moment. Grant said, "No signs of activity now?"

"None."

"We'll come down. Ned?"

"On my way," said Ned Brock.

Jill waited. Several minutes passed. Then Grant's voice told her, "We're in the open, Jill. Come on out."

She saw them as she walked out from under the overhang. They were moving down into the valley from either side. She pointed to the place where the biped had disappeared, and they angled toward it, Suesvants held ready. Jill went on as far as the aircar, waited there. Ned and Grant joined up, edged into the undergrowth and were gone from sight. After some seconds, Ned's voice said, "Jill?"

"Yes?"

"You hit it all right. Heavy blood spoor . . . But it didn't stay down. It's gone."

She said incredulously, "The explosive took it in the head—I saw it! It wasn't hauled off by others?"

"One set of tracks," his voice said. "Only one. But it may not get far. We'll follow. You get in the car and cut across the forest. Find out if Witter's got a guncar in the area that might help intercept."

She took a last look around, swung into the car and ripped it up out of the valley. She felt heavy with disappointment and apprehension. To be tracking something that had picked itself up off the ground after being hammered by a Suesvant wasn't pleasant work in forest growth! But the bipeds weren't invulnerable; she'd proved that much. As for herself, she'd be waiting with the car between forest and stream, to catch it in the open if it tried to retreat along its former route. It seemed reasonable to expect it would do that, if its strength didn't ebb out before it got that far.

She turned on the communicator, signaled the Star Union Base, and asked to be connected with Crowell.

The biped didn't appear in the open.

It vanished in the forest. The blood trail led to a narrow creek, deep and swift-moving. There it ended. They couldn't have been many minutes behind it, and if it had turned upstream, Ned's biotracker should have registered traces of its blood in the water. There were no such traces; so they checked both banks, then turned down the creek, again working back and forth across it to search both banks for an emerging spoor. There was none. Their previous experience in tracking the creature indicated it might be an expert swimmer, and there were deep pools in the creek, too deep to be probed visually in the dim forest light, and possibly caves under the rocky banks into which it could have withdrawn. But, again, there should have been traces of blood and scent in the water at such places, and the tracker registered none.

It was awkward time-consuming work. But eventually they came to the point where the forest ended and the creek ran into the stream which led down to the lake. Jill had long since been waiting there, the car hovering above a shallow section of the creek where the biped couldn't have passed without being seen by her. Three hundred feet away, Crowell's guncar, crewed by Crowell and Ilken, hung in the air.

The cars came down. Grant and Ned reported their experience. It remained unexplained. They hadn't passed overhanging tree branches strong enough to let so large a creature clamber up out of the water without touching the banks. "My best guess is," said Ned finally, "that it holed up in some deep tunnel under the creek banks—up above the waterline. Then the creek could have carried away any indications of it before we got that far." He looked at Crowell. "The main point, aside from knowing that the things can be hurt and brought down, is that the biped Jill wounded isn't the one that broke into Station Three and carried off Farquhar. The tracker shows they were of the same species but distinct individuals."

Crowell said, "So there should be at least one living biped still in the area?"

"That's what we think," Grant said. "And if the wounded one doesn't die, it isn't going to stay holed up indefinitely. Our trick isn't likely to work again around here, so we'll pull out for the rest of the day to let things settle down. We'll come back early in the morning and start working through the forest on foot. If we don't hit fresh spoor, there should be old trails the tracker can pick up, and under the trees they'll be less washed out by the rain. They might lead us to where one of the bipeds is hiding out, or draw another attack."

Crowell nodded. "By morning I can have most of the Base's guncars cleared of other duties and stationed around this part of the country. They'll keep watch on the open areas."

They discussed it further. A joint operation could be successful now. If the biotracker indicated points where a biped might be holed up, the heavy energy beams of the guncars could blast through forest cover, soil and rock, to force the creature to view. With luck, they'd have their specimen tomorrow.

They got back into the cars and left. Crowell was having the stations cleared systematically of records and other significant and movable project material during the day, for storage or use on the Base. The survey team would return to its ship.

The Galestral aircar was still an hour's flight away from the ship when it signaled an alert from the ship computer. Something that wasn't a recorded species of the local fauna was skirting the ship's defense perimeter. "Better check!" said Grant quickly.

Jill slid into her seat at the communicator console. The alert was no longer being indicated. She cut in a report order, said after a moment, "Unidentified Disturbance . . . Now it's recording again . . .

Ned said, "Some of Captain Witter's planetbound swimmer friends? We might be on their schedule."

It seemed the most likely explanation, but it remained puzzling. The ship scanners could identify an aircar almost as far as they could sense one. But the report tape kept reiterating that the disturbance was of unidentifiable nature. They had the impression of something moving about the defense zone, touching it and withdrawing again. The alert indicator went on and off.

Then, perhaps five minutes later, the tape registered a brief blast of ship armament. After that, there were no more alerts, and the report tape showed Condition Normal.

Ned shook his head. "Wouldn't stay warned off! We may never know who it was."

They continued toward the ship at high speed, saw it presently suspended above the plain ahead. The aircar's scanners were in action, but there was nothing to suggest the presence of intruders in the area. Grant took the car several times in a wide circle about the ship, then said, "Check condition, Jill."

Jill said after a moment, "Condition Normal. I'm calling for ultimate sensor scan."

"Good idea."

"Condition Normal," Jill said presently again. "If there was something around, it isn't around now, Grant."

"If there was something around?"

"Systems failures aren't unheard of."

"No," Grant acknowledged. "But they haven't happened to us before. And it wouldn't be the best time for problems of that kind to develop." He turned the car in toward the ship. "Well, we'll soon find out!" He tapped the recognition signal.

"Acknowledged," Jill said.

The aircar drove on another three hundred yards toward the ship.

And a glare of brilliant blue light suddenly appeared about the ship, englobing it—its projected defense screens.

Grant whipped the car about, almost end for end, sped back from the defense perimeter. The light winked out.

"Unidentified Disturbance!" Jill read from the report tape, an instant later. "That was us!"

"Must have been." Systems failure? The faces of all three had paled. At normal approach speed, they should have triggered ship armament. Grant said, "Let's repeat the procedure . . ."

They did. The results were the same. The ship recognized the aircar's signal, but prepared to attack when the car came up to the defense perimeter. For the computer mind in there, they remained an Unidentified Disturbance.

"See if you can find out what the problem is," Grant said.

Jill shook her head, ran through the standard checks twice. "As far as I can tell from here, there is no problem," she said then. She thought a moment, added, "Let's try riding in on continuous recognition signal. If it's forced to keep acknowledging, that may cancel its alerting sequence."

They moved in slowly. The defense screens came on. Jill said, "At this point, it refuses to acknowledge. The sequences do cancel each other! Pull back and try again, Grant."

On the fifth attempt it worked. The defense screens remained off, and the ship continued to acknowledge the aircar's approach as a non-hostile one. Grant checked the car on the safe side of the attack zone, said, voice absent, "Continue standard procedure!"

Jill cut the recognition signal. The ship stopped acknowledging. Nothing else happened. She gave the "Lock Open" order, said, "It confirms." Her voice was a little shaky.

Grant nodded, said, "Lock's opening! Well, hold your breath, people! Everything looks all right, and we can't expect it to give us a direct invitation."

He edged into the attack zone, turned the car toward the open lock.

12

. . .

THE STAR UNION Base looked almost normal that night. Many of the sections remained lit after the official work period had been over for some hours. Round-the-clock operations were nothing unusual, and Dr. Sutton had told the department heads to set up new schedules to keep the people who'd been withdrawn from the stations and other outposts usefully occupied.

In the recreation area Crowell noted considerable serious drinking going on. He wasn't surprised. For more than two thirds of the expedition's members, the surface of any planet remained starkly alien territory. They were norm-g walkers, had been trained for the work they were doing, but they'd been born and raised in enclosures. Vast enclosures sometimes, but always and obviously limited. Under the open sky, consciously or not, they felt exposed.

Cencom, Crowell thought, had put the expedition force together precisely with that in mind. It was testing Kulkoor. Not with seasoned planeteers, because there weren't enough seasoned planeteers in the Star Union to man the major operations planned here. It was testing Kulkoor with the approximate level of walker manpower it would have available for planetwide mining work. And if it seemed that level of manpower couldn't take whatever strains Kulkoor might impose, Cencom would resort, however reluctantly, to the use of swimmer domes. The move would involve major concessions to the Swimmer League, but Cencom would pay the price to retain overall control of the Kulkoor operations.

Meanwhile he'd have a growing case of general nerves on his hands if it couldn't be quickly proved that the bipeds, at least, weren't more than a containable local problem. He'd let it be known that one of the creatures had been seriously wounded by the Galestral survey team that morning, and that the Base guncars were to take part in a continuing intensive hunt tomorrow. He wasn't sure how much good that information had done. Evacuation of most of the personnel to the sentinel ship's freezer bay, simply to get them out of the way for the time being, might become the best solution. He'd decide on that when he heard from Captain Bymer that preparations for the process had been concluded. It wasn't a solution Cencom would like at this point—they'd prefer to test the expedition to the point of emotional disintegration. But they hadn't specifically told Crowell that; and they'd put him in charge. The decision was his. Cencom would have to buy it.

The morale of the defense team, at any rate, seemed well above norm. As Herrick had put it, they were men trained to fight and they now had at least the illusion that there was something outside the Base to fight. The energy cannons were connected to the defense screen mechanisms, permitting them to fire through the screens in any direction. Search beams swept about in changing patterns, illuminating the landscape beyond the uncertain glimmering of the screens. Technically it was a drill. If it also served to remind the personnel of the Base's formidable armament, so much the better.

Crowell went to his quarters, had been asleep about an hour when the intercom buzzer alerted him. He switched on, acknowledged.

"Captain Witter," said Dr. Bates' voice, "would you come to my office immediately?"

"What's happened?"

"We've had a . . . well, a disturbance. A case of acute hysteria. There's a chance the hysteria might spread. I think you'd better hear at firsthand what it's about."

"Yes, I'd better do that. I'll be there."

When Crowell arrived with Ilken in Dr. Bates' office, they found Herrick, Hansen and Dr. Sutton already present. Another door opened as they came in, and Dr. Kimberley, Bates' assistant, appeared in it.

"The patient's asleep," Kimberley said. He looked at Crowell. "Under sedation. Of course, she can be aroused again if you want to speak to her."

"I don't at the moment," Crowell said. "Just tell me what's happened."

Dr. Bates said, "The patient is Nancy Watson, a biotechnician.

She was a close friend of Wilma Howard, the young woman who was killed in Station Three."

Crowell nodded.

"Nancy has been terribly upset by Wilma's death," Dr. Bates said. "We had her under treatment for a while yesterday, but she wanted to go back to work then, and I let her do it. It seemed good therapy. What I'm trying to emphasize is that she's been under severe emotional stress. Well—a short while ago, she was coming through one of the south area passages."

"Corridor Forty-eight," said Herrick. "It is, or was, almost unlit. There was no one with her."

"All right," Crowell said. "She was coming alone through a dark corridor. And?"

"She thinks she saw ghosts," said Dr. Bates.

Crowell stared at him. "Ghosts?" he repeated. "The ghosts of Wilma Howard and the others killed in Station Three?"

Dr. Bates frowned. "No," he said. "Though that's what one might have expected in the circumstances."

"Then whose ghosts?"

"No one she knew. The ghosts of three men. According to Nancy, they were three of the men who disappeared from that mysterious mining camp."

Crowell grunted. "Did she give any details?"

"Yes," Dr. Bates said. "She said she was coming along the corridor and saw three men standing together, staring in her direction as if waiting for her to come up. She couldn't make them out clearly at first, so she kept walking toward them until she realized suddenly that they weren't people of the Base at all but, in her terms, ghosts—three dead men. She turned, screaming, and ran back the way she'd come."

Herrick said, "I happened to be in the area and heard the commotion. I and some others investigated the corridor at once. There was no one there or in the structures behind it."

"Dr. Bates," Crowell said, "when you called me, you indicated we might be having to deal with more than one case of hysteria."

"I'm afraid that's quite possible," Dr. Bates said.

Hansen said, "Nancy was audible all over that section, Crowell. At least two dozen people heard her directly. What she was screaming about was that the creatures which killed Alex Hays and the staff of Station Three were devils . . . that this was their world and we shouldn't have come here. And that you'd made the matter worse by letting the Galestrals shoot one of them. So they'd showed her ghosts of earlier victims as a sign they were going to kill all of us now." Hansen shrugged. "We got her quieted as quickly as possible, but I could see she'd been getting reactions from at least some of those who were listening."

Dr. Bates nodded. "Symptoms of agoraphobic disturbance have been frequent here, though so far they haven't significantly affected the efficiency of the expedition. Sleep problems, general tensions... that kind of thing. Usually the patient didn't know what really was bothering him. If the bipeds hadn't appeared, that's all it might have amounted to. But now the pattern will be reinforced by the feeling that the world around us has become actively hostile. We should expect further trouble and—"

He checked himself as the intercom buzzer sounded. A voice inquired, "Is Captain Witter in the Medical Section?"

Dr. Bates turned to his desk, pressed the intercom button. "Yes, he is."

"We have a message for him from the Public Servant Betheny of Varien. She would like to see him in her quarters as soon as possible. The matter is urgent."

Crowell glanced at Ilken, said, "Witter speaking. Tell the Public Servant I'll be there in a few minutes." Dr. Bates released the response button, and Crowell went on, looking at Dr. Sutton, "I've told Captain Bymer to ready the emergency sections of the ship's personnel freezer for occupancy. Some time early tomorrow, he should be prepared to process large groups through on half an hour's notice. You might let it be known in the departments that those who want to go into freeze on the ship will be able to do it then. That should take off a good deal of pressure. If required, we will, in fact, evacuate all personnel except for the combat and security teams and maintenance crews until things have been straightened out down here."

He added, "Dr. Sutton, I don't like to interfere with your Base projects to that extent, but it seems preferable to taking chances with a general panic."

Dr. Sutton smiled wryly. "I find myself in agreement with you!"

"And, Herrick," Crowell went on, "light up the Base for the rest of the night, except for personal quarters. No more dim corridors or darkened work areas. Don't overload your men, but you might keep a few patrols circulating."

Herrick nodded, started for the door.

"Guy," Crowell said, "what's the soonest you can get the surveillance equipment back in action?"

Hansen shrugged.

"If I forget about sleeping—day after tomorrow."

"Captain Witter," said Betheny, "I've decided it can serve no good purpose to continue my attempts to modify Cencom's plans for the Kulkoor operation. I'm abandoning them completely. And I wish to be transferred at once from these quarters to the sentinel ship, to remain there until arrangements can be made to return me to Varien."

The main room of the null-g structure blazed bright with lights. Betheny's two attendants had drifted out through a section exit when Crowell and Ilken came in and took guide rods from the wall of the entrance hall. The two had closed the exit behind them. Betheny wanted this discussion to be private.

Crowell said, "What brought you to that decision?"

"Does it matter?"

"It might matter." He was watching her expression. So, off to one side of the support web, holding her position with a slow fanning motion of the guide rod, was Ilken. "You have a group of followers out there," Crowell remarked, "who haven't received instructions from you for a while."

"What difference could that make?"

"I'm wondering whether one of your instructions to them might have been to launch a strike at the Base at a specified time. The understanding being, of course, that at that time you wouldn't be on the Base."

Betheny's face worked. "They've been given no such instructions!" she said. "Nor are they equipped to carry out a strike against the Base. Since I'm ending the operation here, I'm willing to tell them to come in and surrender. Will that be satisfactory?"

"I couldn't be sure they'd all surrendered, could I?"

She hesitated. "You have your interrogation instrument. It will show you I'm telling the truth. I waive immunity."

"I'll want that on record." Crowell glanced toward Ilken. She nodded, was already in motion, diving toward the entrance hall. After a moment, they heard the entry door close behind her. Crowell looked about the quiet, brilliantly lit area, back at Betheny.

"What are you afraid of?" he asked.

"Afraid?" She shook her head. "I simply wish to be—"

"You're frightened to death." But he was puzzled. He knew some of Betheny's sympathizers on the Base were still keeping her informed of outside events. It was quite possible she'd already heard of Nancy

Watson's hysterical report of an encounter with ghosts. What seemed unlikely was that Betheny of Varien would allow such a story to drive her off the Base or change her plans in any way—unless she had reason to see some significance in it which wasn't obvious to Crowell.

She said, "Your statement is impertinent, Captain Witter! And you're exceeding your authority."

Crowell shook his head. "If I decide it's in Cencom's interest to keep you on the Base, you stay."

"No!" Betheny said shakily. "I must be transferred to the ship."

"Then give me a reason."

She moved her head from side to side. "My mind tells me the planet beast was here. I know it's impossible. But if I'm forced to remain on the surface of Kulkoor, I'll lose my sanity."

There was a chill for an instant along Crowell's spine. "The planet beast?"

She stared at him. "The creature which killed the people in the Station. Or another like it."

"Just what happened?" Crowell said.

She'd been asleep in her darkened rest section, and had come awake at some sound which she couldn't now describe. It wasn't a loud sound. Then she saw something large near the wall of the section. It was vague, shadowy. But in a general way it was man-like except for its great size. It seemed to be watching her. Then it gradually faded away. For a minute or two after she no longer could see it, she still sensed it nearby, still watching her. She remained too frightened to move or make a sound. Then, abruptly, she knew it was gone, and called her bodyguard and Dr. Torres. They'd been unaware of any disturbance.

Ilken returned in the middle of the account. Betheny seemed hardly to notice her or the instruments she carried. Crowell got the immunity waiver recorded, let Betheny go on talking, asked occasional questions. Ilken's face remained impassive as she watched the interrogator's readings. Betheny might have had a vivid nightmare, but she was telling Crowell no more than she believed to be true.

He said at last, "All right, you'll get transferred. Now call in your group."

Betheny took the transmitter Ilken handed her, carefully adjusted the settings, turned the switch.

They waited.

"Did you ever," Crowell asked Ilken, "get a feeling that you're about to discover you're out of your depth?"

"Now and then," Ilken acknowledged. "Is that how you're feeling?"

"I'm not sure." They'd called Dr. Bates to Betheny's quarters, had her and her two attendants drugged and placed in an enclosed null-g carrier of the Medical Section, in which they'd be transferred to the sentinel ship as soon as Captain Bymer's shuttle arrived for them. Bymer then would have the three processed immediately into a freezer. He believed now he might be able to meet Crowell's forty-hour schedule on evacuation preparations. He'd report on that as soon as all checks had been completed. Crowell hadn't yet told anyone that Betheny's group on Kulkoor, eighteen men, seemed to have disappeared. At least, they'd been given their code signal for fifteen minutes without responding, though the transmitter indicated the signal was being recorded. Betheny had been in near-shock by then.

"You going to start evacuation when Bymer's set for it?" Ilken asked.

"We'll clear out the people we don't need here and who want to go tomorrow, yes. Volunteers can stay—so far, it doesn't seem there'll be many of those!" Crowell scratched his scalp, scowling. "There's simply been nothing concrete enough to justify an overall evacuation. We can't very well let the expedition get run out of Kulkoor by ghosts!"

Ilken observed that ghosts were as good a reason as she could think of to get run out of Kulkoor or any place else. Mailliards had a lively respect for the supernatural. "What about Betheny's men vanishing like that?"

Crowell shrugged. "We don't know they've vanished. We only know that the transmitter didn't raise them. And since she doesn't know where they've been hiding, we can't check on it physically . . . Let's go find Herrick, make sure he has the freezer candidates ready to move out in groups as soon as Bymer gives the word and starts running down shuttles for them. Then we'll tighten things up some more, get set for anything we can think of or imagine, and wait for developments."

Later in the night then, about an hour before dawn, there was a development.

Herrick had left a guard posted at a small side lock in the energy screen. A passing patrol noticed the guard wasn't at his station, and informed Herrick. It was established presently that the man was nowhere on the Base.

The aircars were accounted for, and the overhead aircar lock hadn't been used during the night. Which left two possible ways in which the guard could have left the Base. One, voluntarily or otherwise, was through the disposal unit. The other was through the lock he'd been set to watch. It couldn't be employed as a means of entry until it was released by the tower controls. But a man could cycle out through it. There was no trace of the guard outside, and no tracks showed on the rocky ground surrounding the Base. The sentries in the towers, behind their shifting searchlights, had seen nothing of significance in the area.

"But he might have left that way," Crowell told Grant Gage by communicator. "If he did, he went somewhere. Can you give us a hand with your biotracker?"

"We'll be there as soon as we can," Grant's voice told him. "We were about to start out, as it happens."

"Among the Galestral superbeasts," Crowell went on, "is there something that could affect humans mentally—give them hallucinations, produce irrational behavior, insanity?"

Grant said hesitantly, "A number of those species have been known to produce mental effects of various kinds in human beings."

"Mental effects that might explain our reported ghostly visitations—or induce a man to walk off the Base at night?"

"It seems possible. The processes aren't well understood."

"What's the defense against that kind of thing?"

"Generally," said Grant, "killing the responsible creature. There are drugs that give partial protection. And some people simply aren't affected." He added, "We've had a problem of our own. Our ship can't be considered wholly dependable at present." He described their difficulties in attempting to come on board the day before. "Jill and I were up half the night trying to determine what's wrong. The trouble is that nothing seems to be wrong. If it hadn't been for that, we'd have been on our way an hour ago. But we'll leave for your Base within the next ten minutes now."

Captain Bymer called to report that processing preparations on the sentinel ship definitely would be completed in not much more than an hour. Herrick had notified the people who were to maintain the Base. Others were being organized into evacuation groups. There were no protests from department heads; and very few expedition members had decided on their own to remain planetside.

Crowell sent off another drone to Cencom, reporting the current state of affairs on Kulkoor.

13
· · ·

CAPTAIN BYMER'S VOICE said from the communicator, "The reason for the delay is a malfunction in the ship lock to the shuttle launching deck. The lock won't open. Our engineers have been working on it for the past half hour. It can't be too serious a difficulty. I'll call you as soon as a shuttle is ready to start down."

"We'll wait for the call," Crowell said.

He turned off the communicator, grimaced at Ilken. "Let's say nothing about that at present. They're edgy enough here!"

There was fear on the Base that morning, something that went beyond uneasiness, and was strengthened, if anything, by the fact that no one seemed willing to voice it now. Evacuation personnel were gathered in their various sections. Herrick had designated the sequence in which the groups were to leave. The Base's guncars had been withdrawn to the side of their area to leave room for the shuttles. Defense teams had taken up positions; the locks were under guard. There was nothing to do but wait.

Fifteen minutes passed before another call came from the ship. "Yes?" Crowell said.

Captain Bymer's voice was strained. "I have no explanation for this," he said. "It's just been reported to me that there has been an explosion in the shuttle launch section."

Crowell glanced quickly at Ilken, said, "What's the damage?"

"Captain Witter, we don't know. The shuttle lock remains jammed. But the explosion appears to have been a fairly heavy one. I'm afraid we won't—"

He broke off. There was a spluttering sound in the communicator.

"Captain Bymer?"

"A second explosion," Bymer's voice said thinly. "This one apparently in the engine room. I—"

The communicator went dead.

Crowell and Ilken stared at each other. The shock in her face was replaced quickly by a cold set expression. "Another coincidence?" she said.

"Hardly! But what—"

"Crowell, something got the ship! Something wasn't going to let the Base be evacuated. It'll be after the Base next!"

He nodded. "Come on! We'll get off a drone to Cencom—let them know what they'll be up against when they come back to Kulkoor. May not be much time left—"

As they turned toward the door of the communicator room, there was the thud of explosion. The flooring shook. They ran out the door. Black smoke poured up from the far end of the Base.

Crowell caught Ilken by the arm.

"The drone storage area!" he said harshly. "They've started to show their hand—and now they don't want us to be sending messages to Cencom. Go back—call the Galestrals! Tell them the Base is under attack and they're to lift their ship off the planet while they can!"

Ilken turned back toward the computer room. Light blasted inside it. The shock of the explosion sent her stumbling backward toward Crowell, arms lifted to shield her face. As he caught and steadied her, screaming began all about the Base.

Kulkoor flowed by below the survey team's aircar. Flat tableland here, sparkling with pools formed by the recent rains. The mountains were gliding up, great snow-capped ranges enclosing chilled glacier lakes. To the south beyond the mountains lay the area of the Star Union Base.

Jill Hastings' gaze roved ceaselessly, methodically, over what was in view. Her fingers on the scanner scales adjusted magnification automatically. Her thoughts followed their own somber and apprehensive courses, which in no way diminished the effectiveness of her watch. If the scanners should pass over something that called for further attention, she'd be aware of it instantly. That ability was as practiced and reflexive as adjusting the instruments.

They'd dispatched a drone to the Galestral Company just before leaving the ship. It contained the information Crowell had given Grant by communicator, the fact that he had decided on a partial evacuation of the Star Union Base. It contained a detailed report on the unexplained malfunctioning of the team's ship computer. There'd been nothing, absolutely nothing, to show why the ship had failed to recognize their aircar as a non-hostile object after acknowledging their recognition signal. When they'd played back the scanner tapes, there'd again been nothing to explain the ship's use of defensive and offensive armament which they'd recorded previously in the aircar.

They'd moved the ship forty miles to the west then, left it stationed two miles above the ground. They'd entered its new location in the drone message, and the recognition signals by which it might be approached and boarded, with caution. They'd added finally that they were leaving for the Star Union Base to see what they could do there, dispatched the drone, and left.

All that, of course, was in case somebody else would be sent along by the Galestral Company presently to pick up the Kulkoor Problem at the point where they'd failed to solve it.

Failure had begun to seem quite possible.

Jill bent over the ground scanners, shutting the voices of her companions from her mind. Like most of those born on Galestral, she had few illusions about man's absolute superiority in the scheme of things. Their world had been an object lesson. Life was unpredictable; its possible final expressions seemed beyond all estimation. Man was a competitor who had remained in the lists until now. It could not be said safely that he was, or would be, anything else.

It seemed there might be a major competitor on Kulkoor. Was it the biped, the great brown-black ogre of this world, with its appearance of savage cunning and near-indestructibility?

Or something else—something that so far had manifested itself only indirectly?

They came speeding presently down the southern slopes of the mountains. The car crossed the area where they had ambushed the biped, and Jill saw the abandoned structure of Station Three to the left below.

"Grant!" she exclaimed suddenly. "There's somebody down there!"

"What? Where?"

"At the Station. I saw him just a moment . . . there he is again!" She twisted a dial. Her breath caught sharply.

"What is it?"

Jill, face quite white now, said in a low, strained voice, "Keep moving—but slowly! It can't be, of course . . . but that's Farquhar standing down there beside the Station. Frank Farquhar!"

"It can't be Farquhar," Grant said. "What is it? Are you having trouble keeping it clear in the viewer?"

"Yes," said Jill. The impossible figure down there seemed to blur slightly from moment to moment, then solidify again. It wasn't a matter of adjusting the scanners; the rocky ground around it remained unblurred.

She heard Ned Brock say, "Looks like somebody's playing ghost . . . Same sort of game as last night on the Base?"

"Probably," said Grant. "Let's start down."

Jill looked around at him. "That's what we're supposed to do!"

"Of course it's what we're supposed to do. But this—whatever it is—is Kulkoor showing its face. We'll take a look."

Jill didn't answer, kept her attention on the figure at the Station as the aircar swung about, went gliding down. Ned was at the communicator, signaling the Star Union Base to let Crowell know what they'd come across. Base comm hadn't responded so far. Something, Jill thought, had seen their car coming back over the mountains on the route they'd taken before. Something that knew it was their car, knew they were connected with Farquhar, knew it was they who had shot down and tried to collect a biped.

So an image of Farquhar had been produced near Station Three. Something knew they would see it, would come to it. It was a trap, but she didn't say that aloud. Grant and Ned knew it, too. And Grant was right; it was necessary to find out what this was.

The thought came again then: that mankind could not expect to win every round, and might already have lost this one.

Grant checked the aircar four hundred yards from the image, fairly close to the ground. To the left, the forest line lifted above the car, not much more than two hundred feet away. Ned had shut off the communicator, was crouched with his Suesvant at the opened car door, attention on the forest. If there were watchers nearby, they should be there. The only place of concealment on the rocky slopes below was the Station; and the Station supposedly had been sealed inside its force screen.

Grant was keeping a more general watch on the area. His hands remained on the car controls, ready to swing the car into full acceleration in any direction. The nose of the car was pointed at Farquhar's image, and Jill's attention was on that, as it showed in the scanners.

It appeared to be there not much more than twenty feet from

her. Jill had experienced an increasing sense of revulsion as they moved down toward it from the sky. Most of that feeling was gone now; she was trying to define what this thing, this simulacrum of a dead man, one she'd known slightly in life, might be. It wasn't a perfect likeness; there were minor discrepancies and it didn't have the appearance of life, might be intended not to have it. There was no motion. The expression was frozen. The eyes seemed blind.

She reported tonelessly, "The figure appears to touch the ground only with one foot. If it had any weight, it should topple over in that position."

"You can't make out anything else about it?"

"Not a thing."

"Ned?"

"Nothing stirring in the shrubbery," Ned said briefly.

"I'll move in closer," said Grant.

Jill sighed softly. They meant to spring the trap. Perhaps it couldn't be avoided. The image, its mere presence, whatever its nature, already had made a number of things joltingly clear.

Her eyes remained on the viewer, but she was aware of the slope starting to move past on the left as the car slid slowly forward. Perhaps a minute passed. The image of Farquhar came steadily closer in the viewer. Suddenly, it vanished.

"It's gone, Grant!"

"I saw." He'd checked the car as Jill spoke. She switched the scanners to a wider view of the slope. They remained silent then, waiting. The disappearance of the image should have some meaning.

There was a sound about them. Not at all loud, but steady. It hung like a shivering in the air, neither grew nor faded.

"You hear that?" Grant asked.

Ned grunted. "You get a feeling that something's pulling at you?"

"Yes. An odd . . . Jill?"

Jill didn't reply. Grant swung around in the seat, felt the blood drain from his face, shouted at the top of his lungs: "*Jill!*"

In the seat behind him was a shape. It showed Jill's outlines, but they were a hazy gray, almost smokily unsubstantial. At his shout, the face seemed to turn toward him, her features still faintly discernible. He heard Ned's shocked gasp. Then the shape moved, turned solid, color flowing into it; and she was there again, blinking, startled.

"Grant . . . what—"

"Just hang on! Stay *here!* Watch her, Ned!" Grant slapped in acceleration, swung the car around in a sharp arc, and upward.

"You were fading out like a ghost!" he said a minute later, face still white. "What happened to you?"

The car was circling half a mile above the Station and south of it. The image of Farquhar was again in sight down there. Apparently, it became invisible if the viewer moved close enough, reappeared as he withdrew.

Jill shook her head. "I'm not sure! There was a kind of fog. I mean a literal kind of fog. It was getting thicker. I seemed to be moving into it. Your voices began to go away. Then I heard you yell—and I was back."

"Why didn't you do something?"

She shrugged helplessly. "Do what? I wasn't worried. I don't know why. I was aware of what was happening, but it didn't seem very real. More like a dream."

"The trap mechanism," Grant said after a moment. "It almost got you. And if we hadn't seen you going, it should have got us. We were feeling a pull—"

"It fits in with other things," Ned said.

It did. The trails of the two bipeds they'd tracked had appeared to end in water. "They got picked up," Ned said, "by—well, whatever this is!"

Grant nodded. "They can focus the effect on some given spot. The second biped was hurt—he yelled for help, and they lifted him out of the creek just ahead of us." As a man had vanished without trace from the Star Union Base during the night.

"And the ghosts, human and biped, they saw on the Base earlier," Grant went on. "It works both ways. A form of transportation. You fade out here; you fade in there. Hold the effect before you're all the way there, and you'll look like a ghost. As Jill did, sitting here."

"And defense screens are giving Witter's Base no protection at all," Ned added.

"Not a bit," Grant agreed. "Now—what will they do next?"

Jill said soberly, "They must be ready to come in for the kill! They've been trying to scare humans off the planet. They tried it first by pretending to be animals—"

Cunning, savage animals, striking without warning, unharmed by human weapons, vanishing mysteriously when trailed. If the Star Union expedition's losses could be piled up to an intolerable extent, until the survivors fled in panic, humans might decide not to come back to so ferociously inhospitable a world.

"But then Jill shot one of them," Grant said. "Body screens. They'd turn an ordinary energy beam, but the Suesvant punched through. He may have been badly hurt, perhaps dying, when they got him back. That ended the invulnerable superbeast myth—so, last night, they switched to supernatural effects. They'd already set that up by cleaning out the mining camp and letting it stand there to be found."

"If they planned to scare us off the planet, they must have reason to think our minds work pretty much like theirs," said Ned. "There's a civilization here. Underground? In mountain caves?"

Grant said, "Perhaps only while there are humans around. There may not be too many of them, but it has to be a pretty advanced civilization in some respects. Could they have gimmicked our ship yesterday?"

Ned said after a pause, "No need to assume that at present."

Jill said, "I think Farquhar figured it out! He'd been trying to work out a way to communicate with them. That's why he left Station Three. But they don't care about communicating. What do we do now? They saw us coming, set up a trap on the route we've used before. They must know we three had a connection with Farquhar. The trap hasn't worked, and maybe they already know it hasn't worked."

Ned said, "The Base still isn't responding to our signal."

There was silence for a moment. Jill said, "You're thinking there might be a problem on our ship again? The communicator linkup was operational an hour ago. We can find out quickly by going on to the Base..."

"And you two are going there," Grant said. "We have to let Witter know about this at once, so he can get out the information."

"What about you?" said Jill.

Grant tapped his viewer, said, "There's a machine down there, according to our metal scanners. Check it for yourself, Ned. I have it pinpointed. About a hundred and fifty yards from their Farquhar image. Copper, steel, other items. About eighteen by twelve inches across the top. We'll assume it's the image projector."

"What do you want to do?" Jill asked sharply.

"We'll go down, and I'll get out under cover. Then you two leave for the Base. After you're gone, I'll put a bullet in their machine. That should bring one of them here to find out what's happened. I'll be waiting for him."

"Grant, don't do it!" Jill said. "At least, let's stay together!"

"I'd rather we could stay together. There isn't time. They seem to know almost everything there is to know about us, and we still know next to nothing about them. Anything I learn here may be vital. When I'm in the clear, I'll call you by transmitter. Don't try to contact me before I do. You might give away my position."

"Jill, he's right," Ned said, as she was about to reply.

"I suppose so," Jill agreed forlornly. She didn't add that she had a strong conviction she wouldn't see Grant again.

The car turned down, made a wide, wary circle about the Farquhar image, paused above the forest, then slipped down among the trees. If there were watchers about, the idea was to create the impression the Galestrals were searching the forest for them. The car rose back up through the canopy some minutes later, lifted into the air, and sped off in the direction of the Star Union Base. Grant was no longer in it.

"Where's Gage?" Crowell asked.

"He's busy," said Ned.

"On your ship?"

"No. Trying to ambush a biped."

Crowell made a snorting sound. "He could do that here!"

"You've been under siege obviously," Ned said.

"We're still under siege," Crowell told him. "There's a lull right now. Five minutes ago we had some action. They'll be back. We've lost something more than forty people here on the Base. It's hard to keep track. And they got to our sentinel ship. A few of them could have gone up there on the shuttle yesterday. No one would have spotted them."

"What happened?"

"The ship blew up a short while ago. I was talking to Bymer at the time. He reported two preliminary explosions but couldn't give any details."

The Base's guncars were dispersed and grounded in the installation's central open square. The guns were manned. Ned saw Ilken at one of them. She gave no notice to him or to Jill, still in the Galestral car which hovered beside Crowell and Ned. Her eyes shifted about in quick, flicking glances; her hands stayed on the handles of the gun. Several dozen men, armed with a variety of weapons ranging from energy handguns to semi-portables, were stationed along the edges of the square. Some six or seven held shock guns, as did Crowell.

The rest of the Star Union personnel was present but not armed. They were scattered about the square between the guncars, sitting down, singly or in small groups. Some lay facedown, but Ned saw none that looked injured. There was hardly any movement.

"How did you lose your people?" he said.

Crowell jerked his head at the nearest building.

"Around a dozen are lying behind that," he said. "What's left of them. We didn't get them out here in time. They were blasted with some kind of fire. The crew in the south tower saw the biped that did it. They cut loose on him, knocked in the side of the building. But he'd simply disappeared . . . And the rest of the people we've lost have also disappeared. There's a kind of sound—"

"We've heard it," said Ned. "They nearly got Jill that way."

"You look around, and another three or four seem to be gone, eh? Fade out . . . Well, we've fixed that—probably!"

"How?"

"Figured the sound might have something to do with the fading," Crowell said. "When it starts now, we cut in with the siren. Haven't lost anyone since. This defense arrangement"—he indicated the area around them—"is to stall their other approach. We've got everybody out here, covered by the guns. The guns cover one another. When the things start to materialize in the air, they get chopped with a short-beam blast and vanish again. They don't get time to use their weapons."

"They haven't tried materializing elsewhere on the Base and attacking from there?" Ned asked.

"Not after the first time. We got three as they came out. Killed them, I think; but the bodies had faded along with their weapons before we could reach them. They could try it again, but apparently they don't intend to get hurt. Of course, they don't have to take losses." Crowell indicated the north end of the Base. "One explosion back there! Just one. Placed exactly where it would cut through our last contact to Cencom—inside the safe-storage section where the navigational units of the message drones were kept. Nothing salvageable left."

He shook his head. "You get the picture. They could blow up the whole Base any time they like. There's nothing we could do to stop it. But they don't want it that way. They want to clean it out almost as neatly as they cleaned out the mining camp. When investigators arrive, there'll be a new mystery, a much bigger one. What happened? What hit the Base? Where did the sentinel ship go? All our reports mentioned so far were problems with a bipedal animal—and hallucinations. Beautifully timed! You know, it could work. It should drive the Cencom computers crazy." He added, "If you can still get to your ship, you'd better do it, get off the planet. That's the only sure way anybody outside is going to find out what's really happened."

"We don't know if we can still get to the ship," Ned said. He looked over at Jill. "Want me along?"

She shook her head quickly. "I'll travel light! As soon as I'm clear of the Base, I'll jettison everything I can, including spare fuel blocks. Might make it to the ship in thirty minutes then. They can use you here. I'll get a drone off, come back with the ship. Luck, Ned!"

"Luck, Jill! If Grant calls, we'll go get him with one of these cars."

She nodded, gave them both a small scared smile, slammed the car door shut. The car soared quickly back toward the open overhead lock, disappeared beyond the bluish glimmer of the screens.

"She shouldn't bring your ship here," Crowell said disapprovingly.

"She should," said Ned. "It's a damn good ship, and it fights itself. I was never trained to handle them, but Jill was. The bipeds may get more of an argument than they're counting on."

14
. . .

GRANT GAGE STOOD, back against a tree trunk, shoulder-deep in shrubbery, big rocks to his right and left. A natural blind, just beyond the triggering range of the bipeds' projection trap. The device which controlled the projection was eighty yards away, down the slope on the left. It wasn't visible, wouldn't have been visible if he'd been next to it. They'd camouflaged it in some manner: But he had its position fixed mentally—two feet out from the tip of a patch of dark-yellow growth. He could put an explosive into it from where he stood.

Which he would do if whoever had set up the device didn't return within the next ten minutes to pick it up, now that its usefulness must appear to be over. That would be preferable. But Jill and Ned should have reached the Base, and Crowell Witter's message to Cencom might be about on its way. No reason to delay more than another ten minutes before giving them a prod by knocking out their machine.

Perhaps three of those ten minutes had passed then before he saw something . . . a haziness forming gradually above a flat, sloping boulder, twenty yards from the device, on the far side of it. Motionless, Grant watched. The haze could be only one thing, though as yet it had no recognizable shape or definite outline. It was like an upright patch of gray fog which stirred and shifted but stayed where it was. It was large enough to enclose a biped. Jill had said that, in the moment when she almost disappeared, sight and sound seemed to blur out in a kind of fog. The bipeds controlled the process. There was one there now—though also not quite there— on that slab of rock, peering out through its subjective fog at the objective details of the slope, possibly to make quite sure there was no human enemy near the device. They'd shown they were suspicious and cautious creatures in spite of their demonstrated ferocity.

The haze faded gradually again, vanished completely. Grant passed his tongue along his lips, wondering. He hadn't stirred; it didn't seem likely he could have been detected here. But he wasn't certain—

Something stirred on his left, close to the front line of trees. He shifted only his eyes. For an instant, he saw the biped—if it was the same one. No ghost shape now, at any rate, but quite substantial, standing in profile a hundred feet away, looking down the slope. An impressive creature, manlike in the way it stood and held itself. But the head was as Jill had described it, something like that of a short-faced bear or pig, except for the large pointed ears.

The figure blurred and disappeared at once. And that, Grant thought, had been no coincidence. If the biped had been merely conducting a preliminary survey of the area, it should have remained in sight longer. It might be trying to draw a reaction from him. It either suspected or knew he was here, perhaps even exactly where he was. They could have instruments which scanned through the shielding fog. He'd seen no instruments, but there'd been a kind of belt around the furred torso. Aside from that, the lack of visible trappings might have made it seem still an animal.

Perhaps a second or two had passed in these reflections. Grant's attention was now chiefly on the area at his right. So he saw the biped reappear. Abruptly in sight, some fifty feet away and slightly below him on the slope, faced toward him, half crouched, one great furred arm extended, giant hand holding a glassy tube pointed at the thicket where he stood—

Grant pitched sideways through the shrubs, down over the rock to his left, flattened out.

Fire exploded the thicket beyond the rock, surged furiously up the tree trunk against which Grant had been standing, flowed out down the slope.

A furnace of heat closed about him. He thrust himself forward, saw, through blazing vegetation, the biped still crouched on the slope, staring at the thicket, weapon held watchfully pointed. Grant rolled sideways, bringing the Suesvant around and forward in the motion, sighted and triggered. The second shot crowded the first, the third the second, reports merging into a howl of sound. The biped staggered backward along the slope, the glassy weapon arcing high through the air above it. Grant pumped three more shots into the big head, saw the creature strike the ground and begin to blur, got to his feet and leaped across the burning shrubbery.

The biped vanished. Then, as Grant stood still in a shock of disappointment, it reappeared—sprawled out in midair, a few yards above the ground, and a dozen feet from where it had last been. It fell heavily, struck the slope, vanished again—and reappeared again, almost in its previous position. Now it lay still.

Grant flicked a fresh set of shells into the Suesvant, watching the biped, then started downhill toward it. The fire's explosive fury had spent itself; it was making no more headway in the wet vegetation. His left hand went to the wrist transmitter on his right. He looked down, swore softly and fervently.

The face of the little device was crushed, mashed into uselessness against some rock surface in his dive for safety. No way now to contact the others.

A few things became obvious almost at once. The biped wore a kind of vest, made of a material which so closely matched its own shaggy hide in appearance that Grant became aware of it only as he began to investigate the fallen creature. The vest ended at the broad belt he'd seen when the biped first appeared. There were sealed pockets in it, and he could feel various devices in the pockets.

The next discovery wasn't unexpected. The biped's skin was no natural armor; it was enclosed in a personal energy field. Grant prodded here and there at the giant, found the protective field seemed to cover everything but the hands and feet. Vest and belt were fastened over it. The field yielded slightly to a steady push but could not be depressed enough to touch the flesh immediately beneath. Obviously it couldn't hamper either the wearer's breathing or his motions, but it seemed almost impervious to forces from without. All Grant's bullets had pierced it; but the body within could have experienced only a fraction of the Suesvant's monstrous jolting effect. Still, that had been enough to kill.

Grant found what turned out to be the field switch on the side of the belt, fumbled at the fastening, got it unlocked, and pulled the switch down. The field went off; and the fur vest, which had seemed to be seamless, opened along the center of the chest. Grant pulled it free of the belt and stared down at the cause of the lumpy deformity of the chest area in these creatures.

They were four-armed. The second pair of arms was set forward on the chest and, while sinewy and well muscled, was much smaller and relatively shorter than the principal pair, in fact barely the size of the arms of an average adult human male. The hands had long, thin, deft-looking fingers. In spite of its bulk, the biped should have been capable of doing very delicate work. The secondary arms had been carried folded on the chest; and one of the hands was closed on something. Grant lifted the arm, and the hand unfolded in the limp submission of death, releasing the object.

Grant picked it up without immediate interest, still staring at the dead biped.

Six-limbed . . . The dominant pseudo-mammalian fauna of Kulkoor, to which the bipeds had appeared to belong, was four-limbed. He was looking at the explanation of the Kulkoor Mystery.

No hidden civilization here! The bipeds weren't part of the native life. They'd come from another world, almost certainly for the same reason men had come—to work the planet's heavy metal deposits. They hadn't been here long, or evidence of their mining operations would have been detected. They had a concealed base somewhere; but there might be no more of them on Kulkoor at present than there were humans.

And they'd been trying to drive away a competitive civilized species without revealing what they were . . .

However technologically advanced they might be, they must feel vulnerable here.

Grant looked down at the object that had been clasped in the biped's hand. Apparently, it had been of value to the biped—it might be of value to him. About three inches long, gray, smooth, pear-shaped with a shallow indentation at the narrow end, rather heavy for its size. A personal amulet, without other significance? Creatures which tried to play on superstition in others should have their own share of it.

He glanced at the lifelessly open hand of the biped. The thick end of the gray pear had been enclosed by the palm. He laid it in his own palm. At its touch, he felt a faint tingling which immediately faded. And now his interest had increased sharply. The thing was powered—powered for some purpose.

He looked at the hand again. It seemed to him that the ball of one of the fingers had been clasped against the top of the pear, pressed into the indentation. He placed his own finger in that position. The tingling resumed briefly, faded again.

His vision misted over.

He blinked, shook his head—and realization came suddenly of what was happening. He almost dropped the gray object, then, instead, lifted his finger away from the tip. At once, the foggily dimming air about him cleared again.

Grant sucked in a quick breath, looked at the biped. So he was holding one of their transportation devices! He was quite sure now that when he first saw it, the biped's finger had still been clamped over the indented tip. But that had produced no effect on the device. While shortly before, immediately after being shot, the giant had twice vanished for an instant. Consciously or not, Grant thought, it had been trying to escape back to wherever it had come from, and hadn't quite made it. It was dying then. Dead, it was solidly here.

The device needed contact with a living body in order to function.

Did it need the direction of a living mind to tell it where to go?

15
. . .

JILL HAD SPENT most of the racing drive back to the ship checking on its operating condition as exhaustively as she could from the car. She discovered nothing wrong with it. Condition was normal. Ultimate sensor scan reported the vicinity clear of suspicious objects.

The aircar's scanners showed the same innocuous picture as she approached the ship. She slowed, gave the recognition code, read the ship's acknowledgment on the tape, set the code on continuous repetition, and moved up to the defense perimeter.

The ship's screens remained off. Everything seemed all right. She bit her lip, gave the signal for the entry lock to open for the car, saw it opening in the viewplate.

The car slid forward into the defense zone.

The world seemed to dim, almost imperceptibly. Jill grew aware of a sound.

It hung about her like the half-heard vibration of a bell, a shuddering in the air. Dreaminess settled on her. Then came jarring fright.

"No!"

The dreaminess was gone. But the aircar was growing vague, fading out in a gray haze. She tried to wrench herself back into its reality, knew she was failing, reached out automatically for the hazy Suesvant on the car door. For an instant, she seemed to touch nothing; then the stock grew firm and cool against her palm, and she snatched the rifle to her. The car controls—

She was no longer in the car. She saw its shadow shape ahead of her in a darkening fog, moving toward the ship. And the ship expanded suddenly into a ball of yellow fire. An explosion which had no sound for Jill. The shadow car vanished in the fire, and the fog closed all around.

She was in nothingness. But *she* was real. The Suesvant she held had remained real with her.

Otherwise—no sight, no sound. The fog was no fog but the absence of other realities. It had no substance, no temperature. Nothing.

But she was there. She could look down and see herself as if by daylight, hands gripping the rifle. Her lungs breathed, ignoring the fact that logically they should find nothing to breathe. She cleared her throat, heard the sound.

In its way, it began to make sense. If the bipeds used this as a form of transportation, the process itself mustn't hurt her, was nothing to fear. Danger wouldn't develop until it released her again.

A little time passed. Then the fog seemed to be thinning. Jill had waited for that. She pressed the alert button on her wrist transmitter. "Ned?"

No response. Light of sorts appeared gradually about her.

She was within something now. A structure. A long hall with metal walls. Nothing else to be seen. It was like looking through water. She was in motion, drifting along the hall, then slanting toward one of the walls. She touched the wall without sensing the touch, went through it—

And was in a vast room. Again there was the metal gleam of enclosing walls, great sleek engines below, moving shapes vaguely seen in the distance beyond the engines. Sound reached her here, the surging hum of power. She turned over and over like a tumbling leaf, was swirled down toward the central engine and into it. Light blazed briefly through her closed lids; furious energies quivered about her . . . then she was out of that incredible hell, unhurt, untouched. Moving on. More swiftly. A biped appeared suddenly ahead, standing on a catwalk, staring at her. He raised a big arm as if startled by her approach and trying to ward her off. Four-armed? Was he four-armed? She couldn't be certain in a momentary blurred glance. As she swung up the Suesvant, she'd passed through him, gone on through another wall.

A ghost. Moving through sections of the subterranean Kulkoor civilization they'd theorized? It didn't seem so. What she saw here suggested a vital, powerful technology, one that stood openly and boldly on its world, prepared to face any intruder—not the remnants of an advanced but failing culture which must skulk spitefully underground when visitors arrived from the stars. She began to get glimpses of other bipeds. Sometimes they seemed briefly aware of her, sometimes not. Four-armed they were. Why had she failed to notice so significant a detail about the one she'd shot? She had the impression that most of these were smaller, slighter creatures than the giants they'd stalked, though unmistakably of the same species.

Which, of course, could no longer be considered a Kulkoor species . . . Had she been transferred to a different world? It seemed possible. At the moment, perhaps almost anything would have seemed possible.

Abruptly the fog grew dense again. For moments only. When it began to fade, Jill knew what the aimless drifting had been about. A temporary delay only because they'd been busy with other matters. Other prisoners.

For here was an execution chamber.

It was a small room compared with most of the rest she'd passed through, long and low-ceilinged. Something like a great ventilator grille stretched overhead. One of the big bipeds stood at the far end of the room, looking in her direction. He held a short tubular device in one hand. Against the side of the room was a pile of contorted charred objects. Jill looked at them once and didn't look again.

Did the executioner recognize the Suesvant as a weapon which might be dangerous to him? With her first understanding of where she was, why she was here, Jill had let the rifle down at her side, holding it loosely in one hand, as she stared at the watching biped.

He turned his head; she heard a muted bellowing. The fog thinned farther; she felt a lurch, stood suddenly on the hard flooring of the room, smelled the stench of burned flesh the air rushing through the chamber hadn't yet carried off. The biped was leveling his fire tube.

The Suesvant was leveled much faster. The executioner didn't wear a body screen. He was dead as two slugs smashed him back against the wall.

Now what? Jill thought.

In answer, the fog enclosed her again. Again, things went swirling past, vaguely glimpsed. She was back in the immaterial half-world. The chamber had vanished instantly, but now a landscape was emerging about her, below her. A wraith of a landscape, pale, without color. Nevertheless, she recognized the formation of those shadowy mountain ranges at once and knew she was on Kulkoor. When she looked down, there was a lake below her—far down, at least two thousand feet. The glacier lake which formed the northern border of the area where they'd tracked two bipeds and she'd shot one. She looked in the direction from which she seemed to have come. There, within the shadow bulk of a mountain ridge, lay a shape, a huge oblong shape, tapering to a point at one end.

A ship, Jill thought. A gigantic spaceship, lying within the mountain. Four-arms had come to Kulkoor from a world of a distant star . . .

As she stared at the ship, its outlines faded. The mountains about her, the lake below, began to acquire color and solidity. For an instant, there was the brush of cold wind, a flash of brilliant daylight. She reached quickly for the alert button of the wrist transmitter, pressed it. She'd been returned to the world of reality, to die there. A two-thousand-foot drop to the lake would be a simple way to dispose of an unexpectedly recalcitrant prisoner.

But there might be time . . .

Somewhere then, somebody's mind changed; and the fog enclosed her again.

And this then was the control deck of the great ship. It could be nothing else. It was correspondingly huge, about a fifth of it filled with instrument banks, arranged before a curving viewscreen along wall and ceiling. The wall on the left showed what seemed to be outlines of the layered decks of the ship, about forty, their shifting light and color patterns signaling information to the control deck. A relative few of the instruments were manned. In all, around thirty bipeds were in sight, two of them the giant type. The others weren't of much more than human height. With their lighter build, their weight might be barely a fourth that of the giants.

Jill had been stopped near the center of the deck. A number of bipeds stood about, staring at her. The fog effect seemed very slight, but she knew she was still separated from them. Her feet seemed to be touching the floor, but when she took a step forward, her position on the deck didn't change. She held the Suesvant ready for use. The two big bipeds were armed. The others weren't.

Within a minute, the reason she was here was made apparent. The entire wall on the right side of the control deck became a viewscreen. Through it, Jill was looking into another room, as high-ceilinged as this one, though less wide. A dozen of the smaller bipeds stood and moved about there. Behind them was a specimen of a third biped variety—one which shrank the mighty ogres into insignificance. Seated human fashion in a great chair, it had the bulk of one of Earth's dinosaurs. Standing, it would have topped twenty-five feet.

She'd been brought here to be looked over by this four-armed entity—Ship's Captain, Being in Charge, sitting in a command room before a set of instruments designed for its proportions. Did it ever leave the room? Probably. Much of the ship was shaped for hugeness. It was the Suesvant they were interested in, of course. She'd demonstrated again what it could do, in executing their executioner. They wanted the weapon for study. The Being in Charge eyed her a long minute from the screen; then its voice boomed briefly. The viewscreen went blank, became again a wall of the control deck. Her fate had been decided.

The control deck faded from sight.

Grant picked up the dead biped's heat weapon. It was heavy; he needed both hands to hold it and aim it at the body above him on the slope. He thumbed down the stud, and the body and the ground about it blazed furiously. When the biped's fellows came searching for it, they should find something of a mystery to brood about, for a change. Grant shut off the device, clipped its end to his belt. It was an awkward weight; but the thing could be useful again. He picked up the fur vest he'd pulled off the body. Its sealed pockets were crammed with a variety of articles which might be investigated in detail at another time. Two of them, however, were gray pear-shaped instruments of the kind the biped had been holding in its hand. Emergency spares. It wouldn't have cared to find itself suddenly without a working device of that type available to it.

Their personal transportation method. Grant didn't know what limitations there might be on its effective range, but that information wasn't important now. He'd found out what he needed to know. The brain supplied directions; the gray instrument did what it did. You visualized the place you wanted to be, or you'd find yourself simply floating in the fogs of nowhere as your finger came down into the instrument's hollowed tip, closed contact. But visualize the place, and you went there. You emerged quickly or slowly, as you chose. Or you didn't emerge at all, remained just within nowhere, a ghost, a near-invisibility, peering out into a shadow world.

A very practical device. He'd tested it during the past few minutes, had made a number of longer shifts back and forth across the slope. Ready now for a purposeful jump . . . He hung the biped's vest over his left arm, took the gray instrument in his right hand, closed contact.

Fog swept in, thinned. He halted the process mentally. He was inside a room, vaguely defined but recognizable. It was in the Medical Section of the Star Union Base; he and Jill and Ned had been taken there to see the bodies of the people killed in Station Three. No one around at present. Grant came out of the fringes of nowhere into the room . . .

Into a storm of sound! Siren blaring in the air, sinking to an angry whine. Thud of energy bolts. A Suesvant's flat hard crack—

"Jill was to bring the ship here," Ned said, wiping sweat from his face. "They may have got her."

"What makes you think so?"

"Grant, I'm not saying they have! I don't know! I had an alert signal from her not more than ten minutes ago. I couldn't acknowledge. The bipeds were trying to break through—forcing it. They're getting impatient. I tried to contact Jill first chance I got. I've kept the alert button down. She hasn't replied."

"Ten minutes . . . how long can you hold out here?"

Crowell said, "They'll finish it any time they quit worrying about what it costs. Four car guns and the north turret left. At the present level of attack, we might last half an hour or more."

"One of you come along," Grant told them. "I have two spares of that space jumping gadget. We can do something with that."

"Your job," Ned said to Crowell. He looked at Grant, tapped the Suesvant. "This could make an additional quarter hour's difference here. You go after Jill."

Crowell and Grant ran across the square, past the living and dead, almost ignored by the Base's diminished survivors. Only a few faces—pale, sweat-streaked, shocked—turned to look after them. In the room in the Medical Section, Grant took the biped's two spares from the fur vest, handed one to Crowell, snapped the heat weapon back on his belt.

"I'll see about Jill as soon as you know how to use it," he said. "Here's what you do—"

When Grant went back into the nowhere fog, visualizing the Galestral ship's control room, nothing happened immediately. Then the fog darkened. A rumbling earthquake sensation began, building up quickly in violence. Grant had an awareness of imminent, ultimate danger. His mind snatched at another visualization. For a moment, that seemed to alter nothing. Then the rumbling faded. The fog thinned, vanished. The dangling fire weapon slapped heavily against his thigh. Grant slipped the transporting device into his pocket, looked quickly around.

He stood under the overhang of a great cliff, fallen boulders about him, a rounded shallow valley below, mountains lifting above the forest beyond the valley.

This was the point where they'd left Jill stationed when they prepared to ambush the biped. He'd needed a place to which he could retreat safely; and his mind had produced this picture, brought him here. It seemed a good choice. A familiar area, free at the moment of bipeds, screened from the observation of bipeds. Animals were in view in the valley, browsing undisturbed. The cliffs and the tumbled boulders concealed him.

He should have gone to their ship's control room. He had a strong conviction that instead he'd nearly been projected into a final nothingness. The control room no longer existed. Their ship no longer existed. He was being drawn into nonexistence when he'd veered away to this other place . . .

Ghost biped, prowling about the ship's defense perimeter as their aircar approached. It could look into the ship's opening lock. It could project itself later into the lock. From then on, an unseen presence moved occasionally about the ship. The ship had become alien property. When the aliens no longer had a use for it, it was destroyed.

And Jill—

He couldn't think of Jill as dead, as nonexistent. The bipeds took captives, had tried to take her captive earlier today.

Grant slipped his hand back into his pocket, closed it about the transporting device. He brought Jill's face into his mind, pictured it a few feet from his own. He kept the picture there as he pressed his finger into the indentation at the tip of the instrument.

Fog condensed, thinned.

The first thing he saw then wasn't Jill. It was the round black muzzle of a Suesvant pointed at him. The Suesvant was jerked aside.

"Grant!" A thin whisper.

Small bare cube of a room with seamless metal walls and nothing that looked like a door. Jill was staring at him, eyes huge in a chalk-white face.

16

. . .

GRANT HADN'T KNOWN it was going to work, but he thought it should work. It did. He'd simply picked Jill up instantly and visualized the overhang above the valley. The transporting instrument took them there. He set her down, took the biped's second spare from his pocket. Jill learned how to use it.

Then she talked.

"*Inside* a mountain?" Grant said.

"But outside our space." Jill added, "It must work along the same general lines as their transporters, on a huge scale. If we were standing by the lake, I could show you the mountain."

"They've got other prisoners," said Grant then.

She shook her head. "We won't have to consider that." Before being left in the exitless cell, she'd been shifted to another part of the ship, a large laboratory devoted to the study of the human enemy. The enemy had been thoroughly studied. Something floated in a transparent container. Most of its organs were suspended in the container beside it but still connected to it. The extracted heart beat steadily away, and the thing might be conscious because its eyes turned to Jill when she appeared in the laboratory, and remained fixed on her. There was a large number of other study subjects.

Jill evidently was destined for the laboratory after they got the Suesvant from her without harming her. The three bipeds on duty there looked her over in her semi-material state for a minute or two; then one of them waved a hand and she was shifted off to the cell. "They experimented with the first human group they picked up," she said. "What's left of them isn't salvageable. The

527

528   *James H. Schmitz*

people transported in from the Star Union Base were killed on arrival. A simple way to dispose of them."

"Then that's it," Grant said. "You go ahead. I'll come in beside you."

They unslung the Suesvants. Jill took the alien instrument in her left hand. She vanished.

The ship's great control deck appeared before Grant. Jill was standing four feet to his right.

The wide door space behind them was empty. They moved farther apart. The wall on the right was a wall at present, not a viewscreen. Two big-armed bipeds stood halfway between them and the instrument section, watching a scattering of smaller bipeds at work. One of the smaller ones was moving along the rows of consoles, but it didn't look around. No one had seen them appear. No biped as yet—unless they'd happened to check Jill's cell in the last few minutes—should have reason to suspect that a human had obtained some of their transportation devices, had found out how to use them.

They fired together. The big bipeds were hurled forward, struck the floor ponderously, already dead. On the ship, they'd had no reason to wear body screens. Until now.

Grant gave no attention to the smaller bipeds. They were Jill's business. Except for the first one, the shells he'd be using here were explosives and incendiaries. Their targets were the instrument banks.

He fired as quickly as he ever had in his life. A continuous crashing moved along the stands; flames and smoke erupted. Biped voices howled briefly through the commotion, went silent. Jill stopped firing. She stood half-turned to Grant, gaze sweeping the deck. Then she flicked the Suesvant up suddenly, firing past Grant toward the entry. A few seconds later, she fired again.

Grant didn't turn. That was still Jill's department unless she indicated she needed help. He continued his work of demolition. There were secondary explosions at the end of the control deck, other sounds. One of the vast ship's nerve centers was being shredded. How effectively, he couldn't tell.

Then Jill lifted her hand, shouted his name. They hadn't known how long it would take others in the ship to become aware of the destruction being wreaked on the control deck and to alert defenders; but staging a final fight here was no part of their plan. Time to move—

The first shift was a short one, to the far side of the deck, beyond the control stands. Looking back toward the entrance, Grant saw four big biped forms on the floor, one struggling to rise. Weapons lay about them.

"The last one had a body screen!"

"Did he transport in?"

Jill shook her head. "Came in from the hall with the others!"

So the counterattack wasn't organized yet. But it couldn't be long in coming. Grant slung the Suesvant over his shoulder, took the biped heat weapon from his belt. At close range, it should complete the wreckage caused by the rifle.

It did. Great gouts of white fire crashed through the stands. There were renewed explosions and arcing energy bolts about the consoles. Through the racket, Grant heard Jill's shout again, glanced quickly over at her, saw Crowell standing beside her, a heavy shock gun in his hands. Jill caught Crowell's arm, said something, yelled to Grant, "Three just transported in—other side of the deck! Witter can follow us."

She was gone. Grant snapped the fire weapon back on his belt, took the Suesvant in his left hand, the transporter in his right.

Fog washed in, cleared away. Jill there, on his left—and Crowell materializing abruptly a few steps to the right. The gigantic biped Jill had described, arms like shaggy brown tree trunks braced against the table before it, was leaning forward, attention on a screen from which rose a blurred gabbling. The guns lashed out together.

It was like assaulting a god, an animal deity.

The huge body staggered. The head, swinging toward the intruders, was instantly blinded. The giant took a swaying step and began turning. An arm flailed, smashed into the screen. The great biped kept turning, falling, went down.

"Let's go—" And Jill was gone again.

Four more vulnerable points struck, briefly, ruinously. Surprise still on their side—no other armed bipeds had appeared to dispute their presence, prevent what they were doing. Then a sixth shift; and Crowell said, "Why here?" Jill had guided them to a narrow gallery above a wide hallway. They heard biped voice sounds, though no biped was in sight.

Jill said, "They won't look for us here."

"But there's nothing to—"

"When that engine went, I felt something else! The ship might be beginning to go."

"The ship?" Crowell said. "This is a *ship*?"

Jill nodded. "A very big one. But we may have hurt it enough. That was like a series of explosions on the decks beneath us—or some distance away."

Grant said, "We'd better be sure! I didn't notice anything." They looked at one another a moment, faces pale and taut. Grant asked Crowell, "How did you find us?"

Crowell grunted. "Mental fix on your Suesvant. Easy to visualize! Where it was, you'd be. You seemed to have an idea on how we could use their gadgets. You did. But shouldn't we—"

He broke off. A biped had materialized in the hall beneath them. It lifted its great arms in the air, uttered blaring cries, turning this way and that. Other voices responded. A group of aliens ran past. Somewhere not far off, an intercom cut in. What they heard then might have been the voice of the giant they had brought down— a huge ululating; mournful noise. It ended abruptly.

Now the hall below suddenly filled with the alien creatures. They seemed to be pouring out of other passages, went streaming by in both directions, milling aimlessly, squalling, clasping their heads.

The gallery swayed. The tumult below swelled up. Jill caught her breath. "Stronger now!" she said. "But that's what it felt like!"

There was a distant thudding of explosion. Shrieks rose from the hall. Crowell said shortly, "*They* seem to believe the ship's going!"

Another explosion came, heavier or more close than the previous one. Grant said, "All right. Let's get out!" He looked at Crowell. "We'll meet you at the Base. Jill and I have one more stop to make."

"Huh?"

"Frank Farquhar's aircruiser," said Grant. "We can go to it now wherever he hid it. He had a store of message drones there."

The alien ship went five minutes later. There might have been frantic work on board to contain the chain of destructive reactions surging through it. If so, they were unsuccessful. The remaining defenders of the Star Union Base saw a sheet of brilliant purple light leap from the northern mountain ranges to the sky. Kulkoor's surface shuddered. Presently there came the faraway thunderings of a great explosion.

Grant and Jill had returned by then with the sack of drones they'd scooped up in Farquhar's cruiser. The Base remained on alert. The biped group attacking it apparently had been recalled to the stricken ship; but others could have been left on Kulkoor. Survivors might seek revenge.

Then Grant made a discovery. He'd decided to transport back to the cruiser and fly it in to the Base. Farquhar could have had records of deductions he'd made about the bipeds. Grant found that the transporting instrument would no longer transport him. It did nothing, seemed dead. They tried out the other two devices and had the same experience with them. Evidently they'd been powered by the ship and wouldn't operate now it was gone.

That ended any concern about bipeds who might still be around. If they were, they had no more mobility now than that provided by their legs. They couldn't become a problem. A guncar sent to check reported that the whole hump of mountain inside which the great ship had been concealed had vanished with it.

So then it was time at last to count the dead and missing. There were almost no wounded. Where biped weapons had struck, they'd killed.

It was a long, long list of names.

"Most of the stuff may not be too important," Crowell remarked late that night. He was in his office with Ilken and the Galestrals, and the assortment of articles which had been found in the furred biped vest were spread out on a table. They'd been going over them together. "I'm hardly much of a physicist, but I doubt any very significant new discoveries will be made when specialists take the things apart."

There were thoughtful nods. Ned said, "That seems probable. Nothing too exciting there."

"These, of course," Crowell went on, touching one of the three lifeless transporters lying aside from the rest, "should be a different matter . . ."

"Quite different!" Ned agreed again, dryly.

Crowell regarded his companions. They gazed reflectively back at him. Jill, relaxed in a chair, knees crossed, seemed unaware of the Suesvant laid casually across her lap. Grant's and Ned's rifles were slung as casually from their shoulders. Of course, Galestrals reputedly rarely were seen separated from their deadly pets. Ilken's pale eyes were alert and she carried her brace of tarsh knives well forward on her belt. But there was nothing really unusual about that either.

Crowell tilted back in his chair, hands clasped behind his head. "One thing we do know about the bipeds," he observed, "is that they came a long way to reach Kulkoor. A civilization like theirs couldn't exist in an area touched by our exploration ships without being noticed. It's reasonable to assume they wouldn't have come that far on a mining operation unless the range and efficiency of their warp drive makes anything we've developed look pathetic."

"That does seem a quite reasonable assumption," Jill told him.

"You think so, too, eh?" Crowell brought his chair forward, nudged the transporters. "Would you say the warp drive and these gadgets should operate on the same basic principles?"

Jill nodded. "Uh-huh. Except for range, they must do much the same thing. And range might depend mainly on controllable power."

Crowell remarked to Grant, "You took the transporters from the biped you killed. Technically, they're yours, you know—spoils of war!"

Grant smiled briefly. "Except for another technicality! I'm an employee-shareholder of the Galestral Company and obtained those items on a Company assignment. That makes them Company property."

Crowell grunted. "What do you think the Company will do with them?"

Jill said judiciously, "Well, to begin with, of course, it will clamp on complete secrecy. Then try to work out the principles. Apply them to ship drives. Build a few ships. Keep on improving the drives."

"What kind of ships?"

She studied him, shrugged. "Battlewagons, with at least the mass the bipeds had here. If they happen to come back in force, the Galestral Company will want to be ready for them."

"Cencom would figure it like that," Crowell agreed. "And Cencom will be breaking its neck to get at those principles!"

"I imagine it will," Jill said. "If a warp drive is developed, the Company won't want it to become generally available within any foreseeable time. It'll limit its use to support its own overall policies."

Ned said mildly, "The drive's existence in itself would force those policies to change, Jill!"

"In three, four decades, yes. It needn't change them basically then."

"Captain Witter," Grant said, "what would Cencom do if it had possession of the transporters?"

"Oh, about the same!" Crowell leaned back in his chair again.

"Just about the same thing. Try to develop the warp drive and keep control of it. As long as possible. If Star Union citizens could warp away out of contact whenever they felt like it, what would become of Cencom's authority?"

"Then isn't this a somewhat theoretical discussion?" Ned asked him. "Of the two, naturally, I'd prefer the Galestral Company to wind up with the transporters. Everyone left alive on the Base knows we have them. Unless they're destroyed—which would make no sense at all—who actually does get control of them should depend primarily on whose relief expedition manages to get here first. That could turn into a rather close race!"

"It won't matter who wins it," Crowell said, "if we send the transporters off by message drone tonight."

No one spoke for a few seconds. "One to the Company, one to Cencom?" Ned said then. "And let both know it's been done? It would put them in another race against each other—but it should avoid any head-on trouble." He added, "But it still won't make the warp drive available to individual Star Union citizens or Galestral employees. You won't have affected that."

"They'd keep it from us by tacit agreement," Crowell acknowledged. "So a third drone and the third transporter go simultaneously to the headquarters of the Swimmer League on Varien. A three-way race then—one the swimmers should win. They have the newest and most sophisticated technology, but so far they haven't had a drive good enough to make their mobile cities independent of the Star Union and Cencom. They'll work hard to get it. When they have it, they'll start moving out. And they have the same motive for wanting a warp drive to become generally available that Cencom and your Company have for not wanting it. It will break up the present systems of control. Everything becomes fluid again; and Cencom and the Company have to go along with a new situation. The swimmers will broadcast those principles as soon as they know what they are!" Crowell looked around the group. "Well?"

Ned Brock shook his head. "Everything becomes fluid again . . . If I acted as a Company man should about this, I'd simply find myself outvoted. I won't bother to do it. Let's set the drones up to go out!"

Afterword

by Eric Flint

And . . . that's it.

Well, not quite. There is still one more story to go, in this reissue of the complete writings of James H. Schmitz. That, of course, is *The Witches of Karres.* We will be reissuing that novel a few months from now, as the seventh and final volume of the Baen edition.

But leaving aside *The Witches of Karres,* and the one (and only) collaboration Schmitz ever wrote—"Operation Alpha," with A.E. Van Vogt—the publication of this volume puts every story James Schmitz ever wrote back in print. And this is the first time, ever, that they've *all* been in print simultaneously.

I began this project almost three years ago, as the culmination of what had been a lifelong daydream to see James H. Schmitz restored to the place I believe he deserves in SF's roster of great writers. The fact that he fell almost completely out of print for so many years after his death in 1981 was, in my opinion, the single most outstanding "injustice" of this sort in the science fiction genre. (Though by no means the only one—there are many other fine writers who have suffered the same fate.)

It was my hope—and certainly my intention and goal—that with this Baen edition the so-called historical verdict might be overturned. Of course, I doubt if it will happen again that *everything* James Schmitz wrote will be in print at any one time. But if this edition revitalizes his reputation, and gains him a generation of new fans, that'll be enough. Sooner or later, as they always do, this edition will also start fading away into the used book stores. But . . .

someone, perhaps Baen Books itself, will do another edition of some kind. Someone always does, with those few authors who gain a permanent place in SF's pantheon.

Was I successful in my aim?

I don't know, and I never will. These things can only be measured in decades, not years. I'm fifty-five years old, and (sad to say, but there it is) I won't live long enough to find out.

So be it. For me, the project is now over, and that's sufficient. There is a satisfaction in doing a job as well as you can, whether or not you ever learn its final result. Just as there is a satisfaction in paying a debt forward because you can't pay it back to the man, now long gone, who did so much to introduce a teenage boy named Eric Flint to the joys of science fiction.

That was forty years ago. If, forty years from now, something of James H. Schmitz is still in print, somebody can wake up my ghost and give me the good news.

How?

I don't know. Ask Telzey. Or Pilch. Or track down Trigger and see if her on-and-off husband, Heslet Quillan, has run into another odd monster-that-isn't. Maybe they'll understand how to talk to a ghost.

If all else fails, consult the witches of Karres.

That might be a bit difficult, I admit. Forty years from now, they'll probably have moved their planet again.

James H. Schmitz Chronography

by Guy Gordon

Title	Date	First Pub	Vol
Greenface	Aug 1943	Unknown	5
Agent of Vega	Jul 1949	Astounding	5
The Witches of Karres	Dec 1949	Astounding	*
The Truth About Cushgar	Nov 1950	Astounding	5
The Second Night of Summer	Dec 1950	Galaxy	5
Space Fear (aka The Illusionists)	Mar 1951	Astounding	5
Captives of the Thieve Star	May 1951	Planet Stories	6
The End of the Line	Jul 1951	Astounding	5
The Altruist	Sep 1952	Galaxy	6
We Don't Want Any Trouble	Jun 1953	Galaxy	6
Caretaker	Jul 1953	Galaxy	6
The Vampirate (aka Blood of Nalakia)	Dec 1953	SF Plus	1
Grandpa	Feb 1955	Astounding	4
The Ties of Earth	Nov 1955	Galaxy (2-part serial)	6
Sour Note on Palayata	Nov 1956	Astounding	3
The Big Terrarium	May 1957	Saturn	6
Harvest Time	Sep 1958	Astounding	3
Summer Guests	Sep 1959	IF	6
Gone Fishing	May 1961	Analog	5
Lion Loose . . .	Oct 1961	Analog	3
The Star Hyacinths (aka The Tangled Web)	Dec 1961	Amazing	1
A Tale of Two Clocks (aka Legacy)	1962	SFBC/Torquil	3

An Incident on Route 12	Jan 1962	IF	6
Swift Completion	Mar 1962	Alfred Hitchcock's	6
Novice	Jun 1962	Analog	1
The Other Likeness	Jul 1962	Analog	4
Rogue Psi	Aug 1962	Amazing	5
Watch the Sky	Aug 1962	Analog	5
These Are the Arts	Sep 1962	F&SF	6
The Winds of Time	Sep 1962	Analog	4
Left Hand, Right Hand	Nov 1962	Amazing	6
Beacon to Elsewhere	Apr 1963	Amazing	5
Oneness	May 1963	Analog	6
Ham Sandwich	Jun 1963	Analog	6
Undercurrents	May 1964	Analog	
		(2-part serial)	1
Clean Slate	Sep 1964	Amazing	6
The Machmen	Sep 1964	Analog	4
Spacemaster	1965	New Writings	
		in SF 3	6
A Nice Day for Screaming	Jan 1965	Analog	4
Planet of Forgetting (aka Forget It)	Feb 1965	Galaxy	3[†]
The Pork Chop Tree	Feb 1965	Analog	2[‡]
Balanced Ecology	Mar 1965	Analog	4
Goblin Night	Apr 1965	Analog	1
Trouble Tide	May 1965	Analog	4
Research Alpha	Jul 1965	IF	[§]
Sleep No More	Aug 1965	Analog	1
The Witches of Karres	1966	Chilton	7
Faddist	Jan 1966	Bizarre Mystery	6
The Searcher	Feb 1966	Analog	4
The Tuvela (aka The Demon Breed)	Sep 1968	Analog	
		(2-part serial)	4
Where the Time Went	Nov 1968	IF	6
The Custodians	Dec 1968	Analog	5
Just Curious	Dec 1968	Alfred Hitchcock's	6
Attitudes	Feb 1969	F&SF	4
Would You?	Dec 1969	Fantastic	6
Resident Witch	May 1970	Analog	2
Compulsion	Jun 1970	Analog	2
The Telzey Toy (aka Ti's Toys)	Jan 1971	Analog	2
Company Planet	May 1971	Analog	2
Glory Day	Jun 1971	Analog	2
Poltergeist	Jul 1971	Analog	1

The Lion Game	Aug	1971	Analog (2-part serial)	1
Child of the Gods	Mar	1972	Analog	2
The Symbiotes	Sep	1972	Analog	2
The Eternal Frontiers		1973	G.P Putnam's Sons	6
Crime Buff	Aug	1973	Alfred Hitchcock's Mystery Magazine	6
One Step Ahead	Apr	1974	IF	6
Aura of Immortality	Jun	1974	IF	3

Notes:

* The original 1949 "The Witches of Karres" novelette became the first two chapters of the 1966 novel of the same name.

† "Forget It" (Vol. 3) is a slightly modified version of "Planet of Forgetting."

‡ "The Pork Chop Tree" appears in Vol. 2 as the prologue to "Compulsion."

§ "Research Alpha" was written in collaboration with A.E. Van Vogt, and is not reprinted in these volumes. It can be found in the collection "More Than Superhuman."

"Volume" refers to the volumes of the current Baen edition. By title, as follows:

1) *Telzey Amberdon*
2) *T'n T: Telzey & Trigger*
3) *Trigger & Friends*
4) *The Hub: Dangerous Territory*
5) *Agent of Vega & Other Stories*
6) *Eternal Frontier*
7) *The Witches of Karres* (forthcoming)